THE GOOD SOLDIER ŠVEJK

Jaroslav Hašek was born on 24 April 1883, the son of a teacher of mathematics. Forced by the dictates of necessity to earn some sort of a living he became a bank clerk, but soon abandoned it in favour of an eccentric and wandering life. He spent a good deal of time tramping off the beaten track in Central and South-Eastern Europe. He also did various jobs as a journalist and soon became known as a comic character and a practical joker who was fond of associating with the devotees of taverns. He wanted to write, and before the catastrophic years of the First World War he had published sixteen volumes of short stories. Taken prisoner on the Eastern Front he spent several years in Russian prison camps. On his return he began to write *The Good Soldier Švejk*, his Gargantuan book which was to inflame a nation to resistance and sweep all Europe with the virility of its satire. According to his original plan, 'Švejk' was to be completed in six volumes. He died, however, in 1923 at Lipnice in Czechoslovakia, with only four volumes written.

JAROSLAV HAŠEK

The Good Soldier Švejk

AND HIS FORTUNES IN THE
WORLD WAR

*

A new and unabridged
translation from the Czech by
CECIL PARROTT
with the original illustrations by
Josef Lada

PENGUIN BOOKS
in association with William Heinemann

PENGUIN BOOKS

Published by the Penguin Group
27 Wrights Lane, London w8 5tz, England
Viking Penguin Inc., 40 West 23rd Street, New York, New York 10010, USA
Penguin Books Australia Ltd, Ringwood, Victoria, Australia
Penguin Books Canada Ltd, 2801 John Street, Markham, Ontario, Canada l3r 1b4
Penguin Books (NZ) Ltd, 182–190 Wairau Road, Auckland 10, New Zealand

Penguin Books Ltd, Registered Offices: Harmondsworth, Middlesex, England

This complete text in English
first published by William Heinemann in association with Penguin Books 1973
This edition first published in the United States of America
by Thomas Y. Crowell 1974
Published in Penguin Books in the United States of America
by arrangement with Harper & Row, Publishers, Inc.
Published in Penguin Books 1974
11 13 15 17 19 20 18 16 14 12

Made and printed in Great Britain by
Richard Clay Ltd, Bungay, Suffolk
Set in Monotype Ehrhardt

Contents

THE GOOD SOLDIER ŠVEJK

Part I · Behind the Lines

Part II · At the Front

Introduction

JAROSLAV HAŠEK, the author of *The Good Soldier Švejk*, was a true bohemian within the meaning of the term 'La Bohème' but a very untypical Czech. The son of an impoverished schoolmaster who drank himself to death, he was left at the age of thirteen without adequate parental control and quickly acquired the tastes and habits of a hobo or beatnik.

This born truant first saw the light of day in Prague on 30 April 1883 in a house in a street called appropriately enough Školská, or 'School Street'. At school he was idle and in the family's straitened circumstances after his father's death he was offered employment in a chemist's shop belonging to a Mr Kokoška. This brief episode in his life is reflected not only in *The Good Soldier Švejk* but also in his stories *From an Old Chemist's Shop*. Thus already in his teens Hašek was beginning to store up material for later literary use.

In 1899 at the age of sixteen he was admitted to the recently founded Czechoslavonic Commercial Academy, where for the first time he appears to have done a little study and to have acquitted himself creditably. But he also began to develop a taste for what were to be the main occupations of his life – writing and vagrancy. A Prague newspaper, *Národní listy*, published anonymously his first story at a time when the young author was making vacation trips in Moravia, Slovakia, Hungary and Galicia. He set off without a penny in his pocket and supported himself by begging, consorting with gipsies, tramps and vagabonds and acquiring many bad habits from them.

His good record at the Commercial Academy won Hašek a place in the Slavia Bank in 1902 but he threw it up and went off to Slovakia instead. A few weeks later he returned and was indulgently taken back, but when a month later he absconded on another jaunt he was justifiably given notice. From then on he resolved to try to live by his writing, but in the course of the eight years from 1900 to 1908 he was only able to get published 185 short feuilletons – a quite insufficient number to enable him to support himself in a regular existence.

Not only was Hašek a true bohemian: he was a born mischief-maker and hoaxer as well. As a schoolboy he had taken part in the anti-German riots in Prague in 1897, tearing down proclamations of martial law, damaging emblems of the Austro-Hungarian monarchy, breaking windows of government offices and joyfully helping to set fire to the yard of a Prague German. In 1906 he systematized these perverse proclivities by joining the anarchist movement, which naturally led to further conflicts with the police and short periods of arrest and imprisonment. But in the same year he encountered a new and un-expected influence. He met Jarmila Mayerová, the daughter of a Prague stucco decorator, and fell deeply in love with her. But there was trouble in store for him because his vagabond life and radical convictions were unlikely to find favour with her respectable bourgeois parents.

In 1907 his anarchist activities increased. He became editor of the anarchist journal *Komuna* and gave lectures to miners and textile workers in the provinces. Austrian police informers reported that he was particularly dangerous and his movements were closely watched. During an anarchist demonstration he was arrested for assaulting a police constable and sentenced to a month's imprisonment. From gaol he sent out love poems to Jarmila, as a result of which her father tried to prevent her from seeing any more of him and instructed her to warn him that any further anarchist involvement on his part would make it impossible for them to see each other again, let alone think of marriage. Hašek promised to give up anarchism, but continued to go about in such ragged clothes that his future father-in-law insisted that if he was to be a serious contender for Jarmila's hand he must at least dress himself decently and find some permanent employment. Again Hašek promised to obey. His conflicts with the police became fewer. The following year he was only summonsed twice, once because he tried to tear down a flag on the Wenceslas Square and another time for breach of public order. But this was more than Jarmila's parents could tolerate and they took their daughter away from Prague. Her undesirable but importunate suitor followed her all the way into the country and when he had no money for his railway ticket back to Prague he tramped the whole sixty miles on foot.

In 1909 he seemed to be making a genuine effort to prove to Jar-mila's parents that he was capable of maintaining himself and her. In this year he wrote sixty-four stories, most of which were published in the paper *Karikatury*, which was edited by the artist Josef Lada, the illustrator of the present edition of *The Good Soldier Švejk*. Later he succeeded a journalist friend of his as editor of a journal called *The Animal World*, but was soon dismissed for writing articles about non-existent animals which he had invented – in fact exactly what Marek claimed to have done in the present book.

Preparations for the wedding were now under way and Jarmila's parents insisted that it must be celebrated in a church. For this purpose Hašek had to agree to return to the Catholic fold, which he had deserted some three years earlier. The wedding finally took place on 13 May 1910. Hašek now had his Jarmila, but his marriage with her inevitably brought him into circles where he was unlikely to feel at his ease. Nevertheless 1910 was a bumper year for his literary output and he wrote and published seventy-five stories.

In 1911 he published in *Karikatury* the first of his stories about 'The Good Soldier Švejk'. They consisted of a number of tales about a soldier who had not quite yet developed into the famous character of the present book but bore a strong resemblance to him. The next year they were included in a book of short stories under the title of *The Good Soldier Švejk and Other Strange Stories*, although the Švejk stories only took up twenty-nine pages. Meanwhile Hašek had shown himself utterly incapable of living a regular life or of keeping up to the standards which Jarmila and her parents demanded of him. He had already perpetrated little hoaxes on the readers of *The Animal World*. He now carried this art a stage farther by pretending one day to commit suicide by jumping off the Charles Bridge at the spot where the legendary St John of Nepomuk was thrown into the water. The police were called and took him off to a mental home. Here he was able to gather material for the passages in the present book which describe Švejk's adventures among the lunatics. After that Hašek took it into his head to form his own 'cynological institute' (his own pretentious name for a dog-fancier's shop). He was helped in the business by Jarmila and again his experiences in this pursuit are to be found in the pages not only of this book but of others of his works too. A year or two later he was to publish an article, 'Cynological Institute', in the fashionable Prague illustrated, *Světozor*. He explained how he had found the word 'cynological' in an encyclopedia, and had hit on the name 'institute' after walking past the Agricultural Institute. 'I am now at last the owner of an Institute,' he wrote.

His next escapade was to found a new political party called '*The Party of Moderate and Peaceful Progress Within the Limits of the Law*'. It was the time of the elections to the Austro-Hungarian parliament and he stood as a candidate for it, publicly debunking the monarchy, its institutions and its social and political system. Of course it was only another hoax, designed partly to satisfy Hašek's innate thirst for exhibitionism and partly to bolster the finances of the pub where the election meetings were held.

In 1912 Jarmila bore him a son, Richard, but the marriage had not proved a happy one and was soon to break up. Hašek lost a promising job with a leading Prague paper after publicly attacking the leaders of the political party controlling it. Jarmila left him and went to live with her parents, while Hašek reverted to his former bohemian existence. He continued to write prolifically and could now draw on his experiences of married life. His breach with Jarmila led to his almost total alienation from society and from now on he lived in the 'underground'. He was not registered anywhere and the police searched for him in vain.

The outbreak of the First World War found him living spasmodically with the cartoonist Lada, who afterwards related that Hašek wrote many stories and cooked many wonderful meals during his stay with him. Indeed, he had the reputation of being as talented a cook as he was a writer, and the culinary details in *The Good Soldier Švejk* merit serious study.

It was at this time that Hašek perpetrated what was probably his most daring hoax. He has collected around him as many legends as the saints, and one version of what happened is as follows. He decided to fool the authorities by taking a room at U Valšů, which was notorious for being half-hotel and half-brothel, and registering himself there as a Russian. The name he wrote in the visitor's book sounded Russian enough, but when read backwards in Czech it became 'Kiss my arse.' When required to state what he was doing in Prague he wrote that he was looking into the activities of the Austrian general staff. At the time war fever was at its height and the police were at once alerted and the hotel surrounded. They thought they had caught an important spy and were disappointed and embarrassed when they found that it was none other than the by now notorious hooligan Hašek. Asked why he had done it Hašek replied in all innocence that he had wanted to assure himself that the Austrian police were operating effectively. He got off lightly with only five days' imprisonment.

In 1915 he was called up and drafted to the 91st Infantry Regiment in České Budějovice – the very same regiment to which Švejk himself belonged. Like Marek in *The Good Soldier Švejk* he was admitted as a one-year volunteer and the privileges of his rank were later withdrawn from him. In his case it was because it had been subsequently discovered that he was entered on the police records as a dangerous anarchist. From Southern Bohemia the 91st soon moved to Király-hida in Hungary and from there to the front.

During his brief spell in the regiment Hašek carefully observed the officers, N.C.O.s and men he came into contact with – especially his battalion commander, Captain Ságner, his company commander, Lieutenant Lukas, the lieutenant in the reserve, Mechálek, and finally Lieutenant Lukas's batman, a private called Strašlipka. The names of all these men, who were to appear later under the same or different names in *The Good Soldier Švejk*, could afterwards be found in the records of the 91st regiment. Hašek was particularly attached to Lieutenant Lukas. He was not in fact Lukas's batman but served under him, admired him greatly and wrote a number of poems to him. The lieutenant, who lived in retirement in the Czechoslovak Republic after the war, kept the poems long after Hašek's death, but after his own death they unaccountably disappeared.

Hašek also saw a lot of the quartermaster sergeant-major, Vaněk, whom he assisted with the accounts and whose office he shared. Lieutenant Mechálek was the model for the notorious Lieutenant Dub. There is mention too of a Cadet Biegler and a Major Wenzel in the records, but no trace of any Josef Švejk or of a one-year volunteer Marek. It appears that Hašek took the name of Josef Švejk from a respectable parliamentary deputy of that name. It is to be presumed that for the characters of Švejk and Marek he drew on his own personal experiences, except that Strašlipka, the real batman, seems to have been part model for Švejk. Photographs are preserved of these various members of the regiment and they have little in common with the illustrations which Lada drew and are included in this volume. The photograph of Strašlipka is much closer to the image the reader forms of Švejk than Lada's brilliant but farcical caricatures. Hašek himself never saw any of the illustrations contained in the present volume but they have now become inseparable from the book.

Hašek's long trek by train and on foot from Királyhida to the front in Galicia provided him with the material for the journey he describes in the book. But he did not stay long at the front. He was taken prisoner on 23 September 1915 after having been cut off in a dug-out as the result of a sudden Russian breakthrough. Although Lieutenant Lukas personally tried to persuade him to retreat with the others he would not follow them and gave himself up to the Russians.

Conditions in the Russian prisoner-of-war camps at that time were terrible, not least for the Czechs. The Russians regarded their fellow Slavs as the least privileged category among the prisoners and considered them devoted enough to Mother Russia to be proud to undergo the worst suffering and take upon themselves the most arduous labours. Hašek was sent first to a camp near Kiev and later to another one at Totskoye near the southernmost point of the Urals. Here he was fortunate to be able to escape the worst rigours of the camp by working in the very comfortable office of one of the camp commanders. Like most of the other prisoners he caught spotted typhus but the attack was not a serious one.

One day the news reached him that a military volunteer unit was about to be formed drawn from the Czechs and Slovaks in Russia. It was to be the nucleus of the future Czech Legion and he at once applied to serve in it. He was accepted and immediately employed on recruiting service by the Union of Czech Associations in Russia. His literary gifts predisposed him for journalistic and propaganda work and it was natural that he should be employed in this capacity. In his spare time he worked on a journal, *Čechoslovan*, which was published by the Czech colony in Kiev, and it was here that he began to write a second series of stories about Švejk which bore the title *The Good Soldier Švejk In Captivity*. It was published in Kiev in book form in 1917.

It was hardly to be expected that Hašek would be a very reliable employee of the Union and he often caused them embarrassment by his freelance writings. He lampooned the leadership in an article in the *Čechoslovan* called 'The Pickwick Club' and was disciplined for it. He was not only strongly pro-Czech and anti-Austrian but very Russophil as well. He greeted the news of the coronation of the new Austrian emperor in 1916 with the words: 'We started our revolution to overthrow the Hapsburg dynasty and call to the Czech throne a member of the great family of the Romanovs.' Even after the Russian February Revolution Hašek continued to express pro-monarchical views and attack the Bolsheviks. But after the October Revolution his views became more radical. He was strongly opposed to plans to send the Legion away from Russia to fight on the Western Front, believing that it should remain on Russian soil and fight the Germans there. When the Legion left Kiev to move into the interior of Russia in preparation for its later transhipment to the West, Hašek did not go with it. At the end of February 1918 he left for Moscow to join the Red Army. A month later he had become a member of the Bolshevik Party. Hašek could no longer agitate for the Legion to fight the Germans in Russia, as the Bolsheviks had signed a peace treaty with the Central Powers on 3 March. The Legion proclaimed him a traitor and issued an order for his arrest. Later Hašek was sent to the town of Samara to work for the Bolsheviks, but after it fell into the hands of the Legion he had hastily to disappear into the Central Asian provinces of Russia disguised as a German colonist. When the Red Army established control in Russia and the Legion was gradually withdrawn Hašek started to make a career for himself in the Russian Bolshevik Party organization – to become in fact an *apparatchik*. In December 1918 he was appointed Deputy Commandant of the town of Bugulma. The Czech Red Army man became the Soviet Commissar Gashek (the Russians, having no 'h' in their alphabet, spell and pronounce his name in this way). The little town has since been immortalized in the amusing stories about Soviet life which the author published on his return to Prague. In 1919 he was appointed Secretary of the Committee of Foreign Communists in the Russian town of Ufa, in the same year Secretary of the Party Cell of the printing office of *The Red Arrow*, and a year later Head of the International Section of the Political Department of the 5th Army. He is also said to have completed a course at the Soviet Communist Party School. More significant was the surprising fact that he gave up drinking and led an orderly and sober life for thirty months.

It seems improbable that Hašek – bohemian and anarchist as he was – would have been able to adapt himself to the rigidities of the Soviet system for any length of time but fortunately he had other options open to him. And when a visiting Czechoslovak Social Democratic delegation invited him to come back and help the party in his own country, he readily agreed. On 19 December 1920 he suddenly turned up in Czechoslovakia and began to write articles in *Rudé Právo*, the organ of the Left Wing of the Social Democratic Party. He could not return to Jarmila, because he had brought another wife with him from Russia. Some say that she was an aristocrat, a relative of Prince Lvov, but it is possible that this was another of Hašek's yarns. None the less he was anxious to re-establish contact with Jarmila and enlist her help in finding permanent employment. But this was no simple task. In the new Republic Hašek was not highly thought of nationally, politically or socially. He was branded as a traitor, a Bolshevik and finally a bigamist. Unable to secure a steady job he drifted back into his drunken vagabond existence of the pre-war years. However, he had to maintain himself and his new Russian wife and this spurred him to try his hand at a complete novel for the first time. Early in 1921 he started writing *The Good Soldier Švejk* and in the summer of the same year moved to Lipnice on the Sázava which lies some hundred miles to the east of Prague and where in its beautiful surroundings he hoped to be able to concentrate on his writing with least disturbance. The novel was to extend to four volumes and no publisher was anxious to handle it. Consequently Hašek was forced to publish the first volume privately and distribute it himself together with his friend, Franta Sauer. But after the success of the initial volume a publisher was found who was ready to take over the remaining parts. Although Hašek did not make much money out of the first volume he earned enough to buy a cottage at Lipnice, where he could begin to dictate the subsequent volumes.

But his renewed irregular life coming on top of his hard existence in Russia had taken a severe toll of his health. After the abstemiousness of thirty months his system could ill support a return to the orgies and excesses of his youth. He fell seriously ill and died on 3 January 1923. The only mourners at his funeral were his eleven-year-old son, Richard, and a few friends. The fourth volume of his book remained unfinished. A friend of his, Karel Vaněk, completed it but the ending, although illustrated by Lada, has been omitted from recent versions because it is not only spurious but generally considered to be of inferior quality. It is not included in the present volume.

Although *The Good Soldier Švejk* was a popular success from the beginning it was not taken seriously by the literary critics for many years. Indeed, books on the First World War did not begin to attract serious notice until some ten years after it had ended. In the immediate post-war years people were still under the spell of the emotions it had unleashed. It had been grand and heroic, from whichever side you looked at it. Only after a distance of years were people able to free themselves from this obsession and to view it critically and dispassionately. And for the Czechs it was particularly difficult to do so. Even if they had been forced to fight on the wrong side many of them had 'done their bit' and were not unproud of it. Some on the other hand had later deserted to the Russians and helped to form the Czech Legion there. For a short time the Legion had become the most formidable force in Russia and had even inflicted defeats on the Red Army. When the legionaries eventually returned home after the war they became part of the national legend. And there were many Czechs who thought then and still do now that Švejk himself is not a good advertisement for the Czech character. When the new Republic was trying to establish its identity and reputation abroad patriots did not wish to be associated in the minds of foreign readers with the qualities which seemed to characterize Švejk. But these fears were unjustified. Although 'Schweikism' is a word often used to characterize the passive resistance of the Czechs, anyone who reads the book carefully and knows the Czechs will perceive that Švejk is not necessarily a Czech figure. He might be any Central European and is in fact a 'Mr Everyman', in the sense that he resembles any 'little man' who gets caught up in the wheels of a big bureaucratic machine.

A true appreciation of the book requires a full understanding of Švejk's character. It is a complex one. Although he was discharged from military service for patent idiocy, as he proudly tells everyone, he is far from being a fool. He is quite capable of making himself *appear* a fool to save a situation, and it was probably to this resourcefulness that he owed his discharge from the army. Švejk speaks most of the time in double-talk. He pretends to be in agreement with anyone he is dealing with, particularly if he happens to be a superior officer. But the irony underlying his remarks is always perceptible. Not only are his observations and explanations ironical, but so too are many of his actions. One example of this is his *apparent* efforts to get to the front by protesting his patriotism and devotion to the monarchy, when it is clear that his actions only impede the achievement of his proclaimed objective.

Švejk is no ignoramus. He is the brother of a schoolmaster and is clearly an educated man. Although he expresses himself in the Prague vernacular he has a rich literary vocabulary combined with an almost encyclopedic knowledge, no doubt derived from considerable reading of newspapers and journals. He is a close observer of human nature and some of his deductions are penetrating. In dealing with his superiors he masks his real views and, indeed, even when talking to people of his own class he rarely reveals his true thinking. At the end of Part I, in conversation with a soldier he says exactly what he thinks of Austria-Hungary: 'A monarchy as idiotic as this ought not to exist at all.' None the less he accepts with resigned and even cheerful equanimity all the struggles and privations of army life in wartime. Although he evidently has no high opinion of most of his superiors he is capable of personal devotion at least to the officer whose batman he originally was, Lieutenant Lukáš. In situations where he has the upper hand he can be decisive to the point of ruthlessness. The way he punishes Baloun for cheating his master contrasts strikingly with the picture some people may have formed of him as a slippery and refractory orderly. Švejk grows in stature as he proves his superiority to those around him. He is a complete match for any of the soldiers or N.C.O.s who are unlucky enough to be his escorts. He is capable of reducing Lieutenant Dub to a state of speechlessness. At the same time he has a disarming way of attracting the admiration and approval of some stupid general or colonel. He has 'a way with him'. Few people, not even stern judge advocates, can resist his good-natured but un-flinching blue eyes.

Moreover, unlike his creator, Švejk is no anarchist. He believes in law and order and means what he says when he asserts that discipline must be preserved. At the same time he is full of human feeling and compassion. 'Mistakes must occur,' he says, and he is always ready to excuse or defend, when others attack or complain. These can be the characteristics of Czechs but are not necessarily such. Some of the characteristics are common to many who are placed in the position in which Švejk finds himself. But the combination of all these traits makes Švejk unique.

One writer who recognized the greatness of Hašek's novel soon after it was written was Max Brod, the man who had diagnosed the genius of Kafka and Janáček. 'Hašek was a humorist of the highest calibre,' he wrote. 'A later age will perhaps put him on a level with Cervantes and Rabelais.' Max Brod saw that there was something of the Sancho Panza in Švejk. There is some truth in this. Lieutenant Lukáš might well have said to his batman, and in fact did say in so many words, what Don Quixote said to Sancho Panza: 'If you tell your story that way, Sancho, and repeat everything you have to say twice over, you will not be done in two days. Tell it consequentially like an intelligent man, or else be quiet.' And Švejk might well have replied like Sancho, although he did not: 'The way I am telling it is the way all stories are told in my country, and I don't know any other way of telling it.' But while Sancho is the foil to Don Quixote, Švejk is the main character of the Czech novel. And Sancho has neither the education nor the courage of Švejk. 'I've never read any histories at all, because I can't read or write,' says Sancho, who also admits to his master that he is very peaceable by nature and 'all against shoving himself into brawls and quarrels'. But Švejk is certainly not the man to pull his punches, as can be seen by the way he joins Vodička in the brawl with the Hungarians or eggs Kunert on to complain against Lieutenant Dub.

The parallel with Rabelais is more valid. In this book Hašek comes near to scraping the barrel in coarseness and nastiness. Here of course he is showing his true colours as the anarchist who wants to shake the bourgeoisie out of its comfortable complacency and hypocritical respectability, and he does not scruple to rake about in the dirt just for the sake of the stench. There were times in Prague when to invent a new anecdote all one had to do was to mention the name of the wife of a prominent political leader and add to it as much filth as possible. This is exactly Hašek's method of treating the Catholic Church. Some of the episodes dealing with the army chaplain can hardly be said to embellish the work. Hašek was consumed with such a bitter hatred of the Church and religion that in this book and many of his other stories he shot wide of the mark and the reader soon becomes surfeited, if not nauseated. One should note that he was more tolerant towards the Orthodox Church.

Nor should one blind oneself to Hašek's shortcomings as a writer. He is certainly a master of character-drawing and dialogue. Indeed, it is his dialogue which often provides the material for the characterization. And he displays considerable ingenuity, inventiveness and imagination too in devising the innumerable stories which Švejk and the characters tell in the course of the book. But his own comments and descriptions are less successful. He was good at recording what he had heard in life, especially over a drink at the pub – the stories, the conversations, the adventures. But he can be surprisingly lame in his descriptions and unconvincing in his narrative style. His greatest achievement is to maintain the momentum of the book and the raciness of the narrative in spite of introducing so many stories which hold back the action. He wrote carelessly and quickly. Sometimes it is apparent that he must have been drunk when he was writing, so confused do his thoughts and sentences become. But with all its imperfections *The Good Soldier Švejk* is a classic and I know of no novel which conveys so poignantly not only the ugliness of war but the utter futility of anything connected with it.

This rendering of *The Good Soldier Švejk* into English for the first time in an unabridged and unbowdlerized version will give English-speaking readers the chance of reviewing their opinions of the author and his leading character. But it is of course impossible to convey to a reader who does not know Czech or German finer points which must inevitably be lost in translation. Josef Švejk is inseparable from the manner in which he expresses himself. The language of Švejk *is* Švejk himself. Unfortunately it is impossible to reproduce this in English without running the risk of distorting his image, his period and his milieu.

THE ILLUSTRATIONS

Although Josef Lada (1887–1957) had been Hašek's friend since 1907 and had published in 1911 some of his stories in the humorous journal *Karikatury*, which he was then editing, it was not until 1921 that Hašek asked him to design a cover for the weekly parts in which *The Good Soldier Švejk* was then making its first appearance. Lada accepted the commission and did the drawing. He relates that it was approved by Hašek and his friend Sauer, who were the joint private publishers, but not only was the promised payment for it never made but Lada had to foot the bill for the meal over which the transaction was concluded.

This sketch was the first illustration which Lada made of Švejk. It bore little resemblance to the later illustrations with which we are now so familiar, but it was the only Lada illustration which Hašek personally approved.

It was not until 1924 – a year after Hašek's death – that Lada was commissioned to draw 540 pictures of Švejk for the Sunday supplement of the Czech daily *České Slovo*. These appeared each week in serial form, and each illustration was accompanied by a much shortened text adapted from the book by the artist himself. In these pictures Lada changed the figure of Švejk and created other characters after his own fancy. He also invented a brief ending for the unfinished book and illustrated it accordingly. This 'strip' version of Švejk was very popular and soon led to the appearance of a new edition of the book with about a quarter of Lada's original illustrations. But there were some changes in the drawings. Švejk was now shown with his head shaven from the very beginning. In fact he became less and less like Strašlipka, on whom he was probably modelled, and more a figure of Lada's own. The present translation reproduces 156 of these drawings.

If none of them were seen or approved by Hašek, and if many of the figures depicted bear little resemblance to the living persons who inspired Hašek's characters, they are now as inseparable from his *Švejk* as Tenniel's drawings are from *Alice in Wonderland*. For all their deviations, they reproduce very faithfully in caricature the picture which many Czechs had of Austro-Hungarian officialdom. But if Lada seems to have had no mercy on Austrian officials he is hardly more indulgent when he depicts his own countrymen – high or low. In this he was at one with Hašek, for the biggest *blbec* in the book ('idiot' – to use Hašek's favourite word), Lieutenant Dub, is a Czech and is caricatured without mercy.

Although Lada was a serious artist who achieved fame in his water-colours, *paysages*, animal pictures and book illustrations, he is known today mainly as the illustrator of the characters in Hašek's tales. He is said to have made 1,339 sketches to accompany Hašek's various works and 909 for *The Good Soldier Švejk* alone. His clear-cut drawings in bold strokes, which immortalize the humorous gestures of the people of that period and region, effectively combine the primitive and the popular. They are as much a revolt against the glorification of Czech history and legend, as shown by Mánes and Aleš in their innumerable heroic visions of Libuše, Žižka or Jiří of Poděbrady, as Hašek's writings are against national romanticism in Czech literature from Jirásek to Medek.

NOTE ON THE TRANSLATION

The translator of *The Good Soldier Švejk* is faced with a number of problems at the very outset. First there is no authorized text of the work. Only the first and second editions were seen by the author during his lifetime, but there is no certainty that even these texts represent what he actually wrote or approved. Only a part of the manuscript has been preserved. The author, it appears, cared little about what he had written once he had sent it off to the printer.

Broadly speaking there are two groups of texts – the texts published before the war, which were assumed to be what the author himself had written, and the texts published from the 1950s onwards which were revised in orthography, grammar and syntax. In making this translation I have drawn on both groups and have chosen whichever version seemed clearer and more consistent. Discrepancies between the texts, except in spelling and syntax, are not substantial, the only major difference being the omission in the post-war editions of a 'message' from Hašek to President Masaryk which was to be found in the pre-war editions, and which is included in this translation. (See footnote on p. 680.)

I have already referred to the language in which Švejk expresses himself and the impossibility of reproducing this in English. Švejk and many of the other characters in the book use what is called 'obecná čeština' or *common* Czech, which is not quite the same as *literary* or *book* Czech. The use of common Czech in Bohemia and Moravia is by no means confined to the uneducated. The Czechs are a democratic people and when they get together and let their hair down, whether they are educated or not, they speak a more or less common vernacular. This cannot be adequately rendered in English, since the only thinkable equivalent would be dialect or bad English. Either would be false and out of place in this context. We also have to remember that the action is taking place during the First World War in the Austro-Hungarian Empire among Czechs and it will create a wrong atmosphere if the language used in the English translation is associated with people and conditions of a very different kind. Much of the charm of Švejk's narration lies in his use of common Czech.

Another problem is that although in the Austro-Hungarian army the nationalities spoke their own languages among themselves, the language of command was German. Thus in the book there are a large number of German words and phrases, some of which are distorted by Czech mispronunciation, and this adds a peculiar colour and humour to the language. It also has some significance whether the characters speak German or Czech and what kind of German or Czech they speak. This too cannot be adequately conveyed in translation.

A further complication is the richness of Czech 'bad language' as compared with our own. In common with other Slavic languages and with German, Czech can boast a wide range of words of abuse in all shades of intensity. We cannot match these in Britain, where – no doubt under the influence of puritanism – the bulk of our terms of abuse are too mild and our strong expressions are limited to one or two hackneyed obscenities. Czech words of abuse generally involve domestic animals, excrement or the parts of the body connected with it. The English relate mainly to sexual functions or perversions, although there is in this respect a narrow area of common ground between the two languages. If the reader finds a certain monotony in the words chosen by the translator I hope he will realize that the bandsman has to operate within the limits of his instrument.

It is characteristic of Švejk's way of telling a story that he does not bother about syntax. This of course is an indication of his mentality and a part of his character, but it is also a reflection of the author's disregard of grammatical rules. In translating Švejk's lengthy anecdotes it has been found necessary to break up some of his sentences so that the reader can understand their drift and get the point of the story. In doing this the translator risks incurring the charge of having tried to 'edit' Hašek. In fact any translator of Hašek has to exercise very considerable self-restraint, since it is often tempting completely to re-write him. But if this were carried too far the book would not be Hašek's any more. It follows from what has been written above that there are passages in the original of *The Good Soldier Švejk* which may be not too intelligible. In these cases the translator has had to try to make them so. Fortunately these cases are very few and not of vital importance.

This is the first unabridged and unbowdlerized version of *The Good Soldier Švejk* in English. The only previous translator reduced the book to less than two-thirds of this volume. There is no doubt that Hašek was writing to make money and that he spun out the book to increase his earnings. No one would deny that it needs pruning. But it is a different matter when censorship is applied to it. Hašek regaled his readers with words which had never appeared in Czech literature before. In his postscript to the first volume he explains why he did this and how important it was to him. As far as the translation goes the omission of anecdotes because they are 'dirty' or of references to monarchs or the deity because they might be treasonable or blasphemous could hardly be justified in 1930 and would certainly be indefensible in 1973. Today 'The Good Soldier Švejk' must stand as he is, without any fig-leaf.

I owe a great debt to Dr Dana Kňourková for the invaluable assistance she gave me in reading my manuscript and helping to solve the many problems connected with the translation.

CECIL PARROTT

Guide to the Pronunciation of Czech Names

The first syllable always bears the stress. However, the unstressed syllables are not swallowed as in English. Each syllable is pronounced clearly, whether stressed or not.

Baloun = Bah-lohn

České Budějovice = Che-skeh Boo-dye-yo-vi-tseh

Dub = Doop

Konopiště = Kon-o-pish-tyeh

Lukáš = Loo-kaahsh

Matušič = Mah-too-shich

Na Bojišti = Nah Bo-yish-tyee

Palivec = Pah-li-vets

Piešt'any = Pee-ye-shty-ah-nee

Písek = Pee-sek

Putim = Poo-tyim

Ságner = Saah-gnehr

Švejk = Shvayk

Vaněk = Vah-nyek

Vodička = Vo-dyich-kah

Vršovice = Vrr-sho-vi-tseh

Czech vowels are short or long. The diacritic marks which look like acute accents and the small circle occurring on 'u' (ů) indicate that the vowel is long.

The use of a hook (or an apostrophe) on a consonant letter has the effect of softening it:

ť (or t') sounds like 't' in '*t*une' in contrast with hard 't' in '*t*op'

ď (or d') sounds like 'd' in '*d*uke' in contrast with hard 'd' in '*d*one'

ň sounds like the French 'gn' in 'Champa*gn*e'

The same effect, i.e. softening of the previous consonant, is produced by 'i' or 'í' or 'ě' when following 'd', 't', or 'n'.

Otherwise Czech 'č' sounds like 'ch' in 'chop';

'š' sounds like 'sh' in 'short';

'ž' resembles the sound denoted by 's' in 'plea*s*ure'.

The most difficult Czech sound is probably 'ř', which sounds somewhat like 'rzh' (compare 'Dvořák' – Dvo-rzhaahk).

Czech 'r' is pronounced exactly like the Scottish 'r', and Czech 'ch' like 'ch' in 'loch'.

GI

Prague

BOHEMIA

SEE MAP B

České
Budějovice

MORAVI

S

Bratisla

Vienna

Bruck an der Leitha

SWITZERLAND

GERMANY

Királyhida

River Leitha

H

AUSTRIA

Venice

CROATIA

SL

BOSNIA

ITALY

Adriatic Sea

HERZEG

DALMATIA

SVEJK'S JOURNEY WITH HIS REGIMENT TO THE FRONT

RUSSIAN POLAND

Żółtańce

SEE MAP C   Przemyśl   Lwów

Cracow

Sanok

Stara Sól

Lupka Pass   GALICIA

Medzilaborce

Humenné

Sátoraljaújhely

Miskolc

Füzesabony

Budapest

G   A   R   Y

River Danube

TRANSYLVANIA

BUKOVINA

RUSSIAN UKRAINE

RUMANIA

SERBIA

A.

THE
AUSTRO-
HUNGARIAN
MONARCHY

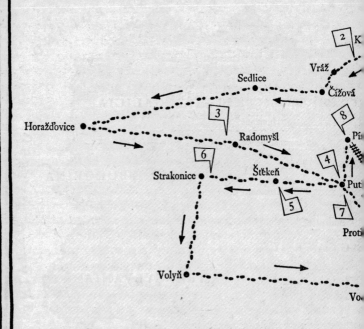

(1) Five minutes before the train reached Tábor Švejk and a railwayman had their hands on the handle of the alarm signal and it is really a mystery how it happened that the train came to a halt. When he finally reached Tábor Švejk sat drinking, missed all the trains to České Budějovice and was told by the lieutenant on duty to walk there.

(2) Here Švejk was helped by a motherly old woman.

(3) Here Švejk met Farmer Melichárek who took him for a deserter.

(4) Here at Putim Švejk slept in the haystack in gay company.

(5) Here Švejk met a resourceful and garrulous tramp.

(6) Here Švejk and the tramp were feasted by an even more garrulous shepherd in the Schwarzenberg sheep-fold.

(7) Here Švejk found himself back again at Putim. He was arrested by the gendarmerie and taken for a Russian spy.

(8) Švejk was escorted to Písek by the corporal (or rather Švejk escorted him!) and was then sent to České Budějovice by train.

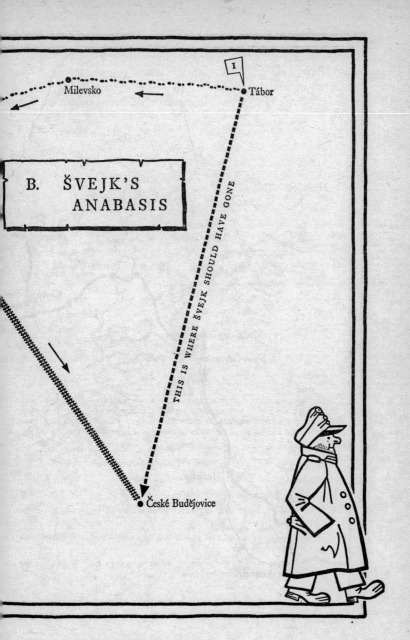

Milevsko

Tábor

B. ŠVEJK'S ANABASIS

THIS IS WHERE ŠVEJK SHOULD HAVE GONE

České Budějovice

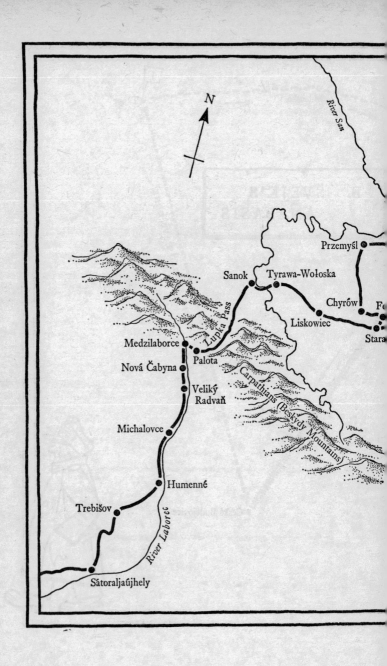

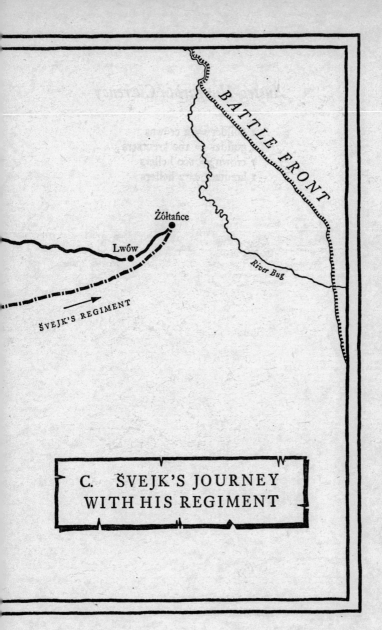

BATTLE FRONT

Żółtańce

Lwów

River Bug

ŠVEJK'S REGIMENT

C. ŠVEJK'S JOURNEY
WITH HIS REGIMENT

Austro-Hungarian Currency

1 guilder = 2 crowns
1 guilder = 100 kreutzers
1 crown = 100 hellers
1 kreutzer = 2 hellers

THE GOOD SOLDIER ŠVEJK

AND HIS FORTUNES IN THE
WORLD WAR

*

Part I

BEHIND THE LINES

Preface

GREAT times call for great men. There are unknown heroes who are modest, with none of the historical glamour of a Napoleon. If you analysed their character you would find that it eclipsed even the glory of Alexander the Great. Today you can meet in the streets of Prague a shabbily dressed man who is not even himself aware of his significance in the history of the great new era. He goes modestly on his way, without bothering anyone. Nor is he bothered by journalists asking for an interview. If you asked him his name he would answer you simply and unassumingly: 'I am Švejk . . .'

And this quiet, unassuming, shabbily dressed man is indeed that heroic and valiant good old soldier Švejk. In Austrian times his name was once on the lips of all the citizens of the Kingdom of Bohemia, and in the Republic his glory will not fade either.

I am very fond of the good soldier Švejk and in relating his adventures during the world war I am convinced that this modest, anonymous hero will win the sympathy of all of you. Unlike that stupid fellow Herostrates he did not set fire to the temple of the Goddess in Ephesus just to get himself into the newspapers and school books.

And that is enough.

THE AUTHOR

I

The Good Soldier Švejk Intervenes in the Great War

'AND so they've killed our Ferdinand,'[1] said the charwoman to Mr Švejk, who had left military service years before, after having been finally certified by an army medical board as an imbecile, and now lived by selling dogs – ugly, mongrel monstrosities whose pedigrees he forged.

Apart from this occupation he suffered from rheumatism and was at this very moment rubbing his knees with Elliman's embrocation.

'Which Ferdinand, Mrs Müller?' he asked, going on with the

1. The Archduke Franz Ferdinand, nephew of the Austrian Emperor, Franz Joseph, was assassinated with his wife at Sarajevo by the Serbian nationalist, Gavrilo Princip, in 1914.

massaging. 'I know two Ferdinands. One is a messenger at Průša's, the chemist's, and once by mistake he drank a bottle of hair oil there. And the other is Ferdinand Kokoška who collects dog manure. Neither of them is any loss.'

'Oh no, sir, it's His Imperial Highness, the Archduke Ferdinand, from Konopiště, the fat churchy one.'

'Jesus Maria!' exclaimed Švejk. 'What a grand job! And where did it happen to His Imperial Highness?'

'They bumped him off at Sarajevo, sir, with a revolver, you know. He drove there in a car with his Archduchess.'

'Well, there you have it, Mrs Müller, in a car. Yes, of course, a gentleman like him can afford it, but he never imagines that a drive like that might finish up badly. And at Sarajevo into the bargain! That's in Bosnia, Mrs Müller. I expect the Turks did it. You know, we never ought to have taken Bosnia and Herzegovina from them.[1] And so you see, Mrs Müller. His Imperial Highness now rests with the angels. Did he suffer l ong?'

'His Imperial Highness was done for at once, sir. You know, a revolver isn't just a toy. Not long ago there was a gentleman in Nusle, where I come from, who fooled about with a revolver too. And what happened? He shot his whole family and the porter too who came up to see who was doing the shooting there on the third floor.'

'There are some revolvers, Mrs Müller, that won't go off even if you bust yourself. There are lots of that type. But for His Imperial Highness I'm sure they must have bought something better. And I wouldn't mind betting, Mrs Müller, that the chap who did it put on smart togs for the occasion. Potting at an Imperial Highness is no easy job, you know. It's not like a poacher potting at a gamekeeper. The question is how you get at him. You can't come near a fine gentleman like that if you're dressed in rags. You've got to wear a topper, so the cops don't nab you beforehand.'

'They say there were a lot of them, sir.'

'Well, of course, Mrs Müller,' said Švejk, finishing massaging his knees. 'If you wanted to kill His Imperial Highness or for that matter even His Imperial Majesty the Emperor, you'd certainly need advice. Several heads are wiser than one. One chap advises you this, another

---

1. After the Russo-Turkish war of 1877–8 Austria-Hungary occupied Bosnia and Herzegovina. They remained under Turkish suzerainty until 1908 when Austria-Hungary annexed them.

that, and then "the deed is crowned with success", as our national anthem says. The main thing is to watch out for the moment when a gentleman like that rides past. Just like old Luccheni, if you remember, who stabbed our late lamented Elizabeth[1] with a file. He just went for a stroll with her. Who's going to trust anybody now? After that there'll be no more strolls for empresses! And a lot of other persons'll have it coming to them too, you know. You mark my words, Mrs Müller, it'll be the turn of the Tsar and the Tsarina next and maybe, though God forbid, even of His Imperial Majesty the Emperor, now they've started with his uncle.[2] He's got a lot of enemies, the old gentleman has. Even more than Ferdinand. Not long ago a gentleman was telling us in the pub that a time would come when all these emperors would get done in one after the other, and all the king's horses and all the king's men wouldn't save them. After that he hadn't any money to pay his bill and the landlord had to have him arrested. And he hit the landlord across the jaw once and the policeman twice. So after that they took him away in a drunks' cart to sober him up again. Well, Mrs Müller, what a world we live in, to be sure! What a loss for Austria again! When I was in the army an infantryman once shot a captain. He loaded his rifle and went into his office. They told him he had no business there, but he went on insisting he must speak to the captain. The captain came out and at once gave him "confined to barracks!" But he took up his rifle and bang it went, plum through the captain's heart. The bullet flew out of his back and damaged the office into the bargain. It smashed a bottle of ink which messed up the official documents.'

'Oh, goodness, and what happened to that soldier?' asked Mrs Müller later, while Švejk was dressing.

'He hanged himself on his braces,' said Švejk, cleaning his bowler. 'And what's more they weren't even his. He'd borrowed them from the warder on the excuse that his trousers were falling down. Do you think he should have waited until they shot him? You know, Mrs Müller, in a situation like that anyone would be in a flap. They reduced the warder to the ranks because of it and gave him six months. But he didn't sit them out. He ran away to Switzerland and today he's a preacher of some church or other. Today there are very few honest

1. The Empress Elizabeth of Austria was stabbed by an anarchist in 1898 in Switzerland.
2. In fact Franz Ferdinand was the Emperor's nephew.

people about, Mrs Müller. I can imagine that His Imperial Highness, the Archduke Ferdinand, made a mistake in Sarajevo about that chap who shot him. He saw a gentleman and thought, "He must be a decent fellow who's giving me a cheer." And instead of that he gave him bang! bang! Did he give him one bang or several, Mrs Müller?'

'The newspaper says, sir, that His Imperial Highness was riddled like a sieve. He emptied all his cartridges into him.'

'Well, it goes jolly quickly, Mrs Müller, terribly quickly. I'd buy a Browning for a job like that. It looks like a toy, but in a couple of minutes you can shoot twenty archdukes with it, never mind whether they're thin or fat. Although, between you and me, Mrs Müller, a fat archduke's a better mark than a thin one. You may remember the time they shot that king of theirs in Portugal? He was a fat chap too. After all, you wouldn't expect a king to be thin, would you? Well, now I'm going to the pub, The Chalice, and if anyone comes here for that miniature pinscher, which I took an advance on, tell them I've got him in my kennels in the country, that I've only just cropped his ears, and he mustn't be moved until they heal up, otherwise they'll catch cold. Would you please give the key to the house-porter.'

There was only one guest sitting at The Chalice. It was the plain-clothes police officer, Bretschneider, who worked for the State Security. The landlord, Palivec, was washing up the glasses and Bretschneider was vainly endeavouring to engage him in serious conversation.

Palivec was notorious for his foul mouth. Every second word of his was 'arse' or 'shit'. But at the same time he was well read and told everyone to read what Victor Hugo wrote on this subject when he described the last answer Napoleon's Old Guard gave to the British at the Battle of Waterloo.[1]

'Well, it's a glorious summer!' said Bretschneider, embarking on his serious conversation.

'Shit on everything!' answered Palivec, putting the glasses away into a cupboard.

'It's a fine thing they've done to us at Sarajevo,' said Bretschneider with a faint hope.

'Which Sarajevo?' asked Palivec. 'Do you mean the wine cellar at

[1]. When the British Commander called upon Marshal Cambronne to surrender he is reputed to have said: '*Merde!* The guard dies but does not yield.'

Nusle? They're always fighting there, you know. Of course it's Nusle.'

'At Sarajevo in Bosnia, Mr Palivec. They've just shot His Imperial Highness, the Archduke Ferdinand, there. What do you say to that?'

'I don't poke my nose into things like that. They can kiss my arse

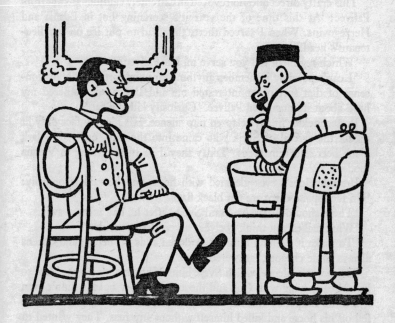

if I do!' Palivec replied politely, lighting his pipe. 'Nowadays, if anyone got mixed up in a business like that, he'd risk breaking his neck. I'm a tradesman and when anyone comes in here and orders a beer I fill up his glass. But Sarajevo, politics or the late lamented Archduke are nothing for people like us. They lead straight to Pankrác.'[1]

Bretschneider lapsed into silence and looked disappointedly round the empty pub.

'Hallo, there used to be a picture of His Imperial Majesty hanging here once,' he started up again after a while. 'Just where the mirror hangs now.'

1. The Prague prison.

'Yes, you're right,' Palivec replied. 'It did hang there, but the flies used to shit on it, so I put it away in the attic. You know, somebody might be so free as to pass a remark about it and then there could be unpleasantness. I don't want that, do I?'

'In Sarajevo it must have been a pretty ugly business, Mr Palivec.'

This crafty direct question evoked an extremely cautious answer from Palivec: 'At this time of the year it's scorching hot in Bosnia and Herzegovina. When I served there, they had to put ice on our lieutenant's head.'

'Which regiment did you serve in, Mr Palivec?'

'I can't possibly remember anything so unimportant. Bloody nonsense of that sort never interested me and I've never bothered my head about it,' answered Palivec. 'Curiosity killed a cat.'

Bretschneider finally relapsed into silence. His gloomy face only lit up on the arrival of Švejk who came into the pub, ordered a dark black beer and remarked: 'Today they'll be in mourning in Vienna too.'

Bretschneider's eyes gleamed with hope, and he said laconically: 'On Konopiště there are ten black flags.'

'There should be twelve,' said Švejk, after he had taken a swig.

'What makes you think twelve?' asked Bretschneider.

'To make it a round number. A dozen adds up better, and dozens always come cheaper,' answered Švejk.

There was a silence, which Švejk himself broke with a sigh: 'And so he's already lying with God and the angels. Glory be! He didn't even live to be Emperor. When I was serving in the army a general once fell off his horse and killed himself without any fuss. They wanted to help him back onto his horse, to lift him up, but to their surprise he was completely dead. And he was going to be promoted Field Marshal. It happened at a review. These reviews never come to any good. In Sarajevo there was a review too. I remember once at a parade like that I had twenty buttons missing from my uniform and they sent me into solitary confinement for a fortnight, where I lay for two days trussed up like Lazarus. But in the army you must have discipline, otherwise why would anyone bother at all? Our Lieutenant Makovec always used to say: "There's got to be discipline, you bloody fools, otherwise you'd be climbing about on the trees like monkeys, but the army's going to make human beings of you, you god-forsaken idiots." And isn't that true? Just imagine a park, let's say at Charles Square, and on every tree an undisciplined soldier! It's enough to give you a nightmare!'

'At Sarajevo,' Bretschneider resumed, 'it was the Serbs who did it.'

'You're wrong there,' replied Švejk. 'It was the Turks, because of Bosnia and Herzegovina.' And Švejk expounded his views on Austrian foreign policy in the Balkans. In 1912 the Turks lost the war with Serbia, Bulgaria and Greece. They had wanted Austria to help them, and when this didn't happen, they shot Ferdinand.

'Do you like the Turks?' said Švejk, turning to Palivec. 'Do you like those heathen dogs? You don't, do you?'

'One customer is as good as another,' said Palivec, 'never mind a Turk. For tradesmen like us politics doesn't enter into it. Pay for your beer, sit down in my pub and jabber what you like. That's my principle. It's all the same to me whether our Ferdinand was done in by a Serb or Turk, Catholic or Moslem, anarchist or Young Czech.'[1]

'All right now, Mr Palivec,' resumed Bretschneider, who was again beginning to despair of catching either of them out, 'but all the same you'll admit that it's a great loss for Austria.'

Švejk replied for the landlord: 'Yes, it's a loss indeed, there's no denying it. A shocking loss. You can't replace Ferdinand by any twopenny-halfpenny idiot. Only he ought to have been still fatter.'

'What do you mean?' Bretschneider livened up.

'What do I mean?' Švejk answered happily. 'Just this. If he'd been fatter then of course he'd certainly have had a stroke long ago, when he was chasing those old women at Konopiště when they were collecting firewood and picking mushrooms on his estate, and he wouldn't have had to die such a shameful death. Just imagine, an uncle of His Imperial Majesty and shot! Why, it's a scandal! The newspapers are full of it. Years ago in our Budějovice a cattle-dealer called Břetislav Ludvík was stabbed in the market place in a petty squabble. He had a son called Bohuslav, and wherever that lad came to sell his pigs, no one wanted to buy anything from him and everyone said: "That's the son of that chap who was stabbed. He's probably a first-class bastard too!" There was nothing for him to do but to jump into the Vltava from that bridge at Krumlov, and they had to drag him out, resurrect

1. A member of the Czech National Liberal Party led by Dr Kramář, later to be the first Premier of the Czechoslovak Republic.

him, pump water out of him, and of course he had to die in the arms of the doctor just when he was giving him an injection.'

'You do make strange comparisons, I must say,' said Bretschneider significantly. 'First you talk about Ferdinand and then about a cattle-dealer.'

'Oh, no, I don't,' Švejk defended himself. 'God forbid my wanting to compare anyone to anybody else. Mr Palivec knows me very well. I've never compared anyone to anybody else, have I? But I wouldn't for the life of me want to be in the skin of that Archduke's widow. What's she going to do now? The children are orphans and the family estate at Konopiště has no master. Marry a new Archduke? What would she get out of that? She'd only go with him to Sarajevo again and be widowed a second time. You know years ago there was a game-keeper in Zliv near Hluboká.[1] He had a very ugly name – Pind'our.[2] Some poachers shot him, and he left a widow and two little babes. Within a year she married another gamekeeper, Pepík Šavel from Mydlovary. And they shot him too. And then she married a third time, again a gamekeeper, and said: "Third time lucky. If it doesn't succeed this time, then I don't know what I shall do." Well, of course, they shot him too, and with all these gamekeepers she had six child-ren altogether. She even went to the office of His Highness the Prince at Hluboká and complained that she'd had trouble with those game-keepers. And so they recommended her a fellow called Jareš[3] who was a water bailiff in the watch tower at Ražice. And, can you imagine it? He was drowned when they were fishing the lake out. And she had two children by him. And then she took a pig-gelder from Vodňany and one night he hit her over the head with his axe and went and gave himself up voluntarily. And when they hanged him afterwards at the district court at Písek he bit the priest's nose and said he didn't regret anything. And he also said something extremely nasty about His Imperial Majesty.'

'And you don't happen to know what he said?' Bretschneider asked hopefully.

'I can't tell you, because no one dared repeat it. But I'm told that it was something so dreadful and horrible that one of the magistrates went mad, and they keep him to this very day in solitary confinement,

1. Famous estate of Prince Schwarzenberg in Southern Bohemia.
2. 'Little cock'.
3. Hašek's grandfather was called Jareš and was a water bailiff.

so that it shan't get out. It wasn't the usual sort of insulting remark which people make about His Imperial Majesty when they're tight.'

'And what sort of insulting remark do people make about His Imperial Majesty when they're tight?' asked Bretschneider.

'Now come, gentlemen, please change the subject,' said Palivec. 'You know, I don't like it. Somebody might talk out of turn and we'd be sorry for it.'

'What sort of insulting remarks do people make about His Imperial Majesty when they're tight?' Švejk repeated. 'All kinds. Get drunk, have the Austrian national anthem played and you'll see what you start saying! You'll think up such a lot about His Imperial Majesty, that if only half of it were true it would be enough to disgrace him all his life. But the old gentleman really doesn't deserve it. Just think! His son Rudolf[1] – lost in tender years, in full flower of his manhood. His wife Elizabeth – stabbed with a file. And then Jan Orth – also lost. His brother, the Emperor of Mexico[2] – put up against a wall and shot in a fortress somewhere. And now again in his old age they've shot his uncle. A chap needs iron nerves for that. And then some drunken bastard starts to swear at him. If the balloon went up today I'd go as a volunteer and serve His Imperial Majesty to my last drop of blood.'

Švejk took a deep draught of beer and continued:

'Do you really think His Imperial Majesty is going to put up with this sort of thing? If so, you don't know him at all. There'll have to be a war with the Turks. "You killed my uncle and so I'll bash your jaw." War is certain. Serbia and Russia will help us in it. There won't half be a blood bath.'

Švejk looked beautiful in this prophetic moment. His simple face, smiling like a full moon, beamed with enthusiasm. Everything was so clear to him.

'It may be,' he said, continuing his account of Austria's future, 'that if we have war with the Turks the Germans'll attack us, because the Germans and the Turks stick together. You can't find bigger bastards anywhere. But we can ally ourselves with France which has had a down

1. Rudolf, the son of the Emperor Franz Joseph and heir to the throne, died mysteriously at his hunting lodge of Mayerling.

2. Archduke Johann gave up his Hapsburg title and called himself Johann Orth. Ferdinand Maximilian, the brother of the Emperor, was crowned Emperor of Mexico. He was taken prisoner and executed in 1867.

on Germany ever since 1871. And then the balloon'll go up. There'll be war. I won't say any more.'

Bretschneider stood up and said solemnly:

'You don't need to. Just come along with me into the passage. I've got something to say to you there.'

Švejk followed the plain-clothes police officer into the passage where a little surprise awaited him. His drinking companion showed him his eaglet[1] and announced that he was arresting him and would take him at once to police headquarters. Švejk tried to explain that the gentleman must be mistaken, that he was completely innocent and that he had not uttered a single word capable of offending anyone.

However, Bretschneider told him that he had in fact committed several criminal offences, including the crime of high treason.

Then they returned to the pub and Švejk said to Palivec:

'I've had five beers, a couple of frankfurters and a roll. Now give me one more slivovice and I must go, because I'm under arrest.'

1. The two-headed eagle was the warrant of the Austrian State Security.

Bretschneider showed Palivec his eaglet, stared at him for a moment and then asked:

'Are you married?'

'I am.'

'And can Madam carry on the business for you during your absence?'

'She can.'

'Then it's all right, Mr Palivec,' said Bretschneider gaily. 'Call your wife here, give the business over to her, and in the evening we'll come for you.'

'Take it easy,' Švejk consoled him. 'I'm only going there for high treason.'

'But what am I going for?' moaned Palivec. 'After all, I've been so careful.'

Bretschneider smiled and said triumphantly:

'Because you said the flies shitted on His Imperial Majesty. They'll certainly knock His Imperial Majesty out of your head there.'

And so Švejk left The Chalice under the escort of the plain-clothes police officer. When they went out into the street his face lit up with its good-natured smile and he asked:

'Should I step down from the pavement?'

'What do you mean?'

'I thought as I'm under arrest I've no right to walk on the pavement.'

When they passed through the door of police headquarters Švejk said:

'Well, the time passed very pleasantly for us there. Do you often go to The Chalice?'

And while they were escorting Švejk to the reception office Palivec at The Chalice handed over the running of the pub to his weeping wife, consoling her in his own inimitable way:

'Don't cry, don't howl. What can they do to me because of some shit on a picture of His Imperial Majesty?'

And thus it was that the good soldier Švejk intervened in the great war in his own sweet, charming way. It will interest historians that he saw far into the future. If the situation subsequently developed otherwise than he had expounded it at The Chalice we must bear in mind that he had never had any preparatory training in diplomacy.

2

The Good Soldier Švejk at
Police Headquarters

THE Sarajevo assassination had filled police headquarters with numerous victims. They were brought in one after another, and the old inspector at the reception office said in his kindly tone:

'That Ferdinand is going to cost you dear.'

When they had locked Švejk up in one of the numerous cells on the first floor, he found six persons already assembled there. Five of them were sitting round the table, and in a corner a middle-aged man was sitting on a bunk, as though trying to avoid the company of the others.

Švejk started asking them in turn why they had been arrested.

From the five sitting at the table he received almost exactly the same answer:

'Because of Sarajevo.' 'Because of Ferdinand.' 'Because of the murder of His Imperial Highness.' 'For Ferdinand.' 'Because they did away with His Imperial Highness at Sarajevo.'

The sixth, who was avoiding the company of the other five, said he did not want to have anything to do with them, in case any suspicion should fall on him. He was only detained here for attempted robbery with murder on a farmer Giles from Holice.

Švejk sat down at the table with the conspirators, who were recounting for at least the tenth time how they had got there.

All, except one, had been taken in a pub, a wine cellar or a café. The exception was an unusually fat gentleman with glasses and tear-stained eyes, who had been arrested in his apartment, because two days before the murder at Sarajevo he had stood drinks to two Serbian students of engineering at the pub U Brejšky and had been seen by detective Brixi drunk in their company in Montmartre in Řetězová Street where, as he had already confirmed by his signature on the police report, he had stood them drinks too.

In reply to all questions during the preliminary investigation at police headquarters he repeated the stereotyped moan:

'I keep a stationer's shop.'

Whereupon he received the equally stereotyped reply:

'That's no excuse.'

The short gentleman, who had been taken in the wine cellar, was a professor of history and was expounding to the landlord the history of various assassinations. He was arrested at the very moment when he had completed a psychological analysis of every assassination and was saying:

'The idea of an assassination is as simple as Columbus's egg.'

'Yes, just as simple as you're for Pankrác,' said the police inspector during the interrogation, capping his remark.

The third conspirator was the president of the charity organization Dobromil at Hodkovičky. On the day the assassination took place Dobromil had organized a garden party with a concert. The sergeant of the gendarmerie came to ask the public to go home, as Austria was in mourning, whereupon the president of Dobromil said good-naturedly: 'Just wait a moment until we have finished playing "Hej Slované".'[1]

Now he was sitting there with bowed head and lamenting:

1. Famous patriotic song in Bohemia calling for the wider use of the Czech language.

'In August we have new elections for the presidency. If I'm not home by then I may not be elected. It's the tenth time I'm president. I'll never survive the shame.'

The late lamented Ferdinand played an odd trick on the fourth detainee, a man of sterling character and blameless reputation. For two whole days he had avoided any talk about Ferdinand until in the evening in the café, while playing mariáš[1] and trumping the king of spades with the seven of clubs, he said:

'Seven pips like at Sarajevo.'

The fifth man, who as he said himself was detained there 'because of that murder of His Imperial Highness at Sarajevo', was so scared that his hair and beard were still standing on end and his head reminded one of a stable pinscher.

This man had not uttered a single word in the restaurant where he had been arrested. He had not even read the newspapers about the murder of Ferdinand and was sitting alone at the table, when a gentleman came up to him, sat down opposite him and said to him quickly:

'Have you read it?'

'No.'

'Do you know about it?'

'No.'

'And do you know what it's about?'

'No, I'm not interested.'

'But you ought to be interested.'

'I don't know what I ought to be interested in. I just smoke my cigar, drink my few glasses, have my supper and don't read the newspapers. The newspapers tell lies. Why should I get excited?'

'And so you're not even interested in the murder at Sarajevo then?'

'I'm not interested in any murder at all, whether it's at Prague, Vienna, Sarajevo or London. For that there are authorities, courts and police. If at any time anywhere they kill anybody it only serves him right. Why is he such a bloody careless fool to let himself get killed?'

Those were his last words in this conversation. From that moment he went on repeating aloud at intervals of five minutes:

'I'm innocent. I'm innocent.'

He screamed out these words at the gate of police headquarters; he is going to repeat them when he is transferred to the criminal court in Prague; and with these words he will enter his prison cell.

1. A popular Czech card game.

When Švejk had heard all these dreadful conspiratorial tales he thought it right to explain to the others the utter hopelessness of their position.

'We're all of us in a nasty jam,' he began his words of comfort. 'You're not right when you say that nothing can happen to you or any of us. What have we got the police for except to punish us for talking out of turn? If the times are so dangerous that archdukes get shot, no one should be surprised if he's carried off to police headquarters. They're doing all this to make a splash, so that Ferdinand can have some publicity before his funeral. The more of us there are here, the better it'll be for us, because it'll be all the jollier. When I was in the army half a company of us were sometimes locked up together. And how many innocent people used to be condemned! And not only in the army but in the civil courts too. I remember once a woman was sentenced for strangling her newly-born twins. Although she swore on oath that she couldn't have strangled twins, when she'd given birth to only one little girl, which she had succeeded in strangling quite painlessly, she was sentenced for double murder all the same. Or that innocent gipsy in Záběhlice, who broke into a greengrocer's shop on Christmas Day in the night. He swore that he'd gone there to get warm, but it didn't help. Once it gets into the hands of the courts it's bad. But that bad has to be. Perhaps all people aren't such scoundrels as you'd think them to be. But how can you tell the good chap from the rotter, especially nowadays at such a serious time as this when they've bumped off Ferdinand? When I served in the army in Budějovice the captain's dog got shot in a forest behind the parade ground. When he learnt about it he summoned us all, made us fall in and ordered every tenth man to step forward. Of course it goes without saying that I was one of the tenth men. And so we stood at attention without batting an eyelid. The captain went along our ranks and said: "You bastards, you, you swine, you, you brutes, you spotted hyenas, you, because of that dog I'd like to send every bloody one of you into solitary confinement, make macaroni out of you, shoot you up and make kedgeree out of you. And to show you I'm not going to be soft with you I'm giving all of you fourteen days c.b." And so there you see. Then it was all because of a mangy cur and now it's all because of no less a person than His Imperial Highness. You have to have some horror, to make the mourning worth while.'

'I'm innocent, I'm innocent,' repeated the man with his hair on end.

'Jesus Christ was innocent too,' said Švejk, 'and all the same they crucified him. No one anywhere has ever worried about a man being innocent. *Maul halten und weiter dienen*![1] – as they used to tell us in the army. That's the best and finest thing of all.'

Švejk lay down on the bunk and fell asleep contentedly.

Meanwhile they brought in two new detainees. One of them was a Bosnian. He walked up and down the cell grinding his teeth and every time he opened his mouth said: '*Jebem ti dušu.*[2] He was tortured by the thought that his pedlar's basket would get lost at police headquarters.

The other new guest was the landlord Palivec. When he saw his friend Švejk, he woke him up and called out in the most tragic tones:

'Now I'm here too!'

Švejk shook his hand cordially and said:

'I'm glad about that, really I am. I knew that gentleman would keep his word when he said that they'd come for you. Punctiliousness like that is a good thing.'

But Palivec remarked that punctiliousness of that sort was not worth a shit and lowering his voice asked Švejk whether the other gentlemen under arrest were thieves, because it might harm his business.

Švejk explained to him that all of them belonged to the same party arrested because of the Archduke, except the man who had been arrested for attempted robbery with murder on a farmer Giles from Holice.

Palivec took umbrage at this and said that he was not here for any pip-squeak of an Archduke but because of His Imperial Majesty. And because the others began to show interest he told them how his flies had defiled His Imperial Majesty.

'They fouled him up for me, the vermin,' he said, ending the description of his adventure, 'and finally they got me locked up. I'll never forgive those flies for that,' he added menacingly.

Švejk went back to bed, but he did not sleep long because they came to take him away for questioning.

And so, mounting the staircase to the 3rd Department for questioning, Švejk carried his cross up on to the hill of Golgotha, sublimely unconscious of his martyrdom.

Observing the notice that spitting in the corridors was prohibited,

1. Famous phrase of Švejk: 'Grin and bear it and get on with the job.'
2. A common obscene oath in Serbian: 'Fuck your soul!'

he asked the policeman to allow him to spit in the spittoon, and, beaming with his natural simplicity, said as he came into the office:

'A very good evening to you all, gentlemen.'

Instead of a reply, someone pummelled him under the ribs and stood him in front of a table, behind which there sat a gentleman with a cold official face and features of such bestial cruelty that he might have just fallen out of Lombroso's book, *Criminal Types*.

He gave Švejk a bloodthirsty look and said:

'Take that idiotic expression off your face.'

'I can't help it,' replied Švejk solemnly. 'I was discharged from the army for idiocy and officially certified by a special commission as an idiot. I'm an official idiot.'

The gentleman of the criminal type ground his teeth:

'What you're accused of and you've committed proves you've got all your wits about you.'

And now he proceeded to enumerate to Švejk a whole series of different crimes, beginning with high treason and ending with abuse of His Majesty and members of the Imperial Family. The central gem of this collection was Švejk's approval of the murder of the Archduke Ferdinand, from which there branched out a string of fresh crimes, among which the shining light was the crime of incitement, as it had all happened in a public place.

'What do you say to that?' the gentleman with features of bestial cruelty asked triumphantly.

'There's a lot of it,' Švejk replied innocently. 'You can have too much of a good thing.'

'So there you are, then, you admit it's true?'

'I admit everything. You've got to be strict. Without strictness no one would ever get anywhere. When I was in the army . . .'

'Shut your mug!' shouted the police commissioner, 'and speak only when you're questioned! Do you understand?'

'Of course I understand,' said Švejk. 'Humbly report, I understand and am able to orientate myself in everything you are pleased to say, sir.'

'Whom are you in contact with?'

'My charwoman, your honour.'

'And you don't have any friends in political circles here?'

'Yes, I do, your honour. I subscribe to the afternoon edition of *Národní Politika* – "The Bitch".'[1]

    1. A famous Prague conservative daily which ceased to appear in 1945.

'Get out!' the gentleman with the bestial appearance roared at Švejk. As they were leading him out of the office, Švejk said:

'Good night, your honour.'

Back in his cell Švejk told all the detainees that this kind of interrogation was fun. 'They shout at you a bit and finally they kick you out.

'In the old days,' continued Švejk, 'it used to be worse. I once read in a book how the accused had to walk on red-hot iron and drink molten lead, to prove whether they were innocent or not. Or else they put their legs into Spanish boots or strung them up on the ladder if they wouldn't confess. Or they burnt their hips with a fireman's torch like they did to St John of Nepomuk.[1] They say that when they did it to him he screamed like blue murder and didn't stop until they had thrown him from Eliška's bridge in a watertight sack. There were many cases like that and even after that they went and quartered the chap or stuck him on a stake somewhere near the Museum. And if a chap like that was only thrown into a dungeon he felt as if he were reborn.

'Nowadays it's fun being locked up,' Švejk continued with relish. 'There's no quartering, no Spanish boots. We've got bunks, a table, a bench. We're not all squashed together like sardines: we get soup; they give us bread and bring us a jug of water. We've got our latrines right under our snouts. You can see progress in everything. It's true that it's a bit far to the interrogation room. You've got to go along more than three corridors and up one staircase, but on the other hand it's clean and lively in the corridors. They bring one person here, another there – young, old, male and female. You can be glad that at least you're not alone here. Everyone goes his own sweet way and no one need be afraid that in the office they'll tell him: "Well, we've considered your case and tomorrow you'll be quartered or burnt. The choice is up to you." That certainly wasn't an easy choice to make, and I think, gentlemen, that many of us at a time like that would be completely flummoxed by it. Yes, nowadays things have improved for our good.'

He had just finished his defence of the modern way of imprisoning citizens, when a warder opened the door and shouted:

'Švejk, get dressed and come for interrogation.'

1. A Czech prelate who was tortured and thrown into the Vltava by order of Wenceslas IV in 1398. He was later canonized and became the symbol of the Counter-Reformation.

'I shall indeed,' answered Švejk. 'I've got no objection, but I'm afraid that there may be some mistake here. I've already been thrown out from interrogation once. And I'm afraid that these other gentlemen who are here with me will be cross with me if I go twice for interrogation when they haven't been there even once the whole evening. They might be jealous of me.'

'Get out and stop talking drivel,' was the reply to Švejk's gentlemanly utterance.

Švejk again found himself face to face with the gentleman of criminal type, who without beating about the bush asked him harshly and irrevocably:

'Do you confess to everything?'

Švejk fixed his good blue eyes on the ruthless man and said softly:

'If you want me to confess, your worship, I shall. It can't do me any harm. But if you say: "Švejk, don't confess to anything", I'll wriggle and wriggle out of it until there isn't a breath left in my body.'

The severe gentleman wrote something on the documents and handing Švejk a pen invited him to sign it.

And Švejk signed Bretschneider's deposition with the following addition:

All the above-named accusations against me are founded on fact.

Josef Švejk

When he had signed, he turned to the severe gentleman:

'Have I got to sign anything else? Or am I to come back in the morning?'

'In the morning you'll be taken off to the criminal court' was the answer.

'At what time, your worship? So that I don't oversleep, for Christ's sake.'

'Get out!' For the second time that day there was a roar from the other side of the table in front of which Švejk was standing.

Returning to his new home behind bars Švejk told the policeman who was escorting him:

'Everything here goes like a house on fire.'

As soon as the door closed behind him, his fellow prisoners deluged him with questions of all kinds, to which he replied clearly:

'I've just admitted that I might have murdered the Archduke Ferdinand.'

Six men crouched in horror under the lice-ridden blankets. Only the Bosnian said:

'*Dobro došli.*'[1]

As he lay down on the bunk Švejk said:

'It's stupid that we haven't got an alarm clock here.'

But in the morning he was woken up without an alarm clock, and at six o'clock sharp he was carried away to the criminal court in the Green Antony.[2]

'The early bird catches the worm,' said Švejk to his fellow travellers when the Green Antony drove out of the gates of police headquarters.

1. 'Welcome.'
2. Black Maria.

3

Švejk before the Medical Experts

THE clean, cosy cubicles of the regional criminal court made the most favourable impression on Švejk – the white-washed walls, the black-painted bars and the fat Mr Demartini, the chief warder for the prisoners on remand, with his purple facings and purple braid on his government-supplied cap. Purple is the colour prescribed not only here, but also at religious services on Ash Wednesday and Good Friday.

The glorious times of Roman rule over Jerusalem were coming back. The prisoners were led out and brought before the Pontius Pilates of 1914 down on the ground floor. And the examining magistrates, the Pilates of modern times, instead of honourably washing their hands, sent to Teissig's for goulash and Pilsen beer and passed more and more indictments to the Director of Prosecutions.

Here all logic mostly disappeared and the § triumphed. The § strangled, went mad, fumed, laughed, threatened, murdered and gave no quarter. The magistrates were jugglers with the law, high priests of its letter, devourers of the accused, tigers of the Austrian jungle, who measured their spring on the accused by the number of clauses.

The exception were a few gentlemen (as at police headquarters) who did not take the law quite so seriously, for everywhere wheat can be found among the tares.

It was to one of these gentlemen that they conducted Švejk for questioning. He was an elderly gentleman of affable appearance who, when he was once interrogating the notorious murderer, Valeš, never failed to tell him: 'Be so good as to sit down, Mr Valeš. There is an empty chair just here.'

When they led Švejk before him, with his natural amiability he asked him to sit down and said:

'So you are this Mr Švejk, then?'

'I think I must be,' answered Švejk, 'because my papa was Mr Švejk and my mamma was Mrs Švejk. I can't disgrace them by denying my own name.'

A kindly smile flitted across the face of the examining magistrate:

'Well, you've been up to a fine lot of things. You've certainly got a great deal on your conscience.'

'I've always got a great deal on my conscience,' said Švejk, smiling even more affably than the magistrate. 'I've probably got more on my conscience than Your Worship is pleased to have.'

'Well, that's clear from the statement you've signed,' said the magistrate in a no less affable tone. 'They didn't bring any pressure on you at the police station, did they?'

'Why, of course not, Your Worship. I asked them myself if I had to sign it, and when they told me to do so I obeyed. After all, I wouldn't want to quarrel with them just because of my signature, would I? It certainly wouldn't be in my interest to do that. There must be law and order.'

'Do you feel completely well, Mr Švejk?'

'Not completely well, no, I wouldn't say that, Your Worship. I've got rheumatism and I rub myself with Elliman's embrocation.'

The old gentleman again gave a kindly smile. 'What would you say if we were to have you examined by our medical experts?'

'I don't think that I can be so bad that these gentlemen need unnecessarily waste their time on me. I was examined by one doctor already at police headquarters to see if I'd got V.D.'

'You know, all the same, Mr Švejk, we'll try with these medical experts. We'll set up a nice commission and keep you in remand under investigation. In the meantime you'll have a nice rest. Now just one more question: is it true, as it is stated in the report, that you declared and widely disseminated the view that war would soon break out?'

'Oh, yes, Your Worship, and it will break out very soon indeed.'

'And you don't occasionally feel run down by any chance?'

'Oh, no, sir, I was only once nearly run down by a car on Charles Square but that was many years ago.'

That concluded the interrogation. Švejk shook hands with the magistrate and after having returned to his cell said to his neighbours:

'Now all because of that murder of His Imperial Highness, the Archduke Ferdinand, they're going to have me examined by the medical experts.'

'I've been examined by those medical experts too,' said a young man. 'That was when I had to come before a jury about some carpets. They certified me as feeble-minded. Now I've embezzled a steam threshing machine and they can't do anything to me. My lawyer told me yesterday that once I've been certified feeble-minded, I'll have the benefit of it for the rest of my life.'

'I don't trust those medical experts at all,' observed the man with the intelligent appearance. 'Once when I forged some bills of exchange I prepared myself for all eventualities and went to lectures by the psychiatrist Dr Heveroch, and when they caught me, I pretended to be a paralytic, exactly as Dr Heveroch had described one. I bit one of the medical experts on the commission in the leg, drank ink out of the ink pot and relieved myself, if you'll pardon the expression, gentlemen, in the corner in the view of the whole commission. But because I bit one of them through the calf they certified me as completely fit and so I was done for.'

'I'm not a bit afraid of these gentlemen's examinations,' said Švejk.

'When I was in the army a vet examined me and it didn't turn out at all badly.'

'Medical experts are swine,' the short man with a stoop broke in. 'Not long ago quite by chance they dug up a skeleton in my meadow, and the medical experts said that it was murdered forty years ago by some blunt object on the head. I'm thirty-eight and I've been gaoled, although I have my birth certificate, an extract from the parish register and my identity card.'

'I think that we should be fair about everything,' said Švejk. 'After all, anybody can and must make a mistake, the more he thinks about a thing. Medical experts are human beings and human beings have their faults. Once in Nusle, just by the bridge across the Botič, a gentleman came up to me in the night, when I was coming back from U Banzetů, and hit me over the head with a knout. And when I was lying on the ground he flashed his torch on me and said: "It's a mistake. It's not him." And he got so angry because he'd made a mistake that he hit me on the back again. It's only human nature that a chap should go on making mistakes until he dies. It's just like that gentleman who one night found a mad, half-frozen dog, took it home with him and put it in his wife's bed. As soon as it had got warmed up it bit the whole family and tore to pieces and devoured the baby in the cradle. Or I can give you an example of a mistake a turner who lives in our house once made. He opened the chapel at Podolí with his key, because he thought it was his kitchen, and lay down on the altar because he thought that he was home in bed. And then he pulled over himself some cloths with holy inscriptions and put the New Testament and other sacred books under his head to make it higher. In the morning he was found by the sexton and when he came to himself he told him quite good-humouredly that it was only a little mistake. "A nice little mistake," said the sexton, "when all because of it we shall have to have the church re-consecrated." After that the turner came before the medical experts and they proved to him that he had been completely sensible and sober, because if he had been tight, they said, he wouldn't have been able to fit the key into the lock of the chapel door. Afterwards that turner died in Pankrác. I can also give you another example of how a police dog at Kladno made a mistake. It was an Alsatian which belonged to the famous cavalry captain, Rotter. Captain Rotter bred these dogs and experimented with them on tramps, until all the tramps began to avoid the district of Kladno. And so he gave orders that the gendarmes must bring in some suspicious individual without fail. Well, once they brought him a quite respectably dressed man, whom they'd found in the Forest of Lány sitting on a tree stump. The captain at once had a piece of his coat-tails cut off and given to his police dogs to sniff. And then they took the man away to a brick works behind the town and set their trained dogs on to his tracks. The dogs found him and brought him back again. Then the man had to climb up a ladder to a loft, leap over a wall and jump into a lake with the dogs after him. In the end it turned out that he was a deputy of the Czech Radical Party who had gone for an outing in the woods of Lány after having got bored with parliament. And that's why I say that people are erring creatures by nature, they make errors, never mind whether they're learned people or stupid uneducated idiots. Even ministers make mistakes.'

whose mistake

The commission of medical experts, which had to decide whether Švejk's mental horizon did or did not correspond to all the crimes with which he was charged, consisted of three unusually solemn gentlemen whose views were such that the view of each differed gloriously from any of the views of the other two.

Three different scientific schools and psychiatric views were represented there.

If in the case of Švejk complete agreement had been reached between these opposing scientific camps, it can be explained purely and simply by the stunning impression he produced upon them when he entered the room where his mental state was to be examined and, observing a picture of the Austrian monarch hanging on the wall, cried out:

'Long live our Emperor, Franz Joseph I, gentlemen.'

The case was clear as daylight. Švejk's spontaneous declaration disposed of a whole range of questions, and there only remained a few very important questions which were needed so that from Švejk's answers the initial opinion of him could be confirmed according to the system of the psychiatrist Dr Kallerson, Dr Heveroch and the Englishman, Weiking.

'Is radium heavier than lead?'

'Please, sir, I haven't weighed it,' answered Švejk with his sweet smile.

'Do you believe in the end of the world?'

'I'd have to see that end first,' Švejk answered nonchalantly. 'But certainly I shan't see it tomorrow.'

'Would you know how to calculate the diameter of the globe?'

'No, I'm afraid I wouldn't,' answered Švejk, 'but I'd like to ask you a riddle myself, gentlemen. Take a three-storied house, with eight windows on each floor. On the roof there are two dormer windows

and two chimneys. On every floor there are two tenants. And now, tell me, gentlemen, in which year the house-porter's grandmother died?'

The medical experts exchanged knowing looks, but nevertheless one of them asked this further question:

'You don't know the maximum depth of the Pacific Ocean?'

'No, please sir, I don't,' was the answer, 'but I think that it must be definitely deeper than the Vltava below the rock of Vyšehrad.'

The chairman of the commission asked briefly: 'Is that enough?', but nonetheless another member requested the following question:

'How much is 12,897 times 13,863?'

'729,' answered Švejk, without batting an eyelid.

'I think that that will do,' said the chairman of the commission. 'You can take the accused back where he came from.'

'Thank you, gentlemen,' replied Švejk deferentially. 'For me it will do too.'

After his departure the three agreed that Švejk was a patent imbecile and idiot according to all the natural laws invented by the luminaries of psychiatry.

The report which was passed to the examining magistrate contained *inter alia* the following:

The undersigned medical experts certify the complete mental feebleness and congenital idiocy of Josef Švejk, who appeared before the aforesaid commission and expressed himself in terms such as: 'Long live our Emperor Franz Joseph I', which utterance is sufficient to illuminate the state of mind of Josef Švejk as that of a patent imbecile.

The undersigned commission accordingly recommends:
1. That the investigation of Josef Švejk be quashed.
2. That Josef Švejk be sent to a psychiatrical clinic for observation to establish how far his mental state is a danger to his surroundings.

While this report was being compiled Švejk was telling his fellow prisoners: 'They didn't care a hoot about Ferdinand, but talked to me about even stupider nonsense. Finally we agreed that what we talked about was quite enough for us and we parted.'

'I don't believe anyone,' observed the short man with a stoop on whose meadow a skeleton happened to have been dug up. 'They're all of them a gang of crooks.'

'There have to be crooks in this world too,' said Švejk, lying down on his straw mattress. 'If everyone were honest with each other, they'd soon start punching each other's noses.'

4

Švejk Thrown out of the Lunatic Asylum

WHEN Švejk subsequently described life in the lunatic asylum, he did so in exceptionally eulogistic terms: 'I really don't know why those loonies get so angry when they're kept there. You can crawl naked on the floor, howl like a jackal, rage and bite. If anyone did this anywhere on the promenade people would be astonished, but there it's the most common or garden thing to do. There's a freedom there which not even Socialists have ever dreamed of. A chap can pass himself off as God Almighty, the Virgin Mary, the Pope, the King of England, His Imperial Majesty or St Wenceslas, although the chap who said he was St Wenceslas was tied up naked all day long and lay in solitary confinement. There was also a chap who shouted out that he was the Archbishop, but all he did was to eat, and, if you'll pardon the expression, do something else which rhymes with it – excrete – but no one's ashamed of doing that there. One chap even pretended to be St Cyril and St Methodius just to get a double portion. And there was one gentleman there who was pregnant and invited everyone to the christening. There were many people shut up there who were chess players, politicians, fishermen and scouts, stamp collectors and amateur photographers. One person was there because of some old pots which he called funerary urns. One was in a straitjacket all the time so that he shouldn't be able to calculate when the world would come to an end. And I also met a certain number of professors there. One of them used to follow me about all the time and expatiate on how the cradle of the gipsy race was in the Krkonoše, and the other explained to me that inside the globe there was another globe much bigger than the outer one.

'Everyone there could say exactly what he pleased and what was on the tip of his tongue, just as if he was in parliament. Sometimes they used to tell each other fairy stories and started fighting when something very bad happened to a princess. The wildest of them all was a gentleman who pretended to be the sixteenth volume of *Otto's Encyclopedia* and asked everybody to open him and to find the entry:

"Cardboard box stapling machine", otherwise he would be done for. He only quietened down when they put him in a straitjacket. Then he was happy, because he thought he had got into a bookbinder's press and begged to be given a modern trim. It was really like living in paradise there. You could kick up a row, fight, sing, cry, bleat, yell, jump, say your prayers, turn somersaults, crawl on all fours, hop, run about, dance, skip, squat all day on your haunches and climb up the walls. No one would come to you and tell you: "You mustn't do that, sir. It's not decent. You should be ashamed of yourself. Aren't you properly brought up?" It's true however that there are loonies there who are quite quiet. There was one well brought-up inventor, for instance, who continually picked his nose and said only once a day: "I've just discovered electricity." As I say it was very pleasant there and those few days which I spent in the lunatic asylum are among the loveliest hours of my life.'

And indeed the very welcome which awaited Švejk in the asylum, when they had taken him away from the criminal court and brought him there for observation, surpassed his expectations. First they stripped him naked, then they gave him a hospital gown and led him off to have a bath, holding him familiarly under his arms, while one of the male nurses entertained him by telling him some jokes about Jews. In the bathroom they immersed him in a tub of warm water, and then pulled him out and put him under a cold douche. They repeated this three times and then asked him how he liked it. Švejk said that it was better than in the baths near the Charles Bridge, and that he liked bathing very much. 'If you'll only cut my nails and my hair too, I'll have everything I need to make me completely happy,' he added with a pleasant smile.

And this request of his was granted too, and after they had thoroughly rubbed him down with a sponge as well, they wrapped him in a sheet, carried him off to the first ward, put him on to a bed, covered him with a quilt and asked him to go to sleep.

And even today Švejk talks about it with affection: 'Just imagine, they carried me, really carried me off. I was in a state of utter bliss at that moment.'

And indeed he fell blissfully asleep on the bed. Then they woke him to offer him a mug of milk and a roll. The roll was already cut up into little pieces and while one of the warders held both his arms, the other dipped the pieces of roll into the milk and fed him like a goose is

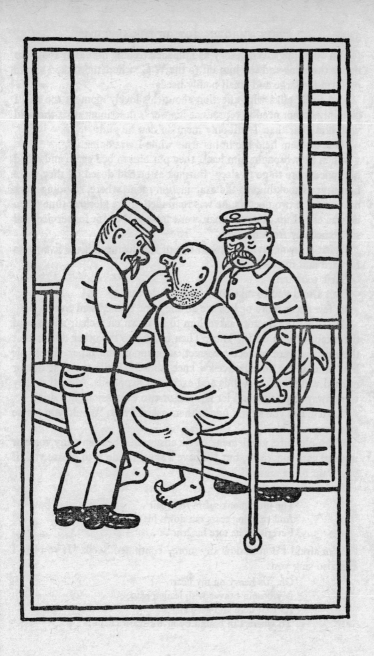

fed on dumplings. When they had finished feeding him, they took him under the arms and led him off to the W.C., where they asked him to perform his large and small bodily needs.

And Švejk talks with affection about this lovely moment too and I certainly do not need to reproduce his words describing what they did with him after that. I will only mention that he said:

'One of them held me in his arms while I was doing it.'

When they brought him back, they put him to bed again and asked him once more to go to sleep. But just as he had dozed off they woke him up and took him to the examination room, where, standing stark naked before two doctors, he was reminded of the glorious time when he was called up. The German word '*tauglich*' or 'fit for service' fell spontaneously from his lips.

'What are you saying?' asked one of the doctors. 'Take five paces forward and five to the rear.'

Švejk took ten.

'But I told you to take five,' said the doctor.

'A few paces more or less are all the same to me,' said Švejk.

After that the doctors asked him to sit down on a chair and one of them tapped him on the knee. Then he said to the other doctor that the reflexes were perfectly correct, whereupon the other shook his head and began to tap Švejk's knee himself, while the first doctor opened wide Švejk's eyelids and examined his pupils. After that they went away to a table and let fall one or two expressions in Latin.

'Listen, can you sing?' one of them asked Švejk. 'Would you please sing us a song?'

'With pleasure, gentlemen,' Švejk answered. 'I haven't any voice or musical ear, you know, but I'll have a shot. I'll do it to please you, if you want to be amused.'

And Švejk struck up:

> 'The little monk sat in the chair
> And scalding tears ran down his cheeks.
> Feverishly he tore his hair . . .

'I'm afraid I don't know any more,' continued Švejk. 'If you like I can also sing you:

> 'Oh, 'tis heavy on my heart,
> My bosom heaves with leaden pain,
> As I sit here and gaze afar,
> To where I'm bound by love's sweet chain . .

'And I can't remember any more of that either,' sighed Švejk. 'I also know the first verse of "Where is my home?"[1] and "General Windischgrätz as the cock did crow". And a few folk songs too, like "God save our Emperor and land", "When we marched to Jaroměř" and "Hail to Thee, Holy Virgin, hail a thousand times" . . .'

The learned doctors exchanged glances, and one of them put the following question to Švejk:

'Have you ever had your mental condition examined?'

'In the army,' Švejk replied solemnly and proudly, 'I was officially certified by military doctors as a patent idiot.'

'I believe you're a malingerer!' the other doctor shouted at Švejk.

'What, me, gentlemen?' said Švejk, defending himself. 'No, I assure you I'm no malingerer. I'm a genuine idiot. You only have to ask at České Budějovice or at the reserve command at Karlín.'

1. Afterwards the Czech national anthem.

The elder of the two doctors waved his hand in a gesture of despair and pointing to Švejk said to the nurses: 'Give this man back his clothes and send him to the third class in the first corridor. Then one of you come back and take all his papers to the office. And tell them there to settle the case quickly, so that we don't have him round our necks for long.'

The doctors cast another devastating look at Švejk who backed deferentially to the door, bowing politely. When one of the nurses asked him what nonsense he was up to now, he answered: 'As I'm not dressed, I'm naked and I wouldn't like to show these gentlemen anything, in case they should think me rude or vulgar.' From the moment the nurses received orders to return Švejk's clothes to him, they no longer showed the slightest concern for him. They told him to get dressed, and one of them took him to the third class where, during the few days it took the office to complete his discharge formalities, he had an opportunity of carrying on his agreeable observations. The disappointed doctors gave him a certificate that he was a 'malingerer whose mind was affected', but as they discharged him before he was given any lunch it led to a minor scene.

Švejk declared that if they threw anyone out of a lunatic asylum they had no right to do so without giving him lunch.

This breach of the public peace was stopped by a police officer who had been summoned by the asylum porter and who took Švejk off to the police station in Salmova Street.

5

Švejk at the Police Station in Salmova Street

AFTER Švejk's beautiful, sunny days in the asylum came hours full of persecution. Police Inspector Braun set the scene for his meeting with Švejk with all the cruelty of Roman lictors in the time of the charming Emperor Nero. With the same ruthlessness as they said: 'Throw this scoundrel of a Christian to the lions', Inspector Braun said: 'Put him behind bars.'

Not a word more or less, except that Inspector Braun's eyes shone with a peculiarly perverted lust.

Švejk bowed and said proudly: 'I'm ready, gentlemen. I believe behind bars means the same as a prison cell, and that's not too bad.'

'Don't make yourself too much at home here,' answered the police officer, whereupon Švejk piped up: 'I'm quite modest and grateful for anything you do for me.'

In the cell a man was sitting on a plank-bed deep in thought. He sat listlessly, and it was clear from his expression that when the key grated in the lock of the cell he did not believe that the door would open to set him free.

'My compliments, Your Honour,' said Švejk, sitting down beside him on the plank-bed. 'What time might it be?'

'Time is not my master,' the thoughtful man answered.

'It's not too bad here,' Švejk continued: 'They've at least planed the wood on this plank-bed.'

The solemn man made no reply. He stood up and began to rush about in the tiny space between the door and the bed, as if he were hurrying to save something.

In the meantime Švejk observed with interest the writings scrawled upon the walls. There was one inscription in which an unknown prisoner solemnly pledged to heaven a fight to the death with the police. It read: 'You won't half catch it.' Another prisoner had written: 'Buzz off, you cops.' Another merely recorded the plain fact: 'I was locked up here on 5 June 1913 and wasn't too badly treated. Josef Mareček, tradesman from Vršovice.' And there was another inscription which was earth-shaking in its profundity: 'Have mercy, Almighty God . . .' And underneath: 'Kiss my a—.' The letter 'a' had been crossed out however and instead was written in capitals: 'COAT TAILS'. Beside it some poetical soul had written the lines: 'I sit in

sorrow by the stream. The sun is hid behind the fells. I watch the radiant mountain tops, Where my best beloved dwells.'

The man who was rushing between the door and the plank-bed as though he was trying to win a marathon race stopped and breathlessly resumed his seat. He plunged his head in his hands and suddenly screamed: 'Let me out!'

'No, they won't let me out,' he said to himself. 'They won't. They won't. I've been here since six o'clock this morning.'

He then had a fit of expansiveness, stood up erect and asked Švejk:

'You don't by any chance have a strap on you, so that I can end it all?'

'That's something I can very gladly help you with,' answered Švejk, undoing his belt. 'I've never yet seen anyone hang himself on a strap in a prison cell.

'Only it's a nuisance that there's no hook here,' he went on, looking around him. 'The window latch won't bear your weight, unless you hang yourself kneeling by the plank-bed, like the monk did in the Emmaus monastery, when he hanged himself on a crucifix because of a young Jewess. I'm very fond of suicides, so just carry on. Well begun is half done.'

The gloomy man, into whose hands Švejk had pushed the strap, gave it one look, threw it into the corner and burst out crying, smearing his tears with his black hands and shrieking out: 'I've got little children! I'm here for drunkenness and immoral practices. My God, my poor wife, what will they say to me in the office? I've got little children! I'm here for drunkenness and immoral practices' etc. etc. *ad infinitum*.

At last, however, he calmed down a little, went to the door and began to kick it and pound it with his fists. From behind the door could be heard steps and a voice: 'What do you want?'

'Let me out,' he said in a voice which sounded as if he had nothing left to live for. 'Where to?' came the answer from the other side.

'To my office,' answered the unfortunate father, official, drunkard and libertine.

Laughter could be heard in the quiet of the passage, horrible laughter, and the steps went away again.

'It seems to me that that gentleman must hate you if he laughs at you like that,' said Švejk, when the despairing man sat down beside him again. 'A policeman like that might do a lot of harm when he gets angry, and when he gets angrier still he might do anything. Just sit down quietly, if you don't want to hang yourself, and wait and see how things develop. If you're an official, you're married and you have little babes, it's frightful, I must admit. If I'm not mistaken you're probably convinced that they'll sack you from the office.'

'I can't say,' he sighed, 'because I don't remember myself what I was up to. I only know that I got thrown out from somewhere and that I wanted to get back there to light a cigar. But it started splendidly. Our departmental chief was celebrating his name day and invited us to a wine restaurant. Then we went to a second, a third, a fourth, a fifth, a sixth, a seventh, an eighth, a ninth . . .'

'Wouldn't you like me to help you count?' asked Švejk. 'I'm a bit of an expert. One night I was in twenty-eight pubs. But, God's truth, I never had at the most more than three glasses of beer in any one of them.'

'In short,' continued the unfortunate subordinate of the departmental chief who had celebrated his name day in such magnificent style, 'when we'd been in about a dozen different night dens we discovered we'd lost our chief, although we'd tied him with string and led him with us like a little dog. And so we went to look for him everywhere and finally we all lost each other until in the end I found myself in one of those night cafés in Vinohrady, a very decent place, where I drank a liqueur straight out of the bottle. What I did afterwards I can't remember. I only know that when they brought me to the police station here two policemen reported that I was drunk, had been behaving immorally, had hit a lady, taken down somebody else's hat from the peg and cut it in shreds with my penknife, chased away the ladies' orchestra, accused the head waiter in front of everyone of stealing twenty crowns, smashed the marble slab at the table where I was sitting and intentionally spat into the black coffee of a stranger at the next table. I didn't do anything else. At least I can't remember having done so. And, believe me, I'm a decent, intelligent man who hasn't a thought for anything except his family. What do you say to that? I'm certainly not a hooligan!'

Švejk made no reply but asked with interest: 'Did you have much trouble smashing that marble slab or did you do it at one go?'

'At one go,' answered the intelligent gentleman.

'Then you're for it,' said Švejk pensively. 'They'll prove to you that you coached yourself for it with intensive training. And that stranger's coffee which you spat into, was it with rum or not?'

And without waiting for an answer he explained:

'If it was with rum, then it'll be worse for you, because it's more expensive. In the court they reckon up every item and add them together so that it amounts at least to a crime.'

'In the court ...' the conscientious paterfamilias whispered dejectedly and, hanging his head, lapsed into that unpleasant state in which a man is devoured by the reproaches of his conscience.[1]

---

1. Some writers use the expression: 'gnawed by the reproaches of his conscience'. I do not regard this expression as altogether appropriate. After all, a tiger devours a man and does not gnaw him. (Author's note.)

'And do they know at home that you're in gaol,' Švejk asked, 'or will they wait till it's in the paper?'

'Do you think it will be in the paper?' was the naïve question of the victim of the name day party of his departmental chief.

'Why, it's a dead certainty,' was the frank answer, for Švejk was never one to conceal anything from others. 'All the newspaper readers will get a great kick out of what you did. I also like to read that column about drunks and their escapades. Not long ago at the pub The Chalice one of the guests didn't do anything more than break his own head with a glass. He threw the glass up into the air and then stood underneath it. But they carried him off and the very next morning we read it in the papers. Or in Bendlovka I once slapped an undertaker's mute and he slapped me back. To restore peace between us they had to arrest us both, and at once it was in the afternoon paper. Or when that Councillor smashed two cups in the café The Corpse, do you imagine they spared him? It was immediately in the newspapers the day after. All you can do is to send a correction to the papers from gaol saying that the information published about you has nothing to do with you, and that you're no relative of the person of that name and have no connection with him. And you must write home and tell them to cut your correction out of the paper and keep it, so that you can read it when you've served out your sentence.

'Aren't you cold?' asked Švejk, who was full of compassion when he saw that the intelligent gentleman was shivering. 'This year the summer has turned very cold.'

'I am done for,' sobbed Švejk's companion. 'I've lost my promotion now.'

'You certainly have,' Švejk agreed readily. 'And if they don't take you back in to the office after you've served out your sentence I don't know whether you'll find another job so quickly, because anyone at all you wanted to work for, even if it was a skinner, would require from you a certificate of good conduct. No, a moment of debauchery like what you've indulged in costs you dear. And will your wife and children have anything to live on while you're sitting in gaol? Or will she have to go and beg and teach the babes all sorts of vices?'

A sob could be heard:

'My poor little babes! My poor wife!'

The conscienceless penitent stood up and started talking about his babes: he had five. The eldest was twelve and was one of those scouts.

He only drank water and ought to have been an example to his father, who had misbehaved like this for the first time in his life.

'A scout?' exclaimed Švejk. 'I like hearing about those scouts. Once in Mydlovary near Zliv, district Hluboká, police district České Budějovice, just when we of the 91st were doing our training, the peasants from the neighbourhood started a hunt for scouts who were swarming in the parish wood. They caught three of them. When they tied up the smallest of them, he moaned, squealed and wailed so much that we hardened soldiers could not bear the sight of it and thought it better to clear off. While these three scouts were being tied up they bit eight peasants. Afterwards under the torture of the birch they confessed before the mayor that there wasn't a single meadow in the region they hadn't flattened out while they lay sunbathing. And then again they said that it was only by pure accident that the field of standing corn near Ražice burnt down. It was just before the harvest and they only happened to be roasting a deer on a spit in the middle of it – one they'd stalked and killed with their knives in the parish wood. In their hide-out in the wood were found more than half a hundred-weight of gnawed bones of poultry and game, an enormous quantity of cherry stones, heaps of cores of unripe apples and other good things.'

The scout's poor father was not to be comforted, however.

'What have I done?' he wailed. 'My reputation is ruined.'

'It certainly is,' said Švejk with his characteristic frankness. 'After all you've done your reputation will certainly be ruined for life. When your friends have read all about it in the newspapers they'll certainly add something to it of their own. They always do that, but don't be worried about it. There are ten times more people in the world with blemished reputations than there are with unblemished ones! That's just a very unimportant trifle.'

In the passage energetic steps could be heard, the key grated in the lock, the door opened and a policeman called Švejk's name.

'Excuse me,' said Švejk chivalrously, 'I've only been here since twelve noon, but this gentleman has been here since six o'clock this morning. I'm not in any hurry anyway.'

Instead of getting an answer Švejk was dragged into the passage by the powerful arm of a policeman and silently led up the stairs to the first floor. In the second room a police inspector was sitting at a table. He was a fat gentleman of amiable countenance and said to Švejk:

'So you're this Švejk, then? And how did you get here?'

'The most common or garden way in the world,' answered Švejk. 'I came here under the escort of a police officer, because I wasn't going to put up with them throwing me out of the lunatic asylum without any lunch. It was as though they took me for a kicked-out whore.'

'All right, Švejk,' said the inspector affably, 'why should we have to be bothered with you here at Salmova Street? Wouldn't it be better to send you to police headquarters?'

'You're master of the situation, as the saying goes,' said Švejk with composure. 'A walk to police headquarters now in the evening would be quite a pleasant little stroll.'

'I am glad that we agree about that,' said the inspector cheerfully. 'It's much better when we agree, isn't it, Švejk?'

'And I'm always awfully glad to take advice from anyone too,' replied Švejk. 'I'll never forget your kindness to me, inspector. Believe me I won't.'

Bowing deferentially he went down to the guardroom accompanied by the police officer, and a quarter of an hour later could be seen at the corner of Ječná Street and Charles Square under the escort of another police officer who was carrying under his arm a voluminous book of prisoners' records with the German title *Arrestantenbuch*.

At the corner of Spálená Street Švejk and his escort met a crowd of people who were surging round a placard that had been hung up.

'That's His Imperial Majesty's proclamation on the declaration of war,' said the police officer to Švejk.

'I prophesied it,' said Švejk, 'but in the lunatic asylum they still don't know about it, although they should have got it from the horse's mouth.'

'What do you mean?' the police officer asked Švejk.

'Because they've got a lot of officer gentlemen locked up there,' Švejk explained, and when they reached another crowd of people surging in front of the proclamation, Švejk shouted out:

'God save our Emperor Franz Joseph! We shall win this war!'

Someone in the enthusiastic crowd banged his hat over his ears, and so the good soldier Švejk, surrounded by a crowd of people, stepped once more through the gates of police headquarters.

'Quite definitely we'll win this war. I repeat it once more, gentlemen!'

And with these words Švejk took leave of the crowd which accompanied him.

And somewhere from the dim ages of history the truth dawned upon Europe that the morrow would obliterate the plans of today.

6

Švejk Home Again after having Broken through the Vicious Circle

THE spirit of alien authority pervaded the building of the police headquarters – an authority which was ascertaining how enthusiastic the population were for the war. With the exception of a few people who were ready to admit that they were sons of a nation which had to bleed for interests completely alien to it, police headquarters presented the finest collection of bureaucratical beasts of prey, to whom gaols and gallows were the only means of defending the existence of the twisted clauses of the law.

They treated their victims with malicious affability, weighing every word carefully in advance.

'I am very sorry that you've fallen into our hands again,' said one of these black and yellow striped vultures, when they brought Švejk before him. 'We thought that you'd reform, but we've been disappointed.'

Švejk mutely nodded his head and assumed so innocent an expression that the black and yellow vulture looked at him inquiringly and said emphatically:

'Take that imbecile expression off your face.'

But he immediately went over to an amiable tone and continued:

'Of course it's very disagreeable for us to keep you in custody, and I can assure you that in my opinion your guilt can't be so enormous. With your absence of intelligence you must obviously have been led astray. Tell me, Mr Švejk, who was it really who led you to commit such stupidities?'

Švejk coughed and replied:

'Begging your pardon, sir, I know nothing of any stupidities.'

'But wasn't it stupidity, Mr Švejk,' he said in an artificially paternal tone, 'when, according to the deposition of the police officer who brought you here, you caused a crowd of people to collect in front of the war proclamation which was posted up at the corner, and you incited people with shouts of: "God Save Our Emperor Franz Joseph! This war is already won!"?'

'I couldn't hang back,' declared Švejk, fixing his honest eyes on the eyes of the inquisitor. 'I was so angry when I saw how they were all reading this proclamation and none of them were expressing any joy. There were no shouts of "God Save Our Emperor", no hurrahs, nothing at all, inspector. It was just as if they didn't care. An old soldier of the 91st regiment like me couldn't go on looking at it and so I shouted out those words. And I believe that had you been in my place you'd have done exactly the same as I did. If there's a war it must be won and people must call out "God Save Our Emperor." No one will talk me out of that!'

Crushed and overcome the black and yellow wolf could not withstand the gaze of the pure and innocent lamb, Švejk. He lowered his gaze on to the official documents and said:

'I give you full marks for your enthusiasm, but if only it had been displayed in different circumstances! After all you know very well that you were under police escort and that a patriotic pronouncement like that could and must have been regarded by the public as ironic rather than serious.'

'When a chap is being led under police escort,' answered Švejk, 'it's a very hard moment in his life. And if a man, even in such a difficult moment as that, doesn't forget what he ought to do when there's a war on, I think he's not so bad after all.'

The black and yellow wolf growled and looked Švejk in the eyes once more.

Švejk parried with the innocent, gentle, modest and tender warmth of his gaze.

For a moment they both went on staring fixedly at each other.

'Go to hell, Švejk,' said the official at last, 'and if you ever come here again, I shan't ask you any questions but march you straight off to the military court at Hradčany. Do you understand?'

But before he could say Jack Robinson, Švejk had stepped towards him, kissed his hand and said:

'May the good Lord reward you for everything! If at any time you should need a thoroughbred little dog, just ask me. I deal in dogs.'

And so Švejk found himself at liberty again and on his way home.

He could not make up his mind whether he should stop first at The Chalice. Finally he decided he would and opened the door through which he had gone out some time ago under the escort of detective Bretschneider.

A deathly silence reigned in the bar. A few guests sat there, including the sexton from St Apollinaire. They looked very gloomy. Behind the serving counter sat Mrs Palivec and stared dully at the beer taps.

'Well, here I am back again,' said Švejk gaily. 'May I have a glass of beer, please? What's happened to Mr Palivec? Is he home again too?'

Instead of replying Mrs Palivec burst into tears and concentrating all her misery on to a special stress on every word groaned out:

'A week ago he – got – ten – years.'

'There you are, then,' said Švejk, 'so he's already served seven days of it.'

'He was always so careful,' sobbed Mrs Palivec. 'He always said that about himself.'

The customers in the bar maintained a stubborn silence, as though the spirit of Palivec was haunting the room and urging them to even greater caution.

'Caution is the mother of wisdom,' said Švejk, sitting down at a table to a glass of beer. In the foam there were little holes made by Mrs Palivec's tears as they fell into it when she brought the glass to the table for Švejk. 'We're living in such times that we are forced to be cautious.'

'Yesterday we had two funerals,' said the sexton of St Apollinaire, changing the subject.

'That means somebody must have died,' said another customer, whereupon a third added:

'Were they funerals with a catafalque?'

'I'd like to know,' said Švejk, 'what military funerals are going to be like now there's a war on.'

The customers rose, paid and went out noiselessly. Švejk was left alone with Mrs Palivec.

'I never imagined that they'd sentence an innocent man to ten years,' he said. 'Sentencing an innocent man to five years, that's something I've heard of, but ten, that's a bit too much.'

'Well, you see, he confessed everything, my old man,' sobbed Mrs Palivec. 'What he was saying here about those flies and that picture he repeated at police headquarters and before the court. I was a witness at the trial, but what evidence could I give when they told me that as I was in a state of relations with my husband I could forgo giving evidence? I was so scared of that "state of relations", in case it might lead to something else, that I got out of giving evidence and he, poor dear, gave me such a look! I shall never forget that look to my dying day. And after the sentence had been passed and they were leading him off he shouted to them in the passage, as though he'd gone off his head: "Long live Free Thinking!"'

'And Mr Bretschneider doesn't come here any more?' asked Švejk.

'He's been here several times,' answered Mrs Palivec. 'He drank a beer or two, asked me who comes here and listened to the customers talking about football. As soon as they catch sight of him they start talking about nothing else but football. And he had the jerks as though any moment he'd go mad and have a fit. And all that time he only succeeded in catching an upholsterer from Příčná Street.'

'It's all a matter of training,' observed Švejk. 'Was that upholsterer a stupid fellow?'

'Rather like my husband,' she replied, weeping. 'Mr Bretschneider asked him if he would fire against the Serbs. And he said he couldn't shoot, that he was once at the shooting range and shot through a whole crown. Then we all heard how Mr Bretschneider took out his notebook and said: "Aha, and here's another nice case of treason!", and he went away with that upholsterer from Příčná Street, who never came back.'

'Lots of them never come back,' said Švejk. 'Can I have a rum, please?'

Švejk was just having a second glass of rum, when Bretschneider came into the bar. Throwing a quick glance at the bar and the empty rooms he sat down next to Švejk and ordering a beer waited to see what he would say.

Švejk took down a newspaper from the hanger and looking at the last page of advertisements said:

'Well, I never! Look at that! A Mr Čimpera of Straškov no. 5, near Račiněves, is selling a farm with nine acres of land convenient for school and railway station.'

Bretschneider drummed his fingers nervously and turning to Švejk said:

'I'm surprised that you're interested in farming, Mr Švejk.'

'Oh, it's you, is it?' said Švejk, shaking his hand. 'I couldn't recognize you at first. I have a very bad memory. The last time we parted, if I remember aright, was in the reception office at police headquarters. What have you been doing since then? Do you come here often?'

'I've come here today because of you,' said Bretschneider. 'I was told at police headquarters that you sell dogs. I need a nice miniature pinscher or a pom or something of that kind.'

'I can get any for you,' replied Švejk. 'Do you want a thoroughbred animal or a common cur?'

'I think I'll plump for a thoroughbred,' replied Bretschneider.

'And why don't you have a police dog?' asked Švejk. 'Wouldn't you like one that picks up the scent at once and leads you to the scene of the crime? There's a butcher in Vršovice who has one and he uses it for drawing his cart. You might very well say that that dog has missed its vocation.'

'I should like a pom,' said Bretschneider with quiet obstinacy, 'a pom that doesn't bite.'

'Do you want a pom without teeth then?' asked Švejk. 'I know of one. It belongs to a pub keeper in Dejvice.'

'Then I'd rather have a miniature pinscher,' replied Bretschneider, whose cynological capacities were very elementary and who would never have learnt anything about dogs at all, if he had not got those orders from police headquarters.

But the instructions were precise, clear and firm – to get on to familiar terms with Švejk on the basis of his dog-dealing; for which purpose he had the right to choose assistants and dispose of funds for the purchase of dogs.

'There are bigger and smaller miniature pinschers,' said Švejk. 'I know of two small ones and three big ones. You can nurse all five of them on your lap. I can recommend them to you very warmly.'

'That's what I'd like,' said Bretschneider. 'And how much would it be if I only took one?'

'It goes by sizes,' answered Švejk. 'It depends on the size, you see. A miniature pinscher's not a calf. With miniature pinschers it's just the opposite, the smaller they are the dearer they come.'

'I'm considering getting larger ones which would be good watch-dogs,' answered Bretschneider, who was beginning to fear that he might overburden the secret funds of the State Police.

'All right, then,' said Švejk. 'I can sell you the bigger ones for fifty crowns and bigger ones still for forty-five crowns. But we've forgotten one thing. Are they to be puppies or grown dogs, dogs or bitches?'

'It's all the same to me,' answered Bretschneider, who was here on unfamiliar ground. 'Get them for me and I'll come and fetch them tomorrow at seven o'clock in the evening. Is that all right?'

'Come along and it'll be all right,' answered Švejk drily, 'but in this case I must ask you for a deposit of thirty crowns.'

'By all means,' said Bretschneider, paying out the money, 'and now let's have a quarter-litre of wine on me.'

When they had drunk it up Švejk stood Bretschneider another quarter and then Bretschneider invited Švejk not to be afraid of him, saying that today he was not on duty and that it was all right to speak to him about politics.

Švejk declared that he never spoke about politics in a pub, that politics in general were only for babies.

Bretschneider's views were, on the contrary, more revolutionary. He said that every weak state was doomed to extinction and asked Švejk what were his views on this subject.

Švejk said that he had nothing to do with the state, but that he had once had to look after a St Bernard puppy in a weak state. He had fed it on army biscuits but it had pegged out all the same.

When each of them had had a fifth quarter-litre Bretschneider declared that he was an anarchist and asked Švejk what organization he would recommend him to join.

Švejk said that an anarchist once purchased from him a Leonberger dog for a hundred crowns and never paid him the last instalment.

During the sixth quarter-litre Bretschneider talked about revolution and against mobilization, whereupon Švejk leaned towards him and whispered in his ear:

'A customer's just come in. Be careful he doesn't hear you otherwise you might be in trouble. You see the landlord's wife's already in tears.'

Mrs Palivec was indeed crying on her chair behind the service counter.

'What are you crying for, Mrs Palivec?' asked Bretschneider. 'In three months' time we'll have won the war, there'll be an amnesty, your husband'll return and then we'll have a fine celebration.

'Or don't you think that we shall win?' he asked, turning to Švejk.

'Why keep on always playing that gramophone record?' said Švejk. 'We've got to win and that's that. And now I must go home.'

Švejk paid his bill and returned to his old charwoman, Mrs Müller, who was scared when she realized that the man who was opening the door of the flat with his latch key was Švejk.

'O Lord, sir, I thought you wouldn't be returning here for many years,' she said with her usual frankness. 'And so in the meanwhile out of charity I took a porter from a night club as a lodger, because we've had a police search here three times, and when they couldn't find anything they said it was all up with you because you were so cunning.'

Švejk was at once able to convince himself that the unknown lodger had made himself very much at home. He was sleeping in his bed and was indeed so noble as to be content with only half of it, having placed in the other half a long-haired creature, who gratefully slept embracing him round the neck, while articles of male and female attire were scattered higgledy-piggledy round the bed. From this chaos it was evident that the night-club porter had returned with his lady in a jocund mood.

'Sir,' said Švejk, shaking the intruder. 'Make sure that you're not late for lunch. I should hate it if you had to say that I had thrown you out after you'd lost your chance of getting any lunch.'

The porter from the night club was very sleepy and it took a long

time before he understood that the owner of the bed had returned home and was making a claim to it.

Like all night-club porters this gentleman declared that he would smash anyone who woke him up, and tried to go on sleeping.

In the meantime Švejk collected parts of his clothing, brought them to his bed and, shaking him energetically, said:

'If you don't dress, I'll try to fling you out just as you are on to the street. It'll be a great advantage for you if you're properly dressed when you fly out.'

'I wanted to sleep until eight o'clock in the evening,' said the porter in a startled voice as he put on his pants. 'I am paying the mistress two crowns a day for the bed and I'm allowed to bring here young ladies from the club. Mařena, get up!'

As he was putting on his collar and tying his tie he recovered sufficiently to be able to assure Švejk that the night club Mimosa was really one of the most respectable night clubs and that ladies were only admitted there who had a clean police book and he cordially invited Švejk to come and visit it.

On the other hand his female companion was not at all pleased with Švejk and used some very choice expressions, of which the choicest of all was:

'You son of an archbishop, you!'

After the departure of the intruders Švejk went to settle accounts with Mrs Müller but found no trace of her except for a scrap of paper, upon which with unusual ease in her scrawly handwriting she had recorded her thoughts about the unfortunate episode of the loan of Švejk's bed to the porter from the night club.

'Excuse me, sir, if I don't see you any more, because I am going to jump out of the window.'

'She's lying,' said Švejk and waited.

Half an hour later the unfortunate Mrs Müller crept into the kitchen and it was clear from her distraught expression that she was expecting words of consolation from Švejk.

'If you want to jump out of the window,' said Švejk, 'go into the sitting-room. I've opened the window for you. I wouldn't advise you to jump out of the kitchen window, because you'd fall on to the rose bed in the garden, damage the bushes and have to pay for them. From the window of the sitting-room you'll fall beautifully on to the pavement and if you're lucky you'll break your neck. If not you'll only break all your ribs, arms and legs, and you'll have to pay for hospital charges.'

Mrs Müller burst into tears, went quietly into the sitting-room and shut the window. Then, coming back, she said: 'It's terribly draughty there and it wouldn't be good for your rheumatism, sir.'

Then she went to make the bed, put it all in order with unusual care and, returning to Švejk in the kitchen, remarked with tears in her eyes: 'Those two puppies, sir, which we had in the court-yard have pegged out. And that St Bernard, it ran away when the police made their search.'

'Oh, my God,' shouted Švejk, 'he'll get himself into a fine mess. The police will be after him soon.'

'He bit one police inspector when they pulled him out from underneath the bed during the search,' continued Mrs Müller. 'Before that, one of those gentlemen said that there was somebody under the bed, and so they called that St Bernard to come out in the name of the law and, when he wouldn't, they dragged him out. And he was going to gobble them up, but then he bolted out of the door and never returned. They also cross-questioned me about who comes to see us, whether we get any money from abroad, and then they started insinuating that I was a fool, when I told them that we only get money from abroad very rarely, the last being from the headmaster in Brno, that advance of sixty crowns for an angora cat which you advertised in *Národní Politika* and instead of which you sent him that blind fox-terrier puppy in a date box. After that they talked to me very affably and recommended me that porter from the night club, so that I shouldn't be afraid of being alone in the flat, that very man you've just thrown out . . . .'

'I've always had bad luck with those authorities, Mrs Müller. Now you'll see how many of them are going to come here to buy dogs,' sighed Švejk.

I don't know whether those gentlemen who examined the police archives after the overthrow of the Austro-Hungarian monarchy succeeded in deciphering the items of the secret funds of the State Police, where it was written: B . . . forty crowns, F . . . fifty crowns, L . . . eighty crowns etc., but they certainly were deceived if they thought that B, F, L were the initials of any gentlemen who for forty, fifty, eighty etc. crowns sold the Czech nation to the black and yellow eagle.

'B' stands for St Bernard, 'F' for fox-terrier and 'L' for Leonberger. All these dogs Bretschneider took from Švejk to police headquarters. They were ghastly mongrels, which had no connection whatsoever with any thoroughbred race which Švejk pretended them to be, when he sold them to Bretschneider.

The St Bernard was a mixture of mongrel poodle and a common street cur; the fox-terrier had the ears of a dachshund and was the size of a butcher's dog, with bandy legs as though it had suffered from rickets. The head of the Leonberger recalled the hairy muzzle of a stable pinscher. It had a stubbed tail, was the height of a dachshund and had bare hindquarters like the famous naked American dogs.

Later detective Kalous came to buy a dog and returned with a wildly staring monster which was reminiscent of a spotted hyena with the mane of a collie, and in the accounts of the secret fund came a new item: M ... ninety crowns.

That monster was passing itself off as a mastiff ...

But not even Kalous succeeded in getting any information out of Švejk. He fared the same as Bretschneider. Švejk diverted the deftest political conversations to the curing of distemper in puppies and the most cunningly prepared traps always ended in Bretschneider bringing back from Švejk another unbelievable mongrel monster.

And that was the end of the famous detective Bretschneider. When he had seven monsters of this kind in his flat, he shut himself up with them in the back room and starved them so long that they finally gobbled him up.

He was so honourable that he saved the state the expense of a funeral.

In his personal file at police headquarters there were recorded under the column 'Advancement in service' the following poignant words: 'Devoured by his own dogs.'

When Švejk learnt later about this tragic event he said:

'It gives me a headache to think how they are going to put all his pieces together when the day of the last judgement comes.'

7

Švejk Goes to the War

AT the time when the forests on the river Raab in Galicia saw the Austrian armies fleeing across the river and when down in Serbia one after the other of the Austrian divisions were taken with their pants down and got the walloping they had long deserved, the Austrian Ministry of War suddenly remembered Švejk. Why, even he might help to get the Monarchy out of the mess.

When they brought Švejk the order to report within a week for a medical examination on Střelecký Ostrov, he happened to be lying in bed, stricken once more by rheumatism.

Mrs Müller was making coffee for him in the kitchen.

'Mrs Müller,' Švejk called softly from his room, 'Mrs Müller, come here for a moment.'

When the charwoman stood by his bed, Švejk repeated in the same soft voice: 'Sit down, Mrs Müller.'

There was something mysterious and solemn in his voice.

When she had sat down, Švejk drew himself up in bed and announced: 'I'm going to the war!'

'Holy Mother!' shrieked Mrs Müller. 'What ever are you going to do there?'

'Fight,' answered Švejk in sepulchral tones. 'Things are going very badly for Austria. Up above they're already creeping on us at Cracow and down below on Hungary. They're crushing us like a steam-roller on all sides and that's why they're calling me up. I read you yesterday from the newspaper, didn't I, that dark clouds were enveloping our dear fatherland.'

'But you can't move.'

'That doesn't matter, Mrs Müller, I shall go to the war in a bath-chair. You know that confectioner round the corner? Well, he has just the right kind of bathchair. Years ago he used to push his lame and wicked old grandfather about in it in the fresh air. Mrs Müller, you're going to push me to the war in that bathchair.'

Mrs Müller burst into tears: 'Oh dear, sir, shouldn't I run for the doctor?'

'You'll not run anywhere, Mrs Müller. Except for my legs I'm completely sound cannon-fodder, and at a time when things are going badly for Austria every cripple must be at his post. Just go on making the coffee.'

And while Mrs Müller, tear-stained and distraught, poured the coffee through the strainer, the good soldier Švejk started singing in bed:

> 'General Windischgrätz as the cock did crow
> Unfurled his banner and charged the foe.
> Rataplan, rataplan, rataplan.
>
> Charged the foe and brandished his sword
> Calling to Mary, Mother of the Lord.
> Rataplan, rataplan, rataplan.'

The panic-stricken Mrs Müller under the impact of this awe-inspiring war-song forgot about the coffee and trembling in every limb listened in horror as the good soldier Švejk continued to sing in bed:

> 'With Mary Mother and bridges four,
> Piedmont, strengthen your posts for war.
> Rataplan, rataplan, rataplan.
>
> At Solferino there was battle and slaughter,
> Piles of corpses and blood like water.
> Rataplan, rataplan, rataplan.
>
> Arms and legs flying in the air,
> For the brave 18th were fighting there.
> Rataplan, rataplan, rataplan.
>
> Boys of the 18th, don't lose heart!
> There's money behind in the baggage cart.
> Rataplan, rataplan, rataplan.'

'For God's sake, sir, please!' came the piteous voice from the kitchen, but Švejk was already ending his war-song:

> 'Money in the cart and wenches in the van!
> What a life for a military man!
> Rataplan, rataplan, rataplan.'

Mrs Müller burst out of the door and rushed for the doctor. She returned in an hour's time, while Švejk had slumbered off.

And so he was woken up by a corpulent gentleman who laid his hand on his forehead for a moment and said:

'Don't be afraid. I am Dr Pávek from Vinohrady – let me feel your pulse – put this thermometer under your armpit. Good – now show me your tongue – a bit more – keep it out – what did your father and mother die of?'

And so at a time when it was Vienna's earnest desire that all the peoples of Austria-Hungary should offer the finest examples of loyalty and devotion, Dr Pávek prescribed Švejk bromide against his patriotic enthusiasm and recommended the brave and good soldier not to think about the war:

'Lie straight and keep quiet. I'll come again tomorrow.'

When he came the next day, he asked Mrs Müller in the kitchen how the patient was.

'He's worse, doctor,' she answered with genuine grief. 'In the night he was singing, if you'll pardon the expression, the Austrian national anthem, when the rheumatism suddenly took him.'

Dr Pávek felt obliged to react to this new manifestation of loyalty on the part of his patient by prescribing a larger dose of bromide.

The third day Mrs Müller informed him that Švejk had got even worse.

'In the afternoon he sent for a map of the battlefield, doctor, and in the night he was seized by a mad hallucination that Austria was going to win.'

'And he takes his powders strictly according to the prescription?'

'Oh, no, doctor, he hasn't even sent for them yet.' Dr Pávek went away after having called down a storm of reproaches on Švejk's head and assured him that he would never again come to cure anybody who refused his professional help and bromide.

Only two days remained before Švejk would have to appear before the call-up board.

During this time Švejk made the necessary preparations. First he sent Mrs Müller to buy an army cap and next he sent her to borrow the bathchair from the confectioner round the corner – that same one in which the confectioner once used to wheel about in the fresh air his lame and wicked old grandfather. Then he remembered he needed crutches. Fortunately the confectioner still kept the crutches too as a family relic of his old grandfather.

Now he only needed the recruit's bunch of flowers for his buttonhole. Mrs Müller got these for him too. During these last two days she got noticeably thinner and wept from morning to night.

And so on that memorable day there appeared on the Prague streets a moving example of loyalty. An old woman pushing before her a bathchair, in which there sat a man in an army cap with a finely polished Imperial badge and waving his crutches. And in his button-hole there shone the gay flowers of a recruit.

And this man, waving his crutches again and again, shouted out to the streets of Prague: 'To Belgrade, to Belgrade!'

He was followed by a crowd of people which steadily grew from the small group that had gathered in front of the house from which he had gone out to war.

Švejk could see that the policemen standing at some of the crossroads saluted him.

At Wenceslas Square the crowd around Švejk's bathchair had grown by several hundreds and at the corner of Krakovská Street they beat up a student in a German cap who had shouted out to Švejk:

'*Heil! Nieder mit den Serben!*'[1]

At the corner of Vodičkova Street mounted police rode in and dispersed the crowd.

When Švejk showed the district police inspector that he had it in black and white that he must that day appear before the call-up board, the latter was a trifle disappointed; and in order to reduce disturbances to a minimum he had Švejk and his bathchair escorted by two mounted police all the way to the Střelecký Ostrov.

The following article about this episode appeared in the *Prague Official News*:

A CRIPPLE'S PATRIOTISM

Yesterday afternoon the passers-by in the main streets of Prague were witnesses of a scene which was an eloquent testimony to the fact that in these great and solemn hours the sons of our nation can furnish the finest examples of loyalty and devotion to the throne of the aged monarch. We might well have been back in the times of the ancient Greeks and Romans, when Mucius Scaevola had himself led off to battle, regardless of his burnt arm. The most sacred feelings and sympathies were nobly demonstrated yesterday by a cripple on crutches who was pushed in an invalid chair by his aged mother. This son of the Czech people, spontaneously and regardless of his infirmity, had himself driven off to war to sacrifice his life and possessions for his emperor. And if his call: 'To Belgrade!' found such a lively echo on the streets of Prague, it only goes to prove what model examples of love for the fatherland and the Imperial House are proffered by the people of Prague.

The *Prager Tagblatt* wrote in the same strain, ending its article by saying that the cripple volunteer was escorted by a crowd of Germans who protected him with their bodies from lynching by the Czech agents of the Entente.

Bohemie published the same report and urged that the patriotic cripple should be fittingly rewarded. It announced that at its offices it was ready to receive gifts from German citizens for the unknown hero.

If in the eyes of these three journals the Czech lands could not have produced a nobler citizen, this was not the opinion of the gentlemen at the call-up board – certainly not of the chief army doctor Bautze, an utterly ruthless man who saw in everything a criminal attempt to evade military service, the front, bullets, and shrapnel.

1. 'Down with the Serbs.'

This German's stock remark was widely famous: 'The whole Czech people are nothing but a pack of malingerers.'

During the ten weeks of his activities, of 11,000 civilians he cleaned out 10,999 malingerers, and he would certainly have got the eleven thousandth by the throat, if it had not happened that just when he shouted 'About turn!' the unfortunate man was carried off by a stroke.

'Take away that malingerer!' said Bautze, when he had ascertained that the man was dead.

And on that memorable day it was Švejk who stood before him. Like the others he was stark naked and chastely hid his nudity behind the crutches on which he supported himself.

'That's really a remarkable fig-leaf,' said Bautze in German. 'There were no fig-leaves like that in paradise.'

'Certified as totally unfit for service on grounds of idiocy,' observed the sergeant-major, looking at the official documents.

'And what else is wrong with you?' asked Bautze.

'Humbly report, sir, I'm a rheumatic, but I will serve His Imperial Majesty to my last drop of blood,' said Švejk modestly. 'I have swollen knees.'

Bautze gave the good soldier Švejk a blood-curdling look and roared out in German: 'You're a malingerer!' Turning to the sergeant-major he said with icy calm: 'Clap the bastard into gaol at once!'

Two soldiers with bayonets took Švejk off to the garrison gaol.

Švejk walked on his crutches and observed with horror that his rheumatism was beginning to disappear.

Mrs Müller was still waiting for Švejk with the bathchair above on the bridge but when she saw him under bayoneted escort she burst into tears and ran away from the bathchair, never to return to it again.

And the good soldier Švejk walked along unassumingly under the escort of the armed protectors of the state.

Their bayonets shone in the light of the sun and at Malá Strana before the monument of Radetzky Švejk turned to the crowd which had followed them and called out:

'To Belgrade! To Belgrade!'

And Marshal Radetzky looked dreamily down from his monument at the good soldier Švejk, as, limping on his old crutches, he slowly disappeared into the distance with his recruit's flowers in his buttonhole. Meanwhile a solemn-looking gentleman informed the crowd around that it was a 'dissenter' they were leading off.

8

Švejk the Malingerer

IN these great times the army doctors took unusual pains to drive the devil of sabotage out of the malingerers and restore them to the bosom of the army.

Various degrees of torture had been introduced for malingerers and suspected malingerers, such as consumptives, rheumatics, people with hernia, kidney disease, typhus, diabetes, pneumonia and other illnesses.

The tortures to which the malingerers were subjected were systematized and the grades were as follows:

1. Strict diet, a cup of tea each morning and evening for three days, during which, irrespective, of course, of their complaints, aspirin to be given to induce sweating.

2. To ensure they did not think that war was all beer and skittles, quinine in powder to be served in generous portions, or so-called 'quinine licking'.

3. The stomach to be pumped out twice a day with a litre of warm water.

4. Enemas with soapy water and glycerine to be applied.

5. Wrapping up in a sheet soaked in cold water.

There were stalwart men who endured all five degrees of torture and let themselves be carried off to the military cemetery in a simple coffin. But there were also pusillanimous souls who, when they reached the stage of the enema, declared that they were now well and desired nothing better than to march off to the trenches with the next march battalion.

In the garrison prison Švejk was put into the sanatorium hut among pusillanimous malingerers of this very type.

'I can't stand it any longer,' said his neighbour in the next bed, who was brought in from the consulting room after having had his stomach pumped for the second time.

This man was shamming short-sightedness.

'Tomorrow I'll join the regiment,' decided his other neighbour on the left, who had just had an enema and who had been shamming deafness.

In the bed by the door a consumptive who was wrapped up in a cold wet sheet was slowly dying.

'That's the third this week,' observed his neighbour on the right. 'And what's your trouble?'

'I've got rheumatism,' answered Švejk, upon which there was a hearty guffaw all round. Even the dying consumptive, who was shamming tuberculosis, joined in the laughter.

'Don't try and climb in here with rheumatism,' a fat man warned Švejk solemnly. 'Rheumatism here doesn't mean more than a chilblain. I'm anaemic, I've lost half my stomach and five of my ribs, but no one believes me. We even had a fellow here who was deaf and dumb. For a fortnight they wrapped him up every half-hour in a cold wet sheet and every day they gave him an enema and pumped his stomach. All the nurses thought he'd won through and would go home, when the doctor prescribed him an emetic. It could have torn him in half and so he lost courage. "I can't go on being deaf and dumb," he said. "My speech and hearing have returned." All the patients urged him not to ruin himself but he insisted that he could hear and speak just like other people. And he reported to this effect at the doctor's visit next morning.'

'He kept it up for quite a long time,' remarked a man, who was pretending to have one leg four inches shorter than the other. 'Not like that chap who shammed a stroke. All they had to do was to give him three doses of quinine, one enema and a day's fasting. He confessed and by the time they started pumping out his stomach there wasn't a trace left of his stroke. The chap who held out longest of all was the one who had been bitten by a mad dog. He bit, he howled – it's true he could do it splendidly – but he just couldn't manage to foam at the mouth. We did our best to help him. Several times we tickled him for a whole hour before the doctor's visit until he had convulsions and got blue all over, but the foam wouldn't come and didn't in fact come at all. It was really terrifying. When he gave in one morning at the doctor's visit we were quite sorry for him. He stood by his bed erect as a candle, saluted and said: "Humbly report, sir, the dog I was bitten by may not have been mad after all." The doctor gave him such a queer look that he began to tremble all over and went on: "Humbly report, sir, I wasn't bitten by a dog at all. It was I who bit myself in the arm." After that confession they put him under investigation for self-mutilation on the charge that he had tried to bite off his arm to get out of going to the front.'

'All those kinds of illnesses where you have to foam at the mouth are difficult to sham,' said the fat malingerer. 'Take for instance epilepsy. We had an epileptic here who always used to tell us that one fit wasn't enough and so he put on some ten a day. He writhed in convulsions, clenched his fists, rolled his eyes wildly, flung himself about on the floor, stuck out his tongue, in short, I can tell you, it was a magnificent first-class epilepsy, the genuine thing. But suddenly he got boils, two on the neck and two on the back, and it was all over with his writhing and flinging himself about on the floor, when he couldn't move his head and wasn't able either to sit or lie down. He got fever and in delirium he let out everything at the doctor's visit. He gave us a lot of trouble over his boils, because he had to lie here with them another three days and got another diet – coffee and rolls in the morning, soup, dumplings and gravy for lunch, and porridge or soup in the evening. And with our hungry, pumped-out stomachs and strict diet we had to watch this fellow bolting the food, smacking his lips, panting and belching with repletion. In this way he broke down another three who confessed as well. They had been suffering from heart disease.'

'The best thing to sham,' said one of the malingerers, 'is insanity. There are two of our teachers lying in the ward next door and one of them shrieks out incessantly day and night: "Giordano Bruno's stake is still smouldering. Reopen the trial of Galileo." And the other one barks, first three times slowly: bow—wow—wow, then five times quickly in succession: bowwowwowwowwow, and then once more slowly, and so it goes on without a break. They've managed to keep it up for over three weeks now. Originally I wanted to be insane too, have religious mania and preach about papal infallibility, but in the end I fixed myself up with cancer of the stomach from a barber in Malá Strana for fifteen crowns.'

'I know a chimney-sweep in Břevnov,' remarked another patient. 'For ten crowns he'll give you such a fever that you'll jump out of the window.'

'That's nothing,' said another. 'In Vršovice there's a midwife who for twenty crowns will dislocate your leg so well that you'll be a cripple until your death.'

'I had my leg dislocated for ten crowns,' came a voice from the row of beds by the window, 'for ten crowns and three glasses of beer.'

'My illness has cost me more than two hundred already,' announced his neighbour, a dried-up stick. 'You tell me any poison I haven't taken. You won't find it. I'm a living repository of poisons of all kinds. I've taken mercury chloride, I've breathed in mercury fumes, I've chewed arsenic, I've smoked opium, I've drunk tincture of opium, I've sprinkled morphine on bread, I've swallowed strychnine, I've drunk a solution of phosphorus in carbon sulphide as well as picric acid. I've destroyed my liver, my lungs, my kidneys, my gall-bladder, my brain, my heart and my intestines. No one knows what kind of illness I have.'

'The best thing to do,' explained somebody from the door, 'is to inject paraffin under the skin of your arm. My cousin was so fortunate as to have his arm cut off under the elbow and today he has no trouble for the rest of the war.'

'So you see,' said Švejk, 'everyone has to go through all that for His Imperial Majesty – even stomach-pumping and enemas. When I served years ago in my regiment it was even worse. In those days they used to truss the patient and throw him into a hole to recuperate him. There weren't any bunks like there are here or spittoons either. Just a bare plank-bed and the patients lay on it. Once one had a genuine typhus and the other next to him had smallpox. Both were trussed, and the regimental doctor kicked them in the belly for being malingerers. And when both these soldiers died it came up in parliament and was in the newspapers. They immediately forbade us to read those newspapers and searched our boxes in case we had them. And as I always have bad luck, I was the only one in the whole regiment they found them on. So I was taken off on regimental report and our colonel, who was a bloody half-wit, God help him, started to roar at me to stand straight and to tell him who it was who wrote that in the newspapers or he'd break my jaw wide open and have me locked up till I was black in the face. Then came the regimental doctor, brandishing his fist under my nose and shouting in German: "You dirty hound, you lousy scab, you miserable turd, you Socialist sod!" I looked them all squarely in the eyes without blinking and kept quiet, my right hand at the peak of my cap and my left on the seam of my trousers. They ran around me like dogs and yapped at me, but I did nothing. I kept mum, saluted, left hand on the seam of my trousers. When they had been raging like this for about half an hour, the colonel rushed at me and roared: "Are you a half-wit or aren't you?" – "Humbly report, sir, I'm a half-wit." – "Very well then. Twenty-one days strict confinement for imbecility, two days a week fasting, a month confined to barracks, forty-eight hours in handcuffs, immediate arrest, don't let him eat, truss him, show him that the monarchy doesn't need half-wits. We'll flog those newspapers out of your head, you bastard," the colonel decided after flying around for a long time. But while I was sitting in jug miracles were happening in the barracks. Our colonel forbade our soldiers to read anything at all, even the *Prague Official News*. In the canteen they weren't even allowed to use the newspapers for wrapping up frankfurters or bits of cheese. From that time all the soldiers started to read, and our regiment became the best educated. We read all the newspapers and in every company they made up rhymes and songs against the colonel. And when anything happened in the regiment you'd always find some public benefactor who sent it to the newspapers under the title: "Maltreatment of the troops". And they didn't stop at that. They wrote to the parliamentary deputies in Vienna, asking them to take up their case, and the deputies began to make interpellations one after the other, saying that our colonel was a monster and suchlike. A minister sent a commission to us to investigate the case and a Franta Henčl from Hluboká got two years for being the chap who got on to the deputies in Vienna, because of the knock across the jaw he got from the colonel on the drill-ground. Later when the commission went away our colonel made us all fall in, the whole regiment, and told us that a soldier is a soldier, that he must shut his mug and do his job, and if he doesn't like anything then it's a breach of discipline. "So you, you bloody bastards, thought that that commission would help you?" said the colonel. "A shit they helped you! And now every company will march past me and repeat aloud what I've said." And so we marched to where the colonel stood, one company after the other, eyes right, and our hands on our rifle slings and shouted at him: "And so we, we bloody bastards, thought that that commission would help us. A shit they helped us!" The colonel doubled up with laughter until the eleventh company marched up. They marched, they stamped, but when they reached the colonel – nothing at all, not the faintest sound! The colonel got red as a turkey-cock, marched the eleventh company back and made them repeat the operation once more. They marched past in silence and each rank after the other stared the colonel insolently in the eyes. "Stand at ease!" said the colonel and paced up and down the yard, lashing his boots with his riding crop and spitting about the place. Then he suddenly stopped and roared out "Dismiss!", mounted his old crock and away he was out of the gate. We waited to see what would happen to the eleventh company, but still there was nothing. We waited one day, then another and then a whole week, but still nothing happened. The colonel never appeared in the barracks at all, which gave great joy to the men, the N.C.O.s and the officers. After that we got a new colonel and it was rumoured that the old one was in a sanatorium because he had written a letter in his own hand to His Imperial Majesty telling him that the eleventh company had mutinied.'

The time for the doctor's afternoon round approached. Dr Grünstein went from bed to bed, followed by the medical orderly officer with his notebook.

'Macuna?'

'Present!'

'Enema and aspirin! Pokorný?'

'Present!'

'Stomach pump and quinine! Kovařík?'

'Present!'

'Enema and aspirin! Kot'átko?'

'Present!'

'Stomach pump and quinine!'

And so it went on, one after the other, mercilessly, mechanically, briskly.

'Švejk?'

'Present!'

Dr Grünstein looked at the new acquisition.

'What's the matter with you?'

'Humbly report, I've got rheumatism!'

In the course of his practice Dr Grünstein had grown accustomed to be gently ironical, which was much more effective than shouting.

'Aha, rheumatism,' he said to Švejk. 'Then you've got a jolly serious illness. It's really a coincidence getting rheumatism just at a time when there is a world war on and you've got to go to the front. I think you must be awfully sorry.'

'Humbly report, sir, I am awfully sorry.'

'Well, there you are, you see, he's awfully sorry. It's really awfully nice of you that with your rheumatism you've not forgotten us just at this particular moment. In peacetime a poor chap like him runs about like a young goat, but as soon as war breaks out he immediately gets rheumatism and suddenly his knees don't work. Your knees hurt, I suppose?'

'Humbly report, they do, sir.'

'And you can't sleep a wink the whole night, can you? Rheumatism's a very dangerous, painful and grave illness. We've already had good experience with rheumatics here. Strict diet and other treatment of ours have proved very effective. Here you'll be fit quicker than in Piešt'any[1] and you'll march to the front like greased lightning.'

Turning to the hospital orderly he said:

'Write this down: Švejk, strict diet, stomach pump twice a day, enema once a day, and we'll see how it goes after that. For the time being take him to the consulting room, pump his stomach and when he comes to, give him an enema, but a real good one, until he screams blue murder and his rheumatism gets frightened and runs away.'

Then turning to all the beds the doctor made a speech full of noble and rational moral maxims: 'Don't imagine that I'm just a bloody half-wit who swallows all your bull. Your tricks don't rattle me in the least. I know you're all malingerers and you want to desert from the war. And I'll treat you as such. I've survived hundreds and hundreds of soldiers like you. Masses of people have lain on these beds here who had nothing wrong with them at all except that they hadn't got a soldier's guts. While their comrades were fighting on the battlefield they thought they'd lounge about in bed, get hospital rations and wait until the war flew by. But they all found they'd made a bloody mistake, and all of you'll find you've made a bloody mistake too. In twenty years time you'll be still screaming in your sleep, when you dream of how you tried it on with me.'

'Humbly report, sir,' came a gentle voice from the bed at the window, 'I'm well again. I noticed in the night that my asthma's gone.'

'Your name?'

'Kovařík. Humbly report, I have to have an enema.'

'Good, you'll still get an enema for the road,' Dr Grünstein decided, 'so that you don't complain that we didn't give you treatment here. Now, all the patients whose names I've read out, fall in and follow the orderly, so that each can get what's due to him.'

1. A famous spa in Slovakia for the treatment of rheumatism.

And each one got a handsome dose of what had been prescribed. And if any of them tried to work on those who were executing the orders by means of prayers or threats that they might too once join the medical corps and the executioners might fall into their hands, Švejk at least bore himself with steadfastness.

'Don't spare me,' he invited the myrmidon who was giving him the enema. 'Remember your oath. Even if it was your father or your own brother who was lying here, give him an enema without batting an eyelid. Try hard to think that Austria rests on these enemas and victory is ours.'

The next day on his round Dr Grünstein asked Švejk how he was enjoying being in the military hospital.

Švejk answered that it was a fair and high-minded institution. In reward he received the same as the day before plus aspirin and three quinine powders which they dissolved into water so that he should drink them at once.

And not even Socrates drank his hemlock bowl with such composure as did Švejk his quinine, when Dr Grünstein was trying out on him all his various degrees of torture.

When they wrapped Švejk up in a wet sheet in the presence of the doctor his answer to the question how he liked it now was: 'Humbly report, sir; it's like being in a swimming pool or at the seaside.'

'Have you still got rheumatism?'

'Humbly report, sir, it doesn't seem to want to get better.'

Švejk was subjected to new tortures.

At that time the widow of the infantry general, Baroness von Botzenheim, took great pains to find that soldier about whom *Bohemie* had recently published a report that, cripple as he was, he had had himself pushed in a bathchair shouting: 'To Belgrade!'; which patriotic pronouncement induced the editorial staff of *Bohemie* to invite their readers to organize collections in aid of the loyal and heroic cripple.

Finally, after inquiries at police headquarters it was ascertained that the man in question was Švejk and after that it was easy to make a search for him. Baroness von Botzenheim went to the Hradčany taking with her her lady companion and her footman with a hamper.

The poor baroness had no idea what it meant for someone to be lying in the hospital of the garrison gaol. Her visiting card opened the prison door for her, in the office they were awfully nice to her, and in five minutes she learnt that 'the good soldier Švejk', whom she was looking for, lay in the third hut, bed number seventeen. She was accompanied by Dr Grünstein himself, who was quite flabbergasted by it.

Švejk was just sitting up in bed after the usual daily procedure prescribed by Dr Grünstein, surrounded by a group of emaciated and starved malingerers, who had not yet given up and were stubbornly struggling with Dr Grünstein on the battlefield of strict diet.

Anyone who had listened to them would have had the impression that he was in the company of epicures, in a school of *cordon bleu* cuisine or a course for gourmets.

'You can even eat ordinary suet cracklings if they are warm,' a patient with 'inveterate stomach catarrh' was just telling the others at this moment. 'As the suet boils, you squeeze the cracklings dry, add salt and pepper, and I can tell you that goose cracklings are not in the same class.'

'You leave goose cracklings alone,' said a man with 'cancer of the stomach'. 'There's nothing to touch them. What are pork cracklings in comparison? Of course you must fry them until they're golden brown, like the Jews do. They take a fat goose, draw the fat off with the skin and fry it.'

'You know, you're quite wrong as far as pork cracklings are concerned,' Švejk's neighbour put in. 'Of course I'm talking about cracklings of home-made fat, what they call home-made cracklings. They're not brown and they're not yellow. They must be something between the two shades. These kinds of cracklings mustn't be either too soft or too hard. And they mustn't be crunchy or they're over-cooked. They must melt on the tongue and you mustn't feel the fat dripping on your chin.'

'Which of you have eaten horse cracklings?' chimed in a new voice, but there was no answer because at that moment the medical orderly ran in:

'Everybody in bed! An archduchess is coming here. Don't anyone dare show his dirty legs outside the bed.'

And not even an archduchess could have entered the ward with such dignity as did Baroness von Botzenheim. After her the whole suite poured in, including even the quartermaster sergeant-major of the hospital who saw in all this the mysterious hand of Accounts Control, which was going to tear him away from his fat feeding trough at the base and deliver him to the tender mercies of the shrapnel some-where under the barbed wire posts.

He was pale, but Dr Grünstein was even paler. Before his eyes there danced the old baroness's small visiting card with her title, 'Widow of a general', and everything which could be associated with it like connections, protection, complaints, transfer to the front and other frightful things.

'Here you have Švejk,' he said, endeavouring to preserve an arti-ficial composure and leading the Baroness von Botzenheim to Švejk's bed. 'He behaves with great patience.'

Baroness von Botzenheim sat down on the chair prepared for her at Švejk's bed and said: 'Tshech zoldier, goot zoldier, krippl – zoldier iss brafe zoldier. I lof fery moch Tshech Austrian.'

At that she stroked Švejk on his unshaven cheeks and went on:

'I reat eferyzink in ze newspapers, I brink you yum yum, zomzink to bite, to shmoke, to zuck, Tshech zoldier, goot zoldier. Johann, come here!'

Her footman, whose bristly side-whiskers recalled the notorious killer Babinský, dragged a voluminous hamper to the bed, while the old baroness's companion, a tall lady with a tearful face, sat down on Švejk's bed and smoothed out his straw pillow under his back with the fixed idea that this was what ought to be done for sick heroes.

In the meantime the baroness drew presents out of the hamper: a dozen roast chickens wrapped up in pink silk paper and tied with a yellow and black silk ribbon, two bottles of a war liqueur with the label: '*Gott strafe England*.'[1] On the back of the label was a picture of Franz Joseph and Wilhelm clasping hands as though they were going to play the nursery game: 'Bunny sat alone in his hole. Poor little bunny, what's wrong with you that you can't hop!'[2]

Then she took out of the hamper three bottles of wine for the con-valescent and two boxes of cigarettes. She set out everything elegantly on the empty bed next to Švejk's, where she also put a beautifully bound book, *Stories from the Life of our Monarch*, which had been written by the present meritorious chief editor of our official *Czechoslovak Republic* who doted on old Franz. Packets of chocolate with the same inscription, '*Gott strafe England*', and again with pictures of the Austrian and German emperors, found their way to

1. 'God punish England.'
2. Czech children's game.

the bed. On the chocolate they were no longer clasping hands; each was acting on his own and turning his back to the other. There was a beautiful toothbrush with two rows of bristles and the inscription '*Viribus unitis*',[1] so that anyone who cleaned his teeth should remember Austria. An elegant and extremely useful little gift for the front and the trenches was a manicure set. On the case was a picture showing shrapnel bursting and a man in a steel helmet rushing forward with fixed bayonet. And underneath it was written in German: 'For God, Emperor and Fatherland!' There was a tin of biscuits without a picture on it but with a verse in German instead, together with a Czech translation on the back:

> Austria, thou noble house,
> Thy banners wide unfurl!
> Thy flags shall flutter proud on high.
> Austria shall never die!

The last gift was a white hyacinth in a flower-pot.

When all of this lay unpacked on the bed the Baroness von Botzenheim could not restrain her tears for emotion. Several famished malingerers felt their mouths water. The baroness's companion propped up the seated Švejk and wept too. There was a silence of the grave which was suddenly broken by Švejk who said with his hands clasped in prayer:

'Our Father, which art in heaven, hallowed be Thy name. Thy kingdom come. . . . Pardon me, your ladyship, it's not right. I mean to say: O God our Father in heaven, bless for us these gifts that we may enjoy them thanks to Thy goodness. Amen.'

After these words he took a chicken from the bed and started to devour it under the horrified gaze of Dr Grünstein.

'Ach, how he enjoys it, poor soldier,' the old baroness whispered enthusiastically to Dr Grünstein. 'He's certainly well again and can go to the battlefield. I'm really very glad that my gifts stand him in such good stead.'

Then she walked from bed to bed, distributing cigarettes and chocolate creams. When she came back again to Švejk after her promenade, she stroked his hair, said in German: 'God protect you all!' and went out of the door with her whole escort.

Before Dr Grünstein could return from below, where he had gone

---

1. 'With united forces'. The device of the Emperor Franz Joseph.

to see the baroness out, Švejk had distributed the chickens. They were bolted by the patients so quickly that Dr Grünstein found only a heap of bones gnawed cleanly, as though the chickens had fallen alive into a nest of vultures and the sun had been beating down on their gnawed bones for several months.

The war liqueur and the three bottles of wine had also disappeared. The packets of chocolate and the box of biscuits were likewise lost in the patients' stomachs. Someone had even drunk up the bottle of nail-polish which was in the manicure set and eaten the toothpaste which had been enclosed with the toothbrush.

When Dr Grünstein returned he resumed his belligerent pose and delivered a long speech. A stone fell from his heart now that the visitors had gone. The pile of gnawed bones confirmed his belief that they were all incorrigible.

'Men,' he burst out, 'if you'd had a little sense, you'd have left it all untouched and said to yourselves: "If we eat it all up, then the doctor won't believe that we're very ill." Now you've yourselves provided me with proof that you don't appreciate my kindness. I pump your stomachs, I give you enemas, I try to keep you on strict diet and you go and stuff up your stomachs again. Do you want to get stomach catarrh? You're making a great mistake. Before your stomach tries to digest all this I'll clean it out for you so thoroughly that you'll remember it to your dying day and tell your children how you once gobbled up chickens, and gorged yourself on various other delicacies, and how they didn't stay in your stomach fifteen minutes, because they pumped it out while it was still warm. And now fall in all of you, one after the other, so that you don't forget that I'm not a bloody fool like you are, but a little bit cleverer than the whole lot of you together. In addition I want to inform you that tomorrow I'm going to send a commission to you, because you've been lazing around here far too long and there's nothing wrong with any of you if in those five minutes you could pig it and stuff your stomachs up so chock-full as you did just now. One, two, three, march!'

When it was Švejk's turn Dr Grünstein looked at him and a memory of the mysterious visit of the day prompted him to ask: 'You know Her Excellency?'

'She's my stepmother,' Švejk answered calmly. 'In tender years she abandoned me and now she's found me again. . . .'

And Dr Grünstein said tersely: 'Afterwards give Švejk an extra enema.'

In the evening melancholy reigned among the bunks. A few hours earlier all of them had had in their stomachs various good and tasty things and now they only had weak tea and a slice of bread.

From the window could be heard the voice of no. 21: 'Do you know, chaps, that I prefer fried chicken to roast?'

Somebody growled: 'Give him the blanket treatment', but they were all so weak after the unsuccessful banquet that no one stirred.

Dr Grünstein was as good as his word. In the morning there came several military doctors from the famous commission.

They went solemnly past the rows of beds and said nothing else but 'Put out your tongue!'

Švejk put his tongue out so far that his face made an idiotic grimace and his eyes screwed up:

'Humbly report, sir, I don't have a longer tongue than that.'

And an interesting discussion arose between Švejk and the com-

mission. Švejk asserted that he had made this observation in case they might think he was trying to hide his tongue from them.

The members of the commission, however, were remarkably divided in their conclusions about Švejk.

Half of them insisted that Švejk was 'a half-wit', while the other half insisted he was a scoundrel who was trying to make fun of the war.

'It'll be a bloody miracle,' roared the chairman of the commission at Švejk, 'if we don't get the better of you.'

Švejk looked at the whole commission with the godlike composure of an innocent child.

The senior staff doctor came up close to Švejk:

'I'd like to know, you swine, what you're thinking about now?'

'Humbly report, sir, I don't think at all.'

'Himmeldonnerwetter,' bawled one of the members of the commission, rattling his sabre. 'So he doesn't think at all. Why in God's name don't you think, you Siamese elephant?'

'Humbly report, I don't think because that's forbidden to soldiers on duty. When I was in the 91st regiment some years ago our captain always used to say "A soldier mustn't think for himself. His superiors do it for him. As soon as a soldier begins to think he's no longer a soldier but a dirty, lousy civilian. Thinking doesn't get you anywhere..."'

'Shut your mug!' the chairman of the commission interrupted Švejk in fury. 'We know all about you already. The swine thinks he'll be taken for a genuine idiot. You're not an idiot at all, Švejk. You're cunning, you're foxy, you're a scoundrel, you're a hooligan, you're a lousy bastard, do you understand...?'

'Humbly report, sir, I understand.'

'I've already told you to shut your mug. Did you hear?'

'Humbly report, sir, I heard that I must shut my mug.'

'Himmelherrgott, then shut it! When I've given you orders, you know very well that you must stop talking rot!'

'Humbly report, sir, I know well I must stop talking rot.'

The military gentlemen exchanged glances and called the sergeant-major:

'Take this man to the office,' said the senior staff doctor pointing to Švejk, 'and wait for our announcement and report. At the garrison they'll knock all this drivel out of his head. The fellow's as fit as a fiddle. He's only shamming and into the bargain he talks rot and tries to make fun of his superiors. He thinks they're only here for his amusement and that the whole war's a joke, a laughing matter. At the garrison, Švejk, they'll soon show you that war's no picnic.'

Švejk went off with the sergeant-major to the office and on the way through the courtyard hummed to himself:

> 'I always thought
> That war was fun.
> A week or two
> And home I'd run . . .

And while in the office the duty officer was bellowing at Švejk that bastards like him ought to be shot, in the wards upstairs the commission was making short shrift with the malingerers. Of seventy patients only two got through. One had had a leg torn off by a shell and the other suffered from genuine bone decay.

These two were the only ones who did not hear the word '*Tauglich*'. All the others, including even the three dying of consumption, were certified fit for service at the front, whereupon the senior staff doctor did not deny himself the opportunity of making a speech.

His speech was interlarded with the most variegated oaths and was brief in content. They were all swine and dung and only if they were to fight valiantly for His Imperial Majesty would they be fit to return to human society and after the war be forgiven for having tried to get out of military service and been malingerers. He himself however didn't believe that this would happen and thought the gallows were in store for them all.

A youngish army doctor whose soul was still pure and uncorrupted asked the senior staff doctor if he might say a few words too. His speech distinguished itself from that of his superior by its optimism and naïvety. He spoke in German.

He dwelt long on the fact that each of them who was leaving the hospital to join their regiments at the front must be conqueror and knight. He was convinced they would be skilful in handling their weapons on the battlefield and honourable in all their dealings in war and in private life. They would be unconquerable warriors, mindful of the glory of Radetzky and Prince Eugène of Savoy. With their blood they would fertilize the vast fields of glory of the monarchy and victoriously accomplish the task to which history had predestined them. With fearless courage, despising their lives, they would charge forward under the bullet-ridden ensigns of their regiments towards new glories and new victories.

Later in the corridor the senior staff doctor said to this naïve man: 'My dear colleague, I can assure you it's all a complete waste of time. Why, not even Radetzky or your Prince Eugène of Savoy could make soldiers out of bastards like them. Whether you speak to them like an angel or a devil, it all comes to the same thing. They're a gang of crooks.'

9

Švejk in the Garrison Gaol

FOR people who did not want to go to the front the last refuge was the garrison gaol. I once knew a probationary teacher who was a mathematician and did not want to serve in the artillery and shoot people. So he stole a lieutenant's watch to get himself into the garrison gaol. He did this deliberately. War neither impressed nor enchanted him. Shooting at the enemy and killing with shrapnel and shells equally unhappy probationary teachers of mathematics serving on the other side seemed to him sheer idiocy.

'I don't want to be hated for my brutality,' he said to himself, and calmly stole the watch. First they examined his mental condition but, when he said he wanted to get rich quick, they sent him off to the garrison gaol. There were a lot more people like that sitting there for theft or fraud – idealists and non-idealists. There were people who saw the war as a way of increasing their income, those various quarter-master sergeants at the base or at the front who were up to all possible kinds of fiddles with messing and pay, and also petty thieves who were a thousand times more honest than the blackguards who sent them there. And soldiers sat there who had committed various other offences of a purely military kind such as insubordination, attempted mutiny or desertion. Then came the political prisoners who were in a special class; eighty per cent of them were utterly innocent and of these ninety-nine per cent were sentenced.

The whole establishment of the office of the judge advocate was magnificent. Every state on the brink of total political, economic and moral collapse has an establishment like this. The aura of past power and glory clings to its courts, police, gendarmerie and venal pack of informers.

In every military unit Austria had her snoopers who spied on their comrades, sleeping on the same bunks with them and sharing their bread on the march.

In addition the garrison gaol was supplied with material by the

State Security, Messrs Klíma, Slavíček and Co. The military censorship consigned here the writers of letters exchanged between the men at the front and the despairing ones they had left behind at home. The gendarmes even brought here poor old peasant pensioners who had written letters to the front, and the court-martial jugged them for twelve years as a punishment for their words of consolation and their descriptions of the misery at home.

From the Hradčany garrison the road led through Břevnov to the drill-ground at Motol. Along it a procession would pass, headed by a man under military escort with his hands manacled and followed by a cart with a coffin on it. On the drill-ground was heard the curt order: 'Fire!' And then in all the regiments and battalions they read out the regimental order that one more man had been shot for mutiny during call-up, when his wife, not bearing to be parted from him, had been slashed by the captain's sabre.

And in the garrison gaol the triumvirate – Staff Warder Slavík, Captain Linhart and Sergeant-Major Řepa, alias 'the hangman', were getting on with the job! How many did they flog in solitary confinement? Perhaps in the Republic today Captain Linhart is still a captain. I hope for his sake his years of service in the garrison gaol will count towards his pension. They do in the case of Slavíček and Klíma from the State Security. Řepa has returned to civilian life and carries on with his profession as a master builder. Perhaps he is a member of one of the patriotic societies in the Republic.

Under the Republic Staff Warder Slavík became a thief and is today in gaol. The poor man could not set himself up so comfortably in the Republic as the other military gentlemen did.

It was quite natural that when he took charge of Švejk Staff Warder Slavík gave him a look of mute reproach, as much as to say:

'So you've got a tarnished reputation too, if you've got yourself here? Well, love, we'll sweeten your stay here, as we do for anyone who's fallen into our hands, and you know that our hands aren't exactly the ladies' kind.'

And to add weight to his look he thrust his muscular fat fist under Švejk's nose and said:

'Sniff that, you bastard!'

Švejk sniffed it and observed:

'I wouldn't like to get that in the nose. It smells of the graveyard.'

This calm, considered remark appealed to the staff warder.

'Hey,' he said, prodding Švejk in the stomach with his fist, 'stand straight! What's that you've got in your pockets? If it's cigarettes, you can leave them here. And hand over your money too so that they don't

steal it off you. Haven't you got anything else? Honest to God? Don't tell lies, now. You'll be punished for lying.'

'Where shall we put him?' asked Sergeant-Major Řepa.

'In no. 16,' the staff warder decided, 'among the pants. Don't you see that Captain Linhart has marked his papers: "Guard and watch closely!"'

'Oh, yes, indeed,' he declared solemnly to Švejk, 'vermin are treated like vermin. If anyone gets awkward we drag him off to the solitary. There we break all his ribs and leave him until he's a goner. That's our right. Like we did with that butcher, eh, Řepa?'

'Yes, he gave us a lot of trouble, sir,' replied Sergeant-Major Řepa dreamily. 'What a body! I stamped on him for more than five minutes, until his ribs began to crack and blood poured out of his mouth. And he lived for another ten days. A really tough customer.'

'So you see, you bastard, what happens here when anyone starts getting awkward or trying to escape,' said Staff Warder Slavík, concluding his pedagogical discourse. 'It's sheer suicide, and by the way suicide's punished too. And God help you, you miserable shit, if when there's an inspection you take it into your head to complain about anything. When there's an inspection and you're asked: "Have you any complaints?" you have to stand at attention, you stinking vermin, salute and answer: "Humbly report, none. I'm completely satisfied." Now what are you going to say, you lousy oaf? Repeat what I said!'

'Humbly report, none. I'm completely satisfied,' Švejk repeated with such a sweet expression on his face that the staff warder was misled and took it for honest zeal and decency.

'Now strip down to your pants and go to no. 16,' he said affably, without adding either 'shit', 'stinking vermin' or 'lousy oaf' as he usually did.

In no. 16 Švejk encountered twenty men in their pants. They were all men whose papers had been marked 'Guard and watch closely!' and who were now being watched very carefully so that they should not escape.

If those pants had been clean and there had been no bars on the windows, you might at first glance have supposed that you were in the dressing-room of some bathing establishment.

Sergeant-Major Řepa handed Švejk over to the 'cell commander', a hairy fellow in an unbuttoned shirt. He wrote Švejk's name down on a piece of paper which was hanging on the wall and said to him:

'Tomorrow we're going to have a show. They'll take us to the chapel to hear a sermon. We shall all of us be standing in our pants right under the pulpit. There'll be some fun.'

As in all prisons and penitentiaries the local chapel was very popular in the garrison gaol too. Not that enforced attendance at it brought the congregation nearer to God or that the prisoners learned more about morality. There could be no question of any nonsense of that kind.

The service and sermons were a marvellous thrill in the boredom of the garrison gaol. It was not a question of getting nearer to God, but of the hope of finding on the way in the corridor or in the courtyard a fag-end or a cigar-end. A little fag-end, lying about hopelessly in a spittoon or somewhere in the dust on the floor, stole the show and God was nowhere. That little stinking object triumphed over God and the salvation of the soul.

Then on top of that came the sermon, which was a rare picnic, for the chaplain, Otto Katz, was really a lovely man. His sermons were unusually exciting and amusing and they refreshed the boredom of the garrison gaol. He could drivel so beautifully about the infinite grace of God, and give uplift to the abandoned prisoners and disgraced men. He could let off such resounding oaths from the pulpit and the altar. He could roar out his '*Ite, missa est*' so gorgeously at the altar, conduct the whole service in such an original way and turn the whole order of the Holy Mass upside down. When he was thoroughly drunk he could invent entirely new prayers and a new Holy Mass, even a liturgy of his own, something which was quite unheard of here.

And then, what a scream when he sometimes slipped and fell over with the chalice, the holy sacrament or the missal, loudly accusing the server from the prison unit of having purposely tripped him up and dealing him out solitary confinement or irons before the Holy Communion itself.

And the recipient was happy because it was an inseparable part of the whole pantomime in the prison chapel. He played a leading part in the piece and acquitted himself honourably in it.

The chaplain, Otto Katz, the most perfect of army chaplains, was a Jew. By the way, there's nothing odd about that. Archbishop Kohn was a Jew too and a friend of Machar[1] into the bargain.

Chaplain Otto Katz had an even more colourful past than the famous Archbishop Kohn.

He studied at the Commercial Academy and served in the forces as a one-year volunteer. He mastered so thoroughly bills of exchange and the laws about them that within a year he brought the firm of Katz and Co. Ltd to such a glorious and successful bankruptcy that old Mr Katz went off to North America, pulling off a kind of settlement unbeknown to his creditors or his partner, who went off to the Argentine.

And so after having disinterestedly bestowed the firm of Katz and

[1]. At the turn of the century the Czech poet J. S. Machar (1864–1942) defended Dr Theodor Kohn, Archbishop of Olomouc, against attacks on his Jewish origin.

Co. upon North and South America, young Otto Katz found himself in the position of a man who had no hopes of inheriting anything, had nowhere to lay his head and must therefore join the army.

Before this, however, Otto Katz had hit upon an awfully fine idea. He had himself baptized. He turned to Christ to help him make a career. He applied to him in absolute confidence that this was a business transaction between him and the Son of God.

He was solemnly baptized in the Emmaus monastery in Prague. Father Alban himself[1] dipped him in the font. It was a magnificent spectacle; it was attended by a pious major from the regiment where Otto Katz served, an old maid from the Institute of Gentlewomen on the Hradčany and a large-jowled representative of the consistory, who acted as his godfather.

The officers' examination went off well, and the newly-fledged Christian Otto Katz stayed in the army. At first he thought he was going to do well and even wanted to study on staff courses.

But one day he got drunk and went into a monastery, gave up the sword and donned the cassock. He was received by the archbishop on the Hradčany and managed to get himself into the seminary. Before his ordination he got drunk as a fish in a very respectable house served by ladies in the alley behind U Vejvodů, and straight from a whirl of voluptuous pleasures and delights went to have himself ordained. After his ordination he went to his regiment to try and get them to help him get a job. After he was appointed chaplain, he bought a horse, rode through the streets of Prague and took a merry part in all the drinking bouts with the officers of his regiment.

In the corridor of the house where he lived the curses of dissatisfied creditors could very often be heard. He also brought home tarts from off the streets or sent his orderly to fetch them. He loved playing färbl,[2] and there were certain conjectures and presumptions that he cheated, but nobody caught him out with an ace hidden in the wide sleeves of his chaplain's cassock. In officer circles they called him 'Holy Father'.

He never prepared his sermons beforehand and in this he differed from his predecessor who also used to visit the garrison gaol. The latter was possessed by the fixed idea that the men in the garrison gaol

1. Alban Schachleitner, a Benedictine monk, said later to have emigrated to Germany and become a Nazi.
2. An illegal Austrian card game.

could be reformed from the pulpit. This venerable chaplain piously rolled his eyes, explaining to the prisoners that prostitutes should be reformed and care for unmarried mothers improved, and held forth about the bringing up of illegitimate children. His sermons were of an abstract character with no connection whatsoever with life today. They were very boring.

Chaplain Otto Katz, on the contrary, delivered sermons which everybody looked forward to.

It was a festive moment when they led the 'number sixteens' to the chapel in their pants, because to allow them to be dressed entailed the risk that one of them might escape. They put these twenty angels in white pants right under the pulpit. Some of them, upon whom fortune had smiled, were chewing fag-ends which they had found on the way, because as was only natural they had no pockets and there was nowhere to put them.

Around them stood the rest of the garrison prisoners and gazed with relish at the twenty men in pants beneath the pulpit. The chaplain climbed up in to it, clinking his spurs.

'Attention!' he shouted. 'Let us pray, forward after me, repeating what I say! And you at the back there, you bastard, don't snot into your hands! You're in the temple of the Lord, and I'll have you locked up for it. I wonder if you haven't forgotten the Lord's Prayer, you oafs? All right, let's try it – well, I knew it wouldn't go. What the hell does the Lord's Prayer mean to you? All you care about is two helpings of meat and bean salad, stuffing yourself up, lying on your backsides on your bunk and picking your nose without a thought for the Lord. Isn't that right?'

He stared down from the pulpit at the twenty white angels in pants, who were thoroughly enjoying themselves like all the rest. At the back they were playing 'flesh'.[1]

'This is first-class,' Švejk whispered to his neighbour, who was suspected of having taken an axe and chopped off all his mate's fingers to get him out of military service – at the price of three crowns.

'You wait,' was the answer. 'Today he's properly oiled again. He'll tell us once more about the thorny path of sin.'

True enough the chaplain was in an excellent mood that day. He did

---

1. A game among soldiers where one soldier bares his buttocks and the others hit him from behind. If he can guess which of the others has hit him, that soldier has to change places with him.

not know himself why he was doing it, but he continually leaned out
of the pulpit and nearly overbalanced.

'Sing something, boys,' he shouted down to them, 'or do you want
me to teach you a new song? Now sing with me:

> 'Of all people in the world,
> I love my love the best.
> I'm not her only visitor;
> I queue up with the rest.
> Her lovers are innumerable.
> Now, tell me, pray, her name?
> It is the Virgin Mary —

'You'll never learn it, you bastards,' continued the chaplain. 'I'd
like to have you all shot, do you understand? I state this from this
holy place of God, you scoundrels, because God's a thing that's not
afraid of you and'll give you hell, and all because you hesitate to turn
to Christ and you'd rather go along the thorny path of sin.'

'Now it's coming. He's properly oiled,' whispered Švejk's neighbour
delightedly.

'The thorny path of sin, you bloody half-wits, is the path of the
battle against vice. You are the prodigal sons who prefer to loll about
in quod rather than return to the bosom of Our Father. But lift up
your eyes to heaven on high, and you will be victorious and peace will
abide in your souls, you gutter-snipes. I'd be glad if the person at the
back would stop snorting. He's not a horse and he's not in a stable.
He's in the Temple of the Lord. Let me tell you that, ducks. Now then,
where was I? Yes,' he continued in German, 'about peace in your
souls. Very good. Bear in mind, you cattle, that you're human beings
and that you must look through the dark clouds into the wide spaces
and know that everything here lasts only for a moment, while God is
for eternity. Very good, wasn't it, gentlemen?' (He lapsed into German
again.) 'I ought to pray for you day and night, that merciful God, you
bloody imbeciles, may infuse your cold hearts with His spirit and wash
away your sins with His holy mercy, that you may be His for evermore
and that He may love you for ever, you blackguards. But that's just
where you're wrong. I'm not going to lead you into paradise.' The
chaplain hiccoughed. 'No, I won't,' he repeated obstinately. 'I won't
do anything for you. I wouldn't dream of it, because you are incorrigible
scum. On your ways you will not be guided by the grace of the

Lord, the breath of God's love will not be wafted on to you, because the Lord would not dream of having anything to do with such twisters as you. Do you hear that, you down there below in those pants?'

Twenty pairs of pants looked up and said as with one voice:

'Humbly report, sir, we hear.'

'It's not enough just to hear,' the chaplain continued. 'Dark is the cloud of life and God's smile will not take away your woe, you bloody apes, for God's goodness has its bounds too. And don't choke yourself, you bounder at the back there, or I'll have you locked up until you're black in the face! And you down there, don't think that you're in the tap room! God is supremely merciful, but only to decent people and not to the scum of human society who won't be guided by His laws or by service regulations. That's what I wanted to tell you. You don't know how to pray, and you think that going to chapel is some kind of entertainment like being at a theatre or cinema. But I'll knock that out of your heads so that you don't think that I'm here to amuse you and bring pleasure to your lives. I'll send each one of you into solitary confinement, that's what I'll do, you sods. I'm wasting my time on you and I see it's all quite useless. If the field marshal himself or the archbishop had been here you wouldn't reform, you wouldn't incline to the Lord. But all the same one of these days you'll remember how I was trying to do you some good.'

Among the twenty pants a sob could be heard. It was Švejk, who had burst into tears.

The chaplain looked down. There stood Švejk rubbing his eyes with his fist. Round him were signs of gleeful appreciation.

Pointing to Švejk the chaplain continued:

'Let every one of you take an example from this man. What is he doing? He's crying. Don't cry, I tell you, don't cry! Do you want to reform? That's not so easy for you, my lad. You're crying now, but when you go back to your cell you'll be just as big a bastard as you were before. You'll have to think a lot about the unending grace and mercy of God. You'll have to work hard to see that your sinful soul finds the right path to tread in this world. Just now we saw a man who wants to be reformed bursting into tears. And what do the rest of you do? Nothing at all. Over there someone's chewing something, as though his parents had been ruminants, and over there they're searching for lice in their shirts in the Temple of the Lord. Can't you do your scratching at home? Must you reserve it just for the divine service?

And, Staff Warder, you never notice anything either. After all, you're all soldiers and not a lot of half-witted civilians. You've got to behave as befits soldiers even if you're in a church. For Christ's sake, get on with searching for God, and do your searching for lice at home. That's all I've got to say, you gutter-snipes, and I request you to behave yourselves at Mass, so that it doesn't happen as it did last time, when people in the back rows were bartering government linen for bread and then gorging it during the elevation of the Host.'

The chaplain came down from the pulpit and went off to the vestry, followed by the staff warder. After a while the staff warder came out, went straight up to Švejk, pulled him out of the group of twenty pants and led him away to the vestry.

The chaplain was sitting very comfortably on a table and rolling a cigarette.

When Švejk came in, the chaplain said:

'Oh, here you are! I've been thinking it all over and I believe I've seen through you. D'you understand, you bastard? It's the first case I've had of anyone blubbing in the church here.'

He jumped down from the table and, standing beneath a huge gloomy painting of St Francis of Sales, jerked at Švejk's shoulder and shouted:

'Confess that you only blubbed for fun, you sod.'

And St Francis of Sales gazed inquiringly down from his portrait at Švejk. From another painting on the other side, a martyr gazed openmouthed at him, while Roman mercenaries were sawing through his buttocks. During this operation no suffering could be detected on the martyr's face, nor the joy nor the glory of martyrdom either. He only stared, open-mouthed, as though he wanted to say: 'How on earth did this happen to me? What on earth are you doing to me, gentlemen?'

'Humbly report, sir,' said Švejk deliberately, staking everything on a single card, 'I confess to God Almighty and to you, venerable Father, who are God's deputy, that I was really only blubbing for fun. I saw that for your preaching you needed a reformed sinner, and that you were looking for him in vain in your sermon. And so I really wanted to give you a pleasure, so that you shouldn't think that there weren't any just men left, and at the same time I wanted to have a little fun on my own to get some relief.'

The chaplain looked searchingly at Švejk's artless countenance. A sunbeam played on the melancholy face of St Francis of Sales and warmed the staring eyes of the martyr on the opposite wall.

'I'm beginning to take a fancy to you,' said the chaplain, sitting on the table again. 'Which regiment do you belong to?' He began to hiccough.

'Humbly report, sir, I belong and don't belong to the 91st regiment and I haven't the faintest idea how I really stand.'

'And what are you in gaol here for?' inquired the chaplain, continuing to hiccough.

From the chapel were wafted in this direction the sounds of a harmonium which was a substitute for an organ. The musician, a teacher who had been gaoled for desertion, wailed out on the harmonium the most mournful hymn tunes. With the hiccoughing of the chaplain these sounds blended to form a new Doric scale.

'Humbly report, sir, I really don't know why I am in gaol here, but I don't complain. It's just my bad luck. My intentions are always the best, and in the end I always get the worst of it, just like that martyr there in the picture.'

The chaplain looked at the picture, smiled and said:

'Yes, I've really taken to you. I must ask the judge advocate about you and I won't stay talking to you any longer. I must get that Holy Mass off my chest! About turn! Dismiss!'

When Švejk returned to his family group of pants beneath the pulpit, he replied very drily and laconically to their questions about what the chaplain had wanted of him in the vestry:

'He's sozzled.'

The chaplain's new performance, the Holy Mass, was followed by all with close attention and unconcealed enjoyment. One man under the pulpit even bet that the monstrance would fall out of the chaplain's hands. He wagered his whole portion of bread against two across the jaw and won his bet.

What inspired the souls of everyone in the chapel at the sight of the chaplain's ministration was not the mysticism of the faithful or the piety of true Catholics; it was the feeling we have in the theatre when we do not know what the play is about, when the plot develops and we breathlessly wait to see how it is going to end. They were absorbed in the scene which the chaplain with great devotion presented to them before the altar.

They surrendered completely to the aesthetic enjoyment of the vestments which the chaplain had put on inside out and watched all the happenings at the altar with ardent sympathy and enthusiasm.

The red-haired server, a deserter from the ranks of the sextons, a specialist in petty larcenies in the 28th regiment, was doing his level best to conjure up in his memory the whole ritual, technique and text of the Holy Mass. He was both server and prompter to the chaplain, who quite frivolously turned whole sentences upside down and instead of getting to the ordinary Mass found himself at that point of the prayer book where the Advent Mass came. He then began to sing this to the general satisfaction of the congregation.

He had neither voice nor musical ear, and under the vaulting of the chapel there resounded such a squealing and caterwauling as could only be heard in a pig-sty.

'He's really well sozzled today,' those sitting in front of the altar said with great joy and relish. 'He isn't half oiled. He's been at it again! He must have got tight with some tarts somewhere.'

And now for about the third time the strains of '*Ite, missa est!*' rang out from the altar like a Red Indian war-whoop until the windows rattled.

Then the chaplain looked once more into the chalice, in case there should still be a drop of wine left in it, made a gesture of annoyance and addressed his listeners:

'Well, now you can go home, you bastards. It's all over. I observed that you don't show that true piety you ought to have when you are in church in the presence of the Holy of Holies, you cads. When you're face to face with God Almighty you're not ashamed to laugh aloud, cough and snigger, shuffle your feet, even in my presence, who represent here the Virgin Mary, Jesus Christ and God the Father, you bloody imbeciles. If you do this again next time you'll get the hell you deserve and you'll learn that there's not only that hell which I preached to you about in my last sermon but one, but a hell on earth as well. And if you should by any chance save yourself from the first one, I'll see you don't escape from the second. Dismiss!'

The chaplain, who had just given such a wonderful practical demonstration of that damnable old custom – prison visiting – went into the vestry, changed his clothes, poured out some sacramental wine from the cask into a flagon, drank it up and with the help of the red-haired server mounted his horse which was tied up in the courtyard. Then he remembered Švejk, dismounted again and went to the office of Judge Advocate Bernis.

Judge Advocate Bernis was a man who liked society. He was an elegant dancer and a rake who was frightfully bored here and spent his time writing German verses for girls' autograph albums so as to have a supply always at hand. He was the most important element in the whole apparatus of military justice, and because he had such a tremendous pile of unfinished cases and muddled documents he was held in respect by the whole military court on Hradčany. He kept losing the documents for the indictment and was compelled to invent new ones. He mixed up names, lost the threads of the indictments and spun new ones just as they happened to come into his head. He tried deserters for theft and thieves for desertion. He brought in political cases which he had fabricated himself. He invented all kinds of hocus-pocus to convict men of crimes they had never even dreamt of. He invented insults to the monarch and always attributed fabricated incriminating state-ments to anyone, if the indictment and informers' reports had got lost in the unending chaos of documents and official correspon-dence.

'Hallo,' said the chaplain, shaking his hand. 'How are you?'

'Not very well,' answered Bernis. 'They've mucked up my papers and I can't make bloody head or tail of them. Yesterday I put up the material I'd processed on a fellow had up for mutiny, and they sent it back saying that in this case it wasn't a question of mutiny but of stealing a tin. And I'd taken the trouble to give it a completely different number, and it beats me how they managed to discover it.'

The judge advocate spat.

'Are you still playing cards?' asked the chaplain.

'I've lost everything I had at cards. The last time it happened I was playing makao with that bald-headed colonel and I had to throw everything I'd got down his bloody maw. But I know of a nice young bird. And what are you doing, Holy Father?'

'I need a batman,' said the chaplain. 'Last time I had an old book-keeper without academic education but a prize bastard. He kept on snivelling and praying that God would save him, and so in the end I drafted him off to the front with a march battalion. They say it was cut to pieces. Then they sent me a little chap, who did nothing but sit in the pub and drink at my expense. He was quite a tolerable cove, but had sweaty feet. So I drafted him off too. Today when I was preaching I found a bastard who started blubbing just for fun. That's the kind of cove I need. He's called Švejk and sits in no. 16. I'd like to know why they've put him there and whether it wouldn't be possible somehow to arrange for me to get him out.'

The judge advocate started looking in the drawers for the files on Švejk, but as usual he couldn't find anything.

'Captain Linhart'll have them,' he said after a long search. 'God knows where all these files of mine get to. I must have sent them to Linhart. I'll telephone to him at once – Hallo! It's Lieutenant Bernis speaking, sir. Please, have you by any chance some files about a man called Švejk. . . . They must be with me? I'm surprised. . . . I took them over from you? Well, I'm very surprised. . . . He's at present in no. 16 . . . I know, sir, that I've got the no. 16 file with me. But I thought that Švejk's papers must be lying around somewhere in your tray. . . . You'd be glad if I didn't speak to you in that tone? Papers don't lie around in your tray? . . . Hallo, hallo . . .'

Bernis sat down at the table and angrily condemned the disorderly way the investigations were being carried out. There was a long-standing feud between him and Captain Linhart in which they were both very consistent. If Bernis got hold of papers belonging to Linhart, he arranged them in a way that no one could make head or tail of them. Linhart did exactly the same with papers belonging to Bernis. And of course they lost each other's enclosures.[1]

(The papers on Švejk were not found until after the war. They were in the archives of the Army Legal Department and were minuted: 'Planned to throw off his hypocritical mask and come out publicly against our ruler and our state.' The papers had been stuck into files dealing with a certain Josef Koudela. On the file cover was a cross and underneath it 'Action completed' with the date.)

'So I've lost Švejk,' said Bernis. 'I'll have him sent for, and if he doesn't confess to anything, I'll let him go and have him drafted to you and you can settle it with his regiment.'

After the chaplain had gone Bernis had Švejk brought before him but left him standing at the door, because he had just received a telephone message from police headquarters that the material which was required for prosecution document no. 7267 about infantryman

---

1. Thirty per cent of the people who sat in the garrison gaol went on sitting there throughout the whole war without once being brought up for interrogation. (Author's note.)

Maixner, had arrived in office no. 1 and been signed for by Captain Linhart.

Meanwhile Švejk inspected the judge advocate's office.

One could not say that it made a very favourable impression, especially the photographs on the walls. They were photographs of various executions carried out by the army in Galicia and Serbia. They were artistic photographs of charred cottages and trees with branches sagging under the weight of bodies strung up on them. Particularly fine was a photograph from Serbia of a whole family strung up – a small boy and his father and mother. Two soldiers with bayonets were guarding the tree, and an officer stood victoriously in the foreground smoking a cigarette. On the other side in the background a field kitchen could be seen in full operation.

'Well, what's the trouble with you, Švejk?' asked Bernis, when he had filed away the telephone message. 'What have you been up to? Are you going to confess or wait until a charge is brought against you? It can't go on like this. Don't imagine that you're before a court where you'll be tried by lunatic civilians. Ours are courts-martial – the Imperial and Royal Military Court. The only way you can save yourself from a severe and just punishment is to confess.'

Bernis had a special method when he had lost the material against the accused. As you can see, there was nothing special about it and so we need not be surprised if the results of such an examination and cross-questioning always amounted to nix.

And Bernis felt he was always so clairvoyant that, without having any material against the accused and without knowing what he was accused of or why he was imprisoned in the garrison gaol but simply by observing the behaviour and physiognomy of the man who had been brought before him for interrogation, he could deduce why they had imprisoned him.

His clairvoyance and knowledge of human nature was so great that a gipsy who was sent by his regiment to the garrison gaol for stealing a few dozen shirts (he was helping the storekeeper in a store) was accused by him of political crimes; allegedly he had spoken in a pub somewhere with some soldiers about the setting up of an independent national state made up of the lands of the Bohemian crown and Slovakia and ruled by a Slav king.

'We have material evidence,' he said to the unfortunate gipsy. 'There's nothing left for you but to confess in which pub you said it, which regiment those soldiers came from, who listened to you and when it took place.'

The unfortunate gipsy invented not only the date but the pub and the regiment which his alleged listeners came from, and when he left the interrogation he ran away from the garrison altogether.

'So you won't confess to anything,' said Bernis, when Švejk remained deathly silent. 'You won't say why you're here and why they've put you in gaol? You could at least have told me, before I tell you it myself. I warn you once more that you'd better confess. It will be easier for you because it helps the investigation and alleviates the punishment. In that respect it's just the same here as in a civil court.'

'Humbly report, sir,' Švejk piped up good-naturedly, 'I am here in garrison gaol because I'm a foundling.'

'What do you mean by that?'

'Humbly report, sir, I can explain it quite simply. In our street there's a coal merchant and he had an entirely innocent two-year-old little boy. This laddie once walked all the way from Vinohrady to Libeň, where a policeman found him sitting on the pavement. So he took him to the police station and locked him up there – a two-year-old child. The little boy was, as you see, quite innocent and yet he was locked up. And if he'd been able to speak and anyone had asked him why he was locked up there, he wouldn't have known either. And it's rather like that with me. I'm a foundling too.'

The keen gaze of the judge advocate passed swiftly over Švejk's figure and face and foundered on them. Such unconcern and innocence radiated from the whole of the being which stood before him that Bernis began to pace nervously up and down his office and, if he had not given his word to the chaplain, God knows what might have happened to Švejk.

Finally he came to a standstill again by his table.

'Listen,' he said to Švejk, who was gazing unconcernedly in front of him. 'If ever I meet you again, you'll never forget it. Take him away!'

When they took Švejk back to no. 16 Bernis had Staff Warder Slavík called before him.

'Until further orders,' he said laconically, 'Švejk is sent to Chaplain Katz for his disposal. Prepare his discharge papers and have him escorted to the chaplain by two men!'

'Is he to be put in handcuffs for the journey, sir?'

The judge advocate banged his fist on the table.

'You're an oaf. I told you quite distinctly to make his discharge papers out.'

And all the bile which had accumulated in the judge advocate's soul in the course of that day because of Captain Linhart and Švejk poured out like a wild torrent on the head of the staff warder. At the end of it Bernis said:

'And now do you understand that you are a prize royal oaf?'

This is something which should only be said to kings and emperors, but even this simple staff warder, who was no royal personage, was not very pleased about it. On his way back from the judge advocate's office he gave a cruel kicking to a prisoner on fatigue duty who was cleaning the corridor.

As for Švejk, the staff warder made up his mind that he must spend at least one night more in the garrison gaol so as to derive a little more benefit from it.

The night spent in the garrison gaol will always rank among Švejk's most affectionate memories.

Next to no. 16 was the 'black hole', a murky pit for solitary confinement, from which could be heard during that night the howls of a soldier whose ribs were being broken by Sergeant-Major Řepa at the orders of Staff Warder Slavík because of a disciplinary offence.

When the howling stopped there could be heard in no. 16 the smashing of lice which got in between the fingers of the prisoners during their search.

Above the doors in an aperture in the wall a paraffin lamp, fitted with a protective grille, emitted a feeble light and smoked. The smell of paraffin mingled with the natural exhalations of unwashed human bodies and the stench of the bucket, which every time it was used had its surface stirred up and added a new wave of stink to no. 16.

The bad food made the digestive process difficult for everyone, and the majority suffered from wind, which they released into the stillness of the night, answering each other with these signals to the accompaniment of various witticisms.

In the corridors could be heard the measured tread of the sentries. From time to time the aperture in the door opened and a warder peered through the peephole.

From the middle bunk could be heard a voice quietly saying:

'Before I tried to escape and before they brought me here among you I was in no. 12. There they keep the light cases. Once they brought in a chap from somewhere in the country. The good fellow had got fourteen days because he allowed soldiers to stay overnight with him. At first they thought that it was a plot but then it turned out that he did it for money. He should have been locked up among the lightest cases but because it was full there he came to us. And you can't imagine all the things he brought with him from home and what they sent him, because he somehow got permission to order his own food and make things cosy for himself. And he got permission to smoke. He had two hams, giant loaves of bread, eggs, butter, cigarettes – well, in short he had in his two knapsacks everything you could dream of. And the bastard thought that he must guzzle it all up himself. We started begging him to share it with us, when he didn't hit on the idea himself, like others did when they got something. But he was a mean bastard and said no: he'd be locked up for fourteen days and the cabbage and rotten potatoes, which they gave us for mess rations, would ruin his stomach. He said he'd give us all his mess rations and army bread: it wasn't worth having and we could share it among ourselves or have it in turns. I tell you that he was such a gent that he didn't even want to sit on the bucket and waited until the next day for the exercise hour so that he could do it in the latrine in the courtyard. He was so spoiled that he even brought his own toilet paper. We told him that we didn't care a damn about his rations and we braved it out one, two, three days. The bastard guzzled ham, spread butter on his bread, shelled his eggs – in short he lived like a pig in clover. He smoked cigarettes and wouldn't give anyone even a puff. He said that we weren't allowed to smoke and if the warder were to see him giving us a puff they'd lock him up. As I said we stood it for three days. But on the fourth day in the night we did it. The bastard woke up early, and I forgot to tell you that in the early morning, at noon and in the evening, before he began to stuff himself, he always prayed and prayed for a very long time. And so this time he prayed and then looked for his knapsacks under his bunk. Yes, the knapsacks were there, but they were dried up and shrunk like dried prunes. He began to shriek that he had been robbed and that we'd only left him his toilet paper. And then for about five minutes he thought that we were only joking and that we had hidden it somewhere. He said still quite merrily: "I know you're only teasing. I know you'll give it back to me, but it was neatly done." There was a chap among us from Libeň and he said, "Look, cover yourself with your blanket and count up till ten. And then look in your knapsacks." And he covered himself and counted one, two, three, like an obedient little boy . . . and then the chap from Libeň said again: "You mustn't do it so quickly, you must do it very slowly." And there he was under the blanket counting slowly at intervals: one – two – three – . . . and when he got to ten he climbed out of his bunk and looked into his knapsacks. "Jesus Mary, chaps," he began hollering, "they're just as empty as they were before." And all the time his face was so bloody silly that we could all have split our sides with laughter. And then that chap from Libeň went on: "Try once more." And believe me he was so crazy after all this that he tried again, and when he saw that there was still nothing there except toilet paper he began to bang on the door and to shout out: "They've robbed me, they've robbed me, help, open, for Christ's sake, open." And then they all came rushing in and called the staff warder and Sergeant-Major Řepa. We all said with one voice that he had gone mad, that the day before he gorged far into the night and guzzled everything up. But he just wept and kept on saying: "Surely there must be some crumbs left somewhere." And then they started looking for the crumbs and couldn't find any because we were quite clever too. What we had not been able to guzzle ourselves we sent by rope-post up to the second storey. They couldn't prove anything on us, although that stupid fool kept on with his: "But surely there must be some crumbs left." The whole day he ate nothing and looked carefully to see whether anyone ate or smoked anything. And at lunch the next day again he didn't touch his rations, but in the evening the rotten potatoes and cabbage seemed to appeal to him, only he didn't pray as much as he did when he used to tuck into his ham and eggs. Then one of us somehow got some fags from outside, and then he began talking to us for the first time, asking us to give him a puff. But we didn't give him anything.'

'I was afraid you'd give him a puff,' remarked Švejk. 'That would've spoiled the whole story. You only find noble actions like that in novels, but in the garrison gaol in such circumstances it would be sheer lunacy.'

'And you didn't give him the blanket treatment?' someone asked.

'We didn't think of it.' Then a discussion began in hushed tones as to whether he should have had the blanket treatment or not. The majority were for it.

The conversation gradually died out. They were falling asleep, scratching themselves under their armpits, on their chests and on their bellies – at those points in their underclothes where the lice congregated most. They went to sleep, drawing the lice-ridden blankets over their heads, so that the light of the paraffin lamp shouldn't disturb them ...

At eight o'clock in the morning they called Švejk to go to the office.

'On the left-hand side of the door leading into the office there's a spittoon and they throw fag-ends into it,' one man informed Švejk. 'And on the first floor you'll pass another one. They don't sweep the passages till nine o'clock, so something may still be there.'

But Švejk disappointed their hopes. He never came back to no. 16. The nineteen pairs of pants made various deductions and conjectures about him.

A freckled soldier belonging to the Landwehr who had a very lurid imagination spread the news that Švejk had shot his captain and would be led away the same day to the drill-ground at Motol for execution.

10

Švejk Batman to the Chaplain

I

ŠVEJK'S odyssey began anew under the honourable escort of two soldiers with fixed bayonets who had to conduct him to the chaplain.

His escort were men who complemented each other. If one was lanky, the other was small and tubby. The lanky one limped with his right foot and the small tubby one with his left. Both served behind the lines because sometime before the war they had been totally exempted from military service.

They walked solemnly alongside the pavement and from time to time looked sideways at Švejk, who strode in the middle and saluted everyone he saw. His mufti and the military cap he got when he joined up had got lost in the garrison stores. Before they discharged him they had given him an old military uniform which had belonged to some pot-bellied fellow who was taller than him by a head.

As for the trousers three more Švejks could have got into them. An endless succession of baggy folds from his feet up to where his trousers reached over his chest involuntarily evoked the admiration of the spectators. A vast tunic with patches on the elbows, covered with grease and dirt, dangled around Švejk like a coat on a scarecrow. His trousers hung on him like a circus clown's costume. The military cap, which they had also changed in the garrison gaol, came down over his ears.

Švejk answered the smiles of the spectators with a sweet smile of his own and the warm tender look of his good-natured eyes.

And so they marched to the chaplain's apartment at Karlín.

The first of the two to speak to Švejk was the small tubby one. They were just at that moment in Malá Strana down under the arcades.

'Where do you come from?' asked the small tubby one.

'From Prague.'

'And you're not going to run away?'

Now the lanky one joined the conversation. It is a very remarkable phenomenon that people who are small and fat are generally good-humoured optimists, whereas people who are lanky and spindly are on the contrary sceptics.

And so the lanky one said: 'He'd run away if he could.'

'But why should he?' replied the small tubby one. 'Now he's out of the garrison gaol he's practically free. I'm carrying it in the bundle here.'

'What's in that bundle for the chaplain?' asked the lanky one.

'I don't know.'

'There, you see. You don't know and yet you talk about it.'

They crossed the Charles Bridge in complete silence. In Charles Street the small tubby one spoke to Švejk again:

'Do you know why we're taking you to the chaplain?'

'For confession,' said Švejk nonchalantly. 'Tomorrow they're going to hang me. This is what they always do on these occasions and they call it spiritual consolation.'

'And why are they going to. . . ?' the lanky one asked cautiously, while the tubby one looked pityingly at Švejk.

Each was a small tradesman from the country, a paterfamilias.

'I don't know,' replied Švejk, with his good-natured smile. 'I haven't the faintest idea. It must be fate.'

'Perhaps you were born under an unlucky star,' remarked the little fellow with a knowing air and in sympathy. 'At home in Jasenná near Josefov during the war with Prussia they hanged someone just like that. They came to fetch him, didn't say anything to him, and hanged him in Josefov.'

'If you ask me,' said the lanky one sceptically, 'they don't hang a person for nothing at all. There must always be some reason for it, so they can justify it.'

'When there isn't a war on,' remarked Švejk, 'they justify it, but when there is, they don't worry about you. You could just as well fall at the front or be hanged at home – six of one or half a dozen of the other.'

'I say, you're not a "political", are you?' asked the lanky one. The tone of his question indicated that he was beginning to take to Švejk.

'Yes, I'm much too political,' replied Švejk with a smile.

'You aren't a National Socialist?'[1] Now it was the turn of the small

1. A Czech political party dating from Austrian times. Later Eduard Beneš became one of its leaders.

tubby one to start being cautious. Breaking in on the conversation he said: 'What's that got to do with us anyway? There are lots of people around everywhere and they're watching us. If we could only take off our bayonets in a passage somewhere without attracting attention. You won't run away from us, will you? We'd have trouble if you did. Aren't I right, Toník?' he said to the lanky one, who answered quietly: 'We could take off our bayonets. After all, he's one of us.'

He ceased being a sceptic and his heart filled with compassion for Švejk. They looked for a suitable passage where they could take off their bayonets and the tubby one allowed Švejk to walk alongside him.

'You'd like a smoke, wouldn't you?' he said. 'I wonder whether . . .' He wanted to say: 'I wonder whether they allow you to have a smoke before they hang you', but he did not complete the sentence, realizing that it might be tactless.

They all had a smoke and Švejk's escort began to tell him about their families in the country near Hradec Králové, their wives and children, their plot of land and their cow.

'I'm thirsty,' said Švejk.

The lanky one and the small tubby one exchanged glances.

'We might drop in somewhere for a quick one,' said the little fellow, feeling he could count on the lanky one's consent, 'but somewhere where it won't attract attention.'

'Let's go to Kuklík,' Švejk suggested. 'You can put your rifles in the kitchen there. The landlord, Serabona, is a Sokol[1] and you don't need to be afraid of him.

'They play the violin and the accordion there,' continued Švejk, 'and tarts come in and various other members of good society who aren't allowed in at the Represent'ák.'[2]

The lanky one and the small one exchanged glances once more and then the lanky one said: 'Very well, then, let's go. It's still a long way to Karlín.'

On the way Švejk told them various stories, and they arrived at Kuklík in a good mood and did exactly as Švejk had advised. They put

1. Czech patriotic sports club whose members wore falcon feathers on their hats. (Sokol = falcon.)
2. The Representational Hall – a complex in the centre of Prague containing a café, a restaurant, several reception rooms and the Smetana Hall, the largest concert hall.

their rifles in the kitchen and went into the bar, where the violin and accordion filled the room with the strains of the popular song:

> At Pankrác there's a hill
> And on that hill there stands
> A lovely row of trees . . .

A young lady who was sitting on the knees of a jaded youth with smoothly parted hair was singing in a hoarse voice: 'I had a girl lined up and now another's pinched her.'

At one table a drunken sardine-hawker was asleep. He woke up from time to time, struck the table with his fist, stuttered out: 'It's no good', and fell asleep again. Under a mirror behind the billiard table sat three other young ladies who shouted at a railway guard: 'Young man, stand us a glass of vermouth.' Near the orchestra two people were quarrelling about whether Mařka had been caught the previous night by the patrol or not. One of them saw it with his own eyes and the other maintained that she had gone to bed with a soldier at the hotel U Valšů.[1]

By the door a soldier was sitting with a number of civilians and telling them how he had been wounded in Serbia. He had a bandaged arm and his pockets were full of cigarettes they had given him. He said that he couldn't drink any more, but one of the company, a bald-headed old man, kept on offering him something: 'Have another, soldier. Who knows if we'll ever meet again. Shall I get them to play something for you? Do you like "The Orphan Child"?'

This was the bald-headed old man's favourite song, and sure enough presently the violin and accordion started to wail it out, while tears came into his eyes and he started to sing in a tremulous voice: 'When it grew to wiser years, it asked about its mamma, it asked about its mamma . . .'

From the other table somebody said: 'Stop it, can't you? Go and stuff it up! String yourself up on a hook! Get to bloody hell with your orphan child!'

And as a final trump the rival table began to sing: 'To part, to part, It breaks my heart, my heart . . .'

'Franta,' they called to the wounded soldier when they had out-sung and drowned the 'Orphan Child', 'leave them and come and sit

1. A louche house in Prague where rooms could be rented by the hour.

with us. They can go to hell. You come and bring the cigarettes here. You won't amuse those mugs.'

Švejk conjured up memories of the time when he often used to sit here before the war. The police inspector, Drašner, used to raid the place and the prostitutes were scared of him and made up songs about him full of *double-entendres*. He remembered how once they sang in a chorus:

> When Drašner made his raid
> Mařena wasn't afraid.
> In all the hullaballoo
> She'd knocked back quite a few.

Just at that moment who should have come in but the terrible and ruthless Drašner himself, accompanied by his men. It was like shooting into a flock of partridges. The plain-clothes police herded all the people together in a bunch. And Švejk found himself in it too, because with his usual bad luck he had said to Inspector Drašner when he was asked to show his papers: 'Have you got permission for this from police headquarters?' Švejk also remembered a poet who used to sit there under the mirror, and in the general uproar of Kuklík amidst the strains and sounds of the accordion used to write poems and recite them to the prostitutes.

On the other hand Švejk's escort had no such reminiscences. For them it was a quite new experience and they began to like it. The first who found complete satisfaction here was the small tubby one, because people of his type tend to be not only optimists but epicures. The lanky one struggled with himself for a short time. And just as he had already lost his scepticism, so he now began gradually to lose his self-control and the rest of his good sense also.

'I'm going to have a dance,' he said after his fifth beer, when he saw how couples were dancing the 'Šlapák'.

The little one abandoned himself completely to dissipation. A young lady sat next to him and told him dirty stories. His eyes sparkled.

Švejk drank. The lanky one finished his dance and returned with his partner to the table. Then they sang, danced, drank without interruption and spanked their lady companions. And in the atmosphere of venal love, nicotine and alcohol there was ever present, if barely perceptible, the old slogan: '*Après nous le déluge!*'

In the afternoon a soldier came up to them and offered them a boil with blood poisoning for five guilders. He had with him a hypodermic

syringe and could inject paraffin into their legs or arms.[1] With this they would be in bed for at least two months and if they fed the wound with saliva they could perhaps spin it out to half a year and be completely discharged from the army.

The lanky one, who had completely lost his mental balance, had himself injected intravenously in the leg with paraffin. The soldier did it for him in the W.C.

As it was already getting towards evening Švejk proposed that they resume their journey to the chaplain. The small tubby one, who was already beginning to wander, tried to persuade Švejk to stay a little longer. The lanky one was also of the opinion that the chaplain could wait. But Švejk was not enjoying it any more at Kuklík and threatened to go on alone.

And so they left, but he had to promise them that they would all stop somewhere again.

They stopped at a small café at Florence, where the tubby one pawned his silver watch so that they could go on having fun.

When they left, Švejk was already leading them by the arm. It gave him an awful lot of trouble. Their feet kept on slipping, and they were all the time wanting to go somewhere. The small tubby one almost lost the bundle for the chaplain, and so Švejk was forced to carry it himself.

Švejk had continually to alert them when an officer or an N.C.O. came by. After superhuman efforts and struggles he managed to bring them to the house in Královská Avenue where the chaplain lived.

He fixed the bayonets on their rifles himself and by poking them in the ribs forced them to lead him instead of his leading them.

On the first floor, where there was a visiting card on the door: 'Otto Katz, Chaplain', a soldier came to open. From the drawing-room could be heard voices and the clinking of bottles and glasses.

'Hum – bly – report – sir,' said the lanky one with an effort in broken German and saluting the soldier: 'One – bundle – and one man delivered.'

'Come in,' said the soldier. 'However did you manage to get into that state? The chaplain's the same way . . .' The soldier spat.

[1]. This is a fairly well proved method of getting into hospital. But the smell of the paraffin, which remains in the boil, gives it away. Petrol is better, because it evaporates quicker. Subsequently a mixture of ether and petrol used to be injected and later other improvements were introduced. (Author's note.)

The soldier went off with the bundle. They waited in the hall for a long time until the door opened and through it there flew rather than walked the chaplain himself. He was in his waistcoat and held a cigar in his hand. 'So you're here already,' he said to Švejk, 'and these people brought you. Hey, have you got any matches?'

'Humbly report, sir, I haven't.'

'Hey, and why haven't you got any? Every soldier should have matches so that he can light up. A soldier who hasn't got any matches is . . . what is he?'

'Humbly report, sir, he's without matches,' answered Švejk.

'Very good. He's without matches and can't give anyone a light. Well, that's one essential point and now here's another. Do your feet stink, Švejk?'

'Humbly report, sir, they don't.'

'Well, that was the second point. And now for the third. Do you drink spirits?'

'Humbly report, sir, I don't drink spirits, only rum.'

'Good. Just have a look at this soldier here. I borrowed him for the day from Lieutenant Feldhuber. He's his batman. And he doesn't drink anything. He is a t- t- total abstainer, and that's why he is going to be drafted to the front. Be- because a man like him is no use to me. He's not a batman, he's a cow. A cow also drinks only water and lows like an ox.

'You're a teetotaller,' he said, addressing the soldier. 'You ought to be ashamed of yourself, you nincompoop. You deserve a few across the jaw.'

The chaplain addressed himself to those who had escorted Švejk and who in their endeavour to stand straight were wobbling about, vainly trying to prop themselves up on their rifles.

'You are dr- drunk,' said the chaplain. 'You got drunk while on duty, and I'm going to have you l- locked up for that. Švejk, remove their rifles and take them into the kitchen. You're to guard them until the patrol comes to fetch them. I shall teleph- teleph- telephone to the barracks.'

And so on this occasion too the truth of Napoleon's saying, 'In war the situation changes every moment', was entirely borne out.

In the morning these two had led Švejk under bayonet escort and had been afraid he might run away. Then he led them and now finally had to guard them.

They were not at first fully aware of this rapid change of fortune and it only dawned on them when they were sitting in the kitchen and saw Švejk standing at the door with rifle and bayonet.

'I could do with a drink,' sighed the little optimist, while the lanky one again had a fit of scepticism and said that the whole thing was a

piece of lousy treason. He started loudly accusing Švejk of having landed them in this mess and reproached him that he had promised them that he would be hanged the next day. And now they could see that it was all a trick with his confession and his hanging.

Švejk was silent and walked up and down by the door.

'We've been bloody asses!' shouted the lanky one.

In the end, having listened to all the accusations, Švejk declared:

'Now at any rate you can see that the army's no picnic. I'm only doing my duty. I got into this just the same way as you did, but as the saying is: Fortune smiled on me.'

'I could do with a drink,' repeated the optimist in desperate tones.

The lanky one got up and reeled towards the door. 'Let's go home,' he said to Švejk. 'Chum, don't be a bloody fool.'

'Get back,' answered Švejk. 'I've got to guard you. Now we don't know each other any longer.'

The chaplain appeared in the door: 'I – I – can't get through on the phone to the barracks, so you go home and remem-mem-member that when you're on duty you can't go and get yourselves sozzled. Quick march!'

To the honour of the chaplain may it be said that he did not get through to the barracks because he had no telephone at home and in fact was talking to a lamp-stand.

11

Švejk had been the chaplain's batman for three days, but during all this time he had seen him only once. On the third day Lieutenant Helmich's batman arrived to tell Švejk to come and fetch his chaplain.

On the way he told Švejk that the chaplain had had a quarrel with the lieutenant, had smashed the piano, was dead drunk and refused to go home.

Lieutenant Helmich was also drunk and had thrown the chaplain out into the corridor, where he was sitting on the floor by the door-way and dozing.

When Švejk reached the spot he shook the chaplain, and when the latter began to growl and opened his eyes, Švejk saluted and said:

'Humbly report, sir, I'm here.'

'And what do you want – here?'

'Humbly report, sir, I have to come and fetch you.'

'So you have to come and fetch me, have you? And where are we going?'

'To your apartment, sir.'

'Why do I have to go to my apartment – aren't I in my apartment?'

'Humbly report, sir, you're in the corridor of somebody else's house.'

'And how – did – I – get here?'

'Humbly report, sir, you were here on a visit.'

'N- n- not on a v- visit. You're m- m- making a mistake.'

Švejk lifted the chaplain and propped him up against the wall. The chaplain lurched from side to side and rolled over on him saying: 'I'm falling on you!

'Falling on you,' he repeated with an idiotic grin. Finally Švejk managed to press the chaplain to the wall, where in this new position he started to doze again.

Švejk woke him up. 'What can I do for you?' said the chaplain making a vain attempt to drag himself along by the wall and sit on the floor. 'Who are you, anyhow?'

'Humbly report, sir,' replied Švejk, pushing the chaplain back against the wall once more, 'I'm your batman, Your Reverence, sir.'

'I haven't got any batman,' said the chaplain with an effort, making another attempt to fall on to Švejk. 'And I'm not a Reverence.

'I'm a pig,' he added with the sincerity of a drunkard. 'Let me go, sir, I don't know you.'

The little tussle ended in a complete victory for Švejk. He took advantage of it to drag the chaplain down the stairs into the carriage entrance, where the chaplain tried to stop him from dragging him into the street. 'I don't know you, sir,' he kept on saying to Švejk during the struggle. 'Do you know Otto Katz? That's me.

'I've been with the archbishop,' he shouted, clinging to the gate in the carriage entrance. 'The Vatican's interested in me, do you understand?'

Švejk dropped the 'humbly report, sir' and spoke to the chaplain in very familiar tones.

'Drop it, I tell you,' he said, 'or I'll bash your flipper. We're going home and no more nonsense. Just shut up.'

The chaplain let go of the door and rolled over on to Švejk: 'Well, let's go somewhere, but I won't go to U Šuhů.[1] I've got debts there.'

Švejk pushed him and carried him out of the carriage entrance and dragged him along the pavement in the direction of his home.

'Who is that gentleman?' asked one of the spectators in the street.

'He's my brother,' answered Švejk. 'He got leave and came to visit me. He was so happy that he got drunk. You see he thought I was dead.'

The chaplain, who caught the last words, hummed a tune from an operetta which no one would have recognized, rose up and addressed the spectators: 'Whoever of you is dead must report to Army Corps headquarters within three days so that his corpse can be sprinkled with holy water.'

1. A notorious brothel.

And he lapsed into silence, endeavouring to fall nose-first on the pavement, while Švejk held him under the arm and dragged him home.

With his head thrust forward and his legs trailing behind and dangling like those of a cat with a broken backbone, the chaplain was

humming to himself: '*Dominus vobiscum – et cum spiritu tuo. Dominus vobiscum.*'

When they reached the droshky rank Švejk propped the chaplain against the wall and went to haggle with a droshky driver about his transport.

One of the drivers said he knew the gentleman very well, had had him as a passenger once and wouldn't ever take him again.

'He spewed over everything,' he stated bluntly, 'and didn't even pay for the ride. I drove him for more than two hours before he found where he lived. Only after a week, when I had been to see him at least three times, did he give me anything and then it was only five crowns for all that.'

After long haggling one of the drivers agreed to take them.

Švejk returned to the chaplain, who was sleeping. Someone had removed and carried off his bowler (for he generally went about in mufti).

Švejk woke him up and with the help of the driver got him to the droshky. Once inside the chaplain fell into a state of complete torpor. Mistaking Švejk for Colonel Just of the 75th infantry regiment he repeated several times: 'Don't be angry, old chap, if I call you by your Christian name. I'm a pig.'

At one moment it seemed that the jolting of the droshky on the cobbles was bringing him to his senses. He sat up straight and began to sing a snatch of an unknown song. Perhaps it was only his fancy:

> 'I recall that lovely time
> When he rocked me on his knee
> We were living in those days
> At Merklín near Domažlice-e-e.'

After a while he fell again into complete torpor. Then turning to Švejk he winked an eye and asked: 'How are you today, madam?...

'Are you going somewhere for the summer?' he said after a short pause, and seeing everything double he asked: 'So you already have a grown-up son, have you?' Saying this he pointed to Švejk.

'Sit down!' shouted Švejk, when the chaplain tried to climb on to the seat. 'Otherwise I'll teach you how to behave!'

The chaplain became quiet and stared out of the droshky with his little piggy eyes. He had not the faintest idea what was actually happening to him.

He no longer had a clue and turning to Švejk said dejectedly: 'Madam, give me first class.' Then he tried to take his trousers down.

'Button yourself up at once, you swine!' Švejk shouted at him. 'All the droshky drivers know you only too well already. You spewed all over yourself once, and now this! Don't imagine you'll get away with it without paying like last time!'

The chaplain with a melancholy expression propped his head on his hands and began to sing: 'No one loves me any more...' but he broke off his song suddenly and remarked in German: 'Excuse me, old man. You're a bloody idiot. I can sing what I like.'

He appeared to want to whistle some tune, but instead he emitted from his mouth such a powerful 'Whoa' that the droshky came to a standstill.

When afterwards at Švejk's order they continued their journey further, the chaplain began to try to light his cigarette holder.

'It doesn't burn,' he said despondently, when he had used up a whole box of matches. 'You're blowing at it.'

But at that moment he lost the thread again and started to laugh: 'This is a lark. We're alone in the tram, aren't we, my dear colleague?' He began to rummage in his pockets.

'I've lost my ticket,' he shouted. 'Stop, I must find my ticket!'

He waved his hand resignedly: 'All right, let's go on . . .'

He then began to wander: 'In the vast majority of cases. . . . Yes, all right. . . . In all cases. . . . You're quite wrong. . . . Second floor? . . . That's just an excuse. . . . It's not my concern, but yours, my dear madam. . . . Bill, please. . . . I had a black coffee!'

In a half dream he began to squabble with an imaginary enemy who was disputing his rights to sit by the window in a restaurant. Then he began to mistake the droshky for a train and, leaning out of the window, shrieked at the street in Czech and German: 'Nymburk, all change!'

Švejk pulled him back and the chaplain forgot about the train and began to give various animal imitations. He spent longest over the cock and his cock-a-doodle-do resounded triumphantly from the droshky.

For some time he was very active and restless and tried to fall out of the droshky, swearing at the passers-by and calling them gutter-snipes. Then he threw his handkerchief out of the droshky and shouted that they must stop because he had lost his luggage. Then he began to tell a story: 'In Budějovice there was once a drummer. He got married. A year later he died.' He burst out laughing: 'Isn't that a good story?'

All this time Švejk treated the chaplain with ruthless severity.

On the various occasions when the chaplain tried some tricks on him such as falling out of the droshky, or breaking the seat, Švejk gave him one or two punches under the ribs, which the chaplain accepted with unusual apathy.

Only once did he make an attempt to mutiny and jump out of the droshky, saying that he wouldn't go any further and that he knew that they were going to Podmokly instead of Budějovice. In the course of one minute Švejk had liquidated his mutiny completely and forced him to return to his previous position on the seat, taking care that he did not fall asleep. The mildest thing he said during all this was: 'Don't fall asleep, you death's-head!'

Suddenly the chaplain had an attack of melancholy and began to sob, asking Švejk whether he had a mother.

'Folks, I'm all alone in this world,' he shouted from the droshky. 'Take care of me!'

'Don't make a scandal,' Švejk rebuked him. 'Stop or else everyone will say you're tight.'

'I haven't touched a drop, old man,' answered the chaplain, 'I'm completely sober.'

But suddenly he stood up, saluted, and said in German: 'Humbly report, sir, I'm sozzled.

'I'm a filthy hog,' he repeated ten times in succession in hopeless and sincere despair.

And turning to Švejk he persistently begged and entreated: 'Throw me out of the car. Why are you taking me with you?'

He sat down again and muttered: 'Rings are forming round the moon. Captain, do you believe in the immortality of the soul? Can a horse get to heaven?'

He started to laugh aloud, but in a moment again grew sad and looked apathetically at Švejk, saying: 'Excuse me, sir, I've seen you somewhere before. Were you ever in Vienna? I remember you from the seminary.'

He amused himself for a while by reciting Latin verses: '*Aurea prima sata est aetas, quae vindice nullo* . . .

'I can't go on,' he said. 'Throw me out. Why won't you throw me out? I won't do anything to myself.

'I want to fall on my nose,' he announced in a resolute tone.

'Sir,' he continued again imploringly, 'dear old man, give me one across the jaw.'

'One or several?' asked Švejk. 'Two? Here you are . . .'

The chaplain counted the blows aloud as they came, beaming blissfully all the time.

'That does one a lot of good,' he said. 'It helps the stomach and promotes the digestion. Give me another one.'

'Thank you very much,' he called, when Švejk immediately obliged him. 'I'm completely satisfied. Tear open my waistcoat please.'

He expressed the most varied wishes. He wanted Švejk to dislocate his leg, to throttle him for a bit, to cut his nails and to pull out his front teeth.

He exhibited yearnings for martyrdom, asking him to cut off his head and throw him in a sack into the Vltava.

'Some stars round my head would suit me very well,' he said with enthusiasm. 'I should need ten.'[1]

Then he began to speak about the races and quickly went over to the ballet, which however did not detain him for long either.

'Do you dance the czardas?' he asked Švejk. 'Do you know the bear dance? Like this . . .'

He tried to jump in the air but fell on Švejk, who began to box him and then laid him out on the seat.

'I want something,' shouted the chaplain, 'but I don't know what. Don't you know what I want?' He hung his head in complete resignation.

'What business of mine is it what I want?' he said solemnly. 'And it's no business of yours either, is it, sir? I don't know you. How dare you rebuke me? Do you know how to fence?'

For a moment he became more aggressive and tried to push Švejk off the seat.

Then when Švejk had calmed him down and had not scrupled to give him a taste of his physical superiority, the chaplain asked: 'Is it Monday or Friday today?'

He was anxious to know too whether it was December or June and exhibited a great aptitude for asking the most diverse questions such as: 'Are you married? Do you like gorgonzola? Did you have bugs at home? Are you all right? Has your dog had distemper?'

He became communicative. He told how he owed money for riding breeches, a whip and a saddle, that he'd had V.D. some years ago and had cured it with permanganate.

'There was no idea of trying anything else, no time for it,' he said with a belch. 'It may seem to you pretty drastic, but tell me, hic, hic, what am I to do, hic, hic? You must forgive me.

'Thermos flask,' he continued, forgetting what he had been talking about a moment ago, 'is the name for receptacles which keep drinks and food in their original warmth. Which do you think, my dear colleague, is the fairer game, färbl or vingt-et-un?

1. Another reference to St John of Nepomuk. The statue of the saint has stars over the halo, which symbolize the miracles which took place at his martyrdom.

'Really, I've seen you somewhere before,' he called out, trying to embrace Švejk and kiss him with salivary lips. 'We were at school together. You're a good chap,' he said, tenderly stroking his own leg. 'How you've grown from the time when I saw you last. The pleasure of seeing you makes up for all my sufferings.'

A poetic mood came over him and he began to speak of going back to the sunshine of happy faces and warm hearts.

Then he knelt down and began to pray 'Ave Maria', laughing to split his sides.

When they stopped before his apartment, it was very difficult to get him out of the droshky.

'We aren't there yet,' he shrieked. 'Help! They're kidnapping me! I want to go on.' He was literally torn out of the droshky like a boiled snail from its shell. At one moment it seemed as if he would be pulled apart, because his legs got stuck behind the seat.

He laughed loudly when this was happening, saying he had diddled them: 'You are tearing me apart, gentlemen.'

Then he was dragged through the carriage entrance up the steps to his apartment and, once inside, thrown like a sack on to the sofa. He declared that he wouldn't pay for the car which he hadn't ordered, and it took more than a quarter of an hour for them to explain to him that it was a droshky.

And even then he did not agree, objecting that he only drove in a fiacre.

'You're trying to diddle me,' he declared, winking knowingly at Švejk and at the droshky driver. 'We walked here.'

And suddenly in an outburst of generosity he threw his purse to the driver: 'Take it all. I can pay. A kreutzer more or less doesn't make any difference to me.'

He should really have said 'thirty-six kreutzers' because that was all the purse contained. Fortunately the driver subjected him to an exhaustive search, talking of swipes over the jaw as he did so.

'All right, then, give me one,' the chaplain answered. 'D'you think I couldn't take it? I could manage five from you.'

In the chaplain's waistcoat pocket the driver found ten crowns. He went away cursing his fate and the chaplain for wasting his time and ruining his business.

The chaplain took some time to fall asleep because he kept on

making new plans. He wanted to do all sorts of things, play the piano, take dancing lessons and fry fish.

Then he promised Švejk his sister, although he did not have one. And he also asked to be taken off to bed, and finally he fell asleep, asserting that he wished to be regarded as a human being, which was just as valuable an entity as a pig.

III

When Švejk entered the chaplain's room in the morning, he found him lying on the sofa and puzzling hard how it could happen that someone had wetted him in such a peculiar way that he had got stuck to the leather couch with his trousers.

'Humbly report, sir,' said Švejk, 'that in the night you . . .'

In a few words he explained to the chaplain that he was terribly mistaken if he thought that he had been wetted. The chaplain, who had an unusually heavy hangover, was in a depressed mood.

'I can't remember,' he said, 'how I got from the bed on to the sofa.'

'You never were in the bed, sir. As soon as we got here we laid you on the sofa. That's as far as we could manage.'

'And what have I been up to? Was I up to anything at all? Wasn't I perhaps drunk?'

'Not half!' answered Švejk, 'to-hotally you were, sir. A little delirium came over you. I hope it'll help you if you change your clothes and wash.'

'I feel as if someone had given me a drubbing,' complained the chaplain. 'And I'm thirsty too. Did I have a brawl yesterday?'

'It wasn't too bad, sir. The thirst is the result of the thirst you had yesterday. A chap doesn't get over it so quickly. I knew a cabinet-maker who got drunk for the first time on New Year's Eve in 1910 and on the morning of the first of January he had such a thirst and felt so bad that he bought a salted herring and started drinking again. And he has gone on doing that every day for four years and no one can help him because he always buys his salted herrings on Saturday for the whole week. It's a proper merry-go-round, as our old sergeant-major in the 91st regiment always used to say.'

The chaplain was suffering from a hundred-per-cent hangover and was in a state of utter depression. Anyone who had been listening to him at that moment would have been convinced that he regularly attended the lectures of Dr Alexander Batěk ('We must declare war to the death on the demon of alcohol, who slaughters our best men') and had been reading his 'Hundred ethical sparks'.

He modified it slightly, it's true. 'If,' he said, 'you drank noble drinks like arak, maraschino, cognac – all right! But yesterday I drank some frightful borovička.[1] I'm surprised I could swill that stuff like I did. It had a disgusting taste. If it had only been griotte. People think up different kinds of filth and drink them like water. A borovička like that doesn't even taste good, it doesn't have any colour and burns your throat. If it had only been the genuine article, distilled from juniper, like what I once drank in Moravia. But it was made out of some kind of wood alcohol and scented oils. Look how I am belching.

'Alcohol's poison,' he decided. 'It must be original and genuine and not manufactured synthetically in a factory as the Jews do it. It's the same with rum. Good rum's a rarity.

'If we only had here genuine ořechovka,'[2] he sighed. 'That would put my stomach right. The sort of ořechovka which Captain Šnábl in Bruska has.'

He began rummaging in his pockets and examining his purse.

'I've only got thirty-six kreutzers. What about selling the sofa?' he reflected. 'What do you think? Would anyone buy it? I'll tell the landlord that I've lent it to somebody or that somebody's stolen it. But no, I'll keep the sofa. I'll send you to Captain Šnábl to ask him to lend me a hundred crowns. The day before yesterday he had a win at cards. If you don't get anything from him, then go to the barracks at Vršovice to Lieutenant Mahler. If you don't succeed with him, you can go to the Hradčany to Captain Fišer. You can tell him that I've got to pay for my horse's fodder and I've spent the money on drink. And if you don't have any luck with him we'll pawn the piano and damn what happens. I'll write you a few general lines. Don't let yourself get fobbed off. Say that I need it and that I'm quite broke. Think up whatever you like, but don't return empty-handed, otherwise I'll march you off to the front. Ask Captain Šnábl where he buys his ořechovka and buy two bottles of it.'

Švejk discharged his mission brilliantly. His sincerity and honest

1. Schnaps made out of juniper.
2. The same, made out of walnut.

countenance won him complete confidence and no one doubted the truth of what he was saying.

He considered it appropriate, in the presence of Captain Šnábl, Captain Fišer and Lieutenant Mahler, not to say that the chaplain had to pay for his horse's fodder, but to support his request for a loan

by saying that the chaplain had to pay paternity alimony. He was given money at all three places.

Having acquitted himself honourably on his expedition and brandishing on return the three hundred crowns, the chaplain, who had by this time taken a bath and put on clean clothes, was very surprised.

'I took the whole lot at one go,' said Švejk, 'so that we shouldn't have to worry our heads about money again tomorrow or the day after tomorrow. It went pretty smoothly, but I had to go on my knees to

Captain Šnábl. He's a real swine. But when I told him that we have to pay alimony . . .'

'Alimony?' the chaplain repeated in horror.

'Yes, alimony, sir, compensation for the women, you know. You told me that I should think up something and I couldn't hit on anything else. Where I come from, a cobbler paid alimony to five different girls. He was quite desperate about it and had to go and borrow money too. But everybody was ready to believe that he was in a frightful situation. They asked me what the girl was like and I said she was very pretty and not yet fifteen. And so they wanted her address.'

'You certainly made a nice mess of it, Švejk,' sighed the chaplain and began to walk up and down his room.

'That's another nice scandal,' he said, clutching his head. 'I've got a terrible headache.'

'I gave them the address of an old, deaf lady in the street where I live,' explained Švejk. 'I wanted to do the thing properly, because an order is an order. I wouldn't let myself be fobbed off, and I had to think up something. And now they're waiting in the hall for the piano. I brought them here, so that they could take it away to the pawnshop, sir. It won't be a bad thing when that piano's gone. There will be more room here and we shall have more money altogether. And we shall have peace for a day or two. And if the landlord asks what we're going to do with the piano, I'll say that there are strings broken in it and that we've sent it to the factory for repair. I've already told the concierge so that she won't think it strange when they take away the piano and load it on the van. And I also have a purchaser for the sofa. He's a friend of mine, a dealer in second-hand furniture, and he's coming here this afternoon. A leather sofa fetches a good price today.'

'Is that all you've done, Švejk?' asked the chaplain, continuing to clutch his head and looking desperate.

'Humbly report, sir, instead of two bottles of ořechovka which Captain Šnábl buys, I've brought five so that we can have something in reserve to drink. Can they come and take the piano before they shut the pawnshop?'

The chaplain waved his hand hopelessly and a few minutes later they were already loading the piano on to the van.

When Švejk returned from the pawnshop, he found the chaplain sitting in front of an open bottle of ořechovka and swearing, because the cutlet he had got for lunch had been underdone.

He was again half-seas over. He declared to Švejk that from to-morrow he would lead a new life. Drinking alcohol was vulgar materialism and one must live a spiritual life.

He spoke philosophically for about half an hour. When he opened the third bottle, the furniture-dealer arrived, and the chaplain sold him the sofa for a song. He invited him to talk to him and was very discontented when the furniture-dealer excused himself on the grounds that he had still to go and buy a bedside table.

'It's a pity that I haven't got one,' said the chaplain reproachfully. 'A man can't think of everything.'

After the furniture-dealer had gone the chaplain started up a friendly conversation with Švejk, with whom he drank another bottle. Part of his talk was taken up with his personal attitude to women and cards.

They were sitting for a long time. And evening found them deep in friendly conversation.

In the night however their relationship changed. The chaplain returned to his condition of the day before, mixed Švejk up with someone else and said to him: 'Oh no, please don't leave now! Do you remember that red-haired cadet from the baggage train?'

This idyll continued until Švejk said to the chaplain: 'Look, I'm fed up. Now you'll climb into bed and snooze, do you understand?'

'I'm climbing in, my dear boy, I'm climbing in – why shouldn't I climb in?' babbled the chaplain. 'D'you remember how we were in the fifth form together and I used to do your Greek exercises for you? You've got a villa at Zbraslav. And you can go by steamer on the Vltava. Do you know what the Vltava is?'

Švejk forced him to take off his boots and undress. The chaplain obeyed with a protest directed to some unknown persons.

'You see, gentlemen,' he said to the cupboard and to the ficus, 'how my relations treat me.

'I don't know my relations,' he suddenly decided, getting into bed. 'Even if heaven and earth were to conspire against me, I don't know them . . .'

And the room resounded with his snoring.

IV

It was during these days too that Švejk went to visit his old charwoman, Mrs Müller. In his apartment Švejk found her cousin, who told him in tears that Mrs Müller had been arrested the same evening that she pushed Švejk off to the war in a bathchair. They had court-martialled the old lady and, finding no evidence against her, had taken her off to a concentration camp at Steinhof. A card had already come from her.

Švejk took this precious household relic and read:

Dear Aninka,
We are enjoying ourselves very much here. We are all well. The woman in the next bed to me has spotted ———— and also there are here people with small ————. Otherwise everything is in order.

We have plenty to eat and collect potato ———— for soup. I have heard that Mr Švejk is already ———— so find out somehow, where he is laid, so that after the war we can decorate his grave. I forgot to tell you that in the right-hand corner in the attic there is a little dog in a box, a miniature pinscher puppy. But he hasn't had anything to eat for several weeks, ever since they came to fetch me because of————. So I suppose that it's already too late and the little dog is also resting with ————.

And across the whole letter there was a pink stamp in German: 'Censored, Imperial and Royal Concentration Camp, Steinhof.'

'And the little dog was really dead,' sobbed Mrs Müller's cousin, 'and you'd never recognize your apartment either. I've got some dress-makers lodging there. And they've turned it into a real lady's fashion parlour. Everywhere there are fashion pictures on the walls and flowers in the windows.'

Mrs Müller's cousin was not to be comforted.

Amid continuous sobbing and lamentations she finally expressed the fear that Švejk had deserted from the army and wanted to ruin her too and bring her into misery. Finally she spoke to him as though he were an infamous adventurer.

'That's really priceless,' said Švejk. 'I really love that. And let me tell you, Mrs Kejř, that you are absolutely right about my getting out. I had to kill fifteen sergeants and sergeant-majors. But don't tell anybody . . .'

And Švejk left his home, which was so unwelcoming to him, saying: 'Mrs Kejř, I've got some collars and shirt-fronts at the laundry. Please fetch them for me so that when I come back from the war I'll have some mufti to put on. And please see too that the moths don't get at my suits in the wardrobe. And give my love to those young ladies who are sleeping in my bed.'

And then Švejk went to pay a visit to The Chalice. When Mrs Palivec saw him she declared that she wouldn't serve him, as he had probably deserted.

'My husband,' she started the same old gramophone record, 'was

so careful and he's there; he's locked up, poor dear, all for nothing. And people like you are free to roam about and desert from the army. They were looking for you here again only last week.

'We are more cautious than you,' she concluded, 'and all the same we're in the soup. Not everyone has your luck.'

This conversation was overheard by an elderly man, a locksmith from Smíchov, who came up to Švejk and said: 'Excuse me, sir, do you mind waiting for me outside? I've got something to talk to you about.'

In the street he talked confidentially to Švejk, believing him to be a deserter on the basis of Mrs Palivec's opinion.

He told him that he had a son, who had deserted too and was with his grandmother at Jasenná near Josefov.

Disregarding Švejk's assurances that he was not a deserter, he pressed a twenty-crown piece into his hand.

'That's a bit of first aid,' he said, dragging him into a wine restaurant at the corner. 'I understand you. You don't need to be afraid of me.'

Švejk returned late at night to the chaplain who had not yet come home.

He did not come till next morning, when he woke up Švejk and said: 'Tomorrow we're going to celebrate a drumhead mass. Make some black coffee and put some rum in it. Or, still better, make some grog.'

Švejk Goes with the Chaplain to Celebrate a Drumhead Mass

I

PREPARATIONS for the slaughter of mankind have always been made in the name of God or some supposed higher being which men have devised and created in their own imagination.

Before the ancient Phoenicians cut a prisoner's throat they also performed religious ceremonies just as solemnly as did new generations some thousand years later before marching to war and destroying their enemies with fire and sword.

The cannibals of the Guinea Islands and Polynesia sacrifice to their gods and perform the most diverse religious rites before ceremoniously devouring their captives or unnecessary people like missionaries, travellers, agents of various business firms or persons who are just inquisitive. As the culture of vestments has not yet reached them they decorate the outsides of their thighs with bunches of gaudy feathers of forest birds.

Before the Holy Inquisition burnt its victims, it performed the most solemn religious service – a High Mass with singing.

When criminals are executed, priests always officiate, molesting the delinquents with their presence.

In Prussia the unfortunate victim was led to the block by a pastor, in Austria to the gallows by a Catholic priest, in France to the guillotine, in America to the electric chair by a clergyman and in Spain to a chair where he was strangled by an ingenious appliance. In Russia the revolutionary was taken off by a bearded Orthodox priest etc.

Everywhere on these occasions they used to march about with a crucified Christ figure, as if to say: 'They're only cutting your head off, they're only hanging you, strangling you, putting fifteen thousand volts into you, but think what that chap there had to go through.'

The great shambles of the world war did not take place without the blessing of priests. Chaplains of all armies prayed and celebrated drumhead masses for victory for the side whose bread they ate.

When mutineers were executed a priest appeared. A priest could also be seen at the execution of Czech legionaries.

Nothing has changed from the time when the robber Vojtěch,[1] whom they nicknamed 'the Saint', operated with a sword in one hand and a cross in the other, murdering and exterminating the Baltic Slavs.

Throughout all Europe people went to the slaughter like cattle, driven there not only by butcher emperors, kings and other potentates and generals, but also by priests of all confessions, who blessed them and made them perjure themselves that they would destroy the enemy on land, in the air, on the sea etc.

Drumhead masses were generally celebrated twice: once when a detachment left for the front and once more at the front on the eve of some bloody massacre and carnage. I remember that once when a drumhead mass was being celebrated an enemy aeroplane dropped a bomb on us and hit the field altar. There was nothing left of the chaplain except some bloodstained rags.

Afterwards they wrote about him as a martyr, while our aeroplanes prepared the same kind of glory for the chaplains on the other side.

We had a great deal of fun out of this, and on the provisional cross, at the spot where they buried the remains of the chaplain, there appeared overnight this epitaph:

> What may hit us has now hit you.
> You always said we'd join the saints.
> Well, now you've caught it at Holy Mass.
> And where you stood are only stains.

II

Švejk brewed a splendid grog which eclipsed the grogs of old sea-dogs. Pirates of the eighteenth century might have drunk a grog like that and been satisfied with it.

The chaplain was delighted. 'Where did you learn to make such a marvellous thing?' he asked.

'Years ago as a wandering apprentice,' answered Švejk, 'I learned it

1. St Adalbert – a Czech patron saint.

in Bremen from a debauched sailor, who used to say that grog must be so strong that if anyone fell into the sea he could swim across the whole English Channel. After a weak grog he'd drown like a puppy.'

'After a grog like this, Švejk, we'll be able to celebrate a marvellous drumhead mass,' reflected the chaplain. 'I think I ought to say a few farewell words first. A drumhead mass is not such fun as a mass in the garrison gaol or preaching to those rascals. You have to have all your wits about you. We have a field altar. It's a folding one – a pocket edition.

'Jesus Mary, Švejk,' he cried, holding his head in his hands, 'we're bloody idiots. Do you know where I used to keep that folding field altar? In the sofa which we sold.'

'Oh dear, that's really a misfortune, sir,' said Švejk. 'As a matter of fact I know that furniture-dealer, and the day before yesterday I met his wife. He's in jug because of a stolen wardrobe and a teacher in Vršovice has got our sofa. It's going to be a disaster if we don't have that field altar. The best thing we can do is to drink up the grog and go and look for it, because I think that without a field altar you can't celebrate a mass.'

'A field altar's really the only thing that's missing,' said the chaplain in a melancholy voice. 'Everything's ready on the parade ground. The carpenters have already made a platform for it. The monstrances are being lent to us from Břevnov monastery. I ought to have a chalice of my own, but where on earth is it . . . ?'

He reflected: 'Suppose I've lost it. Then we'll get the sports cup from Lieutenant Wittinger of the 75th regiment. Years ago he ran in races and won it for "Sport-Favorit". He used to be a good runner. He did the forty-kilometre stretch from Vienna to Mödling in 1 hour 48 minutes, as he always boasted about it. I arranged this with him already yesterday. I'm a bloody fool leaving everything till the last moment. Why didn't I look inside that sofa? Bloody ass!'

Under the influence of the grog, prepared after the recipe of the debauched sailor, he began torpidly to swear at himself and explained in the most diverse maxims where he really belonged.

'Well, we'd better go and have a look for that field altar,' suggested Švejk. 'It's already daybreak.'

'I still have to put on my uniform and drink another grog.'

At last they went out. On their way to the wife of the furniture-dealer the chaplain told Švejk that the day before he had won a lot of money gambling at 'God's blessing' and that if all went well he'd buy the piano back from the pawnbroker.

It was rather like when heathens promise to bury an offering. From the sleepy wife of the furniture-dealer they learnt the address of the teacher in Vršovice, the new owner of the sofa. The chaplain displayed unusual generosity. He pinched her cheek and tickled her under the chin.

They went to Vršovice on foot, as the chaplain avowed that he must have a turn in the fresh air to distract his thoughts.

An unpleasant surprise awaited them in the apartment of the teacher at Vršovice who was a pious old gentleman. Finding the field altar in the sofa the old gentleman had thought that this must be some divine dispensation and had given it to the vestry of the local church in Vršovice, stipulating that on the other side of the folding altar there should be the inscription: 'Presented for the honour and praise of God by Mr Kolařík, retired teacher, in the year of our Lord 1914'. He displayed great embarrassment because they came on him in his underclothes.

From their conversation with him it was clear that he attributed to the discovery the significance of a miracle and a divine direction. He said that when he bought the sofa an inner voice said to him: 'Look at what's in the drawer of the sofa.' He claimed he had also had a vision of an angel who gave him the direct command: 'Open the drawer of the sofa.' He obeyed.

And when he saw the miniature folding altar in three sections with a recess for a tabernacle he had knelt down in front of the sofa and prayed long and fervently and praised God. Regarding it as a direction from heaven he adorned the church in Vršovice with it.

'We don't think this at all funny,' said the chaplain. 'An object of this kind which didn't belong to you, you should at once have taken to the police and not to any blasted vestry.'

'Because of that miracle,' added Švejk, 'you may face a lot of trouble. You bought a sofa and not the altar, which belongs to the army authorities. A divine dispensation like that can cost you dear. You ought not to have paid any attention to the angels. There was a man in Zhoř who dug up a chalice in a field. It had been stolen from a church and kept there for better times until it was forgotten. He also took it as a divine dispensation and instead of melting it down went to the vicar with it and said he wanted to present it to the church. And the vicar thought that he had been moved by pangs of conscience and sent for the mayor. The mayor sent for the gendarmerie and, although he was innocent, he was sentenced for stealing church property, just because he kept on babbling about some miracle. He wanted to defend himself and also

talked about an angel, but he mixed the Virgin Mary into it and got ten years. You'd do best to come with us to the local vicar here and get him to return us the army property. A field altar isn't a cat or a sock that you can give away to anyone you like.'

The old gentleman trembled all over and his teeth chattered as he put on his clothes: 'I really meant no harm. I thought that with a divine dispensation like that I could use it for the adornment of our poor Church of our Lord in Vršovice.'

'At the expense of the army authorities, no doubt,' Švejk said sternly and harshly. 'Thank God for a divine dispensation like that! A fellow called Pivoňka of Chotěboř also thought it was a divine dispensation when a halter with somebody else's cow in it got into his hand by accident.'

The poor old gentleman was quite confused by these remarks and made no further attempts to defend himself, trying to dress as quickly as possible and settle the whole business.

The vicar at Vršovice was still asleep and when he was awoken by the noise started to swear, because in his drowsiness he thought that he had to go and administer the last rites to somebody.

'They shouldn't bother people with this extreme unction,' he growled, dressing himself unwillingly. 'People take it into their heads to die when a chap's having a really good sleep. And afterwards you have to haggle with them about the fee.'

And so they met in the hall. One, the representative of the Lord for the Catholic civilians of Vršovice, the other, the representative of God on earth for the military authorities.

Altogether, however, it was nothing more than a dispute between a civilian and a soldier.

When the vicar asserted that the field altar did not belong to the sofa, the chaplain declared that in that case it belonged all the less to the vestry of a church which was attended only by civilians.

Švejk made various remarks to the effect that it was an easy job to fit up a poor church at the expense of the army authorities. He pronounced the word 'poor' in inverted commas.

Finally they went to the vestry of the church and the vicar handed over the field altar in return for the following receipt:

Received a field altar which accidentally found its way into the church at Vršovice.   *Chaplain Otto Katz*

The famous field altar came from the Jewish firm of Moritz Mahler in Vienna, which manufactured all kinds of accessories for mass as well as religious objects like rosaries and images of saints.

The altar was made up of three parts, liberally provided with sham gilt like the whole glory of the Holy Church.

It was not possible without considerable ingenuity to detect what the pictures painted on these three parts actually represented. What was certain was that it was an altar which could have been used equally well by heathens in Zambesi or by the Shamans of the Buriats and Mongols.

Painted in screaming colours it appeared from a distance like a coloured chart intended for testing colour-blind railway workers. One figure stood out prominently – a naked man with a halo and a body which was turning green, like the parson's nose of a goose which has begun to rot and is already stinking. No one was doing anything to this saint. On the contrary, he had on both sides of him two winged creatures which were supposed to represent angels. But anyone looking at them had the impression that this holy naked man was shrieking with horror at the company around him, for the angels looked like fairy-tale monsters and were a cross between a winged wild cat and the beast of the apocalypse.

Opposite this was a picture which was meant to represent the Holy Trinity. By and large the painter had been unable to ruin the dove. He had painted a kind of bird which could equally well have been a pigeon or a White Wyandotte. God the Father looked like a bandit from the Wild West served up to the public in an American film thriller.

The Son of God on the other hand was a gay young man with a handsome stomach draped in something that looked like bathing drawers. Altogether he looked a sporting type. The cross which he had in his hand he held as elegantly as if it had been a tennis racquet.

Seen from afar however all these details ran into each other and gave the impression of a train going into a station.

What the third picture represented was quite impossible to make out. The soldiers always argued about it and tried to solve the enigma. One even thought that it was a landscape from the Sázava valley. But underneath it was the inscription in German: 'Holy Mary, Mother of God, have mercy on us.'

Švejk deposited the field altar safely in the droshky and seated himself next to the driver on the box. The chaplain made himself comfortable inside the droshky with his feet on the Holy Trinity.

Švejk chatted with the driver about the war. The driver was a rebel. He made various remarks about the victory of the Austrian forces such as: 'They made it hot for you in Serbia', etc. When they crossed the customs point the official asked them what they were taking with them. Švejk answered:

'The Holy Trinity and the Virgin Mary together with the chaplain.'

Meanwhile on the parade ground the march detachments were waiting impatiently. And they had waited a long time. For they had had to fetch the sports cup from Lieutenant Wittinger and then the monstrance, the pyx and other accessories of the mass, including a bottle of sacramental wine, from the Břevnov monastery. From this one may conclude that it is no simple matter to celebrate a drumhead mass.

'We muddle along as we can,' said Švejk to the driver.

And he was right. For when they reached the drill-ground and were at the platform with the wooden framework and table, on which the field altar was to be placed, it turned out that the chaplain had forgotten the server.

Before it had always been an infantryman who served, but he had preferred to get himself transferred to telephones and had gone to the front.

'Never mind, sir,' said Švejk, 'I can manage that too.'

'But you can't serve?'

'I've never done it,' answered Švejk, 'but there's no harm in having a shot. Today there's a war on and in wartime people do things which they never dreamed of doing before. I'll manage to cope with that stupid "*et cum spiritu tuo*" to your "*dominus vobiscum*". And I think it's not very difficult to walk around you like a cat round hot porridge, and wash your hands and pour wine out of the flask . . .'

'All right,' said the chaplain, 'but don't go and pour me out any water. Better put wine in the other flask too. As to the rest I'll always tell you whether you have to go to the right or to the left. If I whistle once very softly that means go to the right. Twice means to the left. And you don't need to drag the missal about much. It's great fun really. Got stage fright?'

'I'm not frightened of anything, sir, not even of serving.'

The chaplain was right when he said: 'It's great fun really.'

Everything went like a house on fire.

The chaplain's address was very brief.

'Soldiers! We have met here, so that before we go to the battlefield we may incline our hearts to God, that he may grant us victory and keep us safe and sound. I won't detain you long and wish you all the best.'

'Stand at ease!' shouted an old colonel on the left flank.

A drumhead mass is called a 'drumhead' mass because it comes under the same rules as military tactics in the field. During the long manoeuvres of the armies in the Thirty Years' War drumhead masses were apt to be extremely lengthy too.

In modern tactics, where the movements of armies are rapid and brisk, drumhead masses must be equally rapid and brisk.

And so this one lasted exactly ten minutes and those who were close by wondered very much why the chaplain whistled during it.

Švejk quickly mastered the signals. Now he walked to the right of the altar and now he was on the left; and he said nothing else but: '*Et cum spiritu tuo.*'

It looked like a Red Indian dance round a sacrificial stone, but it made a good impression, for it banished the boredom of the dusty melancholy drill-ground with its avenue of plum trees behind and its latrines, the odour of which replaced the mystical scent of incense in Gothic churches.

Everyone enjoyed themselves immensely. The officers standing round the colonel were cracking jokes with each other and so everything was as it should be. Here and there among the rank and file could be heard the words: 'Give me a puff.'

And from the companies blue clouds of tobacco smoke rose to heaven as from a burnt offering. All the N.C.O.s started smoking when they saw that the colonel himself had lit a cigarette.

At last the words 'Let us pray' were heard. There was a whirl of dust and a grey rectangle of uniforms bowed their knees before Lieutenant Wittinger's sports cup, which he won for 'Sport-Favorit' in the Vienna–Mödling race.

The cup was filled full and the general opinion in the ranks of the chaplain's manipulations was: 'He's swilled it all right!'

This performance was repeated twice. After that once more: 'Let us pray', whereupon the band did its best with the Austrian national anthem. Then came 'attention' and 'quick march'.

'Collect all this stuff,' said the chaplain to Švejk, pointing to the field altar, 'so that we can take it all back where it belongs!'

So they drove off with their droshky, returned everything like good boys, except for the bottle of sacramental wine.

And when they were home again and had told the unfortunate droshky driver to apply to the regimental command for payment for the long drive Švejk said to the chaplain: 'Humbly report, sir, must a server be of the same confession as the man he's assisting?'

'Of course,' answered the chaplain, 'otherwise the mass wouldn't be valid.'

'Then, sir, a great mistake has been made,' said Švejk. 'I'm a man without confession. It's always me that has the bad luck.'

The chaplain looked at Švejk, was silent for a moment, then patted him on the shoulder and said: 'You can drink up what's left in the bottle of sacramental wine and imagine that you've been taken back into the bosom of the Church.'

12

A Religious Debate

IT happened that for whole days at a time Švejk never saw the man who had the cure of army souls. The chaplain divided his time between duties and debauchery and came home very rarely; when he did he was filthy and unwashed like a mewing tom-cat when it makes its amorous expeditions on the tiles.

When he came back, if he was able to express himself at all, he talked to Švejk for a bit before falling asleep. He spoke of lofty aims, inspiration and the pleasure of meditation.

Sometimes too he tried to speak in verse and quoted Heine.

Švejk and the chaplain celebrated one more drumhead mass for the sappers, to which another chaplain had been invited by mistake, a former catechist. He was an extraordinarily pious man, who stared at his colleague in amazement when he offered him a sip of cognac out of the field-flask which Švejk always carried with him for religious functions of this kind.

'It's a good brand,' said Chaplain Katz. 'Have a drink and go home. I'll do the job myself, because I need to be in the open air. I've got a bit of a headache.'

The pious chaplain went away shaking his head, and as usual Katz acquitted himself nobly of his task.

This time it was wine and soda water which was transubstantiated into the blood of our Lord, and the sermon was longer, every third word being 'and so forth and of course'.

'Today, my men, you are going to the front and so forth. Incline your hearts now to God and so forth and of course. You don't know what's going to happen to you and so forth and of course.'

And from the altar there continued to thunder: 'And so forth and of course', alternating with God and all the saints.

In his enthusiasm and rhetorical flights the chaplain presented Prince Eugène of Savoy as a saint who would protect them when they built bridges over the rivers.

Nonetheless the drumhead mass ended without any untoward incident. It was pleasant and amusing. The sappers enjoyed themselves very much.

On the way back the chaplain and Švejk were not allowed into the tram with their folding field altar.

'I'll break this saint on your head,' Švejk said to the conductor.

When they finally got home they found that somewhere on the way they had lost the tabernacle.

'It doesn't matter,' said Švejk. 'The early Christians served Holy Mass without a tabernacle. If we advertised for it somewhere, the honest man who found it could ask us for a reward. If it had been money, then I don't suppose any honest finder would have been found, although such people do exist. In our regiment at Budějovice there was a soldier, a dear old fathead, who once found six hundred crowns in the street and gave it up to the police. In the newspapers they wrote about him as an honest finder, but it only brought discredit on him. No one would talk to him; everyone said: "You half-wit, what's this bloody nonsense you've done? Why, you must be quite disgusted with yourself, if you've still any sense of honour left." He had a girl and she wouldn't speak to him any more. When he came home on leave his friends threw him out of the pub during a dance-party because of it. He got ill and took it all so much to heart that he finally threw himself under a train. And then again in our street there was a tailor who found a golden ring. People warned him not to give it up to the police, but he wouldn't listen. He got an unusually kind reception there and was told that the loss of a golden ring with a diamond had already been notified to them. But then they looked at the stone and said to him: "My good man, you know very well that it's glass and not diamond. How much did they give you for that diamond? We know very well *your* kind of honest finder." In the end it came out that another man had lost a gold ring with a false diamond, a kind of family heirloom, but the tailor sat three days in prison all the same, because he got het up and insulted a policeman. He was given the legal reward of ten per cent, which was one crown twenty hellers because that trash was worth twelve crowns, but he threw it in the gentleman's face. The gentleman then sued him for insulting his honour, so he got another ten crowns fine. Afterwards he used to say everywhere that every honest finder deserves twenty-five strokes, let them flog him black and blue, flog him publicly so that people should remember and take a lesson from it. I don't think that anyone'll bring our tabernacle back, even though it has the regimental crest on the back, because <u>no one wants to have anything to do with army property. They'd rather throw it in the water somewhere, so as not to have further complications with it.</u> Yesterday at the pub, The Golden Wreath, I spoke to a man from the country. He was fifty-six and was going to the office of the district hejtman[1] in Nová Paka to ask why they had requisitioned his carriage. On the way back, when they had thrown him out of the hejtman's office, he had a look at the baggage train which had just come in and was standing on the square. A young man asked him to wait a moment by the horses, which were to fetch tinned goods for the army, and then he never came back. When the baggage train moved off this chap had to go with them and found himself in Hungary, where he in his turn asked someone to wait by the baggage train in his place. It was only in this way that he saved himself, otherwise they'd have dragged him off to Serbia. When he arrived he looked absolutely terrified and would never have anything to do with army property any more.'

In the evening they received a visit from the pious chaplain who had wanted to serve the drumhead mass for the sappers that morning. He was a fanatic who wanted to bring everyone close to God. When he had been a catechist he had developed religious feelings in children by slapping their faces and there had appeared from time to time in various journals articles about 'the sadistic catechist', 'the slapping catechist'. He was convinced that a child learns the catechism best with the help of the birch.

He limped a little on one foot, which had been caused by a visit made to him by the father of one of his pupils, whose face he had slapped for having expressed certain doubts about the Holy Trinity. He got three slaps on the face himself. One for God the Father, a second for God the Son and a third for the Holy Ghost.

Today he had come to lead his colleague Katz on to the right path and to have a heart-to-heart talk with him. He began it with the remark: 'I'm surprised that you've got no crucifix hanging here. Where do you say your breviary prayers? And there's not a single portrait of the saints on the walls of your room. What's that hanging over your bed?'

Katz smiled: 'That's Susanna and the Elders, and that naked woman underneath is an old friend of mine. On the right there's something Japanese, depicting the sexual act betweeen a geisha and an old Japan-

1. Representative of the central government in a district.

ese Samurai. Very original, isn't it? The breviary's in the kitchen. Švejk, bring it here and open it on the third page.'

Švejk went away, and from the kitchen could be heard the sound of corks being drawn from three bottles of wine.

The pious chaplain was aghast when the three bottles made their appearance on the table.

'It's a light sacramental wine, brother,' said Katz, 'of very good quality, a Riesling. It tastes like Moselle.'

'I'm not going to drink,' said the pious chaplain stubbornly. 'I've come to have a heart-to-heart talk with you.'

'That'll dry up your throat, my dear colleague,' said Katz. 'Have a drink and I'll listen. I'm a very tolerant fellow and can listen to other views.'

The pious chaplain drank a little and rolled his eyes.

'It's a devilish good wine, my dear colleague, isn't it?'

The fanatic said sternly: 'It has not escaped me that you are swearing.'

'That's habit,' answered Katz. 'Sometimes I even catch myself blaspheming. Pour the chaplain out some more, Švejk. I can assure you that I also say: "Himmelherrgott, krucifix and sakra." I think that when you've served in the army as long as I have you'll find yourself doing it too. It isn't at all difficult or complicated and it's very familiar to us clergy – heaven, God, the cross and the holy sacrament. Doesn't that sound marvellously professional? Drink a bit more, my dear colleague.'

The former catechist sipped mechanically. It was obvious that he wanted to say something, but could not. He was collecting his thoughts.

'My dear colleague,' continued Katz, 'cheer up! Don't sit there so miserably, as though they were going to hang you in five minutes' time. I've heard about you, how once on a Friday by mistake you ate a pork cutlet in a restaurant, because you thought that it was Thursday, and how you stuck your finger down your throat in the W.C. to get rid of it, because you thought God would obliterate you . I'm not afraid of eating meat in Lent and I'm not afraid of hell-fire either. Excuse me, please go on drinking. Are you better now? Or do you have progressive views about hell and keep up with the spirit of the times and the reformists? I mean, instead of ordinary cauldrons with sulphur for poor sinners, there are Papin's pots[1] and high-pressure boilers. The sinners are fried in margarine, there are grills driven by electricity, steam rollers roll over the sinners for millions of years, the gnashing of the teeth is produced with the help of dentists with special equipment, the howling is recorded on gramophones, and the records are sent upstairs to paradise for the entertainment of the just. In paradise sprays with eau de cologne operate and the Philharmonic Orchestra plays Brahms so long that you prefer hell and purgatory. The cherubs have aeroplane propellers in their behinds so as not to have to work so hard with their wings. Drink, my dear colleague! Švejk, pour him out some cognac. I don't think he's feeling well.'

When the pious chaplain came round he started to whisper: 'Religion is a matter of rational reasoning. Whoever does not believe in the existence of the Holy Trinity . . .'

'Švejk,' Katz interrupted him, 'pour out one more cognac for the chaplain, so as to bring him round! Tell him something, Švejk!'

'Humbly report, sir,' said Švejk, 'near Vlašim there was a dean who

1. Quick-boiling kettles invented by the French physicist Papin in 1781.

had a charwoman, when his old housekeeper ran away from him with the boy and the money. And this dean in his declining years started studying St Augustine, who is said to be one of the Holy Fathers, and he read there that whoever believes in the Antipodes will be damned. And so he called his charwoman and said to her: "Listen, you once told me that your son was a fitter and that he went to Australia. That would be in the Antipodes and according to St Augustine's instructions everyone who believes in the Antipodes is damned." "Reverend sir," the woman answered, "after all my son sends me letters and money from Australia." "That's a snare of the devil," replied the dean. "According to St Augustine Australia doesn't exist at all and you are just being seduced by the Anti-Christ." On Sunday he anathematized her publicly and shouted out that Australia didn't exist. So they took him straight out of the church into the lunatic asylum. More people like him ought to be put there. In the Convent of the Sisters of St Ursula they have a bottle of the Holy Virgin's milk with which she suckled the baby Jesus, and in the orphanage at Benešov, after they'd brought them water from Lourdes, the orphans got diarrhoea the like of which the world has never seen.'

Black spots were dancing in front of the pious chaplain's eyes and he only came to himself after another cognac, which went to his head.

Blinking his eyes he asked Katz: 'Don't you believe in the Immaculate Conception of the Virgin Mary? Don't you believe that the thumb of St John the Baptist, which is preserved in the Piarists' monastery, is genuine? Do you believe in the Lord at all? And if you don't, why are you a chaplain?'

'My dear colleague,' answered Katz, patting him familiarly on the back, 'until the state recognizes that soldiers who are going to their death at the front don't need the blessing of God for it, the chaplaincy remains a decently paid profession, where a chap isn't overworked. It was better for me than running about on the drill-ground and going on manoeuvres. Then I used to get orders from my superiors but now I do what I like. I represent someone who doesn't exist and myself play the part of God. If I don't want to absolve anybody's sins then I don't, even if they beg me on their bended knees. But you'd find bloody few people nowadays who'd go that far.'

'I love God,' declared the pious chaplain, beginning to hiccough. 'I love him very much. Give me a little wine. I respect God,' he continued.

'I respect and honour him very much. I respect no one as much as I respect him.'

He struck the table with his fist until the bottles jumped. 'God is an exalted being, something unearthly. He's honourable in his dealings. He's a radiant revelation, and no one's going to convince me of the contrary. I respect St Joseph too, I respect all the saints, except St Serapion. He's got such an ugly name.'

'He ought to apply to have it changed,' observed Švejk.

'I love St Ludmila and St Bernard,' continued the former catechist. 'He saved many pilgrims in St Gothard. He carries a bottle of cognac around his neck and looks for people caught in snow drifts.'

The conversation took a new turn. The pious chaplain started getting completely muddled. 'I honour the Innocents. They have their Saints' day on the twenty-eighth of December. I hate Herod. When the hens sleep, you can't get any new-laid eggs.'

He gave a guffaw and began to sing 'Holy, Holy, Holy, Lord God of Sabaoth.'

He broke off at once, and turning to Katz and getting up asked him sharply: 'You don't believe that the fifteenth of August is the day of the Assumption of the Virgin Mary?'

The fun was in full swing. More bottles appeared, and from time to time Katz could be heard saying: 'Say that you don't believe in God, otherwise I won't let you have a drop!'

It was as though the times of the persecution of the early Christians had returned. The former catechist sang a song of the martyrs of the Roman arena and yelled out: 'I believe in God. I won't forswear him. You can keep your wine. I can send for some myself.'

Finally they put him to bed. Before he fell asleep he proclaimed, raising his right hand in a solemn oath: 'I believe in God the Father, Son and Holy Ghost. Bring me the breviary.'

Švejk put into his hand a book which was lying on the night table. The pious chaplain then fell asleep with Boccaccio's *Decameron* in his hand.

13

Švejk Administers Extreme Unction

CHAPLAIN OTTO KATZ sat glumly over a circular which he had just brought from the barracks. It contained secret instructions from the War Ministry.

For the duration of the war the War Ministry suspends all operative regulations concerning the administering of extreme unction to soldiers of the army and lays down the following regulations for army chaplains:

§*1*. At the front extreme unction is cancelled.

§*2*. Those who are seriously ill and wounded are forbidden to go back to the base for extreme unction. Army chaplains are required at once to hand over such cases to the appropriate military authorities for further action.

§*3*. In army hospitals at the base extreme unction can be administered *en masse* on the basis of a certificate from the army doctors, provided it does not entail difficulties for the appropriate military institutions.

§*4*. In exceptional cases the Military Hospitals Command at the base may allow individuals to receive extreme unction.

§*5*. Army chaplains are obliged, if called on by the Military Hospitals Command, to administer extreme unction to those designated by the Command.

After that the chaplain read once more the order informing him that the next day he must go to the army hospital at Charles Square to administer extreme unction to the seriously wounded.

'Listen, Švejk,' the chaplain called out, 'isn't this a bloody nuisance? Just as if I was the only chaplain in the whole of Prague! Why don't they send that pious priest who slept here the other day? We've got to go and administer it at Charles Square. I've already forgotten how to do it.'

'Then we'll buy a catechism, sir. It'll be there,' said Švejk. 'It's a kind of Baedeker for spiritual pastors. In the Emmaus monastery a gardener's assistant, who worked there once, wanted to join the ranks of the lay brothers and get a cowl so as not to tear his clothes. He had to buy a catechism and learn how to make the sign of the cross, who alone is preserved from original sin, what it means to have a clean conscience, and other trifles like that. And after that he secretly flogged half the cucumbers from the monastery garden and left the monastery in disgrace. When I met him he said: "I could have flogged those cucumbers just as well without the catechism." '

When Švejk brought the catechism, which he had purchased, the chaplain turned the pages in it and said: 'Look, extreme unction can only be administered by a priest and then only with oil which has been consecrated by a bishop. So you see, Švejk, you yourself can't administer extreme unction. Read out to me how one does it.'

Švejk read out: 'It's done like this: the priest anoints the sick man on all his senses, at the same time praying as follows: "By this Holy Unction and by His Holy Mercy may God forgive thee for all the sins thou hast committed through thine eyes, thine ears, thy smell, thy taste, thy words, thy touch and thy gait." '

'I'd like to know, Švejk,' said the chaplain, 'how a man can sin with his touch. Can you tell me?'

'In lots of ways, sir. You can put your hands into someone else's pocket, or on the dance floor – well, you know what goes on there!'

'And by his gait, Švejk?'

'When he begins to limp so as to arouse people's pity.'

'And by his smell?'

'When he doesn't like stink or stinkers.'

'And his taste, Švejk?'

'When he has a taste for somebody.'

'And his words?'

'That goes together with ears. When someone chatters a lot and someone else listens to him.'

After these philosophical reflections the chaplain was silent and said: 'And so we need oil consecrated by a bishop. Here's ten crowns. Go and buy a bottle. Obviously they won't have this kind of oil at the military stores.'

Švejk set out on his journey in search of oil which had been consecrated by a bishop. This errand was more difficult than looking for the water of life in Božena Němcová's fairy tales.[1]

He went into various chemists and as soon as he said: 'Please, I want a bottle of oil consecrated by a bishop', they either burst out

1. Božena Němcová, one of the greatest Czech writers and a collector of Czech and Slovak fairy tales.

laughing or hid in a panic under the counter. All this time Švejk's countenance was unusually solemn.

And so he decided to try his luck at surgeries. In the first they had him thrown out by a dispenser. In the second they wanted to telephone for an ambulance. And in the third the head of the surgery said that Poláks Ltd in Dlouhá Avenue, a firm dealing in oil and lacquers, would certainly have in stock the oil he wanted.

Poláks Ltd in Dlouhá Avenue was a very efficient firm. They never let a customer go without satisfying his requirements. If he wanted copaiba balsam they poured out turpentine for him and that did just as well.

When Švejk came in and asked for ten crowns' worth of oil consecrated by a bishop, the manager said to the assistant: 'Pour him out a gill of hempseed oil number three, Mr Tauchen.'

And the assistant, wrapping the bottle up in paper, said to Švejk in a completely business-like way: 'It's of the finest quality. If you would like a paint-brush, lacquer or varnish, don't hesitate to apply to us. We shall serve you reliably.'

In the meantime the chaplain was learning up again in the catechism what he had forgotten from his time at the seminary. He enjoyed very much some unusually witty sentences which made him laugh heartily: 'The name "extreme" or "last unction" derives from the fact that this unction is usually the last of all the unctions which the church administers to anyone.'

Or: 'Extreme unction may be received by every Catholic Christian who is seriously ill and has at last come to his senses.'

'The patient is to receive extreme unction, if possible, while his memory still holds.'

Then an orderly came with a packet, in which the chaplain was informed that the next day extreme unction would be attended by the Association of Gentlewomen for the Religious Education of the Troops.

This association consisted of hysterical old women who distributed to the soldiers in the hospitals icons of saints and stories about a Catholic warrior dying for His Imperial Majesty. These stories had a coloured illustration of a battlefield. There were lying about everywhere human corpses and horse carcasses, overturned munition trains and gun carriages. On the horizon villages were burning and shrapnel bursting. In the foreground lay a dying soldier with his leg torn off. An angel was bending over him and bringing him a wreath with the inscription on the ribbon: 'This very day you will be with me in paradise.' And the dying man was smiling blissfully, as though they were bringing him an ice cream.

When Otto Katz had read the contents of the packet he spat and reflected: 'Tomorrow is going to be some day.'

He knew the harpies, as he called them, from the church of St Ignatius, where years ago he used to preach to the troops. At that time he used to put a lot of feeling into his sermons, and the 'Association' used to sit behind the colonel. Two tall and skinny women in black dresses with rosaries once came up to him after the sermon and talked to him for two hours about the religious education of the troops, until he got angry and said to them: 'Excuse me, my good ladies, the captain's expecting me for a game of färbl.'

'And so here's the oil,' said Švejk solemnly, when he returned from Poláks Ltd. 'Hempseed oil number three, finest quality. We can anoint a whole battalion with it. The firm is a reliable one. It sells varnish, lacquer and brushes as well. Now we only need a bell.'

'Why a bell, Švejk?'

'We have to ring it on the way, so that people take their hats off to us when we transport the Lord, sir, with this hempseed oil number three. It's always done, and very many people, to whom it meant nothing, have been put in gaol because they didn't take their hats off. On a similar occasion in Žižkov a vicar once beat a blind man because he didn't take his hat off and he was put in gaol too, because they proved to him before the courts that he was not deaf and dumb, but only blind, and that he had heard the ringing of the bell and caused a scandal, although it was at night time. That's just like at Corpus Christi. At another time people would never look at us, but now they'll take their hats off to us. If you don't mind, sir, I'll fetch it at once.'

Having obtained permission Švejk produced a bell in half an hour.

'It's from the door of the roadside inn U Křížků,' he said. 'It cost me just five minutes' panic, and I had to wait a long time, because people never stopped going by.'

'I'm going to the café, Švejk. If anybody should come, tell him to wait.'

About an hour later there arrived an elderly grey-haired gentleman of erect carriage and stern countenance.

His whole appearance exhaled cold anger and rage. He looked as if he had been sent by fate to destroy our miserable planet and to obliterate all traces of it in the universe.

His words were harsh, dry and severe: 'Not at home? So he's gone to a café, has he? So I've got to wait, have I? Very well, I'll wait till the morning. He's got money for a café, but not to pay his debts. Calls himself a priest! Lousy rat!'

He spat in the kitchen.

'Sir, don't spit here!' said Švejk, looking at the stranger with interest.

'I shall spit once more, as you see, like this,' said the severe gentleman obstinately, spitting on the floor a second time. 'He should be ashamed. An army chaplain. What a disgrace!'

'If you've had any education,' Švejk reminded him, 'then you should have cured yourself of spitting in someone else's house. Or do you think that when there's a world war on, you can do what you please? You've got to behave decently and not like a hooligan. You've got to act politely, talk decently and not carry on like a damned scoundrel, you bloody fool of a civilian, you!'

The stern gentleman got up from his chair, began to shake with fury and shouted: 'You dare tell me I'm not a decent man? Then what am I, tell me . . .'

'You're a dirty pig,' answered Švejk, looking him straight in the eye. 'You spit on the floor as though you were in a tram, a train or a public place. I've always wondered why there are notices hanging everywhere that spitting is prohibited, and now I see it's all because of you. They must know you very well everywhere.'

The stern man began to change colour and tried to answer with a torrent of oaths directed at Švejk and the chaplain.

'Have you finished your speechifying?' Švejk asked composedly (when the gentleman had delivered himself of his last: 'You're both scoundrels. Like master like dog'), 'or would you like to say something more before you fly down the stairs?'

As the stern gentleman had exhausted himself to such an extent that no valuable and effective oath came to his mind, he fell silent, and Švejk took it as a sign that there was no point in waiting for anything further.

And so he opened the door, placed the stern gentleman at it with his face towards the corridor and gave him a kick worthy of the shoot of the best player in an international football championship team.

And behind the stern gentleman Švejk's voice carried all the way down the steps:

'Next time when you visit decent people, see you behave decently.'

The stern gentleman walked for a long time up and down underneath the windows and waited for the chaplain.

Švejk opened the window and watched him.

At last the chaplain came back. He took the stern gentleman into his room and sat him down on a chair opposite him.

Švejk silently brought in a spittoon and placed it in front of the guest.

'What are you doing, Švejk?'

'Humbly report, sir, there's already been some unpleasantness here with this gentleman concerning spitting on the floor.'

'Leave us alone together, Švejk. We have business to transact.'

Švejk saluted.

'Humbly report, sir, I'm leaving you.'

He went into the kitchen and in the next room a very interesting conversation took place.

'You've come for the money for that bill of exchange, if I am not mistaken?' the chaplain asked his guest.

'Yes, and I hope . . .'

The chaplain sighed.

'A man is often brought into a situation where hope is the only thing left. How beautiful is that little word "hope", from that three-leafed clover, which exalts man above the chaos of life: faith, hope, charity.'

'I hope, chaplain, that the sum . . .'

'Of course, worthy sir,' the chaplain interrupted him. 'Allow me to repeat once more, that the word "hope" is a great strength to man in his struggle with life. And you don't lose hope. How wonderful it is to have a definite ideal, to be an innocent, clean being, who lends money on bills of exchange and has the hope that he will be paid back at the right time. To hope, to hope unremittingly that I shall pay you twelve hundred crowns, when I haven't even a hundred in my pocket!'

'And so you . . .' stammered the guest.

'Yes, and so I,' answered the chaplain.

The guest's face again assumed an obstinate and wrathful expression.

'Sir, this is fraud!' he said, getting up.

'Calm yourself, worthy sir.'

'It's fraud,' the visitor shouted obstinately. 'You have disgracefully abused my confidence.'

'Sir,' said the chaplain, 'a change of air will certainly do you good. It is too sultry here.

'Švejk!' he called to the kitchen. 'This gentleman wants to go out in the fresh air.'

'Humbly report, sir,' came the answer from the kitchen, 'I've already thrown that gentleman out once.'

'Repeat the operation!' came the order, which was executed quickly, briskly and ruthlessly.

'It's good, sir, that we got rid of him before he caused a scandal,' said Švejk, when he returned from the entrance hall, 'In Malešice there was once a pub-keeper, a literary fellow, who always had a quotation from the Holy Bible for all occasions, and when he flogged anybody with a knout he always used to say: "He that spareth his rod hateth his son, but he that loveth him chasteneth him betimes. I'll teach you to fight in my pub."'

'You see, Švejk, what happens to a fellow who doesn't honour priests,' smiled the chaplain. 'St John Chrysostom said: "Whoever honours a priest honours Christ. Who humiliates a priest humiliates Christ the Lord, whose representative the priest is!" We must make thorough preparations for tomorrow. Make some fried eggs and ham. Brew a claret punch, and then we'll devote ourselves to meditation, for, as it is said in the evening prayer, "By God's mercy all the snares of the enemy have been turned aside from this dwelling." '

There are people in the world who are very obstinate and to their number belonged the man who had twice been thrown out of the chaplain's apartment. Just as supper was ready someone rang the bell. Švejk went to open the door and returned after a moment to report: 'He's here again, sir. I've shut him up for the moment in the bathroom, so we can eat our supper in peace.'

'That's not right, Švejk,' said the chaplain. ' "A guest in the house is God in the house." At banquets in old times they used to entertain themselves with monsters. Bring him here so that he can amuse us.'

Švejk returned in a moment with the obstinate man who stared sullenly in front of him.

'Sit down,' the chaplain invited him politely. 'We're just finishing our supper. We've had lobster, salmon and now fried eggs and ham as well. We have marvellous blow-outs when people lend us money.'

'I hope that I am not here just for your amusement,' said the sullen man. 'This is the third time I've come. I hope now that everything will be explained.'

'Humbly report, sir,' observed Švejk, 'he's a real leech, like that fellow Boušek from Libeň. Eighteen times in one evening they threw him out of Exners and he always came back saying he'd forgotten his pipe. He crept in through the window, through the door, from the kitchen, over the wall into the saloon, through the cellar to the bar, and he would have come down the chimney if the firemen hadn't pulled him down off the roof. He was so persistent that he would have made a good minister or parliamentary deputy. They did for him what they could.'

The obstinate man, as though taking no notice of what was being said, repeated stubbornly: 'I want to have this matter cleared up and I demand a hearing.'

'That's granted to you,' said the chaplain. 'Speak, worthy sir. Speak as long as you like and we shall meanwhile continue our feast. I hope it won't disturb your story. Švejk, bring in the food.'

'As you well know,' said the obstinate man, 'a war is raging. I lent you the sum before the war and if there had not been a war I should not have insisted on the repayment. But I have had unfortunate experiences.'

He took a notebook from his pocket and continued: 'I have it all recorded here. Lieutenant Janata owed me seven hundred crowns and had the cheek to fall at the battle of the Drina. Lieutenant Prášek was captured on the Russian front and owes me two thousand crowns. Captain Wichterle, owing me the same amount, got himself killed by his own soldiers at Ruska Rava.[1] Lieutenant Machek, taken prisoner in Serbia, owes me fifteen hundred crowns. There are more people like that here. One falls in the Carpathians with an unpaid bill of exchange of mine; another gets taken prisoner; another gets drowned in Serbia; and a fourth dies in a hospital in Hungary. Now you can understand my fears that this war will ruin me if I'm not energetic and ruthless. You could say that you are in no direct danger. But look.'

He thrust his notebook under the nose of the chaplain. 'You see, Chaplain Matyáš at Brno died in an isolation hospital a week ago. I could have torn my hair out. He owed me eighteen hundred crowns and went into a cholera ward to administer extreme unction to a man who meant nothing to him.'

'That was his duty, my dear sir,' said the chaplain; 'I'm going to administer extreme unction tomorrow too.'

'And in a cholera ward too,' observed Švejk. 'You can go with us so that you can see what it means to sacrifice oneself.'

'Chaplain,' said the obstinate man, 'believe me, I am in a desperate situation. Is this war being waged to put out of the way all who owe me money?'

'When they call you up and you go to the front,' observed Švejk again, 'the chaplain and I will celebrate Holy Mass, so that it may please God in heaven that the first shell should tear you to pieces.'

'Sir, this is a serious matter,' the leech said to the chaplain. 'I request that your servant should not intervene in our business, so that we can settle it at once.'

'Just as you wish, sir,' replied Švejk. 'Be so good as to order me specifically not to interfere in your affairs, otherwise I shall continue to defend your interests as it befits a decent soldier. This gentleman

1. A railway junction in Galicia where there was heavy fighting between the Russian and Austrian troops in 1914–15.

is quite right. He wants to go away from here alone. I don't like scenes either. I'm a social man.'

'Švejk, I'm getting bored with this,' said the chaplain, as though he did not notice the presence of his guest. 'I thought this chap would amuse us, tell us some stories, and instead he asks me to order you not to interfere, although you've had to deal with him twice already. On an evening like this when I have in front of me such an important religious rite, when I have to turn all my thoughts to God, he bothers me with a stupid story about a wretched twelve hundred crowns, distracts me from searching my conscience and from God and wants me to tell him once more that I'm not going to give him anything at the moment. I don't want to speak to him any longer, so that this holy evening is not ruined. You say to him, Švejk: "The chaplain is not going to give you anything!"'

Švejk discharged the order, bawling it into the guest's ear.

The obstinate guest continued to sit there, however.

'Švejk,' suggested the chaplain, 'ask him how long he intends to sit gaping here?'

'I won't move from here until I get my money!' the leech retorted obstinately.

The chaplain got up, went to the window and said: 'In that case I give him over to you, Švejk. Do with him what you like.'

'Come here, sir,' said Švejk, seizing the unwelcome guest by the shoulder. 'Third time lucky.'

And he repeated his performance quickly and elegantly, while the chaplain drummed a funeral march on the window.

The evening, which was devoted to meditation, passed through several phases. The chaplain drew close to God with such piety and ardour that at midnight the following strains could be heard from his apartment:

> 'When we marched away,
> The girls all cried their eyes out . . .

And the good soldier Švejk sang with him.

In the military hospital two men were longing for extreme unction – an old major and a bank manager who was an officer in the reserve. Both had got bullets in the stomach in the Carpathians and lay in adjoining beds. The officer in the reserve considered it his duty to have

extreme unction administered to him, because his superior officer was longing for it too. He regarded it as a breach of discipline not to have it. The pious major did it out of calculation, imagining that a prayer could cure an invalid. However, the night before the extreme unction both of them died, and when in the morning the chaplain arrived with Švejk, both the officers lay underneath a sheet with black faces, like all those who die of asphyxiation.

'We were making such a splash, sir, and now they've gone and spoilt things,' Švejk grumbled, when they told them in the office that these two no longer needed anything.

And it was true that they had made a great splash. They had driven there in a droshky. Švejk had rung the bell, and the chaplain had held in his hands the bottle with the oil, which was wrapped up in a table napkin. He solemnly blessed all the passers-by with it and they took off their hats.

There were not many of them, it is true, although Švejk tried to make a tremendous row with the bell.

One or two innocent street urchins ran behind the droshky, and one of them seated himself behind, whereupon his comrades broke out in unison: 'After the carriage, after the carriage!'

And Švejk rang the bell, the droshky driver hit backwards with his whip, in Vodičkova Street a woman concièrge who was a member of the congregation of the Virgin Mary trotted after the droshky and caught up with it. She received a blessing on the way, made the sign of the cross, spat and shouted: 'They're driving like Jehu with the Lord! It's enough to give you T.B.!' after which she returned breathlessly to her old place.

It was the droshky driver's mare which was most worried by the sound of the bell. It must have reminded her of something that had happened in the past, because she continually looked behind and from time to time tried to dance on the cobbles.

And so this was the great splash which Švejk talked about. In the meantime the chaplain went into the office to settle the financial side of the extreme unction and calculated to the quartermaster sergeant-major that the army authorities owed him one hundred and fifty crowns for the consecrated oil and the journey.

Then followed a quarrel between the commandant of the hospital and the chaplain, in the course of which the chaplain hit the table several times with his fist and said: 'Don't imagine, captain, that extreme unction is *gratis*. When an officer of the Dragoons is ordered to go to the stud farm for horses, they pay him subsistence too. I am really sorry that these two did not live to get their extreme unction. It would have been fifty crowns more.'

In the meantime Švejk waited down in the guardhouse with the bottle of holy oil which aroused genuine interest among the soldiers.

One expressed the view that this oil could be used very successfully for cleaning rifles and bayonets.

A young soldier from the Bohemian-Moravian Highlands, who still believed in God, asked them not to talk about these things and not to bring into discussion the mysteries of the sacrament. We must, he said, live in hope, like Christians.

An old reservist looked at the raw recruit and said: 'Nice hope that a shrapnel tears off your head! They've pulled the wool over our eyes. Once a deputy from the Clerical Party came to our village and spoke to us about God's peace, which spans the earth, and how the Lord did not want war and wanted us all to live in peace and get on together like brothers. And look at him now, the bloody fool! Now that war has broken out they pray in all the churches for the success of our arms, and they talk about God like a chief of the general staff who guides and directs the war. From this military hospital I've seen many funerals go out and cartfuls of hacked-off arms and legs carried away.'

'And the soldiers are buried naked,' said another soldier, 'and into the uniform they put another live man. And so it goes on for ever and ever.'

'Until we've won,' observed Švejk.

'And that bloody half-wit wants to win something,' a corporal chimed in from the corner. 'To the front with you, to the trenches! You should be driven for all you're worth on to bayonets over barbed wire, mines and mortars. Anyone can lie about behind the lines, but no one wants to fall in action.'

'I think that it's splendid to get oneself run through with a bayonet,' said Švejk, 'and also that it's not bad to get a bullet in the stomach. It's even grander when you're torn to pieces by a shell and you see that your legs and belly are somehow remote from you. It's very funny and you die before anyone can explain it to you.'

The young soldier gave a heartfelt sigh. He was sorry for his young life. Why was he born in such a stupid century to be butchered like an ox in a slaughterhouse? Why was all that necessary?

A soldier, who was a teacher by profession and seemed to read his thoughts, observed: 'Some scientists explain war by the appearance of sun spots. As soon as a sun spot like that appears, something frightful always happens. The conquest of Carthage . . .'

'To hell with your learning,' the corporal interrupted him. 'Go and sweep the room instead. Today it's your turn. What the hell do we care about any bloody sun spots? Even if there were twenty of them I wouldn't buy them.'

'Those sun spots are really very important,' put in Švejk. 'Once there was a sun spot like that and the very same day I was beaten up at U Banzetů at Nusle. From that time whenever I went anywhere I always looked in the newspapers to see if a sun spot hadn't appeared. And as soon as one did, then count me out, I said. I didn't go anywhere and that was the only way I managed to survive. At the time when the volcano Mont-Pellé destroyed the whole island of Martinique, a professor wrote in *Národní Politika* that he had long ago told readers about a big sun spot. But *Národní Politika* didn't get to the island in time, and so the people on it caught it proper.'

Meanwhile upstairs in the office the chaplain met a lady from the Association of Gentlewomen for the Religious Education of the Troops, an old repulsive siren, who went round the hospital from the early morning and distributed everywhere icons of saints, which the wounded and the sick soldiers threw into the spittoons.

And when she went round she infuriated everybody with her stupid chatter about their having honestly to repent their sins and really reform so that after death God could give them everlasting salvation.

She was pale when she talked with the chaplain. She said that the war instead of ennobling soldiers made beasts of them. Downstairs the patients had stuck their tongues out at her and told her she was a scarecrow and a frightful skinny old frump. 'Oh, how dreadful, chaplain,' she said in German. 'The people have been corrupted.'

And she described how she saw the religious education of a soldier. Only when he believes in God and has religious feelings can a soldier fight bravely for His Imperial Majesty and not fear death, because then he knows that paradise awaits him.

She babbled on and said a few more stupid things like this, and it was clear that she was resolved not to let the chaplain go. But he excused himself in a rather ungallant way.

'We're going home, Švejk!' he called to the guardhouse. On the way back they made no splash.

'Next time anyone who likes can administer extreme unction,' said the chaplain. 'Fancy having to haggle about money for every soul you want to save. Their accounts are the only thing they think about.'

Seeing a bottle of 'consecrated' oil in Švejk's hand, he frowned: 'It would be better, Švejk, if you polished my boots and your own with this.'

'I'll see if I can't oil the lock with it,' added Švejk. 'It squeaks frightfully when you come home at night.'

Thus ended the extreme unction which never was.

14

Švejk Batman to Lieutenant Lukáš

I

ŠVEJK'S good fortune did not last long. Unrelenting fate severed the friendly relations between him and the chaplain. If until this event the chaplain had been a likeable person, what he now did was calculated to strip from him his likeable image.

The chaplain sold Švejk to Lieutenant Lukáš, or, to be more correct, gambled him away at cards, just as they used to sell serfs in Russia in the old days. It happened quite unexpectedly. Lieutenant Lukáš gave a splendid party and they played vingt-et-un.

The chaplain lost everything and said in the end: 'How much will you advance me on my batman? He's a screaming half-wit and an interesting personality, a kind of *non plus ultra*. You never had a batman like him before.'

'I'll advance you a hundred crowns,' Lieutenant Lukáš offered. 'If I don't get them back the day after tomorrow, you can send me this rare specimen. My own batman is a disgusting fellow. He's always groaning, writes letters home and at the same time steals what he can lay his hands on. I've already beaten him, but it doesn't do any good. I box his ears whenever I meet him, but that doesn't help either. I've knocked out some of his front teeth, but even that hasn't improved the bastard.'

'Agreed, then,' said the chaplain light-heartedly. 'Either a hundred crowns the day after tomorrow or Švejk.'

And he gambled away those hundred crowns too and went home sadly. He knew for certain and had never doubted that in two days he could not possibly rustle up those hundred crowns and that he had actually bartered Švejk away basely and despicably.

'I might just as well have said two hundred,' he said to himself angrily, but when he changed on to the tram which would soon take him home he had an attack of conscience and sentimentality.

'It wasn't gentlemanly of me to do it,' he thought, as he rang at the door of his apartment. 'How can I look into his stupid, kind eyes?'

'My dear Švejk,' he said, when he was home. 'Today something unusual happened. I had awfully bad luck in cards. I went "banco"[1] and had the ace in my hand, and then a ten came. But the banker had the knave in his hand and made twenty-one too. I drew an ace or a

ten several times but the banker always had the same. I went through all my money.'

He paused: 'And finally I gambled you away. I borrowed a hundred crowns on you and if I don't return it by the day after tomorrow you won't belong to me any longer but to Lieutenant Lukáš. I'm really very sorry . . .'

'If it's only a hundred crowns,' said Švejk, 'I can lend it to you.'

'Give it to me,' said the chaplain, brightening up. 'I'll take it at once to Lukáš. I should really hate to have to part with you.'

1. i.e. staked the whole contents of the bank.

Lukáš was very surprised when he saw the chaplain again.

'I'm coming to repay my debt,' said the chaplain, looking around triumphantly. 'Let me join the game.'

'Banco,' shouted the chaplain when it was his turn. 'I'm only one pip over,' he announced.

'All right, then. Banco again,' he said, when the second round came. 'And blind.'

'Paying twenty,' announced the banker.

'I've got nineteen altogether,' said the chaplain quietly and paid the bank the last forty crowns of the hundred which Švejk had lent him to ransom himself from his new serfdom.

On his way home the chaplain came to the conclusion that it was all finished, that nothing could save Švejk, and that it was predestined that he should be Lieutenant Lukáš's batman.

And when Švejk opened the door he told him: 'It's all up, Švejk. No one can escape his fate. I have lost you and your hundred crowns too. I did my utmost, but fate was stronger than me. I've thrown you into the clutches of Lieutenant Lukáš and the time is coming when we must part.'

'And was there a lot in the bank?' asked Švejk calmly. 'Didn't you get a chance of being Forehand very often? If the right card doesn't come it's very bad, but sometimes it's awful when the cards are too good. At Zderaz there was once a tinsmith called Vejvoda and he always used to play mariáš in a pub behind the Century Café. Once the devil whispered into his ear: "How about a game of vingt-et-un at ten-heller stakes?" And so they played vingt-et-un at ten hellers and he held the bank. They all joined the game and then the bank grew to ten crowns. Old Vejvoda wanted to help the others and so he kept on saying: "Low and bad is safe." But you can't imagine what bad luck he had. However low his card was it was never worse than what the others had. The bank grew and grew and there was already a hundred crowns in it. None of the players had enough to go "banco" and Vejvoda sat there sweating. You couldn't hear anything except his "Low and bad is safe." One after another people joined in with ten-crown stakes and all of them burst. A master chimney-sweep got furious and went home for more money. He went "banco" when there was already more than a hundred and fifty in the bank. Vejvoda wanted to get himself out of the game and, as he confessed afterwards, he tried to push the bidding up to as much as thirty just so as not to

win. But instead he got two aces. He pretended he had nothing and said on purpose: "Paying sixteens." And that chimney-sweep had only fifteen. Wasn't that bad luck? Old Vejvoda was quite pale and miserable. All around they were swearing and muttering that he was cheating and that he'd already been flogged for card-sharping, although he was really a very honest player. And so they all of them paid him crown after crown and there was already five hundred crowns there. The landlord couldn't stand it any longer. He had money ready to pay to the brewery and so he took it, sat down, pushed forward two hundred and then two hundred again. After that he shut his eyes, spun the chair round for luck and said he'd go "banco". "And we'll play 'Ouvert',"[1] he declared. I don't know what old Vejvoda wouldn't have given to have lost. Everybody was amazed when he drew a card from the pack and it was a seven and he took it. The landlord was smiling up his sleeve, because he had twenty-one. Old Vejvoda drew a second seven and still he took it. "Now an ace or ten will come," said the landlord maliciously. "I bet my last shirt, Mr Vejvoda, that you'll burst." There was a deathly silence. Vejvoda drew again and a third seven appeared. The landlord turned white as a sheet, because it was his last sou. He went into the kitchen and a short time afterwards his apprentice boy ran in and called us to come and cut the landlord down, because he was hanging on a window-handle. And so we cut him down, revived him and the game went on. No one had any money left at all. Everything was in the bank, in front of Vejvoda, who only went on saying: "Low and bad is safe." And he would have given everything in the world to burst but because he had to expose his hand on the table he couldn't cheat and intentionally overbid. They were all furious over his good luck and arranged that when they had no more money left they would give him I.O.U.s. It went on for several hours and thousands and thousands heaped up in front of old Vejvoda. The chimney-sweep was already more than one and a half million in debt to the bank, a coalman from Zderaz about a million, a porter from the Century Café eight times a hundred thousand and a medico over two million. In the pool alone there was more than three hundred thousand on little bits of paper. Old Vejvoda tried all different tricks. He went continually to the W.C. and always asked someone else to draw for him and when he returned they told him that he had drawn and got twenty-one. They

---

1. The player has to expose his hand before the opening lead and permit his opponents to see all his cards.

sent for new cards, but still that didn't help. When Vejvoda stopped at fifteen, the other had only fourteen. They all looked furiously at old Vejvoda and the man who swore at him most was a paver who had only put in eight crowns in cash. He stated openly that a man like Vejvoda shouldn't be allowed to go about free but deserved to be beaten up, thrown out and drowned like a puppy. You can't imagine old Vejvoda's despair. Finally he had an idea. "I'm going to the W.C.," he said to the chimney-sweep. "Draw for me, will you?" And then he went out just as he was without a hat on to the street and straight to Myslíkova Street for the police. He found a patrol and told them that in such and such a pub they were playing gambling games. The police ordered him to go ahead and they would follow immediately after. He came back and was told that in the meanwhile the medico had lost over two million and the porter over three. In the pool there were I.O.U.s for five times a hundred thousand crowns. After a while the policemen burst in; the paver screamed out, "Everyone for himself!" but it was no good. They confiscated the bank and took all the players off to the police station. The coalman from Zderaz resisted and so they brought him along in the drunks' cart. In the bank there were I.O.U.s for over half a milliard and fifteen hundred crowns in cash. "I've never copped as much as that before," said the police inspector, when he saw such dizzy sums. "It's worse than in Monte Carlo." All of them except old Vejvoda had to stay there till morning. He was released for turning king's evidence and was promised that he would get as his lawful reward a third of the money confiscated in the bank, about one hundred and sixty million or more. But before the morning he was already off his head and was going about Prague ordering burglar-proof safes by the dozen. That's what they call success at cards.'

And then Švejk went off to brew some grog. And it happened that when with some difficulty he succeeded in getting the chaplain into bed that night the latter burst into tears and cried: 'I've bartered you, my friend, I've shamefully bartered you. Curse me, beat me, I'll take it. I let you down. I can't look you in the eyes. Tear me, bite me, destroy me. I don't deserve anything better. Do you know what I am?'

And the chaplain pressing his tear-stained face into the pillow said gently in a soft tender voice: 'I'm a bastard without any character at all,' and fell asleep like a log.

The next day, shunning Švejk's gaze, the chaplain went out early and returned late at night with a fat infantryman.

'Show him, Švejk, where everything is so that he can get his bearings,' he said, again avoiding his gaze. 'And show him how to make
grog. Tomorrow you are to report to Lieutenant Lukáš.'

Švejk spent the night agreeably with the new man making grog. By
the morning the fat infantryman could hardly stand on his legs and
was humming a strange pot-pourri of various national songs, which he
mixed up together: 'Around Chodov there runs a stream, My love
serves red beer there, Mountain, mountain, thou art high, Maidens
went along the path, On the White Mountain a peasant is ploughing.'

'I'm not worried about you,' said Švejk. 'With a talent like that you'll
keep your job with the chaplain.'

And so it happened that in the morning Lieutenant Lukáš saw for
the first time the decent and honest countenance of the good soldier
Švejk, who announced to him: 'Humbly report, sir, I am Švejk whom
the chaplain gambled away at cards.'

II

The institution of officers' orderlies is of very ancient origin. It seems
that even Alexander the Great had his batman. What is certain,
however, is that in the period of feudalism the knights' hirelings performed this role. What else was Don Quixote's Sancho Panza? I am
surprised that no one has yet written up the history of army orderlies.
If anyone had, we should read in it how at the siege of Toledo the Duke
of Almavira was so hungry that he ate his orderly without salt, which
the duke himself mentions in his memoirs, relating that his orderly had
fine, tender, succulent meat tasting like something between chicken
and donkey.

In an old German book about the art of war we find directions for
orderlies. The batman of the old days had to be pious, virtuous, truthful, modest, brave, courageous, honest and industrious. In short he
had to be a model man. Modern times have changed this type considerably. The modern batman is usually not pious or virtuous or truthful. He tells lies, cheats his master and very often turns his superior's life
into sheer hell. He is a cunning slave, who thinks out the most varied
forms of treacherous ploys to embitter his master's life. In this new
generation of batmen you will not find such self-sacrificing creatures
as would let themselves be eaten by their masters without salt, like the
noble Fernando, batman of the Duke of Almavira. On the other

hand we find that commanders who wage a life and death struggle with their orderlies of modern times adopt the most varied methods to preserve their authority. It is a certain kind of terror. In 1912 there was a trial in Graz in which the leading figure was a captain who had kicked his batman to death. He was acquitted then because it was only the second time he had done it. In the eyes of gentlemen like this the life of a batman has no value at all. He is only an object, often an Aunt Sally, a slave, a maid of all work. It is not surprising that such a position requires of the slave that he should be crafty and cunning. His position on this planet can be compared only with the sufferings of the pot-boys of old days, who were trained to be conscientious by means of blows and torture.

There are however cases where a batman rises to the position of a favourite, and then he becomes the terror of the company or the battalion. All the N.C.O.s try to bribe him. He decides questions of leave and can use his influence and see that it goes well with those who are sent on report. These favourites were usually rewarded in wartime with the large and small silver medals for bravery and valour.

In the 91st regiment I knew several of them. One batman received the large silver medal because he was an adept in roasting the geese he had stolen. Another got the small silver medal because he used to get from his home wonderful food hampers so that in the time of the most acute famine his master stuffed himself up so much that he could hardly walk.

And his master formulated the citation for his decoration as follows:

'For displaying unusual bravery and courage in battle, despising death and not abandoning his superior officer for a moment under the powerful fire of the advancing enemy.'

But in fact he was plundering hen coops somewhere in the base.

The war changed the relationship between the batman and his master and made him the creature who was most hated by the rank and file. The batman always got a whole tin of meat, where otherwise it would be divided among five. His field-flask was always full of rum or cognac. The whole day this type of creature munched chocolate and devoured sweet biscuits reserved for officers, smoked his master's cigarettes, cooked for hours on end and wore an extra tunic.

The batman was on the closest terms with the company orderly and gave him fat pickings from his table and from all those privileges which he enjoyed. He allowed into the triumvirate the quartermaster sergeant-major. This trio lived in direct contact with the officer and knew all the operations and war plans.

The unit whose corporal was friendly with the batman was always best informed about when things would start.

When he said: 'At 2.35 we shall start hopping it,' then at 2.35 exactly the Austrian soldiers began to disengage from the enemy.

The batman was on the most intimate terms with the field-kitchen and always liked to hang around the cauldron and give orders as though he were in a restaurant and had the menu before him.

'I'd like a rib,' he would say to the cook. 'Yesterday you gave me the tail. And add a piece of liver to my soup. You know I don't eat milt.'

But the batman was always in best form when starting a panic. When the trenches were being bombed his heart ran down into his pants. In such times he was always in the most secure cover together with his luggage and that of his master. He covered his head with a rug, in case a shell should find him, and he had no other wish than that his master should be wounded and that he could go with him to the base as far as possible behind the front line.

He cultivated panic systematically by the use of a certain measure of secrecy. 'I've got a hunch that they're packing the telephone up,' he would say confidentially to the units. And he was happy when he was able to say: 'Now they've packed it up.'

No one loved a retreat as much as he did. In such moments he forgot that shell and shrapnel were flying over his head and pushed on indefatigably with the luggage to staff headquarters, where the baggage train was standing. He loved the Austrian baggage train and was very happy when he could travel on it. In emergencies he would use the ambulance two-wheelers. When he had to go on foot he gave the impression of being a completely broken man. In that case he abandoned his master's luggage in the trenches and took only his own property with him.

Should it happen that the officer escaped capture by running away and the batman was caught, he never forgot under any circumstances to take his master's luggage with him into captivity. It then passed into his ownership and he clung to it with might and main.

I once saw a captured batman who had gone on foot with others from Dubno to Darnica beyond Kiev. Besides his own haversack he had with him the haversack of his superior officer who had escaped capture, five handcases of different shape and size, two blankets and a pillow, apart from another piece of luggage which he carried on his head. He complained that the Cossacks had stolen two of his cases.

I shall never forget that man who dragged himself in this way across the whole of the Ukraine. He was a walking removal van, and I can

never understand how he was able to carry off this luggage and drag it for so many hundreds of kilometres and then go with it as far as Tashkent, look after it and die of spotted typhus on it in a prison camp.

Today batmen are scattered over the whole of our republic and they tell of their heroic deeds. It was they who stormed Sokal, Dubno, Niš and the Piave. Every one of them is a Napoleon: 'I told our colonel to ring staff headquarters and say it can start.'

Most of them were reactionaries and the rank and file hated them. Some of them were informers and it was their special delight to watch someone being seized and bound.

They developed into a special caste. Their selfishness knew no bounds.

III

Lieutenant Lukáš was a typical regular officer of the ramshackle Austrian monarchy. The cadet school had turned him into a kind of amphibian. He spoke German in society, wrote German, read Czech books, and when he taught in the course for one-year volunteers, all of whom were Czechs, he told them in confidence: 'Let's be Czechs, but no one need know about it. I'm a Czech too.'

He equated being a Czech with membership of some sort of secret organization, to which it was wiser to give a wide berth.

Otherwise he was a decent man, who was not afraid of his superiors and looked after his company at manoeuvres, as was seemly and proper. He always found them comfortable quarters in barns and often let the soldiers roll out a barrel of beer at the expense of his own modest salary.

He liked it when his men sang songs on the march. They had to sing even when they went to and from drill. And walking by the side of his company he sang with them:

> 'And when it was midnight black
> The oats jumped out of the sack,
> Tantantara! Zing! Bum!'

He enjoyed the affection of his men because he was unusually just and was not in the habit of bullying anyone.

The N.C.O.s trembled before him and in a month he could reduce the most brutal sergeant-major to a perfect lamb.

He could shout, it is true, but he never swore. He used choice expressions and sentences. 'You see,' he said, 'I really don't like punishing you, my boy, but I can't help it, because the efficiency and courage of an army depends on discipline, and without discipline an army is a reed swaying in the wind. If you don't have your uniform in order and your buttons properly sewn on or if they're missing it is obvious that you are neglecting the responsibilities you owe to the army. Perhaps it may seem incomprehensible to you that you are being put in detention just because yesterday at an inspection there was one button missing on your tunic, in other words, a tiny unimportant matter which in civil life would be completely overlooked. But, you see, in the army neglect of your personal appearance like that must result in your punishment. And why? It's not a question here of a missing button but of your having to get used to order. Today you forget to sew on a button and start getting slack. Tomorrow you'll already find it a bore to dismantle your rifle and clean it. The day after you'll forget your bayonet in a pub somewhere, and finally you'll fall asleep at your post, because with that unfortunate button you already started on the downward career of a scrimshanker. So that's it, my boy, and I am punishing you to save you from an even worse punishment for things you might do if you slowly but surely began to forget your duties. I am sending you to detention for five days, and over your bread and water I want you to reflect that punishment is not revenge but just a means of education. Its object is to reform and improve the soldier who is being punished.'

He should have been a captain long since but his cautiousness in the nationality question had not helped him, because he always behaved towards his superiors with complete frankness and any kind of bootlicking in official relations was beneath him.

This is what he had retained of the character of a peasant from South Bohemia, where he was born in a village among dark forests and lakes.

Although he was just to the soldiers and did not bully them he had one special trait in his character. He hated his batmen, because he always had the bad luck to get the most disgusting and mean ones imaginable. He hit them across the jaw, boxed their ears and tried to train them by precept and deed, not looking upon them as soldiers. He struggled with them hopelessly for a number of years, changed them continually and finally sighed: 'Now I've got another filthy bastard.' He regarded his batmen as the lowest form of animal life.

He was very fond of animals. He had a Harz canary, an Angora cat and a stable pinscher. All the batmen in turn treated these animals no worse than Lieutenant Lukáš treated them when they too did something mean.

They starved the canary. One batman knocked one of the Angora cat's eyes out. They beat the stable pinscher every time they saw it, and finally one of Švejk's predecessors took the wretched animal off to Pankrác to the skinner, where he had him put away, paying ten crowns for it from his own pocket without any regrets. Then he simply told the lieutenant that the dog had run away from him on a walk. The very next day that batman was marching with the company to the drill-ground.

When Švejk came to report to Lukáš that he was starting his duties the latter took him into the sitting-room and said: 'The chaplain recommended you and I hope you won't disgrace his recommendation. I've already had a dozen batmen and not one of them has ever settled down with me. I must warn you that I'm strict and that I punish terribly any meanness or lying. I require you always to tell me the truth and to carry out all my orders without grumbling. If I say to you: "Jump into the fire", then you must jump into the fire, even though you don't want to. What are you looking at?'

Švejk was looking with interest sideways at the wall where a cage hung with a canary in it, and fixing his kindly eyes on the lieutenant he answered in a gentle, good-natured tone: 'Humbly report, sir, there's a Harz canary there.'

And after having interrupted in this way the flow of the lieutenant's words Švejk adopted a military stance and looked him straight in the eyes without blinking.

The lieutenant wanted to say something sharp, but observing the innocent expression on Švejk's face said nothing more than 'The chaplain recommended you as a frightful idiot and I think he was not wrong.'

'Humbly report, sir, he certainly was not wrong. When I was serving as a regular I got a complete discharge for idiocy and for patent idiocy into the bargain. In our regiment only two of us were discharged in this way, me and a Captain von Kaunitz. And whenever that captain went out in the street, if you'll pardon me, sir, he always at the same time picked his left nostril with his left hand, and his right nostril with his right hand, and when he went with us to the parade ground he always made us adopt a formation as though it was going to be a march past and said: "Men, ahem, remember, ahem, that today is Wednesday, because tomorrow will be Thursday, ahem." '

Lieutenant Lukáš shrugged his shoulders, like a man who did not know how to express a certain thought and could not immediately find words to do so.

He went from the door to the window on the other side of the room past Švejk and back again. All this time Švejk did 'eyes right' or 'eyes left' wherever the lieutenant was and did it with such a marked expression of innocence on his face that the lieutenant lowered his gaze to the carpet and said something which had no connection at all with Švejk's observation about the stupid captain: 'Yes. With me there's got to be order, cleanliness and no lying. I like honesty. I hate lies and I punish them mercilessly. Do you understand?'

'Humbly report, sir, I understand. There's nothing worse than when someone tells a lie. As soon as he starts getting tied up he's done for. In a village behind Pelhřimov there was once a teacher called Marek who used to keep company with the daughter of the gamekeeper

Špera. The gamekeeper gave him to understand that if ever he had a rendezvous with the girl in the forest and he found him there, he'd shoot a brush full of salt into his backside. The teacher sent him a message that it was not true, but once when he was going to meet the girl the gamekeeper caught him, and was just about to carry out the operation on him when the teacher excused himself by saying that he was only picking flowers. And then after that he said he had gone to catch some beetles and got more and more tied up until finally he got into a panic and swore that he had gone out to set traps for hares. And so the good gamekeeper seized him and took him away to the gendarmerie station, and from there the case went to the courts and the teacher might easily have been sent to prison for it. If he'd said just the bare truth he'd only have got the brushes with the salt. I'm of the opinion that it's always best to confess, to be open and, if I've done something, to come and say: ' 'Humbly report, I've done this and that.'' And as for honesty that's always a jolly good thing because it's always the best policy. It's just like in those walking races. As soon as a chap begins to cheat and run he's already disqualified. That happened to my cousin. An honest man's respected everywhere, he's honoured, satisfied with himself and feels new-born when he can go to bed and say: ''Today I've played the game again!'' '

While he was speaking Lieutenant Lukáš sat for a long time on his chair, looking at Švejk's boots and thinking: 'My God! I often talk drivel like this too and the only difference is the form I serve it up in.'

Nonetheless, not wishing to lose his authority, he said when Švejk had ended:

'With me you must clean your boots, have your uniform in order, your buttons properly sewn on and give an impression of being a soldier and not a miserable civvy. It's extraordinary how none of you seem to be able to carry yourselves like soldiers. Only one of all my batmen looked like a real warrior and in the end he went and stole my full-dress uniform and sold it in the Jewish quarter.'

He was silent and then continued, explaining to Švejk all his duties, in the course of which he did not forget to lay the main emphasis on the fact that he must be loyal and never talk about what was happening at his home.

'Ladies pay me visits,' he added. 'Sometimes one of them stays overnight, if I'm not on duty the next day. If that happens you'll bring us our coffee in bed, when I ring. Do you understand?'

'Humbly report, I understand, sir. If I should come to the bed without warning it might perhaps be disagreeable for a lady. I once brought a young lady home and my charwoman brought us coffee in bed just when we were enjoying ourselves immensely. She got frightened and poured the coffee all over my back and said into the bargain: "A very good morning to you." I know what is seemly and proper, when there's a lady sleeping somewhere.'

'Good, Švejk, we must always show exceptional tact to the ladies,' said the lieutenant, who was getting into a better temper, because the conversation was touching a subject which filled his leisure hours between the barracks, the parade ground and card-playing.

Women were the life and soul of his apartment. It was they who made his home for him. There were several dozen of them and many tried during their stay to adorn his flat with various bric-à-brac.

One lady, the wife of a café proprietor, who lived with him for a whole fortnight until her husband came for her and took her home, embroidered for him a delightful table runner, put monograms on all his underclothing and might indeed perhaps have completed the embroidery of the wall hangings, if her husband had not destroyed the idyll.

Another lady, whom her parents fetched after three weeks, wanted to turn his bedroom into a lady's boudoir and placed everywhere various fancy things and little vases and hung a picture of the guardian angel over his bed.

In all corners of his bedroom and dining room the traces of a feminine hand could be felt. And this extended to the kitchen, where could be seen the most varied kitchen implements and utensils, which had been the magnificent gift of the lovesick wife of a factory-owner. Together with her passion she brought with her a gadget for cutting all kinds of greens and cabbages, a machine for making breadcrumbs and scraping liver, various casseroles, roasters, frying pans, basting ladles and God knows what else.

But she went away after a week, because she could not reconcile herself to the thought that the lieutenant had besides her some twenty other loves, which left certain traces on the performance of the noble male in uniform.

Lieutenant Lukáš also carried on a voluminous correspondence. He had an album of his lady loves and a collection of various relics, because for the last two years he had evinced a tendency to fetishism. Thus he had a number of different ladies' garters, four delightful pairs of ladies' knickers with embroidery and three transparent fine thin chemises, cambric kerchiefs and even a corset and a number of stockings.

'Today I'm on duty,' he said. 'I shan't come back till night. Have everything ready and put the apartment in order. My last batman went off today to the front in the march column because of his skulduggery!'

After giving further orders concerning the canary and the Angora cat he went away without forgetting to make a few remarks about honesty and order while still in the doorway.

After his departure Švejk put everything into the finest order, so that when Lieutenant Lukáš returned to his home at night he could report to him:

'Humbly report, sir, everything is in order. Only the cat has got into mischief and eaten up your canary.'

'What?' thundered the lieutenant.

'Humbly report, sir, it was like this: I knew that cats hate canaries and like to insult them. And so I thought I'd introduce them to each other, and if the brute tried anything on I'd flay her so that she'd remember to her dying day how to behave towards canaries, because I'm very fond of animals. In the house where I live there's a hat-maker and he trained his cat so well that after eating up three of his canaries she didn't eat any more – a canary could sit on her if it liked. And I wanted to try that out too and so I took the canary out of its cage and let her smell it, and she, the little monkey, bit its head off before I realized it. I really never expected such caddishness from her. If it had been a sparrow, sir, I wouldn't have said anything, but a lovely canary like that from the Harz. And how greedily she gobbled it up, feathers and all, and at the same time purred out of sheer joy. They say cats have no musical education and can't stand it when a canary sings, because the brutes don't understand it. I swore at the cat, but I swear to God that I didn't do anything to her and waited for you to come to decide what's to be done with her, the scabby beast.'

While saying this Švejk looked into the lieutenant's eyes with such sincerity that although the latter approached him at first with certain cruel intentions he moved away from him again, sat down on a chair and asked:

'Listen, Švejk, are you really God's prize oaf?'

'Humbly report, sir,' Švejk answered solemnly, 'I am! Ever since I was little I have had bad luck like that. I always want to put something right, to do good, but nothing ever comes out of it except trouble for me and all around. I really wanted these two to get to know each other so that they would understand each other, and I can't help it if she ate it up and it was the end of the acquaintance. In a house called U Štupartů some years ago a cat even ate up a parrot, because it laughed and mimicked her miaowing. But cats cling pretty obstinately to their lives. If you want me to do her in, sir, then I'll have to crush her in the door. Otherwise she'll never be finished.'

And Švejk with the most innocent of countenances and his gentle good-humoured smile gave the lieutenant an account of how cats are executed, the content of which would certainly send any society for the prevention of cruelty to animals into a lunatic asylum.

In telling this he revealed such expert knowledge that Lieutenant Lukáš forgot his anger and asked:

'So you know how to look after animals? Have you got some feeling for them? Do you love them?'

'I like dogs best of all, sir,' said Švejk, 'because they offer a profitable business for anyone who knows how to sell them. I wasn't able to do it, because I've always been honest. But all the same people used to be after me and say I'd sold them a lame duck instead of a healthy thoroughbred, as though all dogs must be thoroughbred and healthy. And everyone at once asked for a pedigree, so that I had to have pedigrees printed and turn some mongrel from Košíře, which had been born in a brickworks, into the most thoroughbred aristocrat from the Bavarian kennels of Armin von Barheim. And really people were only too happy if it turned out so well that they had a thoroughbred at home. I could perhaps have offered them a Vršovice pom as a dachshund, and they would only have been rather surprised that such a rare dog, coming all the way from Germany, was shaggy and didn't have bow legs. They do that in all kennels. You should see, sir, the fiddles which go on with these pedigrees in the big kennels. There are really very few dogs existing which could say of themselves: "I'm a thoroughbred." Either its mamma forgot herself with some frightful monstrosity, or its granny did, or else it's had several papas and inherited a bit from each. From one its ears, from another its tail, from another again the tufts on its snout, from a third its muzzle, from a fourth its hobbling legs and from a fifth its size. And if it had had twelve such papas, you can imagine, sir, what such a dog looks like. I once bought a dog like that called Balabán. After all his papas he was so ugly that all dogs avoided him and I only bought him out of pity because he was so abandoned. And he always used to sit at home in a corner and was so unhappy, till I had to sell him as a stable pinscher. What gave me the most trouble was dyeing him, so that he had a pepper and salt colour. In this condition he went with his master to Moravia and from that time on I've never set eyes on him any more.'

The lieutenant began to be extremely interested by this cynological lecture and Švejk was able to continue without interruption.

'Dogs can't dye their hair like ladies do. This always has to be done by the person who wants to sell them. If a dog is so old that it's completely grey and you want to sell it as a year-old puppy or pretend that the old dodderer is only nine months old, then you must buy some silver nitrate, dissolve it and paint the dog black so that it looks quite new. And you must feed it like a horse with arsenic, so that it gains strength, and you must clean its teeth with sand paper like they use for cleaning rusty knives. And before you lead it out to be sold to a customer, you must pour some slivovice down its throat, so that it gets a bit tipsy. Then it'll immediately get lively, gay, bark joyfully and make friends with anyone, like a drunken town councillor. But the main thing is this: you must talk to people, sir, and go on talking to them until the customer gets completely crazy. If anyone wants to buy a miniature pinscher off you and you have nothing else at home but a pointer, you must be able to talk him into taking away with him a pointer and not a miniature pinscher, and if by chance you only have a miniature pinscher at home and someone comes to buy a fierce German mastiff for a watch dog, you must fool him so that he takes away in his pocket the tiny little miniature pinscher instead of the mastiff. When I used to be in the dog business, a lady came in to tell me that her parrot had flown out into her garden, so she said, and that some little boys who were playing Indians in front of her villa had just seized it, torn all the feathers from its tail and decked themselves up in them like police. And this parrot, out of the shame of being tailless, fell ill, and the vet finished it off with some powders. And so she wanted to buy a new parrot, a respectable one, not a vulgar one which would do nothing but swear. What could I do when I hadn't a parrot at home and didn't know of one? I only had at home a savage bulldog, which was completely blind. And so, sir, I had to spend from four o'clock in the afternoon to seven o'clock in the evening talking that lady into buying that blind bulldog instead of a parrot. It was worse than any diplomatic situation, and when she was going out I said: "Now let the boys try to pull *his* tail out", and I never spoke to this lady any more, as she had to leave Prague on account of that bulldog, because it bit everyone in the house. Believe me, sir, it's very difficult to get hold of a decent animal.'

'I'm very fond of dogs,' said the lieutenant. 'Some of my friends at the front have their dogs with them there and have written to me that the war passes very pleasantly when you have as a companion such a faithful and devoted animal. And so I see you know all breeds of dogs very well, and I hope that if I ever should have a dog you'd look after it properly. Which breed do you think is the best? I mean as a companion, you know? I once had a stable pinscher, but I don't know . . .'

'In my opinion, sir, a stable pinscher is a very nice dog. Not everyone likes them, it is true, because they have wire hair and very stiff whiskers on their muzzle, so that they look like a released convict. They are so ugly that they're beautiful and at the same time they're very clever. What's an idiotic Great St Bernard in comparison? They're even cleverer than fox-terriers. I knew one . . .'

Lieutenant Lukáš looked at his watch and interrupted Švejk's conversation:

'It's getting late. I must have a good sleep. Tomorrow I'm on duty again and you can spend the whole day finding a stable pinscher for me.'

He went to bed, and Švejk lay down on a sofa in the kitchen and read the newspaper which the lieutenant had brought with him from the barracks.

'Well, here you are then,' said Švejk to himself, following with interest the summary of the day's news. 'The sultan has decorated Kaiser Wilhelm with the War Medal, and I haven't even got the small silver medal yet.'

He thought for a moment and then jumped up: 'I nearly forgot . . .'

He went into the bedroom of the lieutenant who was already fast asleep and woke him:

'Humbly report, sir, I've no orders about that cat.'

And the sleepy lieutenant, half-awake, turned over on the other side, and growled: 'Three days confined to barracks!' and went on sleeping.

Švejk went softly out of the room, dragged the wretched cat from underneath the sofa and said to her: 'You've got three days confined to barracks. Dismiss!'

And the Angora cat crawled back under the sofa again.

IV

Švejk was just starting to go and look for a stable pinscher when a young lady rang the bell and asked to speak to Lieutenant Lukáš. Beside her stood two heavy suitcases, and Švejk caught a glimpse of a porter's cap disappearing down the stairs.

'He's not at home,' said Švejk firmly, but the young lady was already in the hall and gave the categorical order to Švejk: 'Carry the suitcases in!'

'Not without the lieutenant's permission, madam,' said Švejk. 'The lieutenant gave express orders that I must never do anything without his permission.'

'You're dotty,' the young lady cried. 'I've come to stay with him.'

'I have no information at all about that,' answered Švejk. 'The lieutenant is on duty today. He won't be back before night and I've had orders to go and find him a stable pinscher. I know nothing about any suitcases or any lady. Now I'm going to lock up the apartment and I'd be glad if you would kindly go away. I've not been informed and so I can't leave in the apartment any strange person whom I don't know. Once they left someone in the house of the pastry cook Bělčický in our street and he opened their wardrobe and ran away.

'I've nothing against you,' continued Švejk, when he noticed that the

young lady was getting desperate and beginning to cry, 'but you definitely can't stay here, you must admit that, because the apartment has
been put in my charge and I'm responsible for every little thing in it.
And so I must ask you again if you would very kindly spare yourself
the effort. Until I receive orders from the lieutenant I don't even know
my own brother. I'm sincerely sorry that I have to talk to you in this
way, but in the army there's got to be order.'

In the meantime the young lady had pulled herself together a little.
She took out of her bag a visiting card, wrote a few lines on it in pencil,
put it into a charming little envelope and said dejectedly: 'Take this to
the lieutenant. Meanwhile I shall wait here for an answer. Here's five
crowns for your trouble.'

'That's not going to help,' answered Švejk, offended by the obstinacy
of the unexpected guest. 'Keep those five crowns. They are here on the
chair, and, if you like, come with me to the barracks and wait for me
there. I'll deliver your letter and bring you the answer. But I'm afraid
that it's not possible for you to wait here.'

With these words he dragged the suitcases into the hall and
rattling the keys like the turnkey of a castle said significantly at the door:
'We're locking up!'

The young lady went out dejectedly into the corridor. Švejk shut the
door and went ahead. The visitor trotted behind him like a little dog
and caught up with him when he went to buy some cigarettes at a
tobacconist.

Now she walked beside him and tried to start a conversation with
him.

'You'll really deliver it?'

'Of course I'll deliver it, if I said so.'

'And you're sure you'll find the lieutenant?'

'That I don't know.'

They walked side by side again in silence until after quite a long time
his companion began to speak again:

'Do you think, then, that you won't find the lieutenant?'

'No, I don't think that.'

'And where do you think he might be?'

'I don't know.'

Then the conversation was interrupted for a long time until it was
resumed once more by a question from the young lady:

'You haven't lost that letter?'

'I haven't lost it yet.'

'And so you'll be sure to give it to the lieutenant?'

'Yes.'

'And you'll find him?'

'I've already said I don't know,' answered Švejk. 'It amazes me how people can be so inquisitive and continually ask the same question. It's just as though I stopped every second person on the street and asked them what was the date today.'

In this way her attempts to make a deal with Švejk came to a definite end and the rest of the journey to the barracks passed in complete silence. It was only when they stopped at the barracks that Švejk invited the young lady to wait and started to chat with the soldiers at the gate about the war, which must have made the young lady awfully happy, because she walked up and down the pavement nervously and appeared extremely miserable when she saw that Švejk was persisting in his talk, with just as stupid an expression on his face as could be seen on the photograph published at that time in the *World War Chronicle* under the headline: 'The Heir to the Austrian throne in conversation with the two pilots who shot down a Russian aeroplane'.

Švejk sat down on a bench at the gate and explained that on the Carpathian battle front the army's attack had failed, but on the other hand the commander of Przemyśl, General Kusmanek, had reached Kiev and that behind us in Serbia there remained eleven bases and that the Serbs would soon be too tired to go on running after our troops.

And then he started criticizing certain famous battles and made the truly Archimedean discovery that a detachment has to give itself up when it is encircled on all sides.

When he had been talking long enough, he thought it right to go out and tell the desperate lady that he would be back again at once, and that she shouldn't go anywhere. Then he went upstairs to the office, where he found Lieutenant Lukáš, who was just at that moment solving for a subaltern a trenches exercise and was reproaching him for not being able to draw and for having no idea at all about geometry.

'Look, this is how you have to draw it. If on a given straight line we have to draw a perpendicular line, we must draw it so that it makes a right angle with it. Do you understand? If you do it this way, you will have your trenches running in the right direction and not in the direction of the enemy. You will be six hundred metres away from him. But the way you've drawn it you'd be pushing our positions into the enemy's line and you'd be standing with your trenches perpendicular over the enemy, whereas you need an obtuse angle. It's really quite simple after all, isn't it?'

And the lieutenant in reserve, who in civil life was a bank cashier, stood in complete despair over these plans. He could not understand anything and heaved a sigh of relief when Švejk advanced towards the lieutenant:

'Humbly report, sir, a lady sends you this letter and is waiting for an answer.' And as he said this he gave a knowing and familiar wink.

What the lieutenant read did not make a favourable impression on him. It was written in German.

Dear Heinrich,
My husband is persecuting me. I absolutely must stay a few days with you. Your batman is a proper swine. I am unhappy.

> Your Katy

Lieutenant Lukáš sighed, took Švejk into an empty office next door, shut the door and began to walk up and down between the tables. When he finally stopped by Švejk he said: 'The lady writes that you're a swine. What on earth have you done to her?'

'I haven't done anything to her, humbly report, sir. I've behaved very respectably, but she wanted to install herself in the apartment at once. And because I had not had any orders from you I didn't leave her alone there. Into the bargain she brought two suitcases with her, as if she was coming home.'

The lieutenant gave another loud sigh and Švejk did the same.

'What did you say?' shouted the lieutenant menacingly.

'Humbly report, sir, it's a difficult case. Two years ago a young lady came into an upholsterer's in Vojtěšská Street and he couldn't get her out of the apartment and had to gas both her and himself, and that was the end of the fun. It's difficult with women. I can see right through them.'

'A difficult case,' repeated the lieutenant after Švejk, and he had never uttered a more truthful word. Dear Heinrich was definitely in an ugly situation. A wife, persecuted by her husband, comes to him on a visit of several days, just when he's expecting to have Mrs Micková from Třeboň. She is coming to him for three days to repeat what she regularly offers him every quarter, when she comes to Prague to do her shopping. And then the day after, a young lady is going to come.

She had definitely promised him that she would let herself be seduced after having thought it over for a whole week, as she was going to be married to an engineer a month later.

The lieutenant now sat on the table with his head in his hands. He pondered in silence, but for the time being he could think of nothing else except at last to sit down at the table, take official paper and envelope and write as follows:

Dear Katy,

On duty until nine p.m. Back at ten. Please make yourself at home with me. As for my batman, Švejk, I've already given him orders to oblige you in everything.

Your Heinrich

'Take this letter to the lady,' said the lieutenant. 'Your orders are to behave to her politely and tactfully and to fulfil all her wishes, which you must regard as a command. You must behave gallantly and serve her decently. Here's a hundred crowns, for which you must account to me, in case she may want to send you for something and you can order her lunch, dinner and so on. Then buy three bottles of wine and a packet of cigarettes. All right, then. Nothing more for the present. You can go, and once more let me impress upon you that you must obey her slightest whim.'

The young lady had already lost all hope of seeing Švejk and was therefore very surprised when she saw him coming out of the barracks in her direction with a letter.

After saluting her he handed her the letter and reported: 'By orders of the lieutenant, madam, I am to behave to you politely and tactfully, serve you decently and obey your slightest whim. I am to feed you and buy for you whatever you wish. I have received from the lieutenant a hundred crowns, but out of it I have to buy three bottles of wine and a packet of cigarettes.'

When she had read the letter her resolution returned, which was manifested by her ordering Švejk to call a fiacre, and when this was done, she bade him sit on the box-seat with the driver.

They drove home. When they were in the apartment the lady was excellent in playing the role of mistress of the house. Švejk had to carry her suitcases into the bedroom and beat the carpets in the court-yard, and a tiny little spider's web behind a mirror brought her to a state of fury.

Everything seemed to confirm that she intended to dig herself in for a long time in the position she had won.

Švejk sweated. After he had beaten the carpets, she took it into her head that the curtains had to be taken down and beaten too. Then he got orders to clean the windows in the sitting-room and in the kitchen. After that she began to move the furniture about, doing

so very nervily, and when Švejk moved it all from corner to corner she was not pleased and made new plans and thought out new arrangements.

She turned everything in the apartment upside down but gradually her energy in building the nest began to peter out and she stopped harrying him.

She took clean bed linen out of the linen cupboard and put the covers on the pillows and eiderdown. It was clear that she did this with

affection for the bed, which object induced in her a sensual trembling of the nostrils.

Then she sent Švejk to get lunch and wine. And before he came back she changed into a transparent gown, which made her exceptionally alluring and attractive.

At lunch she consumed a bottle of wine, smoked many cigarettes and got into bed, while Švejk in the kitchen was enjoying his army bread, which he soaked in a glass of some sweet spirit.

'Švejk!' could be heard from the bedroom, 'Švejk!'

Švejk opened the door and saw the young lady in an alluring position on the pillows.

'Come in!'

Švejk walked towards the bed. With a peculiar smile she measured up his stocky figure and powerful thighs.

Pulling aside the delicate material which veiled and concealed everything, she said severely: 'Take off your boots and trousers! Come on! . . .'

And so it happened that the good soldier Švejk could report to the lieutenant when he returned from the barracks: 'Humbly report, sir, I've fulfilled all the lady's wishes and served her decently according to your orders.'

'Thank you, Švejk,' replied the lieutenant. 'And did she have lots of wishes?'

'About six,' answered Švejk. 'And now she is sleeping as though quite exhausted by the ride. I *did* obey her slightest whim, sir.'

V

While masses of armies, pinned to the forests by the Dunajec and the Raab, stood under a rain of shells, and artillery of heavy calibre was tearing to pieces whole companies and burying them in the Carpathians, and while the horizons on all the battlefields blazed with burning villages and towns, Lieutenant Lukáš and Švejk went through an unpleasant idyll with the lady who had run away from her husband and had now made herself mistress of the house.

When she went out for a walk Lieutenant Lukáš held a council of war with Švejk on how to get rid of her.

'It would be best, sir,' said Švejk, 'if her husband, who she's run away from and who's looking for her, as you said was stated in the letter which I brought you, got to know where she was and came to fetch her away. We could send him a telegram that she's with you and that he could come and fetch her. There was a similar case last year in a villa in Všenory. But then the telegram was sent to the husband by the wife herself, and he came for her and boxed them both across the ears. Then they happened to be both civilians but in this present case the husband wouldn't dare to assault an officer. Besides, you're not guilty at all, because you never invited anybody, and when she ran away from home she did it at her own risk. You'll see that a telegram like that'll do a power of good. Even if there are a few swipes across the jaw . . .'

'He's very intelligent,' Lieutenant Lukáš interrupted him. 'I know him. He's a wholesaler in hops. I must definitely speak to him. I'll send a telegram.'

The telegram he sent was very laconic and commercial: 'The present address of your wife is . . .' Then followed the address of Lieutenant Lukáš's apartment.

And so it happened that Mrs Katy had a very unpleasant surprise when the hop-merchant burst in through the door. He looked very circumspect and careful when Mrs Katy, who did not lose her composure at this moment, introduced both gentlemen to each other: 'My husband – Lieutenant Lukáš.' She couldn't think of anything else.

'Please sit down, Mr Wendler,' Lieutenant Lukáš said in a welcoming tone and took a cigarette case from his pocket. 'May I offer you one?'

The intelligent hop-merchant took a cigarette with great propriety and puffing smoke from his mouth said in measured tones: 'Will you soon be going to the front, lieutenant?'

'I've applied to be transferred to the 91st regiment at Budějovice, where I shall probably be sent as soon as I have finished the one-year volunteers' training school. We need a lot of officers and it is an unhappy feature of the situation today that young people who are qualified to be accepted as one-year volunteers don't apply for it. They prefer to remain ordinary infantrymen rather than try to become cadets.'

'The war has inflicted considerable damage on the hop trade, but I don't think it can last long,' remarked the hop-merchant, looking now at his wife and now at the lieutenant.

'Our situation is very good,' said Lieutenant Lukáš. 'Today no one doubts any longer that the war will end in a victory of the Central Powers. France, England and Russia are too weak against the Austro-

Turco-German granite. It's true that we have suffered some small reverses on some fronts. But as soon as we break through the Russian front between the Carpathian ridge and the middle Dunajec, there's no doubt at all that it will mean the end of the war. And the French too will very soon be threatened with the loss of the whole of Eastern France and the penetration of the German army into Paris. That's now quite certain. Apart from that our manoeuvres in Serbia continue very successfully, and the departure of our troops, which is in fact only a redeployment, has been misinterpreted by many people in a way which is in complete conflict with what cool reason demands in time of war. We shall very soon see that our well-calculated manoeuvres on the southern front are bearing fruit. Please look here.'

Lieutenant Lukáš took the hop-merchant gently by the arm, led him to a map of the battlefields which was hanging on the wall and showed him certain points, explaining: 'The Eastern Beskyds are an excellent base for us. As you can see here we have great support in the Carpathian sector. If we make a powerful strike on this line we shan't stop until we're in Moscow. The war will end before we think.'

'And what about Turkey?' asked the hop-merchant, thinking all the time how he could come to the point which he had come for.

'The Turks are holding well,' replied the lieutenant, leading him to the table again. 'The President of the Turkish parliament, Hali Bej, and Ali Bej have come to Vienna. Marshal Liman von Sanders has been appointed commander of the Turkish Dardanelles army. Goltz Pasha has just come from Constantinople to Berlin, and Enver Pasha, Vice Admiral Usedom Pasha and General Dzevad Pasha have been decorated by our Emperor. This is a fairly considerable number of decorations in such a short time.'

They all sat in silence opposite each other, until the lieutenant considered it appropriate to interrupt the embarrassing situation with the words: 'When did you arrive, Mr Wendler?'

'This morning.'

'I'm very glad that you found me at home, because in the afternoon I always go to the barracks and I have night duty. Because my flat is actually empty the whole day I have been able to offer madame hospitality. She is not troubled by anyone during her stay in Prague. Being an old acquaintance . . .'

The hop-merchant gave a cough: 'Katy is certainly a strange

woman, lieutenant. Please accept my warmest thanks for everything which you've done for her. She took it into her head to go to Prague out of the blue, because, so she said, she had to take a cure for her nerves. I was away, I came home and found the house empty. Katy had gone.'

Trying to put on as agreeable an expression as possible he shook his finger at her and asked her with a forced smile: 'And so you thought, did you, that when I was travelling you could travel too? Of course you didn't realize . . .'

Lieutenant Lukáš, seeing that the conversation was taking an awkward turn, led the intelligent hop-merchant back to the map of the battlefields again and showed him places which had been underlined, saying: 'I forgot to point out to you one very interesting circumstance – this great bend which is facing south-west, where this group of mountains forms a major bridgehead. It is just against this spot that the Allies' offensive is directed. By closing this railway line, which links the bridgehead with the enemy's main defence line, communication between the right flank and the Northern Army on the Vistula must be broken. Is that quite clear to you now?'

The hop-merchant answered that everything was quite clear to him and fearing with his natural tact that what he said might be taken up as a hint he mentioned on returning to his place: 'During the war our hops have lost their markets abroad. France, England, Russia and the Balkans are now lost for hops. We're still sending hops to Italy but I'm afraid that Italy will get drawn into it soon. But when we've won it'll be we who will dictate the prices for our goods.'

'Italy is keeping strictly neutral,' the lieutenant said to him to cheer him up. 'She's . . .'

'Then why doesn't she admit that she's bound by the Triple Alliance with Austria-Hungary and Germany?' the hop-merchant suddenly burst out in anger. His head became suddenly full of everything – hops, his wife, the war. 'I expected that Italy would march against France and Serbia. The war would then have been over. The hops in my stores are rotting, in the home market trade is poor, export amounts to nothing, and Italy is keeping strictly neutral. Why did Italy renew her Triple Alliance with us in 1912? Where is the Italian Minister of Foreign Affairs, the Marquis of San Giuliano? What's that gentleman doing? Is he asleep or what? Do you know what annual turnover I had before the war and what I have now?

'You mustn't think that I don't follow events,' he continued. He looked furiously at the lieutenant, who was calmly blowing from his mouth rings of cigarette smoke which caught and broke each other up while Mrs Katy followed the operation with close interest. 'Why did the Germans go back to the frontier, when they'd already been near

Paris? Why is such heavy gunfire going on again between the Maas and Moselle? Do you know that at Combres and Woevre near the Marche three breweries have been burnt down, where we used to send every year more than five hundred sacks of hops? And in the Vosges the Hartmansweiler brewery has burnt down and the enormous brewery in Niederaspach near Mülhausen has been razed to the ground. That means the loss of twelve hundred sacks of hops for my firm every year. Six times the Germans have fought the Belgians for the Klosterhoek brewery. There you have a loss of 350 sacks of hops a year.'

He was so furious that he couldn't go on speaking, but only stood up, advanced towards his wife and said: 'Katy, you come home with me at once. Put on your things.

'All these happenings irritate me very much,' he said a moment later in an apologetic tone. 'Before, I used to be completely calm.'

And when she went away to put on her things he said in a low voice to the lieutenant: 'This is not the first time she's behaved like this. Last year she went away with a probationary teacher and I found them as far away as Zagreb. I used the opportunity to make a contract with the city brewery in Zagreb for 600 sacks of hops.

'Yes, the south used to be a gold mine. Our hops went as far as Constantinople. Today we are half-ruined. If the government limits production of beer at home it will deal us the final blow.'

And lighting the cigarette which had been offered to him he said in despair: 'Warsaw alone used to buy 2,370 sacks of hops. The largest brewery there is the Augustinian. Its representative used to visit me regularly each year. It is enough to make one desperate. It's a good thing I've got no children.'

This logical deduction from the yearly visit of the representative from the Augustinian brewery in Warsaw caused the lieutenant to give a gentle smile which the hop-merchant noticed and so he went on in his explanation: 'The Hungarian breweries in Sopron and in Gross-Kanisza bought from my firm for their export beer, which they exported as far as Alexandria, an average of a thousand sacks of hops a year. Now they refuse to order anything on account of the blockade. I offer them hops thirty per cent cheaper but they don't order a single sack. Stagnation, decay, misery and on top of that domestic troubles.'

The hop-merchant was silent for a moment, but his silence was interrupted by Mrs Katy, who was ready for the journey: 'What are we to do with my suitcases?'

'They'll come and fetch them, Katy,' said the hop-merchant with relief. He was glad in the end that everything had gone off without a row and a scandalous scene. 'If you want to do any more shopping, it's high time that we went. The train goes at 2.20.'

Both took friendly leave of the lieutenant and the hop-merchant was so glad that it was all over that on his way to the hall he said to the lieutenant: 'If you should be wounded at the front, and God forbid that you should, come and convalesce with us. We'll look after you with every care.'

Returning to the bedroom where Mrs Katy had dressed for the

journey, the lieutenant found on the wash-basin four hundred crowns and the following letter:

Lieutenant, you didn't stand up for me before that gorilla of a husband of mine, that prize blockhead. You allowed him to drag me away with him like some chattel he had forgotten in your apartment. And in doing so you took the liberty to observe that you had offered me hospitality. I hope that I have not caused you more expense than the enclosed four hundred crowns, which please share with your servant.

Lieutenant Lukáš stood for a moment with the letter in his hand and then slowly tore it in pieces. With a smile he looked at the money lying on the wash-basin and, seeing that when she was doing her hair before the mirror in her agitation she had forgotten her comb on the table, he placed it among his fetish relics.

Švejk returned in the afternoon. He had gone to look for a stable pinscher for the lieutenant.

'Švejk,' said the lieutenant, 'you're in luck. That lady who stayed with me has gone. Her husband took her away. And for all the services which you performed for her she left four hundred crowns on the wash-basin. You must thank her nicely or rather her husband, because it's his money which she took with her on the journey. I shall dictate to you a letter.'

He dictated:

'Honoured Sir,
Please convey my most cordial thanks for the four hundred crowns which madam, your wife, gave me for the services which I performed for her during her visit to Prague. Everything which I did for her I did with pleasure and therefore I cannot accept this sum but send it . . .

'Now then, just go on writing, Švejk. What are you fidgeting about? Where did I stop?'

'But send it . . .' said Švejk with a trembling voice full of tragic emotion.

'Good, then:

'. . . but send it back with the assurance of my deepest respect. Respectful greetings and a hand-kiss to madam. Josef Švejk, officer's orderly to Lieutenant Lukáš.

'Finished?'
'Humbly report, sir, the date is missing.'

'20 December 1914. Now write the envelope, take these four hundred crowns, carry them to the post office and send them to that address.'

And Lieutenant Lukáš began happily to whistle an aria from the operetta *The Divorced Lady*.

'One thing more, Švejk,' he called out when Švejk was going to the post office. 'What about that dog which you went to look for?'

'I've got my hands on one, sir, a jolly pretty animal, but it'll be difficult to get it. Tomorrow I hope that I'll be able to bring it after all. It bites.'

VI

Lieutenant Lukáš had not heard the last word, though it was so important. 'The beast bit for all it's worth,' Švejk had wanted to repeat, but in the end he thought: 'What business is it of the lieutenant's? He wants a dog, and he'll get one!'

It's of course an easy thing to say: 'Get me a dog!' Dog-owners are very careful about their dogs even if they are not thoroughbreds. And a mongrel whose only function in life is to warm the feet of an old woman is adored by its owner and no one is allowed to hurt a hair of its head.

But the dog, especially if it is a thoroughbred, must feel instinctively that one fine day it will be purloined from its master. It lives in continual fear that it will and must be stolen. For instance, when a dog is out for a walk it goes away from its master for a moment. At first it's happy and skittish. It plays with other dogs and climbs on their backs for immoral purposes and they climb on his. It smells the kerbstones, lifts its leg at every corner and even over the greengrocer woman's basket of potatoes: in short it has such *joie de vivre* and the world seems just as wonderful to it as it does to a young man when he has passed his school-leaving examination.

But suddenly you notice that its gaiety vanishes and it feels that it's got lost. And now it is assailed for the first time by real despair. It runs in a panic about the streets, sniffs, whines and drags its tail between its legs in utter hopelessness. It puts its ears back and rushes along in the middle of the street no one knows where.

If it could speak it would cry: 'Jesus Mary, someone's going to steal me!'

Have you ever been in a kennel and seen dogs which are panicky? They've all been stolen. The large city has evolved a special class of thief who lives exclusively on the theft of dogs. There exist tiny breeds of drawing-room dogs, tiny miniature pinschers which fit like a very small glove into the pocket of an overcoat or a lady's muff. And they even get pulled out from there, poor things. The savage German spotted mastiff gets kidnapped at night while it is ferociously guarding a villa in the suburbs. The police dog is whisked off under the detective's nose. You take a dog out on a lead, someone cuts the lead in two, the dog's gone and you are left looking idiotically at an empty strap. Fifty per cent of the dogs which you meet in the streets have changed their masters several times, and very often after years you may buy back your own dog which someone had stolen from you as a puppy once when you took it for a walk. The danger of being stolen is worst when dogs are led out to perform their small and large bodily needs. It is just when they are engaged in doing the latter that most of them get lost. That is why every dog, when it is so occupied, looks cautiously around itself.

There are various modes of operation resorted to by dog-thieves. They steal dogs either directly in pickpocket fashion or by cunningly enticing the unfortunate creature. It is only in a school reader or natural history primer that a dog is a faithful animal. Once allow even the most faithful of dogs to smell a fried horsemeat sausage and it's lost. It forgets its master by whose side it is walking, turns round and follows you with its mouth watering, and in anticipation of the great joy over the sausage it wags its tail in a very friendly way and distends its nostrils like the wildest stallion when it is being led off to the mare.

In Malá Strana near the Castle Steps there is a small pub. Two men were sitting there one day in the back in the dusk. One was a soldier and the other a civilian. Leaning forward to each other they whispered mysteriously. They looked like conspirators from the days of the Venetian Republic.

'Every day at eight o'clock,' the civilian whispered, 'the maid takes it out to the corner of Havlíček Square on the way to the park. But it's a real brute and bites for all it's worth. You can't stroke it.'

And leaning closer to the soldier he whispered in his ear: 'It doesn't even touch sausage.'

'Not even fried?' asked the soldier.

'Not even fried.'

Both spat.

'Well, what does the brute eat?'

'God knows. These dogs are as spoiled and pampered as an arch-bishop.'

The soldier and the civilian clinked glasses and the latter whispered again: 'Once a black pom which I needed for some kennels over the Klamovka wouldn't look at sausage either. I followed it for three days, until I couldn't hold out any longer and asked the lady who was leading it straight out what it actually was fed on, because it was so beautiful. The lady was flattered and said that it liked cutlets best. And so I bought it a schnitzel. I thought a schnitzel was better. And do you know the brute wouldn't even look at it, because the schnitzel was veal and it was used to pork. So after all I had to buy it a pork cutlet. I let the dog smell it first, and then I ran away with the dog following me. The lady shouted: "Puntík, Puntík!", but where was her dear Puntík? It ran after the pork cutlet as far as the corner and beyond. Then I put a lead round its neck and the next day it was already in the kennels over the Klamovka. It had a patch of white tufts under its neck and they blacked it over and nobody recognized it. But the other dogs, and there were a lot of them, all went for fried horsemeat sausage. It would be best if you asked the maid what the dog likes to eat most; you're a soldier, you've a fine figure and she's more likely to tell you. I've already asked her, but she looked at me as though she wanted to stab me and said: "What business is it of yours?" She isn't very pretty, she's like a monkey but with a soldier like you she'll certainly talk.'

'Is it really a stable pinscher? My lieutenant doesn't want anything else.'

'It's a very natty stable pinscher. Pepper and salt, real thoroughbred just as you're Švejk and I'm Blahník. What I want to know is what it eats and I'll give it that and bring it to you.'

Both friends clinked their glasses again. When before the war Švejk was still making his living on the sale of dogs Blahník used to supply him with them. He was an experienced man and it was said of him that he bought suspicious dogs illegally from the skinner's yard and resold them. He even once had rabies and was quite at home in the Pasteur Institute in Vienna. Now he considered it his duty to give his disinterested help to the soldier Švejk. He knew all the dogs in the whole of Prague and its surroundings and spoke quietly because he had to be careful not to betray himself to the landlord. Six months ago he had carried away from him a dachshund puppy concealed under his coat, and given it a baby's bottle to suck, so that the stupid puppy obviously regarded him as its mummy and never made a sound.

On principle he only stole thoroughbreds and might have been a legal expert on them. He supplied all kennels and private persons as opportunity offered, and when he walked along the street all the dogs which he had once stolen growled at him. It sometimes happened that when he stood somewhere near a shop window a dog, anxious to pay him back, would lift its leg over him and besprinkle his trousers.

At eight o'clock the next morning the good soldier Švejk could be seen walking at the corner of Havlíček Square by the park. He was waiting for the maid with the stable pinscher. Finally she came and a whiskered, bristly dog with a rough coat and wise black eyes ran past him. It was skittish like all dogs are when they have performed their needs and ran after sparrows which were breakfasting on horse dung in the street.

Then the woman who was looking after the dog came past Švejk. She was an elderly spinster and her hair was neatly plaited into a crown. She whistled to the dog and brandished a chain and an elegant whip.

Švejk spoke to her:

'Excuse me, miss, would you please tell me which is the way to Žižkov?'

She stopped and looked at him, to see whether the question was honestly meant and the good-natured face of Švejk told her that actually this soldier perhaps really wanted to go to Žižkov. The expression of her face softened and she gladly explained how to get there.

'I've only recently been transferred to Prague,' said Švejk. 'I don't come from here. I'm from the country. You aren't from Prague either, are you?'

'I'm from Vodňany.'

'Then we're not far away from each other,' answered Švejk. 'I'm from Protivín.'

This knowledge of the topography of South Bohemia, which Švejk had acquired once during manoeuvres there, filled the good lady's heart with a local patriotic glow.

'Then you certainly know the butcher Pejchar in the square at Protivín?'

'Why, of course I do! He's my brother. At home they all like him very much,' said Švejk. 'He's very good and helpful. He has good meat and gives good weight.'

'You aren't by chance one of Jareš's sons?' asked the maid, beginning to feel drawn to the unknown soldier.

'I am.'

'And which Jareš, the one from Krč near Protivín or from Ražice?'

'From Ražice.'

'Does he still deliver beer?'

'Yes, he does still.'

'But he must be a long way past sixty already?'

'He was sixty-eight last spring,' answered Švejk composedly. 'Now he has got a dog and it goes around with him. It sits on his cart. It's just the same kind of dog as that one there running after the sparrows. A lovely little dog, very lovely.'

'That's ours,' Švejk's new friend explained to him. 'I work for the colonel here. Don't you know our colonel?'

'I do. He's bally intelligent,' said Švejk. 'In Budějovice we had a colonel like that.'

'Our master is very strict, and when people were recently saying that we'd been beaten in Serbia, he came home in a frightful rage, threw all the plates around in the kitchen and wanted to give me notice.'

'So that's your doggie?' Švejk interrupted her. 'It's a pity that my lieutenant can't stand dogs, because I'm very fond of them myself.' He was quiet for a moment and suddenly blurted out: 'But not every dog will eat anything.'

'Our Fox is very faddy. At one time he wouldn't eat any meat at all, but now he does again.'

'And what does he like to eat best?'

'Liver, boiled liver.'

'Veal or pork?'

'It's all the same to him.' Švejk's 'fellow countrywoman' smiled, since she took his last question for an unsuccessful attempt to be funny.

They walked together for a little and then they were joined by the stable pinscher which was put on to the chain. It was very friendly to Švejk and tried to tear his trousers with its muzzle. It jumped up at him, but suddenly stopped as though it sensed what Švejk was planning for it, and walked sadly and despondently, looking sideways at Švejk as though it wanted to say: 'And so now it's coming to me too?'

Then she told him as well that she came here with the dog every evening at six o'clock and that she didn't trust any of the men in Prague; she had once put an advertisement in the newspaper, to which she received an answer from a locksmith offering to marry her. But he had wheedled eight hundred crowns out of her for some invention of his and disappeared. In the country people were definitely more honest. If she were to marry she would only take a man from the country, and only after the end of the war. She regarded war marriages as stupid, because a war bride was generally left a widow.

Švejk gave her good reason to hope that he would come at six o'clock and went away to tell his friend, Blahník, that the dog ate liver of any kind.

'I'll treat him to ox liver,' Blahník decided. 'That was how I got the St Bernard belonging to the company director, Vydra, which was a jolly faithful animal. Tomorrow I'll bring you the dog safe and sound.'

Blahník was as good as his word. When Švejk had finished cleaning the apartment in the morning he heard a barking at the door and Blahník dragged in the protesting stable pinscher, which was even more bristly than nature had bristled it. It rolled its eyes wildly and looked so surly that it recalled a hungry tiger in a cage in a zoological garden when it sees a well-fed visitor standing before it. It ground its teeth and growled, as though it wanted to say: 'I'll tear you to pieces. I'll gobble you up.'

They tied the dog to the kitchen table and Blahník described how he had purloined it.

'I went purposefully past it and held the boiled liver wrapped up in paper. It began to sniff and to jump up on me. I didn't give it anything, but just walked on, the dog following me. By the park I turned into Bredovská Street and there I gave it its first piece. It ate it while it was going along so as not to lose sight of me. I turned into Jindřišská Street, where I gave it another portion. And when it'd eaten that up, I put it on a chain and dragged it through Wenceslas Square to Vinohrady and then on to Vršovice. On the way it played me some fantastic tricks. When I crossed the tram lines it lay down and wouldn't move. Perhaps it wanted to be run over. I've brought with me a blank pedigree, which I bought at Fuchs the stationers. Do you know how to forge the pedigree, Švejk?'

'It must be written in your hand. Write that the dog comes from the kennels of von Bülow at Leipzig. Its father was Arnheim von Kahls-berg, its mother Emma von Trautensdorf, descended on the father's side from Siegfried von Busenthal. Its father won the first prize at the Berlin Exhibition of stable pinschers in 1912. The mother was decorated with the gold medal of the Nuremberg society for the breeding of thoroughbred dogs. How old do you think it is?'

'Two years by its teeth.'

'Write down that it's one and a half.'

'It's badly cropped, Švejk. Look at its ears.'

'We can put that right. We can if necessary clip them when it gets used to us. Now it could only make it more angry.'

The stolen animal growled furiously, panted, rushed around and then lay down. With tongue hanging out it waited, tired and exhausted, to see what was going to happen to it next.

Gradually it grew calmer and only occasionally whined piteously.

Švejk offered it the remains of the liver, which Blahník had given him. But it took no notice of it, gave it a defiant look and gazed at it as though it meant to say: 'I burnt my fingers once. You can eat it your-selves.'

It lay down in resignation and pretended to doze. Suddenly it got something into its head, jumped up and began to stand on its hind legs and beg with its front paws. It had capitulated.

But this moving scene had no effect on Švejk.

'Lie down,' he shouted at the wretched animal, which lay down again and whined piteously.

'What name shall I put on its pedigree?' asked Blahník. 'It was called Fox, so we must find something like it, which it will understand at once.'

'Why not perhaps "Max"? Look, Blahník, how it pricks up its ears. Get up, Max!'

The unfortunate stable pinscher, which had been robbed of its home and name, stood up and waited for further orders.

'I think we ought to untie it,' Švejk decided. 'We shall see what it'll do then.'

When it was untied, it made its way to the door, where it barked three times at the handle, obviously relying on the generosity of these evil men. Seeing however that they had no understanding for its yearning to get out, it made a little pool by the door, convinced that they would throw it out as people used to do to it when it was young and the colonel was teaching it in a strict military fashion to be house-trained.

Instead Švejk observed: 'It's a cunning one, to be sure, a bit of a Jesuit.' He gave it a blow with his belt and dipped its muzzle in the puddle, so that it had a hard time licking itself clean.

It whined at this humiliation and began to run round the kitchen, desperately sniffing at its own tracks. Then out of the blue it went to the table, ate up the rest of the liver which was lying on the floor, lay down near the stove and fell asleep after all this adventure.

'How much do I owe you?' Švejk asked Blahník, when the latter took his leave of him.

'Don't mention it, Švejk,' said Blahník gently. 'For an old friend I'd do anything, especially when he's serving in the army. Goodbye, my boy, and don't ever lead it across Havlíček Square, in case any misfortune should happen. If you should ever need another dog, you know where I live.'

Švejk let Max sleep very long and in the meantime bought half a pound of liver at the butcher's, boiled it and waited until Max woke up, letting it smell a piece of warm liver.

Max began to lick its lips in its sleep, then it stretched, sniffed the liver and ate it up. After that it went to the door and repeated its experiments with the door handle.

'Max!' Švejk called to it. 'Come here!'

It came distrustfully. Švejk took it on his lap, stroked it, and Max for the first time wagged the remains of its clipped tail in a friendly way, snapped gently at Švejk's hand, held it in its jaws and looked very wisely at Švejk, as though it was going to say: 'There's nothing to be done. I know I've lost.'

Švejk went on stroking it and began to talk to it in a tender tone:

'There was once a doggie who was called Fox and it lived with a colonel. The maid took it for a walk and a gentleman came and stole it. Fox came to the army to a lieutenant and they gave it the name of Max. Max, give me your paw! Now you see, you bastard, that we shall be good friends if you'll be obedient and good. Otherwise you'll have a hell of a war.'

Max jumped down from Švejk's lap and began happily to jump up on him. By the evening when the lieutenant returned from the barracks Švejk and Max were the very best of friends.

Looking at Max Švejk thought philosophically: 'After all, by and large every soldier's stolen from his home too.'

Lieutenant Lukáš was very agreeably surprised when he saw the dog, which also manifested great pleasure when it again saw a man with a sabre.

In reply to the question where it came from and how much it cost, Švejk said with perfect composure that the dog had been given him by a friend, who had just been called up.

'Good, Švejk,' said the lieutenant, playing with Max. 'On the first of the month you'll get fifty crowns from me for the dog.'

'I can't accept that, sir.'

'Švejk,' said the lieutenant sternly, 'when you began your service with me I explained to you that you must obey all my orders. When I tell you that you'll get fifty crowns, you must take them and spend them on drink. What will you do, Švejk, with these fifty crowns?'

'Humbly report, sir, I shall spend them on drink according to your orders.'

'And in case I should forget this, Švejk, I order you to report to me that I have to give you fifty crowns for the dog. Do you understand? Are you sure the dog hasn't got fleas? You'd better give it a bath and comb it. Tomorrow I'm on duty, but the day after I'll take it for a walk.'

While Švejk was giving Max a bath, its former owner, the colonel, was thundering at home and threatening that he would bring the thief before a court-martial and have him shot, hung, gaoled for twenty years and quartered.

'Bugger that blasted bloody swine,' could be heard in German all over the colonel's apartment so that the windows rattled. 'I'll be even with that murderous assassin.'

Over the heads of Švejk and Lieutenant Lukáš a catastrophic storm was brewing.

15

Catastrophe

COLONEL FRIEDRICH KRAUS, who bore the additional title of von Zillergut after a village in the district of Salzburg which his ancestors had already completely fleeced in the eighteenth century, was a most venerable idiot. Whenever he was relating something, he could only speak in platitudes, asking whether everybody could understand the most primitive expressions: 'And so a window, gentlemen, yes. Well, do you know what a window is?'

Or: 'A track which has a ditch on each side of it is called a road. Yes, gentlemen. Now, do you know what a ditch is? A ditch is an excavation on which several people work. It is a hollow. Yes. They work with picks. Now, do you know what a pick is?'

He suffered from a mania for explanations, which he gave with the enthusiasm of an inventor expounding his work.

'A book, gentlemen, is a number of squares of paper cut in different ways and of varying format which are printed on and put together, bound and gummed. Yes. Well, do you know, gentlemen, what gum is? Gum is adhesive material.'

He was so colossally stupid that the officers avoided him from afar so as not to have to hear from him that the pavement divided the street from the carriage-way and that it was a raised paved strip along the façade of the house. And the façade of the house was that part of it which we see from the street or from the pavement. We cannot see the rear part of the house from the pavement, a fact we can immediately prove to ourselves by stepping into the carriage-way.

He was ready to demonstrate this interesting fact at once. Fortunately however he was run over. From that time he became even more raving mad. He stopped officers on the street and engaged them in unendingly long conversations about omelettes, the sun, thermometers, doughnuts, windows and postage stamps.

It was really remarkable how this fat-head managed to be promoted so quickly and to have behind him such very influential people as a general of the Supreme Command who backed him up in spite of his utter military incompetence.

At manoeuvres he performed miracles with his regiment. He never arrived at any position in time, led his regiment in column formation against machine-guns, and once many years ago at the Imperial man-oeuvres in South Bohemia he and his regiment got completely lost and finally reached Moravia, where they wandered about with him for several days after the manoeuvres were over and the troops were back in the barracks. But he got away with it.

His friendly relations with the general and other no less fat-headed military dignitaries of old Austria brought him various decorations and orders, by which he felt extraordinarily honoured and considered him-self to be the best soldier under the sun and the best theoretician in strategy and all military sciences.

At regimental reviews he used to start talking with the men and always asked them the same question:

'Why are the rifles which have been introduced into the army called "manlichers"?'[1]

In the regiment he was nicknamed 'the manlicher lunatic'. He was extraordinarily vindictive, ruined his subordinate officers if he did not like them, and when they wanted to get married sent up very bad reports attached to their applications.

He had lost half his left ear, which had been cut off in his youth by a rival in a duel fought merely to establish the truth of the fact that Friedrich Kraus von Zillergut was an utter imbecile.

If we analyse his mental capacities, we reach the conclusion that they were not one wit better than those which had made the big-lipped Franz Joseph Hapsburg celebrated as a patent idiot.

In each you found the same torrent of words, the same store of colossal naïvety. At a banquet in the officers' club Colonel Kraus von Zillergut said quite out of the blue, when there had been mention of Schiller: 'Now, gentlemen, I saw a steam plough yesterday. It was driven by a locomotive, but mark my words, gentlemen, not just by one locomotive, but by two. I see the smoke, I come nearer and there is one locomotive and on the other side another. Tell me, gentlemen, isn't that funny? Two locomotives, as though one were not enough.'

He was silent for a moment and then remarked: 'When the petrol in the car is used up it has to stop. I saw that yesterday too. And then

1. The old-fashioned repeater rifle called after the name of its inventor.

they talk nonsense about perpetual motion, gentlemen! It doesn't go, it stands still, it doesn't move, it hasn't got petrol. Isn't that funny?'

With all his stupidity he was immensely pious. In his apartment he had a house altar. He often went to the church of St Ignatius for confession and communion and after the outbreak of the war prayed for the success of the Austrian and German arms. He mixed Christianity with dreams of German hegemony. God had to help them seize the wealth and lands of the conquered.

He flew into a passion when he read in the newspaper that prisoners had been taken again.

He said: 'What's the point of taking prisoners? They all ought to be shot. No mercy. Dance among the corpses. All the civilians in Serbia should be burnt to a man and the children finished off with the bayonet.'

He was no worse than the German poet Vierordt, who published during the war verses demanding that Germany should have a soul of iron and hate and kill millions of French devils.

> Let the piles of human bones and burning flesh
> Rise to the clouds over the mountains . . .

Having finished his teaching at the course for one-year volunteers Lieutenant Lukáš took Max out for a walk.

'I take the liberty of warning you, sir,' said Švejk solicitously, 'that you must be very careful with that dog in case it runs away. It may perhaps be homesick for its old home and take to its heels if you let it off the lead. And also I wouldn't advise you to take it along Havlíček Square. That's the beat of a savage butcher's dog from The Image of the Virgin, which bites frightfully. As soon as it sees a strange dog in its area it's at once jealous of it for fear it should eat up something. It's like the beggar of St Haštal.'[1]

Max jumped about merrily and got under the lieutenant's feet, wound its lead round his sabre and expressed unusual joy at going for a walk.

They went out on to the street, and Lieutenant Lukáš went with the dog in the direction of Příkopy. He was to meet a lady at the corner of

1. A church in Prague where a beggar, who had made its porch his permanent beat, was arrested by the police for driving away other beggars.

Panská Street. He was deep in thoughts about his work. What should he lecture on to the volunteers in the school tomorrow? How do we determine the height of a given hill? Why do we reckon the height from sea level? How can we establish from its height above sea level the height of a mountain from its foot? Damn it! Why does the Ministry of War put such things into the school programme? Clearly it's a matter for the artillery. And there are after all general staff maps. When the enemy is on elevation 312 it's no use thinking why the height of the hill should be reckoned from sea level or calculating how high the hill is. We look at the map and we have it there.

He was jerked out of these thoughts by a severe 'Halt!', just when he came near Panská Street.

Simultaneously with the 'Halt!' the dog tried to wriggle out of its lead and threw itself with a joyful bark on the man who had just said severely 'Halt!'

In front of the lieutenant stood Colonel Kraus von Zillergut. Lieutenant Lukáš saluted the colonel and stood before him, apologizing that he had not seen him.

Colonel Kraus was known among the officers for his passion for halting people.

He regarded saluting as something on which the success of the war depended and on which the whole power of the army was built.

'A soldier must put his soul into his salute,' he used to say. It was the finest kind of corporal's mysticism.

He saw to it that those who saluted did so according to the smallest niceties of the instructions, accurately and with dignity.

He lay in wait for all who passed him, from infantryman up to lieutenant-colonel. If any infantryman saluted casually as though when he touched his cap he were saying 'God bless' the colonel took him straight off to the barracks for punishment.

For him it was no excuse to say: 'I did not see you, sir.'

'A soldier,' he used to say, 'must pick out his superior officer in a crowd and think of nothing else but carrying out the duties which are prescribed in service orders. When he falls on the battlefield he must salute before he dies. Anyone who doesn't know how to salute, pretends he doesn't see me, or salutes casually I regard as vermin.'

'Lieutenant,' said Colonel Kraus in an awesome voice, 'the lower ranks must always pay respect to the higher. This order has not been rescinded. And next: since when do officers promenade about with stolen dogs? Yes, with stolen dogs. A dog which belongs to someone else is a stolen dog.'

'This dog, sir . . .' Lieutenant Lukáš objected.

'Belongs to me, lieutenant,' the colonel interrupted him harshly. 'It's my Fox.'

And Fox or Max remembered its old master and drove the new one entirely out of its heart. It tore itself loose, jumped up on the colonel and showed such joy as only a love-sick sixth former is capable of when he finds understanding on the part of his beloved.

'Promenading with stolen dogs, lieutenant, is not compatible with the honour of an officer. Didn't you know that? An officer may not buy a dog unless he has assured himself beforehand that he can do so without consequences!' Colonel Kraus thundered on, stroking Fox-Max, who began to growl meanly at the lieutenant and to bare its teeth, as though the colonel had pointed to the lieutenant and said: 'Seize him!'

'Lieutenant,' continued the colonel, 'would you consider it right to ride about on a stolen horse? Did you not read the advertisement in *Bohemie* and in the *Tagblatt* about the loss of my stable pinscher? You didn't read the advertisement which your superior officer put into the newspaper?'

The colonel clapped his hands.

'Really, these young officers! Where has discipline gone? The colonel puts in advertisements and the lieutenant doesn't read them.'

'If only I could give you a few across the jaw, you bloody old dotard,' Lieutenant Lukáš thought to himself, looking at the colonel's side whiskers which were reminiscent of an orang-outang.

'Come with me for a moment,' said the colonel. And so they walked along and had a very pleasant conversation:

'At the front, lieutenant, a thing like this cannot happen to you again. Promenading with stolen dogs behind the lines is certainly very agreeable. Yes, walking about with your superior officer's dog at a time when every day we are losing a hundred officers on the battlefield. And advertisements are not read! For a hundred years I could insert notices that my dog is lost. Two hundred years! Three hundred years!'

The colonel blew his nose noisily, which with him was always a sign of great fury, and said: 'You can go on with your walk.' Then he turned round and went away, angrily striking with his riding whip across the ends of his officer's greatcoat.

Lieutenant Lukáš crossed to the opposite pavement and heard once more: 'Halt!' The colonel had just stopped an unfortunate infantry-man in the reserve, who was thinking about his mother at home and had not noticed him.

The colonel took him in person to the barracks for punishment and swore at him for being a swine and bastard.

'What shall I do with Švejk,' thought the lieutenant. 'I'll smash his jaw, but that's not enough. Even tearing his skin from his body in little strips would be too good treatment for that blackguard.' Disregarding the fact that he was due to meet a lady, he set off home in a fury.

'I'll kill him, the dirty hound,' he said to himself as he got into the tram.

Meanwhile the good soldier Švejk was deep in conversation with an orderly from the barracks. The soldier had brought the lieutenant some documents to sign and was now waiting.

Švejk treated him to coffee and they discussed together how Austria would be smashed.

They carried on this conversation as though it could be taken for granted. There was an endless series of utterances which would certainly have been defined in the court as treasonable and for which both of them would have been hanged.

'His Imperial Majesty must be completely off his rocker by this time,' declared Švejk. 'He was never bright, but this war'll certainly finish him.'

'Of course he's off his rocker,' the soldier from the barracks asserted with conviction. 'He's so gaga he probably doesn't know there's a war on. Perhaps they're ashamed of telling him. If his signature's on the manifesto to his peoples, then it's a fraud. They must have had it printed without his knowledge, because he's not capable of thinking about anything at all.'

'He's finished,' added Švejk knowingly. 'He wets himself and they have to feed him like a little baby. Recently a chap at the pub told us that His Imperial Majesty has two wet nurses and is breast-fed three times a day.'

'If only it was all over,' sighed the soldier from the barracks, 'and they knocked us out, so that Austria at last had peace!'

And both continued the conversation until finally Švejk condemned Austria for ever with the words: 'A monarchy as idiotic as this ought not to exist at all', whereupon the other, to complete his utterance by adding something of a practical kind, said: 'When I get to the front I'll hop it pretty quick.'

And when both continued to interpret the views of the average Czech about the war, the soldier from the barracks repeated what he had heard that day in Prague, that guns could be heard at Náchod and that the Tsar of Russia would soon be in Cracow.

Then they related how our corn was being carted away to Germany and how German soldiers were getting cigarettes and chocolate.

Then they remembered the times of the old wars, and Švejk solemnly argued that when in the olden days they threw stink-pots into a beleaguered castle it was no picnic to have to fight in such a stink. He had read that they had besieged a castle somewhere for three years and the enemy did nothing else except amuse themselves every day in this way with the beleaguered inside.

He would certainly have added something else interesting and informative if their conversation had not been interrupted by the return of Lieutenant Lukáš.

Casting at Švejk a fearful, crushing glance, he signed the documents and after dismissing the soldier motioned Švejk to follow him into his sitting-room.

Frightful lightning shafts darted from the lieutenant's eyes. Sitting on the chair he looked at Švejk and pondered how he should start the massacre.

'First I'll give him a few across the jaw,' he thought. 'Then I'll break his nose and tear off his ears. And after that we'll see.'

But he was confronted by the honest and kindly gaze of the good and innocent eyes of Švejk who dared to interrupt the calm before the storm with the words: 'Humbly report, sir, you've lost your cat. She ate up the boot polish and permitted herself to pass out. I threw her into the cellar – but next door. You won't find again such a good and beautiful Angora cat.'

'What shall I do with him?' flashed through the lieutenant's mind. 'For Christ's sake, what an idiotic expression he has.'

And the kindly innocent eyes of Švejk continued to glow with gentleness and tenderness, combined with an expression of complete composure; everything was in order and nothing had happened, and if something had happened, it was again quite in order that anything at all was happening.

Lieutenant Lukáš jumped up, but did not hit Švejk as he had originally intended to do. He brandished his fist under his nose and roared out: 'Švejk, you *stole* the dog!'

'Humbly report, sir, I know of no such case recently and I would like to observe, sir, that you yourself took Max this afternoon out for a walk and so I couldn't have stolen it. I saw at once when you came back without the dog that something must have happened. That's called a situation. In Spálená Street there is a bag-maker named Kuneš and he couldn't take a dog out for a walk without losing it. Usually he left it somewhere at a pub or someone stole it from him or borrowed it and never returned it . . .'

'Švejk, you bastard, you, Himmellaudon, hold your tongue! Either you're a cunning blackguard or else you're a camel and a fat-headed idiot. You're a real object lesson, but I tell you you'd better not try anything on me! Where did you get that dog from? How did you get hold of it? Do you know that it belongs to our colonel, who took it off with him when we happened to meet? Do you realize that this is a colossal world scandal? So speak the truth now! Did you steal it or not?'

'Humbly report, sir, I didn't steal it.'

'Did you know that it was a stolen dog?'

'Humbly report, sir, I knew it was stolen.'

'Švejk, Jesus Mary, Himmelherrgott, I'll have you shot, you bastard, you cattle, you oaf, you pig. Are you really such a half-wit?'

'Humbly report, sir, I am.'

'Why did you bring me a stolen dog? Why did you put that beast into my apartment?'

'To give you a little pleasure, sir.'

And Švejk's eyes looked kindly and tenderly into the face of the lieutenant, who sat down and sighed: 'Why did God punish me with this bastard?'

The lieutenant sat on the chair in quiet resignation and felt he had not the strength even to roll a cigarette, let alone give Švejk one or two across the jaw, and he had no idea why he sent Švejk to get *Bohemie* and *Tagblatt* so that Švejk could read the colonel's advertisement about the stolen dog.

With the newspaper open on the advertisement pages Švejk returned.

He beamed and proclaimed joyfully: 'It's there, sir. The colonel describes that stolen stable pinscher so beautifully that it's a pure joy, and into the bargain he offers the finder of it a hundred crowns. That's quite a handsome reward. Generally they only give fifty. A chap called Božetěch from Košíře made a business just out of this. He always stole dogs, then looked in the advertisements to see whether one had run away and at once went there. On one occasion he stole a beautiful black pom, and because the owner didn't advertise it in the newspapers, he tried to put an advertisement in himself. He spent ten crowns on advertisements until finally a gentleman announced that it was his dog, that he had lost it and that he had thought that it would be useless to try and look for it, as he didn't believe any longer in people's honesty. But now he saw that all the same there were honest people to be found, and this gave him tremendous pleasure. He said he was opposed on principle to rewarding honesty, but as a souvenir he would give him his book on indoor and outdoor plant cultivation. The good Božetěch took that black pom by its back legs and hit the gentleman over the head with it and from that time he swore he wouldn't put in any more advertisements. He'd rather sell a dog to a kennel, if no one wanted to advertise for it.'

'Go to bed, Švejk,' the lieutenant ordered. 'You are capable of drivelling on like this till tomorrow morning.' And he went to bed too. In the night he dreamt of Švejk, how Švejk had also stolen the horse of the Heir to the Throne and brought it to him, and how the Heir to the Throne had recognized the horse at a review, when the unfortunate Lieutenant Lukáš rode on it at the head of his company.

In the morning the lieutenant felt as if he had gone through a night of debauch during which he had been knocked many times over the head. An unusually oppressive nightmare clung to him. Exhausted by the frightful dream he fell asleep towards the morning, only to be woken by a knocking on the door. The kindly face of Švejk appeared and asked when he should wake the lieutenant.

The lieutenant groaned in bed: 'Get out, you monster, this is sheer hell!'

But when he was already up and Švejk brought him his breakfast, the lieutenant was surprised by a new question from Švejk: 'Humbly report, sir, would you wish me to look for another nice doggie for you?'

'You know, Švejk, that I feel like having you court-martialled,' said the lieutenant with a sigh, 'but they'd only acquit you, because they'd never have seen anything so colossally idiotic in all their lives. Do look at yourself in the mirror. Doesn't it make you sick to see your own drivelling expression? You're the most idiotic freak of nature that I've ever seen. Now, tell me the truth, Švejk, do you really like yourself?'

'Humbly report, sir, I don't. In this mirror I am somehow lopsided or something. But the glass is not properly cut. At the Chinaman, Staněk's, they once had a convex mirror and when anybody looked at himself in it he wanted to spew. A mug like this, a head like a slop-pail, a belly like a sozzled canon, in short a complete scare-crow. Then the Governor of Bohemia passed by and saw himself in it and the mirror had to be removed at once.'

The lieutenant turned away, sighed and thought it right to pay attention to his coffee rather than to Švejk.

Švejk was already pottering about in the kitchen, and Lieutenant Lukáš heard him singing:

> 'Grenevil is marching through the Powder Gate.
> Swords are flashing, pretty girls are weeping . . .'

And then there came from the kitchen another song:

> 'We're the boys who make the noise,
> Win the hearts of all the tarts,
> Draw our pay and then make hay.'

'You certainly make hay, you bastard,' the lieutenant thought to himself and spat.

Švejk's head appeared in the doorway: 'Humbly report, sir, they've come here for you from the barracks. You're to go at once to the colonel. His orderly officer is here.'

And he added confidentially: 'Perhaps it's because of that dog.'

'I've already heard,' said the lieutenant, when the orderly officer wanted to report to him in the hall.

He said this dejectedly and went out casting an annihilating glance at Švejk.

This was not regimental report. It was something worse. When the lieutenant stepped into his office the colonel sat in his chair frowning frightfully.

'Two years ago, lieutenant,' said the colonel, 'you asked to be transferred to the 91st regiment in Budějovice. Do you know where Budějovice is? It's on the Vltava, yes, on the Vltava, where the Ohře or something like that flows into it. The town is big, so to speak, and friendly, and if I'm not mistaken it has an embankment. Do you know what an embankment is? It is a wall built over the water. Yes. However, this is not relevant here. We had manoeuvres there.'

The colonel was silent, and looking at the ink pot passed quickly to another subject: 'My dog's ruined after having been with you. He won't eat anything. Look, there's a fly in the ink pot. It's very strange that flies should fall into the ink pot in winter. That's disorderly.'

'Well, say your say, you bloody old dodderer,' thought the lieutenant to himself.

The colonel got up and walked once or twice up and down the office.

'I've thought for a long time, lieutenant, what I ought to do with you to prevent this *recurring*, and I remembered that you wanted to be transferred to the 91st regiment. The high command recently informed us that there is a great shortage of officers in the 91st regiment because they have all been *killed by the Serbs*. I give you my word of honour that within three days you will be in the 91st regiment in Budějovice, where they are forming *march battalions for the front*. You don't need to thank me. The army requires officers who . . .'

And not knowing what else to say he looked at his watch and pronounced: 'It's half past ten and high time to go to regimental report.'

And with this the agreeable conversation came to an end, and the lieutenant felt very relieved when he left the office and went to the volunteers' school, where he announced that very soon he would be going to the front and was therefore organizing a farewell evening party in Nekázanka.

Returning home he said significantly to Švejk: 'Do you know, Švejk, what a march battalion is?'

'Humbly report, sir, a march battalion is a *maršbaťák* and a march company is a *marškumpačka*. We always use abbreviations.'

'Very well then, Švejk,' said the lieutenant in a solemn voice. 'I wish to tell you that you are going with me on the *maršbaťák*, if you like such abbreviations. But don't think that at the front you'll be able to drop such bloody awful clangers as you've done here. Are you happy?'

'Humbly report, sir, I'm awfully happy,' replied the good soldier Švejk. 'It'll be really marvellous when we both fall dead together for His Imperial Majesty and the Royal Family . . .'

Epilogue to Part I,
'Behind the Lines'

As I finish the first part of the book *The Good Soldier Švejk and his Fortunes in the World War* ('Behind the Lines') I should like to announce that two further volumes will be published in quick succession: 'At the Front' and 'In Captivity'. And in these two further volumes the soldiers and civilian population will go on talking and acting as they do in real life.

Life is no finishing school for young ladies. Everyone speaks the way he is made. The protocol chief, Dr Guth, speaks differently from Palivec, the landlord of The Chalice, and this novel is neither a handbook of drawing-room refinement nor a teaching manual of expressions to be used in polite society. It is a historical picture of a certain period of time.

Where it is necessary to use a strong expression which was actually said, I am not ashamed of reproducing it exactly as it was. I regard the use of polite circumlocutions or asterisks as the stupidest form of sham. The same words are used in parliament too.

It was once said, and very rightly, that a man who is well brought-up may read anything. The only people who boggle at what is perfectly natural are those who are the worst swine and the finest experts in filth. In their utterly contemptible pseudo-morality they ignore the contents and madly attack individual words.

Years ago I read a criticism of a novelette, in which the critic was furious because the author had written: 'He blew his nose and wiped it.' He said that it went against everything beautiful and exalted which literature should give the nation.

This is only a small illustration of what bloody fools are born under the sun.

Those who boggle at strong language are cowards, because it is real life which is shocking them, and weaklings like that are the very people who cause most harm to culture and character. They would like to see the nation grow up into a group of over-sensitive little people – masturbators of false culture of the type of St Aloysius, of whom it is said in the book of the monk Eustachius that when he heard a man breaking wind with deafening noise he immediately burst into tears and could only be consoled by prayers.

People like that proclaim their indignation in public but take unusual pleasure in going to public lavatories to read obscene inscriptions on the walls.

In using a few strong expressions in my book I have done nothing more than affirm *en passant* how people actually talk.

We cannot expect the inn-keeper Palivec to speak with the same refinement as Mrs Laudová, Doctor Guth, Mrs Olga Fastrová[1] and a whole series of others who would like to turn the whole Czechoslovak Republic into a big salon with parquet flooring, where people go about in tail-coats, white ties and gloves, speak in choice phrases and cultivate the refined behaviour of the drawing-room. But beneath this camouflage these drawing-room lions indulge in the worst vices and excesses.

I use this opportunity to draw your attention to the fact that Palivec is still alive. He survived the war, which he spent in gaol, and has remained just as he was when he had that spot of trouble with the portrait of the Emperor Franz Joseph.

He came to see me when he read that he was in the book, and he bought more than twenty copies of the first instalment and distributed them to his friends, thus contributing to its dissemination.

It gave him sincere pleasure that I wrote about him and described him as being renowned for his foul mouth.

'No one's likely to change me,' he said. 'I've always spoken all my whole life just as bawdily as I think, and I shall go on doing so. I'm not going to put a table napkin over my mug just for the sake of some cow or other. Today I'm famous.'

His self-confidence has indeed grown considerably. His fame rests on a number of strong expressions. This is enough to make him happy and if in reproducing his speech faithfully and accurately it had perhaps been my intention to warn him that he shouldn't talk like that (which of course it was not) I should certainly have insulted this good man.

In unrefined language he unconsciously expressed in a simple and honest way the detestation the ordinary Czech feels for Byzantine

1. People of Hašek's time who wrote on morals and behaviour.

methods. It was in his blood – this lack of respect for the Emperor and for polite phrases.

Otto Katz is also still alive. He is the real personification of the chaplain. When the monarchy collapsed he threw everything over, left the Church and today is manager in a bronze and dye factory in North Bohemia. He wrote me a long letter, in which he threatened to pay me out for what I'd done. A certain German newspaper published a translation of that chapter where he is described as he actually looked. And so I went to see him and it all went off very well. At two o'clock in the morning he could no longer stand on his legs but preached and said: 'I am Otto Katz, chaplain, you plaster-cast blockheads.'

Lots of people of the type of the late Bretschneider, who under old Austria was a member of the secret police, are still knocking about today in the Republic. They are extremely interested in what people are talking about.

I do not know whether I shall succeed in achieving my purpose with this book. The fact that I have already heard one man swear at another and say 'You're about as big an idiot as Švejk' does not prove that I have. But if the word 'Švejk' becomes a new choice specimen in the already florid garland of abuse I must be content with this enrichment of the Czech language.

                                                    JAROSLAV HAŠEK

Part II

AT THE FRONT

Švejk's Misadventures in the Train

IN a second-class compartment of the Prague-České Budějovice express there were three people: Lieutenant Lukáš, an elderly gentleman opposite with a completely bald pate, and Švejk, who stood modestly at the door to the corridor and was just braving himself to receive a new volley of oaths from Lieutenant Lukáš, who, disregarding the presence of the bald civilian, kept thundering at Švejk throughout the journey that he was the Almighty's choicest quadruped and so on.

It all concerned a mere trifle – the number of pieces of luggage which Švejk was supposed to be looking after.

'So they've stolen one of our cases, have they?' the lieutenant reproached Švejk. 'Anyone can say that, you bastard!'

'Humbly report, sir,' Švejk put in gently, 'they really did steal it. On the station there are always a lot of crooks like that knocking about and I imagine that one of them *undoubtedly* took a liking to your case. This chap *undoubtedly* took advantage of the moment when I slipped away from our luggage to tell you that everything was all right with it. He probably stole our case just at that favourable opportunity. They're always waiting for such an opportunity, you know. Two years ago at the North West station they robbed a young lady of a pram and a little girl in swaddling clothes and were so decent as to hand the little girl in at the police station in our street, saying that they had found her abandoned in the carriage entrance. Then the press tried to make out that the poor young lady was an unnatural mother.'

And Švejk underlined: 'At stations there always have been thefts and always will be. It can't be otherwise.'

'I'm convinced, Švejk,' the lieutenant put in, 'that one day you'll come to a really sticky end. I still don't know whether you're just pretending to be a mule or whether you were born one. What was in the suitcase?'

'Nothing in particular, sir, really,' answered Švejk, keeping his eyes fixed on the bald cranium of the civilian opposite, who appeared to take no interest whatsoever in the whole business and went on reading his *Neue Freie Presse*. 'In the whole suitcase there was only the mirror from the sitting-room and the iron clothes-rack from the hall, so we've really not suffered any loss at all, because the mirror and the clothes-rack both belonged to the landlord.'

Seeing the lieutenant's threatening gesture, Švejk continued in an amiable tone: 'Humbly report, sir, I really didn't know beforehand that the suitcase would be stolen, and as for the mirror and the clothes-rack I told the landlord that we would return them to him when we came home after the war. In enemy countries there are lots of mirrors and clothes-racks, so that even in this case neither the landlord nor us'll suffer any loss. As soon as we conquer a city . . .'

'Hold your tongue, Švejk!' the lieutenant interjected in an awe-inspiring voice: 'Some time I'm going to have you court-martialled. Think carefully whether you aren't the bloodiest fool and bastard in the whole world. In a thousand years no one else could make such a prize idiot of himself as you have done in these few weeks. I hope you've noticed that too?'

'Humbly report, I have, sir. I've got, as they say, a well-developed talent for observation when it's already too late and some unpleasant-ness has happened. I have the same sort of luck as a chap called Nechleba from Nekázanka, who went into the pub there called The Bitches' Grove. He always wanted to do good and start to lead a new life from Saturday onwards, but he always said the next day: "And in the small hours, chaps, I observed that I was lying on a plank-bed." And it always happened to him when he intended to go home respect-ably that in the end it turned out that he broke a fence somewhere, unharnessed some droshky driver's horse or wanted to clean his pipe with a cock's feather from the hat of a police patrol. He was quite desperate about it, and what worried him most of all was that this bad luck had been handed down from generation to generation. His grand-father once went out on his apprentice travels . . .'

'Oh, for God's sake, Švejk, don't pester me with your stories.'

'Humbly report, sir, everything I tell you is holy truth. His grand-father went out on his apprentice travels . . .'

'Švejk!' the lieutenant burst out in fury. 'Once more I order you not to tell me any more stories. I don't want to hear them. I'll deal with you when we get to Budějovice. Do you know, Švejk, that I'm going to have you gaoled?'

'Humbly report, sir, I don't know,' said Švejk gently. 'You haven't mentioned it yet.'

The lieutenant involuntarily ground his teeth, gave a deep sigh, took out from his coat a copy of *Bohemie* and read reports of the great victories and the activities in the Mediterranean of the German submarine 'E'. But when he got to the news of a new German invention for blowing up towns by special bombs dropped from aeroplanes which exploded three times in succession, he was roused by the voice of Švejk addressing himself to the bald-headed gentleman:

'Excuse me, your honour, don't you happen to be Mr Purkrábek, the representative of the Slavia Insurance Company?'

When the bald-headed gentleman did not reply, Švejk said to the lieutenant:

'Humbly report, sir, I once read in the newspapers that a normal man ought to have on his head an average of sixty to seventy thousand hairs and that dark-haired people have less, as can be seen from many examples.'

And he continued inexorably on: 'Once a medico in the café U Špírků said that loss of hair was caused by emotional excitement in childbed.'

And now something frightful happened. The bald-headed gentleman jumped up, roared at Švejk in German: 'Outside with you, you swine, you', kicked him out into the corridor and returned to the compartment, preparing a nice little surprise for the lieutenant by introducing himself to him.

There had been a little mistake. The bald-headed individual was not Mr Purkrábek of the Slavia Insurance Company, but only Major-General von Schwarzburg. The major-general, dressed in mufti, was just making a journey of inspection of the garrisons and was on his way to give Budějovice a surprise.

He was the most frightful inspecting general ever born, and if he found anything that was not in order he spoke with the garrison commander like this:

'Have you got a revolver?' 'Yes, I have.' 'Good! In your place I should certainly know what to do with it, because what I see here is not a garrison but a bloody piggery.'

And indeed after his inspections someone always shot himself somewhere or other, which induced Major-General von Schwarzburg to conclude with satisfaction: 'That's how it should be! That's a soldier for you!'

It seemed that he was not at all happy if anyone remained alive after his inspection. He had a mania for drafting an officer to the most unpleasant places. On the slightest provocation an officer would have to take leave of his garrison and make a pilgrimage to the Montenegrin frontier or to some drunken desperate garrison in a filthy corner of Galicia.

'Lieutenant,' he said, 'where were you at cadet school?'

'In Prague.'

'And so you've been to a cadet school and don't even know that an officer is responsible for his subordinate. That's a fine state of affairs. Next you talk with your servant as though he were your intimate friend. You allow him to speak without first being spoken to. That's still finer. Thirdly you allow him to insult your superiors. That's finest of all. As a result of all this I shall take the consequential measures. What's your name, lieutenant?'

'Lukáš.'

'And what regiment do you serve in?'

'I was . . .'

'Thank you. We're not talking about where you were. I want to know where you are now.'

'In the 91st infantry regiment, sir. They transferred me . . .'

'Transferred you? That was very sensible of them. It won't do you any harm to go as soon as possible with the 91st regiment and have a look at the front somewhere.'

'That's already been decided, sir.'

The major-general now gave a lecture on how he had observed in recent years that officers were in the habit of talking with their subordinates in a familiar tone, in which he saw the danger of a spread of democratic principles. A soldier must be kept in a state of terror; he must tremble in front of his superior; he must be in mortal dread of him. Officers must keep the men ten paces from their person and not allow them to think independently or even think at all. That had been the tragic mistake of recent years. In the old days the men feared their officers like fire and brimstone, but nowadays . . .

The major-general waved his hand in a hopeless gesture: 'Nowadays most officers spoil their soldiers. That's what I wished to convey.'

The major-general took up his newspaper again and immersed himself in it once more. Lieutenant Lukáš turned deadly pale and went out into the corridor to settle accounts with Švejk.

He found him standing by the window with such a blissful and contented expression as could only grace a month-old baby which had drunk and sucked its fill and was now enjoying its bye-byes.

The lieutenant stopped, nodded to Švejk and showed him an empty compartment. He followed Švejk into it and closed the door.

'Švejk,' he said solemnly, 'the moment has finally come when you are going to get the most colossal swipe across the jaw the world has ever seen. Why on earth did you attack that bald-headed gentleman? Do you realize he is Major-General von Schwarzburg?'

'Humbly report, sir,' replied Švejk, assuming the expression of a martyr, 'I never in my life had the slightest intention of insulting anybody and I never had any idea or even dreamed of any major-general. He really is the spit and image of Mr Purkrábek, the representative of the Slavia Insurance Company. He used to come to our local pub and once when he fell asleep at the table some charitable person wrote in an indelible pencil on his bald head: "Allow us to propose to you our scheme for safeguarding your children's dowries and trousseaux by means of an insurance policy as per schedule 3c enclosed." Of course everybody went away, leaving me alone with him and, because I always have bad luck, when he woke up and looked at himself in the mirror he got furious and thought that it was me who had done it. He wanted to give me one across the jaw too.'

The little word 'too' dropped so touchingly, so gently and so reproachfully from Švejk's lips that the lieutenant's poised hand fell back into its place.

But Švejk continued: 'That gentleman ought not to have got so angry over a tiny little mistake like that. He really should have sixty to seventy thousand hairs, as it was stated in that article on what every normal man should have. It had never in my life occurred to me that there could exist a bald major-general. It's a tragic mistake, as they say, and it can happen to anybody when he makes a remark and the other party at once catches on to it. Years ago a tailor called Hývl told us how he travelled from the place where he was working in Steiermark to Prague via Leoben and had with him a ham which he had bought in Maribor. While he was travelling in the train he thought he was the only Czech among all the passengers, and when somewhere near St Moritz he started to slice up the ham, the gentleman sitting opposite him began to cast loving eyes on it and his mouth started to water. When the tailor noticed this he said aloud to himself: "You'd like to have a bite, wouldn't you, you old bastard?" And the gentleman replied in Czech: "Of course I would if you'd only let me." And so both of them together wolfed up the ham completely before they reached Budějovice. That gentleman's name was Vojtěch Rous.'

Lieutenant Lukáš gave Švejk a look and went out of the compartment. When he was sitting in his place again after a little time the honest face of Švejk appeared in the door.

'Humbly report, sir, we shall be in Tábor in five minutes' time. The train stops there for five minutes. Have you any orders for food? In the old days they used to have here some very good . . .'

The lieutenant jumped up in fury and said to Švejk in the corridor: 'Once more I must warn you that the less I see of you the more pleased I shall be. I'd be happiest of all if I never set eyes on you again, and you can be sure I'll see to that. Keep out of my sight altogether. Don't let me catch even a glimpse of you, you mule, you oaf, you half-wit.'

'Just as you order, sir.'

Švejk saluted, turned round and marched in military step to the end of the corridor, where he sat down in the corner in the guard's seat and started a conversation with a railwayman: 'May I ask you something, please?'

The railwayman, who obviously manifested no desire for conversation, gave a faint and uninterested nod.

'I used to see a lot of a good man called Hofmann,' Švejk went on expansively, 'and he always maintained that these alarm signals never work. In other words they don't function properly when you pull that handle. To tell you the truth I've never taken any interest in such things, but when I saw this alarm signal here I felt I'd like to know what the position is if by any chance I needed to use it at any time.'

Svejk stood up and walked with the railwayman towards the alarm brake: 'For use in emergency'.

The railwayman considered it his duty to explain to Švejk the working of the whole mechanism of the alarm signal: 'He was right when he told you that you have to pull it by this handle, but he was lying when he said that it doesn't work. It always brings the train to a halt, because it is connected with the engine through all the carriages. The alarm brake must function.'

Both of them had their hands on the handle at this moment and it is really a mystery how it happened that they pulled it and the train came to a halt.

They could neither of them agree on who had actually done it and given the alarm signal.

Švejk asserted that it couldn't be him, because he wasn't a hooligan.

'I'm very surprised myself that the train suddenly stopped,' he said

good-humouredly to the guard. 'It was going and then suddenly it stopped. It really annoys me more than it does you.'

A solemn gentleman came to the defence of the railwayman and asserted that he had heard that it was the soldier who first began the conversation about alarm signals.

As against that Švejk spoke continually of his honesty and how he had no interest in making the train late, because he was going to the front.

'The station master will explain that to you,' the guard decided. 'It will cost you twenty crowns.'

Meanwhile one could see passengers getting out of the carriages, the chief guard blowing his whistle and a lady running madly with her case across the line into the fields.

'It's really worth twenty crowns,' said Švejk with equanimity and perfect calm. 'And that's really very cheap. Once when His Imperial Majesty was on a visit to Žižkov, a chap called Franta Šnor stopped his carriage by kneeling before His Imperial Majesty in the middle of the road. Then the police commissioner of that district told Mr Šnor with tears in his eyes that he ought not to have done that to him in his district. He ought to have done it in a street lower down, which was in the district of Chief Commissioner Kraus. It was there that he should have made his obeisance. After that they put Mr Šnor in gaol.'

Švejk looked around just when the circle of listeners was swelled by the arrival of the chief guard.

'Well, let's go on now,' said Švejk. 'It's not at all nice when a train is late. If it were in peacetime, who the hell would care, but when there's a war on, everyone has to know that in every train there are military personalities – major-generals, lieutenants and batmen. Every single delay of this kind can be touch and go. Napoleon was five minutes late at Waterloo and after that he and all his glory went down the drain . . .'

At that moment Lieutenant Lukáš pushed through the group of listeners. He was ghastly pale and could utter nothing but: 'Švejk!'

Švejk saluted and said: 'Humbly report, sir, they're shoving the blame on to me for having stopped the train. The State Railways have very peculiar seals on their emergency brakes. A chap shouldn't really come anywhere near them, otherwise he might have an accident, and they might demand twenty crowns from him as they're now doing from me!'

The chief guard was already outside. He gave the signal and the train went off again.

The audience went back to their places in the compartments. Lieutenant Lukáš did not utter another word and went to sit down too.

There remained only the guard, Švejk and the railwayman. The guard took out a notebook and made a report of the whole incident. The railwayman looked spitefully at Švejk, who asked calmly: 'Have you been long with the railway?'

Because the railwayman did not answer, Švejk declared that he knew a certain Mlíčko František from Uhříněves near Prague. He too once pulled the alarm brake and was so frightened that for a whole fortnight he lost his power of speech and regained it only when he came to see a certain Vaněk, a gardener, at Hostivař. There he got into a brawl and they broke a knout across him. 'That happened in May 1912,' Švejk added.

The railwayman opened the door of the W.C. and locked himself inside.

The guard remained with Švejk and tried to get a twenty crowns' fine out of him, stressing that if he didn't pay it he'd have to take him to the station master at Tábor.

'All right,' said Švejk. 'I'm always glad to talk to educated people and it will be a great pleasure for me when I see that station master at Tábor.'

Švejk took a pipe out of his tunic, lit it and, emitting the pungent smoke of army tobacco, continued: 'Years ago the station master at Svitava was a Mr Wagner. He was a devil to his subordinates and gave them hell whenever he could, but the chap he was most down on was the points-man Jungwirt. Finally in despair the wretched man went and drowned himself in the river. But before doing so, he wrote a letter to the station master saying that he'd come and haunt him in the night. And to tell you the honest truth, that was exactly what he did. In the night the good station master was sitting at his telegraph receiver when the bell rang and he received the following telegram: "How are you, you old bastard? Jungwirt." This lasted a whole week and the station master began to send official telegrams across all the lines to answer the ghost: "Forgive me, Jungwirt." And in the night the receiver knocked out the following reply: "Go and hang yourself on the signals at the bridge. Jungwirt." And the station master obeyed. Afterwards they gaoled the telegraphist from the station before Svitava. You see, there are more things in heaven and earth than are dreamt of in our philosophy.'

The train went in to the station at Tábor and Švejk, before leaving the train in the company of the guard, reported to Lieutenant Lukáš as was proper: 'Humbly report, sir, they're taking me to the station master.'

Lieutenant Lukáš did not answer. He was overcome by general apathy to everything. It dawned on him that the best thing to do was not to give a damn for the whole business, either for Švejk or for the bald-headed major-general opposite. It would be better to sit still, get out of the train at Budějovice, report to the barracks and go to the front with a march company. At the front he could get himself killed if necessary and be quit of this miserable world, in which a hideous brute like Švejk was rampaging about.

When the train moved off Lieutenant Lukáš looked out of the window and saw Švejk standing on the platform, absorbed in a serious conversation with the station master. He was surrounded by a crowd of people in which could be seen several railway uniforms.

Lieutenant Lukáš sighed. It was not a sigh of compassion. It was a relief to him that Švejk had remained on the platform. Why, even that bald-headed major-general no longer seemed to him such a loathsome monster.

The train had long ago wheezed its way in the direction of České Budějovice but on the platform the number of people around Švejk did not grow any less.

Švejk spoke of his innocence and was so successful in convincing the crowd of it that a lady exclaimed: 'Another case of a poor soldier being harried.'

The crowd accepted this verdict and one gentleman announced to the station master that he would pay Švejk's twenty crowns' fine. He was convinced that the soldier had not done it.

'Just look at him,' he said, drawing his deduction from the very innocent expression on the face of Švejk, who, turning to the crowd, declared: 'Folks, I'm innocent.'

Then the gendarmerie sergeant appeared, took a citizen out of the crowd, arrested him and led him off with the words: 'You'll answer for this; I'll teach you to incite people! If you handle soldiers like this no one can expect of them that Austria'll win the war.'

The unfortunate citizen could do nothing else but aver frankly that he was a master butcher from the Old Gate and had no such intentions.

Meanwhile the good man who believed in Švejk's innocence paid the fine for him in the office and took him off to the third-class restaurant where he treated him to a glass of beer. Discovering that all his papers and his railway warrant were with Lieutenant Lukáš, he generously gave Švejk ten crowns for his ticket and further expenses.

When he went away he said to Švejk in confidence: 'All right, my good soldier, if, as I said, you're taken prisoner in Russia, give my regards to the brewer Zeman at Zdolbunov. You've got my name written down, haven't you? Only keep your wits about you and see you don't stay long at the front.'

'You needn't worry about that,' said Švejk. 'It's always interesting to see foreign parts free.'

Švejk remained sitting at the table and, while he quietly drank away the ten crowns given to him by the generous benefactor, people on the platform who had not been present at Švejk's interview with the station master and only saw the crowd from a distance were telling each other that a spy had just been caught there and had been photographing the station. But this was contradicted by a lady who declared that it wasn't a spy, but that she had heard how a dragoon had beaten up an officer by the ladies' lavatory, because he'd pursued there the dragoon's girl-friend who had come to see him off.

However, these adventurous speculations, which were characteristic of the wartime nerviness, were nipped in the bud by the gendarmerie who cleared the platform. And Švejk went on drinking quietly, thinking tenderly of his lieutenant. What would he do when he came to České Budějovice and could not find his batman anywhere in the train?

Before the arrival of the passenger train the third-class restaurant filled up with soldiers and civilians. They were predominantly soldiers of various regiments and formations and the most diverse nationalities whom the whirlwinds of war had swept into the Tábor hospitals. They were now going back to the front to get new wounds, mutilations and pains and to earn the reward of a simple wooden cross over their graves. Years after on the mournful plains of East Galicia a faded Austrian soldier's cap with a rusty Imperial badge would flutter over it in wind and rain. From time to time a miserable old carrion crow would perch on it, recalling fat feasts of bygone days when there used to be spread for him an unending table of human corpses and horse carcasses, when just under the cap on which he perched there lay the daintiest morsels of all – human eyes.

One of these candidates for suffering who had been released from a military hospital after an operation came and sat next to Švejk in a dirty uniform covered with traces of blood and mud. He was somehow shrivelled, skinny and miserable. He put on the table a small package, took out a shabby purse and counted his money. Then he looked at Švejk and asked him: '*Magyarúl?*'[1]

'I'm a Czech, old chap,' answered Švejk. 'Would you like a drink?'
'*Nem tudom, barátom.*'[2]

---

1. 'Do you speak Hungarian?'
2. 'I don't understand, my friend.'

'That doesn't matter, old boy,' Švejk said invitingly, putting his own full glass in front of the unhappy soldier. 'Just have a good drink.'

He understood, drank and thanked Švejk: '*Köszönöm szivesen.*'[1] Then he went on to examine the contents of his purse and finally gave a sigh. Švejk understood that the Hungarian would like to order a beer

but did not have enough money and so he ordered a glass for him, whereupon the Hungarian thanked him again and tried to explain something to him with the help of gestures. He pointed to his shot arm and said in international language: 'Pif, paf, poof!'

Švejk shook his head in sympathy and the crippled convalescent explained further to Švejk, by holding his left hand half a metre above the ground and then raising three fingers, that he had three little children.

'*Nincs ham, nincs ham,*' he continued, wishing to tell him that they had nothing to eat at home, and he wiped the tears from his eyes with the dirty sleeve of his military greatcoat, where there was a hole from a

1. 'Thank you very much.'

bullet which had penetrated his body – all for the sake of the King of Hungary.[1]

It was not surprising that in a conversation like that Švejk gradually parted with every one of those ten crowns and was slowly but surely cutting himself off from České Budějovice, losing the possibility of buying a railway ticket with every glass of beer which he stood himself and the Hungarian convalescent.

Another train to Budějovice passed through the station but Švejk went on sitting at the table and listening to the Hungarian repeating his: 'Pif, paf, poof! *Három gyermek nincs ham, éljen!*'[2]

He said the last words when Švejk clinked glasses with him.

'Just go on drinking, you Hungarian bastard,' replied Švejk. 'Soak yourself! You wouldn't treat us like this . . .'

From the next table a soldier said that when they came to Szeged with the 28th regiment the Hungarians had pointed at them and put their hands up.[3]

This was the honest truth, but this soldier had obviously been insulted by it, although it was a common occurrence among all Czech soldiers and in the end the Hungarians did the same themselves, when they had got tired of brawling for the sake of the King of Hungary.

Then this soldier sat down next to Švejk and told how they had given the Hungarians a rough time in Szeged and beaten them out of several pubs. Saying this he gave full credit to the Hungarians for their ability to brawl and said that he had got a knife wound in the back, so that he had to be sent to the base to be cured.

But now when he returned the captain of his battalion would obviously put him in gaol, because he had not had time to pay the Hungarian back for the knife wound as was only fit and proper. The fellow should have got his due and the honour of the whole regiment have been preserved.

But Švejk was suddenly set upon by the commander of the army control, a sergeant-major, accompanied by four soldiers with bayonets, who began: '*Ihre Dokumenten*, your tokuments? I zees, you zits, not goes, zits, trinks, keep on trinks, zoldier!'

'Haven't got any documents, *miláčku*,'[4] answered Švejk. 'Lieu-

---

1. The Emperor Franz Joseph was also King of Hungary.
2. 'Three children, nothing to eat, here's how!'
3. A dig at the Czech troops for surrendering and deserting to the enemy.
4. Czech for 'sweetheart'.

tenant Lukáš, regiment number 91, took them with him and I stayed here on the station.'

'What does the word *milatschku* mean?' the sergeant-major said in German to one of his soldiers, an old Landwehr man, who seemed to do everything to spite him because he replied calmly in the same language:

'*Miláčku*? That's the same as "Mr Sergeant-Major".'

The sergeant-major went on talking to Švejk: 'Efrey soldat most haf tokuments. Vizout tokuments I lock him op at Bahnhofs-Militärkommando,[1] like a mad dog, ze lousy brute.'

They took Švejk to the station army headquarters where in the guard-room the men sat looking exactly like the old Landwehr man who had been able to find such an excellent translation in German for the word '*miláčku*' for the benefit of his born enemy, His Lordship, the sergeant-major.

The guard-room was decorated with lithographs, which the Ministry

1. Army headquarters at the station.

of War had had distributed at that time to all offices which were visited by the troops as well as to schools and barracks.

The good soldier Švejk was welcomed by a picture which, according to the title, showed how Sergeant František Hammel and Corporals Paulhart and Bachmayer of the Imperial and Royal 21st Artillery Regiment encouraged the men to endurance. On the other side there hung a picture with the inscription: 'Sergeant Jan Danko of the 5th regiment of the Honvéd Hussars reconnoitring the position of an enemy battery.'

On the right side lower down hung the placard: '*Rare examples of valour.*'

With the aid of placards like this, in which the examples and texts were invented and written up by various conscripted German journalists, idiotic old Austria tried to inspire troops who never read them; and when these examples of valour were sent to them at the front bound in books, they rolled cigarettes out of them from pipe tobacco or disposed of them still more appropriately, so that their use could correspond to the value and spirit of the rare examples of valour which had been so glowingly written up.

While the sergeant-major went off to find an officer, Švejk read on a placard:

BRAVE DRIVER JOSEF BONG

The men of the Ambulance Corps transported the seriously wounded to carts prepared in a sheltered ravine. As soon as a cart was full they drove away with it to the first-aid post. When the Russians discovered these carts they began to shell them. The horse of driver Josef Bong of the Imperial and Royal 3rd Army Service Squadron was killed by shrapnel. Bong moaned: 'My poor Dobbin, it's all over with you!' At that very moment he was hit himself by a piece of shrapnel. In spite of this he unharnessed his horse and dragged the three-span cart back to safe shelter. After that he returned for the harness of his slaughtered horse. The Russians went on shooting. 'Just go on shooting, you blasted devils! I'm not going to leave the harness here!', and he went on unfastening the harness from the horse muttering these words. At last he finished and dragged himself back to the cart with the harness. Here he had to listen to a thundering rebuke from the ambulance men for his long absence. The brave soldier excused himself: 'I did not want to abandon the harness. It's practically new. It would have been a pity, I thought. We don't have too many of these things.' He then went to the first-aid post and only then reported himself wounded. His captain later decorated his breast with the silver medal for bravery.

When Švejk had finished reading this and the sergeant-major had not yet returned he said to the Landwehr men in the guard-room: 'That's a very fine example of valour. If we go on doing that we shall have nothing but new harness in the army. But when I was in Prague I read in the *Prague Official Gazette* of an even finer example – a one-year volunteer, Dr Josef Vojna. He was in Galicia in the 7th battalion of the Field Rifles, and when it came to a bayonet charge he got a bullet in his head. When they took him away to the first-aid post he shouted at them that he didn't need to be bandaged for a slash like that. And he wanted to advance again immediately with his company, but a shell cut off his ankle. Again they were going to carry him away, but he began to hobble towards the battle line with a stick and defended himself with it against the enemy. But a new shell came flying at him and tore off the arm in which he held the stick. And so he transferred the stick to his other arm and shouted out that he'd never forgive them that. God knows what might have happened to him if, after a short time, a piece of shrapnel hadn't finally murdered him. Perhaps if they hadn't finished him off he too might have got the silver medal for bravery. When his head had been blown off and it was rolling down it still went on shouting: "Never mind if death is near! Do your job and never fear!"'

'That's what they write in the newspapers,' said one of the men, 'but if the writer saw all this he'd be off his chump in an hour.'

The Landwehr man spat: 'In Čáslav, where I live, there was an editor from Vienna, a German. He was serving as an ensign. He refused to speak Czech with us, but when he was drafted to the march company, where there were nothing but Czechs, he was suddenly able to speak it.'

The sergeant-major appeared in the door, gave a furious look and fired off:

'If man go avay tree minute, zen of course he hear nozing but "Tschech, Tschechs".'

Going outside, obviously to the restaurant, he pointed at Švejk and told the corporal of the Landwehr to bring the lousy bastard at once before the lieutenant when he arrived.

'The lieutenant's fooling around again with the telegraph girl at the station,' said the corporal, after he had gone. 'He's been running after her for a fortnight and he's always frightfully furious when he comes from the telegraph office and he says about her: "She's a whore. She won't sleep with me!"'

And now he was obviously in just such a furious temper, because when shortly afterwards he came in he could be heard banging some books about on the table.

'Can't be helped, old man. You've got to go to him,' the corporal said to Švejk in sympathy. 'Lots of people have passed through his hands, old and young soldiers.'

And he led Švejk into the office, where behind a table on which there was a mess of papers a young lieutenant sat looking extremely furious.

When he saw Švejk and the corporal he said very promisingly: 'Ha!' Then followed the report of the corporal: 'Humbly report, sir, this man was found on the station without any documents.'

The lieutenant nodded, as though wishing to indicate that he had calculated years ago that on this very day and at this very hour Švejk would be found on the station without any documents, since anyone who looked at Švejk at this moment could not escape the impression that a man with such a face and figure as his could not possibly have any documents on him. At that moment Švejk looked as if he had fallen down from the sky from some other planet and he was now looking with naïve wonder at a new world where people were demanding from him idiotic nonsense which he had never heard of before, like documents.

The lieutenant looked at Švejk and reflected for a moment on what he should say to him and what questions he should put to him.

In the end he asked: 'And what were you doing at the station?'

'Humbly report, sir, I was waiting for the train to České Budějovice, so that I could rejoin my 91st regiment, where I am serving as batman to Lieutenant Lukáš. I had to leave him behind, when I was brought before the station master for a fine. I was under suspicion of having used the safety and emergency brake and stopped the express in which we were travelling.'

'You're driving me up the wall,' shouted the lieutenant. 'Speak connectedly and to the point and cut out all this drivel.'

'Humbly report, sir, we had bad luck from the very first moment that Lieutenant Lukáš and I got into that express, which was to take us away and convey us as quickly as possible to our 91st Imperial and Royal Infantry Regiment. First we lost a suitcase and then again, so as to get it quite straight, a major-general, who was completely bald . . .'

'Himmelherrgott,' sighed the lieutenant.

'Humbly report, sir, it's got to be shaken out of me like out of a hairy rug in order to get a proper view of all the events, if I'm permitted to quote the favourite words of the late lamented cobbler Petrlík, when he ordered his apprentice to take down his trousers before he started flogging him with a strap.'

And while the lieutenant snorted Švejk continued:

'Well, somehow or other I didn't find favour in the eyes of that bald-headed major-general and so I was sent out into the corridor by Lieutenant Lukáš, whose batman I am. And then in the corridor I was accused of doing what I've just told you. Before that matter could be settled I had to stay behind alone on the platform. The train had gone, the lieutenant and the suitcases and all my documents had gone too, and I was standing there gaping like an orphan without any documents.'

Švejk looked at the lieutenant with an expression of such moving tenderness that the latter was at once clear in his mind that it was the complete truth he was hearing from this bastard, who gave the impression of being a congenital idiot.

The lieutenant now recited to Švejk all the trains that had left for Budějovice after the express and asked him why he had missed all of them.

'Humbly report, sir,' answered Švejk, smiling affably, 'while I was waiting for the next train I suffered the misfortune that I sat down at a table and started drinking one glass of beer after another.'

'I've never seen such a bloody coot as this before,' the lieutenant thought to himself. 'He admits everything. When I think of all the people who I have had before me and who have all denied the charges, and this one calmly says: "I missed all the trains, because I drank one glass of beer after another." '

He put all these thoughts together in one sentence, and pronounced them to Švejk: 'You're degenerate, you bastard. Do you know what it means when you call somebody degenerate?'

'Humbly report, sir, at the corner of Na Bojišti and Kateřinská Street, where I live, there was once a degenerate. His father was a Polish count and his mother a midwife. He used to sweep the streets but in the bars he never allowed anyone to call him anything else than "My Lord".'

The lieutenant thought it proper to find a way of liquidating the case and so he said with emphasis: 'Let me tell you, you blasted fool, you bloody oaf, that you're going to the booking office and you'll buy a ticket and go to Budějovice. If ever I find you here again I'll deal with you as a deserter. Dismiss!'

Because Švejk failed to move but continued to stand with his hand at the peak of his cap the lieutenant shouted out in German: 'Clear

out! Don't you hear? Dismiss! Corporal Palánek, take this bloody half-wit to the booking office and buy him a ticket to České Budějovice!'

Corporal Palánek appeared a moment later in the office again. In the half-open door the good-natured face of Švejk peeped in behind Palánek.

'Well, what's the matter now?'

'Humbly report, sir,' Corporal Palánek whispered mysteriously, 'he hasn't any money for the ticket and I haven't either. They wouldn't take him free, because he hasn't got any military documents to show he's going to his regiment.'

The lieutenant did not hesitate to solve this difficult question with the judgement of Solomon.

'Then let him walk,' he decided. 'Let them gaol him at his regiment for coming late. Who on earth wants to be plagued with him here?'

'There's nothing to be done, old chap,' said Corporal Palánek to Švejk when they left the office. 'You must go to Budějovice on foot, old man. In the guard-room we've got an army loaf, and we'll give it you for the journey.'

And half an hour later, when they had treated Švejk to black coffee and given him a packet of army tobacco and an army loaf for his journey to the regiment, Švejk walked out of Tábor in the darkness of the night through which his singing resounded.

He was singing an old army song:

> 'When we marched to Jaroměř,
>   Believe it, if you like, or not . . .'

And God knows how it happened, but the good soldier Švejk instead of going south to Budějovice went on marching straight to the west.

He trudged through the snow along the road in the frost wrapped up in his military greatcoat, like the last of Napoleon's old guard returning from the Moscow campaign, with the only difference that he sang merrily to himself:

> 'I went out for a little stroll
> Into the green, green grove.'

And in the snowed-in forests in the stillness of the night the echo resounded until the dogs started to bark in all the villages.

When he got tired of singing, he sat down on a heap of gravel, lit his pipe and after a rest trudged on towards the new adventures of his Budějovice anabasis.

Švejk's Budějovice Anabasis

XENOPHON, that warrior of ancient times, travelled through the whole of Asia Minor and got to God knows where without any maps at all. And the Goths of old too made their expeditions without any knowledge of topography. Marching forward all the time is what is called an anabasis: penetrating into unknown regions: being cut off by enemies who are waiting for the first convenient opportunity to wring your neck. If anyone has a good brain, like Xenophon or all those thieving tribes who came to Europe from God knows where in the Caspian or Sea of Azov, he can work real wonders on a march.

Caesar's Roman legions penetrated somewhere to the north by the Gallic Sea and they had no maps either. Once they said they would march back to Rome again by another route so that they could get more out of it. And they got there too. And it is obviously from that time that people say that all roads lead to Rome.

And all roads lead to České Budějovice too. The good soldier Švejk was fully convinced of this when instead of the Budějovice region he saw villages in the Milevsko region.

All the same he went steadily forward, for no good soldier can allow a Milevsko to stop him from getting to České Budějovice.

And so Švejk turned up west of Milevsko at Květov, after having rung all the changes in the repertoire of army songs which he knew from his various marches, and so just before Květov he was compelled to start again with the song:

> 'When we marched away,
> All the girls began to cry . . .'

An old woman who was returning from church on the way from Květov to Vráž, which was still in a westerly direction, hailed Švejk with the Christian greeting: 'Good morning, soldier, where are you bound for?'

'I'm going to my regiment at Budějovice, mother,' answered
Švejk, 'to the war.'

'Then you're going wrong, soldier,' said the old woman in a scared
voice. 'You'll never get there this way through Vráž. If you go straight
on you'll get to Klatovy.'

'I believe that a man can get to Budějovice even from Klatovy,'
said Švejk resignedly. 'It's certainly a tidy walk, if a chap's hurrying
to get to his regiment to avoid any trouble through not being punctual
at his destination for all his goodwill.'

'We've already had a chap like you here. He had to go to Pilsen
to the Landwehr. He was called Toníček Mašků,' the old woman
said with a sigh. 'He was a relation of my niece and he went away. And
a week later the gendarmerie were looking for him, because he hadn't
reported to his regiment. After another week he turned up here in
mufti saying he had been allowed home on leave. But the mayor went

to the gendarmerie and they pulled him out of that:"leave". Now he's written from the front that he's wounded and that he's lost a leg.'

The old woman looked pityingly at Švejk: 'You can wait in that spinney there, soldier. I'll bring you some of our potatoes. They'll warm you up a bit. You can see our cottage from here. It's just to the right behind the spinney. You mustn't go through our village of Vráž. The gendarmes there are like hawks. You can go afterwards from the spinney towards Malčín. But after that, soldier, avoid Čížová. The gendarmerie there would flay you and they always catch dissenters. Go straight through the wood to Sedlec by Horažd'ovice. There's a very good gendarme there who lets everybody through the village. Have you got any papers on you?'

'I haven't, mother!'

'Then don't go there. It's better you go to Radomyšl, but see that you get there by evening. Then all the gendarmes are in the pub. And there in the Lower Street behind St Florian you'll find a house painted blue below and you can ask for Farmer Melichárek. That's my brother. You can give him my love and he'll show you how to get to Budějovice from there.'

For over half an hour Švejk waited in the spinney for the old woman. When he had warmed himself with the potato soup which she had brought him in a pot covered with a pillow so as not to get cold, she took out of her kerchief a hunk of bread and a piece of bacon, stuck all of it into Švejk's pocket, made the sign of the cross on him and said that she had two grandsons in the army.

Then she repeated to him in detail through which villages he had to go and which he had to avoid. Finally she took a crown out of the pocket of her coat so that in Malčín he could buy some spirit for his journey, because Radomyšl was very far away.

Following the instructions of the old woman Švejk walked from Čížová towards Radomyšl to the east and thought to himself that he could not help getting to Budějovice from any point of the compass.

From Malčín he was accompanied by an old accordion player, whom he had found in a pub when he bought the spirit for that long journey to Radomyšl.

The accordion player took Švejk for a deserter and advised him to go with him to Horažd'ovice, where he had a married daughter whose husband was a deserter too. The accordion player had obviously had a drop too much in Malčín.

'She has been keeping her husband hidden in a stable for two months already,' he confided to Švejk, 'so she can hide you too and you'll be able to stay there until the end of the war. And if there are two of you it'll be jollier.'

When Švejk politely declined this invitation the accordion player suddenly got very angry and went off to the left over the fields, threatening Švejk that he would denounce him to the gendarmerie in Čížová.

Towards evening in Radomyšl in the Lower Street behind St Florian Švejk found Farmer Melichárek. When he conveyed greetings from his sister in Vráž it did not have any effect on the farmer.

He insisted repeatedly on seeing Švejk's papers. He was rather a prejudiced person, talking all the time about robbers, vagabonds and thieves, masses of whom were infesting the whole district of Písek.

'They run away from the army, they don't want to serve in it and then they roam about the whole district and steal,' he said with emphasis to Švejk, looking him straight in the eyes. 'And they all look as innocent as lambs.

'Yes, of course, people always get worked up when it's a question of telling the truth,' he added, when Švejk got up from the bench. 'If a chap has a clean conscience, he sits still and lets his papers be examined. But if he hasn't got any . . .'

'Well, goodbye to you, grandfather.'

'And goodbye to you too, and next time try and catch someone who isn't quite as sharp as me.'

When Švejk went off into the darkness, the old man still went on grumbling for quite a time: 'He says he's going to Budějovice to join his regiment. From Tábor. And the rascal goes first to Horažd'ovice and only then to Písek. Why, he's making a trip round the world.'

Švejk went on walking almost the whole night until somewhere near Putim he found a haystack in a field. As he was scratching the straw apart he heard a voice quite near him saying: 'What's your regiment? Where are you off to?'

'The 91st. I'm going to Budějovice.'

'Why should you be going there?'

'I've got my lieutenant there.'

He could hear close to him not just one person laughing but three. When the laughter died down Švejk asked what regiment they belonged to. He discovered that two of them were from the 35th and one from the artillery, also from Budějovice.

A month ago the 35th had deserted just before they should have marched to the front, and the artilleryman had been on the tramp from the day he was called up. He was from here at Putim and the haystack belonged to him. At night he always slept in the haystack. The day before he had found the other two in the wood and had taken them with him to his rick.

All cherished the hope that the war must be over in a month or two. They imagined that the Russians were already beyond Budapest and in Moravia. This was what people were saying everywhere in Putim. In the morning before dawn the dragoon's wife would bring them breakfast. After that the men of the 35th would go on to Strakonice, because one of them had an aunt there, and she again had a friend in the mountains beyond Sušice. He had a saw mill and they would find good shelter there.

'And you of the 91st can go with us too, if you like,' they offered Švejk. 'Shit on your lieutenant!'

'That won't be so easy,' answered Švejk and he squeezed and crawled deeper into the haystack.

When he woke up next morning they were all of them gone and one of them, obviously the dragoon, had placed at his feet a slice of bread for the journey.

Švejk walked through the forests and near Štěkno he met a tramp, an old gaffer, who welcomed him like an old friend with a nip of brandy.

'Don't walk about in that,' he told Švejk. 'That army uniform of yours could cost you hell. Now it's full of gendarmes everywhere and there's no chance of doing any begging in those clothes. Today, of course, it's not us the gendarmes chase like they did before. Now it's only you they're after.

'It's only you they're after,' he repeated in a tone of such conviction that Švejk thought it wiser not to tell him anything about the 91st regiment. Let him take him for what he thought him to be. Why destroy the good old fellow's illusions?

'And where are you bound for?' the tramp asked after a while, when they had both lit their pipes and were slowly walking round the village.

'To Budějovice.'

'For the love of Christ!' the tramp said in horror. 'They'll round you up there in a jiffy, before you can say Jack Robinson. You must wear mufti and be in rags. You must hobble about like a cripple.

'But don't be afraid. Now we'll go to Strakonice, Volyň, and Dub, and it'll be hellishly bad luck if we don't scrounge some mufti there. In Strakonice the people are still so idiotically honest that they often leave their doors open for you at night and in the daytime they don't lock them at all. In winter when they go off and have a chat with a neighbour you can pick up some mufti straight away. What do you need? You have boots, so all you want is something to put over you. Is your army greatcoat old?'

'Yes, it is.'

'Well, keep it. People go about in that in the country. You need trousers and a jacket. When we get that mufti we'll sell your army trousers and tunic to the Jew Herrman at Vodňany. He buys everything that's army and sells it again in the villages.

'Today we'll go to Strakonice,' he unfolded his plan further. 'Four hours from here is the old Schwarzenberg sheep-fold. The shepherd there is a friend of mine. He's an old gaffer too. And so we'll stay the night there and in the morning we'll move on to Strakonice to see if we can't scrounge some mufti somewhere in the neighbourhood.'

In the sheep-fold Švejk found the nice old gaffer, who remembered how his grandfather used to tell him stories about the French wars. He was about twenty years older than the old tramp and called him 'lad' just as he did Švejk.

'Well, you see, lads,' he explained, when they sat round the stove, on which potatoes were boiling in their jackets, 'at that time my grandfather dissented too just like your soldier here is doing. But they caught him in Vodňany and flogged his arse so much that strips flew off it. But he had luck after all. Jareš's son, the grandfather of old Jareš, the water bailiff from Ražice near Protivín, got some powder and lead in him at Písek for desertion. And before they shot him on the ramparts at Písek he ran the gauntlet of the soldiers in the street and got six hundred blows with sticks, so that when death came it was a relief and redemption for him. But when did you run away?' he turned to Švejk with tearful eyes.

'After call-up, when they took us away to the barracks,' answered Švejk, realizing that a soldier must not shatter the illusions of the old shepherd.

'Did you climb over the wall?' the shepherd asked curiously, obviously recalling how his grandfather used to tell of how he too climbed over the barrack wall.

'There was no other way, granddad.'

'And the guard was strong and they shot at you?'

'Yes, they did, granddad.'

'And where are you off to now?'

'He's off his head,' the tramp answered in place of Švejk. 'He insists on going to Budějovice. You know, he's a foolish young puppy and goes to his ruin. I must give him a few lessons. We'll try and scrounge some mufti for him and then everything'll be all right. We'll manage somehow until the spring and after that we'll go and take work with a farmer. This year there'll be a great shortage of labour, there'll be famine and they say all tramps will be rounded up and put on to farm work. And so I think it's better to go of your own accord. There won't be many farm workers. They'll all be wiped out.'

'You think that it won't be over this year?' asked the shepherd. 'Well, of course you're right, lad! There have been long wars in the past. There was the Napoleonic war and then the Swedish wars and the Seven Years' War, as they used to tell us. And people deserved these wars. The good Lord couldn't stand it any longer; people were getting so uppish, you see. They didn't even want to have mutton under their whiskers, they wouldn't even swallow that, lads. In the old days they used to come queuing up here in the hope I'd sell them some mutton under the counter, but in recent years they've guzzled nothing but pork and poultry, all soaked in butter or lard. And so the good Lord got angry with them because of their pride, but they won't come to their senses again until they're cooking goosefoot like they did in the Napoleonic wars. Our lords and masters too didn't know what to do, they were so debauched. The old Prince Schwarzenberg drove about in an ordinary carriage but the young prince, that greenhorn, does nothing but stink around in a motor-car. The good Lord will rub his nose in petrol one of these fine days.'

The water in which the potatoes were cooking on the stove began to bubble and after a short silence the old shepherd said in prophetic tones: 'And His Imperial Majesty won't win this war. There's no enthusiasm for it at all, because, as our schoolmaster in Strakonice says, he wouldn't have himself crowned. Now he can talk as much soft soap as he likes. When you promised you'd be crowned you should have kept your word, you old bastard!'

'Perhaps he'll manage to do it now,' said the tramp.

'Nobody cares a hell any more about it now, lad,' the shepherd said irritably. 'You ought to be there when the neighbours get together down in Skočice. Everyone has a friend at the front and you should hear how they talk. After this war they say there'll be freedom and there won't be any noblemen's palaces or emperors, and the princes'll have their estates all taken away. The gendarmes already took off a chap called Kořínek because of talk like that. They said it was seditious. Yes, today it's gendarmerie law.'

'But so it was before,' replied the tramp. 'I remember how in Kladno there used to be a captain of the gendarmerie called Rotter. One fine day he began to breed those, what do you call them, police dogs, which are like wolves and follow everything when they're trained. And that captain at Kladno had his arse full with all those trainee dogs. He had a special little house for them, where they lived like lords. And one day he had the idea of experimenting with them on us poor tramps. So he gave orders that the gendarmerie in the whole Kladno district should round up the tramps, every man jack of them, and hand them all over to him. And once I was tramping from Lány and kept deep in the woods so that only a glimmer of me could be seen, but it was no good. I didn't get to the gamekeeper's lodge I was making for before they caught me and took me to the captain. And, chaps, you couldn't think or imagine what I had to go through with that captain and his dogs. First of all he made them all smell me, and then I had to climb up a ladder. And when I was on the top he set one of his monsters after me and the bloody brute pulled me down from the ladder on to the ground and kneeled on me, growling and snarling in my face. Then they took the brute away and told me to hide somewhere – anywhere I liked. I went into the woods towards the valley of Kačák, down into a ravine, and half an hour later two of those wolfhounds caught up with me, knocked me over and, while one of them held me by the throat, the other ran off to Kladno. An hour later Captain Rotter himself came with his gendarmes, shouted at the dogs, gave me five crowns and permission to beg in the Kladno region for two whole days. But did I do it? You bet! I rushed off like a madman towards the Beroun district and didn't show myself any more near Kladno. All the tramps avoided it because that captain made his experiments on all of them. He was frightfully fond of those dogs. At the gendarmerie stations they used to say that when he came on an inspection and saw a wolfhound anywhere he didn't make any inspection at all but spent the whole day happily drinking with the sergeant.'

And while the shepherd sieved the potatoes and poured into the dish sour sheep's milk the tramp continued to impart his memories of gendarmerie justice: 'In Lipnice there was a gendarmerie sergeant down underneath the castle. He lived in the gendarmerie station itself and I, being a simple old chap, was always under the impression that a gendarmerie station must be in some prominent place like in the square or somewhere like that and certainly not somewhere in a side street. And so I kept to the side streets of that little country town and didn't look at the street signs. I took one house after the other until I got to the first floor of an ordinary cottage, opened the door and announced, "Have pity on a poor tramp." Good Lord, chaps, I could have dropped through the floor. It was the gendarmerie station. There were rifles along the wall, a crucifix on the table, a register on the chest and His

Imperial Majesty looked down at me directly over the table. And before I could stammer anything, the sergeant jumped at me and gave me such a blow on the jaw at the door that I flew out down those wooden stairs to the very bottom and only stopped when I got to Kejžlice. That's gendarmerie law.'

They started to eat and soon went to sleep stretched out on the benches in the warm sitting-room.

In the night Švejk quietly dressed and went out. The moon was just rising in the east and in its waking light Švejk marched to the east, repeating: 'It's not possible for me not to get to Budějovice.'

And because when Švejk came out of the woods he saw on the right a town, he took a more northerly course and then turned to the south, where again there could be seen a town of some kind. (It was Vodňany.) And so he moved away in the opposite direction over the meadows and the early sun welcomed him on the snow-covered slopes above Protivín.

'Forward the brave!' said the good soldier Švejk to himself. 'Duty calls. I must get to Budějovice.'

But by an unfortunate chance instead of going from Protivín south to Budějovice Švejk directed his steps to the north towards Písek.

About noon Švejk saw a village in front of him. Coming down from a small hill he thought: 'It's no good going on like this. I'll ask how I can get to Budějovice.'

And going into the village he was very surprised when he saw its name marked on a post by the first house: 'Putim'.

'Jesus Christ,' sighed Švejk. 'Here I am back in Putim where I slept in the haystack.'

And so he was not the slightest bit surprised when he saw behind the little lake a white-washed house on which a 'chicken' was hanging (the name given in some places to the Austrian 'eaglet') and a gendarme walking out of it like a spider guarding its web.

The gendarme went straight up to Švejk and said nothing except, 'Where are you off to?'

'To my regiment at Budějovice.'

The gendarme smiled sarcastically: 'But you're going away from Budějovice. Your Budějovice is far behind you,' and he took Švejk into the gendarmerie station.

The sergeant of the Putim gendarmerie was renowned throughout the whole district for his very tactful and shrewd way of conducting business. He never swore at those he detained or arrested, but subjected them to such a searching cross-examination that even an innocent man could do nothing but confess.

Two gendarmes at the station assisted him and the cross-examination

was always accompanied by the grins of the whole staff of the gendarmerie.

'The secret of criminal investigation lies in shrewdness and good manners,' the sergeant always said to his subordinates. 'Bellowing at anybody doesn't help. You must always be gentle with delinquents and suspects, but at the same time ensure that they are drowned in a flood of questions.'

'Welcome here, soldier,' said the sergeant. 'Sit down and make yourself at home. Anyway, you must be tired after your journey. Tell us where you're going.'

Švejk repeated that he was going to České Budějovice to join his regiment.

'Then of course you've taken the wrong turning,' said the sergeant with a smile, 'because you're now going away from České Budějovice, as I can easily convince you. Over your head there's a map of Bohemia. Have a look at it, soldier. To the south of us is Protivín. South of Protivín is Hluboká and south of that is České Budějovice. And so you see you're not going *to* Budějovice but *away from* it.'

The sergeant looked affably at Švejk, who said with composure and dignity: 'But I'm going to Budějovice all the same.' This was more effective even than Galileo's famous statement, 'But it goes round all the same!', because Galileo must certainly have been furious when he said it.

'You know, soldier,' the sergeant said to Švejk with the same affability, 'I shall disabuse you of that idea, and you yourself will come to share my opinion that every denial only makes a confession more difficult!'

'You're absolutely right,' said Švejk. 'Every denial makes a confession more difficult and vice versa.'

'And so you see, soldier, that you're coming to that conclusion of your own accord. Answer me frankly where you were coming from when you set out for this Budějovice of yours. I say intentionally "of yours", because there must obviously be another Budějovice which lies somewhere to the north of Putim and hasn't yet been recorded on any map!'

'I came from Tábor.'

'And what were you doing in Tábor?'

'I was waiting for a train to Budějovice.'

'And why didn't you take that train to Budějovice?'

'Because I didn't have a ticket.'

'But you were a soldier. Why didn't they give you as a soldier a free railway warrant.'

'Because I didn't have any documents on me.'

'Ah, there we have it,' said the sergeant triumphantly to one of his men. 'He's not nearly as stupid as he pretends to be. He's beginning to shoot a good line.'

The sergeant began again, as though he had not heard the last reply about the documents:

'And so you left Tábor. Where did you go then?'

'To České Budějovice.'

The sergeant's face assumed an expression of some severity and his gaze fell on the map.

'Can you show us on the map by what route you went to Budějovice?'

'I can't remember all the places. All I can remember is that I've already been in Putim once.'

All the staff of the gendarmerie station looked at each other inquiringly and the sergeant continued: 'And so in Tábor you were on the railway station. Have you got anything on you? Take it out.'

When they had made a thorough search of Švejk's person and found nothing except a pipe and some matches, the sergeant asked Švejk: 'Tell me, why do you have absolutely nothing on you?'

'Because I don't need anything.'

'Oh, my God,' sighed the sergeant, 'you really are a martyrdom. You said that you've already been in Putim once. What did you do here then?'

'I walked past Putim to Budějovice.'

'Now see how tied up you're getting. You yourself said that you were going to Budějovice and now we've convinced you that you were coming away from it.'

'I suppose I must have gone round in a circle.'

The sergeant again exchanged a knowing glance with the whole personnel of the station. 'A fine circle, that circle of yours! I think that you must be just loafing about the district. Did you stay long on the station at Tábor?'

'I stayed until the last train left for Budějovice.'

'And what did you do there?'

'I talked to the soldiers.'

Another very knowing look from the sergeant to the staff.

'And what did you talk about, for instance, and what did you ask them about?'

'I asked them their regiment and where they were going.'

'Excellent. And you didn't happen to ask them for example how many men there would be in a regiment and how they were distributed?'

'No, I didn't ask that because I knew it by heart ages ago.'

'And so you're perfectly informed about the composition of our army?'

'Of course, sergeant.'

And the sergeant now played his last trump, looking around triumphantly at his gendarmes:

'Do you speak Russian?'

'No, I don't.'

The sergeant nodded to the lance-corporal and when both of them had gone out into the next room he rubbed his hands with the enthusiasm of complete victory and certainty and said: 'Did you hear that? He doesn't speak Russian! He's a cunning one! He's confessed everything except the most important thing. Tomorrow we shall send him to the district officer in Písek. Criminology depends on shrewdness and good manners. You saw how I drowned him in a flood of questions. Who would have thought that of him? He looks so stupid and idiotic, but it's just with people of his kind that you need to have all your wits about you. Now lock him up somewhere and I'll go and write a report about it.'

And that very afternoon towards evening the gendarmerie sergeant, smiling sweetly, drew up a report in every sentence of which occurred in German: 'Under suspicion of espionage.'

When Sergeant Flanderka had spent a little time writing his odd official German the situation became gradually clearer to him, and when he ended with the words: 'And so I beg humble leave to report that the enemy officer will today be sent to Gendarmerie District Command in Písek,' he smiled over his work and called to the lance-corporal: 'Have you given the enemy officer anything to eat?'

'By your orders, sergeant, we serve food only to those who are brought in and interrogated before twelve o'clock.'

'This is a great exception,' said the sergeant solemnly. 'This is a high-ranking officer, someone from their general staff. You know, the Russians would never send here a mere corporal as a spy. Send to The Old Tom Cat for some lunch for him. If they haven't got anything left they'd better cook something specially. After that let them make tea with rum and send everything here. Don't say who it's for. Don't mention to anybody at all who we've got here. It's a military secret. What is he doing now?'

'He asked for a little tobacco. He's sitting in the guard-room and behaving as contentedly as if he were at home. "It's very cosy and warm in here," he said, "and your stove doesn't smoke. I like being here with you very much. But if the stove should smoke, have the chimney swept. But only in the afternoon and never when the sun's right over it." '

'That's very cunning of him,' said the sergeant, his voice full of enthusiasm. 'He acts as though it didn't concern him. And yet he knows that he'll be shot. We must respect a man like that, even if he is our enemy. A man like that goes to certain death. I don't know whether we would be capable of it in his place. We might perhaps waver or give in, but he sits there calmly and says: "It's very cosy and warm in here and your stove doesn't smoke." That's character, lance-corporal. For that you need iron nerves, self-denial, firmness and enthusiasm. . . . If there were enthusiasm like that in Austria . . . but don't let's talk about that. After all, even we have our enthusiasts. Did you read in *Národní Politika* of that Lieutenant Berger of the artillery who climbed up on a high fir tree and set up an observation post on its branches? When our men retreated he couldn't climb down any more, otherwise he would have been taken prisoner. And so he waited there until our troops drove the enemy out again and it took fourteen days. He was fourteen whole days on top of that tree and so as not to die of hunger he gnawed away the whole crown of the tree and fed himself on little shoots and needles. And when our men arrived he had grown so weak that he couldn't keep himself up on the top any longer and fell down and killed himself. He was posthumously decorated with the Golden Cross of Merit for valour.'

And the sergeant added solemnly: 'That was a sacrifice, lance-corporal, that was heroism! Now see how we've got lost in talking again. Run and order that lunch and meanwhile send the man to me.'

The lance-corporal brought in Švejk and the sergeant motioned him in a friendly way to sit down. Then he started to ask him first of all whether he had any parents.

'No. I haven't.'

It occurred to the sergeant immediately that it was better so, because at least there would be nobody to mourn the unfortunate man. He looked at the good-natured face of Švejk and in a fit of good humour suddenly patted him on the back, leant towards him and asked him in a fatherly tone:

'Well, and how do you like being in Bohemia?'

'I like it everywhere in Bohemia,' answered Švejk. 'On my journey I found very good people everywhere.'

The sergeant nodded his head in agreement: 'Our people are very good and well behaved. A theft or a brawl here or there doesn't affect the overall picture. I've been here already fifteen years and if I reckon up I can say that every year there's only about three quarters of a murder.'

'You mean an uncompleted murder?' asked Švejk.

'No, I don't mean that. In the course of fifteen years we've investigated only eleven murders. Of those five were murders with robbery and the remaining six were just the ordinary kind which are of no importance.'

The sergeant was silent and returned to his interrogation method: 'What did you want to do in Budějovice?'

'Take up my duty in the 91st regiment.'

The sergeant ordered Švejk back to the guard-room and then quickly, so that he should not forget, he added the following entry to his report to the district gendarmerie commander in Písek: 'Having a complete mastery of Czech, he planned to enrol in the 91st infantry regiment in České Budějovice.'

The sergeant rubbed his hands joyfully, delighting in the wealth of collected material and the accurate results of his method of investigation. He recalled his predecessor, Sergeant Bürger, who never spoke with a detainee at all, never asked him anything, but sent him at once to the district court with a short report: 'According to the information of the lance-corporal this man has been detained as a vagabond and beggar.' Was that an investigation?

And the sergeant, looking at the pages of his report, smiled with satisfaction and took out of his writing desk a secret instruction of the gendarmerie headquarters in Prague stamped as usual: '*Strictly confidential!*' and read it over to himself again:

All gendarmerie stations are strictly enjoined to keep exceptionally careful watch on all persons passing through their district. As a result of the movement of our troops in Eastern Galicia some Russian units have crossed the Carpathians and taken up positions within the confines of our Empire, as a consequence of which the front has been pushed deeper to the west of the Monarchy. Thanks to this new situation and to the fluidity of the front, Russian spies have been able to penetrate deeper into the territory of our Monarchy, above all in Silesia and Moravia, from where, according to confidential information, a large number of Russian intelligence agents have found their way into Bohemia. It has been ascertained that among them are many Russian Czechs educated in the higher military staff schools of Russia. They speak perfect Czech and appear to be especially dangerous intelligence agents, because they can and do disseminate treasonable propaganda among the Czech population. The regional High Command therefore orders that all suspicious elements should be detained and that vigilance must be increased particularly in those places which have in their vicinity garrisons, military centres and stations through which army trains pass. Those detained must be subject to an immediate examination and passed on to a higher authority.

Sergeant Flanderka again smiled with a satisfied smile and put the secret instruction away with other documents into the file with the inscription: '*Secret Orders*'.

There were many of them, which the Ministry of the Interior drew up with the collaboration of the Ministry of Regional Defence, to which the gendarmerie was subordinated.

The regional headquarters of the gendarmerie in Prague could not cope with their duplication and distribution.

There were:

Orders for the control of the attitude of the local population.

Directives on how to converse with the local inhabitants and elicit from them what influence the news from the front had on their attitude.

A questionnaire on how the local population reacted to the war loans which had been issued and the collections which had been instituted.

A questionnaire on the morale of those called up and those who were to be called up.

A questionnaire on the morale of the members of the local government and the intelligentsia.

An order for the immediate supply of information about the political party affiliations of the local population and the strength of the various political parties.

An order for the control of the activity of the leaders of the local political parties and information on the degree of loyalty of certain political parties represented in the local population.

A questionnaire on what newspapers, journals and brochures came to the district of the gendarmerie station.

Instructions on how to obtain information on the contacts of people suspected of disloyalty and what their disloyalty consisted in.

Instructions on how to recruit paid denouncers and informers among the local population.

Instructions for paid informers from the local population who were officially registered at the gendarmerie station.

Every day brought new instructions, directives, questionnaires and orders.

Swamped with this flood of inventions emanating from the Austrian Ministry of the Interior, Sergeant Flanderka had amassed an enormous backlog of unprocessed papers and answered the questionnaires in a stereotyped way: everything was in perfect order here and the loyalty of the local population could be graded I.a.

The Austrian Ministry of the Interior invented the following grades for unshakeable loyalty to the monarchy: I.a, I.b, I.c; II.a, II.b, II.c; III.a, III.b, III.c; IV.a, IV.b, IV.c. The last fours in Roman figures meant, in conjunction with 'a', treason and the gallows, with 'b', internment, with 'c', 'keep under observation and behind bars'.

In the sergeant's desk were all sorts of printed papers and lists. The government wanted to know what every citizen thought about it.

Sergeant Flanderka would often wring his hands in desperation over these printed circulars which grew inexorably with every post. As soon as he saw the familiar envelopes with the stamps, 'Official – Postage free', his heart always began to thump and at night, pondering over it all, he came to the conviction that he would not live to see the end of the war; the regional command of the gendarmerie would deprive him of his last remnant of reason and he would not be able to enjoy

the victory of the Austrian arms, since by then he would certainly be completely off his nut. And the district command bombarded him daily with questions as to why questionnaire no. $\frac{72345}{721\,af}$ d had not been answered, what action had been taken on instruction no. $\frac{88\,992}{822gfeh}$ z, and what were the practical results of directive no. $\frac{123456}{1922bir}$ V etc.

He had the greatest trouble over the instructions on how to recruit paid denouncers and informers from the local population. Finally, as he considered it impossible to find anyone in the region of Blata, where the people had very thick skulls, he hit on the idea of taking into his service the village herdsman. He was a village idiot who always jumped in the air when people called out to him: 'Pepek, ups-a-daisy!' He was one of those unfortunate figures whom nature and humanity have neglected, a cripple, who for a few guilders yearly and a little food pastured the village cattle.

And so the sergeant had him fetched and said to him: 'Do you know, Pepek, who old Procházka is?'

'Meaeaea,' Pepek bleated.

'Don't bleat but remember that this is how they call His Imperial Majesty. You know who His Imperial Majesty is?'

'That's Sperial Madesty.'

'Well done, Pepek! Now remember that when you go begging for food from house to house, if you should hear anybody say that His Imperial Majesty is an ox or something like that, then come and inform me at once. You'll get six kreutzers. And if you hear anyone say that we shan't win the war, then you must come to me, you understand, and tell me who said it. Then I'll give you another six kreutzers. But if I hear you're concealing something from me, then it'll be all up with you. I'll have you arrested and sent off to Písek. And, now, ups-a-daisy!' When Pepek had jumped, he gave him twelve kreutzers and happily wrote a report to the district gendarmerie command saying that he had recruited an informer.

The next day the vicar came to him and told him in secret that that very morning outside the village he had met the village herdsman, Pepek Vyskoč, who had told him: 'Your reverence, the sergeant told me yesterday that His Sperial Madesty is an ox and that we shan't win the war. Meaeaea. Ups-a-daisy!'

After further explanation and discussion with the priest Sergeant Flanderka had the village herdsman arrested. Afterwards Pepek was condemned at the Hradčany to twelve years' imprisonment for treasonable subversion, incitement, lese-majesty and several other crimes and offences.

He conducted himself in court as he did on the pastures or among his neighbours. In reply to all questions he bleated like a goat and after the sentence had been pronounced he uttered the sounds: 'Meaeaea. Ups-a-daisy!' and jumped. For this he was given the disciplinary punishment of a hard bunk, solitary confinement and three days' fast.

From that time onwards the gendarmerie sergeant had no informer and had to content himself with inventing one, giving him a fictitious name and raising his own salary by fifty crowns a month, which he spent on drink in The Old Tom Cat. When he had drunk his tenth glass he had a fit of conscience, the beer grew bitter in his mouth and he always heard from his neighbours the same remark: 'Today our sergeant is rather sad, as though he wasn't in a good mood.' Then he went home and after he had left somebody always said: 'Our men must have been caught with their pants down in Serbia somewhere. That's why the sergeant hasn't got anything to say.'

But at home the sergeant could at least fill in one more questionnaire: 'The mood of the population: I.a.'

There were often long sleepless nights for the sergeant. He was always expecting an inspection or an investigation. At night he dreamed of the hangman's rope, how they were taking him to the gallows and how finally at the end the Minister of Regional Defence himself asked him right under the gallows: 'Sergeant, where is your answer to circular no. $\frac{1789678}{23792}$ $X.Y.Z.$?'

And now! It was as if the old German hunting greeting: 'Weidmannsheil!' resounded from all the corners of the gendarmerie station. And Sergeant Flanderka had no doubt that the district commander would pat him on the back and say: 'Sergeant, I congratulate you.'

The sergeant painted in his mind other alluring pictures which had taken shape in some corner of his official brain: decoration, accelerated promotion to the highest rank, appreciation of his criminological capabilities opening the way to a brilliant career.

He called the lance-corporal and asked him: 'Did you get the lunch?'

'They brought him smoked ham with cabbages and dumplings. The soup was already off. He's drunk his tea and wants another cup.'

'Let him have it!' the sergeant agreed magnanimously. 'When he's drunk it, bring him to me.'

'Well then now. Did you enjoy it?' the sergeant asked, when half an hour later the lance-corporal brought in Švejk, who was replete and happy as always.

'It wasn't so bad, sergeant. I could have done with a little more of that cabbage. But never mind! I know you were not prepared for it. The smoked ham was well smoked. It must have been home-smoked from a pig which had been home-reared. The tea with the rum did me good too.'

The sergeant looked at Švejk and began: 'Is it true that in Russia they drink a lot of tea? Have they got rum there also?'

'You can find rum all over the world, sergeant.'

'Don't quibble,' thought the sergeant to himself. 'You ought to have paid more attention before to what you were saying!' And, leaning towards Švejk, he asked him in a confidential tone: 'Are there pretty girls in Russia?'

'You can find pretty girls all over the world, sergeant.'

'Oh, you bastard!' thought the sergeant to himself once more. 'You'd give anything to get out of this now.' And the sergeant came out with his forty-two pounder.

'What did you want to do in the 91st regiment?'

'I wanted to go with them to the front.'

The sergeant looked at Švejk with satisfaction and observed: 'That's right. That's the best way of getting to Russia.'

'Indeed, very well thought out.' The sergeant glowed with satisfaction, observing what effect his words had on Švejk.

But he could not read from the expression of Švejk's eyes anything except the most complete calm.

'This fellow doesn't bat an eyelid,' the sergeant thought to himself in alarm. 'That's their military training. If I were in his situation and someone were saying this to me my knees would begin to shake . . .'

'Tomorrow we'll take you off to Písek,' he mentioned casually. 'Have you ever been to Písek?'

'In 1910 at the Imperial manoeuvres.'

After this answer the sergeant's smile was still more friendly and triumphant. He felt in his heart that he had excelled himself with his system of questioning.

'Did you go through all the manoeuvres?'

'Of course I did, sergeant, as an infantryman.' And then again just as calmly as before Švejk looked at the sergeant, who squirmed with pleasure and could hardly stop himself from immediately making a report of it. He called the lance-corporal to take Švejk away and completed his report: 'His plan was as follows: to insinuate himself into the ranks of the 91st infantry regiment, to volunteer at once for the front and at the first opportunity get to Russia, because he realized that any other way back would be impossible owing to the vigilance of our security organs. That he would have been able to get on very well in the 91st infantry regiment is quite understandable, because by his own admission he confessed after a further cross-examination that in 1910 he took part in all the Imperial manoeuvres in the region of Písek, as an infantryman. From this it is clear that he is very able in his profession. I should like to add that the indictments which I have collected are the result of my own system of cross-examination.'

The lance-corporal appeared in the door: 'Sergeant, he wants to go to the rears.'

'Fix bayonets!' the sergeant decided. 'But wait a moment! No, bring him here.'

'You want to go to the rears?' said the sergeant in a friendly tone. 'Isn't there something else behind this?' and he focused his gaze on Švejk's face.

'Honestly, it's only a question of number two, sergeant,' answered Švejk.

'To make sure there's nothing else behind it,' the sergeant repeated significantly, girding himself with his official revolver, 'I shall accompany you there myself!'

'This is a very good revolver,' he said to Švejk on the way. 'Seven shots and it shoots very accurately.'

But before they went out into the courtyard he called the lance-corporal and said to him mysteriously: 'You must fix bayonets and when he's inside station yourself at the back of the rear, so that he doesn't dig himself a tunnel out through the dung pit.'

The latrine was the usual small wooden shack, standing despondently in the middle of the yard over a pit full of dung water, which oozed out of the heap of manure near by.

It was already an old veteran, into which whole generations had discharged their bodily needs. Now Švejk sat inside it, holding with one hand the door by the cord, while behind him through the window the lance-corporal watched his hind quarters in case he should dig himself out.

And on the door were fixed the hawk-like eyes of the gendarmerie sergeant who was considering into which leg he should shoot if Švejk attempted to escape.

But the door calmly opened and there emerged a satisfied Švejk who remarked to the sergeant:

'I hope I wasn't too long inside? I hope I haven't kept you waiting?'

'Oh, not at all, not at all,' answered the sergeant, thinking in his mind: 'What polite, decent people they are. He knows what's in store for him, but all honour to him. Up to the last he's a gentleman. Would one of our own people be the same in his place?'

In the gendarmerie station the sergeant went on sitting next to Švejk on the empty bunk of the gendarme Rampa, who was on duty until the next morning. He had to go the rounds of the villages and at that very moment was sitting peacefully in The Black Horse in Protivín

playing mariáš with the master cobblers and explaining in the intervals that Austria was bound to win.

The sergeant lit his pipe and offered Švejk to fill his, the lance-corporal put a log in the stove, and the gendarmerie station changed into the most agreeable spot on the globe, into a quiet corner, a warm nest in the approaching winter twilight when it was time for friendly chat.

Nevertheless no one spoke. The sergeant was pursuing a certain line of thought and at last expressed it, turning to the lance-corporal: 'In my view it's not right to hang spies. A man who sacrifices himself for his duty, for his, let us say, fatherland, ought to be dispatched in an honourable fashion, with powder and lead. What do you think, lance-corporal?'

'Certainly he should only be shot and not hanged,' the lance-corporal agreed. 'Let's say that they sent us and told us: "You must find out how many machine-guns the Russians have in their machine-gun detachment." And then we had to disguise ourselves and go. Why should they have to hang me like some robber and murderer?'

The lance-corporal got so excited that he stood up and called out: 'I insist on being shot and buried with full military honours.'

'But the snag is,' said Švejk, 'that if a chap's clever nobody can ever prove anything against him.'

'Oh yes they can!' said the sergeant emphatically, 'if they are clever too and have *their method*. You'll see for yourself.

'You'll see,' he repeated in a placid tone and gave a friendly smile. 'No one succeeds in wriggling out of it with us, do they, lance-corporal?'

The lance-corporal nodded in agreement and mentioned that in the case of some people the game was already up in advance and even a mask of complete calm would not help, because the calmer anyone seemed to be the more it was proof against him.

'You are of my school,' the sergeant affirmed proudly. 'Calm, that's a soap bubble. And artificial calm is a *corpus delicti*.' And breaking off the exposition of his theory he turned to the lance-corporal and asked: 'What are we going to have for dinner tonight?'

'Aren't you going to the pub tonight, sergeant?'

With this question there arose for the sergeant a new and difficult problem which had to be solved at once.

What if the man were to take advantage of his absence during the night and run away? The lance-corporal was of course a reliable man and careful, but two tramps already had escaped from him. In fact it had happened because he had not wanted to trudge with them in winter through the snow all the way to Písek, and so he set them free in the fields near Ražice and fired a shot into the air *pro forma*.

'We'll send our old woman to fetch us dinner and she can also bring us beer in a jug,' said the sergeant, solving the difficult problem. 'Let the old woman run about a bit.'

And old Pejzlerka, who served them as a charwoman, certainly did run about.

After dinner the path between the gendarmerie station and The Old

Tom Cat was busy the whole time. The unusually frequent footmarks of the heavy big boots of old Pejzlerka on this connecting line indicated that the sergeant was compensating himself fully for his absence from The Old Tom Cat.

And when old Pejzlerka finally appeared at the bar with the message

that the sergeant sent his compliments and would like a bottle of kontušovka[1] sent up to him the landlord could not control his curiosity.

'Who have they got there?' old Pejzlerka answered. 'Why – some suspicious individual. Just before I went away they both had their arms round his neck and the sergeant was stroking him on the head and saying to him: "My lovely Slav bastard, my little spy!"'

And when it was already long past midnight the lance-corporal fell asleep, stretched out on his bunk in full uniform and snoring deeply.

Opposite him sat the sergeant with the rest of the kontušovka at the bottom of the bottle. He had his arm round Švejk's neck, tears ran

1. A kind of Polish vodka.

down his tanned cheeks and his whiskers were stuck together with
kontušovka. He jabbered: 'Say that in Russia they haven't got such
good kontušovka as this! Say it, so I can go to bed in peace! Confess it
like a man!'

'They haven't.'

The sergeant rolled over on to Švejk.

'You've made me happy. You've confessed. That's how it should be
at a cross-examination. If I'm guilty, why should I deny it?'

He got up and staggering into his room with the empty bottle
babbled: 'If he hadn't taken the wrong t-t-turning everything might
have been di-different.'

Before he threw himself on to his bed in his uniform he took out of
his writing-desk his report and tried to supplement it with the following material:

'I must add in addition that Russian kontušovka on the basis of
paragraph fifty-six . . .' He made a blot and licked it. Smiling idiotically, he threw himself on the bed and fell asleep like a log.

In the morning the lance-corporal, lying on his bed by the opposite
wall, started such a snoring, accompanied by a whistling in the nose,
that it woke Švejk up. He got up, shook the lance-corporal and went
back to bed. But already the cocks had begun to crow, and when afterwards the sun came up, old Pejzlerka, who had also overslept as a result
of her nocturnal running about, came to light the stoves, she found the
door open and everything plunged in deep slumber. The paraffin lamp
in the guard-room was still smoking. Old Pejzlerka raised the alarm,
pulled the lance-corporal and Švejk out of bed and said to the lance-
corporal: 'Aren't you ashamed of going to bed fully dressed like one of
the Lord's cattle?' and she reminded Švejk that he might at least do up
his fly buttons when he saw a woman.

Finally she energetically urged the sleepy lance-corporal to go and
wake the sergeant, since it was not decent for people to sleep so long.

'You've certainly fallen into fine hands,' the old woman grumbled to
Švejk, when the lance-corporal went to wake the sergeant. 'One's as
big a boozer as the other. They'd booze away their nose between their
eyes. They owe me my wages for three years and when I remind them
of it the sergeant always says: "Be quiet, old woman, or I'll have you
put in gaol: we know your son's a poacher and steals wood from the
estate." And so I have been martyring myself with them for four years
now.' The old woman gave a deep sigh and went on grumbling. 'Be

sure to be on your guard with that sergeant. He's as oily as you make them and a first-class bastard into the bargain. Whenever he can he'll do anyone down and have them put in gaol.'

The sergeant was very difficult to wake up. The lance-corporal had hard work convincing him that it was already morning.

Finally he surfaced, rubbed his eyes and began to have a vague memory of what had happened the night before. Suddenly there came to him a frightful thought, to which he gave expression, looking uncertainly at the lance-corporal: 'Has he run away?'

'Why, of course not. He's an honest fellow.'

The lance-corporal began to walk up and down the room, looked out of the window, came back again, tore a piece of paper from the newspapers on the table and rolled a paper pellet out of it between his fingers. It was obvious that he wanted to say something.

The sergeant looked at him in some uncertainty and at last, to confirm for certain what he only suspected, he said: 'I'll help you, lance-corporal. Yesterday I suppose I made an exhibition of myself again, didn't I?'

The lance-corporal looked reproachfully at his superior: 'If you knew, sergeant, all you said yesterday and the sort of conversation you had with him.'

Bending close to the sergeant's ear, he whispered: 'You said that all of us, Czechs and Russians, are of the same Slav blood; that Nikolai Nikolaevich[1] will be in Přerov next week; that Austria can't hold out, and that, when he is interrogated again, he must deny everything and talk nonsense so as to be able to hold out till the Cossacks come and free him; that it must come to breaking point very soon; that it will be just like it was during the Hussite wars; the peasants will come with their flails to Vienna; that His Imperial Majesty is a feeble old dotard and will kick the bucket very soon; that Kaiser Wilhelm is a reptile, and that you'll send him money in gaol to improve his conditions and many other things like that . . .'

The lance-corporal moved away from the sergeant: 'I can remember all that very well, because to begin with I was only a little tipsy. After that I got completely sozzled too and I don't know any more.'

The sergeant looked at the lance-corporal.

'But what I can remember,' he declared, 'is that you said that we're

1. The Grand Duke Nicholas who was commander-in-chief of the Russian armed forces.

pigmies compared with the Russians and that you shouted out in front of our old woman: "Long live Russia!"'

The lance-corporal began to walk nervously up and down the room.

'You bellowed like a bull,' said the sergeant, 'and then you threw yourself on to the bed and began to snore.'

The lance-corporal stopped by the window and drumming with his fingers on it declared: 'Sergeant, you didn't exactly keep your mouth shut in front of our old woman either and I remember how you said to her: "Remember, old woman, that every emperor and king thinks only of his own pocket, and that's why they wage war, even if it's only an old dotard like old Procházka,[1] whom they can't let out of the rears in case he should shit up the whole of Schönbrunn."'

'You mean to say I said that?'

'Yes, sergeant, you said that, before you went out into the courtyard to vomit, and into the bargain you shouted: "Old woman, stick your finger down my throat!"'

'You said some fine things too,' the sergeant interrupted him, 'when you hit on the stupid idea that Nikolai Nikolaevich would be King of Bohemia.'

'I don't remember that,' the lance-corporal said timidly.

'Of course you wouldn't remember it. You were absolutely pickled. You had pig's eyes and when you wanted to go outside, you climbed up the stove instead of going through the door.'

Neither of them spoke until the sergeant broke the long silence: 'I've always told you that alcohol is death. You can't take much and yet you drink. What would have happened if he had run away? How could we have explained it? O God, my head's splitting.

'I tell you, lance-corporal,' the sergeant went on, 'that just because he didn't run away it's quite clear what a dangerous and cunning fellow he is. When they come to cross-examine him he'll say that the door was open the whole night, that we were drunk and that he could have run away a thousand times if he had felt guilty. It's a piece of luck that they won't believe a fellow like him and when we say under official oath that it's all a fabrication and an impudent lie on his part, not even the Lord God himself will help him and he'll have another article of the law round his neck. In his case of course it doesn't make much difference. If only my head didn't ache so much!'

1. Czech nickname for Emperor Franz Joseph.

There was a silence. After a moment the sergeant said: 'Get hold of our old woman.'

'Listen, old woman,' said the sergeant to Pejzlerka, looking her sternly in the eye, 'go and collect a crucifix on a stand from somewhere and bring it here.'

Pejzlerka's questioning look produced an explosion on the part of the sergeant: 'You'd better make sharp!'

The sergeant took out of the table drawer two candles on which there were traces of the sealing wax which he used to seal official documents, and when in fear and trembling Pejzlerka finally came in with the crucifix the sergeant put the cross between both candles on the edge of the table, lit the candles and said in a solemn voice: 'Sit down, old woman.'

The terror-stricken Pejzlerka sank down on the sofa and looked wild-eyed at the sergeant, the candles and the crucifix. Panic seized her and as she had her hands on her apron you could see that they were trembling with her knees.

The sergeant walked gravely round her and stopping a second time in front of her announced in a solemn voice: 'Yesterday evening you witnessed a great event, old woman. It may well be that your feeble mind cannot grasp it. That soldier is an intelligence officer, a spy, old woman.'

'Jesus Mary,' shrieked Pejzlerka. 'Dear Holy Virgin from Skočice!'

'Quiet, old woman! In order to get something out of him we had to say. various things to him. You heard what strange things we said, didn't you?'

'Yes, sir, I did,' Pejzlerka whispered with a quaking voice.

'But everything we said, old woman, was only designed to make him confess, to make him trust us. And we succeeded. We got everything out of him we wanted. We trapped him.'

The sergeant interrupted his address for a moment to adjust the wick on the candles and then he continued gravely, looking severely at Pejzlerka: 'You were present and you are initiated into the whole secret. This secret is an official one. And you must not say a single word about it to anyone. Not even on your deathbed, otherwise they wouldn't be allowed to bury you in the churchyard.'

'Jesus, Mary, Joseph,' whined Pejzlerka, 'why was I so unfortunate ever to set foot here!'

'Don't howl, old woman. Get up. Approach the crucifix. Put up the two fingers of your right hand. You will take an oath. Speak after me!'

Pejzlerka staggered to the table incessantly moaning: 'Virgin Mary of Skočice, why did I ever set foot here.'

And the careworn face of Christ looked down on her from the cross, the candles smoked and everything appeared dreadful and unearthly to Pejzlerka. She was completely lost, her knees knocked and her hands trembled.

She raised the two fingers of her hand and the sergeant solemnly and emphatically recited for her to repeat: 'I swear before God Almighty and you, sergeant, that I shall never to the day of my death mention a word of what I have heard and seen here, even if I were asked by anybody about it. So help me God.

'And now kiss the crucifix too, old woman,' the sergeant ordered, when Pejzlerka had taken the oath to the accompaniment of terrible sobbing and had crossed herself devoutly.

'And now you can take the crucifix back to where you borrowed it from and tell them I needed it for a cross-examination!'

The shattered Pejzlerka went out from the room on tip-toe with the crucifix and from the window she could be seen continually looking back at the gendarmerie station, as though she wanted to convince herself that this was not merely a dream, but that just a moment ago she had really lived through the most ghastly experience in her whole life.

The sergeant meanwhile re-wrote his report, which he had supplemented the night before with the blots he had tried to lick away together with the handwriting, just as if there had been jam on the paper.

Now he re-wrote it completely and remembered that he had not asked one question. He summoned Švejk and asked him: 'Do you know how to take photographs?'

'Yes, I do.'

'Then why don't you have a camera with you?'

'Because I don't have one,' came the honest and clear answer.

'And if you had had one would you have taken photographs?' the sergeant asked.

'If ifs and ans were pots and pans,' Švejk answered simply, and calmly endured the puzzled expression on the face of the sergeant, whose head had just then begun to ache again so that he could not think out any other question except: 'Is it difficult to photograph a station?'

'Easier than anything else,' answered Švejk, 'because it doesn't move but always stands in the same place and you don't have to tell it to smile.'

The sergeant was then able to supplement his report as follows: 'To report no. 2172, I have the honour to add . . .'

And the sergeant went on writing: 'Among other things during my cross-examination he confessed that he knew how to take photographs and that he liked best photographing stations. It is true that no camera was found on him, but one can presume that he has it hidden somewhere and therefore doesn't carry it on him, so as to divert attention away from himself, which is supported by the evidence of his own confession that he would photograph if he had a camera on him.'

The sergeant, having a terrible head after the night before, got more and more mixed up in his report about the photographing and went on writing: 'It is clear that by his own confession only the fact that he didn't have a camera on him prevented him from photographing the station buildings and places of strategic importance in general, and it is indisputable that he would have done so, if he had had that relevant photographic instrument on him which he had hidden somewhere. It is only thanks to the fact that he did not have a camera handy that no photographs were found on him.'

'That's enough,' said the sergeant and signed it.

He was completely satisfied with his work and read it to the lance-corporal with great pride.

'That's a success,' he said to the lance-corporal. 'There you are, that's the way to write reports! Everything must be put in. A cross-examination, my friend, is not a simple matter, and the main thing is that everything is put neatly into the report so that the people at the top are so foxed by it that their eyes boggle. Bring our man in so that we can finish with him.

'And so now the lance-corporal will take you away to the district gendarmerie command at Písek,' he said gravely to Švejk. 'According to the regulations you ought really to be put in handcuffs. But because I think you're a decent fellow we shan't do that. I'm sure you won't try to escape on the way.'

Obviously touched by the sight of Švejk's good-natured face the sergeant added: 'And I hope you won't think badly of me. Take him away, lance-corporal. Here you have the report.'

'Then goodbye and God speed,' added Švejk gently. 'Thank you, sergeant, for everything you've done for me. When I have the chance I'll write to you and if I should ever come round here again I'll drop in on you.'

Švejk went out with the lance-corporal on to the road and anyone who had met them, engaged as they were in friendly conversation, might have taken them for old friends who by chance were going the same way to the town, perhaps to the church.

'I never imagined,' Švejk was saying, 'that the way to Budějovice would involve such difficulties. It reminds me of the case of the butcher Chaura from Kobylisy. Once in the night he came to Palacký's monument at Moráň and went round and round it until morning, because he thought that the wall didn't have any end. He was quite out of his mind about it and by morning he couldn't go on any more and began to shout: "Help, police!" When the cops came he asked them the way to Kobylisy saying that he'd already been walking around a wall for five hours and there was no end to it yet. And so they took him with them and he smashed everything in solitary confinement in his cell.'

The lance-corporal did not say a word but thought to himself: 'What yarns you're spinning! You're starting with your fairy tales about Budějovice again.'

They walked past a lake and Švejk asked the lance-corporal with some interest whether there were many poachers of fish in the region.

'Here everyone's a poacher,' answered the lance-corporal. 'They wanted to throw the last sergeant into the water. The water bailiff on the dam keeps on shooting bristles into their backsides, but it doesn't help. They carry metal plates in their trousers, you see.'

The lance-corporal started to talk about progress, how quickly people get on to everything, and how people cheat each other. He developed a new theory that the war was a great blessing for humanity, because in the battles not only good people were shot but lots of rogues and bastards too.

'In any case there are too many people in the world,' he said reflectively. 'Each one's breathing down the other's neck and it's awful how humanity breeds.'

They approached a roadside pub.

'It's blowing bloody awful,' said the lance-corporal. 'I think that a wee dram won't do us any harm. Don't tell anybody I'm taking you to Písek. It's a state secret.'

Before the eyes of the lance-corporal there danced the instructions of the central authorities about suspicious and conspicuous people and of the duties of every gendarmerie station: 'Keep them away from all contact with the local population and take strict care that on their way to a higher authority there are no unnecessary conversations in the region.'

'It mustn't be let out who you are,' the lance-corporal said again. 'What you've done is nobody's business. We mustn't allow panic to spread. Panic's a very bad thing in these times of war,' he continued. 'You say something and it spreads like an avalanche over the whole region. Do you understand?'

'Well, I shan't spread any panic,' said Švejk, and he was as good as his word, because when the landlord talked to him, he said emphatically: 'My brother here says we'll be in Písek at one o'clock.'

'And so your brother's got leave?' the inquisitive pub-keeper asked the lance-corporal, who without batting an eyelid had the cheek to answer brazenly: 'Today's his last day!'

'We bamboozled him all right,' he said, smiling to Švejk, when the pub-keeper ran out somewhere. 'Only no panic of any kind. It's wartime.'

When the lance-corporal before going into the roadside pub declared that a wee dram would do no harm, he was an optimist, because he forgot about the quantity, and when he had drunk twelve he stated quite firmly that until three o'clock the commander of the district gendarmerie station would be at lunch and that it was useless to come there earlier and in addition a blizzard was starting. If they reached Písek by four o'clock in the afternoon it would be loads of time. Even six would be time enough. It would be dark anyhow as you could see by the weather that day. It was all the same whether they went now or later. Písek couldn't run away.

'Let's be glad that we sit in a warm place,' was his decisive word. 'Out there in the trenches in stinking weather like this those chaps go through a lot more than we do sitting by the stove.'

The big old stove glowed with heat and the lance-corporal found that one could very well top up the outer warmth with an inner warmth attained through the help of various sweet and potent spirits, as they say in Galicia.

In this isolated spot the landlord had eight kinds of spirit; he was bored to death and drank to the sound of the wailing wind which whistled behind every corner of the building.

The lance-corporal went on inviting the landlord to keep in step with him, accusing him of drinking too little, which was obviously an injustice, because he could hardly stand on his legs and wanted all the time to play färbl. He maintained that in the night he had heard gun-fire from the east, upon which the lance-corporal hiccupped: 'Only no panic, for God's sake! About that there are in- in- instructions.'

And he went on to explain that instructions were a collection of immediate orders. In doing so he betrayed some secret directives. But the landlord no longer understood anything. He was only capable of stating that the war could not be won by instructions.

It was already dark when the lance-corporal decided that he and Švejk would now set off on the road to Písek. In the blizzard they could not see more than a step or two in front of them and the lance-corporal kept on saying: 'Go on following your nose until Písek.'

When he had said this for the third time his voice no longer sounded from the road but from somewhere below, where he had slipped down the slope on the snow. With the help of his rifle he scrambled labor-iously up on to the road again. Švejk heard him giggling to himself: 'Skating rink.' After a time he could not be heard any more on the road, because he had again slipped down the slope and was bawling so loud that he drowned the wind: 'I'm falling. Panic!'

The lance-corporal was transformed into a busy ant, which when-ever it falls down anywhere stubbornly tries to climb up again.

Five times the lance-corporal repeated his excursion down the slope and when he was again at Švejk's side he said helplessly and desperately: 'I could easily lose you.'

'Don't be afraid, lance-corporal,' said Švejk. 'We'll get on best if we fasten ourselves together. Then neither of us can lose the other: Have you got handcuffs with you?'

'Every gendarme must always carry handcuffs on him,' said the lance-corporal firmly, stumbling around Švejk. 'That's our daily bread.'

'Then let's link up,' Švejk suggested. 'Why not try?'

With a masterly flick of his hand the lance-corporal fastened the handcuffs to Švejk and the other end of them to the wrist of his right hand; now they were linked together like twins. Stumbling on the road, they could not separate. The lance-corporal dragged Švejk over piles of stones and when he fell down he pulled Švejk down with him. When this happened the handcuffs cut their hands until finally the lance-corporal said that they couldn't go on like this and that he must unfasten them again. After long and vain attempts to free himself and Švejk from the handcuffs he sighed, 'We're linked until kingdom come.'

'Amen,' added Švejk, and they continued their laborious journey.

The lance-corporal was seized with a fit of deep depression and

when late in the evening after terrible trials they got to the gendarmerie headquarters at Písek, he was completely broken and said on the steps: 'Now it'll be frightful. We can't get away from each other.'

And truly it was frightful, when the sergeant sent for the commander of the station, Captain König.

The captain's first words were: 'Breathe on me!

'Now I understand,' said the captain, taking in the situation with his keen experienced nose. 'Rum, kontušovka, čert, jeřabinka, ořechovka, višňovka, vanilková.'[1]

1. Various kinds of schnaps made out of rowan berries, walnuts, cherries, vanilla, etc.

'Sergeant,' he said turning to his subordinate, 'here you see what a gendarme should *not* look like. Conduct like this is an offence on which a court-martial will have to give its verdict. Handcuffing himself to a delinquent! Coming here sozzled, dead drunk. Crawling here like an animal! Take the handcuffs off him!

'Well, what is it?' he said, turning to the lance-corporal who with his free arm was saluting upside down.

'Humbly report, sir, I bring a report.'

'A report on you is going to the court,' said the captain tersely: 'Sergeant, gaol both the men, bring them tomorrow for interrogation, study the report from Putim carefully and send it to me to my house.'

The captain of the gendarmerie at Písek was a very officious man, very thorough in prosecuting his subordinates and outstanding in bureaucratic matters.

In the gendarmerie stations in his district no one could ever say that the storm had passed. It came back with every communication signed by the captain, who spent the whole day issuing reprimands, admonitions and warnings to the whole district.

Ever since the outbreak of war heavy black clouds had loured over the gendarmerie stations in the Písek district.

It was a truly ghostly atmosphere. The thunderbolts of bureaucracy rumbled and struck the gendarmerie sergeants, lance-corporals, men and employees. For every twopenny halfpenny thing there was a disciplinary investigation.

'If we want to win the war,' he said on his inspections of the gendarmerie stations, 'then "a" must be "a", "b" "b"; and everywhere there must be a dot on the "i".'

He felt himself encircled by treason on all sides and was absolutely convinced not only that every gendarme in his district had sins on his conscience as a result of the war, but that everybody at this important time was guilty of some dereliction of duty.

And from above he was bombarded with official communications in which the Ministry of Regional Defence pointed out that according to the information of the Ministry of War soldiers from the Písek district were deserting to the enemy.

And they drove him into testing the loyalty of his district. It looked ghastly. The women from the neighbourhood went to see their husbands off to the war and he knew for certain that their husbands promised them not to let themselves be killed for His Imperial Majesty.

The yellow and black horizon was beginning to become overcast with the clouds of revolution. In Serbia and in the Carpathians battalions went over to the enemy: the 28th and the 11th regiments. In the latter were soldiers from the Písek district and region. In the sultry calm before the storm of the approaching revolution recruits from Vodňany arrived with carnations of black organdie. Soldiers on their way from Prague passed through Písek station and threw back the cigarettes and chocolate which Písek society ladies had given them in their pig trucks.

Then a battalion on its way to the front went past and some Písek Jews bawled out in German: 'God save the Emperor! Down with the Serbs!' They got such a beating up that they could not show themselves in the streets for a week.

And while these episodes took place, showing clearly that when 'God save our Emperor' was played on the organ in the churches it was only a pitiful veneer and universal sham, there came from the gendarmerie stations the familiar answers to the questionnaire *à la* Putim saying that everything was in the best order, that there was no antiwar agitation anywhere and the attitude of the population was I.a, enthusiasm I.a–b.

'You're not gendarmes but village cops,' the gendarmerie captain used to say on his inspections. 'Instead of sharpening your vigilance a thousand per cent you're slowly turning into cattle.'

Having made this zoological discovery, he added: 'You lounge about at home and think: "They can kiss our arses with that war of theirs."'

This was always followed by a list of all the duties of the unfortunate gendarmes, a lecture on the general situation and how to keep everything firmly in hand, so that it should really be as it ought to be. After this description of the glowing image of gendarmerie perfection, aimed at the strengthening of the Austrian monarchy, there followed threats, disciplinary investigations, transfers and oaths.

The captain was firmly convinced that he stood here on guard, that he was preserving something and that all these gendarmes from the gendarmerie stations who were under his orders were a bunch of do-nothing egoists, bastards, crooks for whom nothing else but brandy, beer and wine had any meaning. Because they had low wages they accepted bribes to be able to booze and they were slowly but surely breaking Austria up. The only man he trusted was his own sergeant in the district command, but that sergeant always said at the pub: 'Today that silly old crackpot of ours has been a scream again . . .'

The captain studied the report of the gendarmerie sergeant from Putim about Švejk. Before him stood his gendarmerie sergeant Matějka and thought to himself that as far as he was concerned the captain could go to hell with all his reports because down at the Otava they were waiting for him to take part in a game of 'Schnapsen'.[1]

'I told you last time, Matějka,' the captain said, 'that the biggest bloody fool I've ever known is the gendarmerie sergeant in Protivín, but judging by this report here the sergeant from Putim has gone one better. That soldier, whom that spirit-sodden scoundrel of a lance-corporal brought here, and whom he was linked with like two dogs, is certainly not a spy. He's undoubtedly a common or garden deserter. Here the idiot writes such stupid rubbish that every little child could see at a first glance that he was as tight as a papal prelate.

'Bring that soldier here at once,' he ordered, after he had studied the report from Putim for a while. 'I've never in my life seen such a tissue of bunkum and on top of all this he sends as escort for this suspicious bastard a sod like his own lance-corporal. These people still don't know me. I can be a devil. Until I've made them shit with fright three times a day they seem to think that they can put anything across me.'

The captain began to expatiate on how the gendarmerie nowadays had a negative attitude to all orders and how it was obvious that every sergeant when he wrote his report had a lark with it just to make a bigger mess of things.

When the warning came from above that the possibility could not be excluded of intelligence agents roaming about the countryside, the gendarmerie sergeants began to manufacture them wholesale and if the war lasted any longer it would be a giant madhouse. In the office they must send a telegram to Putim summoning the sergeant to Písek the next day. He'd knock out of his head that 'very important event', which he wrote about at the beginning of his report.

'Which regiment have you deserted from?' were the captain's welcoming words to Švejk.

'I haven't deserted from any regiment.'

The captain looked at Švejk and saw such composure in his calm face that he asked: 'How did you get hold of that uniform?'

1. A card game, also known as 'sixty-six'.

'Every soldier gets a uniform when he's called up,' answered Švejk with a placid smile. 'I serve in the 91st regiment and not only did I not desert from my regiment, but quite the *contrary*.'

He pronounced the word 'contrary' with such emphasis that the captain assumed a piteous expression and asked: 'How do you mean – the *contrary*?'

'It's a terribly simple matter,' Švejk confided. 'I'm going to my regiment, I'm looking for it and not deserting from it. I want nothing better than to get to my regiment as soon as possible. I'm already quite nervy when I think how I'm obviously getting farther and farther away from České Budějovice, and the whole regiment is waiting for me there. The sergeant in Putim showed me on the map that Budějovice is to the south, but instead of sending me there he directed me to the north.'

The captain waved his hand as though meaning to say: 'He perpetrates much worse things than directing people to the north.'

'And so you can't find your regiment?' he said. 'Have you gone to look for it?'

Švejk explained to him the whole situation. He named Tábor and all the places he'd passed through on the way to Budějovice: Milevsko – Květov – Vráž – Malčín – Čížová – Sedlec – Horažd'ovice – Radomyšl – Putim – Štěkno – Strakonice – Volyň – Dub – Vodňany – Protivín and finally Putim again.

With enormous enthusiasm Švejk described his struggle with fate, how he had tried with might and main to get to his 91st regiment at Budějovice disregarding all obstacles and how all his efforts had been in vain.

He spoke passionately and the captain mechanically drew with his pencil on a piece of paper the vicious circle which the good soldier Švejk could not get out of when he set out to join his regiment.

'That was a labour of Hercules,' he said at last, when he had listened with enjoyment to Švejk's description of how irritated he was that it was taking him so long to get to his regiment. 'It must have been a wonderful sight to see you wandering round and round Putim.'

'It could have been decided already then,' Švejk remarked, 'if it hadn't been for that sergeant in that miserable hole. He never asked my name or my regiment and somehow or other everything was frightfully mysterious to him. He should have had me taken away to Budějovice and in the barracks they would have told him whether I was that Švejk who was looking for his regiment or some suspicious individual.

By now I might have already been a whole day with my regiment and be carrying out my military duties.'

'Why didn't you point out in Putim that it was a mistake?'

'Because I saw that it was useless to talk to him. That was what the old pub-keeper Rampa at Vinohrady said when someone wanted to get something from him on tick: there are times when a man is as deaf as a post to everything.'

The captain did not pause long for reflection. He merely concluded that such a round-about journey by a man who wanted to get to his regiment was a sign of the deepest human degeneration and he had the following knocked out on the typewriter in the office, observing all the rules and embellishments of officialese:

To the Illustrious Command of the Imperial and Royal Infantry Regiment no. 91 at České Budějovice.

Enclosed please find Josef Švejk, who according to the statement of the same should be an infantryman of the same regiment, detained on the basis of his statements in Putim, Písek district, by the gendarmerie station under suspicion of desertion. The same asserts that he is making for his above-mentioned regiment. The enclosed has a small stocky figure, a symmetrical face and nose and blue eyes without special characteristics. In annex b.1. is transmitted the account for the messing of the enclosed for kind remittal to the accounts of the Ministry of Regional Defence with the request for confirmation of the receipt of the enclosed. In annex c.1. is sent for confirmation a list of army property which the detained had on him on the day of his arrest.

Švejk's journey from Písek to Budějovice in the train passed off briskly and swiftly. His companion was a young gendarme, a novice whose eyes never left Švejk's face and who was scared to death that Švejk might run away from him. During the whole journey he was trying to solve a difficult problem: 'If I had now to go and do number one or number two, what would I do?'

He solved it by accepting that Švejk must act as his chaperone.

Throughout the whole journey with Švejk, from the station to the Mariánské barracks in Budějovice, he had his eyes fixed convulsively on Švejk, and whenever they came to a corner or to a cross-roads he told Švejk, as though quite casually, how many loaded cartridges they were given for each escort, upon which Švejk answered that he was convinced that no gendarme would shoot anyone on the street, in case he should cause an accident.

The gendarme wrangled with him and in this way they reached the barracks.

On duty in the barracks for the second day was Lieutenant Lukáš. All unsuspecting he sat at his desk in the office, when they suddenly brought Švejk to him with the papers.

'Humbly report, sir, I'm here again,' Švejk said, saluting and putting on a solemn expression.

This whole scene was witnessed by Company Sergeant-Major Kot'átko, who later related that when Švejk announced himself Lieutenant Lukáš jumped up, put his hands to his head and fell backwards on top of Kot'átko, and that when they revived him Švejk, who had been saluting all this time, repeated: 'Humbly report, sir, I'm here again!' Then Lieutenant Lukáš, white as a sheet, took with trembling hands the papers which concerned Švejk, signed them, asked everybody to go out, told the gendarme that everything was all right and locked himself into the office together with Švejk.

And so ended Švejk's Budějovice anabasis. It is certain that if Švejk had been granted liberty of movement he would have got to Budějovice on his own. However much the authorities may boast that it was they who brought Švejk to his place of duty, this is nothing but a mistake. With Švejk's energy and irresistible desire to fight, the authorities' action was like throwing a spanner into the works.

Švejk and Lieutenant Lukáš looked one another straight in the eye.

The lieutenant's eyes had a dreadful, menacing and desperate gleam in them, while Švejk looked at the lieutenant tenderly and kindly, as though he were looking at his dearest one whom he had lost and found again.

In the office it was as still as the grave. Nearby from the corridor someone could be heard walking about. It was some conscientious one-year volunteer, who had had to stay at home because of a cold, as could be told from his voice, since he was giving a very nasal performance of what he had learnt by heart in German: how members of the Imperial Household must be received at fortresses. One could hear clearly: 'As soon as the exalted personages approach the fortress, a salute is to be fired on all bastions and fortifications. The commandant will receive them on horseback with dirk in hand. He will then ride forward.'

'Shut up there,' the lieutenant roared into the corridor. 'Get to hell out of it! If you've got fever, stay at home in bed!'

The eager volunteer could be heard going away and from the end of the corridor was audible the faint echo of his nasal entoning: 'At the moment when the commandant salutes, the firing is to be repeated. It will be repeated a third time when the exalted personages alight.'

And again the lieutenant and Švejk went on staring at each other in silence, until finally Lieutenant Lukáš said with harsh irony: 'Hearty welcome, Švejk, to České Budějovice. He that is born to be hanged will never be drowned. There's already an arrest order out for you and tomorrow you will be at regimental report. I'm not going to be bothered with you any more. I've suffered more than enough from you, and my patience is shattered to smithereens. When I think that I managed to live so long with such a bloody half-wit as you . . .'

He began to walk up and down the office: 'No, it's frightful. Now I'm amazed that I didn't shoot you. What would have happened to me if I had? Absolutely nothing. I'd have been acquitted. Do you realize that?'

'Humbly report, sir, I realize it fully.'

'Don't start again, Švejk, with that bullshit of yours, or something really will happen. In the end we'll put a stop to your tricks once and for all. You have raised your idiocy to the degree of infinity until everything has burst catastrophically.'

Lieutenant Lukáš rubbed his hands: 'It's all up with you, Švejk.' He returned to his table and wrote a few lines on a piece of paper, called the guard in front of the office and ordered him to lead Švejk off to the prison warder and to give him the note.

They led Švejk off across the courtyard and the lieutenant with unconcealed delight watched the prison warder unlock the door with the black and yellow label, 'Regimental arrest'. He saw how Švejk disappeared behind that door and how a moment later the warder emerged from it alone.

'Now, thank the Lord!' the lieutenant thought aloud. 'At last he's there.'

In the dark spaces of the dungeon of the Mariánské barracks Švejk was welcomed cordially by a fat one-year volunteer who was sprawling about on a straw mattress. He was the only prisoner and was bored to death for the second day. To Švejk's question why he was in gaol he answered that it was for nothing. He had boxed the ears of an artillery lieutenant by mistake at night in the square in an archway when he was drunk. Actually he hadn't even boxed his ears but only knocked his cap off. The artillery lieutenant happened to be standing at night under the archway and was apparently waiting for a prostitute. He had his back to him and the volunteer took him for a friend of his, another volunteer called Materna František.

'And he's a little tich, just like him,' he told Švejk, 'so I came up to him nicely from behind and knocked his cap off, saying: "Servus, Franci!" And the bastard was such a bloody fool that he at once started to whistle for the military police and they took me off.

'It may be,' the volunteer admitted, 'that in the course of that scuffle a few blows fell, but I don't think that affects the matter, since it was an obvious case of mistaken identity. He admits himself that I said: "Servus, Franci", and his Christian name is Anton. That's quite clear. The only thing which can get me into trouble is that I ran away from hospital, and if it gets out about that hospital book . . .

'When I joined up,' he went on, 'I first of all rented a room in the town and tried to contract rheumatism. Three times in succession I got myself thoroughly pickled, went and lay down in a ditch outside the town when it was raining, and took my boots off. But that didn't help. And then in the winter I bathed by night in the Malše for a whole week, but I achieved just the opposite results. Old man, I got so hardened that for a whole night I could lie in the snow in the court-yard of the house where I lived, and when the people of the house woke me up in the morning my feet were as warm as if I had been wearing fur slippers. If I had only caught tonsillitis at least, but absolutely nothing came of it. And I couldn't even catch that bloody V.D. Every day I went to The Port Arthur. Some of my colleagues had already got inflammation of the testicles and had their balls cut off, but I still remained immune. It was hellishly bad luck, old man. And then one day at The Rose I met a disabled soldier from Hluboká. He told me to come and see him one Sunday and promised that the next day I'd have legs like cans. At home he had a needle and syringe and really I could hardly get home from Hluboká afterwards. That precious soul hadn't deceived me. And so in the end I got my muscular rheumatism. I was at once taken to the hospital and everything was hunky-dory. And then fortune smiled at me again. My brother-in-law, Dr Masák from Žižkov, was transferred to Budějovice and it's him I have to thank for my being able to stay in hospital so long. He could have spun it out so long as to get me discharged as unfit for service, if I hadn't ruined it with that damned hospital book. The idea was a good one, first class. I got hold of a big book, gummed a label on to it and wrote on it: "Hospital book of the 91st regiment". The headings and so on were all in order. I wrote in false names, temperature readings, diseases, and every afternoon after the doctor's visit I coolly went into the town with this book under my arm. At the gates the Landwehr men were keeping guard and so from that side I was completely secure too. I showed them the book and they even saluted me. Then I went to a chap I knew, an official in the tax office, changed into mufti and went to a pub, where in company I knew we carried on various treasonable conversations. After that I got so cool that I didn't even bother to change into mufti and went in uniform to pubs and about the town. I didn't get back to my bed in the hospital before the early hours and when the patrol stopped me at night I showed them my "Hospital book of the 91st regiment" and after that no one asked me any more. At the gates of the hospital I again silently showed the book and somehow I always managed to get back to my bed. My cheek increased so much that I thought no one could do anything to me. Then came that fatal mistake at night on the square beneath the archway, a mistake that clearly showed that no trees grow all the way up to heaven, old man. Pride goes before a fall. All flesh is as grass and all the glory of man as the flower of grass. Icarus burnt his wings. Man would like to be a giant – and he's nothing but a shit, old man. Don't trust to chance but pinch yourself morning and night to remind yourself that discretion is the better part of valour and that nothing's more harmful than excess. After debauches and orgies there always follows the moral hangover. That's the law of nature, old man. When I think that I ruined my chance of being exempted for life from active service, that I could have been rejected as C3. . . . What a tremendous break! I could have loafed about somewhere in an office in the Reserve Command but my carelessness tripped me up.'

The volunteer solemnly concluded his confession as follows:

'Carthage fell. Nineveh was reduced to ruins, old man, but thumbs up! Don't let anyone imagine that when they send me to the front I'll fire a single shot. Regimental report! Expulsion from the school! Long live Imperial and Royal cretinism! Why should I squat in their school and take their exams? Cadet, ensign, second lieutenant, lieutenant! I'll shit on them! Officers' school! Dealing with those pupils that have to repeat the whole year's course over again! Military paralysis! Should a rifle be carried on the left or right shoulder? How many stars does a corporal have? Checking up on lists of reservists! Himmelherrgott! There's nothing to smoke, old man! Would you like me to teach you to spit on the ceiling? Look, this is how it's done. Wish something while you're doing it and it will be granted. If you like drinking beer I can recommend you the excellent water there in the jug. If you're hungry and you want to enjoy your food I can recommend you the City Club. I advise you to write poetry as a cure against boredom. I've already written an epic:

> 'Is the warder at home? He sleeps the night through.
> We carry the brunt, till we hear from H.Q.
> That the battle is lost.
> And here against the enemy's raid
> From bunks he builds a barricade.
> When he's finished with his wall
> From his lips you hear the story:
> "Austria's might will never fall,
> God preserve its power and glory."

'You see, old man,' the fat volunteer went on, 'to hell with anyone who says that respect for our dear monarchy is disappearing among our people. Here's a man in prison, who has nothing to smoke and is waiting to go on regimental report, and he is giving the finest example of affection for the throne! He pays homage in his songs to his greater fatherland, at a moment when it is threatened with a walloping on all sides. He is deprived of his liberty, but all the same there flow from his lips verses of unswerving devotion. *Morituri te salutant, Caesar!* The dead salute you, Caesar, but the warder's a bastard. You've got bloody good menials in your service. The day before yesterday I gave him five crowns to buy me cigarettes and the bloody swine told me this morning that smoking was forbidden, that he would get into trouble if he' did what I asked and that he'd return those five crowns to me when he got his pay. Yes, old man, I don't believe anything nowadays. The best slogans are turned upside down. Robbing prisoners! And into the bargain the bastard sings the whole day: "Where people sing you can sleep without wrongs. Folk who are wrong-uns have no songs!" Hound, gutter-snipe, scoundrel, traitor!'

The volunteer now asked Švejk what was his offence.

'You were trying to find your regiment?' he said. 'That must have been some hunt. Tábor, Milevsko, Květov, Vráž, Malčín, Čížová, Sedlec, Horažd'ovice, Radomyšl, Putim, Štěkno, Strakonice, Volyň, Dub, Vodňany, Protivín, Putim, Písek, Budějovice. A thorny path! And tomorrow you're on regimental report too? Brother, we'll meet together on the execution ground. Then our Colonel Schröder will have something to chuckle about. You've got no idea how worked up he gets by regimental affairs. He flies round the yard like a mad bloodhound and sticks his tongue out like a dying old pack-horse.

'And then his speeches, his exhortations, while all the time he spits about him like a slavering camel. His speeches never come to an end, and you could expect the whole of the Mariánské barracks to collapse at once. I know him well because I was on his regimental report once before. I joined up in top boots and wore a top hat because my tailor hadn't delivered my uniform in time. And so I came to the parade ground for the one-year volunteers' school dressed in top boots and a top hat and fell into line and marched with the others on the left flank. Colonel Schröder rode straight at me and nearly knocked me down. "Donnerwetter," he roared in German so that you could hear it far away in the Šumava, "what are you doing here, you bloody civilian?" I answered him politely that I was a one-year volunteer and that I was taking part in drill. And you should have seen him! He orated for half an hour and then for the first time he saw that I was saluting in my top hat. All he did was to shout out that the next day I must go on regimental report, after which he spurred his horse God knows where like a mad rider. Then he galloped up again, roared and rampaged once more, beat his breast and ordered me at once to clear out of the drill-grounds and to go to the guard-house. At regimental report he gave me fourteen days confined to barracks, made me put on impossible rags from the store and threatened to tear off my stripes.

' "A one-year volunteer," that bloody fool of a colonel went on drivelling aloud, "is something noble. They are the embryos of glory, military quality, heroism. The one-year volunteer Wohltat was promoted to the rank of corporal after passing the usual examination. He then volunteered for the front and took fifteen enemy prisoners. While he was handing them over he was torn to pieces by a shell. Five minutes later the order came that Wohltat was promoted cadet. And you too could expect the same glorious future, advancement,

decorations. Your name could be inscribed in the golden book of the regiment." '

The volunteer spat: 'You see, old man, what kinds of bastards are born under the sun. I don't care a damn about one-year volunteers' stripes and all the other privileges they give you: "Sir, you are an oaf." How fine that sounds: "Sir, you are . . ." and not just vulgarly, "Bloody oaf!" And after your death you will get the *Signum Laudis* or Great Silver Medal: the Imperial and Royal purveyors of corpses with or without stars. Why, any ox is better off. They kill it in the slaughterhouse and don't drag it beforehand to the drill-ground and to rifle practice.'

The fat volunteer rolled on to the other straw mattress and went on: 'It's obvious that one day it will all collapse. It can't last for ever. Try to pump glory into a pig and it will burst in the end. If I went to the front I should write on the carriage:

> 'Upon the fields your bones they'll put.
> Eight horses or four dozen foot.'

The door opened and the warder appeared, bringing a quarter portion of army bread for both and some fresh water.

Without getting up from the mattress the volunteer apostrophized the warder in the following speech: 'How noble and beautiful it is to visit prisoners, St Agnes of the 91st regiment! Welcome, angel of charity, whose heart is full of compassion. Thou art bowed down under the hampers of food and drinks brought to alleviate our sufferings. We shall never forget the charity thou hast shown us. Thou art a radiant vision in our dark prison.'

'On regimental report you'll soon forget your sense of humour,' the warder grumbled.

'Keep your hair on, you miserable old screw,' the volunteer replied from his plank-bed. 'You'd better tell us what you'd do if you had to lock up ten one-year volunteers? Don't look so bloody silly, you turnkey of the Mariánské barracks. You'd lock up twenty and let out ten, you hamster. Christ, if I were the minister I'd see you had a wonderful war! You know the law that the angle of incidence equals the angle of reflection? I only ask you one thing: Show me and give me a firm point in this universe and I'll lift up the whole world with you in it, you conceited oaf!'

The warder's eyes bulged, he shook himself and banged the door.

'A mutual aid society for removing warders,' said the volunteer, dividing the portion of bread fairly in two parts. 'According to paragraph sixteen of prison regulations prisoners in the barracks have to be served full army rations until sentence is passed on them, but here it's the law of the jungle which rules: lucky the chap who's the first to wolf up the prisoners' rations.'

Švejk and he were sitting on the plank-bed and chewing the army bread.

'You can see best by the warder how war brutalizes a man,' the volunteer went on reflecting. 'No doubt before our warder was called up he was a young man with ideals, a fair-haired cherub, gentle and humane, defending the unfortunate, whom he always stood up for when at revels in his village there was a rough-house because of a girl. No doubt everybody respected him then, but today. . . . My God, how I itch to give him one across the jaw, bang his head on the plank-bed, throw him head-first into the rears. And that too, old man, is a proof of how in the military business your mentality gets completely brutalized.'

He started singing:

> 'Not even the Devil could scare her,
> Till she met an artillery man . . .

'Old man,' he went on, 'if we consider all this from the angle of our dear monarchy, we reach the inescapable conclusion that the situation is just the same as it was with Pushkin's uncle, of whom Pushkin wrote that, as he was a dying duck, there was nothing to do but:

> 'Sigh and keep on wondering,
> When the devil will carry you off!'

The rattle of a key in the door could be heard again and the warder lit the oil lamp in the corridor.

'A ray of light in the darkness!' shouted the volunteer. 'Enlightenment penetrates the army! Goodnight, Mr Warder, give my love to all the higher ranks and I wish you pleasant dreams – perhaps you'll dream that you've returned me those five crowns which I gave you to buy cigarettes with and which you've spent on drinking my health. Sweet dreams, you old monster.'

The warder could be heard muttering something about regimental report the next day.

'Alone once more,' said the volunteer. 'Now I shall devote the time

before sleep to an exposition and lecture on how the zoological knowledge of the N.C.O.s and officers increases every day. In order to dig
out new live war material and militarily conscious morsels for the
cannon's maw, profound studies of natural history are needed or of the
book *The Sources of Economic Prosperity*, published by Kočí, where on
every page crop up the words: cattle, pig, swine. But recently we have
noted however that our progressive military circles have been introducing new nomenclature for recruits. In the 11th company Corporal
Althof uses the word "Engadine goat"; Lance-Corporal Müller, a
German schoolmaster from Kašperské Hory,[1] calls recruits "stinking
Czech swine"; Sergeant-Major Sondernummer "ox-headed toads" or
"Yorkshire porkers", promising in addition that he'll flay and stuff
every recruit. He does it with expert knowledge, as though he came
from a family of taxidermists. All our superior officers try in this way
to instil in us a love for our fatherland by means of special teaching aids
such as bellowing at recruits and dancing round them, a war-cry
reminiscent of the natives in Africa when they are about to skin an
innocent antelope or roast the haunches of a missionary who is being
dressed for the table. Such expressions never apply to Germans of
course. If Sergeant-Major Sondernummer uses the expression "pack
of swine" he always quickly adds the word "Czech", in case the
Germans should be offended and think it was meant for them. Then
all the N.C.O.s of the 11th company roll their eyes like a miserable dog
that has been greedy enough to swallow a sponge dipped in oil and
can't get it out of its throat. Once I heard a conversation between
Lance-Corporal Müller and Corporal Althof about the next steps in
the training of the men of the home defence. In this conversation the
following words stood out: "a couple across the jaw". I thought at
first they were having a row, that the German military monolith was
coming unstuck, but I made a great mistake. They were actually only
referring to the rank and file.

' "When a Czech pig like that" (these were the discreet instructions given by Corporal Althof) "does not learn after thirty 'flat
downs' to stand as straight as a candle it's not enough to give him a
few across the jaw. Deal him a sharp blow in the belly with the fist
of one hand and with the other knock his cap across his ears, saying: 'About turn!' As he turns round give him a kick up his backside

---

1. Bergreichenstein, a town in the Bohemian forest, where the Germans were in
an overwhelming majority.

and you'll see how he'll straighten up and how Ensign Dauerling will laugh."

'And now, old man, I must tell you something about Dauerling,' continued the volunteer. 'The recruits in the 11th company talk about him rather like a lonely old woman on a farm near the Mexican frontiers would romance about some famous Mexican bandit. Dauerling has the reputation of being a man-eater – an anthropophagus from the Australian tribes who devour the members of other tribes when they fall into their hands. His life story is marvellous. Not long after his birth his nurse fell down when she was carrying him, and little Konrad Dauerling knocked his head so hard that even today you can see a flattening on it as though a comet had struck the North Pole. Everybody doubted whether he would ever be fit to do anything, even if he survived the concussion of the brain. Only his father, a colonel, didn't lose hope and said that it wouldn't matter at all because, as a matter of course, when young Dauerling grew up he would go in for a military career. Young Dauerling managed to get into the cadet school at Hainburg after a frightful struggle with four classes of the lower technical school, for which he was coached by private crammers. The first of them grew prematurely grey and went mad, and the second grew so desperate that he wanted to jump off the St Stephen's Tower in Vienna. In the cadet school they never worried about previous education because it was generally unsuitable for Austrian regular officers. Their one military ideal was the Prussian drill-sergeant. Education ennobles the soul and this is useless in the army. The coarser the officers the better.

'In the cadet school Dauerling was no good even in those subjects of which every pupil had at least a smattering. Even there traces could be observed of his having given his head a knock in childhood.

'His answers at examinations spoke eloquently of his unfortunate accident. They were remarkable for their stupidity and were considered classic examples of crass idiocy and mental confusion, so that the professors at the cadet school never called him anything but "our dumb friend". His stupidity was so dazzling that it justified the hope that perhaps after a few decades he might make the Theresian Military Academy or the Ministry of War.

'When the war broke out and all the young cadets were made ensigns, Konrad Dauerling got himself on to the list of Hainburg cadets who were promoted and thus he found his way to the 91st regiment.'

The volunteer paused, and went on: 'The Ministry of War published a book, *Drill or Education*, in which Dauerling read that terror was essential for soldiers. Training had success in proportion to the degree of terror applied. And in this Dauerling always had success. To avoid having to listen to his bellowing whole companies of soldiers reported sick – a practice, however, which didn't exactly come off. Anyone who reported sick received three days "severe". By the way do you know what "severe" means? They chase you on the drill-ground all day and then after that they lock you up at night. So it happened that no one in Dauerling's company reported sick any more. Those who did simply sat in clink. Dauerling always preserves on the drill-ground that casual barracks tone, beginning with the word "swine" and ending with that mysterious zoological enigma "swinehound". But at the same time he's very liberal. He leaves to the soldiers their freedom of decision. He says: "What do you want, you elephant, a few bashes on the nose or three days 'severe'?" If anyone chooses "severe" he gets two bashes on the nose as well, to which Dauerling adds this explanation: "You bloody coward, I suppose you're afraid of your snout? What are you going to do later on when the heavy artillery strikes up?"

'Once, when he knocked out a recruit's eye he declared in German: "Ugh! What a lot of fuss about a bastard that'll peg out anyhow." Field Marshal Konrad von Hötzendorf used to say the same: "All soldiers have to peg out sooner or later."

'A favourite and effective method of Dauerling's is to summon the Czech rank and file and lecture them on Austria's military tasks, where he explains the general principles of army education from handcuffing to hanging and shooting. At the beginning of the winter before I went to hospital we drilled on the drill-ground next to the 11th company, and when there was a rest-pause Dauerling made a speech to his Czech recruits:

' "I know," he began, "that you're scum and that I'll have to knock out of your heads all your Czech bullshit. With Czech you won't even get to the gallows. Our supreme commander is a German too. Are you listening? Hell's bells! Flat down!"

'Everyone fell down flat, and when they were all lying on the ground Dauerling walked in front of them and orated:

' " 'Flat down's' got to be 'flat down', even if you cut yourself to pieces in the mud, you brigands. 'Flat down' existed even in ancient

Rome; in those days everyone had to join up and serve from seventeen to sixty. They had to serve thirty years in the field and weren't allowed to wallow about in the barracks like pigs. And at that time too there was one army language and command. If the men had tried to talk Etruscan to them, those Roman officers would have given them hell, and I too require all of you to reply in German and not in that double-Dutch of yours. You see how nice it is for you to lie in the mud, but just imagine what would happen if one of you didn't want to go on lying there and tried to get up. What would I do? I'd break his jaw up to his ears, because it would be an act of insubordination, mutiny, opposition, dereliction of duty for a good soldier, a breach of order and discipline and contempt for official instructions in general. From this it follows that a bastard like that is destined for the gallows and 'forfeiture of any claim to respect and civil rights'." '

The volunteer lapsed into silence and continued again after having obviously in the interval worked out his theme of the description of conditions in the barracks:

'It was under Captain Adamička. He was completely apathetic. When he sat in the office he usually stared blankly into space like a harmless lunatic and had an expression as though he was going to say: "I couldn't care less." At battalion report God knows what he was thinking about. Once a soldier of the 11th company presented himself on battalion report with the complaint that one evening in the street Ensign Dauerling had called him a Czech pig. He was a book-binder in civil life and a nationally conscious Czech worker.

' "And so that's how it is," said Captain Adamička quietly, because he always spoke very quietly. "He said that to you yesterday in the street. Now we shall have to see whether you had permission to go out of the barracks. Dismiss!"

'Some time later Captain Adamička summoned the man who had lodged the complaint.

' "It has been ascertained," he said again just as quietly, "that you had permission that day to absent yourself from the barracks until ten o'clock in the evening. And so you will not be punished. Dismiss!"

'After that, old man, it used to be said of Captain Adamička that he had a sense of justice, and so they sent him to the front and in his place came Major Wenzl. But he was a devil when people tried to stir up trouble between the nationalities. And it was he who hauled Ensign Dauerling over the coals. Major Wenzl has a Czech wife and is very much afraid of nationality disputes. Years ago when he served as a captain in Kutná Hora and was drunk he swore at a waiter in a hotel and called him "Czech scum". Let me mention that in society Major Wenzl never spoke anything but Czech, just as he did at home, and that his sons study in Czech. But nonetheless he uttered these words, and it got into the local paper. Then a deputy made an interpellation in the Vienna parliament about Captain Wenzl's behaviour in the hotel. Wenzl had a lot of unpleasantness because of it as it was just at the time of the debate on the army estimates, and right into the middle of it all came a sozzled Captain Wenzl from Kutná Hora.

'Later Captain Wenzl learned that all this was a put-up job by Zítko, one of the probationary cadets from the one-year volunteers, who sent it to the newspaper because there had been a feud between him and Captain Wenzl from the time when Zítko at a party in Wenzl's presence started reflecting that one only had to look at Mother Nature to observe how clouds cover the horizon, mountains rise high on the sky-line, waterfalls thunder in the forests and birds sing.

' "You only have to reflect," said probationary cadet Zítko, "what any captain is compared with sublime nature? Just as much of a zero as any probationary cadet."

'Because all the officer gentlemen were at that moment completely pickled, Captain Wenzl wanted to flog the unfortunate philosopher Zítko like a mule, and so the feud increased and the captain bullied Zítko whenever he could and all the more because Zítko's utterance became proverbial.

' "What is Captain Wenzl compared with sublime nature?" It was famous over the whole of Kutná Hora.

' "The bastard! I'll make him hang himself," Captain Wenzl used to say, but Zítko went into civil life and went on studying philosophy. But from then on Major Wenzl conceived a mad loathing for all junior officers. Not even a lieutenant was proof against his raging and raving, not to speak of cadets and ensigns.

' "I'll crush them like bugs!" says Major Wenzl, and woe betide that ensign who would drive anyone on to battalion report for any trifling offence. In Major Wenzl's eyes only an enormous and frightful offence has any significance – like for instance a soldier falling asleep on guard at the powder magazine or when he does something even more frightful like falling asleep when crawling at night over the wall of the Mariánské barracks and letting himself be caught by a patrol of the Landwehr or the artillery – in short, horrible things which would be a blot on the good name of the regiment.

' "For Christ's sake!" I heard him once roar in the corridor, "it's the third time he's been caught by the Landwehr patrol. Throw the reptile into the dungeon at once! The bastard must be sent away from the regiment to the train to cart dung somewhere. And he didn't even fight with them! They're not soldiers, these bastards, they're crossing-sweepers! Don't let him have anything to eat until the day after tomorrow. Take away his straw mattress and shove him into solitary confinement. Don't let him have a blanket, the rat!"

'Now just imagine, my friend, immediately after the major had come here, that idiotic Ensign Dauerling hounded on to battalion report a man who, allegedly, had intentionally failed to salute him when he was driving across the square in a fiacre one Sunday afternoon with a young lady! According to the N.C.O.s' accounts, battalion report on that occasion was like the day of the last judgement. The sergeant-major from the battalion office ran out into the passage with the registers and Major Wenzl roared at Dauerling:

' "I won't have this bloody nonsense, Himmeldonnerwetter! I utterly forbid it! Do you know, ensign, what battalion report is? Battalion report's not a Sunday-school treat! How the hell could he see you when you were driving across the square? Don't you know that you yourself were taught that officers are to be saluted only when met, and that doesn't mean that a soldier has got to gyrate like a top just to keep track of some ensign driving across a square. Be good enough to hold your tongue! Battalion report is a very serious institution. If the soldier has already stated to you that he didn't see you because at that moment he was saluting me on the corso and had turned his eyes in my direction – do you understand, Major Wenzl's, and if he said that he couldn't look behind at the fiacre you were driving in, then I think you've got to believe him. Next time, have the goodness not to bother me with such trifles."

'From that time on Dauerling changed.'

The volunteer yawned: 'We must have a good sleep before regimental report. I only wanted to tell you something of what it's like in the regiment. Colonel Schröder doesn't like Major Wenzl. He's altogether a funny bird. Captain Ságner, who looks after the volunteers' school, sees in Schröder the true type of soldier, although nothing in the world frightens Colonel Schröder more than the idea that he might have to go to the front. Ságner is a very smart customer indeed and hates reserve officers just like Schröder. He calls them "civilian stink". He regards volunteers as wild beasts out of which you have to make military robots, sew stars on their tunics and send them to the front to be liquidated instead of noble active officers who have to be preserved for stud purposes.

'All along the line,' said the volunteer, pulling the blanket over him, 'everything in the army stinks of rottenness. Up till now the wide-eyed masses haven't woken up to it. With goggling eyes they let themselves be made into mincemeat and then when they're struck by a bullet they just whisper, "Mummy!" Heroes don't exist, only cattle for the slaughter and the butchers in the general staffs. But in the end everybody will mutiny and there will be a fine shambles. Long live the army! Goodnight!'

The volunteer was quiet. Then he started to toss and turn under the blanket and asked:

'Are you asleep, old man?'

'No,' answered Švejk from the other bunk. 'I'm thinking.'

'What about, old man?'

'About the Great Silver Medal for valour which at the beginning of the war was conferred on a cabinet-maker from Vávrova Street at Vinohrady, Mlíčko by name, because he was the first in his regiment to have his leg torn off by a shell. He got an artificial leg and began to boast about his medal everywhere and to say he was the first and very first war cripple in the regiment. Once he came to the Apollo at Vinohrady and had a row with butchers from the slaughterhouse. In the end they tore off his artificial leg and clouted him over the head with it. The man who tore it off him didn't know it was an artificial one and fainted with fright. At the police station they put Mlíčko's leg back again, but from then on he was furious with his Great Silver Medal for valour and went and pawned it in the pawnshop, where they seized him and the medal too. He had some unpleasantness as a result. There was a kind of special court of honour for disabled soldiers and it sentenced him to be deprived of his Silver Medal and later of his leg as well...'

'How do you mean?'

'Awfully simple. One day a commission came to him and informed him that he was not worthy of having an artificial leg. Then they unscrewed it, took it off and carried it away.

'Or,' Švejk went on, 'it's awful fun too when the survivors of someone who has fallen in the war suddenly receive a medal like that with
an inscription saying that they are lent it so that they can hang it somewhere in an important place. In Božetěchova Street at Vyšehrad an
infuriated father, who thought that the authorities were making fun of
him, hung the medal up in the rears and a policeman who shared those
rears on the gallery with him denounced him for treasonable activities,
and so the poor fellow got hell.'

'From this we may conclude,' said the volunteer, 'that all flesh is as
grass and all the glory of man as the flower of grass. Now they have
published in Vienna *The diary of a one-year volunteer*, and in it there's
a fascinating poem in Czech translation:

> 'There was once a valiant volunteer
> Who gave his life for his country dear
> Thus showing how, without fear or fright,
> A man should for his country fight.
> They carry his corpse on to the gun.
> Prayers rise to heaven, one by one,
> As they pin an order on to the breast
> Of the man who fell at his monarch's behest.

'And so I think,' said the volunteer after a short silence, 'that our
military morale is declining. I therefore propose, old man, that in the
darkness of the night, in the silence of our prison, we sing a song about
the gunner Jabůrek. That will raise military morale. But we must bawl
it out as loud as we can so it can be heard all over the Mariánské
barracks. I accordingly recommend that we should station ourselves
close by the door.'

And from the prison there soon resounded such a powerful roar that
the windows in the corridor began to shake:

> 'And he stood by his gun
> And loaded on, on, on,
> And he stood by his gun
> And loaded on.
> In the midst of war's alarms
> A shell blew off his arms.
> But he stayed where he was
> And loaded on, on, on,
> And he stood by his gun
> And loaded on.'

In the courtyard could be heard steps and voices.

'That's the warder,' said the volunteer. 'With him is Lieutenant Pelikán who is on duty today. He's a reserve officer, a friend of mine from the Czech Club. In civilian life he's a mathematician in an insurance firm. We'll get cigarettes out of him. Let's go on bawling.'

And again could be heard: 'And he stood by his gun . . .'

When the door opened the warder, obviously upset by the presence of the officer on duty, let fly at them sharply:

'This isn't a menagerie!'

'Excuse me,' answered the volunteer, 'this is the local branch of the Rudolfinum. It's a concert in aid of prisoners. We've just finished the first number in the programme: War Symphony.'

'Stop that,' said Lieutenant Pelikán, pretending to be severe. 'I think you know that you have to be in bed at nine o'clock and not make a noise. Your concert number could be heard as far away as the square even.'

'Humbly report, sir,' said the volunteer, 'we didn't rehearse it properly, and if there's any lack of harmony . . .'

'He does that every evening,' said the warder, trying to put the officer up against his enemy. 'Altogether he behaves frightfully unintelligently.'

'Please, sir,' said the volunteer, 'I'd like to speak to you alone. Let the warder wait outside the door.'

When this was done the volunteer said familiarly:

'All right, then, cough up the cigarettes, Franta . . .

'Only Sportky? You're a lieutenant and you haven't got anything better? All right, then, for the time being, thanks very much. And matches too.'

'Sportky!' said the volunteer contemptuously, when the lieutenant had gone. 'Even in the direst straits a man must keep his spirits up. Have a smoke, old man, for the last time. Tomorrow the last judgement awaits us.'

The volunteer did not forget to sing before he fell asleep 'Mountains, valleys and lofty cliffs are my friends. But they cannot bring back to us what we once loved, my beloved sweetheart . . .'

If the volunteer characterized Colonel Schröder as a brute, he was wrong because Colonel Schröder had a partial sense of justice, which manifested itself clearly after those nights when he had been happy with the company in which he spent his evenings in the hotel. And when he had not been happy?

While the volunteer was delivering his crushing criticism of the conditions in the barracks, Colonel Schröder was sitting in the hotel in the company of officers and listening to Lieutenant Kretschmann, who had returned from Serbia with a wounded leg (a cow had gored him), relating how he saw the attack on the Serbian positions from the staff to which he was assigned.

'Yes, now they fly out of the trenches. Along the whole length of two kilometres they now climb over the barbed wire and hurl themselves on the enemy, hand grenades at their belts, gas-masks, rifles over their shoulders, ready to fire, ready for the attack. The bullets whistle. One soldier who jumped out of the trenches falls; another falls on the rampart which had been blown up; a third falls after a few steps, but his comrades sweep on with shouts of "hurrah!" through smoke and powder! And the enemy shoots from all sides, from the trenches and shell craters, and train their machine-guns on us. Again soldiers fall. A group try to reach an enemy machine-gun. They fall too. But their comrades are already in front. Hurrah! An officer falls. The rattle of rifle-fire can no longer be heard. Something frightful is in store. Again a whole group falls and the enemy machine-guns can be heard: ratatata . . . and there falls. . . . Pardon me, I can't go on, I'm drunk . . .'

And the officer with the wounded leg was silent and sat dully on his chair. Colonel Schröder smiled graciously and listened as Captain Spíra opposite him struck the table with his fist as though wanting to start up a quarrel and repeated something which had no meaning and from which it was impossible to deduce what it was intended to mean or what he wanted to say:

'Consider it carefully, please. We have fully mobilized the Austrian Landwehr Uhlans, the Austrian Landwehr, the Bosnian Rifles, the Austrian Rifles, the Austrian Infantry, the Hungarian Infantry, the Tyrolean Imperial Sharpshooters, the Bosnian Infantry, the Hungarian Honvéd Infantry, the Hungarian Hussars, the Landwehr Hussars, the Mounted Rifles, the Dragoons, the Uhlans, the artillery, the train, the sappers, the medical corps, the marines. Do you understand? And Belgium? The first and second levy form the operational army, the third looks after service at the base . . .'

Captain Spíra struck the table with his fist. 'The Landwehr carries out its duties at the base in time of peace.'

A young officer next to him was earnestly trying to convince the colonel that he was a hardened soldier and asserted very loudly to his neighbour: 'Consumptives should be sent to the front. It does them good and after all it's better for the sick to be killed than the fit.'

The colonel smiled, but suddenly he frowned and, turning to Major Wenzl, said: 'I'm surprised Lieutenant Lukáš avoids our company. Since he came here he has not been with us once.'

'He writes verses,' Captain Ságner remarked scornfully. 'Hardly had he come here when he fell in love with the wife of engineer Schreiter, whom he met in the theatre.'

The colonel frowned and stared into space: 'I've heard he can sing couplets.'

'Yes, in the cadet school he used to entertain us a lot with his couplets,' answered Captain Ságner, 'and he knows a lot of good stories. They're marvellous. I don't know why he doesn't join us.'

The colonel shook his head sadly: 'Today there's no longer the right spirit of comradeship among us. In the old days, as I remember, every one of us officers tried to make some contribution to our entertainment in the officers' club. One of them, as I remember, a Lieutenant Dankl, stripped himself naked, lay on the floor, stuck the tail of a herring in his backside and gave us a performance of a mermaid. Another, Lieutenant Schleisner, could wiggle his ears and whinny like a stallion, imitate the mewing of cats and the humming of bumble-bees. I also remember Captain Skoday. He always brought his girls into the mess whenever we wanted them. They were three sisters and he'd trained them like dogs. He put them on the table and they began to strip for us in time. He had a little conductor's baton with him and, all honour to him, he was a splendid bandmaster. And what didn't he do with them on the sofa! Once he had a tub of hot water brought into the middle of the room and each one of us, one after the other, had to go and take a bath with those girls. And he photographed us.'

Recalling this Colonel Schröder smiled ecstatically.

'And what bets we made in the tub,' he went on, smacking his lips lecherously and squirming in his chair. 'But today? Is there any fun at all? And even that coupletist doesn't appear. And the younger officers today don't even know how to hold their drink. It's not yet twelve o'clock and around this table as you see there are five people drunk already. There were times when we sat for two days and the more we drank the more sober we were. We went on pouring beer, wine and liqueurs into ourselves without stop. Today there's no longer the real military spirit. God knows why. No jokes, only everlasting talk without end. Just listen now how at the table down there they're talking about America.'

From the other end of the table someone's solemn voice could be heard saying: 'America can't come into the war. The Americans and British are at daggers drawn. America's not ready for it.'

Colonel Schröder sighed: 'That's the drivelling of reserve officers. It's enough to make you sick. Only yesterday a man like that was writing in a bank somewhere, making paper bags and selling spice, cinnamon and boot polish, or telling children in the school that hunger drives the wolves from the forests. Today he thinks he can be on the same footing as a regular officer, know everything and poke his nose into everything. And when we have a regular officer like Lieutenant Lukáš, he doesn't come and join us.'

Colonel Schröder went off home in an angry mood, and when he woke up the next morning he was in an even worse temper, because in the newspapers which he read in bed he found several times in the reports from the front the sentence that our troops had withdrawn to positions already prepared in advance. These were glorious days for the Austrian army, as like the days of Šabac[1] as two peas in a pod.

And it was under these impressions that at ten o'clock in the morning Colonel Schröder approached the act which, probably quite rightly, the volunteer had characterized as the last judgement.

Švejk and the volunteer stood in the courtyard and waited for the colonel. Already present were the N.C.O.s, the officer on duty, the regimental adjutant and the sergeant-major from the regimental office with the documents about the delinquents on whom the axe of justice – the regimental report – was about to fall.

At last the colonel appeared, frowning and accompanied by Captain Ságner from the volunteers' school. He was nervously striking the tops of his boots with his riding whip.

After having received the report he walked several times in death-like silence past Švejk and the volunteer, who did 'eyes right' or 'eyes left' according to the side from which the colonel appeared. They did this with unusual thoroughness and could easily have twisted their necks, because it lasted so long.

At last the colonel stopped in front of the volunteer who reported: 'One-year volunteer . . .'

'I know,' said the colonel tersely. 'A one-year volunteer scum and reject. What do you do in civilian life? Do you study classical philosophy? So I suppose you're a boozed intellectual . . .

'Captain,' he called to Ságner, 'bring the whole volunteers' school here.

'Of course,' he went on to the volunteer, 'a Lord High Student of classical philosophy, whom people like us have got to be contaminated with. About turn! Just what I expected! The folds on his greatcoat are not in order. It looks as if he had just left a woman or had been wallowing in a brothel. I'll teach you, you young upstart.'

The volunteers' school marched into the courtyard.

'Form a square!' ordered the colonel. They formed a narrow square round the accused and the colonel.

'Look at that man,' shouted the colonel, pointing to the volunteer with his riding whip. 'He has boozed away the honour of you volun-

1. A town in Serbia which was fought over by the Austrian and Serbian armies in 1914 and 1915.

teers, out of whom we have to train up a cadre of respectable officers who can lead the men to glory on the battlefield. But where would this fellow lead his men to, this drunken sot? From pub to pub. He'd soak up the men's whole rum ration. Have you anything to say in your defence? You haven't. Look at him. He can't even say anything in his own defence and in civilian life he studies classical philosophy. Truly a classic example.'

The colonel pronounced the last words slowly and emphatically and spat: 'A classical philosopher, who in a state of intoxication knocks officers' caps off their heads at night. My God! How lucky that it was only an artillery officer!'

Into that last remark was concentrated all the 91st regiment's loathing for the artillery in Budějovice. Woe betide the artilleryman who fell at night into the hands of the regimental patrols and vice versa. The hatred was frightful and irreconcilable; a vendetta, a blood feud which had been handed down from one year to another, accompanied on both sides with traditional stories, such as how the infantrymen threw the artillerymen into the Vltava or the reverse; how they fought in The Port Arthur, at The Rose and in other numerous places of entertainment in the Southern Bohemian metropolis.

'None the less,' continued the colonel, 'a crime like that must be punished in an exemplary way. The bastard must be expelled from the volunteers' school and morally annihilated. We've quite enough intellectuals of his kind in the army already. Regimental office!'

The sergeant-major from the regimental office advanced gravely with documents and pencil.

There was silence as in a court-room where a murderer is being tried and the judge says: 'I shall now pronounce the sentence.'

And in this very same tone of voice the colonel announced: 'One-year volunteer Marek is sentenced to twenty-one days' "severe". After serving his sentence he is to be sent to the kitchen to peel potatoes.'

Turning to the volunteers' school, the colonel gave the orders to dismiss. They could be heard quickly forming fours and marching off, while the colonel said to Captain Ságner that it was not properly done and in the afternoon he should repeat the march drill with them in the courtyard.

'It must thunder, captain. And one other thing more. I nearly forgot.

Tell them that the whole school has five days confined to barracks, so that they shall never forget their former colleague, the scoundrel Marek.'

But the scoundrel Marek stood by the side of Švejk and looked quite happy. It could not have turned out better for him. It was definitely better to peel potatoes in the kitchen, shape dumplings and take meat

off the bone than stand up to the hurricane fire of the enemy and roar out: 'Form two deep! Fix bayonets!' when one's trousers were full.

Returning from Captain Ságner, Colonel Schröder stopped in front of Švejk and observed him carefully. Švejk's figure at this moment was characterized by his full smiling face, bordered with great ears. They stuck out under his military cap, which was rammed down over his head. The whole created an expression of complete assurance and total ignorance of any offence. His eyes asked: 'Have I done something wrong, please?' His eyes spoke: 'Don't you see that I'm as innocent as a lamb?'

And the colonel concentrated his observations on the question he put to the sergeant-major from the regimental office: 'Idiot?'

And then the colonel saw the mouth of that good-natured face open before him.

'Humbly report, sir, yes, idiot,' Švejk answered for the sergeant-major.

Colonel Schröder nodded to the adjutant and drew him aside. They then called the sergeant-major and looked at the material on Švejk.

'Aha,' said Colonel Schröder. 'So this then is Lieutenant Lukáš's batman who, according to the lieutenant's report, got lost in Tábor. I think that officers must educate their batmen themselves. If Lieutenant Lukáš chose such a patent idiot for his batman he must suffer the consequences. He has plenty of time for it since he doesn't go anywhere. You haven't seen him in our company either, have you? Very well, then. He has quite enough time to train his batman.'

Colonel Schröder walked up to Švejk and looking into his good-natured face said: 'You mentally deficient animal, I give you three days' "severe", and when you have served that, go and report to Lieutenant Lukáš.'

And so Švejk met up again with the volunteer in the regimental prison and Lieutenant Lukáš was able to enjoy the opportunity of being told by Colonel Schröder, who had sent for him: 'Lieutenant, after your arrival in the regiment about a week ago you made an application for a batman, because your servant had got lost on the station in Tábor. Since he has returned . . .'

'Sir . . .' Lieutenant Lukáš answered pleadingly.

'I have decided,' the colonel went on with emphasis, 'to put him in gaol for three days and then send him back to you . . .'

Lieutenant Lukáš staggered out of the colonel's office, completely shattered.

During the three days which Švejk spent in the company of the volunteer Marek he amused himself hugely. Every evening on their plank-beds they made patriotic demonstrations.

In the evening from the prison there could always be heard the strains of 'God save our Emperor' and 'Prince Eugène, the noble

Knight'. They sang also a whole series of military songs and when the warder came in they greeted him with:

> 'Our old warder
> Mayn't give up the ghost,
> Till the devil comes from hell
> And puts him on the roast.
> Comes up with his cart
> And knocks him on the ground.
> Oh, what splendid firewood
> Those devils in hell have found!'

And over the plank-bed the volunteer made a drawing of the warder and wrote underneath it the text of an old song:

> When I went to Prague a sausage for to buy
> Who should I meet but a funny old guy.
> That funny old guy our warder chanced to be,
> And if I hadn't run away he'd have bitten me.

And meanwhile, while they both were teasing the warder, just as in Seville they tease an Andalusian bull with a red cloth, Lieutenant Lukáš was waiting in agony for the moment when Švejk would turn up to report for duty again.

3

Švejk's Adventures in Királyhida

THE 91st regiment moved to Királyhida or Bruck an der Leitha.

Just three hours before Švejk was to be released after three days' confinement he was taken away with the one-year volunteer to the main guard-room and marched to the station under military escort.

'It was known a long time ago,' the volunteer said to him on the way, 'that we'd be transferred to Hungary. There they'll form march battalions, the soldiers'll be trained in field shooting, they'll brawl with the Hungarians and we shall go gaily to the Carpathians. The Hungarians'll come here to Budějovice to do garrison duty and the races'll get mixed. There's a theory that raping girls of another nationality is the best recipe against degeneration. The Swedes and Spaniards did it during the Thirty Years' War, the French under Napoleon and now in the Budějovice region the Hungarians'll do it too, and it won't be rape with gross violence. Everything will be all right in time. Fair exchange is no robbery. A Czech soldier will sleep with a Hungarian girl, an unfortunate Czech girl will take a Hungarian Honvéd into her bed, and centuries later there will be an interesting surprise for the anthropologists: why did people with protruding cheekbones appear on the banks of the Malše?'

'This cross-breeding,' observed Švejk, 'is a very interesting matter altogether. In Prague there is a negro waiter called Kristián, whose father was an Abyssinian king and who had himself exhibited in a circus at Štvanice in Prague. A schoolmistress who used to write verses in *Lada* about shepherds and a forest brook went with him to a hotel and fornicated with him, as it says in the Holy Scripture, and she was awfully surprised when she gave birth to a little boy who was completely white. All right, but after a fortnight the little boy began to get brown. He got browner and browner and then after a month he began to get black. Within half a year he was as black as his grandfather, the Abyssinian king. She went with him to the clinic for skin diseases in the hope that they'd be able to bleach him somehow, but there they told her that it was a real black nigger skin and there was nothing to be done. This drove her off her head; she began to write to the magazines for advice on what to do against niggers, and they took her away to Kateřinky[1] and put the little nigger boy in an orphanage, where they had an awful lot of fun with him. Then he learned to be a waiter and went dancing in night clubs. Today there are Czech mulattoes who have been successfully bred from him and are not as coloured as he was. A medico who used to go to The Chalice once told us that it's not quite as simple as all that. A half-breed like that brings half-breeds into the world again and they can't be distinguished from white people. But suddenly in a later generation a negro turns up. Imagine the catastrophe! You might get married to a young lady. The filly is quite white and suddenly she gives birth to a negro baby. And if before her ninth month she went without you to the Variety Theatre to watch wrestling where a negro was performing, I think the whole thing would give you something to think about.'

'The case of your negro, Kristián,' said the volunteer, 'has to be looked at from a war point of view too. Let's suppose they called that

1. Lunatic asylum at Prague.

negro up. He's from Prague and so he comes under the 28th regiment. But you've heard how the 28th regiment went over to the Russians. How surprised the Russians would be if they found they had taken the negro Kristián prisoner. The Russian newspapers would certainly write that Austria was driving into the war the colonial troops she hasn't got and was already drawing on her nigger reserves.'

'People used to say,' put in Švejk, 'that Austria did have some colonies somewhere in the north. Emperor Franz-Josephs-Land or something . . .'

'Lay off, boys,' said one of the escort soldiers. 'You'd better be careful not to speak about any Emperor Franz-Josephs-Land today. Don't mention any names and it'll be better for you . . .'

'Well, then, look at the map,' the volunteer put in. 'There really does exist a land of our most gracious monarch, the Emperor Franz Joseph. According to the statistics the only thing on it is ice which is exported from it on ice-breakers belonging to the Prague ice works. This ice industry is highly prized by foreigners, because it is a profitable, if dangerous, enterprise. The greatest danger occurs during the transport of the ice from Emperor Franz-Josephs-Land across the polar circle. Can you imagine it?'

The soldier from the escort muttered something unintelligible and the corporal, who accompanied the escort, came nearer and listened to the further remarks of the volunteer, who went on solemnly: 'This one and only Austrian colony can supply the whole of Europe with ice and is an outstanding national economic asset. Colonization is proceeding slowly of course, because colonists partly don't volunteer and partly get frozen to death. None the less, with the help of an adjustment of the climatic conditions, in which the Ministries of Trade and Foreign Affairs have a great interest, there is hope that the great areas of the icebergs will be appropriately exploited. By building several hotels heaps of tourists will be attracted. It will of course be necessary to lay out tourist paths and roads between the ice floes and to paint tourist signs on the icebergs. The only difficulty are the Eskimoes, who make the work of our local authorities impossible . . .

'The bastards won't learn German,' continued the volunteer, while the corporal listened with interest. He was an active man – a farm-hand in civil life. He was stupid and coarse, swallowed everything which he knew nothing about and his ideal was to grow old in Austrian service.

'The Ministry of Education, corporal, built a school for them at great expense and sacrifice. Five of the builders froze to death . . .'

'The bricklayers survived,' Švejk interrupted him, 'because they kept themselves warm with the pipes they lit.'

'Not all of them,' said the volunteer. 'Two of them unfortunately forgot to puff and their pipes went out. And so they had to be buried in the ice. But in the end the school was built out of ice bricks and re-inforced concrete, which holds together very well, but the Eskimoes lit a fire all round it out of the wood from merchant ships which were ice-bound, and achieved what they wanted. The ice on which the school was built melted away and the whole school with the headmaster and the government representative, who was to have been at the solemn consecration of the school the next day, fell into the sea . When he was up to his neck in water you could hear the government representative shout out: "*Gott strafe England!*" Now they'll probably send an army there to restore order among the Eskimoes. Of course it'll be a hard war with them. What will cause our troops the most damage will be the tame polar bears.'

'That would be the last straw,' the corporal observed wisely. 'As though there were not enough war inventions already. Take for instance gas masks for gas poisoning. You put one on your head and you're poisoned, as they told us in the N.C.O.s' school.'

'They're only trying to frighten you,' said Švejk. 'No soldier ought to be afraid of anything. Even if he falls into the rears while fighting he should only lick himself and go back into battle. And everyone's used to poison gas in the barracks, when they serve a ration of new bread and peas with groats. But now they say the Russians have got a new invention against N.C.O.s . . . .'

'Those are probably special electrical currents,' the volunteer added. 'When they are connected to the stars on the N.C.O.s' collars the stars explode because they're made out of celluloid. That'll be a new disaster.'

And although the corporal in civilian life was a cowman and a prize fat-head as well, he perhaps understood in the end that they were pulling his leg, left them, and went away to the head of the patrol.

Moreover they were drawing near to the station where the inhabitants of Budějovice were taking leave of their regiment. It had no official character, but the square in front of the station was filled with people who were waiting for the army.

Švejk's interest was concentrated on the crowds lining the streets. As was usually the case the good soldiers marched in the rear and those under arrest at the head. The good soldiers would later be squashed into cattle trucks and Švejk with the volunteer would be put into a special prisoners' van, which was always attached to the military trains just behind the staff carriage. In a prisoners' van of this kind there was always heaps of room.

Švejk could not help crying out '*Nazdar!*'[1] to the line of people and waving his cap. It worked so suggestively that the crowd repeated it loudly and '*Nazdar*' spread far and wide and thundered in front of the station. Far away people began to say: 'They're coming.'

The corporal from the escort was quite upset and shouted at Švejk to shut his mug. But the shouts spread like an avalanche. The gendarmes pushed the crowds back and made a path for the escort, but people went on shouting '*Nazdar!*' and waved their caps and hats.

It was a regular manifestation. From the windows of the hotel opposite the station some ladies waved their handkerchiefs and cried: '*Heil!*' In the crowd too, '*Nazdar*' mingled with German '*Heil*' and one enthusiast who used the opportunity to shout out in German 'Down with the Serbs' was tripped up and slightly trampled on in the artificial log-jam.

And like an electric spark it flashed along: 'They're coming!'

And they came, Švejk under armed escort waving affably to the crowd and the volunteer solemnly saluting.

It was in this way they went into the station and to the military train appointed for them, where the band of the Sharpshooters, whose conductor was seriously confused by the unexpected manifestation, nearly started to play 'God save our Emperor'. Fortunately in the nick of time the senior chaplain , Father Lacina, from the 7th cavalry division, appeared in a black bowler and began to restore order.

His story was a simple one. He had come to Budějovice the day before and as though by chance attended a small banquet of the officers of the departing regiment. A voracious glutton, the scourge of all the officers' messes, he ate and drank for ten people and went in a more or less intoxicated condition to the officers' mess to try to wheedle some scraps out of the cook. He gulped down dishes of sauces and dumplings, tore the meat from the bones like a wild cat and finally got to the rum in the kitchen. When he had soaked up so much of it that he belched he

1. The greeting used by Czech patriots.

returned to the farewell party and distinguished himself there by a fresh bout of boozing. He had rich experience of this sort of thing and in the 7th cavalry division he always cost the officers a lot of money. In the morning he got the idea that he must clean things up when the first regimental carriages went off and so he sauntered along the whole length of the crowd, and produced such an effect in the station that the officers in charge of the regiment's transport shut themselves up in the station master's office to get away from him.

And so he appeared again in front of the station just in time to tear away the baton from the bandmaster of the Sharpshooters at the moment when he was about to conduct 'God save our Emperor'.

'Stop!' he said. 'Not yet! Wait till I give you the word. Stand at ease until I come back.' He went off into the station and set off after the escort, which he stopped with his shout of 'Halt!'.

'Where are you off to?' he said severely to the corporal, who had no idea what to do in the new situation.

The good-natured Švejk answered for him: 'They are taking us to Bruck. If you'd like to come with us too, sir, you can.'

'Very well, then, I will,' said Father Lacina, and turning to the escort added: 'Who says I can't? Forward march!'

When the senior chaplain found himself in the prisoners' van, he lay down on the bench, and the good-natured Švejk divested himself of his own greatcoat and put it under his head, while the volunteer observed softly to the horrified corporal: 'Nursing service for senior chaplains.'

Father Lacina, now comfortably stretched out on the bench, began to expound: 'Ragout with mushrooms, gentlemen, is better the more mushrooms there are, but the mushrooms must first be fried with onions and only afterwards should bay leaves and onions be added . . .'

'You've put the onions in already, sir,' said the volunteer. The corporal looked at him in desperation, seeing in Father Lacina a drunk indeed but at the same time his superior officer none the less.

The corporal's situation was really desperate.

'Yes,' put in Švejk, 'the senior chaplain is perfectly right. The more onions the better. In Pakoměřice there lived a brewer who used to put onions in the beer, because he said onions provoke thirst. The onion is a frightfully useful thing altogether. Fried onions are used against boils too . . .'

Father Lacina was meanwhile talking in a half-whisper on the bench

as though in a dream: 'Everything depends on the spices, what spices it's seasoned with and the quantity. There shouldn't be too much pepper or too much paprika . . .'

As he went on he talked slower and more softly: 'Not too many cloves, not too much lemon, not too much allspice, not too much muscat . . .'

He never finished and fell asleep whistling through his nose when he stopped snoring from time to time.

The corporal looked at him with a glassy eye, while the men from the escort sat on their benches and laughed quietly.

'He's not going to wake up so quick,' said Švejk after a time. 'He's completely sozzled.

'It doesn't matter,' Švejk went on, when the corporal gave him an anguished sign to keep quiet. 'You can't do anything about it. He's as tight as a lord. He's got the rank of a captain. All these chaplains, never mind whether they're senior or junior, have the special gift from God of getting themselves stinking drunk at every opportunity. I served under Chaplain Katz and he could have drunk his own nose away. What this man's doing here is absolutely nothing compared with what the other used to do. Together we pawned the monstrance to get drink, and we'd have even pawned the Lord God himself, if anyone had advanced us money on him.'

Švejk approached Father Lacina, turned him over towards the wall and said with the confidence of an expert: 'He'll go on snoring until we get to Bruck.' Then he returned to his place, followed by the despairing look of the unfortunate corporal, who observed: 'Perhaps I should go and report it.'

'Don't think of doing so,' said the volunteer. 'You are in command of the escort. You mustn't leave us. And according to regulations you mustn't let any of the escorting guard go away to make a report until you have a replacement. As you see, this is a knotty problem. Nor can you fire a shot as a signal for someone to come, because that's not possible either. Nothing is happening here. On the other hand there's a regulation that apart from the prisoners and the escorts accompanying them no one else is allowed in the prisoners' van. Entrance is strictly forbidden to unauthorized persons. Moreover, if you wanted to cover up the traces of your delinquency and unobtrusively throw the senior chaplain out of the train while it's going you couldn't do that either, because here there are witnesses, who have seen that you let him come into the van where he doesn't belong. You'll certainly get demoted, corporal.'

The corporal replied in confusion that he had not allowed the senior chaplain to come into the van; he had come in of his own accord and he was after all a superior officer.

'You are the only superior here,' the volunteer asserted emphatically. And Švejk completed the utterance: 'Even if His Imperial Majesty wanted to come in you shouldn't let him. It's just like being on guard when an inspecting officer comes to a recruit and asks him to go and fetch cigarettes for him and the recruit asks him what sort he should bring him. For that you'll be put into the fortress.'

The corporal feebly objected that it had after all been Švejk who had been the first to tell the senior chaplain that he could join them.

'I can afford to do that, corporal,' answered Švejk, 'because I'm soft-headed, but no one would expect it from you.'

'Have you been a regular for long?' the volunteer asked the corporal in course of conversation.

'Three years. And now I expect to be promoted platoon sergeant.'

'You can put paid to that,' said the volunteer cynically. 'I tell you, it looks like demotion.'

'It's all the same,' said Švejk, 'whether you fall as an N.C.O. or as an ordinary soldier – but it's true that they push the demoted into the first ranks of the firing line.'

The senior chaplain stirred.

'He's snoozing,' said Švejk, when he had ascertained that everything was in the best order. 'Now he's certainly dreaming about some blow-out. I'm only afraid that he may do something here. When my chaplain Katz got sozzled, he didn't know what he was doing in his sleep. Once he . . .'

And Švejk began to relate his experiences with Chaplain Otto Katz in such detail and in such an interesting way that they did not notice that the train had started.

It was only the roar from the vans behind which interrupted Švejk's narrative. The 12th company, which consisted exclusively of Germans from Krumlov and Kašperské Hory, were bawling out:

> 'When I come, when I come,
> When I come, come again.'

And from another van a desperate fellow howled out towards disappearing Budějovice:

> 'And you, my dear,
> Stay here.
> Holaryo, holaryo, holo!'

It was such a frightful yodelling and screeching that his comrades had to drag him away from the open door of the cattle truck.

'I'm surprised we haven't had any inspection yet,' the volunteer said to the corporal. 'According to regulations, as soon as we got to the station you should have reported us to the commandant of the train and not have wasted your time on a drunken senior chaplain.'

The wretched corporal preserved an obstinate silence and went on staring stubbornly at the disappearing telegraph posts.

'When I think that we've not been reported to anybody,' continued the volunteer maliciously, 'and that at the next station the train commander will certainly come and see us, then all my soldier's blood rises up in protest. Why we're being treated like . . .'

'Like gipsies,' Švejk put in, 'or tramps. It's as though we were afraid of God's light and dared not report anywhere in case they lock us up.'

'Apart from that,' said the volunteer, 'pursuant to the decree of 21 November 1879 the following regulations have to be observed when arrested soldiers are being taken by train: first, the prisoners' van must be furnished with bars. This is as clear as daylight and has been carried out here according to regulations. We are behind perfect bars. And so that's in order. Secondly, supplementary to the Imperial and Royal decree of 21 November 1879 there must be a W.C. in every prison van. If there is not, the van must be fitted with a chamber pot with a lid for the discharge of the great and small bodily needs of the prisoners and the escort. In our case we can't really talk about a prison van where there might be a W.C. We're simply in a reserved compartment, isolated from the whole world. And there's no chamber pot here . . .'

'You can do it through the window,' the corporal said in despairing tones.

'You forget,' said Švejk, 'that no prisoner may approach the window.'

'Then thirdly,' continued the volunteer, 'a vessel with drinking water has to be provided. You haven't bothered about that either. By the way, do you know at what station they'll give us our mess portions? You don't? I knew you hadn't taken the trouble to find out . . .'

'And so you see, corporal,' observed Švejk, 'that conveying prisoners isn't just a Sunday-school treat. We have to be looked after. We're no ordinary soldiers who can look after ourselves. Everything has to be brought to our very noses, because there are decrees and clauses about it which everyone must observe, otherwise there would be no order. "A man under arrest is like a baby in swaddling clothes," a notorious ragamuffin said to me once. "He has to be looked after in case he catches cold or gets excited, so that he's content with his lot and no one insults him, poor little chap."

'By the way,' said Švejk after a moment, looking in a friendly way at the corporal, 'would you be kind enough to tell me when it's eleven o'clock?'

The corporal looked at Švejk inquiringly.

'You obviously wanted to ask me, corporal, why you should tell me when it's eleven o'clock. From eleven o'clock onwards I belong to the cattle truck, corporal,' said Švejk with emphasis and went on in a solemn voice: 'On regimental report I was sentenced to three days. At eleven o'clock I started serving my sentence and today at eleven o'clock I must be released. After eleven o'clock I have no business here. No soldier may be detained longer than he has to be, because in the army discipline and order must be observed, corporal.'

The desperate corporal took a long time to recover from this blow, but finally voiced the objection that he had received no papers.

'My dear corporal,' said the volunteer, 'papers don't go to the escort commander of their own accord. If the mountain won't go to Mahommed the escort commander must go and fetch the papers himself. You're now faced with a new situation. Definitely you have no right to detain anyone who should be set free. On the other hand, according to current regulations no one may leave a prison van. Honestly, I don't know how you're going to get out of this awful situation. The further you go the worse it seems. Now it's half past ten.'

The volunteer pushed his watch back into his pocket: 'I'm very curious to know, corporal, what you are going to do in half an hour's time.'

'In half an hour's time I belong to the cattle truck,' Švejk repeated dreamily, whereupon the corporal, who was by now in a state of complete confusion and demoralization, turned to him and said:

'If it isn't inconvenient to you, I think it's much more comfortable here than in the cattle truck. I believe . . .'

He was interrupted by a shout from the senior chaplain who screamed in his sleep: 'More gravy!'

'Hushaby, hushaby,' said Švejk affably, putting under the senior chaplain's head the corner of his own greatcoat, which was falling from the bench. 'Go on dreaming something nice about guzzling.'

And the volunteer began to sing:

> 'Hushaby baby on the tree-top,
> When the wind blows the cradle will rock.
> When the bough bends the cradle will fall,
> Down comes baby, cradle and all.'

The desperate corporal no longer reacted to anything.

He stared blankly at the countryside and gave full rein to the utter disorganization in the prisoners' van.

By the partition the escort were playing 'flesh', and nimble and hefty swipes were falling on their buttocks. When he looked in their direction his eyes caught the provocative hindquarters of an infantryman. He sighed and turned back to the window again.

The volunteer thought for a moment about something and then addressed the crushed corporal: 'Do you know the magazine *The Animal World*?'

'That magazine,' the corporal answered with an obvious expression of pleasure that the conversation was taking another turn, 'used to be taken by the pub-keeper in our village, because he was frightfully keen on angora goats and they all pegged out. So he asked advice from it.'

'My dear fellow,' said the volunteer, 'the story I am now going to tell will prove to you as clearly as daylight that no one is free from faults! I'm convinced, gentlemen, that you in the back there will stop playing "flesh", because what I'm going to tell you now will be very interesting if for nothing else for the mere fact that you won't be able to understand many technical expressions in it. I'm going to tell you a story about *The Animal World* so that we can forget our war troubles of today.

'How I actually once became editor of *The Animal World*, a very interesting magazine, was for some time a pretty insoluble puzzle for me, until I had reached the conclusion that I could only have accepted the job in the completely demented state of mind into which I had been driven by my friendly affection for my old comrade Hájek. Up to that time he had edited the magazine quite decently, but while doing so he fell in love with the daughter of its owner, Mr Fuchs, who gave him an hour's notice on condition that he found a decent editor for him.

'As you can see there were strange labour relations at that time.

'When I was introduced to the owner of the magazine by my friend Hájek, he received me very courteously and asked me whether I had any idea at all about animals. He was very satisfied with my answer that I had always had a very high respect for animals and saw in them the transition stage to man. Particularly from the point of view of animal protection I had always respected their desires and wishes. No animal has any other wish than to be liquidated as painlessly as possible before it is eaten.

'From the day of its birth the carp is dominated by the idea that it is not nice of the cook to slit its belly while it's still alive. The custom of decapitating a cock is a step towards the principles of the Society for the

Prevention of Cruelty to Animals, that poultry should not have their throats slit bv unprofessional hands.

'The twisted forms of fried roaches prove that in the act of dying they protest against being fried alive in margarine in Podolí. To chase a turkey . . .

'At that moment he interrupted me and asked me whether I knew anything about poultry-keeping, dogs, rabbits, bee-keeping, miscellanea from the animal world; whether I could cut out of foreign magazines pictures for reproduction, translate expert articles in foreign journals about animals, consult the pages of Brehm and cooperate with him in writing leading articles about the life of animals in connection with Catholic saints' days, the varying seasons, horse-racing, hunting and shooting, the training of police dogs, national and church holidays – in short have a journalist's bird's-eye view of the situation and make use of it in a short meaty leader.

'I declared that I had already thought a great deal about how a magazine like *The Animal World* ought properly to be run, and that I could fully cope with all those columns and points, having perfectly mastered all the subjects he'd mentioned. My endeavour would be to raise the magazine to an unusually high standard. I would re-organize its contents and system.

'I would introduce new columns such as for instance: "Gay Animals' Corner", "Animals about Animals", always carefully taking the political situation into account.

'I would offer the readers surprise after surprise, so that they would not be able to recover breath from one animal to the next. A column, "A Day in the Life of the Animals", ought to alternate with "A New Programme for Solving the Question of Farm Animals" and "The Cattle Movement".

'Again he interrupted me and said that this would do perfectly and if I succeeded in carrying out only half of it he would give me a pair of bantam Wyandottes from the last Berlin poultry exhibition. They had won the first prize and their owner had been awarded a gold medal for excellent selective breeding.

'I can say that I did my best and kept to my action programme for running the magazine as far as lay within my powers. But I soon discovered that my articles went beyond my capabilities.

'Wishing to offer the public something completely new I invented animals.

'I proceeded from the basic assumption that animals like, for instance, the elephant, the tiger, the lion, the monkey, the mole, the horse, the pig etc. were already quite familiar creatures to the readers of *The Animal World* and that it was therefore necessary to stimulate the readers with something fresh, with new discoveries. And so I made an experiment with the Sulphur-Bellied Whale. This new kind of whale of mine was the size of a cod and was equipped with a bladder full of formic acid as well as a special cloaca through which it could make an explosive discharge of narcotic poisonous acid on small fishes which it wanted to devour. An English scientist, I've forgotten now what name I gave him, later gave this acid the name of whale acid. Whale blubber was already known to everybody, but the new acid aroused the attention of several readers, who asked for the name of the firm manufacturing it.

'I can assure you that the readers of *The Animal World* are in general very inquisitive.

'Shortly after the Sulphur-Bellied Whale I discovered a whole series of other animals. Among them I would mention the Artful Prosperian, a mammal of the kangaroo family; the Edible Ox, the ancient proto-type of the cow; the Sepia Infusorian, which I characterized as a sort of sewer rat.

'My new animals multiplied daily. I was extremely surprised myself by my successes in these spheres. I never had any idea that it would be necessary to make such copious additions to the animal kingdom and that Brehm had left out so many animals from his book *The Life of Animals*. Did Brehm and all those who followed him know of my bat from Iceland, the Faraway Bat, or of my domestic cat from the peak of Mount Kilimanjaro called the Irritable Bazouky Stag-Puss?

'Did zoologists before have any idea of Engineer Khun's Flea, which I found in amber and which was completely blind, because it lived on an underground prehistoric mole, which was also blind because its great-great-grandmother had mated, as I wrote, with a blind under-ground olm from the Postumia caves, which at that time stretched as far as the Baltic Sea of today?

'From this trifling event there developed an extensive controversy between *Čas* and *Čech*,[1] because the latter in its feuilleton on miscellanea

---

1. *Čas* ('Time') was the newspaper which voiced the ideas of T. G. Masaryk and his 'Realist Party' from 1887 to 1923. *Čech* ('The Czech') was the organ of the con-servative wing of the People's (Clerical) Party.

quoted the article about the flea I had discovered and stated: "What God does he does well." *Čas*, naturally in a purely realistic way, tore my flea to shreds together with the august *Čech*, and from that time it seemed that my lucky star as inventor and discoverer of new creations was deserting me. The subscribers to *The Animal World* began to get worried.

'This was due to my various small news-stories about bee-keeping and poultry-keeping, where I developed my new theories. They caused genuine panic, because after reading my simple pieces of advice the well-known bee-keeper, Mr Pazourek, had a stroke and bee-keeping in the Šumava and Podkrkonoší died out completely. The poultry was attacked by a pest and, in a word, everything began to peg out. The subscribers wrote threatening letters and refused to take the journal.

'I then threw myself into wild birds and I can still today remember my affair with the editor of *Peasant Horizon*, the clerical deputy and director, Josef M. Kadlčák.

'I cut out of the English magazine *Country Life* a picture of a little bird sitting on a walnut tree. I gave it the name of nutcracker, just as I wouldn't have hesitated logically to write that a bird sitting on a juniper tree was a junip or a gincracker.

'And what didn't happen after that? I was attacked by Mr Kadlčák, who wrote to me on an ordinary postcard and said that the bird was a jay and certainly no nutcracker, which was a mistranslation of the German *Eichelhäher*.

'I sent him a letter in which I expounded my whole theory about the nutcracker, interpolating frequent words of abuse and imaginary quotations from Brehm.

'Deputy Kadlčák replied with a leader in *Peasant Horizon*.

'My chief, Mr Fuchs, was sitting as usual in the café and reading the provincial press, because he had recently been spending an awful lot of time looking for references to my thrilling articles in *The Animal World*. When I came in he pointed to a copy of *Peasant Horizon* which was lying on the table and spoke quietly, looking at me with that sad expression which had latterly never left his eyes.

'I read aloud in the presence of all the public in the café:

'Honoured Sir,
I have drawn your attention to the fact that your journal is introducing an unusual and unjustifiable terminology, that it shows scant regard for the purity of the Czech language and that it is inventing animals of various kinds.

I cited as evidence that instead of the generally adopted old-established name of "jay" your editor has introduced the name "acorncracker" which has its origin in a mistranslation of the German name *"Eichelhäher"* – jay.

' "Jay," the owner of the newspaper repeated desperately after me.
'I went on reading calmly:

'Then I received from your editor of *The Animal World* a letter which was insufferably vulgar, personal and impertinent, in which I was criminally referred to as a bloody ignorant mule, which merits the sharpest of rebukes. This is not the way respectable people reply to objective scholarly criticisms. I should like to know which of us two is the bigger mule. It is true, perhaps, that I should not have made my reproaches on a postcard, but rather have consigned them to a letter, but through great pressure of work I overlooked this trifling matter. Now after the vulgar onslaught of your editor of *The Animal World* I am determined to pillory him in public.

'Your editor is making a frightful mistake if he imagines that I am an uneducated mule who has no conception of the nomenclature of this or that bird. I have occupied myself with ornithology for years and not from books but from observation in nature. In my cages I have kept far more birds than your editor has ever seen in all his life, he being a man who spends his life immured in Prague gin-palaces and pubs.

'But these are questions of secondary consideration, although it certainly would have done no harm if before starting to make these sallies with his pen your editor of *The Animal World* had taken the trouble to find out whom he was accusing of being a mule, in case it should be destined for Frýdland near Místek in Moravia, where before the appearance of this article your journal had subscribers too.

'It is not a question of personal polemics with some insane lout but of facts, and so I repeat once more that it is quite impermissible to invent names by translation, when we have in our own language the universally known name of "jay".

' "Yes, jay," said my chief in an even more despondent voice.
'I went on reading calmly without letting myself be interrupted.

'It is plain villainy when this is done by ignoramuses and vandals. Who ever called a jay a "nutcracker"? In the book *Our Birds* on page 148 there is the Latin name: ganulus glandarius[1] B.A. That is my bird – the jay.

'The editor of your journal will certainly acknowledge that I know my own bird better than any layman can know it. According to D. Bayer the nutcracker is called mucifraga carycatectes B.[2] and that "B" does not mean,

1. '*Garrulus* glandarius'.
2. *Nucifraga*.

as your editor wrote to me in his letter, the first letter of a certain word. Czech ornithologists know only the common jay and certainly not your "acorncracker", which is the brain-child of that very gentleman, to whom, in accordance with his theory, the initial letter "B" belongs. It is a piece of crude personal invective which does not alter the facts.

'Jay remains jay, even if the editor of *The Animal World* p—s with rage over it, and it only goes to prove how frivolously and unobjectively people can sometimes write, even if he has cited Brehm in an ostentatiously rude way. The lout has the impudence to write that, according to Brehm, the jay belongs to the family of the crocodiloids, page 452, where the reference is to the lesser grey shrike or common butcher-bird (lanius minor L.). Then this ignoramissimus, if I may use this euphemism, again cites Brehm as the authority for his statement that the jay belongs to the fifteenth family, whereas in fact Brehm assigns the crows to the seventeenth family which includes rooks and the jackdaw family. He is so vulgar as to call me a jackdaw (colaeus) and the genus of magpies, blue crows, the sub-family of moron ineptus, although on the same page the reference is to wood-jays and spotted magpies . . .

'"Wood-jays!" sighed my magazine-owner, putting his hands to his head. "Give it back so that I can finish reading it."

'I was afraid that he had lost his voice when he went on reading: "The ring ouzel or Turkish blackbird will always be in Czech translation ring ouzel, just as fieldfare will always be fieldfare."

'"The fieldfare ought to be called the junip or gincracker, sir," I interposed, "because it feeds on juniper from which you make gin."

'Mr Fuchs threw the newspapers on to the table and crawled under the billiard table, gasping out the last words he had read:

'"Turdus, ring ouzel."

'"No jay," he howled from underneath the billiard table. "Nut-cracker. I bite, gentlemen!"

'He was finally dragged out and two days later he expired from cere-bral influenza in the bosom of his family.

'His last words in his last lucid moment were: "It is not a question of my personal interests but of the common weal. From that point of view be so good as to accept my judgement, which is as objective as . . ." – and he hiccupped.'

The volunteer paused and said maliciously to the corporal:

'I only meant by that that at some time or other everybody finds himself in a dicey situation and makes a blunder!'

All in all the only thing the corporal understood from all this was that he was the one who was making a blunder and so he turned back to the window and stared gloomily at the retreating landscape.

Švejk showed more interest in the story. The escort looked stupidly at each other.

Švejk began: 'Nothing remains hidden in the world. Everything comes to light in the end, as you've heard, and it even turns out that an idiotic jay like that is not a nutcracker. It's really very interesting that anyone could be taken in by a trick like that. It's true that inventing animals is a difficult thing to do, but presenting animals which have been invented is really much harder. Once some years ago in Prague there was a chap called Mestek who discovered a mermaid and exhibited her behind a screen in Havlíček Street in Vinohrady. In the screen there was an opening, and everybody could see in the half-light a common or garden sofa with a woman from Žižkov sprawling on it. Her legs were wrapped up in green gauze, which was supposed to represent a tail. Her hair was painted green and she had gloves on her hands with cardboard fins fitted on them, which were also green. And on her spine she had a kind of rudder fixed with a cord. Young people under sixteen were not allowed in, but all those who were over sixteen and had paid for their tickets were absolutely delighted to find that that mermaid had enormous buttocks on which was the inscription: "Au revoir!" As for her breasts they were nothing to shout about. They flopped down to her stomach like a worn-out trollop's. At seven o'clock in the evening Mestek shut the panorama and said: "Mermaid, you can go home." She changed and already at ten o'clock at night you could see her walking up and down Táborská Street and saying quite unobtrusively to every gentleman she met: "Darling, what about coming and playing philopena with me?" Because she didn't have a registration book Drašner locked her up with other tarts like her he had caught in a raid, and Mestek lost his business.'

At that moment the senior chaplain fell off the bench but went on sleeping on the floor. The corporal stared at him stupidly and then during the general silence lifted him on to the bench again without any help from the others. He had obviously lost all authority and when he said in a weak, hopeless voice: 'You might give me a hand,' all the escort looked woodenly and none of them stirred a finger.

'You should have left him snoozing where he was,' said Švejk. 'I never did anything else with my chaplain. Once I let him sleep in the W.C. Once he slept on top of the cupboard, another time in the washing trough in someone else's house and God knows where else he didn't lie and snooze.'

The corporal was suddenly seized by a fit of determination: he wanted to show that he was master here and so he said rudely: 'Shut your mug and don't drivel! Every batman blathers too much. You're worse than vermin.'

'Yes, of course, and you're God, corporal,' answered Švejk with the composure of a philosopher who wants to bring about universal peace throughout the world and launches into frightful arguments. 'You are the Madonna of the Seven Griefs.'

'Oh, God, our heavenly father,' the volunteer cried, wringing his hands, 'fill our hearts with love for all N.C.O.s, that we may not look upon them with loathing. Bless our congregation in this prison hole on wheels.'

The corporal flushed and jumped up: 'I forbid all remarks, you one-yearer.'

'You can't help it,' continued the volunteer in a soothing tone. 'Nature has denied many breeds and families of animals any intelligence whatsoever. Have you ever heard talk of human stupidity? Wouldn't it have been much better if you'd been born some other kind of mammal and not got the idiotic name of human being and corporal? It's a great mistake for you to think that you're the most perfect and most developed creature. If they take your stars away from you you're a mere cipher to be shot dead in any trench and on any front without anybody caring. If they give you another pip and make you into an animal that's called an "old sweat" it still won't be all right with you. Your mental horizon'll get still narrower and when somewhere on the front you lay down your culturally underdeveloped bones there won't be anyone in Europe to shed a tear for you.'

'I'll have you clapped in gaol,' shouted the corporal despairingly.

The volunteer smiled: 'Of course you'd like to clap me in gaol because I've called you names. But you'd be lying, because your mental faculties are quite incapable of grasping any insults and, apart from that, I'm willing to bet you what you like that you don't remember a single word of our conversation. If I said to you that you were an embryo, you'd forget it not just before we come to the next station but before the next telegraph post flashes past us. You're a piece of defunct grey matter. I can't imagine that you could ever report coherently what you've heard me say. Apart from that, you can ask anybody you like whether my words contain the slightest reference to your mental horizon and whether I have insulted you in any way.'

'Why, of course not,' confirmed Švejk. 'No one here said a single word to you on which you could possibly put a wrong construction. It's always bad when someone feels himself insulted. Once I was sitting in the night café The Tunnel and we talked about orang-outangs. There was a sailor sitting with us and he told us that you often can't tell an orang-outang from an ordinary citizen with a beard. An orang-outang has his chin covered with tufts like . . ."like," he went on, "shall we say, that gentleman sitting there at the next table." We all looked round and that man with the beard went up to the sailor and slapped his face. The sailor then broke his head with a beer bottle and the bearded gentleman fell down and lay unconscious. We said goodbye to that sailor, because he went away at once when he saw he had very nearly slain the man. Then we revived the gentleman, which we certainly shouldn't have done, because as soon as he was revived he called the police against all of us, although we had had absolutely nothing to do with it, and the police took us off to the police station. There he went on saying that we had taken him for an orang-outang and that we had been talking about nothing else but him. And so he went on. But we objected and said he wasn't an orang-outang. And he said, yes, he was one, he'd heard it. I asked the police commissioner if he would explain it to him. And he explained it to him quite good-naturedly, but even then that fellow wouldn't hear of it and told the commissioner that he didn't understand anything about it and was in league with us. And so the commissioner had him locked up to sober him, and we wanted to go back to The Tunnel, but we couldn't because we were put into clink too. So you see, corporal, what can come out of a small and unimportant misunderstanding, which is not worth mentioning. In Okrouhlice, too, there was a citizen who got offended when they told him in Německý Brod that he was an Indian python. There are a lot of other words like that which are not criminal at all. For instance, if we told you that you were a musk-rat, would you really have any reason to be angry with us?'

The corporal squealed. You could not say that he roared. Rage, fury, despair, all this merged in a series of powerful sounds and the concert number was completed by the whistling act which the snoring senior chaplain performed through his nose.

After this squealing total depression set in. The corporal sat down on

the bench and his watery expressionless eyes fixed themselves on the forests and mountains in the distance.

'Corporal,' said the volunteer, 'when you stare at the soughing hills and fragrant forests you remind me of the figure of Dante. The same noble face of the poet, a man of gentle heart and soul, susceptible to noble emotion. Please go on sitting there. It suits you very well. With what inspiration, without any affectation or pompousness, you stare out on the countryside. Certainly you are thinking how beautiful it will be in the spring when in the place of these barren spots a carpet of gaily coloured meadow flowers will unfold . . .'

'And that carpet will be hugged by a little brooklet,' observed Švejk, 'and the corporal will be licking his pencil, sitting on a tree-stump and writing a little poem to *The Young Reader*.'

The corporal became completely apathetic while the volunteer maintained that he had definitely seen the corporal's head modelled at a sculptural exhibition:

'Excuse me, corporal, isn't it true that you once sat for the great sculptor Štursa?'

The corporal looked at him and said sadly:

'No, I didn't.'

The volunteer was silent and stretched himself out on the bench.

The men from the escort were playing cards with Švejk. Out of despair the corporal kibitzed from time to time and even permitted himself the remark that Švejk had led the ace of spades and that it was a mistake. He ought not to have trumped, but kept the seven for the last trick.

'In pubs,' said Švejk, 'there used to be very good notices against kibitzers. I remember one of them: "Kibitzer, go and hold your jaw, or I'll knock you on the floor."'

The army train went into the station, where the vans were to be inspected. The train stopped.

'Well, of course,' said the volunteer mercilessly, giving a knowing glance at the corporal, 'we've got the inspection already . . .'

Inspectors entered the van.

Reserve officer Dr Mráz had been appointed by the staff to be commandant of the military train.

They always pushed reserve officers into stupid jobs like this. Dr Mráz had been driven off his rocker by it. He still could not account for one of the vans, though in civil life he was a teacher of mathematics at a secondary modern school. Besides, the number of men reported in the various vans at the last station did not tally with the number given after they had taken their places in the train at Budějovice. When he looked into his papers it appeared that suddenly out of the blue he had two field-kitchens too many. His discovery that in some mysterious way the horses had multiplied sent unpleasant shivers up his spine. In the list of officers he could not trace two missing cadets. In the first van where there was the regimental office they were all the time looking for a typewriter. All this chaos gave him a headache. He had already taken three aspirins and now he was inspecting the train with a painful expression on his face.

When he entered the prison van with his companion he looked at the papers and, receiving the report of the distraught corporal that he was escorting two prisoners and had such and such a number of men with him, he verified once more from the documents the correctness of the information and looked around him.

'Who on earth are you taking with you?' he asked severely, pointing to the senior chaplain who was sleeping on his belly and whose hindquarters looked up provocatively at the inspectors.

'Humbly report, sir,' stuttered the corporal, 'it's thingum-a-bob . . .'

'What do you mean by "thingum-a-bob"?' growled Dr Mráz. 'Express yourself clearly.'

'Humbly report, sir,' Švejk replied for the corporal, 'this gentleman who is sleeping on his belly is a senior chaplain who is the worse for liquor. He hooked himself on to us and got into the van here and because he is our superior officer we couldn't throw him out in case there should be a breach of *super*ordination. He obviously confused the staff carriage with the prison van.'

Dr Mráz sighed and looked into his papers. There was no mention there of any senior chaplain who had to go by train to Bruck. His eye twitched nervously. At the last station there had suddenly been too many horses, and now senior chaplains sprang up out of the blue in the prisoners' van.

He could not brace himself to do anything more than order the corporal to turn the man over because from his present position where he was sleeping on his belly it was not possible to identify him.

After long efforts the corporal turned the senior chaplain over on his back, during which he woke up, and seeing the officer in front of him said in German: 'Hey, servus, Freddie, what's the news? Is dinner ready?' Then he closed his eyes again and turned to the wall.

Dr Mráz at once saw that it was the glutton from the officers' mess of the previous night, the notorious shark who wolfed up all the officers' mess portions, and he sighed quickly.

'For this you'll go on report,' he said to the corporal. He was just going away when Švejk stopped him:

'Humbly report, sir, I don't belong here. I'm supposed to be incarcerated only till eleven, because it's just today that my term expires. I've been locked up for three days and now I ought to go and sit with the others in the cattle truck. As it's already long past eleven I would ask you, sir, if I could be put out on to the track or sent forward either to the cattle truck where I belong or to Lieutenant Lukáš.'

'What's your name?' asked Dr Mráz, looking again at his papers.

'Švejk, Josef, humbly report, sir.'

'H'm, so you're that famous Švejk,' said Dr Mráz. 'It's true you should have been out by eleven. But Lieutenant Lukáš asked me not to let you out until Bruck. He said it'd be safer, because at least you wouldn't be up to any mischief on the way.'

After the inspectors' departure the corporal could not refrain from making the acid remark:

'So you see, Švejk, that it helped you a shit to apply to higher authority. If I'd have wanted to I could have made it very hot for both of you.'

'Corporal,' said the volunteer, 'throwing shit is a more or less credible form of argument, but an intelligent man shouldn't use such words if he is angry, or if he wants to attack anybody. And then that ridiculous threat of yours that you could make it hot for both of us. Why the hell didn't you do so, when you had the opportunity? This just shows your great intellectual maturity and your rare tact.'

'I've had enough of this!' the corporal said, jumping up. 'I can take you both off to prison!'

'And what for, ducks?' asked the volunteer innocently.

'That's my affair!' said the corporal, summoning courage.

'Your affair,' said the volunteer with a smile. 'Yours and ours. Just like that card game, "My aunt – your aunt!". I should rather say that the mention of your having to go on report has upset you, and that's why you are beginning to shout at us, of course in a way quite contrary to official regulations.'

'You're vulgar swine!' said the corporal screwing up his last courage to make himself appear frightening.

'I'll tell you something, corporal,' observed Švejk: 'I'm an old soldier. I served before the war and I tell you you never get anywhere with bad language. I can remember that when I served years ago there was an old sweat in our company called Schreiter. He served for the soup, as the saying goes. He could have gone home long ago as a corporal, but he was slightly cracked. That chap went for us men. He stuck to us like shit on a shirt. This thing wasn't right and then that was against all regulations. He bullied us like hell and used to say to us: "You're not soldiers but a pack of lousy watchmen." One day I lost my temper and went on company report. "What do you want?" asked the captain. "Humbly report, sir, it's a complaint against our Sergeant-Major Schreiter: after all, we're soldiers of the Emperor and not a pack of lousy watchmen. We serve His Imperial Majesty and we're not guarding fruit trees."

' "Listen, you vermin," the captain replied, "get out of my sight!" And so I asked him obediently if he would put me on battalion report.

'On battalion report, when I had explained to the lieutenant-colonel that we were not just watchmen but soldiers of the Emperor, he had me locked up for two days, but then I asked to be put on regimental report. When I explained things on regimental report the colonel roared at me that I was a bloody idiot and I could go to hell. And so I again countered: "Humbly report, sir, may I be put on brigade report?" He was afraid of that and at once had our Sergeant-Major Schreiter summoned to the office, who had to apologize to me in the presence of all the officers for the words "lousy watchmen". Afterwards he caught up with me in the yard and told me that from that day on he wouldn't swear at me but hound me to the garrison gaol. From then on I was on the look-out as you can imagine but I didn't watch carefully enough. I stood at sentry post by the stores and every sentry always wrote something on the wall. Either they drew female genitals or wrote a little rhyme. I couldn't think of anything and so out of sheer boredom I put my signature under the inscription: "Old sweat Schreiter is an oaf." And that swine of a sergeant-major at once denounced me, because he was tracking me like a bloodhound. By an unfortunate mischance on top of that inscription there was another one: "We're not going to war. We shit on it", and that was in 1912, when we were about to march to Serbia because of that consul

Prochaska.[1] And so they sent me at once to Terezín to the regional court. About fifteen times the gentlemen from the military court photographed that wall by the stores and its inscriptions with my signature on it, and ten times they made me write down: "We're not going to war. We shit on it" so that they could examine my handwriting. Fifteen times I had to write in front of them: "Old sweat Schreiter is an oaf", and in the end an expert in handwriting came and made me write: "It was 29 July 1897 when Dvůr Králové on the Elbe experienced the terrors of the Elbe in wild flood." "That's not enough," the judge advocate said. "What interests us is the shit. Dictate to him something where there are a lot of s's and h's." And so he dictated to me: "Sherry, sheik, shark, pasha, sheriff, shemozzle, shyster, riff-raff." That handwriting expert from the court was driven quite crazy by it. He always looked round at the soldier standing behind him with a bayonet and finally said it would have to go to Vienna and I must write three times in succession: "And the sun begins to scorch too. It is beautifully warm." They sent all the material to Vienna and in the end the result was that as far as those inscriptions were concerned it was not my handwriting, but that the signature was mine because I had confessed to it. So I was sentenced to six weeks because I had signed it while on sentry duty and they said I couldn't be properly on guard at the time that I was doing it.'

'And so it's clear,' said the corporal with satisfaction, 'that all the same you didn't get off without being punished and that you are a proper criminal. If it had been me and not that court I'd have booked you not just for six weeks but for six years.'

'Don't be so awful,' the volunteer interposed, 'and think instead of how you'll end up yourself. Not long ago the inspector told you that you'd have to go on report. For a matter like that you ought to prepare yourself very seriously and ponder on the last moments of a corporal. What are you really in comparison with the universe, when you consider that the nearest fixed star is 275,000 times farther away from this army train than the sun and its parallax can make one second of arc? If you were a fixed star in the universe you'd certainly be too minute for even the best astronomical instruments to identify. Your insignificance in the universe defies definition. For half a year you'd make in the sky a

1. In 1912 the Austrian government unleashed a press campaign against Serbia on the unsubstantiated charge that their consul in Prizren, named Prochaska, had been mishandled. In fact nothing had happened to him.

tiny arc, in a year a very tiny ellipse which would be too small to be expressed in figures. Your parallax would defy measurement.'

'If that's the case,' observed Švejk, 'the corporal should be proud of the fact that no one could measure him, and however it may turn out on report he should be calm and not get excited, because all excitement is dangerous for the health, and now in wartime we must all take care of our health, because these war exertions require of every individual that he shouldn't be a lame duck.

'If they put you in gaol, corporal,' continued Švejk with a sweet smile, 'if you suffer any injustice, then don't lose heart, and if they have their own opinions, you stick to yours. I once knew a coalman who was locked up with me at police headquarters in Prague for high treason at the beginning of the war, František Škvor, and who later might have been executed because of a Pragmatic Sanction or something. When this man was asked at interrogation whether he had anything to object to in the statements, he said:

> ' "However it used to be, it used to be somehow.
> It never happened yet that it was no-how."

'After that they put him into a dark cell and gave him nothing to eat or drink for two days and again brought him back for interrogation. But he continued to insist that however it used to be, it used to be somehow. It never happened yet that it was no-how. Perhaps, after they had court-martialled him, he went with it to the gallows.'

'They say that they hang and shoot people a lot nowadays,' said one of the escort. 'Not long ago on the drill-ground they read us out an order that at Motol they had shot the reservist, Kudrna, because the captain slashed with his sabre his little boy, who was in his wife's arms when she came to say goodbye to him at Benešov and he lost his temper. And "politicals" are locked up as a matter of course. They also shot an editor in Moravia. And our captain said that the same fate's in store for others.'

'Everything has its limits,' said the volunteer ambiguously.

'You're right,' said the corporal. 'It serves editors like that right. They only stir the people up. Last year when I was still only a lance-corporal I had an editor under me and he called me nothing else but a disaster for the army, but when I taught him unarmed drill and he sweated, he always used to say: "Please respect the human being in me." But I gave him hell for his human being when the order was "flat down" and there were a lot of puddles in the barracks courtyard. I took him in front of a puddle like that and the bastard had to fall down into it until the water splashed like in a swimming pool. And in the afternoon he had to have everything on him glittering, his uniform had to be as clean as a new pin, and he rubbed and moaned and muttered. The next day he was again like a pig wallowing in the mud and I stood over him and said to him: "So you see, Mr Editor, what's more important, that disaster for the army or that human being of yours?" He was a regular highbrow, he was!'

The corporal looked triumphantly at the volunteer and continued: 'All because of his being a highbrow he lost his one-year stripes, for he wrote to the newspapers about the maltreatment of soldiers. But how could you help maltreating him when a learned chap like him couldn't even dismantle the breech of his rifle, not even when he was shown how to do it ten times. And when he was told: "Eyes left", he screwed his silly nut to the right as though on purpose and stared all the time like an old crow. And at rifle practice he never knew what to grasp first, the sling or his cartridge-pouch. And when you showed him how his arm had to go down on the sling he goggled at you like a calf at a new gate. He didn't even know which shoulder you carry your rifle on and he saluted like a monkey, and when he had to make turns, God help us, the movements he made when there was a march past and he was learning how to step! When he had to do about-turn it was all the same to him which of his shanks he did it with. Thud, thud, thud! He might take six paces forward and only then turn round like a cock on a swivel. And when he marched his step was like a chap's with gout or he danced about like an old whore at a parish fair.'

The corporal spat: 'He was purposely allocated a very rusty rifle from the store to learn how to clean it and he rubbed it like a dog does a bitch, but even if he had bought two kilos of tow more he wouldn't have been able to clean it properly. The more he rubbed it the worse and rustier it became and on report his rifle was passed from hand to hand and everyone was amazed how it was possible that it could be nothing but rust. Our captain used to tell him that he would never be a soldier, that it would be better if he went and hanged himself and that he was uselessly wasting the army bread. But he just blinked under his glasses. It was a red-letter day for him when he didn't get "severe" or confined to barracks. Then he usually wrote his articles to the newspapers about the manhandling of the troops until one day they searched his baggage. And, my God, all the books he had! Only about disarmament and international peace. Because of that he had to pop off quick to the garrison gaol and from then on he gave us peace until he suddenly reappeared in the office, where his job was to fill in ration forms so that the men shouldn't have any contact with him. That was the sad end of that highbrow. He might have become a very different gentleman altogether if he had not lost his volunteer privileges because of his stupidity. He could have become a lieutenant.'

The corporal sighed: 'He couldn't even get the folds right on his greatcoat. From Prague he ordered various liquids and polish for cleaning buttons and all the same his buttons looked as rusty and red as Esau. But couldn't he half jaw! And when he was in the office he did nothing else but philosophize. He had a liking for that before. As I said, he was always on about his "human being" and nothing else. Once when he was reflecting over a puddle in which he had to plop down when he did his "flat down" I said to him: "When you're always talking about a human being even when you're in the mud remember that man was created out of the dust of the ground and it must have been O.K. for him." '

Having said what he wanted, the corporal was pleased with himself and waited for what the volunteer would say. But it was Švejk who spoke:

'For the same sort of things, for manhandling like that, years ago a certain Koníček stabbed himself and his corporal in the 35th regiment. I read it in the *Courier*. The corporal had about thirty wounds in his body, of which over a dozen were mortal. Afterwards that soldier sat on the body of the dead corporal and stabbed himself on top of it. There was another case years ago in Dalmatia where they cut a corporal's throat and no one knows to this day who did it. It remained shrouded in secrecy and all that was known was that the corporal was called Fiala and came from Drábovna near Turnov. And then I know of another corporal in the 75th regiment called Rejmánek . . .'

This pleasant narration was interrupted by loud groans from the seat where the senior chaplain, Lacina, was sleeping.

The venerable father awoke in all his beauty and dignity. His awakening was accompanied by the same phenomena as the morning awakening of the young giant Gargantua as described by gay old Rabelais.

The senior chaplain farted, belched on the bench and gave an enormous yawn. At last he sat up and asked in surprise:

'Kruzilaudon, where am I?'

The corporal, seeing that the military gentleman had woken up, answered very servilely:

'Humbly report, sir, Your Reverence is pleased to be in the prison van.'

A gleam of astonishment passed over the venerable father's face. He sat for a moment in silence and tried hard to collect his thoughts. It was in vain. There was an ocean of obscurity between what had happened to him in the small hours and his awakening in a van the windows of which were covered with bars.

In the end he asked the corporal who was still standing servilely in front of him: 'And on whose orders am I here – I . . .'

'Humbly report, sir, on nobody's orders.'

The venerable father stood up and began to walk up and down between the benches muttering to himself that he could not understand.

He sat down again and said: 'Where are we actually going?'

'Humbly report, sir, to Bruck.'

'And why are we going to Bruck?'

'Humbly report, sir, the whole of our 91st regiment is transferred there.'

The venerable father tried hard again to ransack his memory of what had actually happened to him, how he got into the van and why on earth he was going to Bruck and of all things with the 91st regiment under an escort.

He had recovered sufficiently from his hangover to be able to distinguish the volunteer and so turned to him to ask:

'You are an intelligent person. Can you explain to me without further nonsense and without suppressing anything how I managed to get into your company?'

'With pleasure,' said the volunteer in an amiable tone. 'When we were getting into the train you joined up with us at the station in the morning because you had taken a drop too much.'

The corporal looked at him severely.

'You got into our van,' continued the volunteer, 'and the thing was done. You lay down on the bench, and Švejk here put his greatcoat under your head. When the train was inspected at the last station you were entered on the lists of officers travelling in it. You were, so to speak, officially discovered and our corporal will have to go on report because of it.'

'I see, I see,' sighed the venerable father. 'See that I am transferred to the staff carriage at the next station. You don't know by any chance whether lunch has already been served?'

'Lunch won't be served until Vienna, sir,' the corporal put in.

'And so it was you who put your coat under my head?' the venerable father said to Švejk. 'Thank you very much indeed.'

'I don't deserve any gratitude,' replied Švejk, 'I only acted as every soldier has to act when he sees that his superior officer has nothing under his head and that he's – what-d'ye-call-it. Every soldier has got to respect his superior, even if he's half-seas over. I have great experience with chaplains because I was the batman to the chaplain, Otto Katz. Chaplains are a merry and good-natured lot.'

The senior chaplain, who had got a fit of democracy as a result of his hangover from the day before, took out a cigarette and offered it to Švejk: 'Have a puff, my boy!'

'And you are going on report because of me, are you?' he said to the corporal. 'Don't worry. I'll get you off that. Nothing will happen to you.'

'And as for you,' he said to Švejk, 'I'll take you with me. You'll live with me like in a feather bed.'

Now he got a new fit of magnanimity and insisted that he would do something for each one of them. He would buy chocolate for the volunteer and rum for the escort. He would have the corporal transferred to the photographic section of the staff of the 7th cavalry division. He would free all of them and never forget them.

He began to distribute cigarettes from his case not only to Švejk but to all of them, and declared that he permitted all the prisoners to smoke, that he would do his best to see that their punishment was reduced and have them returned to normal military life.

'I don't want you to think badly of me. I have many connections and I won't let you down. You all of you impress me as being decent people whom the Lord loves. If you have sinned you are atoning for your acts and I see that you gladly and readily endure what God has visited you with.'

He turned to Švejk: 'On what grounds have you been punished?'

'The Lord visited me with a punishment,' answered Švejk piously, 'on regimental report, sir, as a result of my being late in reaching my regiment through no fault of mine.'

'God is boundlessly merciful and just,' said the senior chaplain solemnly. 'He knows whom he should punish and shows in this his wisdom and omnipotence. And why are you in gaol, volunteer?'

'Because,' answered the volunteer, 'merciful God was gracious enough to visit me with rheumatism and I waxed too proud. After serving my sentence I shall be sent to the kitchen.'

'What God ordains he ordains well,' said the venerable father enthusiastically when he heard about the kitchen. 'Even there a decent chap can make a career. The kitchen is just the place where they should put intelligent people because of all the possible combinations. What is important is not how one cooks but the love with which the food is put together and prepared and so on. Take sauces, for example. When an intelligent person makes onion sauce he takes all kinds of vegetables and fries them in butter. Then he adds spices, pepper, new spices, a little nutmeg and ginger. But an ordinary second-rate cook has the onion boiled and throws into it brown roux made with suet. Best of all I'd like to see you somewhere in an officers' mess. A man can live without intelligence in an ordinary occupation and in life, but in the kitchen he's shown up. Yesterday evening in Budějovice in the officers' mess they gave us among other things kidneys *à la madeira*. May God forgive all the sins of the man who cooked them. That was a really intelligent man and it is true that in the kitchen of that officers' mess there is a teacher from Skuteč. I had eaten the same kidneys *à la madeira* in the officers' mess of the 64th Landwehr regiment. They put caraway seed in them, like they do in an ordinary country pub when they make kidneys with pepper. And who did them? What was that cook in civil life? He was a cattle-fattener on a big estate.'

The senior chaplain stopped and then changed the conversation to culinary problems in the Old and New Testament, where particularly in those times they took a great deal of trouble with the preparation of tasty dishes after divine service and other church ceremonies. He then invited them all to sing something, whereupon Švejk, unfortunately as usual, started up:

> 'Naughty Caroline
> Gave a little sign.
> After her the vicar
> Followed with the wine.'

But the senior chaplain did not get angry.

'If there was only a drop of rum here, we wouldn't need any wine,' he said, smiling in a completely friendly mood, 'and we could dispense with that Caroline too. She leads people to sin anyway.'

The corporal cautiously groped in his coat and drew out a flat bottle with rum in it.

'Humbly report, sir,' he said quietly, so that it could be felt what a sacrifice he was making. 'If you wouldn't take it amiss?'

'I'll certainly not take it amiss, my boy,' answered the reverend father joyfully, his voice assuming a cheery tone. 'I'll drink to our happy journey.'

'Jesus Mary,' gasped the corporal, observing that after a thorough swig half the bottle had disappeared.

'Oh, you rogue, you!' said the chaplain, smiling and winking knowingly at the volunteer, 'you're even taking the name of the Lord in vain into the bargain. The Lord must punish you for this.'

The venerable father again took a swig from the flat bottle and giving it to Švejk gave the imperious order: 'Bottoms up!'

'War is war,' Švejk said good-humouredly to the corporal as he returned him the empty bottle, the emptiness being confirmed by a strange glint in the corporal's eyes such as can only appear in a mental patient.

'And now I shall take forty winks until we get to Vienna,' said the senior chaplain, 'and I should be grateful if you would wake me as soon as we get there.

'You,' he turned to Švejk, 'will go to the kitchen of our mess, collect some knives and forks and fetch me my lunch. Say that it is for the senior chaplain, Lacina. Make sure that you get a double portion. If there are dumplings, don't take them from the ends. You only lose out on that. After that bring me a bottle of wine from the kitchen and take your mess-tin with you, so that they can pour rum into it.'

Father Lacina fumbled in his pockets.

'Listen,' he said to the corporal, 'I haven't any change. Lend me a guilder. Hey, here you are! What's your name? Švejk?

'Here you are, Švejk, here's a tip for you! Corporal, lend me another guilder. Look, Švejk, you'll get that second guilder when you've done your commission properly. And don't forget too to see that they give you cigarettes and cigars for me. If they are also serving out chocolate, bag a double portion and if there are any tins see that they give you smoked tongue or goose liver. If they're giving out Emmental cheese, see that they don't give you a piece from the edge, and when it comes to Hungarian salami don't take an end but a cut from the middle, where it's juicy.'

The senior chaplain stretched himself out on the bench and was asleep in a moment.

'I think that you must be quite pleased with our foundling,' said the volunteer to the corporal to the accompaniment of the reverend father's snores. 'He's alive and kicking.'

'He's already weaned, as the saying goes,' said Švejk. 'He's already taking the bottle.'

The corporal struggled with himself for a moment and suddenly, losing all humility, said harshly: 'Pretty fair sauce!'

'Not having any change he reminds me of a chap called Mlíčko, a mason from Dejvice,' said Švejk. 'He never had any change either, until he was up to his ears in debt and was gaoled for fraud. He ate up big money and never had any small change.'

'In the 75th regiment before the war,' said a man from the escort, 'the captain bust all the regimental funds on drink and was cashiered. Now he's a captain again. And a sergeant-major who robbed the army of cloth for facings – there were more than twenty packages of it – is now a staff sergeant-major. And not long ago they shot an infantryman in Serbia because he ate up his whole tin at one go when it was supposed to last him three days.'

'That's got nothing to do with it,' said the corporal, 'but it's true that to borrow from a poor corporal two guilders for a tip is . . .'

'Here you are. Here's the guilder,' said Švejk. 'I don't want to enrich myself at your expense. And if he gives me a second guilder I'll return that too, so that you shouldn't blub. You ought to be glad when one of your military superiors borrows money from you for his expenses. You are frightfully selfish. It's only a question of two miserable guilders. I'd like to see what you'd do if you had to sacrifice your life for your military superior, if he were lying wounded somewhere in the enemy lines and you had to save him and carry him away in your arms, when they were shooting at you with shrapnel and everything possible.'

'You'd shit with fright,' the corporal defended himself, 'you chicken-livered little batman.'

'There's a lot of shitting in every battle,' the man from the escort chimed in again. 'Not long ago one of the chaps who was wounded told us in Budějovice that when they were advancing he shitted three times in succession: first when they were climbing up from cover to the space before the barbed-wire entanglement; a second time when they started cutting the wire, and a third time when the Russians rushed at them with their bayonets and shouted "Hurrah." Then they began to run back to the trenches and in their unit there wasn't a single man who hadn't shitted. And a dead man, who lay on top of the cover with his legs hanging down and half of whose head had been torn off by shrapnel, just as though he'd been cut in half, he too in the last moment shitted so much that it ran from his trousers over his boots into the trenches mixed with blood. And half his skull together with his brains lay right underneath. A chap doesn't even notice how it happens to him.'

'Sometimes,' said Švejk, 'a chap gets ill in a fight. It nauseates him. A sick re-convalescent from Przemyśl told us in a pub called Outlook at Pohořelec in Prague that there was a bayonet assault somewhere under the fortifications and a Russian suddenly appeared facing him, a mountain of a man who went for him with his bayonet and had a huge drip on his nose. When he looked at that Russian's nose drip, at his snot, he suddenly began to feel sick and had to go to the first-aid post where they diagnosed him as suffering from cholera and sent him to the cholera barracks in Budapest, where he actually caught cholera.'

'Was that a common soldier or a corporal?' asked the volunteer.

'It was a corporal,' Švejk answered calmly.

'That could happen to any volunteer too,' said the corporal stupidly, but as he spoke he looked triumphantly at the volunteer, as if to say: 'One up to me. What d'you say to that?'

But the volunteer made no reply and lay down on the bench.

They drew near to Vienna. Those who were not sleeping observed from the window the barbed-wire entanglements and fortifications around Vienna, which obviously evoked feelings of depression throughout the train.

One could still hear from the vans the incessant roaring of the Boche from Kašperské Hory: '*Wann ich kum*', *wann ich kum*', *wann ich wieda*', *wieda*' *kum*',[1] but now it was hushed under the unpleasant impression of the barbed wire, with which Vienna was lined.

'Everything's in order,' said Švejk, looking at the trenches. 'Everything is in perfect order, except that these Viennese may get their trousers torn when they go out on trips on Sunday. A chap's got to be very careful here.

'Vienna is quite an important city,' he continued. 'Only think of the wild animals they have in their Schönbrunn menagerie! When I was in Vienna years ago I liked best of all to go and look at the monkeys, but when any personality drives out of the Imperial Palace they don't allow anybody through the cordon. I had with me a tailor from the tenth district and they put him in gaol because he was determined to see those monkeys at any price.'

'And have you been to the palace too?' asked the corporal.

'It's very beautiful there,' answered Švejk. 'I haven't been there, but someone who had been there told me all about it. The finest of all is the palace guard. Everyone must be two metres high and afterwards he gets a kiosk to run. As for princesses there are swarms of them.'

They passed through a station. Behind them could be heard the sounds of the Austrian hymn played by a band which had come here probably by mistake, because it took them a long time to get with the

1. When I come, when I come,
   When I come back again . . .

train into the station. They stopped, got their mess portions and a ceremonial welcome.

But it was not the same as it had been at the beginning of the war when soldiers on their journey to the front stuffed themselves at every station and when they were welcomed by maidens in stupid white dresses with still more stupid faces, by desperately stupid bunches of flowers and even stupider speeches from some lady, whose husband today pretends to be a great patriot and republican.

The reception party in Vienna consisted of three lady members of the society of the Austrian Red Cross, two members of a war society of Viennese ladies and girls, an official delegate from the Vienna magistracy and a military representative.

Fatigue could be seen on all these faces. Troop trains passed through day and night, ambulance coaches packed full of wounded every hour. At the stations they continually shunted trains of prisoners from one track to another, and members of all these various corporations and clubs had to be everywhere present. This went on from day to day and the initial enthusiasm degenerated into yawning. People attended in shifts and all who appeared on a Vienna station had exactly the same tired expression as those who were waiting that day for the train with the Budějovice regiment.

Soldiers peered out of cattle trucks with an expression of hopelessness like people going to the gallows.

Ladies came to them and doled them out gingerbread cakes with German inscriptions in sugar: 'Victory and Vengeance', '*Gott strafe England*', 'The Austrian has a Fatherland. He loves it and has good cause to fight for it.'

The men from Kašperské Hory could be seen stuffing themselves with gingerbread cakes, without losing their expression of hopelessness.

Then came the order to go by companies for mess portions to the field-kitchens, which stood behind the station.

There was also an officers' kitchen there, where Švejk went to carry out the orders of the senior chaplain, while the volunteer waited until he was fed, because two of the escort went to fetch the mess portions for the whole prison van.

Švejk carried out his orders correctly, and crossing the track saw Lieutenant Lukáš, who was walking between the lines and waiting to see whether there would be anything left for him in the officers' mess.

His situation was very unpleasant because for the time being he shared Lieutenant Kirschner's batman. The scoundrel only bothered about his own master and carried out complete sabotage when it was a question of anything for Lieutenant Lukáš.

'Who are you carrying that to, Švejk?' the unhappy lieutenant asked when Švejk put on the ground the pile of things which he had succeeded in wheedling out of the officers' mess and which he had wrapped up in his greatcoat.

Švejk was taken aback for the moment but immediately pulled himself together. His face was full of joy and peace when he replied:

'To you, humbly report, sir. Only I don't know where you have your carriage and I also don't know whether the commandant of the train won't make a fuss if I go with you. He must be a fair swine.'

Lieutenant Lukáš looked inquiringly at Švejk, who, however, went on affably and confidentially: 'He really is a swine, sir. When he came to inspect the train I informed him at once that it was already eleven o'clock and that I had by now served the whole of my sentence and should be either in the cattle truck or with you, and he snubbed me quite rudely and said that I must stay where I was, so that I shouldn't disgrace you again on the journey, sir.'

Švejk assumed a martyred expression: 'As though I had ever disgraced you, sir.'

Lieutenant Lukáš sighed.

'I've certainly never disgraced you,' continued Švejk. 'If anything ever happened, it was pure coincidence, nothing but a dispensation of God, as old Vaníček from Pelhřimov used to say when he had served his thirty-sixth sentence. I never meant any harm, sir. I always only wanted to do something helpful, something good, and it's not my fault if neither of us had any good out of it, but only misery and torment.'

'Don't cry so much, Švejk,' said Lieutenant Lukáš in a gentle voice, as they approached the staff carriage. 'I'll do everything to see that you're with me again.'

'Humbly report, sir, I'm not crying. It only dawned on me how sad it was that we are both the most unfortunate people of all in this war and under the sun and we can neither of us help it. It's a terrible fate, when I think that I've tried so hard for the best all my life.'

'Calm yourself, Švejk!'

'Humbly report, sir, if it were not insubordinate of me, I'd like to say I can't calm myself, but as things are I must say that following your instructions I'm already quite calm again.'

'Then go and get into the van, Švejk.'

'Humbly report, I'm getting in, sir.'

Night peace reigned over the military camp in Bruck. In the men's huts the soldiers shivered with cold and in the officers' quarters they were opening the windows because of the overheating.

From the various objects which were under guard there could be heard from time to time the steps of the patrol, who were marching to drive away sleep.

Down in Bruck an der Leitha shone the lights of the Imperial and Royal factory for tinned meat. Here they worked day and night and processed various kinds of offal. Because the wind blew from that quarter towards the alley in the military camp, it brought with it the stink of rotten sinews, hooves, trotters and bones which all went into the tinned soup.

From an abandoned little pavilion, where in peacetime a photographer used to photograph soldiers who were spending their youth here at the military shooting range, one could see down in the valley of the Leitha the red electric light of a brothel, The Maize Cob, which Archduke Stephen honoured with a visit during the great manoeuvres at Sopron in 1908, and where the officers foregathered every day.

It was the finest bawdy-house and ordinary soldiers or one-year volunteers were not permitted to patronize it.

They had to go to The House of Roses, the green light of which was also visible from the deserted photographer's studio.

There was the same class segregation as later at the front, when the monarchy could do nothing else to help its troops than provide them with transportable brothels assigned to the brigade staffs, the so-called 'puffs'.

Consequently there were 'Imperial and Royal Officers' Puffs', 'Imperial and Royal N.C.O.s' Puffs', and 'Imperial and Royal Men's Puffs'.

Bruck an der Leitha was bright with lights and on the other side beyond the bridge there glittered Királyhida, Cisleithania and Transleithania.[1] In both towns, Hungarian and Austrian, gipsy bands were playing, the windows of the cafés and restaurants gleamed with light, there was singing and drinking. The local burghers and officials brought their wives and grown-up daughters to the cafés and restaurants, and Bruck an der Leitha and Királyhida were nothing but one giant brothel.

In one of the officers' huts in the camp at night Švejk was waiting for his Lieutenant Lukáš, who had gone that evening to the theatre in the town and had not yet returned. Švejk had prepared the lieutenant's bed and was sitting on it while Major Wenzl's batman was sitting on the table opposite.

The major had returned to his regiment again, after his utter incompetence had been demonstrated on the Drina in Serbia. It was said that he had given orders for the dismantling and destruction of a pontoon bridge when half his battalion were still on the other side of it. Now he had been assigned to the military rifle range in Királyhida as commandant and also dealt with the camp's catering. The officers said that Major Wenzl would now make a packet. The rooms of Lukáš and Wenzl were in the same passage.

1. Austria was called Cisleithania, i.e. the lands on the nearer side of the Leitha. Hungary was Transleithania, i.e. the lands beyond it.

Major Wenzl's batman, Mikulášek, a pockmarked little fellow, was swinging his legs and swearing: 'I can't think why my old bastard hasn't come yet. I'd like to know where the old dodderer is gadding about all night. If he'd only given me the key of his room I could have gone to bed and had a few drops. He's got oceans of wine.'

'They say he flogs a lot,' Švejk observed, comfortably smoking one of his lieutenant's cigarettes because the latter had forbidden him to puff his pipe in the room. 'But surely you must know where he gets all that wine from?'

'I go where he sends me to,' said Mikulášek in a feeble voice. 'I get a warrant from him and then I go and draw supplies for the hospital and bring them to his home.'

'And if he were to order you to rob the regimental till,' Švejk asked, 'would you do it? You swear at him behind his back, but you tremble in front of him like an aspen leaf.'

Mikulášek blinked with his little eyes: 'I'd think twice about that.'

'There's nothing to think twice about, you silly coot!' Švejk shouted at him, but he suddenly stopped because the door opened and Lieutenant Lukáš came in. As could at once be observed he was in a high humour, because he had his cap on back to front.

Mikulášek was so scared that he forgot to jump down from the table and saluted in a sitting position, forgetting as well that he hadn't a cap on his head.

'Humbly report, sir, everything is in order,' announced Švejk, assuming a firm military appearance according to all regulations. Only the cigarette remained in his mouth.

Lieutenant Lukáš did not notice this however and went straight to Mikulášek who observed every one of his movements with goggling eyes and continued to salute while sitting on the table.

'Lieutenant Lukáš,' said the lieutenant, approaching Mikulášek with a not too firm gait. 'And what's your name?'

Mikulášek was silent. Lukáš brought a chair up for himself in front of Mikulášek, sat down and looking up at him said: 'Švejk, bring me my service revolver from my suitcase.'

The whole time that Švejk was looking for the revolver in the suitcase Mikulášek was staring in silent horror at the lieutenant. If he understood at this moment that he was sitting on the table it made him only the more desperate because his legs now were touching the knees of the seated lieutenant.

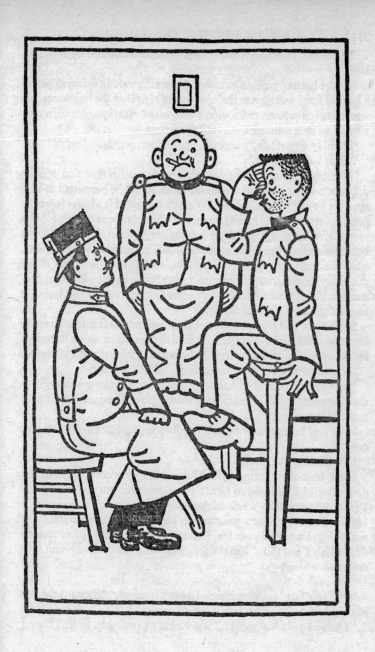

'Hi, what's your name, man?' the lieutenant shouted up to Mikulášek.

But the batman wouldn't answer. As he afterwards explained he had a kind of fit of paralysis at the unexpected arrival of the lieutenant. He wanted to jump down and couldn't, he wanted to reply and couldn't, he wanted to stop saluting but couldn't manage it.

'Humbly report, sir,' Švejk put in, 'the revolver isn't loaded.'

'Then load it, Švejk.'

'Humbly report, sir, we haven't got any cartridges and it'll be difficult to shoot him down from the table. May I be permitted to add, sir, that he is Mikulášek, Major Wenzl's batman. He always loses the power of speech when he sees one of the officer gentlemen. He's too shy to speak. I tell you, the thing's a complete milksop and it's still wet behind the ears. Major Wenzl always leaves it standing in the corridor, when he goes anywhere in the town, and it always moons about miserably from batman to batman in the barracks. You could understand it if it had some reason to be startled, but really, you know, it hasn't done any mischief at all.'

Švejk spat, and from the tone of his voice and the fact that he spoke about Mikulášek in the neuter one could deduce his complete contempt for the cowardice of Major Wenzl's batman and his unmilitary bearing.

'If you permit, sir,' continued Švejk, 'I'll sniff him.'

Švejk dragged down Mikulášek, who went on looking idiotically at the lieutenant from the table, and, having placed him on the ground, sniffed his trousers.

'Not yet,' he asserted, 'but it's already starting. Should I throw him out?'

'Throw him out, Švejk.'

Švejk took the quaking Mikulášek out into the corridor, shut the door after him and said to him: 'There you are, you stupid bastard. I've saved your life. When Major Wenzl returns you'll bring me a bottle of wine and keep your mouth shut, do you understand? I'm not joking. I've saved your life, honestly I have. When my lieutenant's sozzled it's a bad thing. I'm the only chap who can deal with him then and no one else.'

'I'm . . .'

'You're a fart,' Švejk exclaimed contemptuously. 'Sit on the doorstep and wait until your Major Wenzl comes.'

'You've been away enough,' was Lukáš's greeting to Švejk. 'Now I

want to talk to you. You don't have to go on standing at attention like
a stuck pig. Sit down, Švejk, and cut out that "according to orders".
Shut your mug and listen carefully. Do you know where Sopron Street
is in Királyhida? For God's sake cut out your: "Humbly report, sir,

I don't." If you don't know then say: "I don't know", and that's
enough. Write it down on a piece of paper: 16 Sopron Street. In that
house there's an ironmonger's shop. Do you know what an ironmonger's
shop is? Herrgott, don't say "Humbly report". Say "I do" or "I
don't." And so you know what an ironmonger's shop is? You do? All
right, then. That shop belongs to a Hungarian called Kákonyi. Do you
know what a Hungarian is? Now, Himmelherrgott, do you or don't
you? All right. Above the shop there is a first floor and that's where he
lives. Do you know that? You don't know. Hell's bells! I'm telling you
he lives there. Isn't that good enough for you? It is. Good. If it wouldn't
have been good enough for you, I'd have had you clapped in gaol. Have
you got it noted down that that bastard's called Kákonyi? Good. Very

well, then, tomorrow morning at about ten o'clock you'll go down to the town, you'll find that house, you'll go upstairs to the first floor and you'll hand this letter to Mrs Kákonyi.'

Lieutenant Lukáš opened his pocket book and, yawning, put into Švejk's hand a white envelope without an address.

'It's a frightfully important matter, Švejk,' he went on. 'Caution is never out of place, and consequently, as you can see for yourself, there's no address there. I rely completely on your handing this letter over properly. Make a further note that the lady is called Etelka. And so now write "Mrs Etelka Kákonyi". Let me add that you're to hand this letter over discreetly without fail and to wait for an answer. It's already written in the letter that you're to wait for an answer. Anything more?'

'But what am I to do, sir, if they don't give me an answer?'

'Then you'll tell them that you've got to get an answer at all costs,' replied the lieutenant with a terrible yawn. 'Now I'm going to bed. I'm really fagged today. My God, what we haven't drunk! I think anyone'd be as tired as I am after an evening and night like that.'

Lieutenant Lukáš had not originally intended to stay long in the town. Towards the evening he had left the camp and gone to the Hungarian theatre in Királyhida, where they were giving a Hungarian operetta. The leading roles were performed by buxom Jewish actresses, whose fabulous distinction was that when they danced they threw their legs up in the air and didn't wear either tights or drawers, and for the greater gratification of the officers they shaved themselves underneath like Tartar women. If the gallery got no gratification out of this, all the more fell to the share of the officers of the artillery, who were sitting down in the stalls and had taken with them to the theatre their artillery field glasses for this beautiful spectacle.

But this kind of interesting smuttiness had not much of an appeal for Lieutenant Lukáš, because the opera glasses he had hired were not achromatic and instead of thighs he only saw one or two violet patches in motion.

In the interval after the first act he was more attracted by a lady who was dragging to the cloakroom the middle-aged gentleman who escorted her and insisting to him that they should go home at once, because she refused to look at such things. She expressed it rather loudly in German, whereupon her escort replied in Hungarian: 'Yes, my angel, let's go, I agree. It really is a very tasteless spectacle.'

'It's disgusting,' answered the lady in incensed tones, when the gentleman wrapped her theatre cloak around her. Her eyes blazed with indignation over this obscenity – those big black eyes, which went so well with her beautiful figure. As she said this she looked at Lieutenant Lukáš and repeated once more with some passion: 'Disgusting, really disgusting!' This was decisive for a short romance.

He learned from the cloakroom attendant that they were Mr and Mrs Kákonyi, and that the husband kept an ironmonger's shop at 16 Sopron Street.

'And he lives with Mrs Etelka on the first floor,' said the cloakroom attendant with the detailed knowledge of an old bawdy-house keeper. 'She's a German from Sopron and he's a Hungarian. Here everything's mixed.'

Lieutenant Lukáš took his coat from the cloakroom too and went into the town, where he met some officers of the 91st regiment in the large wine restaurant and café, The Archduke Albrecht.

He did not talk much but drank all the more instead, planning what he should write to that severe, moral and pretty lady who definitely attracted him more than all those monkeys on the stage, as the other officers described them.

In a very good mood he went away to a small café, At the Cross of St Stephen, where he went into a small *chambre séparée* and threw out of it a Rumanian woman, who offered to strip naked before him, after which he could do with her what he liked. Then he ordered some ink, a pen, some writing paper and a bottle of cognac. Finally after careful consideration he wrote the following letter which seemed to him to be the loveliest he had ever composed:

Dear Madam,
  Yesterday in the Town Theatre I was present at the play which upset you so much. I watched you during the whole of the first act, you and your husband too. As I could observe . . .

'I won't pull my punches,' said Lieutenant Lukáš. 'What right has that bastard to have such a sweet wife. Why, he looks like a shaven baboon.'

He went on writing:

. . . your husband watched all the lewdness which was shown on the stage with complete understanding. But you, dear madam, were revolted by it because it was not art but disgusting exploitation of the most intimate human feelings.

'What breasts the woman has,' Lieutenant Lukáš thought. 'Why beat about the bush?'

Excuse me, dear lady, for writing so frankly to you, when you do not know me. I have seen many women in my life, but none of them have made such an impression upon me as you have, for your judgement and view of life are completely identical with mine. I am convinced that your husband is a rank egoist and drags you around with him . . .

'No, that won't do,' said Lieutenant Lukáš to himself. He crossed out: 'drags you around' and wrote instead:

. . . and in his own personal interests, dear lady, takes you with him to theatre performances which are on his own level of taste only. It is my custom to be frank. I do not wish to obtrude upon your private life and my only desire is to talk with you privately about pure art . . .

'It'll be no good in the hotels here. I'll have to carry her off to Vienna,' the lieutenant thought again. 'I'll fix up an official journey.'

And so I take the liberty, dear lady, of asking you if we could not meet and get to know each other better in all honour. You will surely not deny this to one who will soon be facing the sufferings of marching to the front and who, if you should accord him your gracious consent, will retain in the turmoil of battle the most beautiful memories of a soul who understood him just as he understood her. Your decision will be my command, your reply the decisive moment of my life.

He signed the letter, drank up his cognac, and ordered another bottle. Then, drinking glass after glass and reading over his last lines, he actually wept over every sentence.

It was nine o'clock in the morning, when Švejk woke Lieutenant Lukáš: 'Humbly report, sir, you've overslept your duty, and I must go with your letter to Királyhida. I called you once at seven, again at half past seven and then again at eight, as they went past for drill practice, but you just turned over on your other side. Sir . . . I say, sir . . . .'

Lieutenant Lukáš murmured something and wanted to turn over on his side again, but he did not succeed, because Švejk quite ruthlessly shook him and bellowed: 'Sir, I'm going with that letter to Királyhida.'

The lieutenant yawned: 'With that letter? Ah, yes, with my letter. This is a very discreet matter, you understand? A secret between us. Dismiss . . .'

The lieutenant wrapped himself up again in his blanket, from which Švejk had dragged him, and went on sleeping while Švejk went on his pilgrimage to Királyhida.

It would not have been difficult to find 16 Sopron Street if he had not by chance met on the way the old sapper, Vodička, who had been drafted to the 'Styrians' whose barracks were down in the camp. Years ago Vodička had lived in Prague at Na Bojišti, and so on the occasion of a meeting like this they both had to go to The Black Lamb in Bruck where the waitress Růženka was a friend of his. She was a Czech and was owed money by all the Czech volunteers in the camp.

Recently Sapper Vodička, who was an old slyboots, had been paying court to her and had a list of all the march battalions which were leaving the camp. He went to see the Czech volunteers at the appropriate time and reminded them that they must not disappear in the tumult of the battle without paying their debts.

'Where exactly are you bound for?' asked Vodička, after they had tasted their first draught of good wine.

'That's a secret,' answered Švejk, 'but I'll tell you, because you're my old friend.'

He explained everything to him in detail, and Vodička declared that he was an old sapper, that he could not desert him and that they would go together to hand the letter over.

They had a wonderful time discussing past times and everything seemed natural and easy to them when at about lunch-time they left The Black Lamb.

Apart from that they had inside them a firm conviction that they were not afraid of anyone. On the way to 16 Sopron Street Vodička expressed tremendous hatred of the Hungarians and told over and over again how he fought with them everywhere, where and when he had had rows with them and what at any time and at any place had happened to prevent him fighting with them.

'Once we had one of those Hungarian bastards by the throat in Pausdorf, where we sappers went for a drink. I wanted to sock him across the coconut with a belt in the dark – you see we had smashed the hanging lamp with a bottle as soon as it started – but all of a sudden he began to shout:

' "Tonda! Why, it's only me, Purkrábek, from the sixteenth Landwehr!"

'A mistake was avoided by a hair's breadth. But instead we gave it fair and proper to those Hungarian clowns at Neusiedler See which we went to look at three weeks ago. In a village near by there was

stationed a machine-gun detachment of a Honvéd regiment, and we all happened to go to a pub where they were dancing their Csardas like mad and shooting their mouths off as they shouted: "*Uram, uram, biró, uram*", or "*Láňok, láňok, láňok a faluba*".[1] We sat opposite them; only we put our belts in front of us on the table and said to ourselves: "You bastards, we'll give it to you hot for your *láňok*", and a chap named Mejstřík who had a paw as big as the White Mountain immediately volunteered to dance and take away a girl from one of these

1. Hungarian songs: 'Mr, Mr, Mr Justice' and 'Girls, girls, girls from the village'.

lousy bastards in the middle of the dance. The girls were bloody neat pieces, you know, with plump calves and fleshy arses, and marvellous thighs and eyes. From the way those Hungarian bastards squeezed them you could see that those girls had breasts as full and firm as rubber balls, that they got a great kick out of it and knew their onions. And then our Mejstřík jumped into the dance and was just going to take the neatest piece away from one of the Honvéds. The Honvéd started to jabber something, but Mejstřík immediately socked him one across the jaw and the bastard fell down. We all of us at once seized our belts, twisted them round our hands so that the bayonets didn't slip out and leaped into the crowd. I shouted out: "Innocent or guilty, finish them off one by one!" From then on it went like a house on fire. They began to jump out of the windows, but we seized them by their legs and dragged them back into the hall again. Anyone who wasn't one of ours didn't half get it. Their mayor and a gendarme tried to intervene, but they got it across the backside. The landlord got a thrashing, because he started to swear in German and accused us of ruining the dance. Afterwards we went through the village and rounded up any who were trying to hide from us, like one of their platoon sergeants who we found buried in the hay in the loft of a farm right down in the village. He was betrayed to us by his girl because he'd gone and danced with another one. She had fallen for our Mejstřík and went with him afterwards on the way up to Királyhida below the forest where the haystacks stand. She dragged him into one of those haystacks and afterwards wanted five crowns from him. But he socked her one across the jaw instead. Afterwards he caught up with us at the top just before the camp and told us that he had always thought that Hungarian women had fire in them, but this cow had been as dead as a log of wood and only jabbered something all the time.

'To put it in a nutshell, the Hungarians are a pack of lousy bastards,' old Sapper Vodička concluded, whereupon Švejk observed: 'Many a Hungarian can't help being Hungarian.'

'Why can't he help it?' Vodička said angrily. 'Of course he can. That's stupid. I'd just like to see you getting into their clutches as I did when I came for courses here the first day. The very same afternoon they drove us into the school like a herd of cattle and some bloody fool started to make drawings and to explain what blindages are, how you lay foundations, how you take measurements and he said that if any-one didn't have it drawn the next morning exactly as he'd explained it, he would be gaoled and trussed. "Bloody hell," I thought. "Did I volunteer at the front for these courses just to get out of serving at the front or did I do it to make bloody silly drawings every evening in a bloody silly exercise book with a bloody silly pencil like a bloody silly schoolboy?" I got so furious, I lost my patience, I couldn't even look at the bloody idiot who was explaining it to us. I wanted to smash everything around me, I was so mad. I didn't even wait for coffee but went straight from the hut to Királyhida and in my fury I had only one thought and that was to find a quiet little pub in the town, drink myself sozzled there, kick up a row, sock someone across the jaw and then go home relaxed and satisfied. Man proposes, God disposes. By the river there among some gardens I found a place exactly like that, quiet as a chapel, just made for a row. There were only two guests sitting there and talking Hungarian which made me madder still, and into the bargain I was already more sozzled than I realized. And so it happened that I didn't notice – sozzled as I was – that next door there was another place where eight hussars came in while I was doing my best. When I socked those two guests across the jaw the hussars set on me. The bastards gave me such a beating up and chased me all over the gardens so I couldn't find my way home until the early morning and had to go at once to the medical depot, where I gave as an excuse that I'd fallen into a brick pit. Then for a whole week they wrapped me up in a wet sheet so that my back didn't get inflamed. O Lord, don't you ever get yourself mixed up with bastards like that! They are not human beings. They're animals.'

'All they that take the sword shall perish with the sword,' said Švejk. 'And so you shouldn't be surprised that they got worked up when they had to leave all their wine on the table and go and chase you all over the gardens in the dark. They should have beaten you up at once on the spot in the pub and then thrown you out. It would have been better for them and for you too if they'd finished with you at the table once and for all. I knew a chap called Paroubek who kept a pub in Libeň. Once a tinker got himself drunk in his bar on jalovcová [1] and began to swear and say that the jalovcová was weak, that Paroubek had put water in it and that if he had been going around as a tinker for a hundred years and for all his earnings had only bought jalovcová and had drunk it all up at one go, he would still be capable of walking on a tight-rope and of carrying Paroubek in his arms over it. After that he told Paroubek that he was a

1. Schnaps made out of juniper berries.

huncut[1] and the monster of Šaščín.[2] Then dear old Paroubek caught hold of him, knocked him across the skull with his mouse-traps and wires, kicked him out of the pub, beat him all the way to the Invalidovna with the pole for pulling down the shop shutters, chased him like a madman across the Invalidovna to Karlín up to Žižkov and from there across the Židovské pece[3] to Malešice, where he finally broke the stick on him and could return to Libeň. But in his blind fury he forgot of course that all the public were still in his pub and that all those thugs would be helping themseves. And when he finally got back he saw for himself that this had really been the case. The shutters were half-closed and two cops were standing there, who got pretty tight as well when they tried to put things in order inside. Half of all the stock was drunk up, in the street was an empty rum barrel, and under the counter Paroubek found two bastards who were completely sozzled. They had escaped the attention of the cops and when he dragged them out they wanted to pay him two kreutzers saying that they had not consumed more schnaps than this. That's the reward for hot-headedness. It's just like in war. First we defeat our enemy, then we pursue him on and on and in the end we can't run fast enough to get away from him.'

'I haven't forgotten those bastards,' said Vodička. 'If a single one of those hussars crossed my path I'd pay him out. We sappers are ugly customers when we get sore. We're not like the Iron Flies.[4] When we were at the front at Przemyśl we had with us a Captain Jetzbacher, a swine, the like of which you won't find again under the sun. He succeeded in bullying us so much that a chap called Bitterlich from our company, a German but a very good fellow, shot himself just because of him. And so we said to ourselves that when it began to whistle from the Russian side it would be all up with our Captain Jetzbacher. And as soon as the Russians started to fire at us we peppered him with five shots in the cross-fire. The monster was still alive after that like a cat with nine lives and we had to finish him with two further shots, so that there wouldn't be any trouble. He just growled but in a comic sort of way so that it was rather funny.'

1. A Hungarian word for a scoundrel.
2. Švejk seems to have got mixed up here but probably is alluding to Elisabeth Báthory of Čachtice who murdered young girls and bathed in their blood in order to make herself beautiful.
3. Literally 'Jewish furnaces' – a suburb of Prague.
4. 'Iron Flies' was a name for the Landwehr.

Vodička laughed: 'That happens every day at the front. One of my friends told me – he's with our company now – that when he was an infantryman at Belgrade his company shot their lieutenant in the middle of a battle. He was a cur of the same sort too who had shot two soldiers on the march, because they hadn't the strength to go on. And when he was about to expire he suddenly started to blow his whistle and give the signal for retreat. All the people around had a good laugh.'

During this absorbing and illuminating conversation Švejk and Vodička finally found the ironmonger's shop of Mr Kákonyi at 16 Sopron Street.

'I think you'd better wait here,' said Švejk to Vodička at the carriage entrance. 'I'll run up to the first floor and hand over the letter. I'll wait for an answer and be down in a moment.'

'Do you really imagine I'd desert you?' said Vodička in astonishment. 'You don't know the Hungarians, I keep on telling you. Here we've got to be very much on our guard with them. I'll sock him one.'

'Listen, Vodička,' said Švejk gravely. 'In this case it isn't to do with a Hungarian but with his wife. I told you everything when we sat together with that Czech waitress, didn't I? I'm carrying a letter from my lieutenant and it's absolutely essential to keep it secret. My lieutenant enjoined me strictly that no living soul must know about it and, after all, your waitress herself said that this was quite right and that it was a very delicate matter. Nobody must know that my lieutenant is corresponding with a married woman. And you approved and nodded your head in agreement. I've explained to you as is right and fitting that I'm faithfully carrying out my lieutenant's order and you suddenly insist at all costs on going upstairs with me.'

'You don't yet know me, Švejk,' answered old Sapper Vodička in very grave tones too. 'When I've once said that I won't leave you, you must remember that my word is my bond. Two are safer than one.'

'I'll talk you out of that, Vodička. Do you know where Neklanova Street is at Vyšehrad? The locksmith, Voborník, had his workshop there. He was a good and just man and when he returned home one day from a spree he brought with him another reveller. And then he lay in bed for a long time and every day when his wife dressed the wound on his head she said to him: "You see, Toníček, if there hadn't been two of you I'd have only given you a wigging and wouldn't have thrown the weighing machine at your head." And later when he was able to speak he said: "You're right, mum, next time when I go anywhere I won't bring anybody back with me." '

'Well, if that Hungarian bastard tried to throw something at our heads it would be the end, really,' said Vodička, starting to get worked up: 'I'll take him by the neck and throw him from the first floor down the steps, so that he'll fly like a piece of shrapnel. You mustn't take any chances with those Hungarian bastards. Kid-gloves are no use.'

'Vodička, you haven't drunk so much after all. I had two quarters of a litre more than you. Please consider carefully that we mustn't make any scandal. I'm responsible for this. Besides, it's a question of a lady.'

'I'll sock the lady one as well, Švejk. It makes no difference to me. You still don't know old Vodička. Once in Záběhlice in The Island of Roses some bitch didn't want to dance with me because I had a swollen jaw, she said. It's true that I did have a swollen jaw, because I'd just come there from a dance-party in Hostivař, but just imagine getting an insult of that kind from that whore. "Well, here's one for you too, noble lady," I said, "so that you shan't complain."

'When I socked her one she pulled down the whole table in the garden with all the glasses where she was sitting with her papa and mamma and two brothers. But I wasn't afraid of the whole Island of Roses; I had friends there from Vršovice and they helped me. We beat up about five families, children as well. It must have been heard all the long way to Michle and after that it was in the newspapers too about that garden party, which was held by a charity association of the citizens of some town or other. And so, as I say, as other people have helped me, so I always help any friend of mine if anything should happen to him. I won't desert you, God help me, I won't. You don't know these Hungarian bastards. . . . You can't surely push me off when we're seeing each other again after so many years and in circumstances like this into the bargain.'

'Very well, then, come with me,' Švejk decided, 'but please act carefully so that we don't have any unpleasantness.'

'Don't worry, old man,' said Vodička quietly, when they approached the steps. 'I'll sock him . . .'

And he added in an even quieter tone: 'You'll see, this Hungarian bastard won't give us any trouble.'

And if there had been anybody in the carriage entrance who understood Czech he would have heard from the stairway Vodička's slogan being loudly proclaimed: 'You don't know these Hungarian bastards

...', a slogan which came to Vodička in the quiet pub above the river Leitha, among the gardens of the famous Királyhida surrounded by mountains. Soldiers will always remember these mountains with curses, recalling all those 'exercises' before the world war and during the world war in which they received theoretical training for practical massacre and slaughter!

Švejk and Vodička stood before the door of Mr Kákonyi's flat. Before pressing the bellpush, Švejk observed: 'Vodička, have you ever heard that discretion is the better part of valour?'

'I'm not bothered,' answered Vodička. 'He mustn't be allowed time even to open his mug...'

'I have no business with anybody here, Vodička.'

Švejk rang the bell, and Vodička said loudly, '*Ein, zwei* and he'll be down the stairs.'

The door opened, a maid appeared and asked in Hungarian what they wanted.

'*Nem tudom*,'[1] said Vodička scornfully. 'Learn to speak Czech, my good girl.'

'Do you understand German?' Švejk asked in broken German.

'A leettle,' the girl replied equally brokenly.

'Then tell lady I want speak lady. Tell her there is letter from gentleman outside in passage.'

'I'm amazed,' said Vodička, following Švejk into the hall, 'that you can waste your time talking to a little squit like that.'

They stood in the hall, shut the door to the passage and Švejk confined himself to observing:

'They're quite nicely set up here, even two umbrellas on the coat stand. And that picture of Jesus Christ isn't too bad either.'

From one of the rooms, from which could be heard the clatter of spoons and the clinking of plates, the maid emerged again and said to Švejk:

'Madam say she have no time. If there is anything you give it me and tell me.'

'Very well,' said Švejk solemnly, 'letter for madam, but mum's the word!'

He took out Lieutenant Lukáš's letter.

'I,' he said, pointing to himself, 'wait for answer in hall here.'

---

1. 'I don't speak [Hungarian].'

'Why don't you sit down?' asked Vodička, who was already sitting on a chair by the wall. 'There's a seat for you. You don't have to stand here like a beggar. Don't demean yourself before that Hungarian. You'll see, we're going to have trouble with him, but I'll sock him.

'Listen,' he said a minute later, 'where did you learn German?'

'I taught myself,' answered Švejk. There was a moment's silence again. Then from the room into which the maid had carried the letter there could be heard a tremendous shouting and uproar. Someone threw something heavy on the ground, then glasses could be clearly heard flying and plates splintering mixed with a bellowing of '*Baszom az anyát, baszom az istenet, baszom a Kristus Máriát, baszom az astyádot, baszom a világot!*'[1]

The door flew open and there flew into the hall a man in his best years with a napkin round his neck waving in his hands the letter which had been delivered a moment before.

Nearest to the door sat old Sapper Vodička, and consequently it was to him that the infuriated gentleman addressed himself first.

'What does this mean? Where is the bloody swine who brought this letter?'

'Gently now,' said Vodička, getting up. 'Don't shout so loud here, unless you want to be chucked out and if you wish to know who brought that letter ask my friend there. But talk to him politely or one, two, three, go, and you'll be out of the door.'

Now it was for Švejk to experience the rich eloquence of the gentleman with the napkin round his neck, who got fearfully tied up and said that they were just having lunch.

'We've heard that you're having lunch,' Švejk agreed in broken German, adding in Czech: 'It could also have occurred to us that we might perhaps be dragging you quite unnecessarily away from your meal.'

'Don't demean yourself!' said Vodička.

The infuriated gentleman, whose napkin as a result of his lively gesticulation hung around him only by one corner, went on to say that he had at first thought the letter contained something about army billeting in this house, which belonged to his wife.

'Quite a lot of soldiers could get in here,' said Švejk, 'but that was not what the letter was about, as you probably now see for yourself.'

1. A string of obscene Hungarian oaths. Literally, 'Fuck your mother, God, Christ, the Virgin Mary, father and the world.'

The gentleman put his hands to his head and uttered a whole series of reproaches, saying that he was also a reserve lieutenant, and that he would like to be serving now but that he had kidney disease. In his day the officers were not so profligate as to disturb the tranquillity of the family. He would send the letter to the regimental commander, to the Ministry of War, he would publish it in the newspapers.

'Sir,' said Švejk with dignity. 'It was me who wrote that letter. I wrote. Not lieutenant. The signature and name are false. I like your wife very much. *Ich liebe Ihre Frau.* I'm up to the ears in love with your wife, as Vrchlický[1] used to say. She's a capital woman.'

The infuriated gentleman wanted to hurl himself at Švejk, who stood calmly and happily in front of him, but old Sapper Vodička following his every movement tripped him up, tore from his hand the letter which he was continually waving and stuck it in his pocket. Then when Mr Kákonyi got up again Vodička seized him, carried him to the door and

1. Famous Czech poet.

opened it with one hand. Then something could be heard rolling down the steps.

It all happened as quickly as in fairy tales, when the devil comes to take someone off.

The only trace which remained of the infuriated gentleman was his napkin. Švejk picked it up, knocked respectfully on the door of the room from which five minutes ago Mr Kákonyi had emerged and where a woman's sobs could be heard.

'I'm bringing you the napkin,' Švejk said gently to the lady, who was weeping on the sofa. 'Someone might trample on it. My compliments, madam.'

He clicked his heels, saluted and went out into the passage. On the stairs no further traces of the struggle could be seen and just as Vodička had forecast the scene passed off quite smoothly. Only afterwards by the gate in the carriage entrance Švejk found a torn-off collar. Evidently the last act of this tragedy was performed here when Mr Kákonyi desperately held on to the house gate so as not to be dragged out into the street.

It was lively in the street however. Mr Kákonyi was dragged off to the carriage entrance of the house opposite, where they poured water on him, and in the middle of the street old Sapper Vodička fought like a lion against some Honvéds and Honvéd hussars who had rallied to their fellow-countryman. He defended himself in a masterly fashion with his bayonet hanging on his belt like a flail. And he was not alone. At his side there fought several Czech soldiers from various regiments who were just passing by in the street.

Švejk, as he later maintained, did not know himself how he came to get mixed up in this, nor how, not having a bayonet, he got hold of the stick of a panic-stricken passer-by.

It lasted quite a long time, but all good things have to come to an end. The military police came along and arrested them all.

Švejk carried with him the stick, which was pronounced by the commandant of the military police to be a *corpus delicti*, and marched side by side with Vodička.

He walked happily, carrying the stick on his shoulder like a rifle.

Old Sapper Vodička was stubbornly silent during the whole journey. It was only when they came to the guard-house that he said in a gloomy tone to Švejk: 'Didn't I tell you that you didn't know those Hungarian bastards?'

4

New Sufferings

COLONEL SCHRÖDER observed with satisfaction the pale countenance of Lieutenant Lukáš who had big rings under his eyes and in his embarrassment avoided the colonel's gaze. Instead, surreptitiously, as though he were studying something he eyed the plan of the disposition of the men in the camp, which was also the only ornament in the whole of the office.

On the table in front of Colonel Schröder lay some newspapers containing articles marked in blue pencil. The colonel scanned them once more and said, looking at Lieutenant Lukáš:

'And so you know already that your batman Švejk is under arrest and will probably be brought before divisional court-martial?'

'I do, sir.'

'But that does not of course close the matter,' the colonel said with emphasis, feasting his eyes on the pale face of Lieutenant Lukáš. 'The local community have certainly been shocked by the whole affair of your batman Švejk, and your name is quoted in that context as well, lieutenant. Divisional headquarters have already sent us certain material. We have here some journals which deal with this case. You may read them aloud to me.'

He handed to Lieutenant Lukáš the newspapers with the marked articles and the lieutenant began to recite them in a monotonous voice, as though he were reading from a child's reading primer the sentence: 'Honey is much more nourishing and more easily digestible than sugar.'

'WHERE IS THE GUARANTEE OF OUR FUTURE?'

'Is that in the *Pester Lloyd*?' asked the colonel.

'Yes, sir,' answered Lieutenant Lukáš and went on reading:

'The conduct of the war demands the cooperation of all classes of the population of the Austro-Hungarian Monarchy. If we are resolved to guarantee the security of the state, all the nationalities must render each other mutual support, and it is just in the spontaneous respect which one nationality feels for another that the guarantee of our future lies. The greatest sacrifices of our doughty warriors at the fronts, where they advance forward without respite, would not be possible if the base, which is the ancillary and political pulse of our glorious armies, were not united – if behind the backs of our troops

there were elements trying to break up the state monolith and by their male-volent propaganda undermine its authority as an integral unit and sow discord in the community of the nationalities of our Empire. In this historic hour we cannot pass over in silence a handful of people who out of local chauvinistic motives would like to try to destroy the unified efforts and struggle of all the nationalities of this Empire for the just punishment of those criminals who have attacked our Empire without just cause or reason with the object of robbing it of the whole heritage of its culture and civiliza-tion. We cannot ignore those disgusting manifestations of the outbursts of a pathological mentality which has no other aim but to disrupt the unanimity reigning in the hearts of our peoples. Already several times we have taken the opportunity to draw attention in our journal to the need for the military authorities to intervene with the utmost severity against those individuals in the Czech regiments, who in disregard of glorious regimental traditions and by their senseless and outrageous conduct stir up hatred in our Hungarian towns against the entire Czech nation, which as a whole is entirely innocent and which has always stood firmly for the interests of this Empire. This is proved by a whole series of outstanding Czech military personalities, among whom we recall the glorious figures of Marshal Radetzky and other defenders of the Austro-Hungarian Monarchy. In contrast to these shining lights there are a few scoundrels drawn from the depraved Czech rabble who in obedience to their lowest instincts have taken advantage of the world war to volunteer for service in the army and to spread chaos in the solidarity of the nationalities of the Monarchy. We have already once drawn attention to the outrageous behaviour of regiment no. . . . in Debrecen, whose disgraceful excesses were the subject of discussion and condemnation by the Budapest Diet and whose regimental standard was later – *confiscated* – at the front. Who is it that has this heinous sin on his conscience? – *confiscated*. Who drove the Czech soldiers to – *confiscated*. The brazen behaviour of this alien vermin in our Hungarian fatherland is best shown by the case in Királyhida, the Hungarian outpost on the Leitha. What was the nationality of those soldiers from the near-by military camp in Bruck an der Leitha who assaulted and tortured the local merchant, Mr Gyula Kákonyi? It is clearly the duty of the authorities to investigate this crime and to demand information from the military command, who must certainly be concerning themselves with this matter. We require to know the exact role played by Lieutenant Lukasch in this unprecedented agitation against citizens of the Kingdom of Hungary. This officer's name is being mentioned in the town in connection with the events of recent days, as we have been informed by our local correspondent, who has already collected voluminous material about the whole affair, which is a crying scandal in today's serious times. The readers of *Pester Lloyd* will certainly follow with interest the developments of the investigation and we wish to assure them that we shall inform them in detail about this affair which is of outstanding importance. Nevertheless we are still expecting official news of the crime at Királyhida, which was committed against the Hungarian population. It is obvious that the Budapest Diet will take the matter up, so that it can be established once and for all that Czech soldiers passing through the Kingdom of Hungary on their way to the front are not permitted to think that they hold the lands of the crown of St Stephen in fee. If however any representatives of that nationality who in Királyhida have so splendidly represented the partnership of all the nationalities of this Monarchy are still unable to understand the situation they had better keep extremely quiet, for in war people of this kind will be taught by the bullet, the gallows, gaol and the bayonet to obey and to subordinate their acts to the highest interests of our common fatherland.'

'Who has signed this article, lieutenant?'

'Béla Barabás, editor and parliamentary deputy, sir.'

'He's a notorious swine, lieutenant; but before the article found its way to the *Pester Lloyd*, it had already been published in the *Pesti Hirlap*. Now please read me the official translation from Hungarian of the article in the Sopron journal *Sopronyi Napló*.'

Lieutenant Lukáš read aloud the article, in which the editor took great pains to ensure that the following hotch-potch of expressions should figure prominently:

'The requirements of state wisdom', 'law and order', 'human degeneration', 'human dignity and feelings trampled underfoot', 'cannibalistic debauches', 'massacre of human society', 'pack of Mamelukes', 'behind the scenes you will recognize them'. And so it went on, as though the Hungarians were the most persecuted element on their own soil – as though the Czech soldiers had come and struck down the editor, trampling on his belly with their boots, while he was howling with pain, and someone had taken it all down in shorthand.

'There is a dangerous silence enshrouding some very important matters, and nothing is written about them,' was the wail of *Sopronyi Napló*, the daily paper of Sopron.

We all know what a Czech soldier is in Hungary and at the front. We all know what things the Czechs do, what is going on here, what the situation is with the Czechs and who is behind it all. The vigilance of the authorities is of course directed towards other important things, which however must not be isolated from the general control of events, so that what has happened these days in Királyhida may never happen again. Our article of yesterday was confiscated in fifteen places. That is why we have no alternative but to state that even today we still do not have on technical grounds many reasons for dealing in detail with the events in Királyhida. The reporter whom we sent out established on the spot that the authorities are showing genuine zeal in the whole affair and that the investigations are proceeding at full steam. The only strange thing is that some participators in the whole massacre are still at liberty. This is particularly the case with one gentleman who according to hearsay still remains unpunished in the military camp and still wears the insignia of his parrot-regiment,[1] and whose name was also published the day before yesterday in the *Pester Lloyd* and the *Pesti Napló*. We refer to the well-known Czech chauvinist, Lükáš, whose outrageous behaviour will form the subject of the interpellation by our deputy Géza Savanyú, who represents the district of Királyhida.

1. The 91st regiment wore parrot-green facings on their uniforms.

'The weekly in Királyhida and the Pressburg papers write just as amiably about you, lieutenant,' Colonel Schröder observed. 'But that won't interest you very much because it's all much of a muchness. There are political reasons for this, because after all we Austrians, whether we're Germans or Czechs, are, if you compare us with the Hungarians, still pretty . . . You understand me, lieutenant, don't you? There's a certain tendency in all this. You might perhaps be more interested in an article in the *Komárno Evening News*, where they assert that you tried to rape Mrs Kákonyi right in her very dining-room during lunch in the presence of her husband, whom you had threatened with your sabre and forced to gag his wife's mouth with a towel to prevent her screaming. That's the latest news of you, lieutenant.'

The colonel gave a smile and went on: 'The authorities have not done their duty. Preventive censorship of the newspapers here is in the hands of the Hungarians too. They do what they like with us. Our officers enjoy no protection from the insults of a swine of a civilian Hungarian editor like this and it was only as a result of our sharp intervention, in other words on the basis of a telegram from divisional court-martial, that the Public Prosecutor's office in Budapest took the necessary steps to see that arrests were carried out among the editorial staffs of all the papers mentioned. The man who's going to catch it hottest is the editor of the *Komárno Evening News*. He will remember his *Evening News* to his dying day. Divisional court-martial has authorized me as your superior officer to hear your side of the case and at the same time has sent me all the documents concerning the investigation. Everything would have turned out all right if it had not been for your unfortunate Švejk. There was with him a certain sapper, Vodička. When they took that man to the guard-house after the brawl they found on him the letter you had sent to Mrs Kákonyi. Your Švejk alleged under cross-examination that it was not your letter, but that he had written it himself. However, when it was shown to him and he was asked to copy it to compare the handwriting in it with his own he ate it up. From regimental office your reports were later sent to divisional court-martial so that they could compare them with Švejk's handwriting and this is the result.'

The colonel turned over the pages of the documents and drew the lieutenant's attention to the following passage:

The accused, Švejk, refused to write the sentences dictated to him, claiming that during the night he had forgotten how to write.

'I really attribute no importance whatsoever to what your Švejk or the sapper said at divisional court-martial, lieutenant. They alleged that it was only a question of a little joke which had been misunderstood, and that they were themselves attacked by civilians and defended themselves to protect their military honour. In the course of the investigation it was ascertained that that Švejk of yours is a fine rascal altogether. Thus for example, when asked why he didn't confess, he answered according to the report: "I'm in just the same position as the servant of the academy painter Mr Panuška once was about some pictures of the Virgin Mary. When it was a question of some pictures he had allegedly embezzled he too couldn't answer anything except: 'Do you want me to spit blood?'" Of course on behalf of regimental command I have seen to it that in the name of divisional court-martial all newspapers must publish corrections of all these rubbishy articles in the local papers here. Today these corrections will be sent out and I hope I have done everything to repair what took place as a result of the rascally conduct of those Hungarian civilian journalist bastards.

'I think I've formulated it well:

'"Divisional court-martial no. N and regimental command no. N state that the article published in the local journals about alleged excesses on the part of the men of regiment N has no basis in fact and is invented from A to Z, and that the proceedings brought against those journals will result in the severe punishment of the guilty."

'Divisional court-martial in its report to our regimental command,' continued the colonel, 'has come to the conclusion that behind all this there is nothing less than a systematic agitation against military units coming from Cisleithania to Transleithania. Just compare how many soldiers have gone to the front from our part of the country and how many from theirs. I tell you that a Czech soldier is much more to my taste than any pack of Hungarian bastards. It's enough for me to remember how at Belgrade the Hungarians shot at our second march battalion, who didn't know that it was the Hungarians who were shooting at them and began to fire at the Deutschmeisters on the right wing. Then the Deutschmeisters got muddled as well and opened fire on the Bosnian regiment which stood alongside them. That was a nice situation! At that very moment I was having my lunch at the brigade staff. The day before we had had to be satisfied with ham and tinned soup but that day we had a proper chicken soup, fillet with rice, and little doughnuts with egg-flip. The evening before we'd hanged a

Serbian wine-merchant in the town and our cooks had found in his cellar wine which was thirty years old. You can imagine how we all looked forward to the lunch. We'd eaten the soup and were just digging into the chicken when suddenly there was a skirmish and a salvo of shots and our artillery, who hadn't the foggiest idea that it was our units who were shooting at each other, began to shoot into our lines and one shell fell quite close to our brigade staff. The Serbs probably thought that a mutiny had broken out on our side and so they began to fire at us from all sides and to cross the river towards us. The brigade general was called to the telephone, and the divisional commander kicked up a tremendous row about the shambles in the brigade sector. He said that he'd just got orders from army staff to begin the attack on the Serbian positions at 2.35 a.m. on the left flank. We were the reserve and we must at once cease fire. But in such a situation how can you hope to have "cease fire". Brigade telephone exchange reported that it couldn't get any connection anywhere but that the staff of the 75th regiment was reporting that it had received from the next division the order "stand firm", that it was not possible to communicate with our division, that the Serbs had occupied points 212, 226 and 327, that a battalion was required to act as liaison and provide telephone communication with our division. We transferred the call to the division but the connection was already broken, because in the meantime the Serbs had got behind us on both flanks and cut up our centre into a triangle. Inside that everything stayed, regiments, artillery and baggage train with the whole column of cars, the stores and the field-hospital. I was two days in the saddle and the divisional commander was captured together with our brigade commander. And that was all the fault of the Hungarians because they shot at our second march battalion. Of course, as you can imagine, they tried to blame it all on our regiment.'

The colonel spat:

'You've been able to see for yourself, lieutenant, what splendid use they have made of your little adventure in Királyhida.'

Lieutenant Lukáš coughed in embarrassment.

'Lieutenant,' the colonel said to him in a familiar tone. 'Hand on your heart, how many times did you sleep with Mrs Kákonyi?'

Colonel Schröder was in a very good mood today.

'Don't say, lieutenant, that you've only just begun to correspond with her. When I was your age, I spent three weeks in Erlau on a geometry course and you should have seen how during all those three weeks I did nothing else but sleep with Hungarian women. Every day with another one. Young ones, single ones, elderly ones, married ones, just as they came. I ironed them out so thoroughly that when I returned to my regiment I could hardly move my legs. It was the wife of a lawyer who took most out of me. She showed me what Hungarian women can do. She bit me on the nose in the process and didn't let me close my eyes the whole night.

'You just began to correspond . . .' the colonel said, patting him familiarly on the shoulder, 'we know that. You don't need to say anything. I have my opinion of the whole matter. You got involved with her, her husband came along, and that stupid Švejk of yours . . .

'But you know, lieutenant, that Švejk of yours must have character after all, when he pulled off such a trick with your letter. One really feels sympathy for such a man. I say it's a matter of upbringing. That's what I like about that bastard. Definitely the proceedings have to be stopped in this respect. Lieutenant, you have been vilified in the newspapers. Your presence here is quite unnecessary. In a week's time a march battalion will be sent to the Russian front. You're the most senior officer in the 11th company and you'll go with it as commander. Everything has been arranged at brigade headquarters. Tell the quartermaster sergeant-major that he should find you another batman instead of that Švejk.'

Lieutenant Lukáš looked gratefully at the colonel, who continued: 'I assign Švejk to you as company orderly.'

The lieutenant turned pale and the colonel got up and offered him his hand saying:

'Well, everything is settled now. I wish you good luck so that you can distinguish yourself on the Eastern front. And if by any chance we should meet again, come and join us. Don't avoid our company as you did in Budějovice . . .'

Lieutenant Lukáš repeated to himself all the way home: 'Company commander, company orderly.'

And vividly before his eyes there loomed the figure of Švejk.

Quartermaster Sergeant-Major Vaněk said, when Lieutenant Lukáš ordered him to find him a new batman instead of Švejk: 'I thought, sir, you were satisfied with Švejk.'

When he learnt that the colonel had nominated Švejk orderly to the 11th company, he cried out: 'God help us all!'

*

At the divisional court in a hut which was fitted with bars they got up according to regulations at 7 a.m. and put in order their straw mattresses which were lying about in the dust on the ground. There were no bunks. In a compartment in the long hall they were folding the blankets and placing them neatly on the straw mattresses according to regulations. The men who had finished their jobs were sitting on benches along the wall and either looking for lice (those who'd come from the front) or amusing themselves by relating various adventures.

Švejk with old Sapper Vodička sat on a bench near the door with a group of soldiers from various regiments and military units.

'Look at that Hungarian fellow there by the window, chaps,' said Vodička. 'See how the bastard prays to God that everything will go well with him. Wouldn't you like to break his mug open from ear to ear?'

'But he's a decent chap,' said Švejk. 'He's only here because he didn't want to join up. He's against the war, belongs to some kind of sect and he's been gaoled because he didn't want to kill people. He keeps God's commandment, but they're going to make God's commandment hot for him. Before the war there was a fellow called Nemrava living in Moravia who didn't even want to take a rifle on his shoulder, and when he was called up he said that it was against his principles to carry a rifle. Because of that he was gaoled until he was blue in the face and then brought up again to take the oath. But he said he wouldn't do it as it was against his principles and he held out so long that he got away with it.'

'He must have been a stupid chump,' said old Sapper Vodička. 'He could have taken the oath and then shitted on everything and the oath too.'

'I've already taken the oath three times,' an infantryman chimed in, 'and this is the third time I'm here for desertion, and if I hadn't got a medical certificate showing that fifteen years ago I beat my aunt to death in a fit of insanity maybe they'd have shot me three times at the front. But my late lamented aunt always helps me out of trouble and in the end I'll probably get out of this war safe and sound.'

'And why did you kill your auntie, old man?' asked Švejk.

'Why do people kill each other?' the pleasant man answered. 'You can guess for yourself. It was for money, of course. She had five savings-bank books, that old frump had, and they had just sent her the interest when I came to visit her and I was completely at the end of my tether. Except for her I didn't have a soul in the whole of God's world. And so I went to ask her if she'd take me into her care and the old bitch said that I was a young, strong, healthy man and ought to go out and work. Well, one word led to another and I only hit her over the head a few times with a poker, but I got her face into such a mess that I didn't know whether she was my aunt or not. And so I sat beside her on the ground and kept on saying to myself: "Is that Auntie or isn't it Auntie?" And that's how the neighbours found me next day, sitting beside her. Then I was put into the madhouse at Na Slupi and, when later, before the war, they sent us before a commission in Bohnice, I was pronounced cured and had at once to go and make up those years' service in the army which I had missed.'

A lean emaciated soldier with a care-worn appearance passed by carrying a broom.

'That's a teacher from the last march company,' said a rifleman who was sitting next to Švejk. 'Now he goes around sweeping up the floor under him. He's an awfully decent chap. He's here because of some stupid rhyme he wrote.

'Hallo, teacher, come here!' he called to the man with the broom, who approached the bench with a solemn expression. 'Tell us the rhyme of yours about the lice.'

The soldier with the broom cleared his throat and began:

> 'The army's all loused up, they're scratching at the front,
> And on our backs a monster louse is creeping.
> The general himself has had to join the hunt.
> The lice have made him toss and spoilt his sleeping.
> The lice are doing finely in the soldiers' huts.
> They're even getting used to the tough N.C.O.s.
> And the bastard Austrian he-louse,[1] if he's still got the guts,
> Can mate with the Prussian she-louse, I suppose.'

The care-worn soldier and teacher sat down on the bench and sighed: 'That's all it was. And because of that I've been examined four times already by the judge advocate.'

'That's really not worth talking about,' said Švejk nonchalantly. 'The question is only this: who will the people in the court think is the bastard Austrian he-louse? It's good that you put in that bit about mating. That'll confuse them completely and knock them off their

1. In Czech *všivák*, which also means (a) someone who has lice on him; (b) a bastard. The reference is of course a veiled one to the Emperor Franz Joseph.

rockers. You've just got to explain to them that the bastard he-louse is the male of the species and that the she-louse can only be mounted by a bastard he-louse. Otherwise you won't get away with it. You obviously didn't write that rhyme to insult anyone. That's quite clear. Just tell the judge advocate that you wrote it for your own personal amusement and that as the male of a pig is called a boar, so the male of a louse is called a bastard.'

The teacher sighed: 'But the trouble is that the judge advocate's Czech isn't very good. I've already tried hard to explain it to him in this way, but he just let fly at me and shouted that a male louse is called "*fešak*" in Czech. "You bloody idiot of a scholar, the feminine is '*ten feš*' and so the masculine is '*ta fešak*'.[1] Go and teach your grandmother to suck eggs!"'

'To put it in a nutshell,' said Švejk, 'you're in a jam, but you mustn't lose hope. It can still change for the better as the gipsy Janeček said in Pilsen when in 1879 they put the cord round his neck for double robbery with murder. He was right in his guess, because at the very last moment they took him away from the gallows, as they couldn't hang him, owing to its being the birthday of His Imperial Majesty which fell on the very same day when he ought to be hanged. And so they hanged him the following day after the birthday had passed. But just imagine the luck that bastard had, because on the third day he got a pardon and his case had to be taken up again, as everything pointed to the fact that it was another Janeček who had committed the crime. So they had to dig him out of the convicts' cemetery and rehabilitate him in the Catholic cemetery at Pilsen. But afterwards it turned out that he had been an evangelical and so they transferred him to the evangelical cemetery. And after that . . .'

'And after that you'll get a sock on the jaw,' said old Sapper Vodička. 'The things that bastard thinks up! A chap has trouble with divisional court-martial and when they took us away for interrogation yesterday the bloody fool starts explaining to me what the Rose of Jericho is.'

'But it wasn't me who explained it. The story comes from Matěj, the painter Panuška's servant, who told an old woman who asked him what the Rose of Jericho looked like:

'Take some dry cow shit, put it on a plate, pour water on it and it

1. The judge advocate, who is a German, gets the meaning and genders wrong, confusing *všivák* (he-louse or bastard) with *fešák* (dandy). The Czechs normally use for both he- and she-louse the word *veš*, which is feminine.

will become green and beautiful: that's the Rose of Jericho,' Švejk said, defending himself. 'It wasn't me who thought up that nonsense, and after all, we had to talk about something when we went to the interrogation. I only wanted to cheer you up, Vodička . . .'

'Wanted to cheer me up!' Vodička spat contemptuously. 'A chap has his head full of worries about how to get out of this jam, how to manage to get free so as to be able to pay out those damned Hungarian bastards and this bloody fool here wants to cheer him up with some cow shit!

'How can I pay those Hungarian bastards out if I'm sitting locked up here, and if into the bargain I've got to pretend to the judge advocate that I don't feel any hatred for the Hungarians? It's a dog's life, my God, really it is, but when I manage to get my paws on one of those Hungarian bastards I'll strangle him like a puppy. I'll teach them their "*Isten, ala meg a magyar*".[1] I'll be even with them. I won't allow them to forget old Vodička, I tell you!'

'Don't let's any of us have any worries,' said Švejk. 'Everything will sort itself out. The main thing is always to say in court what isn't true. Any chap who allows himself to be hoodwinked into confessing is always done for. Nothing good will ever come of that. Once when I worked in Moravská Ostrava there was the following case there: a miner beat up an engineer when he was alone with him so that there were no witnesses. And the lawyer who defended him insisted that if he denied it, nothing could happen to him. But the president of the senate kept on appealing to him that confession would be an extenuating circumstance. But the miner went on asserting that he couldn't confess and so he was acquitted, because he had established his alibi. On the very same day in Brno . . .'

'Jesus Mary,' cried Vodička in a fury. 'I can't stand it any longer. Why he tells all this bloody nonsense I can't understand. Yesterday at the investigation we had just the same sort of a fellow. When the judge advocate asked him what he was in civil life he said: "I blow at crosses." It took more than half an hour before he could explain to the judge advocate that he blew the bellows at a smith's called Cross, and when they asked him afterwards: "So in civil life you're an untrained worker?", he answered them: "Of course I don't work in the train. That's Franta Hybš."'

1. Hungarian for 'God bless the Hungarians' – the first words of the Hungarian national hymn.

From the passage could be heard steps and the shouting of the guard: 'New lot.' 'There'll be more of us again,' said Švejk happily. 'Perhaps these will have managed to keep some cigar stumps.'

The door opened and the volunteer who had sat with Švejk under

arrest in Budějovice, and was now destined for the kitchen of a march company, was pushed in.

'Praised be the Lord Jesus Christ,' he said on entering, upon which Švejk answered in the name of all: 'For ever and ever, amen.'

The volunteer looked happily at Švejk, put the blanket which he had brought with him on the ground and sat down on the bench next to the Czech colony. Then he unwound his puttees, took out the cigarettes which were artfully rolled in the folds and distributed them. Then he took out of his boots the striking part of a box of matches and one or two matches cunningly split down the centre from the top.

He struck a match, carefully lit a cigarette, gave a light to all of them and said nonchalantly: 'I'm accused of mutiny.'

'That's nothing,' said Švejk consolingly. 'That's just fun.'

'Of course it is,' the volunteer agreed. 'But I really don't know if it's the way to win the war with all these courts-martial. If they insist on trying me at any price, let them try me. Generally speaking one trial can't change the situation at all.'

'And how did you mutiny?' asked Sapper Vodička, looking at the volunteer with sympathy.

'I refused to clean the rears in the guard-house,' he answered. 'And so they took me all the way up to the colonel. And he was a pretty fair swine. He started to shout at me that I was locked up on the basis of a regimental report and that I was a common convict, that he was quite amazed that the earth still carried me and didn't stop turning round because of the shame that in the army there was a man with the rights of a volunteer who had claims to officer's rank, but who by his behaviour could only arouse revulsion and contempt in all his superiors. I replied that the rotation of the globe could not be interrupted by the appearance on it of a volunteer like myself, that the laws of nature were more powerful than the shoulder-straps of volunteers and that I would like to know who could compel me to clean a rear, if I had not shitted in it myself, although I might be entitled to do so after the filthy catering there was in the regiment and after all that rotten cabbage and soaked salted mutton they gave us. And then in addition I said to the colonel that his view as to why the earth still carried me was rather odd, since there would surely not be an earthquake because of me. The colonel didn't do anything during the whole of my speech except grind his teeth like a mare when it feels the chill of frozen turnips on its tongue, and then he roared at me:

' "Very well, then, are you going to clean the rear or aren't you?"

' "Humbly report, I'm not going to clean any rear."

' "You are going to clean it, you volunteer!"

' "Humbly report, I'm not."

' "Bloody hell, you're going to clean not only one rear but a hundred rears!"

' "Humbly report, I'm not going to clean either a hundred rears or one rear."

'And so it went on and on: "Are you going to clean it?" "I'm not going to clean it." Rears flew about all over the place as though it was a nursery rhyme by the writer Pavla Moudrá. The colonel ran up and down the office like a madman and finally sat down and said: "Think it over carefully. I'm going to send you to divisional court for mutiny. Don't imagine that you'll be the first volunteer to be shot in this war. In Serbia we hanged two volunteers of the 10th company and shot one of the 9th in cold blood. And why? All because of their pig-headed-ness. Those two who were hanged had hesitated to stab the wife and kid of a comitadji[1] near Šabac, and the volunteer from the 9th company was shot because he wouldn't advance and made the excuse that he had swollen legs and was flat-footed. Very well, then, will you clean the rears or not?"

'"Humbly report, I won't."

'The colonel looked at me and said: "Listen, do you happen to be a Slavophil?"'

'"Humbly report, I don't."

'After that they took me away and declared that I was accused of mutiny.'

'The best thing you can do now,' said Švejk, 'is to pretend to be an idiot. When I sat in the garrison gaol, we had with us a very intelligent and well-educated fellow who was a teacher at a commercial school. He "dissented" from the front and an awfully fine show trial was fixed up for him, so that he could be condemned and hanged as a warning to others. But he managed to get out of the whole mess in an awfully simple way. He started by pretending that he had got some congenital disease and when the staff doctor examined him he said he had not "dissented" but that from his earliest years he had liked to travel and had always had a longing to vanish in some faraway part of the world. Once he had woken up in Hamburg and another time in London and he had not known how he got there. His father had been an alcoholic and had committed suicide before his birth. His mother had been a prostitute who took to drink and died of *delirium tremens*. His younger sister drowned herself; his elder one threw herself under a train; his brother jumped from the railway viaduct at Vyšehrad; his grandfather murdered his wife, poured paraffin on himself and set himself on fire; his other grandmother used to gad about with the gipsies and poisoned herself in prison with matches; one cousin was condemned several times for arson and cut his jugular vein with a glass splinter in the Carthusian monastery prison; a female cousin on the father's side threw herself out of the sixth storey of a building in Vienna. He himself had had a frightfully neglected upbringing and couldn't speak until he was

1. A Balkan guerrilla.

ten, because once when he was six months old and they were changing
his nappies and left him alone on the table, a cat pulled him off it and
he knocked his head in the fall. He also had violent headaches from
time to time and on those occasions he didn't know what he was doing.
It was in a state like this that he went from the front to Prague and it
was only when the military police arrested him at the pub U Fleků
that he came to. My goodness, you should have seen how glad they
were to release him from army service. About five servicemen who
sat with him in the same cell for all eventualities made the following
notes on a piece of paper:

> 'Father alcoholic. Mother prostitute.
> 1st sister (drowned).
> 2nd sister (train).
> Brother (from bridge).
> Grandfather,† wife, paraffin, set fire.
> 2nd grandmother (gipsies, matches)† etc.

'And when one of them started to recite the same story to the staff
doctor he got no further than to the cousin, when the staff doctor, who
had heard it twice before, said: "You bloody bastard, your cousin on
the father's side threw herself out of the sixth storey of a building in
Vienna. You had a frightfully neglected upbringing and so you'll be
put right by 'special' treatment." And so they took him away to the
"special" wing and trussed him and immediately his frightfully neglected upbringing, his alcoholic father and his prostitute mother and all
the rest disappeared and he readily volunteered for the front.'

'In the army nowadays nobody believes any longer in hereditary
taints,' said the volunteer, 'because if they did all the general staffs
would have to be shut up in lunatic asylums, every one of them.'

The key in the reinforced iron door rattled and the warder came in
saying:

'Infantryman Švejk and Sapper Vodička to go to the judge advocate!'

They got up and Vodička said to Švejk: 'You see what these bastards
are like. Every day they have an interrogation and there's never any
result. Himmelherrgott, if only they would sentence us and not keep
on dragging us about. As it is we lie here the whole bloody day and
millions of those Hungarian bastards keep on running around . . .'

Continuing on the way to the interrogation in the office of the
divisional court which was situated in another hut on the other side

of the camp, Sapper Vodička and Švejk wondered when they would actually be brought before a proper court.

'It's always nothing but interrogation,' said Vodička, whipping himself up into a fury. 'If only something would come out of it at last. They waste heaps of paper and a chap doesn't even see the court. He rots behind the bars. Tell me honestly, is the soup eatable? And that cabbage with frozen potatoes? Bloody hell, I've never had such a blasted silly war. I thought it would be quite different.'

'As for me, I'm quite happy,' said Švejk. 'When years ago I was serving as a regular our old sweat Solpera used to say that in the army everybody must be conscious of his duties and he gave you at the same time such a sock on the jaw that you never forgot it. Or the late Lieutenant Kvajser, when he came to inspect the rifles, always lectured us too on how every soldier must show the greatest moral ruthlessness because soldiers were only cattle whom the government fed. They gave them something to guzzle, let them swill coffee and stuff tobacco in their pipes, and for that they had to obey and pull like oxen.'

Sapper Vodička reflected for a moment and said after a time:

'When you come before the judge advocate, Švejk, keep your head screwed on and don't forget to repeat what you said at the last interrogation so that I don't get into a mess. The main thing is that you saw how those Hungarian bastards attacked me. After all, we were together in this.'

'Don't worry, Vodička,' said Švejk consolingly. 'Take it calmly. Don't get nervy. What does it matter being brought before divisional court like this? You should have seen how smartly a court-martial like that worked years ago. There was a teacher called Herál on service with me. Once, when we were lying on our bunks because all of us who shared the room had been confined to barracks, he told us that in the Prague Museum there's a book of records of a military court like that from the time of the Empress Maria Theresa. At that time every regiment used to have its executioner who executed the soldiers of the regiment for one Maria Theresa thaler per head. And according to those records that executioner earned some days as much as five thalers.

'Of course,' Švejk added thoughtfully, 'at that time there were strongly-manned regiments and they were regularly filled with recruits from the villages.'

'When I was in Serbia,' said Vodička, 'some men in our brigade volunteered to hang comitadji for cigarettes. A soldier who hanged a comitadji bastard got ten cigarettes and five for a woman or a child. But later Supplies H.Q started economizing and the shootings took place *en bloc*. There was a gipsy who served in our company and for a long time we didn't know what dirty job he was doing. We only noticed that at nights they always summoned him to go to the office. At that time we were encamped on the Drina. And once in the night when he was away a fellow took it into his head to root about in his things and the swine had in his rucksack three whole cartons each with a hundred cigarettes. Later he returned to our barn towards morning and we made short shrift with him. We knocked him on the ground and a chap called Běloun strangled him with his belt. The bastard had as many lives as a cat.'

Old Sapper Vodička spat: 'You just couldn't strangle him. He shitted, his eyes bulged and still he was as live as a half-decapitated cock. And so they wrenched him in two like a cat. Two chaps took his head and another two took his legs and they broke his neck. After that we put his rucksack on his shoulder with the cigarettes in it and threw him into the Drina. Who would want to smoke those cigarettes? In the morning there was a search for him.'

'You should have reported that he'd "dissented",' said Švejk nonchalantly, 'that he'd already made preparations for it and had been saying every day that he would run away.'

'But who would have thought of that?' answered Vodička. 'We had done our bit and we weren't worried about anything else. It was really quite easy there. Every day somebody was missing and they didn't even fish them out of the Drina. A bloated comitadji floated peacefully down the Drina to the Danube side by side with one of our Landwehr men who had been torn to pieces. People who were new to it became a little feverish when they saw it for the first time.'

'You should have given them quinine,' said Švejk.

They were just entering the hut of the offices of divisional court and the patrol led them at once to office no. 8, where behind a long table with a pile of documents sat Judge Advocate Ruller.

A volume of the legal code lay before him, and a half-consumed glass of tea stood on top of it. On the table on the right stood a crucifix made out of imitation ivory with a dusty Christ, who looked despairingly at the pedestal of his cross, on which there were ashes and cigarette stubs.

To the renewed regret of the crucified Jesus Judge Advocate Ruller was at this very moment flicking the ash from another cigarette on to the pedestal of the crucifix. With his other hand he was raising the glass of tea, which had got stuck to the legal code.

When he had freed the glass from the embrace of the code he turned over the pages of a book which he had borrowed from the officers' club.

It was a book by Franz S. Krause with the promising title: *Research into the History of the Development of Sexual Morals.*

He was staring at the reproduction of naïve drawings of male and female sexual organs with appropriate rhymes which the scholar Franz S. Krause discovered on the walls of the W.C.s of the West Berlin railway station, and so he did not pay any attention to the men who entered the room.

He only pulled himself away from examining the reproductions when Vodička coughed.

'What's the matter?' he asked, turning the pages further and looking for the continuation of the naïve and stupid drawings, sketches and designs.

'Beg to report, sir,' answered Švejk, 'my friend Vodička has caught cold and is now coughing.'

Judge Advocate Ruller only now looked at Švejk and at Vodička. He tried to assume an air of severity.

'And so you've at last come along, you bastards,' he said, ferreting about in the pile of papers on his desk. 'I had you summoned for nine o'clock and now it's almost eleven.

'What do you mean by standing like that, you bloody great ox?' he asked Vodička, who had taken the liberty of standing at ease. 'Only when I say "At Ease" can you do what you like with your shanks.'

'Humbly report, sir, he has rheumatism,' Švejk put in.

'You'd better shut your mug,' said Judge Advocate Ruller. 'You'll only speak when you're given permission. Three times you've come before me for cross-examination and it was like trying to get water from a stone. Well, am I going to find it or aren't I? You've given me a lot of work, you bloody bastards. But you'll pay for having troubled the courts without good reason!

'Now look, you bloody swine,' he said, when he had taken from a heap of documents a voluminous file with the inscription:

'*Schwejk & Woditschka.*'

'Don't think that because of a stupid brawl you'll be able to loll about in the divisional court and get out of front service for a time. All because of you I had to telephone all the way up to the army court, you bloody idiots!'

He sighed.

'Don't look so serious, Švejk. At the front you'll lose your taste for fighting with Honvéds,' he continued. 'The proceedings against you both are quashed. Each of you is going to his unit, where he will be punished at report and after that sent with a march company to the front. If ever you get into my clutches again, you vermin, I'll make such a mess of you that you won't be able to recognize yourselves. Here you have your release warrant and now behave yourselves respectably. Take them to no. 2.'

'Humbly report, sir,' said Švejk, 'we both take your words to heart and we thank you very much for your kindness. If this was in civil life

I would take the liberty of saying that you're a man of gold. And at the same time we must both beg your pardon for giving you so much bother. We really don't deserve your kindness.'

'Well, now get to hell out of it!' the judge advocate shouted at Švejk. 'If Colonel Schröder hadn't put in a word for you both I don't know what might have happened to you.'

Vodička only felt himself the old Vodička again when they were in the corridor and the patrol led them to office no. 2.

The soldier who escorted them was afraid he would be late to lunch and so he said:

'Come on, now, briskly there, you chaps, you crawl along like lice.'

Vodička told him not to open his trap as wide as that. He was lucky to be a Czech. If he had been a Hungarian he'd have torn him to pieces like a salted herring.

As the army writers in the office had already gone to mess, the soldier who had escorted them was obliged to bring them back temporarily to the divisional court gaol. This did not take place without oaths on his part which he addressed to the hated race of army writers.

'The others will have cleaned up all the fat from the soup,' he moaned in tragic tones, 'and instead of meat they'll leave me sinew. Yesterday too I escorted two people into the camp and while I was doing it someone ate up half the loaf which they had drawn for me.'

'It looks as if here in divisional court you only think about filling your bellies,' said Vodička, who was already his old self again.

When they told the volunteer what had happened to them he exclaimed: 'So it's the march company for you, my friends! This is just like in the journal for Czech tourists, "A Fair Wind!" The preliminary preparations for the journey are already completed. Everything has been managed and arranged by the glorious military administration. And you too have been specially picked to join the expedition to Galicia. Set out on your journey with easy minds and light and joyful hearts. Cherish special love for the regions where they will introduce you to the trenches. It's lovely and extremely interesting there. You will feel at home in those distant foreign lands as though you were in familiar parts, yes, almost as though you were in your dear fatherland. With exalted feelings you will begin your pilgrimage to those lands, of which even the good old Humboldt said: "In the whole world I've never seen anything more magnificent than that bloody silly Galicia." The numerous precious experiences which our glorious army acquired in the course of its retreat from Galicia during the first expedition will certainly be very helpful guide lines when we make our programme for the second expedition. Just follow your nose to Russia, and joyfully fire all your cartridges into the air.'

After lunch, before Švejk and Vodička left for the office they were approached by the unfortunate teacher who had written the rhyme about the lice. He took them both aside and said mysteriously: 'Don't forget when you're on the Russian side to say at once to the Russians: "*Zdravstvuite, Russkie bratya, my bratya Chekhi, my nyet Avstritsy*".'[1]

And when they came out of the hut Vodička, wanting to manifest his hatred towards the Hungarians and demonstrate that his confinement had not shaken his convictions, trod on the foot of the Hungarian who didn't want to serve at the front and roared out at him: 'Put on your boots, you bastard!'

'He ought to have said something to me,' Sapper Vodička grumbled afterwards to Švejk. 'He should have piped up and I'd have torn his Hungarian snout from one ear to another. But the idiotic bastard keeps mum and lets me trample on his boots. Herrgott, Švejk, I'm furious that I haven't been convicted. Why, it looks as though they were just laughing at us, as if what we did to the Hungarians was not worth a damn. And yet we fought like lions. It's your fault that they didn't convict us and gave us a clean chit as though we hadn't known how to fight properly. Who do they think we are? Why, it was quite a respectable roughhouse.'

'My dear old boy,' said Švejk affably, 'I can't understand why you're not glad that our divisional court officially recognized us as quite respectable people against whom they could have no charge. It's true that during the investigation I made all sorts of excuses, but that's what you have to do. Its your duty to lie, as the lawyer Bass tells his clients. When the judge advocate asked me why we broke into the apartment of that Mr Kákonyi I simply said to him: "I thought the best way for us to get acquainted with Mr Kákonyi was to go and see him." After that the judge advocate didn't ask me any further questions and had had enough of it.

'Remember,' Švejk continued reflectively, 'that at a court-martial no one must ever confess anything. When I was under arrest at garrison court there was a soldier in the next cell who confessed.

1. 'Hello, Russian brothers, we're your Czech brothers, we aren't Austrians.'

When the others learnt about it they gave him the blanket treatment and ordered him to withdraw his confession.'

'If I'd done something dishonest I wouldn't have confessed, of course,' said Sapper Vodička, 'but when that bastard of a judge advocate asked me straight out: "Did you fight?", I said: "Yes, I did." "Did you manhandle anybody?" "Certainly I did, sir." "Did you

wound anybody?" "Of course I did, sir." He should know who he's dealing with. And the real disgrace is that they acquitted us. It's as though he didn't want to believe that I broke my bayonet-belt over those Hungarian bastards, that I made pea soup, bumps and bruises out of them. You were there, weren't you, at the very moment when I had three of those Hungarian bastards on top of me and you could see after a short time how all of them fell on to the ground and I stamped on them. And after all that the swine of a judge advocate goes and quashes the proceedings. It's just as if he'd said to me: "You fight? Who d'you think you bloody well are?" When the war's over and I return to civilian life I'll find that swine somewhere and show him whether I know how to fight or not. And then I'll come here to Királyhida and make such a roughhouse here as the world has never seen. And people'll go and hide in their cellars when they learn that I have come to have a word with those bastards in Királyhida, those rats, those stinking swine.'

In the office all the formalities were completed very quickly. A sergeant-major with a mouth still greasy from lunch gave Švejk and Vodička their documents with a frightfully solemn expression on his face and did not let the opportunity slip of making a speech to both of them, in which he appealed to their military spirit. In doing so, as he was a *Wasserpolak*, he mixed up several expressions in his dialect, saying things like '*marekvium*', '*glupi rolmopsie*', '*krajcová sedmina*', '*sviňa porýpaná*' and '*dum vám baně na mjesjnuckov vaši gzichty*'.[1]

When Švejk said goodbye to Vodička and each of them was taken off to his unit he said: 'When the war's over come and see me. You'll find me every evening from six o'clock onwards in The Chalice at Na Bojišti.'

'Of course I will,' answered Vodička. 'Will there be any fun there?'

'Every day it goes with a bang there,' Švejk promised, 'and if it should turn out to be too quiet, we'll fix something.'

They parted, and when they were already several paces away from each other, old Sapper Vodička called after Švejk: 'Very well then, but see that you fix some fun when I come to see you!'

Upon which Švejk called back: 'But be sure you come as soon as the war's over!'

After that they went further away from each other and some time later Vodička's voice could be heard from round the corner of the other row of huts: 'Švejk, what kind of beer do they have at The Chalice?'

And Švejk's answer came like an echo: 'Velkopopovický.'[2]

'I thought they had Smíchovský!'[2] Sapper Vodička called from the distance.

'They've got girls there too!' shouted Švejk.

1. *Wasserpolak* (literally 'Water Pole') was a pejorative name for inhabitants of Southern and Western Silesia where a mixture of German and Polish was spoken.
2. Two famous brands of Czech beer.

'Very well, then, at six o'clock in the evening when the war's over!' shouted Vodička from below.

'Better if you come at half-past six, in case I should be held up somewhere,' answered Švejk.

And then Vodička's voice could be heard again this time from a great distance:

'Can't you come at six?'

'Very well then, I'll come at six,' Vodička heard his retreating friend reply.

It was in this way that the good soldier Švejk and the old Sapper Vodička parted. As the German saying goes, '*Wenn die Leute auseinandergehen, da sagen sie "Auf Wiedersehen".*'[1]

1. 'When people part, they say "Till we meet again".'

5

From Bruck an der Leitha to Sokal

LIEUTENANT LUKÁŠ strode angrily up and down the office of the 11th march company. It was a dark hole in the company's hut, partitioned from the corridor by boards. There were a table, two chairs, a can of paraffin and a bunk.

Before him stood Quartermaster Sergeant-Major Vaněk, who here drew up the records of the soldiers' pay, kept the accounts for the men's kitchen, was finance minister for the whole company and spent the whole blessed day in the office, sleeping there as well.

At the door stood a fat infantryman with bushy whiskers like Krakonoš.[1] This was Baloun, the lieutenant's new batman, in civil life a miller from the region of Český Krumlov.

'You've certainly picked me a wonderful batman,' said Lieutenant Lukáš to the quartermaster sergeant-major. 'Thank you very much for this kind surprise. The very first day I send him for my lunch from the officers' mess he wolfs up half of it.'

'I spilled it, please, sir,' said the fat giant.

'Good, you spilled it. But you could only have spilled the soup or the sauce, not the roast with the frankfurter stuffing. Why, you've brought me a speck just small enough to fit in behind a finger-nail, and what did you do with the Apfelstrudl?'

'Sir, I've . . .'

'Now, don't deny it. You've wolfed it up too.'

Lieutenant Lukáš pronounced the last words with such gravity and in such a severe tone that Baloun involuntarily recoiled two steps.

'I asked in the kitchen what there was for lunch today. There was soup with liver dumplings. What have you done with those dumplings? You've filched them on the way, that's certain. And then there was beef with gherkins. What have you done with that? You've bolted that up too. And then there were two slices of roast with frankfurter stuffing. And you've only produced half a slice, haven't you? Two pieces of

---

1. A giant in one of the Czech fairy tales.

Apfelstrudl! What have you done with them? You've stuffed yourself
up with them, you disgusting miserable swine! Speak out! What have
you done with the Apfelstrudl? What do you say? It fell in the mud,
did it? You verminous scab, you! Can you show me the spot where

it's lying in the mud? What do you say? A dog suddenly came up, did
it? By appointment, I suppose? And it seized it and carried it off?
Jesus Christ, I'll give you such a sock on the jaw that you'll have a
head like a wash-tub. And the swine still denies it! Do you know who
saw you? Quartermaster Sergeant-Major Vaněk here. He came to me
and told me: "Humbly report, sir, your swine, Baloun, is wolfing up
your lunch. I looked out of the window and there he was stuffing
himself as if he hadn't eaten for a whole week." Listen, you quartermaster sergeant-major, couldn't you really have picked out some other
animal for me than this prize bastard?'

'Humbly report, sir, Baloun seemed the decentest chap in the whole
of our march company. He's such an idiot that he never can remember

any of the rifle positions. If you put a rifle in his hands there'd certainly be an accident. When we had the last exercise with blanks he nearly shot his neighbour's eye out. I thought that he'd at least be able to do this kind of duty.'

'And he'll wolf up his master's lunch every time,' said Lukáš. 'As if one portion wasn't enough for him. Perhaps you're still hungry?'

'Humbly report, sir, I'm hungry all the time. When anybody has bread to spare I buy it from him for cigarettes, and it still isn't enough. I'm like that by nature. I always think I'm full but it's wrong. In a jiffy, as though it were before a meal, my stomach begins to rumble and there it is again, the beast. Sometimes I think I've really had enough, I couldn't get anything more inside me, but it's no good. If I see somebody eating or if I only smell food my stomach feels at once as if it's been cleaned out. It starts to claim its rights and I could even eat nails. Humbly report, sir, I had already asked whether I could be allowed a double portion. Because of that I went to the regimental doctor at Budějovice and he gave me instead three days in the sick bay, prescribing for me only a little cup of clear soup for the whole day. "I'll teach you to be hungry, you vermin," he said. "Come here again and you'll see how you leave us again. You'll be as thin as a hop pole!" I don't have to look at any specially good things, sir, I've only got to see quite ordinary things and my mouth at once begins to water. Humbly report, sir, I respectfully beg to be allowed a double portion. If there isn't meat, could I at least have the garnishing, potatoes, dumplings, a little sauce. There's always plenty of that left . . .'

'Good. I've listened to these impudences of yours, Baloun,' answered Lieutenant Lukáš. 'Have you ever heard, quartermaster sergeant-major, of a soldier being on top of everything else as insolent as this bastard is? He's wolfed up my lunch and still has the cheek to demand I should give him a double portion. But I'll teach you, Baloun, what it means to be hungry.

'Quartermaster sergeant-major,' he turned to Vaněk, 'take him to Corporal Weidenhofer and tell him to tie him up firmly in the yard by the kitchen for two hours when they serve out goulash this evening. Let him tie him nice and high, so that he can only just stand on tip-toe and see how the goulash is cooking in the cauldron. And make sure that the bastard is kept tied up when the goulash is being doled out in the kitchen, so that his mouth can water like a starving cur's when it's sniffing at a delicatessen shop. Tell the cook to give away the bastard's own portion!'

'Very good, sir. Come along, Baloun!'

Just as they were leaving the lieutenant detained them in the doorway and, looking into the horrified face of Baloun, cried out triumphantly: 'You've done well for yourself, Baloun. I wish you a good appetite! And if you should ever try this on me again, I'll have you mercilessly court-martialled.'

When Vaněk returned and reported that Baloun was already tied up Lukáš said: 'You know me well, Vaněk, and you know I don't like doing things like this, but I can't help it. First you must admit that if you take a bone from a dog it growls. I don't want to have a low fellow about me, and next the fact that Baloun is tied up will have a great moral and psychological impact on all the rank and file. When those bastards are on march companies and know that the next day or the day after they'll go to the front they tend to do what they like.'

Lieutenant Lukáš appeared extremely care-worn and went on in a quiet voice: 'The day before yesterday, when we had night operations, we had as you know to manoeuvre against the volunteer school behind the sugar-refinery. The first group, the advance guard, marched quite noiselessly along the street, because I led them myself, but the second, which was supposed to go to the left and to send advance patrols below the sugar-refinery, behaved as if they were out on a picnic. They sang and stamped, so that they could probably be heard even as far away as the camp. After that on the right flank the third group went to reconnoitre the terrain below the wood. That was about ten good minutes away from us and even at that distance you could see how the bastards were smoking; they were fiery points in the dark. And the fourth group had to form the rear guard and God himself knows how it happened, but they suddenly appeared in front of our advance guard and were taken for the enemy, and I had to retreat from my own rear guard, which advanced against me. That's the 11th march company which I've inherited! What can I do with them? How are they going to show up in a real action?'

Lieutenant Lukáš clasped his hands and assumed a martyr's expression, while the point of his nose seemed to prolong itself.

'Don't worry too much about that, sir,' the quartermaster sergeant-major said, trying to console him. 'Don't let that give you a headache. I've already been on three march companies and every one of them was broken to pieces together with the whole battalion and so we had to go and form another again and again. And every march company was just the same as the other, not a single one of them was a hair better than yours, sir. The worst of all was the 9th. That carried off with it into captivity all the N.C.O.s and the company commander

as well. I was only saved because I had gone to the regimental train to draw rum and wine for the company, so they did their bit without me.

'And you don't know, sir, that during the last night operation, which you were talking about, sir, the volunteer school which was supposed to encircle our company got as far as the Neusiedler See? They went marching on until the next morning and their advance posts got as far as the marshes. It was Captain Ságner who led them. They'd probably have got to Sopron if daylight hadn't come,' continued the quartermaster sergeant-major in a mysterious voice. He took pleasure in such happenings and kept records of them.

'And do you know, sir,' he said, winking confidentially, 'that Captain Ságner is to become battalion commander of our march battalion? Some time ago they all thought, as Staff Sergeant-Major Hegner said, that you would be appointed, because you are the most senior officer we have, but later, they say, the order came from the division to the brigade that Captain Ságner had been appointed.'

Lieutenant Lukáš bit his lip and lit a cigarette. He knew all about that and was convinced that an injustice was being done to him. Captain Ságner had jumped over him twice in promotion; but he said nothing but: 'Well, of course, Captain Ságner . . .'

'I can't say I'm very pleased about it,' said the quartermaster sergeant-major confidentially: 'Staff Sergeant-Major Hegner said that Captain Ságner at the beginning of the war in Serbia wanted to distinguish himself somewhere in the mountains in Montenegro, and drove one company of his battalion after another on to the machine-guns of the Serbian positions, although it was quite unnecessary and the infantry there wasn't any damn use at all because only artillery could have dislodged the Serbs from those cliffs. Out of the whole battalion only eighty men survived; Captain Ságner himself was shot in the hand and later he got dysentery in hospital. And then again he appeared in Budějovice at the regiment and last night they say that he was telling in the officers' club how he was looking forward to the front, and that he'd show what he was worth and get the *Signum Laudis*, even if he had to leave the whole march battalion there. He'd got a ticking off because of Serbia, but now he'd either fall with the whole of the march battalion or be appointed lieutenant-colonel, but the whole march battalion would have to be ready to go west. I think, sir, that we face this risk too. Staff Sergeant-Major Hegner said not long ago that you don't get on very well with Captain Ságner and that he'll send our 11th company first into the attack and place it in the most dangerous positions.'

The quartermaster sergeant-major sighed: 'I believe that in a war like this, where there are so many armies and such a long front, you would gain more merely by proper manoeuvring than by desperate assaults. I saw that at Dukla when I was in the 10th march company. Then everything went off quite smoothly; an order came "Hold fire" and so no one shot and we all waited until the Russians came near to us. We could have taken them without firing a shot, but un-fortunately at that time we had next to us on the left flank the "Iron

Flies", and those stupid Landwehr men were so frightened that
the Russians were coming near us that they started to go down the
slopes of the hills in the snow like on a slide. We got the order that
the Russians had penetrated the left flank and we must try to reach the
brigade. I was then at the brigade itself, having the job of checking
the company catering accounts because I couldn't find our regimental
train. It was just then that the first men of the 10th march company
started coming to the brigade. By the evening 120 had come. The
others apparently lost their way in the retreat and slid down over the
snow like a toboggan somewhere into the Russian positions. It was
really frightful, sir. The Russians had positions in the Carpathians
above and below. And then, sir, Captain Ságner . . .'

'Oh, for God's sake stop talking about Captain Ságner,' said Lieutenant Lukáš. 'I know all that. And, by the way, don't think that next
time when there's an assault and fighting you'll again have the chance
of being somewhere in the regimental train drawing rum and wine.
I've already been told that you're a frightful soaker. Anyone looking
at your red nose can see at once the sort of chap he's dealing with.'

'That comes from the Carpathians, sir. We were forced to drink
there. We really were. By the time the mess portions reached us on top
there they were quite cold. Our trenches were under snow. We weren't
allowed to light fires. And so it was only the rum which kept us alive.
And if it hadn't been for me it would have been the same as in other
companies where they didn't even have rum and people got frozen.
That's why we all of us had red noses from the rum. But that also had
its disadvantage, because an order came from the battalion that only
men with red noses should go on patrols.'

'Now the winter's over,' the lieutenant observed significantly.

'I tell you, sir, rum is an indispensable thing at the front at any
season of the year and wine as well. It makes for good humour, so to
speak. For half a mess-tin of wine and a quarter-litre of rum people
will fight anybody. . . . Who's that mule knocking on the door
again? Can't you read what's written there: "Don't knock. Come in."'

Lieutenant Lukáš turned on his chair towards the door and observed
how it opened slowly and softly. And just as slowly and softly the good
soldier Švejk entered the office of the 10th march company. He was
saluting in the doorway and perhaps he was even doing so when he
knocked on the door and looked at the inscription 'Don't knock.'

His saluting was the full-blooded accompaniment to his everlastingly

contented and carefree face. He looked like the Greek god of theft in the sober uniform of an Austrian infantryman.

Lieutenant Lukáš shut his eyes for a moment at the sight of the good soldier Švejk who embraced and caressed him with his glances.

Probably with the same affection the lost and newly-found prodigal son looked at his father when he roasted a sheep on the spit in his honour.

'Humbly report, sir, I'm here again,' said Švejk with such sincere nonchalance that Lieutenant Lukáš suddenly came to again. From the time when Colonel Schröder had informed him he was going to send Švejk to him and that he would have him round his neck again, Lieutenant Lukáš had mentally tried every day to put off that meeting. Every morning he said to himself: 'He won't come today. He's probably been up to something again and they'll keep him there.'

But Švejk by his sweet and simple entry corrected all these calculations.

Švejk now looked at the quartermaster sergeant-major and turning to him with a pleasant smile handed him some documents which he drew from a pocket of his greatcoat: 'Sergeant-major, I have to give you these papers which they made out for me in the regimental office. They're to do with my pay and messing.'

Švejk moved as freely and sociably in the office of the 11th march company as if he had been Vaněk's best friend, to which the quartermaster sergeant-major reacted simply with the words: 'Put them on the table.'

'It will be best, quartermaster sergeant-major, if you leave me alone with Švejk now,' said Lieutenant Lukáš with a sigh.

Vaněk went away but remained standing outside the door to hear what the two would say to one another.

At first he heard nothing, because Švejk and the lieutenant were silent. Both observed each other closely for a long time. Lukáš stared at Švejk as though he was preparing to hypnotize him like a cock standing in front of a chicken and waiting to spring on it.

Švejk as usual looked at Lieutenant Lukáš with moist tender eyes as though wanting to say: 'United again, heart of mine! Now nothing will separate us, my pet.'

And when the lieutenant remained silent for a long time, Švejk's eyes spoke with sorrowful tenderness: 'Speak, my darling, say what you are thinking.'

Lieutenant Lukáš broke this embarrassing silence with the words into which he tried to inject a considerable dose of irony: 'Hearty welcome to you, Švejk. Thank you for the visit. Well, now, what a precious guest we have!'

He could not contain himself, however, and the anger of the past days exploded into a tremendous blow on the table with his fist, at which the inkstand jumped up and the ink was spilt all over the pay-list.

At the same time Lieutenant Lukáš jumped up, stood directly in front of Švejk and roared at him: 'You animal!' Then he began to march up and down in the restricted space of the office, spitting whenever he came anywhere near Švejk.

'Humbly report, sir,' said Švejk, when Lieutenant Lukáš went on walking up and down and furiously threw into the corner crumpled balls of paper, which he again and again came to the table to pick up, 'I handed the letter over as you instructed me. I was lucky enough to find Mrs Kákonyi and I can say that she's a very pretty woman although I only saw her when she was in tears . . .'

Lieutenant Lukáš sat down on the quartermaster sergeant-major's bunk and cried out in a hoarse voice: 'When is this going to end, Švejk?'

Švejk answered as though he had not heard: 'And then a little disagreeable thing happened to me, but I took the blame for it myself. They didn't believe I had corresponded with the lady and so at the investigation I thought it better to swallow the letter to put them off the scent. Then by pure chance – I can't explain it otherwise – I found myself involved in a small and very unimportant scuffle. But I got out of that too. They recognized my innocence, sent me on regimental report and quashed the whole proceedings in the divisional court. I had only been a few minutes in the regimental office when the colonel came. He swore at me a little, and then said I should at once report to you, sir, as orderly. He ordered me to tell you that he required you to come at once about the march comp. It's already more than half an hour ago, but the colonel didn't know that they would afterwards drag me off to the regimental office and that I would be sitting there another quarter of an hour still. You see the whole time I was under arrest I had my pay left there and I had to be paid by the regiment and not by the company, because I had been put under regimental arrest. Altogether they're in such a God Almighty mess there that it's enough to drive you barmy . . .'

When Lieutenant Lukáš heard that already half an hour ago he should have been with Colonel Schröder he dressed quickly and said: 'You've certainly done me a wonderful service again, Švejk.' He said it in such despairing tones, full of such hopelessness, that Švejk tried to soothe him with a friendly word, which he called out when Lieutenant Lukáš rushed out of the door: 'Don't worry. The colonel'll wait. He hasn't anything to do, anyway.'

A short time after the lieutenant's departure Quartermaster Sergeant-Major Vaněk entered the office.

Švejk was sitting on a chair and feeding the small iron stove, throwing bits of coal inside through its open door. The stove smoked and stank, and Švejk went on with this amusement, taking no notice of

Vaněk, who watched Švejk for a time. Then he kicked the door of the stove shut and told Švejk to remove himself.

'Sergeant-major,' Švejk said with dignity, 'allow me to inform you that even with the best will in the world I cannot carry out your order to remove myself from this room or altogether from the whole camp, as I am subject to higher orders. You see, I am orderly here,' he added

proudly. 'Colonel Schröder assigned me here to the 11th march company, to Lieutenant Lukáš, whose batman I used to be. Thanks to my natural intelligence I have been promoted company orderly. The lieutenant and me are old friends. What are you in civil life, sergeant-major?'

The quartermaster sergeant-major was so surprised by the familiar neighbourly tone of the good soldier Švejk that he forgot his dignity, which he was so fond of showing off to the soldiers of the company, and answered as though he had been Švejk's subordinate:

'I am Vaněk from Kralupy, the chemist.'

'And I was apprenticed to an apothecary too,' said Švejk, 'at a Mr Kokoška's at Na Perštýně in Prague. He was an awfully rum fellow and once when by mistake I set fire to a barrel of petrol in the cellar and the house burnt down he kicked me out. After that the guild wouldn't ever accept me anywhere and so because of that stupid barrel of petrol I couldn't finish my apprenticeship. Do you also manufacture herbs for cows?'

Vaněk shook his head.

'We used to manufacture herbs for cows together with holy images. Mr Kokoška, our chief, was a frightfully religious chap and once he read that St Pelegrinus helped when cattle got flatulent. So he had printed somewhere at Smíchov images of St Pelegrinus and had them consecrated at the Emmaus for two hundred guilders. And then we put them into the boxes of our herbs for cows. The herbs had to be diluted in warm water and given to the cows to drink from the tub, and at the same time a prayer to St Pelegrinus, which Mr Tauchen, our assistant, composed, was recited to the cow. Now, you see, when those images of St Pelegrinus were already printed some little prayer had to be printed on the reverse side. And so in the evening our boss, Kokoška, called Mr Tauchen and told him that by the next morning he must have a prayer written to put on the picture and to be served with the herbs. When he came to the shop at 10 a.m. it must be ready, so that it could be sent to the printers as the cows were already waiting for the prayer. For Mr Tauchen it was "either – or". If he did it well he would be given a guilder in hard cash; if not, he'd get a fortnight's notice. Mr Tauchen sweated the whole night and didn't sleep a wink. In the morning he came to open the shop and had nothing written. He even forgot what the saint for those cow-herbs was called. And so our porter Ferdinand helped him out of the mess. He could do any-thing. When we were drying camomile tea in the attic he always climbed up there, took off his boots and showed us how to stop our feet sweating. He caught pigeons in the attic, knew how to open the cash-drawer in the counter and taught us other small tricks with the goods. At that time I was only a boy and I had at home a chemist's set which I had brought home from the shop. Even the "Brother Hospitallers"[1] didn't have one like it. And Ferdinand helped Mr Tauchen. He just said: "Give it to me, Mr Tauchen, and let me look at it." Mr Tauchen immediately sent me to fetch a glass of beer for

1. A hospital in a monastery at Prague.

him. Before I had brought the beer Ferdinand had already finished
half of it and was reciting:

> "I come from the kingdom above,
>   And bring a message of love.
>   Cow, calf and ox all need
>   On Kokoška's herbs to feed.
>   Kokoška's mixture once a day
>   Keeps the veterinary away."

'And when he had drunk the beer and taken a pretty deep swig of
tincture of amaranth he got on with it quickly and finished it very
neatly in a trice:

> "To Pelegrinus offer vows
>   And he will come and cure your cows.
>   Praise St Pelegrinus who
>   Has blessed this box for guilders two.
>   Worship him in thought and word
>   And beg his blessing on your herd."

'Then Mr Kokoška came and Mr Tauchen went with him to the
office, and when he came out he showed us two guilders, not one as had
been promised, and he wanted to share it fifty-fifty with Ferdinand.
But when Ferdinand saw the two guilders he succumbed to the influence of Mammon. "No," he said, "either I get all or nothing." And
so Mr Tauchen didn't give him anything and kept the two guilders
for himself. Then he took me to the storehouse next door, gave me a
box on the ears and said I would get a hundred more if I ever dared
say that he didn't write it himself, and if Ferdinand should go and
complain to the old man I should say that he was a liar. I had to swear
an oath before some kind of jug of tarragon vinegar. And so that
porter of ours started to revenge himself on those cow-herbs. We mixed
it in big boxes in the attic and whenever Ferdinand was able to sweep
up mouse droppings he brought them up there and mixed them into
the herbs. And then he collected horse manure in the streets, dried it
at home, pestled it in a mortar and threw all that too into our cow-
herbs with the picture of St Pelegrinus. But that was not the end of
it. He pissed into those boxes, shitted into them and stirred it all up
together so that it was like a bran mash . . .'

The telephone rang. The quartermaster sergeant-major jumped to the receiver and threw it away in anger: 'I've got to go to the regimental office. All of a sudden like this! I don't like it at all.'

Švejk was alone again.

After a moment the telephone rang again.

Švejk began to speak into the receiver: 'Vaněk? He's just gone to the regimental office. Who's speaking? The orderly of the 11th march company. Who's calling? The orderly from the 12th march company? Servus, colleague. What's my name? Švejk. And yours? Braun. Are you any relation to the hatter, Braun, in Pobřežní Avenue in Karlín? You aren't? You don't know him . . . ? I don't know him either. I only went past the shop in the tram some time ago and the name of the firm struck me. What's the news? – I don't know anything. – What? When are we going? I haven't spoken with anybody yet about going. Where are we supposed to be going to?'

'With the march company to the front, you ninny.'

'I haven't heard anything about that.'

'Then you're a fine orderly. You don't know whether your lieutenant . . .'

'He's not a lieutenant, he's an *Oberleutnant*.'

'It's all the same. And so your *Oberleutnant* has gone to the colonel for a conference, has he?'

'The colonel called him over.'

'Well, there you are, you see! Ours was called over too and the lieutenant from the 13th march company as well. I've just spoken with the orderly on the telephone. I don't like this flap. And do you know whether the band is packing too?'

'I don't know anything.'

'Don't act like a bloody idiot. Your quartermaster sergeant-major already got the notice about the vans, didn't he? How many men have you got?'

'I don't know.'

'You bloody fool, d'you think I'm going to eat you up?' (The man at the telephone could be heard saying to someone else: 'Franta, take the other receiver, so that you can hear what a bloody mug of an orderly they have in the 11th march company.') – 'Hallo, are you asleep there or what? All right, then, answer when your colleague asks you a question! So you don't know anything yet? Now come clean. Didn't your quartermaster sergeant-major say anything to you about your going to draw tins? You didn't talk to him about any-

thing like that? You bloody oaf, you. It's no business of yours?'
(There was audible laughter.) 'You must have a screw loose. When
you hear anything, ring us in the 12th march company, my sonny
boy, my prize ass! Where do you come from?'

'From Prague.'

'Well, you ought to be brighter. . . . And one more thing: when was
your quartermaster sergeant-major called to regimental office?'

'Only a minute ago.'

'My God, and couldn't you have told me that before? Ours went
away a moment ago too. Something's in the wind. Haven't you
spoken with the train?'

'No.'

'Jesus Christ, and you say you're from Prague? You don't bother
about anything, do you? Where have you been hanging about all this
time?'

'I only came from divisional court an hour ago.'

'Ah, that's another story, old man, then I must come and see you today. Ring off twice.'

Švejk was just going to light his pipe when the telephone rang again.

'To hell with your ringing!' thought Švejk. 'Why should I waste my time on you?'

The telephone went on inexorably ringing until Švejk finally lost his patience. He took the receiver and shouted into the telephone:

'Hello, who's calling? This is Orderly Švejk of the 11th march company.' The answering voice Švejk recognized as belonging to Lieutenant Lukáš:

'What are you doing there? Where's Vaněk? Call him at once to the telephone!'

'Humbly report, sir, a minute ago the telephone was ringing . . .'

'Listen, Švejk, I've no time to waste with you. Telephone conversations in wartime aren't just a gossip like when we invite someone to come and have lunch. They must be clear and concise. There's no time for "Humbly report, sir" on the telephone in wartime. Well, Švejk, I am asking you, is Vaněk there with you? Let him come to the telephone at once!'

'Humbly report, sir, I haven't got him with me. A short time ago he was called away to the regimental office. It might have been less than a quarter of an hour ago.'

'When I'm back I'll deal with you, Švejk. Can't you express yourself concisely? Now, listen very carefully to what I say. Can you understand clearly so that you don't excuse yourself afterwards by saying that there was crackling in the telephone? As soon as you hang up the receiver . . .'

There was a pause and then renewed ringing. Švejk took the receiver and was drowned in a heap of abuse: 'You animal, you gutter-snipe, you blackguard, you. What the hell are you doing? Why do you break the connection?'

'Please, sir, you said I was to hang up the receiver.'

'I shall be back in an hour, Švejk, and then you'll see. . . . Now get cracking at once. Go to the hut and find a platoon sergeant, let's say Fuchs, and tell him at once to take ten men and go with them to the stores to draw tinned food. Now repeat what he's to go and do.'

'He's to go with ten men to the stores to draw tinned food for the company.'

'Now at last you're not talking drivel for once. Meanwhile I'll ring up Vaněk in the regimental office and tell him to go to the stores and take them over. If he should come to our hut in the meanwhile tell him to drop everything and rush at the double to the stores. Now you can hang up the receiver.'

For a long time Švejk vainly searched not only for Platoon Sergeant Fuchs, but for the other N.C.O.s too. They were in the kitchen, gnawing the meat from the bones and enjoying the sight of the tethered Baloun, who stood with his feet firmly on the ground, because they had taken pity on him, but who none the less presented a remarkable spectacle. One of the cooks brought him meat from a rib and pushed it into his mouth and the tethered bearded giant Baloun, who had no possibility of moving his arms, carefully pushed the bone around in his mouth, balancing it with the help of his teeth and his gums, in the course of which he gnawed the meat with the expression of a wild man of the woods.

'Who of you here is Platoon Sergeant Fuchs?' Švejk asked, when he finally got to them.

Sergeant Fuchs considered it beneath his dignity to reply, when he saw that he was being asked for by a common or garden infantryman.

'Hey,' said Švejk, 'how long am I going to stand here asking? Where the hell is Platoon Sergeant Fuchs?'

Sergeant Fuchs stepped forward and in all dignity began to deliver a volley of all kinds of oaths, saying that he wasn't just 'platoon sergeant', he should be addressed as 'sir', and that it was not for Švejk to say 'Where the hell is the platoon sergeant?' but 'Humbly report, sir, where is the platoon sergeant, sir?' In his platoon, if anyone didn't say: 'Humbly report, sir' he immediately got a sock on the jaw.

'Don't try that one on me,' said Švejk deliberately. 'Get cracking immediately. Go to the hut, take ten men and go with them at the double to the storehouse. You are to draw tinned food there.'

Platoon Sergeant Fuchs was so surprised that he could only manage to get out: 'What?'

'I don't permit any "Whats",' answered Švejk. 'I am the orderly of the 11th march company and just a minute ago I was speaking on the telephone with Lieutenant Lukáš and he said: "At the double with ten men to the stores." If you don't go, platoon sergeant, then I shall at once go back to the telephone. Lieutenant Lukáš explicitly wishes that you should go. It is unnecessary to talk about it. "A telephone conversation," says Lieutenant Lukáš, "must be concise and clear. If Platoon Sergeant Fuchs is told to go then he'll go. An order of this kind is not just a gossip on the telephone like when we invite somebody to come and have lunch. In the army, and especially in wartime, being late is a crime. If that Platoon Sergeant Fuchs doesn't go at once when you tell him, then ring me up immediately and I'll deal with him myself. There'll be nothing left of Platoon Sergeant Fuchs." My God, you don't know Lieutenant Lukáš.'

Švejk looked triumphantly at the N.C.O.s, who were really surprised and depressed by his performance.

Platoon Sergeant Fuchs mumbled something unintelligible and went away at a quick pace. Švejk called after him: 'Can I now ring the lieutenant that everything is in order?'

'I'll be at the store with ten men at once,' Platoon Sergeant Fuchs replied from the hut and Švejk without uttering another word left the group of N.C.O.s who were just as surprised as was Platoon Sergeant Fuchs.

'It's already starting,' said little Corporal Blažek. 'We shall be packing.'

When Švejk returned to the office of the 11th march company he again had no time to light his pipe because the telephone rang once more. Again it was Lieutenant Lukáš speaking:

'Where have you been running to, Švejk? It's the third time I've rung and no one's answered.'

'I've fixed it, sir.'

'Have they gone off?'

'You bet they've gone off, but I don't know yet whether they've got there. Shall I run and see once more?'

'Did you find Platoon Sergeant Fuchs?'

'I did, sir. First of all he said: "What?" and only when I had explained to him that telephone conversations must be concise and clear. . . .'

'Don't waste my time, Švejk. . . . Hasn't Vaněk returned yet?'

'He hasn't yet, sir.'

'Don't roar in the telephone. Don't you know where that damned Vaněk could have got to?'

'No, sir, I don't know where that damned Vaněk could have got to.'

'He was in the regimental office and has gone off somewhere else. I think he'll probably be in the canteen. Then go and find him, Švejk, and tell him that he must go at once to the stores. One thing more – find at once Corporal Blažek and tell him to untie Baloun immediately and send him to me. You can hang up the receiver now.'

Švejk really started to make things hum. When he found Corporal Blažek and conveyed to him the lieutenant's order regarding the untying of Baloun, Corporal Blažek growled: 'When it starts to get hot for them they get the jitters.'

Švejk went to see to the release of Baloun and accompanied him on the way, because it led to the canteen, where he was to try and find Vaněk.

Baloun looked on Švejk as his saviour and promised to share with him every packet which he got from home.

'They're going to do some slaughtering at home,' said Baloun in a melancholy voice. 'Do you like Speckwurst with blood or without?

Just say. I'll write home tonight. My pig ought to weigh about 150 kilos. It's got a head like a bulldog and pigs like that are the best. You don't find any duds among pigs like that. They are a very good race and hardy too. It'll have about eight fingers of fat. When I was at home

I used to make the jitrnice[1] myself and I always stuffed myself so full that I could have burst. Last year's pig weighed 160 kilos.

'Oh, that was a pig,' he said with enthusiasm, squeezing Švejk's hand in a powerful grip when they parted. 'I raised it on nothing but potatoes and was amazed myself how well it put on weight. I soaked the hams in brine and, I tell you, a nicely roasted piece of pork, taken out of the brine and served with cabbage and potato dumplings and sprinkled with cracklings, is the finest treat you can have. And then a

1. Jitrnice is a popular variety of Czech sausage, for which there is no translation. It is made of pork liver and various parts of the pig, is highly spiced and fastened at its ends with small wooden sticks.

lot of beer afterwards. A chap's so satisfied. And the war's taken all that away from us.'

The bearded Baloun sighed deeply and went off to the regimental office, while Švejk directed his steps towards the canteen through an old alley of tall lime trees.

Meanwhile Vaněk was sitting happily in the canteen and telling a staff sergeant-major friend of his how much one could make on enamel paints and cement washes before the war.

The staff sergeant-major was already half-seas over. In the morning a rich landowner from Pardubice who had a son in the camp had arrived and given him a respectable bribe, and the whole morning he had been hospitable to him down in the town.

Now he was sitting there in despair, because he had no more appetite; he did not even know what they were talking about and did not react at all to the conversation about the enamel paints.

He was occupied with his own ideas and babbled something about how a local railway line ought to go from Třeboň to Pelhřimov and back again.

When Švejk came in, Vaněk was once more trying to explain to the sergeant-major in figures how much profit could be made out of one kilogram of cement wash for buildings, whereupon the staff sergeant-major answered completely on the other track:

'And on the way back he died, leaving only letters behind him.'

Observing Švejk, he obviously mixed him up with someone whom he did not like and began to swear at him, saying that he was a ventriloquist.

Švejk came up to Vaněk, who was also pretty high but was at the same time very amiable and nice.

'Quartermaster sergeant-major,' Švejk reported, 'you are to go at once to the stores. Platoon Sergeant Fuchs is already waiting there with ten men. Tinned food will be drawn. You are to go at the double. The lieutenant has already telephoned twice.'

Vaněk burst out laughing: 'I'd be a bloody fool if I did, my dear boy. I'd have to swear at myself, my angel. There's plenty of time for everything, sonny boy. There's nothing on fire, my dear boy, is there? When Lieutenant Lukáš has got ready as many march companies as I have he can begin to talk. He won't bother a chap utterly pointlessly with his "at the double". In the regimental office I've already got the order that we are off tomorrow and that we must pack and quickly go and draw provisions for the journey. What have I done? I came here for a quarter-litre of wine and I am sitting here comfortably and letting things slide. Tins'll be tins, and supplies supplies. I know the stores better than the lieutenant does and I know what they talk about at those conferences between the officers and the colonel. It's only the colonel's imagination that there are any tins in the stores. Our regimental stores never had any but only got them from time to time from the brigade or borrowed them from other regiments which they got in touch with. We owe the Benešov regiment alone over three hundred tins. He he! Let them say what they like at their conference, only no flap, please! Why, the storekeeper himself will tell our people when they come there that they've gone mad. Not a single march company has ever got any tins for the journey.

'That's so, isn't it, you old potato,' he said, turning to the staff sergeant-major. But the latter was either falling asleep or getting a little delirious because he answered:

'While she was walking she held an open umbrella over herself.'

'The best thing you can do,' continued Vaněk, 'is to let everything just go its own sweet way. If today they said in the regimental office that we're to go tomorrow, then not even a baby should believe them. Can we go without trucks? While I was there they telephoned to the station. They haven't got a single spare truck there. It was just the same with the last march company. Then we stayed at the station for two whole days and waited till someone would take pity on us and send a train for us. And then we didn't know where we were going. Not even the colonel knew. After that we travelled all over the whole of Hungary and still no one knew whether we were going to Serbia or Russia. At every station we spoke direct to the staff of the division. We were just paper to cover up cracks. Finally we were sent near Dukla. There they cut us to pieces and we marched back to be re-formed. Only no flap, please! Everything will settle itself in time and there's no need for hurry. Yes, that's how it is. Here we are again!'

'Today they've got exceptionally good wine here,' Vaněk went on, not paying any attention to the staff sergeant-major, who was burbling to himself in German: 'Believe me, up to now I've had little from life. I am surprised at this question.'

'Why should I bother myself unnecessarily about the departure of the march battalion? Why, in the first march company I went with, everything was in complete readiness in two hours. In the other companies of our march battalion they took two days to get ready. But we had as company commander a Lieutenant Přenosil, a great dandy, and he said to us: "Don't hurry, boys," and everything went like a house on fire. We only started packing two hours before the departure of the train. Why don't you sit down as well? . . .'

'I can't,' said the good soldier Švejk with frightful self-sacrifice. 'I must go to the office. What if someone telephones?'

'Then go along, sonny boy, but remember for the whole of your life that it's not nice of you. A proper orderly should never be where he's needed. You mustn't be too zealous in your duties. There's really nothing more ugly, love, than a wild orderly who would like to eat up the whole war.'

But Švejk was already out of the door and rushing to the office of his march company.

Vaněk was left in solitude, because no one could possibly claim that the staff sergeant-major provided any company for him.

The latter was living in his own world and babbling the most ridiculous things in Czech and German without any connection and stroking his quarter-litre of wine:

'I walked through this village many times and didn't have an idea that it existed. In a half year's time I'll have passed my state examination and have done my doctorate. I've become an old cripple, thank you, Lucy. They are appearing in finely got-up volumes – perhaps there's someone among you who can remember it.'

Out of boredom the quartermaster sergeant-major drummed a march, but he did not have to be bored for long because the door opened and Jurajda, the cook from the officers' mess, came in and sank into a chair.

'Today we got the order to draw brandy for the journey,' he babbled. 'Because we hadn't a wicker rum bottle empty we had to empty one. That knocked us out! The men in the kitchen just passed out. I was a few portions short in my calculations, the colonel came late and there wasn't anything left for him. Now they're making him an omelette. I can tell you that that was fun and games.'

'It's a marvellous adventure,' observed Vaněk, who always liked beautiful words when he was drinking wine.

The cook Jurajda started to philosophize, which in fact matched his former occupation. Before the war he used to edit an occultist journal and a series of books called *The Mysteries of Life and Death*. When war broke out he shirked his way into the officers' kitchen of the regiment and very often burnt a joint while he was absorbed in reading a translation of the old Indian sutras *Pragnâ – Paramitâ* ('Wisdom Revealed').

Colonel Schröder liked him as a rarity in the regiment; for what officers' kitchen could boast an occultist as its cook? While probing into the mysteries of life and death, he so astounded everyone with his excellent sirloin of beef or ragout that Lieutenant Dufek when mortally wounded near Komarovo continually called for Jurajda.

'Yes,' said Jurajda out of the blue. He could hardly sit on his chair and he stank of rum a mile off. 'When there wasn't anything left for the colonel today and he saw only steamed potatoes he fell into the state of *gaki*. Do you know what *gaki* is? It is the state of starved spirits. And I said to him: "Sir, have you enough strength to overrule the predestination of fate that there's no roast veal left for you? It is written in *karma*, sir, that today you will be served for dinner a wonderful omelette with chopped and stewed calves' liver."

'Dear boy,' he said softly to the quartermaster sergeant-major after a while, involuntarily making a movement with his hand and knocking over all the glasses which stood in front of him on the table.

'There exists the non-being of all phenomena, forms and things,' the occultist cook said gloomily after this act. 'Form is non-being and non-being is form. Non-being is not different from form and form is not different from non-being. Everything that is non-being is also form and everything that is form is also non-being.'

The occultist cook wrapped himself in a shroud of silence, held his head in his hands and looked at the wet, stained table.

The staff sergeant-major continued to babble something which had neither rhyme nor reason: 'The corn has disappeared from the field, disappeared – in this mood he received an invitation and went to her – the Whitsun holidays are in the spring.'

Quartermaster Sergeant-Major Vaněk went on drumming on the table, drank, and occasionally remembered that ten men with a sergeant were waiting for him at the stores.

When this memory came to him he always smiled to himself and dismissed it with a wave of his hand.

When he returned late to the office of the 11th march company he found Švejk by the telephone.

'Form is non-being and non-being is form,' he managed to utter as he climbed fully dressed into his bunk and immediately fell sound asleep.

And Švejk continued to sit by the telephone, because two hours earlier Lieutenant Lukáš had said to him that he was still at the conference with the colonel and he had forgotten to tell him he could leave the telephone.

After that Sergeant Fuchs spoke to him on the telephone. He and his ten men had not only been waiting all that time in vain for the quartermaster sergeant-major but had also found that the stores were shut.

After that he went away and the ten men returned one by one to their hut.

Occasionally Švejk amused himself by taking off the receiver and listening. It was a telephone of a new system which had just been introduced into the army and had the advantage that you could hear quite clearly and intelligibly other people's telephone calls all over the line.

The train was exchanging abuse with the artillery barracks, the sappers were threatening the army post, the military rifle range was growling at the machine-gun section.

And Švejk went on sitting at the telephone . . .

The conference in the colonel's office went on longer and longer . . .

Colonel Schröder was developing his latest theories on field service and was emphasizing particularly the role of trench mortars.

He spoke without rhyme or reason about how the front stood two months ago in the south and east, about the importance of exact communications between individual units, about poison gas, shooting at enemy aeroplanes and catering for the men in the field. Then he passed to conditions among the troops.

He spoke of the relationship of the officers to the men, of the men to the N.C.O.s, of deserting to the enemy at the front, of political events and of the fact that fifty per cent of the Czech soldiers were 'politically suspect'.

'Yes, gentlemen, Kramář, Scheiner and Klofáč.'[1] Most of the officers were wondering all the time when the old dodderer would stop drivelling, but Colonel Schröder burbled on about the new tasks of the new march battalions, of the officers of his regiment who had fallen, of Zeppelins, of 'Spanish riders' and the soldier's oath.

When he reached that point Lieutenant Lukáš remembered that

1. Three Czech political leaders who were imprisoned for treason during the war.

when the whole battalion took the oath, the good soldier Švejk did not take part, because at that time he was under arrest at the divisional court.

And suddenly he couldn't help laughing. It was a kind of hysterical laughter which affected some officers among whom he sat and which caught the attention of the colonel, who just at that moment had gone over to the experiences acquired during the retreat of the German troops in the Ardennes. He got completely muddled and ended: 'Gentlemen, it's no laughing matter.'

Then they all went away to the officers' club because Colonel Schröder had been called to the telephone by brigade staff.

Švejk was still slumbering by the telephone when he was woken up by its ringing.

'Hallo,' he heard, 'regimental office speaking.'

'Hallo,' he answered, 'office of the 11th march company speaking.'

'Don't waste my time,' he heard a voice say. 'Take a pencil and write. Here is a telegram.

'The 11th march company . . .'

Now there followed in succession various sentences in a strange chaos, because they were mixed up with the conversations of the 12th and 13th march companies, which went on at the same time, and the telegram got completely lost in the panic of sounds. Švejk could not understand a single word. Finally everything quietened down and Švejk understood: 'Hallo, hallo, now read it through and don't waste my time!'

'What have I got to read through?'

'What have you got to read through, you bloody fool? The telegram!'

'What telegram?'

'Bloody hell, are you deaf? The telegram which I've just dictated to you, you crazy oaf!'

'I couldn't hear anything. Someone was talking here all the time.'

'You idiotic baboon. Do you think I'm just passing the time of day with you? Well, are you going to take the telegram or not? Have you got a pencil and paper? You haven't, you bastard, and so I've got to wait until you find it? That's a soldier for you, if you like. Well, are you going to take the message or not? Are you ready? At last you've woken up, you bloody bastard. You've been dolling yourself up, I suppose. Now listen. The 11th march company. Repeat that!'

'The 11th march company . . .'

'Company commandant . . . Have you got that? Repeat that.'

'Company commandant . . .'

'For conference tomorrow . . . Are you ready? Repeat that.'

'For conference tomorrow . . .'

'At 9 a.m. "*Unterschrift*." Do you know what "*Unterschrift*" is, baboon? It's "signature". Repeat that!'

'At 9 a.m. *Unterschrift*. Do you know what "*Unterschrift*" is, baboon? It's "signature".'

'Stupid mutt. Well, here you are, here's the signature: Colonel Schröder, bastard. Have you got that? Repeat that!'

'Colonel Schröder, bastard.'

'Good, you bloody mule. Who took the telegram?'

'Me.'

'Himmelherrgott, who's me?'

'Švejk. Anything further?'

'Thank the Lord, nothing. But your name ought to be Cow. What news is there?'

'Nothing. Just the same as before.'

'And you're glad, then, aren't you? One of your men was tied up today, they say?'

'It was only the lieutenant's batman. He guzzled up his lieutenant's mess portion. Do you know when we're going?'

'My dear boy, what a question! Why, even the old man himself doesn't know. Goodnight. Have you got fleas there?'

Švejk hung up the receiver and began to wake Quartermaster Sergeant-Major Vaněk, who furiously resisted. When Švejk began to shake him, he hit him in the nose. Then he lay on his stomach and kicked about in his bunk.

None the less Švejk succeeded in waking Vaněk so far that he rubbed his eyes, turned over on his back and asked in an alarmed voice what had happened.

'Nothing so far,' replied Švejk. 'I'd only like to consult you. We've just got a telegram that tomorrow at 9 a.m. Lieutenant Lukáš is to go to a conference with the colonel again. I don't know now where I stand. Am I to go and deliver the message at once or can I wait till the morning? I hesitated a long time whether I should wake you up when you were snoring so beautifully, but then I thought, never mind, better get his advice . . .'

'For God's sake, please let me sleep,' Vaněk groaned, and gave an enormous yawn. 'Go to him in the morning and don't wake me up.' He rolled over on his side and immediately fell asleep again.

Švejk went back to the telephone, sat down and began to nod at the table. He was woken by the bell.

'Hello, 11th march company?'

'Yes, 11th march company speaking. Who's there?'

'Thirteenth march company speaking. Hallo. What's the time? I can't get hold of the exchange. I've been waiting hours for them to relieve me.'

'Our clock's stopped.'

'Then you're in the same boat as we are. Do you know when we're going? Did you speak to regimental office?'

'There they don't know a shit more than we do.'

'Don't be vulgar, miss. Have you drawn your tins yet? They went there from our company and didn't bring anything back. The stores were shut.'

'Ours came back with nothing too.'

'All this flap is quite pointless. Where do you think we're going?'

'To Russia.'

'I think it's more likely to be Serbia. We'll see when we get to Budapest. If they take us to the right, then it looks like Serbia. If it's to the left it'll be Russia. Have you already got your bread sacks? They say that pay will be increased. Can you play Frische Viere?[1] You can? Then come here tomorrow. We play every evening. How many of you are there at the telephone? Only you? Then damn the telephone and go to bed. You certainly have funny arrangements where you are. What did you say? You got the job by pure fluke? And now at last they've come to relieve me. Have a sweet snore.'

And Švejk indeed fell into a sweet sleep by the telephone, forgetting to hang up the receiver, so that nobody disturbed him in his slumbers on the desk and the telephone operator in the regimental office swore when he could not get any answer from the 11th march company. He had a new telegram requiring that by twelve o'clock the next day the regimental office was to be informed of the number of those who had not been inoculated against typhus.

Meanwhile Lieutenant Lukáš was still sitting in the officers' club with the army doctor, Šancler, who, seated astride a chair, hit the floor

1. A German card game.

at regular intervals with a billiard cue and pronounced the following sentences in succession as he did so.

'The Saracen Sultan, Salah-Edin, recognized for the first time the neutrality of the medical corps.

'The wounded of both sides are to be cared for.

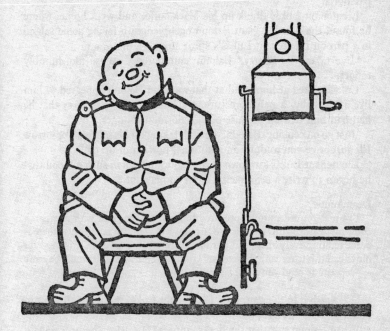

'Drugs and medical care for them are to be paid for against compensation from the other side.

'It should be permitted to send them doctors and their assistants with generals' passports.

'The wounded prisoners are to be sent back under the protection and guarantee of generals or exchanged. But they can afterwards go on serving.

'The wounded on both sides are not to be captured or liquidated but sent to safe shelter in hospitals and it should be permitted to leave them guards who, like the wounded, are to return with generals' passports. This applies also to chaplains, doctors, surgeons, chemists, nurses, assistants and other persons appointed to look after the sick. They may not be taken prisoner but must be sent back in the same way.'

Doctor Šancler had already broken two billiard cues and was still not finished with his peculiar treatise on the care of the wounded in war, continually mixing into it something about some generals' passports.

Lieutenant Lukáš drank up his black coffee and went home, where he found the bearded giant Baloun occupied with frying some salami in a pan on Lieutenant Lukáš's spirit stove.

'I've taken the liberty,' Baloun stammered, 'excuse me, humbly report. . . .'

Lukáš looked at him. And at that moment Baloun appeared to him like a big baby, a naïve creature, and suddenly he was sorry that he had had him tied up because of his enormous hunger.

'Just go on cooking, Baloun,' he said, taking off his sabre. 'Tomorrow I'll authorize you to draw an additional portion of bread.'

Lieutenant Lukáš sat down at the table and was in such a mood that he began to write a sentimental letter to his auntie:

Dear Auntie,

I've just got orders to be prepared to leave for the front with my march company. Perhaps this letter is the last you will get from me because there is fierce fighting everywhere and our losses are great. Therefore it is hard for me to end this letter with the words: 'Until we meet again!' It would be more appropriate to send you a last farewell!

'I'll finish it in the morning,' Lieutenant Lukáš thought and went to bed.

When Baloun saw that the lieutenant was fast asleep he began again to sneak and snoop about the apartment like black-beetles in the night. He opened the lieutenant's suitcase and took a bite of a bar of chocolate. Then when the lieutenant started in his sleep he got scared. He hastily put back into the case the half-bitten chocolate and was quiet.

Then he went noiselessly to see what the lieutenant had written.

He read it and was moved, especially by the 'last farewell!'.

He lay down on his straw mattress by the door and remembered his home and the slaughterings. He could not free himself of the vivid impression that he was making a hole in the Speckwurst to get the air out of it, so that it didn't burst when it was being cooked.

And with the memory of how once at his neighbour's house a whole

Speckwurst had burst and disintegrated he fell asleep in an uneasy slumber.

He dreamed that he had called in a clumsy butcher and that when he was filling the jitrnice with stuffing their guts began to burst. And then again he dreamed that the butcher had forgotten to make blood sausages, and that the fresh boiled pork disappeared and there were not enough little sticks to fasten the jitrnice. After that he dreamed of a drumhead court-martial, because they had caught him when he was taking a piece of meat from the field-kitchen. Finally he saw himself hanging on a lime tree in the alley of the military camp in Bruck an der Leitha.

When Švejk awoke with the breaking dawn, which came to him accompanied by the smell of cooked tinned coffee from all the company kitchens, he hung up the receiver mechanically as if he had only just finished a telephone conversation, and took a little early morning walk round the office, singing while he did so.

He started right in the middle of the text of the song: a soldier dresses up as a girl and goes to find his sweetheart in a mill, where the miller puts him to bed with his daughter, but before that he calls out to his wife:

> Mamma, go and cook some meat
> So the little girl may eat.

The miller's wife gives that mean rascal some food. And then follows the family tragedy:

> The miller and his wife were up by eight
> And found these words upon their gate.
> 'Your daughter, Anne, a maid before,
> Is now, alas, a maid no more.'

Švejk put into the end of the song so much voice that the office came to life: Quartermaster Sergeant-Major Vaněk woke up and asked what the time was.

'Just a moment ago they sounded the reveille.'

'Then I'll get up after I've had coffee,' decided Vaněk, who always had enough time for everything. 'Anyhow, they'll be bound to bully us, get us into a flap and push us around unnecessarily as they did yesterday about those tins . . .' Vaněk yawned and asked whether when he came home he hadn't talked too long.

'Only just a little off the beam,' said Švejk. 'You kept on saying something about some forms, that form wasn't form and what wasn't form was form and that form again wasn't form. But you got over it quite quickly and soon began to snore like a sawmill.'

Švejk was silent, walked to the door and back to the quartermaster sergeant-major's bunk, stopped before him and said:

'As far as I'm personally concerned, sergeant-major, when I heard that you were talking about those forms I remembered a certain Zátka, a gas worker; he had a job at the gas company at Letná and had to light the lamps and put them out again. He was an enlightened man and went to all sorts of pubs at Letná because between the lighting of the lamps and putting them out he had to kick his heels. In the morning when he got back to the gas company he used to talk in the same way as you did yesterday except that he said, "The cube is angularity and that's why the cube is angular." I heard it with my own eyes when a sozzled cop took me to the gas company instead of to the police station for committing a nuisance in the street.

'And after that,' said Švejk quietly, 'that Zátka came to a sad end. He joined the Congregation of the Virgin Mary and went with those sanctimonious nanny-goats to hear the sermons of Father Jemelka[1] at St Ignatius on Charles Square. Once when the missionaries were at St Ignatius he forgot to put out the gas lamps in his district so that the light blazed on the streets uninterruptedly for three days and three nights.

'It's bad,' continued Švejk, 'when a chap suddenly starts to get caught up in philosophizing. That always stinks of *delirium tremens*. Years ago they transferred to us a certain Major Blüher from the 75th. Once a month he always made us fall in and form a square. Then he discussed with us what military superiors were. He never drank anything else but slivovice. "Every officer," he used to tell us in the yard of the barracks, "is, as such, the most perfect being, my men, and has a hundred times more brain than all of you together. You cannot conceive anything more perfect than an officer, my men, even if you were to think about it all your lives. Every officer is a necessary being, whereas you, my men, are only incidental beings. You may exist but you may not. And if, my men, it came to a war and you were to give up your lives for His Imperial Majesty, good, then nothing would change very much. But if before that your officer were to fall, then

[1]. A notorious Jesuit preacher in Prague at the time.

you'd first see how dependent you are on him and what a loss it would be to you. The officer must exist and, in fact, you derive your existence exclusively from the officers; you spring from them. You cannot get on without them. You can't even fart without your military superiors. For you, my men, an officer is your moral law whether you understand it or not, and because every law must have its legislator, my men, it is only the officer to whom you feel and must feel entirely bound and whose every order you must obey unconditionally even if you shouldn't like it."

'Once when he had finished he went round the square and asked the men one by one:

' "How do you feel when you've taken a drop too much?"

'They gave him confused answers such as either they had never taken a drop too much or after drinking they always felt sick. One said he felt as though he was going to be confined to barracks etc. Major Blüher ordered all these to leave the ranks saying that in the afternoon they were going to do unarmed drill in the yard as a punishment for not being able to express what they felt. Before my turn came I remembered what he had discussed with us last time and when he came to me I said quite calmly:

' "Humbly report, sir, when I take a drop too much I always feel inside me a sort of nervousness, a fear and pricking of conscience. But if I'm given extended leave and then return properly to the barracks in time, a feeling of bliss comes creeping over me. I have complete spiritual peace."

'Everyone around me laughed and Major Blüher shouted at me:

' "It's more likely that you've got bugs creeping on you, you bastard, when you snore on your bunk. You miserable swine, you've got the bloody cheek to try to be funny."

'And for that I was put in irons and it wasn't half fun!'

'In the army it's got to be like that,' said the quartermaster sergeant-major, stretching himself lazily on his bed. 'It's an accepted thing that however you answer or whatever you do a dark cloud will always be hanging over you and the thunder will begin to peal. Without that you can't have discipline.'

'Very well said,' said Švejk. 'I shall never forget when they locked up a recruit called Pech. The lieutenant of the company was a chap called Moc and he collected the recruits and asked each of them where he came from.

' "You greenhorns of recruits, you godforsaken bastards," he told them. "You must learn to answer clearly and exactly, like at the crack of a whip. Now let's start. Where do you come from, Pech?" Pech was an intelligent man and answered: "Dolní Bousov, Unter Bautzen, 267 houses, 1936 Czech inhabitants, region Jičín, district Sobotka, former estate of Kost, parish church of St Katherine from the fourteenth century restored by Count Václav Vratislav Netolický, school, post, telegraph, station of the Czech Commercial Railway, sugar refinery, sawmill, an isolated farm called Valcha, and six annual fairs." And at the same moment Lieutenant Moc leaped at him and began to give him one sock after the other across the jaw and to shout: "That'll teach you for one of your annual fairs, here's for the second, here's for the third, the fourth, the fifth, the sixth." And Pech, although he was a recruit, applied to be sent on battalion report. In the office at that time there happened to be a gang of bastards with a sense of humour. They gave as reason for his going on battalion report the annual fairs in Dolní Bousov. The battalion commander was Major Rohell. "Well, what's up?" he asked Pech, who started off: "Humbly report, sir, in Dolní Bousov there are six annual fairs." And then Major Rohell thundered at him, stamped his feet and had him sent at once to the mental section of the military hospital. From that time on Pech became the worst soldier and went from one punishment to another.'

'Soldiers are difficult to educate,' said Quartermaster Sergeant-Major Vaněk, yawning. 'A soldier who has not been punished in the army is no soldier. It was perhaps true in peacetime that a soldier who had completed his service without any punishment could afterwards have an advantage in state service, but today it's different: the worst soldiers, those who in peacetime were never out of prison, become in wartime the best. I remember an infantryman called Sylvanus in the 8th march company. Before the war he always used to get punishment after punishment. And what punishments! He was not above stealing his comrades' last kreutzer. And when he got into action, he was the first to cut through the barbed-wire entanglements, took three chaps prisoner and shot one of them on the way, because he said he couldn't trust him. He was awarded the Great Silver Medal. They sewed on him two stars and if they hadn't later hanged him near Dukla he would have long ago become platoon sergeant. But there you are, they had to hang him because after one action he volunteered for reconnaissance and a patrol of another regiment caught him robbing corpses. They found on him about eight watches and many rings. And so they hanged him at brigade staff.'

'Which only goes to show,' Švejk observed wisely, 'that every soldier must do his utmost to win his place on the ladder.'

The telephone bell rang. The quartermaster sergeant-major went to the telephone and Lieutenant Lukáš's voice could be heard asking what had happened with the tins. After that there could be heard some reproaches.

'But really, there aren't any, sir!' Vaněk shouted into the telephone. 'Of course there aren't, sir. It's only just a flight of imagination from above on the part of Supply H.Q. It was utterly pointless to send those men there. I wanted to ring you up, sir. What, I was in the canteen? Who said that? That occultist cook from the officers' mess? Yes, I took the liberty of going there. You know, sir, what that occultist called that flap about the tins? "The horror of the unborn". Oh no, sir, not at all, I'm completely sober. What is Švejk doing? He's here. Shall I call him?'

'Švejk, come to the telephone!' said the quartermaster sergeant-major, and added in a whisper: 'And if he should ask you what state I was in when I came back say that I was O.K.'

Švejk at the telephone: 'This is Švejk, humbly report, sir.'

'Listen, Švejk, what happened about those tins? Is it all right?'

'No, sir, there isn't any sign of them.'

'Švejk, I want you to report to me every morning, as long as we're in the camp. Otherwise you are to be with me all the time during the journey. What did you do during the night?'

'I was at the telephone the whole night.'

'Was there any news?'

'There was, sir.'

'Švejk, for God's sake, don't start to be an idiot again. Was there anything important reported from anywhere?'

'Yes, sir, there was, but only for nine o'clock.'

'Why didn't you inform me at once?'

'I didn't want to disturb you, sir. It was the last thing I wanted to do.'

'Then for God's sake tell me what was there so important for nine o'clock?'

'A telegram, sir.'

'I don't understand you, Švejk.'

'I've written it down, sir: "Take down the telegram. Who's that at the telephone? Have you got it? Read it or something like that."'

'For God's sake, Švejk, you're the cross I have to bear. Tell me what was in it or I'll leap at you and give you such a sock! Well, what was it?'

'Another conference with the colonel, sir. This morning at nine o'clock. I wanted to wake you in the night, but then I thought better of it.'

'Well, it's your luck that you didn't have the insolence to try to disturb me for any kind of bloody nonsense when there was time enough in the morning. Another conference. To hell with it! Hang up the receiver and call Vaněk to the telephone!'

The quartermaster sergeant-major at the telephone: 'Quartermaster Sergeant-Major Vaněk speaking, sir.'

'Vaněk, find me at once another batman. That rogue Baloun wolfed up all my chocolate in the night. Should you tie him up? No! Let's send him to the medical corps. The bastard's a mountain of a man. He can easily drag the wounded out of the firing line. I'll send him to you at once. Arrange it with the regimental office and come back to the company at once. D'you think we're going to leave soon?'

'There's no hurry, sir. When we had to march off with the 9th march company they fooled around with us for four whole days. It was just the same with the 8th. It was only with the 10th that it was better. Then we were in full state of preparedness for the front. At noon we got the order and by the evening we'd gone. But afterwards they drove us over the whole of Hungary and didn't know which hole on what battlefield they wanted us to bung up.'

Ever since Lieutenant Lukáš had become commander of the 11th march company he had found himself in a state of mind called syncretism; which meant in philosophical terms that he tried to settle conceptual contradictions by means of compromises which were carried to a point when all views merged and lost their identity.

And so he replied: 'Yes, maybe it's like that. You don't think then that we'll be going today, do you? At nine o'clock we have a conference with the colonel. By the way, do you know that you are the sergeant-major on duty? I'm only telling you. Now find out for me. . . . Wait a moment, what should you find out for me? . . . Get a list of the N.C.O.s with information on their length of service. . . . Then the company's stocks. Nationality? Yes, yes, that as well. . . . But first of all send up this new batman. . . . What has Ensign Pleschner to do with the men today? Preparation for departure. Accounts? I'll come and sign them after mess. Don't allow anybody to go into the town. To the canteen in the camp? After mess for an hour. . . . Now call Švejk here! . . .

'Švejk, stay for the moment at the telephone.'

'Humbly report, sir, I've not yet had my coffee.'

'Then bring your coffee and stay in the office at the telephone until I call you. Do you know what an orderly is?'

'Something that runs about, sir.'

'Well, see that you're in your place whenever I call you. Tell Vaněk once more that he must find a batman for me. Švejk, hallo, where are you?'

'Here, sir. They've just brought the coffee.'

'Švejk, hallo!'

'I hear you, sir. The coffee's completely cold.'

'You know very well what a batman is, Švejk. Give him the once-over and then tell me afterwards what sort of fellow he is. Hang up the receiver.'

Vaněk, sipping the black coffee to which he added rum from a bottle with an inscription 'ink' (to take every precaution), looked at Švejk and said: 'Our lieutenant shouts rather into the telephone. I understood every word. You must know the lieutenant very well, Švejk.'

'We're hand in glove,' Švejk replied. 'One palm greases the other. We've gone through a lot together. How often they wanted to tear us apart, but we've always come together again. He always relies on me in everything, so that I'm often really quite surprised myself. And you certainly heard that I've got to remind you once more that you are to find him a new batman and that I must give him the once-over and report on him. The lieutenant won't be satisfied with any kind of batman.'

When Colonel Schröder called all the officers of the march battalion to a conference he did so again with great joy, because it offered him the chance of giving a lecture. Apart from that he had to take some decisions in the case of the volunteer Marek who had refused to clean the latrines and had been sent by him to the divisional court on the charge of mutiny.

Marek had arrived the night before from the divisional court at
the main guard-house where he was held under guard. With him
the regimental office received the report of the divisional court,
which was colossally muddled and in which it was pointed out that in
this case it was not a question of mutiny, because volunteers ought not

to clean latrines. None the less it was a case of 'breach of discipline', a
delinquency which could be condoned on grounds of good conduct in
the field. For this reason the accused volunteer Marek was being sent
back to his regiment and the investigation into the case of breach of
discipline was quashed until the end of the war. It would be taken up
again the next time the volunteer Marek committed an offence.

And then there was another case. Together with the volunteer
Marek the spurious Sergeant Teveles was taken to the main guard-
house from the divisional court. He had appeared recently at the regiment where he had been sent from a hospital in Zagreb. He had the

Great Silver Medal, the stripes of a volunteer and three stars. He told of the heroic acts of the 6th march company in Serbia and said he was the only survivor from it. In the course of investigation it was established that at the beginning of the war a certain Teveles did actually go with the 6th march company, but that he did not have the rights of a volunteer. Information was then sought from the brigade under whose command the 6th march company came when the retreat took place from Belgrade on 2 December 1914, and it was ascertained that in the list of names of those recommended for the award of the Silver Medal or of those awarded it there was no Teveles. It could not, however, be confirmed whether the infantryman Teveles was promoted in the Belgrade war campaign to the rank of sergeant, because the whole of the 6th march company with all its officers disappeared near the church of St Sava in Belgrade. Before the divisional court Teveles defended himself by saying that the Great Silver Medal had really been promised to him and he had therefore bought one in hospital from a Bosnian. As for the volunteer's stripes, he sewed them on when he was drunk and went on wearing them because he was incessantly drunk, his constitution having been weakened by dysentery.

When the conference began Colonel Schröder, before discussing these two cases, announced that they would have to have more frequent contacts before their departure, which would not now be long delayed. He had received information from the brigade that orders were expected from the division. The men must be in a state of alert and company commanders must punctiliously ensure that no one was missing. Then he repeated once more everything that he had said the day before. He again made a survey of the military operations and said that nothing should be allowed to suppress fighting spirit and warlike initiative in the army.

On the table in front of him was fastened a map of the battlefield with flags on pins, but all the flags were overturned and the front lines shifted. Pins with flags were lying about under the table.

The whole battlefield had been frightfully messed up in the night by a tom cat which the writers kept in the regimental office and which, when it performed its own operations on the Austro-Hungarian battlefield, wanting to scratch and cover them over, tore out the flags and smeared the mess over all the positions. It stained the fronts and the bridgeheads and defiled all the army corps.

Colonel Schröder was very short-sighted.

Officers of the march battalion watched with interest as Colonel Schröder's fingers came nearer to these little mounds.

'From here, gentlemen, from Sokal to the Bug,' said Colonel Schröder prophetically and moved his finger from memory towards the Carpathians. In doing this he plunged his finger into one of those

little mounds with which the tom cat had tried to make the map of the battlefield a relief one.

'What's this, gentlemen?' he asked in astonishment when something had stuck to his finger.

'Probably cat droppings, sir,' Captain Ságner answered very politely for all of them.

Colonel Schröder rushed into the office next door, from where there could be heard tremendous thunderings and fulminations with frightful threats that he would make them lick up everything the cat had done.

The cross-examination was brief. It was ascertained that a fortnight ago the cat was brought to the office by the youngest writer, Zwiebelfisch. When this had been ascertained Zwiebelfisch packed himself up lock, stock and barrel and the senior writer took him to the guard-house where he would sit until further orders from the colonel.

With that the whole conference was in fact finished. When Colonel Schröder returned to the officers, crimson in the face, he forgot that he had to discuss the fate of the volunteer Marek and the spurious Sergeant Teveles.

He said quite shortly: 'I request you, gentlemen, to be in a state of alert and to await my further orders and instructions.'

And so the volunteer and Teveles remained under guard at the guard-house and when Zwiebelfisch joined them later they were able to play mariáš together and after mariáš to bother their guards with the request to catch for them the fleas on the straw mattresses.

Then later Corporal Peroutka of the 13th march company was pushed in with them. When the news got around in the camp that they were going to the front, he had got lost and been found in the morning by the patrol at The White Rose at Bruck. He gave as an excuse that before they left for the front he wanted to see the famous greenhouses of Count Harrach at Bruck and on the way back he had lost his way. It was only in the early morning that he got to The White Rose in a state of complete exhaustion. (As a matter of fact he spent the night in bed with Růženka from The White Rose.)

The situation remained unclear. Were they going or weren't they? Švejk at the telephone in the office of the 11th march company heard various pessimistic and optimistic opinions. The 12th march company telephoned claiming that someone in the office had heard that they were waiting to do some shooting practice at moveable targets and that they would only leave after gunnery practice under front conditions. This optimistic view was not shared by the 13th march company which telephoned that Corporal Havlík had just returned from the town and had heard there from a railwayman that the trucks were already at the station.

Vaněk tore the receiver from Švejk's hand and shouted angrily that the railwaymen knew damn all about it and that he had just come back from the regimental office.

Švejk stayed at the telephone with true devotion and his answer to all questions about the news was that nothing definite was yet known.

He answered the lieutenant's question in the same way too when the latter asked:

'What news is there?'

'Nothing definite yet, sir,' Švejk answered in a stereotyped manner.

'You bloody mule. Hang up the receiver.'

Then came a series of telegrams which Švejk took after a lengthy period of misunderstanding. First of all there was the telegram which could not be dictated the night he failed to hang up the receiver and was sleeping. It concerned those who were inoculated and those who were not.

Then there was the delayed telegram about the tins which had been cleared up already the night before.

Finally there was a telegram to all battalions, companies and units of the regiment as follows:

Copy of brigade telegram no. 75692. Brigade order no. 172. In statistical reports about the running of the field-kitchens the following order must be observed in naming articles of consumption: 1 meat, 2 tins, 3 fresh vegetables, 4 dried vegetables, 5 rice, 6 macaroni, 7 groats and semolina, 8 potatoes, instead of previous: 4 dried vegetables, 5 fresh vegetables.

When Švejk read this to Quartermaster Sergeant-Major Vaněk the latter declared solemnly that as a rule telegrams like this are thrown down the rears:

'Some bloody fool on the army staff has thought that one up. Now it's going round all the divisions, brigades and regiments.'

Then Švejk received one more telegram which was so quickly dictated that he managed to get down on the notebook only what sounded like a cipher:

'As a result of more detailed it has been permitted or the same can on the other hand none the less be supplemented.'

'This is all pointless,' said Vaněk, when Švejk was frightfully puzzled by what he had written and read it out aloud three times in succession: 'Sheer stupidity, although God knows it could be in cipher, but in the company we're not equipped to receive cipher. You may throw it away as well.'

'I think so too,' said Švejk. 'If I were to report to the lieutenant that he has as a result of more detailed it has been permitted or the same can on the other hand none the less be supplemented, I think he'd perhaps feel offended.

'You wouldn't believe how frightfully fussy some people are,' continued Švejk, delving deep into his reminiscences again. 'Once I went by tram from Vysočany to Prague and in Libeň a certain Mr Novotný got in. As soon as I recognized him I went to him on the platform and started to get into conversation with him as we both came from Dražov. But he just shouted at me not to molest him and claimed that he didn't know me. I began to explain that he ought to remember, since when I was a kid I used to go and see him with my mother who was called Antonie and that my father was called Prokop and was a bailiff. But even then he didn't want to own that we knew each other. So finally I gave him closer details and said that in Dražov there were two Novotnýs, Tonda and Josef. He was Josef. They had written to me about him from Dražov and said he had shot his wife when she rebuked him for drinking. And then he raised his arm to hit me but I dodged and he broke the windscreen on the front platform – the big one in front of the driver. And so they pushed us both out and took us away. At the police station it turned out that why he had been so touchy was because he was not called Josef Novotný at all but Eduard Doubrava, and had come from Montgomery in America to visit his relatives from whom his family were descended.'

The telephone interrupted his narration and a hoarse voice from the machine-gun section again asked whether they would be going. There was a rumour that there was to be another conference with the colonel the next morning.

In the door there appeared the pale face of Cadet Biegler, who was the biggest ass in the company, because in the volunteers' school he always tried to show off his knowledge. He beckoned to Vaněk to come out in the passage, where he had a long conversation with him.

When Vaněk returned he smiled contemptuously.

'There's a bloody idiot for you,' he said to Švejk. 'We've certainly got some specimens in this march company of ours! He was at the conference too and when it broke up the lieutenant ordered all platoon commanders to make a rifle inspection and to make it a strict one. Now he's come to ask me whether he should tie up Žlábek because he cleaned his rifle with paraffin.'

Vaněk flared up.

'And he asks a bloody stupid thing like that when he knows we're going to the front. Well, the lieutenant thought twice about his having tied up his batman yesterday and I said to this young greenhorn that he should think twice about treating the men like cattle.'

'And while you're speaking about that batman,' said Švejk, 'do you happen to know whether you've found one for the lieutenant?'

'Keep your hair on,' answered Vaněk. 'There's plenty of time for everything. Besides, I believe the lieutenant will get used to Baloun. Now and again he'll guzzle up something of his and then he'll stop. He's bound to when we get to the front. There often neither of them will have anything to eat at all. When I say that Baloun is to stay, then there's nothing to be done about it. This is my business and the lieutenant has no say in it. Take it easy.'

Vaněk lay down on his bed again and said: 'Švejk, tell me a funny story about the army.'

'I might,' answered Švejk, 'but I am afraid someone might ring up again.'

'Then disconnect it, Švejk. Screw off the contacts. Take off the receiver.'

'Good,' said Švejk, taking off the receiver. 'I'll tell you something that's suitable for this situation, except that at that time instead of real war we only had manoeuvres. There was just the same sort of flap as there is today, because no one knew when we would move out of the barracks. Serving with me was a man called Šic from Poříčí, a good chap but religious and funky. He imagined that manoeuvres were something horrible, that people died of thirst on the march and the medical corps would pick them up like rotten fruit. And so he stoked himself up well with drink and when we went out on the manoeuvres from the barracks and came to Mníšek he said: "I can't take it, boys. Only the Lord God can protect me." Then we came to Hořovice and there we had two days' rest because there had been a mistake and we had advanced too quickly, so that we and the other regiments who marched with us on the flank could have taken the whole enemy general staff prisoner. This would have been a disgrace because our army corps was meant to get shat on and the enemy to win, because on the enemy side there was a worn-out old archdukelet. Now this is what that Šic did. When we were encamped there he set out to do some shopping in a village beyond Hořovice, returning to the camp at noon. It was hot and he was quite tight, and on the way he saw a pillar and on the pillar was a box and in it under the glass a small statue of St John of Nepomuk. He prayed in front of St John and said to him: "It must be hot for you here; you ought to drink a little. You're in the sun here. You must certainly be sweating all the time." And so he shook the field-flask, took a sip out of it and said: "I've left you a nip too, St John of Nepomuk." But then he got scared and drank it all up and there was nothing left for St John. "Jesus Mary," he said, "St John of Nepomuk, you must forgive me for this. I'll make it up to you. I'll take you with me to the camp and give you so gloriously much to drink that you won't be able to stand on your feet." And dear Šic, out of pity for St John of Nepomuk, broke the glass, pulled out the statue of the saint, put it under his tunic and carried it off to the camp. After that John of Nepomuk slept with him in the straw, he carried him in his sack on his marches, and he always had tremendous luck at cards. Wherever we were in camp he always won, until we came to the district of Prácheň and lay in Drahenice, and there he lost everything, lock, stock and barrel. When we moved off in the morning St

John of Nepomuk was strung up on a pear-tree by the road. Well, that's your funny story, and now I'll put back the receiver again.'

And the telephone again communicated the quiver of a new nervous activity, after the old harmony of peace in the camp had been disturbed.

During this time Lieutenant Lukáš was in his room studying the ciphers which he had just received from the regimental staff together with the instructions on how they were to be read, as well as secret ciphered instructions about the direction which the march battalion would take on its way to the Galician frontier (first stage):

$$7217 - 1238 - 475 - 2121 - 35 = \text{Mošon}$$
$$8922 - 375 - 7282 = \text{Raab}$$
$$4432 - 1238 - 7217 - 35 - 8922 - 35 = \text{Komárno}$$
$$7282 - 9299 - 310 - 375 - 7881 - 298 - 475 - 7979 = \text{Budapest.}$$

Deciphering this code Lieutenant Lukáš sighed: 'Bugger the whole bloody thing.'

Part III

THE GLORIOUS LICKING

Across Hungary

AT last the moment came when they were stuffed into vans in the ratio of 42 men to 8 horses. The horses travelled more comfortably than the men of course because they could sleep standing, but what did it matter? A military train was again carrying off to Galicia another herd of men driven to the slaughter-house.

But it brought these creatures some relief none the less; when the train moved off it was at last something definite, whereas before there had only been uncomfortable uncertainty and panic as to whether the train would go that day, the next, or the following one. Some felt as though a death sentence had been passed on them and waited in fear and trembling for the moment when the executioner would come. And then calm resignation followed: soon everything would be over.

This was why one soldier shouted from the van like a madman: 'We're off, we're off!'

Quartermaster Sergeant-Major Vaněk was perfectly right when he told Švejk there was no hurry.

Before the moment came for them to get into the vans several days elapsed and all this time there were persistent rumours about tinned goulash. The experienced Vaněk declared that it was only imagination. How could there be any tinned goulash? There might perhaps be a drumhead mass, because there had been one for the previous march company. When there's tinned goulash the drumhead mass is dropped. Conversely, when there's no tinned goulash the drumhead mass is a substitute for it.

And so instead of tinned goulash Senior Chaplain Ibl appeared and killed three birds with one stone. He celebrated a drumhead mass for three march battalions at one go. Two of them he blessed for their march to Serbia and a third for their march to Russia.

On this occasion he delivered a highly inspired address and it was noticeable that he had taken the material from the army almanacs. It was such a moving speech that later, when they went off in the direction of Mošon, Švejk, who travelled with Vaněk in an improvised office in one of the vans, remembered the oration and said to him: 'Won't it be marvellous when, like the chaplain said, the day draws to its close, the sun with its golden beams sets behind the mountains, and on the battle-fields are heard, as he told us, the last breath of the dying, the death-rattle of the fallen horses, the groans of the wounded and the wailing of the population, as their cottages burn over their heads. I love it when people drivel utter bunkum.'

Vaněk nodded his head in agreement. 'It was a damned moving story.'

'It was very beautiful and edifying,' said Švejk. 'I've memorized it perfectly and when I return from the war I'll tell it at The Chalice. When the chaplain was declaiming there he had his shanks so wide apart that I was afraid one of them would slip and he would fall on to the field altar and crack his coconut on the monstrance. He gave us such a wonderful example from the history of our army at the time when Radetzky was still serving in it, the barns on the battlefield were burning and the blaze merged with the glow of sunset. It was just as if he had seen it with his own eyes.'

And the same day the senior chaplain was already back in Vienna telling another march battalion the moving story which Švejk referred to and which he loved so much that he called it 'utter bunkum'.

'My dear men,' the senior chaplain declaimed, 'imagine that it is the year 1848 and the Battle of Custozza[1] has ended in victory, where after a fierce battle lasting ten hours the Italian King Albert has had to aban-don the bloody battlefield to our warrior father, Marshal Radetzky, who in his eighty-fourth year has won such a glorious victory.

'And lo, my dear men, the veteran marshal has stopped on the hill before conquered Custozza! Around him are his faithful generals. The whole circle are held spellbound by the solemnity of the moment, for at no distance at all from the marshal, my dear men, a warrior can be seen wrestling with death. With his limbs shattered on the field of glory the wounded standard-bearer, Hrt, senses that the marshal's eyes are upon him. In a convulsive fit of enthusiasm the valiant wounded standard-bearer still clutches his Gold Medal firmly in his stiffening right hand. At the sight of the noble marshal the pulse of his heart quickens again, the last vestige of his strength suffuses his paralysed

1. In 1848 the Austrians under Marshal Radetzky defeated the army of King Charles Albert of Sardinia who was forced to evacuate Lombardy.

body and in his dying moments he strives with a superhuman effort to crawl towards his marshal.

' "Spare yourself these pains, my brave warrior!" the marshal calls to him, dismounting from his horse and about to shake his hand.

' "It's no good, sir," says the dying warrior. "Both my arms are shot away. But one thing I beg of you. Please tell me the full truth: is it total victory?"

' "Total, dear boy," says the marshal kindly. "It's a pity that your joy is marred by your wounds."

' "Of course, noble sir, my end has come," says the warrior in sombre tones as he smiles sweetly. "Are you thirsty?" asks Radetzky. "The day has been sultry, sir. We have had more than 30 degrees of heat." Radetzky then takes his adjutant's field-flask and hands it to the dying man, who drinks a powerful draught from it. "May God reward you a thousand times, sir!" he cries, striving to kiss the hand of his commander. "How long have you been serving?" the latter asks. "More than forty years, sir! At Aspern[1] I was awarded the Gold Medal. I was at Leipzig[2] too. I have the Artillery Cross also. I was mortally wounded five times but now it's all over with me. Oh, but what a joy and blessing it is that I've lived to see this day. What do I care about death now that we have won this glorious victory and the Emperor's territory is restored!"

'At that moment, my dear men, the mighty and noble strains of our anthem, "God save our Emperor", resound from the camp and are wafted over the battlefield. The fallen warrior, bidding farewell to life, tries once more to rally his strength.

' "*Vivat Austria!*" he shouts enthusiastically. "*Vivat Austria!* May it live on in this jewel of a song! Glory to our Marshal! Long life to our army!"

'The dying man bends once more towards the marshal's right hand and kisses it. Then he sinks down and a quiet last sigh escapes from his noble soul. The marshal stands there with bared head before the body of one of his most valiant warriors.

' "This beautiful passing is indeed to be envied," the marshal says with emotion, lowering his head to his clasped hands.

1. Napoleon was repulsed by the Austrian army in 1809 at the Battle of Aspern when he tried to cross the Danube and march on Vienna.

2. Napoleon was defeated at the Battle of Leipzig in 1813.

'My dear men, let me too wish all of you a beautiful passing like that.'

Remembering this speech by the senior chaplain, Švejk could justifiably, without the least offence to him, call him a driveller of utter bunkum.

After that Švejk began to talk of the famous orders which had been read out to them before they got into the train. One was the army order, signed by Franz Joseph, and another came from Archduke Joseph Ferdinand, the Supreme Commander of the Eastern Army and Group. Both concerned the events on the Dukla Pass on 3 April 1915, when two battalions of the 28th regiment including their officers went over to the Russians to the strains of their regimental band.

Both orders had been read to them in a tremulous voice and ran as follows in Czech translation:

ARMY ORDER OF 17 APRIL 1915

With a heart overflowing with grief it is my command that the Imperial and Royal Infantry Regiment no. 28 be struck off the roll of my army for cowardice and treason. The regimental standard is to be withdrawn from the dishonoured regiment and handed over to the War Museum. This day marks the end of the existence of a regiment which was morally poisoned by the atmosphere at home and went into the field to commit treason.

Franz Joseph I

ORDER OF THE ARCHDUKE JOSEPH FERDINAND

During the campaign in the field the Czech troops failed, especially in the last battles. They failed notably when defending positions where they had lain entrenched for a considerable time. The enemy took advantage of this to make contact and establish links with worthless elements among these troops.

Assisted by these traitors the enemy made a point of directing their attacks against those detachments at the front which were composed of troops of this kind.

The enemy was often successful in surprising our units and was thus able almost without resistance to penetrate our positions and take prisoner a remarkably large number of defence troops.

A thousandfold disgrace, shame and contempt upon these dishonourable wretches, who committed treason against their Emperor and Fatherland, and besmirched the honour, not only of the glorious standards of our noble and valiant army, but also of the nation to which they claim to belong.

Sooner or later they will perish by the bullet or the hangman's rope.

It is the duty of every single Czech soldier who possesses a shred of honour to denounce to his commander every such villain, agitator and traitor.

Anyone who fails to do so is himself a traitor and villain of the same kind. Let this order be read out to all the men of the Czech regiments.

By order of our Monarch the Imperial and Royal Regiment no. 28 has been struck off the roll of the army, and all the deserters from the regiment when they are captured will pay with their blood for their heavy guilt.

Archduke Joseph Ferdinand

'They read it to us a little too late,' said Švejk to Vaněk. 'I'm very surprised they only read it to us now, seeing that His Imperial Majesty issued the order as long ago as on 17 April. It might look as if for some reason or another they didn't allow it to be read to us immediately. If I were His Imperial Majesty I wouldn't let myself be brushed off like this. If I gave an order dated 17 April then on 17 April that order would have to be read out in all regiments, even if the sky fell down.'

Opposite Vaněk on the other side of the van the occultist cook from the officers' mess was sitting and writing. Behind him sat Lieutenant Lukáš's batman, the bearded giant Baloun, and Chodounský, who was assigned to the 11th march company as telephonist. Baloun was chewing a piece of army bread and explaining to Chodounský in fear and trembling that it was not his fault if in the bustle to get into the train he had not been able to reach the staff carriage where his lieutenant was.

Chodounský frightened him by saying that now the fun was over and that Baloun would get a bullet for it.

'If only there could be an end to this misery,' moaned Baloun. 'I was once nearly done for at the manoeuvres near Votice. There we were marching, hungry and thirsty, and when the battalion adjutant came up to us I shouted out: "Give us some water and bread!" He turned his horse on to me and said that if that had happened in war-time I should have had to fall out and he would have had me shot, but as it was he would put me in the garrison gaol. But I had wonderful luck because when he went to report it to the staff, his horse took fright on the way and he fell and broke his neck, thank the Lord.'

Baloun gave a heavy sigh and choked over a bit of bread. When he got over it he looked greedily at Lieutenant Lukáš's two bags, which he was looking after.

'The officer gentlemen have drawn their rations of liver pâté and Hungarian salami,' he said in a gloomy voice. 'How I'd love to have a bit!'

Meanwhile he was looking at his lieutenant's two bags as longingly as a dog which has been abandoned by everyone and sits hungry as a wolf at the door of a delicatessen shop, inhaling the vapour of the delicatessen as it is being cooked.

'It wouldn't do any harm,' said Chodounský, 'if they met us some-where with a good lunch. When we went to Serbia at the beginning of the war we stuffed ourselves at every station because they stood us something everywhere. We took the goose's thighs they gave us, cut little cubes of the very best meat and played draughts with them on bars of chocolate. At Osek in Croatia two gentlemen from the Veterans' Association brought a big cauldron of roast hare into our van and then we couldn't control ourselves and poured all of it over their heads. Wherever we went we did nothing else but spew out of the train. Corporal Matějka in our van stuffed himself so full that we had to put a board across his belly and jump on it, just like when you tread on sauerkraut. That was the only thing that relieved him and it came out of him from on top and underneath. When we went through Hungary they threw roast chickens into our vans at every station. We only ate the brains. In Kaposfalva the Hungarians threw in whole chunks of roast pork and one chap got such a blow on his skull with a whole roast boar's head that he chased the donor across three tracks with his belt strap. In Bosnia on the other hand they didn't even give us water. But on the way there, although it was forbidden, we got various brands of spirit, to our hearts' content, and oceans of wine. I can remember that at one station some young madams and misses treated us to some beer and we went and pissed into their beer jugs. You should have seen how they flew away from the van!

'We were all of us quite muzzy the whole journey. I couldn't even recognize an ace of clubs. We hadn't even finished our game when suddenly before we knew where we were an order came to get out of the vans at once. A corporal, I can't remember what his name was, shouted at his men to sing in German: "And the Serbs must see that we Austrians are victorious, victorious!" But someone gave him a kick from behind and he fell over on to the rails. After that there was a shout that the rifles had got to be stacked in a pyramid, and the train immediately reversed and went back empty. But you know what happens in a flap! It carried off with it all our provisions for two days. And shrapnel began bursting about as close to us as those trees over there. The battalion commander rode up from the other end and called all his officers to a consultation. Then our Lieutenant Macek came up – he was as Czech as they make them, but he only spoke German. He was white as chalk and told us that we couldn't go any farther, because the rails had been blown up. The Serbs had got across the river in the night and were now on our left flank. But that was still far away from us. We should get reinforcements, he said, and then we would cut them

to pieces. If anything should happen no one must surrender; the Serbs, he said, cut off their prisoners' ears and noses and gouged out their eyes. Shrapnel was bursting near us, but we were not to worry about that. It was only our artillery ranging their guns, he said. Suddenly from somewhere behind the mountain there resounded a ta-ta-ta-ta-ta-ta-ta. That was our machine-guns ranging, he said. After that you could hear a cannonade from the left. It was the first time in our lives we'd heard it and we lay down flat on our stomachs at once. Several shells flew over us and set the station on fire. And then from our right side bullets began to whistle over us and in the distance you could hear salvos and the rattle of rifle fire. Lieutenant Macek ordered the pyramids to be unstacked and the rifles to be loaded. The officer on duty came up to

him and said that it couldn't be done as we had no munitions with
us and he knew very well that we were only scheduled to draw our
munitions at the very last staging point before taking up our positions.
The munitions train had gone ahead of us and was obviously now in
the hands of the Serbs. Lieutenant Macek stood for a moment, as
though rooted to the spot, and then gave the order "Fix bayonets!"
without knowing why and only out of desperation for something to do.
Then we stood again on the alert for a long time, and after that lay
down again on the sleepers because an aeroplane had appeared and the
officers roared "Cover, cover, everything under cover!" Then it turned
out that it was one of our own and had been shot down by our artillery
in error. And after that we got up again, but there was no order, only
"At ease!" From one side a cavalryman came galloping towards us.
When he was still far away he shouted out: "Where is Battalion Command?" The battalion commander rode out to meet him. The cavalryman handed him a document and then rode away to the right.
The battalion commander read it on the way and suddenly, as if he'd
gone off his head, drew his sabre and came flying in our direction.

' "General retreat! General retreat!" he roared at the officers. "To
the hollow! Single file!" And then it started. They began to fire at us
from all sides, as if they had only been waiting for that moment. On
the left side was a maize field and that was a hell. Leaving our rucksacks on those blasted sleepers we crawled on all fours to the valley.
Before you could say Jack Robinson Lieutenant Macek had stopped
one in the head from the side. By the time we got away to the valley
there were masses of dead and wounded. We left them there and went
on running until the evening, and there wasn't a single one of our men
left in the region. All of them had cleared out long before we came.
The only thing we saw was a plundered baggage train. In the end
we reached the station, where we got new orders to get into the
train and go back to the staff, which we couldn't do because the whole
staff had been taken prisoner the day before. We only learnt about that
the next morning. After that we were like orphans. No one wanted
anything to do with us and they assigned us to the 73rd regiment so
that we could retreat with them. Of course we were jolly glad to do it,
but first we had to march forward for about a day before we could
get to the 73rd regiment. After that we . . .'

No one was listening to him any longer, because Švejk and Vaněk
were playing two-handed mariáš. The occultist cook from the officers'

mess went on writing a voluminous letter to his wife, who in his absence had begun to publish a new theosophical journal. Baloun slumbered on the bench, and so the telephonist could do nothing but repeat: 'Yes, I'll never forget it . . .'

He got up and started to kibitz those who were playing mariáš.

'You might at least light my pipe for me,' said Švejk in a friendly tone to Chodounský, 'since you're coming to kibitz. Two-handed mariáš is more important than the whole war and that blasted adventure of yours on the Serbian frontier. . . . Oh, my God, what a bloody fool I am! I could kick myself. Why didn't I wait a bit longer with that king? Now the knave has come. I really am a bloody idiot.'

Meanwhile the occultist cook had finished his letter and was reading it to himself, obviously satisfied that he had done a good job with it in face of the military censorship.

My darling wife,

When you get these lines I shall have already been several days in the train, because we are off to the front. I'm not too pleased about it because in the train I have to hang about and I can't be much use. You see, no cooking is done in our officer's mess and we get food at the various staging points. I should have liked to cook a Szeged goulash for our officers on the journey through Hungary, but there was nothing doing. Perhaps when we come to Galicia I shall have a chance of making a real Galician scholet, goose stewed in barley or in rice. Believe me, darling Helenka, I am really doing my utmost to make life more pleasant for our officers and help them overcome their troubles and strain. I have been transferred from the regiment to the march battalion, which was my most ardent desire, because I wanted with the modest resources at my disposal to put the officers' field-kitchen at the front in the best order. You remember, dear Helenka, that when I was called up to the regiment you wished me good superiors. Your wish has been granted. Not only have I nothing whatsoever to complain about, but on the contrary, all the officers are our real friends and to me especially they are like a father. As soon as possible I will let you know the number of our field post . . .

This letter had to be written because of the following circumstances: the occultist cook had got into Colonel Schröder's bad books for good and all. The colonel had protected him for a long time but by a most unfortunate mischance he had again failed to get his portion of rolled roast sirloin of veal at the farewell party with the officers of the march battalion. And so he had sent him with a march company to the front, entrusting the regimental officers' kitchen to an unfortunate teacher from the Institute for the Blind at Klárov.

The occultist cook read over once more what he had written and thought it sufficiently diplomatically phrased to keep him a bit further away from the battlefield, because, you may say what you like, even at the front there are opportunities for an easier life.

This was of course not affected by the fact that while he was still in civil life and working as editor and owner of an occultist journal devoted to knowledge of what was beyond the grave, he had written a long essay on how no one ought to fear death, and another one on the transmigration of souls.

Now he too started to kibitz. At that moment there was no difference in rank between the two players, Švejk and Vaněk. They no longer played two-handed mariáš but three-handed with Chodounský.

Orderly Švejk swore like a trooper at Quartermaster Sergeant-Major Vaněk: 'How can you be such a bloody fool? You do realize, don't you, that he's playing *betl*?[1] I haven't got a bloody diamond and, instead of

1. *Betl* (like *misère* in whist) means that the player must lose every trick in a no-trump game.

playing your eight of diamonds, like a bloody twat you throw away your knave of clubs and give that bastard the game.'

'What a lot of bloody fuss about one lost *betl*,' was the quarter-master sergeant-major's polite answer. 'Why, you're playing like a bloody half-wit yourself. D'you expect me to pull an eight of diamonds out of my hat when I haven't got a single diamond in my hand? I've only got court cards in spades and clubs, you fornicating fool.'

'Then you should have played *durch*, [1] you bloody genius,' said Švejk with a smile. 'It's just like what happened once down at the restaurant, U Valšů. There was a prize oaf there who had a *durch* hand but didn't play it. Instead he always threw away all his lowest cards and made everyone play *betl*. And what hands he had! In every suit he always had the highest cards. And, just as I wouldn't have got anything out of it now, if you had played *durch*, so at that time I couldn't have got anything out of it, nor could anyone of us either. As the game went on we would have paid him all the time. At last I said to him: "Mr Herold, please do play *durch* and don't be a bloody fool." But he flew at me and said he'd play what he liked and I should keep my trap shut since he had had a university education. But he paid dearly for it. The landlord was our friend and the waitress could hardly have been on more familiar terms with us, so we were able to explain to the police patrol that everything was all right. We said first of all that it was a dirty trick of his to disturb the night peace by calling a patrol just because somewhere in front of the pub he had slipped on the ice, fallen on his nose and broken it. We hadn't done anything to him when he cheated at mariáš, but when he had been found out he had rushed out so quickly that he fell full length on the ground. The landlord and the waitress confirmed to us that we'd really been too gentlemanly to him. He had deserved all he got. He had sat from 7 p.m. to midnight, only ordered one glass of beer and one of soda water, and made out that he was a hell of a gentleman because he was a university professor. But he understood as much about mariáš as a goat about parsley. Well, whose turn is it to deal now?'

'Let's play Kaufzwick,'[2] the occultist cook proposed. 'Twenty hellers and two.'

'Much better if you tell us something about the transmigration of

1. *Durch* (like grand slam) means that the player must win every trick.
2. Kaufzwick was a gambling card game forbidden by the Austrian authorities.

souls,' said Vaněk, 'like you told the young lady in the canteen when you got yourself a bloody nose.'

'I've heard something about that transmigration of souls too,' Švejk put in. 'I made up my mind years ago to educate myself, if you'll permit the expression, because I didn't want to be left behind. And so I went to the reading room of the Industrial Union in Prague. But because I was ragged and the light shone through the holes in the seat of my trousers I couldn't educate myself. You see, they wouldn't let me in and showed me the door, because they thought that I had come to steal the overcoats. And so I put on my best suit, went one day to the Museum library, and together with a friend of mine borrowed a book about the transmigration of souls. There I read how an Indian emperor turned after death into a pig, and when they slaughtered that pig he turned into a monkey, and from a monkey he became a dachshund, and from a dachshund a minister. Afterwards when I was in the army I saw that there must be something in it, because everyone who had a star used to call the men swine or some other animal name. From that you might conclude that a thousand years ago these common soldiers had been famous generals. But when there's a war on, a transmigration of souls like that is an awfully silly business. God knows how many changes a man goes through before he becomes, let's say, a telephonist, a cook or an infantryman. Then suddenly he's torn to pieces by a shell and his soul goes into a horse in the artillery, and when the whole battery goes to a point somewhere a new shell bursts into it, and this again kills the horse which the late lamented had become incarnate in. And then his soul immediately moves into a cow in the baggage train, which they make goulash out of for the troops, and from the cow perhaps into a telephonist and from a telephonist . . .'

'I'd really like to know,' said Chodounský, who obviously felt offended, 'why I of all people have to be the butt of your idiotic jokes.'

'Tell me, are you by any chance related to the Chodounský who has a private detective agency with that eye like the Holy Trinity?' asked Švejk innocently. 'I like private detectives very much. I once served years ago in the army with a private detective, a fellow called Stendler. He had such a cockeyed head that our sergeant-major always said that he'd seen many soldiers with cockeyed heads during his twelve years, but a cockeyed head like his he could never have imagined in his wildest dreams. "Listen, Stendler," he always said, "if there didn't happen to be manoeuvres this year, your cockeyed nut wouldn't do for military service, but as it is, the artillery can at least range their guns by it when they come to a locality where there's no better orientation point." He had to put up with a lot of chaff like this from that sergeant-major. Sometimes during the march he sent Stendler five hundred paces in front and then gave the order: "Direction, cockeyed nut."

'But even Mr Stendler had awfully bad luck as a private detective. He often told us in the canteen that he'd had a lot of bother. He got commissions like this one for example: to find out whether the wife of one of his firm's clients, who came to see him in a state of fury, was having an affair with another man and, if she was, who it was she was having the affair with, and where and how. Or again the opposite: a very jealous woman wanted to find out who her husband was having an affair with, so as to make it hotter for him at home. Mr Stendler was an educated man, spoke exquisitely about breach of matrimonial fidelity and was nearly always on the brink of tears when he told us that all his clients wanted him to catch her or him *in flagrante*. Another chap might perhaps get a kick out of it if he came upon a couple *in flag-rante* and his eyes would pop out of his head, but this Mr Stendler, as he told us himself, was quite unhappy because of it. He said very intelligently that he could no longer look at these lewd debauches. When he told us all the various positions in which he'd found those couples our mouths often watered, like a dog slobbers when they carry boiled ham past it. When we were given "confined to barracks" he always used to draw them for us. "This is how," he said, "I saw Mrs So-and-So with this and that gentleman..." And he even told us their addresses. And he used to be so miserable about it. "The slaps on the face I got from both parties!" he always said. "But that didn't upset me half as much as the fact that I stooped to taking bribes. One bribe I shall never forget to my dying day. He was naked; she was naked. It was in a hotel and they hadn't bolted the door, the idiots! They couldn't fit on to the sofa because they were both too fat, and so they made love on the carpet like two kittens. And the carpet was all trampled on and full of dust, and there were cigarette stubs lying about on it. And when I came in both of them jumped up. He stood opposite me and held his hand in front of him like a fig-leaf. And she turned her back to me and you could see the whole network pattern of the carpet printed on her skin and a cigarette stub stuck to her backbone. 'Excuse me,' I said, 'Mr Zemek, I am private detective Stendler, from Chodounský's agency, and it is my official duty to catch you *in flagrante* on the basis of a tip-off from madam, your wife. This lady, with whom you are here maintaining an illicit relationship, is Mrs Grotová.' I've never in my life seen such a calm citizen. 'Excuse me,' he said, as though it were a matter of course, 'I am going to put on my clothes. It is my wife who has the sole responsibility for this. She drives me to this illicit relationship by her groundless jealousy. Goaded on by nothing more than mere suspicion she insults her husband with reproaches and mean distrust. There's no doubt now that this scandal can no longer be hushed up. . . . Where are my pants?' he asked calmly. 'On the bed there.' While he was putting on his pants he went on explaining to me: 'If a scandal cannot be hushed up, people say "divorce", but even in that case the slur of the disgrace cannot be hushed up. A divorce is always a risky thing anyway,' he went on as he dressed. 'The best thing for the wife is to arm herself with patience and do nothing to provoke a public scandal. But do as you like. I'll leave you here alone with the lady.' Meanwhile Mrs

Grotová had climbed into bed. Mr Zemek shook hands with me and left."

'I can't remember any longer how Mr Stendler explained everything and what he talked about after that, because he conversed with the lady in the bed in a very intelligent way. He said that marriage was not instituted to make everyone find happiness immediately and that it was our duty in marriage to suppress lust and to exorcize and sublimate the physical side. "And while I was saying that," Mr Stendler continued, "I gradually began to undress, and just when I was undressed, and was completely bemused and wild as a rutting stag, a Mr Stach whom I knew well came into the room. He was also a private detective from the agency of our rival, Mr Stern, and Mr Grot had turned to him for help over his wife who, he claimed, must have a lover. Stach said nothing more than, 'Ah, Mr Stendler *in flagrante* with Mrs Grotová. My congratulations!' He closed the door again quietly and went away.

' " 'You needn't dress so hastily,' Mrs Grotová said. 'It makes no difference now. There's a place here for you beside me.' 'My good lady, it's just my place that I'm worrying about,' I said and I hadn't any idea any more what I was talking about. I can only remember that I said something about that if there were quarrels between husband and wife, the babes' upbringing suffered through them." And afterwards he told us how he quickly dressed and took to his heels and decided at once to tell everything to his chief, Mr Chodounský, but went first to have a pick-me-up. But before he got back the fat was already in the fire. Stach had been there on orders from his chief, Mr Stern, to give Mr Chodounský a shock by telling him the kind of employee he had in his private detective agency. Mr Chodounský could think of nothing better than at once to send for Mrs Stendler, so that she could deal with her husband herself for having been sent somewhere on official duties and been caught *in flagrante* by a rival agency. "From that time," Mr Stendler always used to say when the subject came up, "my nut is even more cockeyed."

'Now, let's go on playing Five-ten.' And so they did.

The train stopped at the station of Mošon. It was already evening and no one was allowed out of the vans.

When they moved off a powerful voice could be heard from one of the vans. It was as though someone was trying to drown the rattle of the train. In the pious mood of the evening a German soldier from Kašperské Hory in a frightful caterwaul extolled the silent night as it descended on the Hungarian plains:

> 'Good night! Good night!
> To the weary respite.
> As the hushed day closes
> The busy hand reposes
> Till the dawning light.
> Good night! Good night!'

'Shut your trap, you miserable bastard,' someone interrupted the sentimental singer, who then lapsed into silence.

They dragged him away from the window.

But the busy hands did not repose until morning. Just as everywhere else in the train they played cards by candlelight, so here Švejk and the others continued to play Kaufzwick by the light of a small paraffin lamp hanging on the wall. Whenever anyone burst when buying a card Švejk said that Kaufzwick was the fairest of all games, because anyone could swap as many cards as he liked.

'At Kaufzwick,' asserted Švejk, 'it's only the ace and the seven which you have to buy, and after that you can throw your hand in. You don't have to buy the other cards. You do that at your own risk.'

'Let's play "Blessing",'[1] Vaněk suggested amid general agreement.

'Seven of hearts,' said Švejk, cutting the cards. 'Everyone stakes five hellers and gets four cards. Don't waste time so that we can have a good game!'

And their faces looked so happy, as though there were no war on and they were not sitting in a train which was taking them off to positions in the great and bloody battles and massacres but at the card tables in a Prague café.

'I never imagined,' said Švejk after one game, 'when I had nothing in my hand and swapped all four of my cards, that I should pick up an ace. What the hell did you think you would do to me with your king? I smash your king before you know where you are.'

And while here they were smashing the king with the ace, far away at the front kings were smashing each other with their serfs.

In the staff carriage, where the officers of the march battalion were sitting, a strange stillness reigned from the start of the journey. Most of

---

1. A variety of Kaufzwick, where the stakes are higher.

the officers were engrossed in a small book in cloth binding entitled *The Sins of the Fathers*, a novelette by Ludwig Ganghofer, and all were simultaneously busy reading page 161. Captain Ságner, the battalion commander, was standing at the window and holding in his hand this same book, which he also had open at page 161.

He was looking at the landscape and thinking how actually he could explain to everyone in the clearest possible way what they had to do with that book. It was in fact strictly confidential.

Meanwhile the officers were reflecting that Colonel Schröder must have gone off his rocker for good and all. He had been pretty crazy for a long time, but there had surely been no reason to expect that it would take him suddenly like this. Before the departure of the train he called them to a last 'conference' and informed them that each of them would get a copy of the book *The Sins of the Fathers* by Ludwig Ganghofer, which he had had sent to battalion office.

'Gentlemen,' he said with a terribly mysterious expression, 'never forget page 161!' Engrossed as they all were in this page they could not make anything out of it. There a woman called Martha came to a writing-desk, took out a script and reflected aloud that the public must feel sympathy with the hero of the play. And then on the same page there appeared as well a certain Albert, who tried to make jokes all the time, which, divorced from the unknown action which preceded them, seemed such tripe that Lieutenant Lukáš bit his cigarette-holder in fury.

'The old man has really gone barmy,' all of them thought. 'It's all up with him. Now they'll transfer him to the Ministry of War.'

Captain Ságner got up from the window, after he had composed everything in his head to his satisfaction. He did not have much peda-gogical talent, and so it took him a long time before he had in his head the whole plan of a lecture on the importance of page 161.

Before he began to explain he addressed them as 'Gentlemen', just as the old dodderer of a colonel used to do, although before they got into the train he called them 'My dear fellows.'

'Very well, then, gentlemen . . .' And he began to expound how, the evening before, he had received from the colonel instructions about page 161 in *The Sins of the Fathers* by Ludwig Ganghofer.

'Very well, then, gentlemen,' he continued solemnly. 'Strictly con-fidential information about the new system of ciphering telegrams in the field.' Cadet Biegler took out a notebook and a pencil and said in an exceptionally zealous tone: 'I am ready, sir.'

Everybody looked at that idiot, whose zeal in the volunteers' school bordered on imbecility. He volunteered for the army and when the commander of the volunteers' school was looking into the private circumstances of the students he took the first opportunity of letting him know that his ancestors were originally called Bügler von Leuthold and bore in their armorial bearings a stork's wing with a fish tail.

From that time onwards they christened him by the name of his armorial bearings and 'Stork's wing with fish tail' was mercilessly persecuted and became unpopular at once, because it did not in the least fit in with his father's respectable business in hare and rabbit skins. But the romantic enthusiast strove with great earnestness to devour the whole of military science, and not only did he excel in diligence and knowledge of everything which was taught him, but he also crammed his head more and more with the study of writings on military science and the history of warfare, which he always tried to talk about, until he was rapped down and crushed. In officers' circles he considered himself the equal of the senior ranks.

'You cadet there, keep quiet,' said Captain Ságner, 'until I give you permission to speak. No one asked for your opinion. But you're a damned bright soldier all the same. I'm giving you strictly confidential information and you're writing it down in your notebook. If you lose your notes you can expect to be brought before a drumhead court-martial.'

On top of everything else Cadet Biegler had the bad habit of always trying to convince everyone that his intentions were the best.

'Humbly report, sir,' he replied, 'even if I lost the notebook no one could decipher what I've written, because I use shorthand and no one can read my symbols. I use the English system.'

Everyone froze him with a look of contempt. Captain Ságner dismissed his remark with a wave of his hand and continued his lecture.

'I've already referred to the new system of ciphering telegrams in the field, and if it was perhaps not clear to you why you were recommended to read of all things page 161 of Ludwig Ganghofer's novel, *The Sins of the Fathers*, I can tell you, gentlemen, that it is the key to the new ciphering system, operative on the basis of a new directive from the staff of the army corps to which we are assigned. As you will be aware, there are many systems of ciphering important messages in the field. The latest one, which we are using, is the supplementary figure method. This supersedes the ciphers and the deciphering directives given you last week by the regimental staff.'

'Archduke Albrecht's system,' the sedulous Cadet Biegler mumbled to himself, '8922 = R, taken from Gronfeld's method.'

'The new system is exceedingly simple,' the captain's voice rang out through the carriage. 'I have personally obtained from the colonel Book II and the information.

'If, for example, we are to get the order: "On point 228 direct machine-gun fire to the left", we shall receive, gentlemen, the following telegram: "Thing – with – us – that – we – look – in – the – promised – the – Martha – you – that – anxious – then – we – Martha – we – him – we – thanks – well – steering committee – end – we – promised – we – improved – promised – really – think – idea – quite – rules – voice – last." You see, it's frightfully simple, without any unnecessary combinations. From the staff by telephone to the battalion, from the battalion by telephone to the companies. Having obtained this ciphered telegram the commander deciphers it in the following way. He takes *The Sins of the Fathers*, opens it at page 161 and starts from the top to look for the word "thing" on the opposite page, i.e. 160. Very well, then, gentlemen. The first time the word "thing" occurs on page 160 is at the 52nd word, and so he looks for the 52nd letter from the top on the opposite page, no. 161. Please note that it is "O". The next word in the telegram is "with" – that is – now follow me carefully, gentlemen, the 88th word on page 160, corresponding to the 88th letter on the opposite page 161 which is "n". And now we have deciphered "On". And we proceed in this way until we learn the order: "On point 228 direct machine-gun fire to the left." Very ingenious, gentlemen, simple, and impossible to decipher without the key: page 161 of Ludwig Ganghofer: *The Sins of the Fathers*.'

Everyone stared in silence at the unfortunate pages and pondered deeply over them. There was quiet for a moment, until all of a sudden Cadet Biegler called out in a worried voice: 'Sir, humbly report, Jesus Mary! It doesn't fit!'

And it was indeed exceedingly mysterious.

Try as they could, no one except Captain Ságner could find the words on page 160 and the corresponding letters on page 161 with which the key started.

'Gentlemen,' Captain Ságner stammered, when he had realized that

Cadet Biegler's despairing exclamation corresponded to the truth, 'what has happened? In my *Sins of the Fathers* by Ganghofer it's there and in yours it isn't?'

'Permit me, sir,' Cadet Biegler began again. 'May I take the liberty to draw your attention to the fact that the novel of Ludwig Ganghofer is in two parts. You can, if you wish, verify this by looking at the first

title page: "Novel in two parts". We have Part I and you have Part II,' continued the thorough-going Cadet Biegler. 'And so it's as clear as daylight that our pages 160 and 161 do not correspond with yours. We have something completely different. According to you the first word of the deciphered telegram ought to be "On" but ours has come out "Hi".'

Now it was quite clear to everyone that Biegler was not perhaps such an idiot after all.

'I have Part II from brigade staff,' said Captain Ságner, 'and clearly it's a question of a mistake. The colonel ordered Part I for you. Obviously,' he continued, as though it was clear as daylight and he had known it long before he gave the lecture on the very simple system of ciphering, 'there has been a muddle in brigade staff. They didn't inform the regiment that it concerned Part II and that is how it happened.'

In the meantime Cadet Biegler was looking triumphantly at everybody and Lieutenant Dub whispered to Lieutenant Lukáš that 'Stork's wing with fish tail' had put it across Ságner and no mistake – and serve him right!

'What a curious case, gentlemen,' Captain Ságner said again, as though he wanted to start a conversation, because the silence was very embarrassing. 'In brigade office they aren't very bright.'

'Permit me to add,' said the indefatigable Cadet Biegler once more, wanting to show off his knowledge again, 'that matters of this kind which are of a confidential nature, indeed a strictly confidential nature, should not go from division through brigade office. A matter which concerns the most confidential business of the army corps may be communicated by a strictly confidential circular to no one except commanders of divisions, brigades and regiments. I know the cipher systems used in the Sardinian and Savoy wars, in the Anglo-French campaign at Sebastopol, during the Boxer rising in China and in the last Russo-Japanese war. These systems were conveyed . . .'

'We don't care a tuppenny hoot about that, Cadet Biegler,' said Captain Ságner with an expression of contempt and displeasure. 'There's no doubt that the system in question which I have explained to you is not only one of the best but also, we can say, quite unrivalled. All the counter-espionage departments of our enemy staffs can now pack up. Even if they bust themselves, they won't be able to read our cipher. It's something quite new. These ciphers have no precedents.'

The assiduous Cadet Biegler coughed knowingly.

'May I be allowed to take the liberty, sir,' he said, 'to draw your attention to Kerickhoff's book on military ciphering. Anyone can obtain this book from the publishers of the *Encyclopedia of Military Science*. There you will find, sir, described in detail the method which you have just explained to us. Its inventor was Colonel Kircher, who served in the Saxon army in the time of Napoleon. Kircher's word cipher, sir. Every word of the telegram is explained on the opposite page by means of a key. The method was perfected by Lieutenant

Fleissner in his book, *The Handbook of Military Cryptography*, which anyone can buy at the publishers of the Military Academy in Wiener Neustadt. Excuse me, sir.' Cadet Biegler put his hand in his bag, drew out the book to which he was referring and continued: 'Fleissner gives the very same example. You may all wish to confirm it for yourselves. It is exactly the same example as we have just heard.

> 'Telegram: On point 228 direct machine-gun fire to the left.
> Key: Ludwig Ganghofer, *The Sins of the Fathers*, Part II.

'And look further please: "Cipher: Thing – with – us – that – we – look – in – the – promised – the – Martha ..." and so on. Just as we heard a moment ago.'

There was no answer to this. The greenhorn 'Stork's wing with fish tail' was right.

One of the generals in the army staff had hit upon a labour-saving device. He had discovered Fleissner's book about military ciphers and the job was done.

All this time Lieutenant Lukáš appeared to be trying to overcome a strange inner tension. He bit his lip, seemed to want to say something but in the end started to speak about something different from what he had originally intended.

'We need not take this so tragically,' he said in strange embarrassment. 'While we were in camp at Bruck an der Leitha the systems of ciphering telegrams were changed several times. Before we reach the front new systems will again be introduced. But I think that anyhow there's no time for deciphering cryptograms like this in the field. Before any of us had time to decipher a telegram like the example given us the company battalion and brigade would long ago have ceased to exist. It has no practical significance!'

Captain Ságner nodded his head very reluctantly. 'In practice,' he said, 'at least as far as my experiences from the Serbian battlefield go, no one had time to decipher telegrams. I don't mean that ciphers wouldn't have their importance in the course of a prolonged stay in the trenches, when we dig ourselves in and wait. It's also true that ciphers are changed.'

Captain Ságner was retreating all along the line: 'A great deal of the blame for our staffs making less and less use of ciphers when they communicate with the troops in position rests on the inaccuracy and unreliability of our field telephones, particularly during artillery fire when they do not reproduce the individual syllables clearly. You don't hear anything at all and it causes unnecessary chaos.' He paused.

'Chaos is the worst thing that can happen in the field, gentlemen,' he added prophetically and was silent.

'In a moment,' he said, looking out of the window, 'we shall be in Raab. Gentlemen, here the men will get fifteen dekas of Hungarian salami. And there will be half an hour's rest.'

He looked at the schedule: 'At 4.12 we leave. At 3.58 everything must be in the vans. We shall leave the train by companies. The 11th and so on. By platoons. Direction: store number 6. Control over distribution: Cadet Biegler.'

Everyone gave Cadet Biegler a look which meant 'You'll have a nice picnic now, you milksop.'

But the assiduous Cadet Biegler had already taken out of his bag a sheet of paper and a ruler, drawn lines on the paper, divided it according to march companies and asked the commanders of the various companies how many men they had. None of them knew this offhand and they could only give Biegler the required figures from vague jottings in their notebooks.

Meanwhile Captain Ságner in despair began to read the unfortunate book, *The Sins of the Fathers*, and when the train stopped at the station in Raab, he closed it and observed: 'This Ludwig Ganghofer doesn't write at all badly.'

Lieutenant Lukáš was the first to rush out of the staff carriage and go to the van to find Švejk.

Švejk and the others had long ago stopped playing cards and Lieutenant Lukáš's batman, Baloun, was already so hungry that he was beginning to rebel against the military authorities and to tell the others that he knew exactly how those officer gentlemen stuffed their gullets. It was worse now than during serfdom. It hadn't been like that in the army in the old days. As his grandfather who lived at home in retirement always said, the officers in the war of 1866 used to share their chicken and bread with the soldiers. There was no end to his lamentations, until finally Švejk considered it proper to stand up for army life in the present war.

'You must have quite a young grandfather,' he said affably, when they got to Raab, 'if he can only remember the war of 1866. I know a chap called Ronovský, and his grandfather was in Italy under serfdom, and he served his twelve years there and came home as a corporal. As that grandfather had no job, his father took him into his own house to work for him. And once they went to do their *corvée* for their landlord and cart away tree trunks. One trunk, as that grandfather who was working for his father told us, was just like a colossus and they couldn't make it budge. And so he said: "Let's leave the blighter here. Who's going to sweat with it." And a gamekeeper who heard this began to shout at him, raised his stick and told him that he'd got to load that tree trunk. Well, Mr Ronovský's grandfather said nothing but: "You clumsy oaf, you. I'm an old army veteran." But a week later he was served with a summons and called up for service in Italy again. He remained there for another ten years and wrote home that when he came back he'd slog that gamekeeper over the head with an axe. It was a bit of luck that that gamekeeper died.'

At that moment Lieutenant Lukáš appeared in the door of the van. 'Švejk, come here,' he said. 'Stop telling your stupid stories, and come and explain something to me.'

'At your service, humbly report, sir.'

Lieutenant Lukáš took Švejk away and the look he gave him, as he followed him with his eyes, was full of suspicion.

During the whole course of Captain Ságner's lecture, which had ended in such a fiasco, Lieutenant Lukáš had developed a certain aptitude for detective work for which no elaborate speculation was needed, because the day before their departure Švejk had reported to him: 'Sir, there are some books in the battalion for the gentlemen lieutenants. I've fetched them from the regimental office.'

And so when they crossed the second track and got behind an abandoned locomotive, which had been already waiting a week for a munitions' train, Lieutenant Lukáš asked straight out: 'Švejk, tell me, what happened to those books you told me about?'

'Humbly report, sir, it's a very long story and you always are pleased to get angry when I go into a lot of detail. Like the time you wanted to hit me over the jaw when you had torn up the document about the war loan and I told you that I'd read once in a book that in the old days when there was a war on people had to pay for their windows, twenty hellers for every window, and the same amount for their geese . . .'

'Like this we'll never be finished, Švejk,' said Lieutenant Lukáš continuing his cross-examination, during which he resolved that what was strictly confidential must of course be kept completely concealed to prevent that bastard Švejk making some kind of use of it again. 'Do you know Ganghofer?'

'What should he be?' asked Švejk with interest.

'He's a German writer, you stupid bastard,' answered Lieutenant Lukáš.

'Upon my honour, sir,' said Švejk with the expression of a martyr, 'I don't know any German writer personally. I only once knew a Czech writer personally, a certain Ladislav Hájek from Domažlice. He was the editor of *The Animal World*, and I once sold him a mongrel as a thoroughbred pom. He was a very cheery and nice man. He used to go to a pub and always read his stories there, which were so sad that everybody roared with laughter at them. Afterwards he wept and paid for everybody in the pub and we had to sing for him: "The Domažlice gate's in a beautiful state. It's thanks to the art of the amorous heart of a painter I knew who the girls did pursue, and who can't now be found, as he's under the ground ..."'

'You're not on the stage, do you realize that? You're bellowing like an opera singer, Švejk,' shouted Lieutenant Lukáš in horror when Švejk began to sing the last sentence: 'And who can't now be found, as he's under the ground.' 'That's not what I asked you about. I only wanted to know whether you had noticed that those books which you yourself mentioned to me were by Ganghofer. What happened to those books, then?' he burst out angrily.

'Do you mean those I fetched from regimental office and carried to the battalion?' asked Švejk. 'Yes, they were written by that man you asked me whether I knew, sir. I got a telegram phoned straight from regimental office. They wanted to send those books to battalion office, but no one was there. They were all away, even the N.C.O. on duty, because they had to go to the canteen, when they were leaving for the front, as no one knew if they would ever be sitting in the canteen again. And so they were there, sir, they were there and they were drinking. You couldn't get anyone by phone, not even anyone from any of the other march companies, but because you had ordered me to be orderly at the telephone for the time being until they assigned us a telephone operator, Chodounský, I sat there and waited until my turn came. From regimental office they swore and complained that they couldn't get hold of anybody anywhere and that they had a telegram which said that the march battalion office should fetch from regimental office some books for the officers of the whole march battalion. Because I know, sir, that in wartime you have to act quickly, I telephoned to regimental office that I would go and pick up those books myself and take them to battalion office. There I was given such a colossal sack that I could hardly drag it to our company office, where I had a look at those books. But I had ideas of my own about them. The regimental quartermaster sergeant-major at regimental office told me that according to the telegram to the regiment they certainly knew in the battalion which of these books had to be taken and *which part*. You see these books were in *two parts*. The first part separate and the second part separate. I've never laughed so much in my life, because I've read many books in my time, but I've never started a book from the second part. And he said to me once again: "Here you have the first part and there you have the second. The officers know already *which part* they have to read." And so I thought that they must all be tight, because when you have to read a novel from the beginning like the one I've brought about *The Sins of the Fathers* (because I understand German too), you have to begin with the *first* part. After all, we're not Jews and don't read backwards. And that's why I asked you, sir, on the telephone, when you returned from the officers' club and I reported to you about these books, whether perhaps now in wartime it isn't all upside down and whether books aren't read back to front, first the *second* part and only after that the *first* part. And you told me that I was a sozzled ox if I didn't know that in the Lord's Prayer "Our Father" came first and "Amen" afterwards.

'Are you feeling bad, sir?' asked Švejk with concern, when Lieutenant Lukáš, who had turned pale, steadied himself by holding on to the footplate of the boiler of the abandoned locomotive.

There was no sign of anger in his pale face. There was just hopelessness and desperation.

'Go on, go on, Švejk. It doesn't matter. It's quite all right . . .'

'I was, as I've said, sir, of the same opinion myself,' Švejk's soft voice could be heard saying on the abandoned track. 'Once I bought a blood-and-thunder novel about Róža Šavaň from the Bakony Forest and the first part was missing, so I had to guess the beginning, and even in a gangster story like that you really need the first part. And it was quite clear to me that it would have been useless for the officers to start reading the second part first and the first part afterwards, and that it would look very stupid if I had said in the battalion what they told me in regimental office, that the officers would know *which part* they had to read. Altogether with these books I found it frightfully suspicious and mysterious. I knew that the officer gentlemen read very little anyhow and in the tumult of the battle . . .'

'Cut out the drivel, Švejk,' Lieutenant Lukáš groaned.

'And you know, sir, that I asked you by telephone at once, whether you wanted immediately both parts at once and you said to me, just like

now, that I should cut out the drivel and not bother you about carting any books with us. And so I thought that if that was your opinion then the other officers must see it in the same light too. And I also asked our Vaněk, who after all has experience from the front, and he said that at the beginning all the officers thought that the whole war would be just a picnic and took with them to the front whole libraries of books as though they were going on their summer holidays. Archduchesses presented them with complete collections of various poets for the front, so that the wretched batmen doubled up under their weight and cursed the day when they were born. Vaněk said that these books were never of any use for rolling cigarettes, because they were printed on very swell thick paper, and in the W.C. people might, if you excuse the expression, sir, scrape off the whole of their backsides with such poems. But there wasn't a moment for reading, because they had to flee all the time, and so the books were thrown away, and after that it became the usual custom for the batmen to throw away all the light reading at once as soon as they heard the first cannonade. After hearing this I wanted to learn your opinion once again, sir, and when I asked you on the telephone what I was to do with these books you said that when I got something into my bloody stupid noddle I never let go of it until I got one across the jaw. And so, sir, I took only *the first part* of the novel to battalion office, and the second part I left for the time being in our company office. With the best intentions in the world I thought that when the officer gentlemen had read the first part they would be issued with the second part just like at a library, but suddenly there came the news that we had to go and there was a telegram to the whole battalion that everything superfluous must be put into the regimental stores. And so I asked Mr Vaněk again if he regarded the second part of that novel as superfluous and he said to me that after the unhappy experiences in Serbia, Galicia and Hungary no books of light reading were taken to the front, and those boxes which were put in towns for the collection of newspapers for the soldiers were the only things which were any use, because in the newspapers you could roll tobacco or hay, which is what the soldiers smoke when they are in the trenches. They had already distributed to the battalion the first part of that novel and so we carried the second part to the store.'

Švejk paused and at once added: 'There were all sorts of things in that store, sir, even the Budějovice choirmaster's top hat, the one he wore when he was called up to the regiment...'

'I'll tell you something, Švejk,' said Lieutenant Lukáš with a heavy sigh. 'You obviously haven't an inkling of the consequences of your action. I'm quite sick of calling you a bloody half-wit, but there are really no words to describe your idiocy. When I call you a half-wit I'm really paying you a compliment. You've done something so frightful that the most ghastly crimes you've committed while I've known you are like angels' harp-playing in comparison. If you only knew, Švejk, what you've done.... But you will never learn that.... And should there ever be any mention of these books, then don't you dare let out in your chatter that I said something to you about sending the second part. . . . If the subject should ever come up about what happened to the first and second part, just ignore it. You haven't any idea about anything, you don't know anything, you don't remember anything. Don't you dare involve me in anything, you, you . . .'

Lieutenant Lukáš spoke in such tones as though he had a bout of fever and Švejk used the moment when he stopped speaking to ask innocently: 'Humbly report, sir, please forgive me, but why shall I never learn what I've done that's so frightful? I only venture to ask, sir, so that next time I can avoid such a thing, since it's generally said that a man learns from his errors, like that iron-founder Adamec from Daňkovka, when by mistake he drank hydrochloric acid . . .'

He never finished because Lieutenant Lukáš interrupted his example from life with the words: 'You miserable bastard, you! I shan't explain anything to you. Get back into the van again and tell Baloun that when we come to Budapest he is to bring me in the staff carriage a roll and that liver pâté I have in tin foil in the bottom of my bag. Then tell Vaněk that he's a bloody mule. Three times I've asked him to give me the company's exact complement. And when I needed it today I only had the old schedule from last week.'

'At your orders, sir,' Švejk barked in German and slowly withdrew in the direction of his van.

Lieutenant Lukáš walked along the track thinking: 'I ought to have given him a few on the jaw, but instead I've been gossiping with him as though he were a friend.'

Švejk got solemnly into his van. He felt respect for himself. It did not happen every day that he committed something so frightful that he must never be allowed to learn what it was.

'Quartermaster sergeant-major,' said Švejk, when he was sitting in his place again, 'Lieutenant Lukáš seems to me to be in a very good mood today. He asked me to tell you that you are a bloody mule, because he asked you three times to give him the company's correct complement.'

'Herrgott,' said Vaněk in fury. 'I'll give those platoon sergeants hell. How can I bloody well help it if every lazy bastard of a platoon sergeant does what he likes and doesn't send me the correct complement of his platoon? Have I got to pull the complement out of my hat? That's how it is in our company! That can only happen in the 11th march company. But I suspected it, I knew it. I didn't doubt for a moment that things weren't in order with us. One day four portions are missing in the kitchen. The next there are three too many. If only these bloody swine would at least tell me if someone isn't in hospital. Last week I still had on my list a chap called Nikodem and it was only when it came to the issuing of pay that I learnt that that Nikodem had died of galloping consumption in the hospital at Budějovice. All that

time they had gone on drawing rations for him. We drew a uniform for him but God knows what happened to it. And after all that the lieutenant tells me I'm a bloody mule, when he can't himself put right the mess in his own company.'

Vaněk walked up and down the van in fury: 'If I were company commander! Then everything would have to go like clockwork. I'd keep a check on every man jack of them. The N.C.O.s would have to give me the company's complement twice a day. But what can you do when the N.C.O.s are utterly incompetent. The worst of all in our company is that platoon sergeant Zyka. All he does is to make jokes

and tell stories, and when he's told that Kolařík has been assigned away
from his platoon to the baggage train, he reports to me next day the
same complement, as though Kolařík had gone on loafing about in the
company and in his platoon. And when that happens every day and on
top of that I'm told that I'm a bloody mule. . . . The lieutenant isn't
going to make himself popular this way. The quartermaster sergeant-
major in a company isn't just a lance-corporal whom anyone can use
to wipe his . . .'

Baloun, who was listening with his mouth wide open, now spoke for
Vaněk that lovely word which Vaněk did not get round to saying,
wishing with this to contribute to the conversation.

'You shut your mug,' said the infuriated quartermaster sergeant-
major.

'Listen, Baloun,' said Švejk, 'I've got a message for you too. When
we get to Budapest you're to bring to the lieutenant in his carriage a
roll and that liver pâté which he keeps in tin foil at the bottom of his
bag.'

The giant Baloun desperately swung his long chimpanzee-like arms,
bent his back and remained in this position for some time.

'I haven't got it,' he said in a quiet despairing tone, staring at the
dirty floor of the van.

'I haven't got it,' he repeated jerkily. 'I thought . . . I undid it
before we left . . . I smelt it . . . in case it was spoiled . . .

'I tasted it,' he cried out in such genuine despair that it was quite
clear to everybody what had happened.

'You wolfed it all up, tin foil and all,' said Vaněk, stopping in front
of Baloun. He was grateful that he no longer had to defend his view
that he wasn't a bloody mule, as the lieutenant had conveyed to him,
but that the cause of the unknown factor x (the complement of the
men) had deeper roots in other bloody mules. He felt relieved too that
the subject of the conversation had been changed and been shunted to
the guzzler Baloun and to a new tragic event. Vaněk was seized by a
strong desire to say something unpleasant and moralizing to Baloun.
But he was anticipated in this by the occultist cook, Jurajda, who put
down his beloved book, a translation of the old Indian sutras *Pragnâ –
Paramitâ*, and turned to the crushed Baloun, who was bending all the
more under the weight of fate: 'Baloun, you've got to look after yourself and see you don't lose confidence in yourself and your destiny.
You ought not to attribute to yourself what is the merit of others.

Whenever you find yourself faced with a similar problem which you have eaten up, always ask yourself: "In what relation does the liver pâté stand to me?"'

Švejk considered it fitting to round off these reflections with a practical example: 'You yourself, Baloun, recently said that they were going to slaughter and smoke meat at your home, and that as soon as you know the place of your destination and the number of the field post, they are going to send you a piece of ham. Now imagine they sent that ham from the field post to us in the company and we all of us, including the quartermaster sergeant-major, cut off a slice. Let's say we enjoyed it so much that we cut another slice, so that that ham would have incurred the same fate as a postman I knew called Kozel. He had bone decay, so they first cut off his leg under the ankle and then under the knee, and then his thigh, and if he hadn't died in time they'd have cut the whole of him like a broken pencil. And so just imagine, Baloun, that we had wolfed your ham like you did the lieutenant's pâté.'

The giant Baloun looked sadly at all of them.

'It's only thanks to my efforts and my merits,' said the quartermaster sergeant-major to Baloun, 'that you have remained the lieutenant's batman. You were to have been transferred to the medical corps to carry the wounded from the battles. At Dukla our medical corps went out three times for a wounded ensign who got shot in the belly in front of the barbed-wire entanglements, and all of them remained there with their heads shot. Only the fourth pair managed to bring him in, but before they had got him to the first-aid post he'd given up the ghost.'

Baloun could no longer control himself and sobbed loudly.

'Aren't you ashamed?' said Švejk with contempt, 'you, a soldier . . .'

'But I wasn't made for the army,' Baloun lamented. 'It's true I'm a glutton and always unsatisfied, but it's only because I've been torn away from respectable life. We have this in the family. My late papa once wagered in a pub at Protivín that at one go he would eat fifty smoked sausages and two loaves of bread, and he won. Once in a wager I ate four geese and two basins full of dumplings and cabbage. It happened to me at home that after lunch I suddenly felt I'd like to have just a tiny bit more. So I used to go into the larder, cut off a piece of pork, send for a jug of beer and in a minute I'd devoured two kilos of smoked pork. I had at home an old servant, Vomel, and he always warned me not to get so grand, not to stuff myself so full. He remembered how his grandfather told him a long time ago about a gluttonous peasant like that. And how later when there was a war, there was no crop for eight long years, and they used to make bread out of straw and of some odds and ends which were left from the flax seeds; and it was a red-letter day for them when they could crumble a little curd into their milk, when there was no bread. And immediately the famine started that peasant died within a week, because his stomach was not used to such frightful misery . . .'

Baloun raised his anguished face: 'But I believe that even if God punishes people, he doesn't abandon them.'

'God the Father brought gluttons into the world and God the Father will look after them,' observed Švejk. 'You've already been tied up once and now you deserve to be sent to the very front line. When I was the lieutenant's batman he could rely upon me in everything and it never occurred to him that I would have wolfed up anything of his. When something special was issued he always said to me: "You can have it, Švejk," or: "Well, I'm not so keen on it. Give me a bit and do what you like with the rest." And when we were in Prague and he sometimes sent me to a restaurant to get lunch for him, in case he should perhaps think the portion I was bringing him was small because I'd wolfed up half of it on the way, whenever the portion seemed to me to be small I bought an extra one out of my last heller so that he could have enough and not think badly of me. But one day he got to know about it. I always had to bring him the menu from the restaurant and he chose what he wanted from it. And that day he chose stuffed pigeon. And I thought when they gave me only a half that perhaps the lieutenant might think I'd guzzled the other half myself, so I bought an extra portion with my own money and brought such an enormous helping that Lieutenant Šeba, who was trying to find some lunch that day and came to see my lieutenant just before noon, had a good meal out of it as well. And when he'd finished his lunch he said: "Don't tell me that's a single portion. Nowhere in the world would you get on a menu a whole stuffed pigeon. If I manage to get some money today I'll send to that restaurant of yours for some lunch. But tell me honestly, it's a double portion, isn't it?" The lieutenant asked me in his presence to confirm that he had given me money only for one portion, because he had no idea that Lieutenant Šeba was coming. I answered that he had given me money for an ordinary lunch. "So you can see for yourself," said the lieutenant, "this is nothing special. Last time Švejk brought me two whole legs of goose for lunch. Just imagine:

noodle soup, beef with anchovy sauce, two legs of goose, dumplings and cabbage piled up to the ceiling and palatschinken!"'

'Oh, yum-yum-yum-yum!' said Baloun, smacking his lips.

Švejk continued: 'That was the big snag. Of course next day Lieutenant Šeba really did send his batman to that restaurant of ours to get lunch, and he brought him as the main dish only a tiny dab of

chicken pilaf, about as much as a six-week-old baby does in his swaddling clothes, in other words about two spoonfuls. And Lieutenant Šeba accused him of wolfing up half of it himself. But he said he was innocent. And Lieutenant Šeba socked him across the jaw and held me up as an example. He said that the portions I brought Lieutenant Lukáš were decent ones. And so then the next day that innocent soldier, who'd been socked across the jaw, went to the restaurant where he'd gone to get the lunch and asked a lot of questions. And he told it all to his master who told it in his turn to my lieutenant. One evening I was sitting with my newspaper and reading the news from the battlefield reported by the enemy's staffs, when my lieutenant came in deadly pale and went for me at once, telling me to say how many of these double portions I had paid for in the restaurant, that he knew all about it, that it was no use my denying it and that he had long known I was a bloody half-wit but it had never occurred to him that I was a complete lunatic. I had disgraced him so much, he said, that his one desire was to shoot

first me and then himself. "Sir," I said to him, "when you accepted me that very first day you said that every batman was a thief and a low bastard. And when in this restaurant they really gave such small portions of the main dish, you might have thought that I was really one of those low bastards too and that I'd wolfed it all up . . ." '

'My God in heaven,' whispered Baloun. He bent over Lieutenant Lukáš's suitcase and took it with him to the back of the van.

'Then Lieutenant Lukáš began to forage about in all his pockets,' Švejk continued, 'and when that produced nothing he searched in his waistcoat and gave me his silver watch. He was so moved. "When I get my pay, Švejk," he said, "write down how much I owe you. Take this watch as well. And next time don't be so silly." And once after that we were both of us in such straits that I had to take the watch to the pawnbroker's . . .'

'What are you doing there in the back, Baloun?' asked Vaněk.

Instead of answering, the unhappy Baloun began to choke. He had in fact opened the suitcase and was stuffing himself with Lieutenant Lukáš's last roll . . .

Another military train went through the station without stopping. It was crammed from top to bottom with the men of the Deutschmeister regiment, who were being sent to the Serbian front. They had not yet recovered from their enthusiasm at parting with Vienna and had been bawling all the way since without pausing for breath:

> 'Prince Eugène, the noble knight,
> Sought to win for his Emperor's might
> The town and fortress of Belgrade.
> And so he ordered a bridge to be built,
> Over which to ride full tilt
> Into the town with his cavalcade.'

A corporal with an aggressively twisted moustache, leaning out and supporting himself with his elbows on the men who swung their legs out of the van, was beating time and bawling lustily:

> 'And when the mighty bridge was done,
> And man and horse and cart and gun
> Could freely pass o'er the Danube stream,
> They pitched their camps by Semlin's gate
> And sealed the Serbian garrison's fate.'

But then he suddenly lost his balance, flew out of the wagon and with the full force of his flight hit his stomach on the points-lever, on which he remained transfixed and hanging, while the train went on and while in the rear vans they were singing another song:

> 'Count Radetsky, noble sword,
> Swore to sweep the savage horde
> Out of treacherous Lombardy.
> But in Verona he tarried long
> Till reinforcements came along.
> Then no braver Count than he . . .'

Spiked on the stupid points-lever, the bellicose corporal was already dead and a young soldier from the station command was soon standing guard over him with fixed bayonet. He took his responsibility very seriously, stood erect at the points and assumed a triumphant expression, as though the spiking of the corporal on the lever had been his own work.

He was a Hungarian and when the men from the train of the march battalion of the 91st regiment came to have a look he bawled in his mother tongue over the whole track: '*Nem szabat!* Not allowed! Military commission, not allowed!'

'He's had his war,' said the good soldier Švejk, who was also among the curious sightseers, 'and he has the advantage that having a bit of iron in his belly, everybody at least knows where he's buried. It's just on the railway line and you don't have to hunt for his grave all over the battlefields.

'He spiked himself very neatly,' said Švejk, walking round the corporal from the other side and observing him with a professional eye. 'His guts are in his trousers.'

'*Nem szabat, nem szabat!*' shouted the young Hungarian soldier. 'The Military Commission of the station. Not allowed!'

Behind Švejk a severe voice could be heard: 'What are you doing here?'

In front of him stood Cadet Biegler. Švejk saluted.

'Humbly report, we're looking at the late lamented, sir.'

'And what kind of agitation are you up to? What's your business here?'

'Humbly report, sir,' Švejk replied with dignified calm, 'I'm not up to a "gitation" of any kind.'

Behind the cadet several soldiers burst out laughing and Vaněk stepped forward and stood in front of him.

'Sir,' he said, 'the lieutenant sent the orderly Švejk here to tell him what had happened. I was just now in the staff carriage and the battalion orderly Matušič is looking for you with orders from the battalion commander. You are to go at once to Captain Ságner.'

Shortly afterwards the signal to embark was sounded and everybody went off to their vans.

As he went off with Švejk, Vaněk said: 'When there are crowds of people about, do for heaven's sake give up your brainwaves, Švejk. It could get you into real hot water. As that corporal belonged to the

Deutschmeisters they might have made out that you were glad about it. That Biegler's a frightful Czech-eater.'

'But I haven't said anything at all,' answered Švejk in a tone which banished all doubt, 'except that the corporal had spiked himself very neatly and his guts were in his trousers. . . . He could have . . .'

'Well, don't let's talk about it any more, Švejk.' And Vaněk spat.

'As a matter of fact it makes no difference,' Švejk observed once more, 'where exactly his guts come out of his belly for His Imperial Majesty. He did his duty all the same. . . . He could have . . .'

'Listen, Švejk,' Vaněk interrupted him, 'look how Battalion Orderly Matušič is rushing towards the staff carriage. I'm surprised he hasn't fallen over on to the track.'

Shortly before that there had been a very sharp exchange between Captain Ságner and the zealous Cadet Biegler.

'I'm surprised, Cadet Biegler,' said Captain Ságner, 'that you didn't come and inform me at once that those fifteen dekas of Hungarian salami were not being issued. I had to go out myself and find out why the men were returning from the stores. And the officers too, as though an order wasn't an order. Surely you heard me say: "To the stores by platoons, company by company." That meant that if we couldn't get anything at the stores then the men were to return to the vans by platoons, company by company. I ordered you, Cadet Biegler, to make sure that discipline was maintained, but you let everything slide. You were only too glad not to have to bother about counting up portions of salami and as I saw from the window you calmly went to have a look at the Deutschmeisters' corporal who'd spiked himself. And when I had you summoned afterwards you had nothing better to do than to drivel with your cadetish ideas about how you went to find out whether by any chance anyone was up to any agitation near that spiked corporal . . .'

'Humbly report, sir, the orderly of the 11th company, Švejk . . .'

'Shut up about Švejk,' shouted Captain Ságner. 'Don't imagine, Cadet Biegler, that you're going to be allowed to intrigue against Lieutenant Lukáš. We sent Švejk there. . . . You're looking at me as if you thought I had my knife into you. . . . Well, yes, I do have my knife into you, Cadet Biegler. . . . If you don't know how to respect your superior officer, if you try to make a fool of him, then I'll make the war so hot for you that you'll never forget Raab station as long as you live, Cadet Biegler. Swanking about your knowledge of theory! . . . Wait till we get to the front . . . and I order you on officers' patrol through the barbed-wire entanglements. . . . And what about your report? You didn't even submit a report when you came. . . . Not even in theory, Cadet Biegler . . .'

'Humbly report, sir,[1] instead of fifteen dekas of Hungarian salami the men received two picture postcards each. Here you are, sir . . .'

Cadet Biegler handed the battalion commander two of the picture postcards which had been issued by the Office of War Archives in Vienna, where the infantry general, Wojnowich, was in command. On one side there was a caricature of a Russian soldier, a Russian muzhik with a full beard, who was being embraced by a skeleton. Under the caricature was the German text:

'The day when perfidious Russia expires will be a day of salvation for the whole of our Monarchy.'

The other picture postcard came from the German Reich. It was a present from the Germans to the Austro-Hungarian warriors.

On the top there was an inscription: '*Viribus unitis*', and below a picture showing Sir Edward Grey hanging on a gallows. Beneath him were an Austrian and a German soldier saluting gaily.

The poem underneath came from a book by Greinz, *The Iron Fist*, containing jokes against our enemies. The Reich papers wrote that Greinz's verses were like blows with a lash and were full of true un-bridled humour and unsurpassable wit.

The text under the gallows in translation was as follows:

GREY

On these gallows, you might say,
Ought to swing Sir Edward Grey.
It's high time that he did so.
At the same time you should know
That no oak would lend its wood
For the hanging of this Jude.
Aspens tremble on the tree.
They're from France as you can see.

Captain Ságner had not yet finished reading these verses of 'un-bridled humour and unsurpassable wit' when the battalion orderly Matušič charged into the staff carriage.

He had been sent by Captain Ságner to the telegraph exchange at

1. All conversations between the officers, of course, take place in German. (Author's note.)

the station military command in case by any chance there were any other instructions, and he brought with him a telegram from the brigade. It was unnecessary to have recourse to any key for the ciphers. The telegram read quite simply, unciphered: 'Quickly finish cooking and march to Sokal.' Captain Ságner shook his head thoughtfully.

'Humbly report, sir,' said Matušič, 'the station commander asks if he could speak to you. There's another telegram there.'

There then followed a conversation of a very confidential nature between the station commander and Captain Ságner.

The first telegram had to be delivered when the battalion was at the station in Raab, although its contents were very surprising: 'Quickly finish cooking and march to Sokal.' It was addressed unciphered to the march battalion of the 91st regiment with a copy for the march battalion of the 75th regiment, which was still behind. The signature was correct: 'Brigade Commander, Ritter von Herbert.'

'Strictly confidential, sir,' said the station commander mysteriously. 'Here's a secret telegram from your division. Your brigade commander has gone mad. He's been carried off to Vienna after having dispatched from the brigade several dozen telegrams like that in all directions. In Budapest you'll certainly find another telegram. All his telegrams should of course be cancelled, but we haven't received any instructions to this effect yet. I have, as I say, only the order from the division that unciphered telegrams should be disregarded. I have to deliver them because on that point I have not received any answer from *my* authorities. Through *my* authorities I have made inquiries of Army Corps Command and as a result proceedings are being taken against me ...

'I'm a regular officer of the old Engineers,' he added. 'I took part in the construction of our strategic railway in Galicia. ...

'Sir,' he said after a moment, 'for us old rankers it's only the front! Today in the Ministry of War civil engineers from the railways with one-year volunteer examinations are as plentiful as dogs. ... Well, after all, in a quarter of an hour you've got to go on. ... I only remember that once in the cadet school in Prague as a cadet of a senior year I helped you on to the horizontal bar. Then we were neither of us allowed out. You fought then with the Germans in the class.[1] Lukáš was there with you too. You used both of you to be the best of friends. When we got the telegram with the list of the officers of the

---

[1]. In the German conversation which these two carried on: 'At that time you fought with the German fellow cadets too.' (Author's note.)

march battalion who were passing through the station I remembered perfectly.... It's quite a number of years ago.... I liked Cadet Lukáš very much then ...'

The whole conversation made a very painful impression on Captain Ságner. He recognized perfectly well the man who was talking to him and who had led the opposition against 'Austrianism' in the cadet school. Later their preoccupation with their careers knocked all this out of their heads. The most unpleasant thing for him was the mention of Lieutenant Lukáš, who for some reason or other had been always passed over as compared with him.

'Lieutenant Lukáš,' he said emphatically, 'is a very good officer. When is the train leaving?'

The station commander looked at his watch. 'In six minutes' time.'

'I'm going,' said Ságner.

'I thought you'd say something to me, Ságner.'

'All right, then, *nazdar!*'[1] answered Ságner and went out in front of the building of the station command.

When, before the departure of the train, Captain Ságner returned to the staff carriage he found all the officers in their places. They were playing Frische Viere in groups. Only Cadet Biegler was not playing.

He was looking through a heap of unfinished manuscripts about war scenes, because he wanted to make a name for himself not only on the battlefield but also as a literary phenomenom describing the war events. The man with the funny wings and the 'fish tail' wanted to be an outstanding writer on war topics. His literary attempts began with very promising titles, which reflected the militarism of those times, but which were not yet properly worked out, so that on the sheets of paper could only be found the names of the works which were going to emerge:

'The Characters of the Warriors of the Great War. – Who Began the War? – The Policy of Austria-Hungary and the Origin of the World War. – War Notes. – Austria-Hungary and the World War. – Lessons from the War. – Popular Lecture on the Outbreak of the War. – Military Political Reflections. – The Glorious Day of Austria-Hungary. – Slav Imperialism and the World War. – Documents from the War. – Documents for the History of the World War. – A Diary of the World War. – A Daily Survey of the World War. – The First World War. – Our Dynasty in the World War. – Peoples of the Austro-Hungarian

1. Greeting used by Czech patriots.

Monarchy under Arms. – The World Struggle for Power. – My Experiences in the World War. – The Chronicle of My War Campaign. – How the Enemies of Austria-Hungary Fight. – Who Will Be the Victors? – Our Officers and Our Men. – Memorable Acts of My Soldiers. – From the Times of the Great War. – On the Turmoil of Battle. – The Book of Austro-Hungarian Heroes. – The Iron Brigade. – A Collection of My Writings from the Front. – The Heroes of Our March Battalion. – Handbook for Soldiers in the Field.– Days of Battles and Days of Victory.– What I Have Seen and Experienced in the Field. – In the Trenches. – An Officer Relates . . . – Forward with the Sons of Austria-Hungary! – Enemy Aeroplanes and Our Infantry. – After the Battle. – Our Artillery. – Faithful Sons of the Fatherland. – Come All the Devils in the World against Us . . . – Defensive and Offensive War. – Blood and Iron. – Victory or Death. – Our Heroes in Captivity.'

When Captain Ságner came up to Cadet Biegler and scrutinized everything, he asked why he had done this and what was he trying to do.

Cadet Biegler answered with genuine enthusiasm that every title meant a book which he would write – as many books as there were titles.

'If I should fall in battle I should like a memorial to remain after me, sir. My model is the German professor, Udo Kraft. He was born in the year 1870, volunteered for service now in the world war and fell on 22 August 1914 at Anloy. Before his death he published a book: *Self-Education in Dying for the Emperor*.'[1]

Captain Ságner took Cadet Biegler to the window.

'Show me what else you have, Cadet Biegler. Your activities are of great interest to me,' Captain Ságner said with irony. 'What's that notebook you've put under your tunic?'

'That's nothing, sir,' Cadet Biegler replied with a childish blush. 'Please see for yourself.'

The notebook had the following title:

Diagrams of the most outstanding and glorious battles
Of the troops of the Austro-Hungarian army
Compiled according to historical research
By the Imperial and Royal Officer Adolf Biegler.
Furnished with comments and explanations
By the Imperial and Royal Officer Adolf Biegler.

1. Udo Kraft: *Selbsterziehung zum Tod für Kaiser*, C. F. Amelang Publishing House, Leipzig. (Author's note.)

The diagrams were frightfully simple.

From the Battle of Nördlingen, 6 September 1634, to the Battle of Senta, 11 September 1697, the Battle of Caldiero, 31 October 1805, the Battle of Aspern, 22 May 1809, the Battle of the Nations at Leipzig in 1813, the Battle of St Lucia in May 1848 and the Battle of Trutnov, 27 June 1866, up to the taking of Sarajevo, 19 August 1878.

The diagrams and blueprints of the plans of these battles were all the same. Everywhere Cadet Biegler had drawn rectangles, blank on one side and shaded on the other representing the enemy. On both sides were a left flank, a centre and a right flank. Then behind came the reserves with arrows here and there. The Battle of Nördlingen like the Battle of Sarajevo looked like the positioning of players on the field at a football match at the beginning of the game. The arrows seemed to be indicating in which direction each side was to kick the ball.

This at once struck Captain Ságner who asked: 'Cadet Biegler, do you play football?'

Biegler blushed still more and nervously blinked so that he gave the impression that he was going to cry.

Captain Ságner smilingly turned the pages of the notebook further and stopped at a note on the diagram of the Battle of Trutnov during the Austro-Prussian war.

Cadet Biegler had written: 'The Battle of Trutnov should never have been fought, because the mountainous terrain made the deployment of General Mazzucheli's division impossible. It was threatened by powerful Prussian columns which were stationed on the high ground surrounding the left flank of our division.'

'And so in your view,' said Captain Ságner with a smile, returning the notebook to Cadet Biegler, 'the Battle of Trutnov should only have been fought if Trutnov had been on level ground, you Benedek[1] from Budějovice.

'Cadet Biegler, it's very nice of you during the short time of your stay in the ranks of the army to have tried to probe into strategy, except that in your case it's like little boys playing soldiers and giving each other the titles of generals. You have certainly promoted yourself marvellously quickly. It's charming! Imperial and Royal Officer Adolf Biegler! Before we get to Budapest you'll be a field marshal. The day before yesterday you were still somewhere at home with your papa weighing cow-hides. Imperial and Royal Lieutenant Adolf Biegler! Why, man, you aren't even an officer yet. You're only a cadet. You hang in the air between ensign and N.C.O. You're as far from being able to call yourself an officer as a lance-corporal is when in a pub somewhere he lets himself be called staff sergeant-major.

'Listen, Lukáš,' he said, turning to the lieutenant, 'you have Cadet Biegler in your company. Well, make it hot for the lad. He signs himself "officer". Let him win his spurs in battle. When there's a cannonade and we attack, let the brave lad and his platoon cut the barbed-wire entanglements. By the way, Zykán asked to be remembered to you. He's station commander in Raab.'

Cadet Biegler, perceiving that the conversation with him was over, saluted and, purple in the face, marched through the carriage, until he found himself at the very end in the cross corridor.

Like a sleep-walker he opened the door of the W.C. and looking on

1. General Benedek led the Austrian army during its defeat by the Prussians in 1866.

the German and Hungarian inscriptions: 'The W.C. is only to be used while the train is in motion', began to whimper, sob and finally weep silently. Then he took down his trousers. . . . He strained hard, wiping away his tears. After that he used up his notebook with the title: 'Diagrams of the most outstanding and glorious battles of the troops of the Austro-Hungarian army, compiled by the Imperial and Royal Officer Adolf Biegler'. It disappeared dishonoured into the hole. Falling on the track it fluttered between the rails under the disappearing military train.

Cadet Biegler washed his red eyes in the basin of the lavatory and went out into the corridor. He told himself that he must be strong, bloody strong. His head and stomach had been aching since the morning.

He went past the last compartment where the battalion orderly, Matušič, was playing the Viennese game of 'Schnapsen' (sixty-six) with the batman of the battalion commander Batzer.

He looked into the open door of the compartment and gave a cough. They turned round and went on playing.

'Don't you know what is required of you?' Cadet Biegler asked.

'I couldn't help it,' answered Captain Ságner's batman, Batzer, in his frightful German from Kašperské Hory. 'I ran out of trumps.

'It was required of me to play clubs, high clubs and then at once afterwards my King of Spades. . . . That's what I should have done.'

Cadet Biegler did not say a word more and crawled into his corner. When later Ensign Pleschner came to offer him a drink from his bottle of cognac which he had won at cards, he was surprised to see that he was busily reading Professor Udo Kraft's book: *Self-Education in Dying for the Emperor*.

Before they reached Budapest, Cadet Biegler was so drunk that he leaned out of the window of the carriage and kept shouting out to the deserted countryside: 'On, on, ye brave! In God's name, on!'

After that on the orders of Captain Ságner Matušič dragged him off into the compartment, where he and Batzer laid him down on the bench, and Cadet Biegler had the following dream:

CADET BIEGLER'S DREAM ON THE WAY TO BUDAPEST

He had been awarded the *Signum Laudis* and the Iron Cross, was now a major and was going to inspect a detachment of a brigade which had been assigned to him. He could not understand why he was still only a major when he had a whole brigade under him. He suspected that he was to be promoted major-general and that the word 'general' had got lost somewhere in the rush in the field post.

He had to laugh to himself when he thought how in the train on the way to the front Captain Ságner had threatened him with having to go and cut through barbed-wire entanglements. Anyway on his proposal at the division both Captain Ságner and Lieutenant Lukáš had been long ago transferred to another regiment, another division and another army corps.

Someone had also told him how both of them had perished miserably in a bog somewhere while running away.

When he went by car to the front line to inspect the detachment of his brigade everything was clear to him. He had in fact been specially sent from the General Staff of the army.

Soldiers marched past and sang a song which he had read in a collection of Austrian soldiers' songs: 'Our duty'.

> 'Brothers, all your valour show!
> Hold together, crush the foe!
> Let the Emperor's banners fly . . .'

The landscape had the same character as on the pictures in *The Vienna Illustrated*.

On the right side near a barn, artillery could be seen firing at the enemy's trenches beside the road along which the car was travelling. On the left stood a house from which shots were being fired, while the enemy were trying to break open the door with rifle butts. By the side of the road an enemy plane was on fire. On the horizon could be seen cavalry and a burning village, and then the trenches of a march battalion with a small hill, where machine-guns were shooting at the enemy. Farther on the enemy trenches stretched beside the road. The chauffeur drove on with him along the road in the direction of the enemy.

He shouted through his speaking-tube to the chauffeur: 'Don't you know where we're going? That's where the enemy is.'

But the chauffeur answered calmly:

'General, this is the only decent route. The road is in good condition. The tyres would never hold out on those side lanes.'

The nearer they came to the enemy positions the more violent became the fire. Shells blew up the avenue of plum trees over the trenches on both sides of the road.

But the chauffeur calmly answered through the speaking-tube:

'This is an excellent road, general. We're doing swimmingly. If we turned off through the fields our tyres would burst.

'Look, general,' the chauffeur shouted into the speaking-tube, 'this road is so well built that not even a 30½-centimetre mortar could do anything to us. It's like a threshing-floor, but on those stony roads in the fields our tyres would burst. In any case we can't go back now, general!'

'Bzzz – zumm!' Biegler heard, and the car made a tremendous bound.

'Didn't I tell you, general,' the chauffeur roared into the speaking-tube, 'that it's a devilishly well built road? A thirty-eighter has just exploded in front of us, but there's still no hole. The road's like a threshing-floor. But going over the fields would mean the end of the tyres. Now they're firing at us from a distance of four kilometres.'

'But where are we going?'

'That remains to be seen,' answered the chauffeur. 'As long as the road remains as it is, I take responsibility for everything.'

A bound, an enormous bound and the car stopped.

'General,' cried the chauffeur, 'haven't you got a staff map?'

General Biegler lit his electric torch. He saw that he had a staff map on his knees. But it was a naval map of the Heligoland coast from 1864 in the Austro-Prussian war against Denmark over Schleswig-Holstein.

'There's a cross-road here,' said the chauffeur. 'Both the roads lead to the enemy positions. What I am concerned about is a decent road, so that my tyres don't get ruined, general . . . I'm responsible for the staff car . . .'

Then came an explosion, a deafening explosion and there were stars as big as wheels. The Milky Way was as thick as cream.

Biegler was floating through the universe on the seat beside the chauffeur. The car had been cut in two right in front of the back seat as though by scissors. Only the bellicose, aggressive front part of it remained.

'What good luck that you showed me the map from behind,' said the chauffeur. 'You flew towards me and the other part exploded. It was a forty-twoer. . . . I knew at once that as soon as there was a cross-road the road wouldn't be worth a damn. After the thirty-eighter it could only have been a forty-twoer. Nothing bigger has yet been produced, general.'

'Where are you driving to?'

'We're flying to heaven, general, and must avoid the comets. They're worse than the forty-twoers.

'Now we've got Mars underneath us,' said the chauffeur after a long silence.

Biegler felt at ease again.

'Do you know the history of the Battle of the Nations at Leipzig?' he asked, 'when Field Marshal Prince Schwarzenberg marched on Liebertkovice on 14 October 1813 and when on 16 October there was the Battle of Lindenau? Do you know the battles of General Merweldt, when the Austrian army was in Wachau and when Leipzig fell on 19 October?'

At that moment the chauffeur said gravely: 'General, we've just reached the gates of heaven. You must get out, sir. We can't drive in through the gates of heaven. There's a great crowd here. They're all soldiers.'

'Just run over some of them,' he shouted at the chauffeur. 'They're sure to get out of our way.'

And leaning out of the car, he shouted out in German: 'Look out, you pack of swine! What idiotic brutes they are! They see a general and won't do "eyes right".'

The chauffeur calmed him down: 'It's difficult, general. Most of them have their heads blown off.'

It was only then that General Biegler noticed that those who were pressing to get in through the gates of heaven were various disabled soldiers who had lost some parts of their bodies in the war and carried them with them in their rucksacks – heads, arms and legs. A righteous artilleryman, who was pressing at the gates of heaven in a torn greatcoat, had his whole belly and lower extremities folded up in his pack. From another pack, which belonged to a righteous Landwehr man, half of his hind quarters which he had lost at Lwów stared out at General Biegler.

'That's for the sake of order,' said the chauffeur again, driving through the dense crowds. 'It's certainly because of the divine super-inspection.'

At the gates of heaven people were allowed in only after giving the countersign, which came to General Biegler at once: 'For God and the Emperor.' The car drove into paradise.

'General,' said an officer-angel with wings, when they went past the barracks of angel-recruits, 'you must report to supreme command.'

They drove on past a parade ground, where it swarmed with angel-recruits learning to shout: 'Alleluia.'

They drove past a group, where a red-haired angel-corporal was just pitching into a clumsy angel-recruit, thumping him in the belly with his fist and roaring at him: 'Open your mug a bit wider, you swine of Bethlehem. Is that how you shout "Alleluia"? Just as though you had a dumpling in your trap! I'd like to know what bloody ox that was that let cattle like you into paradise. Try it once more. . . . Hlahlehuhya? What, you bastard, so you think we're going to let you whine through your nose here in paradise. . . . Try it once again, you bloody cedar of Lebanon, you.'

They drove on and behind them for a long time they heard the frightened caterwauling of the snuffling angel-recruit: 'Hla – hle – hlu – hja', and the bellowing of the corporal angel: 'A – lle – lu – ja, a – lle – lu – ja, you bloody Jordan cow!'

And then there was an enormous glow over a building as big as the Mariánské barracks in České Budějovice and there were two planes above, one on the left and the other on the right, and in the middle

between them was drawn an enormous banner with the colossal inscription:

IMPERIAL AND ROYAL HEADQUARTERS
OF THE LORD

General Biegler was taken from the car by two angels in the uniform of the field gendarmerie. They took him by the collar and led him up to the first storey of the building.

'Behave yourself in the presence of the Lord,' they said to him, when he was upstairs in front of a door, and pushed him inside.

In the middle of the room, on the walls of which there hung portraits of Franz Joseph and Wilhelm, the heir to the Austrian throne, Karl Franz Joseph, General Viktor Dankel, the Archduke Friedrich and the Chief of the General Staff, Konrad von Hötzendorf, stood the Lord.

'Cadet Biegler,' said the Lord with emphasis, 'don't you recognize me? I am your former Captain Ságner from the 11th march company.'

Biegler was struck dumb.

'Cadet Biegler,' said the Lord again, 'who gave you the right to appropriate for yourself the title of major-general? Who gave you the right, Cadet Biegler, to drive in a staff car on the road through the enemy positions?'

'Humbly report . . .'

'Shut your mug, Cadet Biegler, when the Lord speaks to you.'

'Humbly report,' Biegler blurted out once more.

'And so you're not going to keep your mug shut?' the Lord bawled at him. Then he opened the door and shouted: 'Two angels, come here!'

Two angels entered with rifles hung over their left wings. Biegler recognized in them Matušič and Batzer.

And the lips of the Lord pronounced the words: 'Throw him into the rears!'

Cadet Biegler was falling down somewhere. There was a ghastly stench.

Opposite the sleeping Cadet Biegler, Matušič was sitting with Batzer, Captain Ságner's orderly. They were still playing 'sixty-six'.

'The bastard stinks like a codfish,' remarked Batzer, who observed with interest how the sleeping Cadet Biegler was wriggling gingerly. 'He must have done something. . . .'

'That can happen to anybody,' said Matušič philosophically. 'Leave him alone. You're not going to change his clothes anyhow. Go on and deal instead.'

The glow of the lights above Budapest came into view. A searchlight was moving about above the Danube.

Cadet Biegler was already having another dream, because he said in German in his sleep: 'Tell my brave army that they have built in my heart an imperishable monument of love and gratitude.'

Because, as he said this, he began to fidget again, Batzer caught a strong whiff in his nose. Spitting, he observed: 'He stinks like a lat cleaner, like a shitted-up lat cleaner.'

But Cadet Biegler began to wriggle all the more restlessly and his

new dream was exceedingly fantastic. He was defending Linz in the War of the Austrian Succession.

He saw redoubts, entrenchments and palisades around the town. His G.H.Q. had been turned into an enormous hospital. All around there were wounded lying about and holding their bellies. Below the palisades of the town of Linz the French dragoons of Napoleon I were riding by.

And he, the commander of the town, was standing over this havoc and holding himself by the belly too, shouting at a Frenchman who had come to parley: 'Tell your Emperor that I refuse to yield . . .'

And then it was as though his bellyache had suddenly stopped and he was rushing with his battalion over the palisades out of the town on the road to glory and victory. He saw Lieutenant Lukáš being dealt a blow on the chest by a French dragoon's sword. The blow was really meant for him, Biegler, the defender of beleaguered Linz.

Lieutenant Lukáš was dying at his feet and crying out in German:

'A man like you, colonel, is much more use than a completely useless lieutenant!'

Overcome with emotion the defender of Linz turned away from the dying man. At that moment a piece of shrapnel flew at him and hit him in the muscles of his buttocks.

Biegler mechanically reached with his hands to the seat of his trousers and felt something damp. There was something sticky on his fingers. He shrieked: 'Ambulance! Ambulance!' and fell off his horse . . .

Batzer and Matušič lifted Cadet Biegler up from the floor, where he had fallen from the bench, and put him back in his place again.

Then Matušič went to Captain Ságner and told him that queer things were happening to Cadet Biegler.

'It's probably not after the cognac,' he said. 'It's more likely to be cholera. Cadet Biegler drank water at every station. At Mošon I saw that he . . .'

'Cholera doesn't work as quickly as that, Matušič. Tell the doctor in the next compartment to go and have a look at him.'

The battalion had had assigned to it a 'war doctor', the old medico and former German student, Welfer. He knew how to drink and brawl and at the same time had medicine at his fingertips. He had gone through the medical faculties of various university towns in Austria-Hungary and had practised in the most diverse hospitals, but he never took his doctorate for the simple reason that in the will which his uncle left to his heirs it was stipulated that the medical student, Friedrich Welfer, was to be paid a yearly grant until he obtained his doctor's qualifications.

This grant was about four times as much as the salary of a junior doctor in a hospital and Welfer did his honourable best to postpone taking a doctorate till the Greek calends.

The heirs were furious. They declared him an imbecile, and tried to foist wealthy brides on him so as to get rid of him. But to annoy them all the more, Welfer, who was a member of about twelve German student clubs, published in Vienna, Leipzig and Berlin one or two collections of quite decent poems. He contributed to *Simplicissimus* and went on studying as if nothing had happened.

But then came the war, which was a shameful stab in the back for him.

The student of medicine, Friedrich Welfer, the poet and author of the collections, *Laughing Songs*, *Tankard and Learning* and *Fairy Tales and Parables*, was taken off to the war without further ado and one of the inheritors in the Ministry of War saw to it that the valiant medico was awarded a 'war doctorate'. It was done by correspondence. He had to fill out a questionnaire and everywhere wrote down the stereotyped answer in German: 'Kiss my arse!' After three days he was informed by the colonel that he had been awarded the Diploma of Doctor of General Medicine, that he had long ago been ripe for a doctorate, that the chief staff doctor would assign him to the reserve hospital and that rapid advancement would depend upon his conduct. The colonel added that it was true that he had had duels with officers in various university towns and that this was well known, but that now there was a war on and it was all forgotten.

The author of the collection of poems, *Tankard and Learning*, bit his lip and went off to the army.

Certain cases came to light where the doctor had behaved unusually indulgently to soldier patients, prolonging their sojourn in the hospital as long as possible at a time when the mottos were: 'Rather peg out in the trenches than hang about in hospital' and 'Rather peg out in the front line than in hospital.' As a result Welfer was sent with the 11th march battalion to the front.

The regular officers in the battalion looked upon him as an inferior creature. The reserve officers took no notice of him either and did not make friends with him, for fear that the gulf between them and the regular officers should grow wider.

Captain Ságner naturally felt himself frightfully superior to this former student of medicine who, during the long time of his studies, had slashed a number of officers with his sabre. When the 'war doctor' went past him he did not even honour him with a glance but went on talking to Lieutenant Lukáš about something quite unimportant, such as for instance that vegetable marrows were grown around Budapest. Lieutenant Lukáš answered that when he was in his third year as a cadet he went with some friends in mufti to Slovakia and visited an evangelical vicar, a Slovak. He served marrow with the roast pork and afterwards poured them out wine, saying:

> 'Marrow's a swine
> And likes plenty of wine.'

As a result of this Lieutenant Lukáš felt frightfully insulted.[1]

'We shan't see much of Budapest,' said Captain Ságner. 'They're taking us round it. According to the schedule we should stay here two hours.'

'I think they're shunting the vans,' answered Lieutenant Lukáš. 'We're coming on to the transit siding. Military transport station.'

At that moment the 'war doctor' went by.

'It's nothing,' he said with a smile. 'Those gentlemen who aspire in the course of time to become army officers and who already in the officers' club in Bruck boasted their knowledge of history and strategy ought to be warned that it is dangerous to eat at one go a whole consignment of sweets which their mummy has sent them at the front. Cadet Biegler, who, as he has confessed to me, has eaten thirty cream rolls since we left Bruck and has only drunk boiled water everywhere on the stations, captain, reminds me of a verse of Schiller's: ". . . Who speaks of . . ."'

'Listen, doctor,' Captain Ságner interrupted him. 'It's nothing to do with Schiller. What is in fact the matter with Cadet Biegler?'

The 'war doctor' smiled. 'The candidate for officer's rank, *your* Cadet Biegler, has shitted his trousers. . . . It's not cholera, it's not dysentery, it's just a common or garden shitting. He has drunk a little too much cognac, has *your candidate for officer's rank*, and he has

1. Captain Ságner's conversation with Lieutenant Lukáš was carried on in Czech. (Author's note.)

shitted his trousers. . . . He would certainly have shitted his trousers even without your cognac. He gorged all the cream rolls which were sent him from home. . . . He's a baby. . . . In the club, as I know for a fact, he always drank one quarter of a litre of wine. A teetotaller.'

Doctor Welfer spat. 'He used to buy Linzertorte.'

'And so it's nothing serious?' asked Captain Ságner, 'but at the same time a case like this. . . . What if it were to spread?'

Lieutenant Lukáš stood up and said to Ságner: 'Thank you for a platoon commander like this . . .'

'I helped him a little bit on to his legs,' said Welfer, whose smile did not leave his lips. 'You, sir, as battalion commander, will decide further action. . . . I mean, I shall send Cadet Biegler to a hospital here. . . . I shall write out a certificate that it's dysentery. A severe case of dysentery. Isolation. . . . Cadet Biegler will go to the disinfection hut . . .

'It's definitely better,' continued Welfer with the same detestable smile. 'You can have either a cadet who has shitted his trousers or a cadet who has contracted dysentery . . .'

Captain Ságner turned to Lukáš and said in a completely official tone: 'Lieutenant, Cadet Biegler of your company has gone down with dysentery and will stay in Budapest for treatment . . .'

Captain Ságner thought that Welfer was laughing frightfully provocatively but when he looked at the 'war doctor' he saw that he had assumed a completely disinterested expression.

'Then everything's in order, sir,' answered Welfer calmly. 'The candidate for officer's . . .'

He made a dismissing gesture with his hand: 'With dysentery everybody shits in his trousers.'

And so it happened that the valiant Cadet Biegler was carried off to the military isolation hospital at Új Buda.

His shitted trousers got lost in the vortex of the world war.

His dreams of great victories were confined in a hospital ward in the isolation huts.

When he learned that he had dysentery he was genuinely delighted.

It was immaterial whether in the course of carrying out his duties for His Imperial Majesty he was wounded or sick.

Then he had a piece of ill luck. As all the places for dysentery cases were full they transferred him to the cholera hut.

They gave him a bath and when they put a thermometer under his arm a Hungarian staff doctor shook his head: '37°!' With cholera the worst symptom is a serious fall in temperature. The patient becomes apathetic.

Cadet Biegler, it was true, betrayed no excitement. He was unusually calm, telling himself over and over again that in any case he was suffering for His Imperial Majesty.

The staff doctor gave instructions to put the thermometer into Cadet Biegler's rectum.

'It's the last stage of cholera,' thought the staff doctor to himself. 'Symptoms of the final collapse, extreme weakness when the patient is losing consciousness of his surroundings and his mind is clouded. He smiles in dying convulsions.'

During these manipulations Cadet Biegler was indeed smiling like a martyr, acting like a hero, when they thrust a thermometer up his rectum. But he did not move.

'Symptoms which in cholera lead gradually to death,' thought the staff doctor to himself. 'A passive state . . .'

He asked the Hungarian medical N.C.O. whether Cadet Biegler had vomited and had diarrhoea in the bath.

Receiving a negative answer he stared at Biegler. With cholera, when diarrhoea and vomiting cease, it is again like the previous symptoms, a replica of the course cholera takes in the last hours before death.

Cadet Biegler felt frozen when he was being carried stark naked from the hot bath to his bed. His teeth started to chatter and he had goose flesh all over his body.

'You see,' said the staff doctor in Hungarian, 'violent ague fit. His extremities are cold. This is the end.'

Leaning over Cadet Biegler he asked him in German: 'Well, how do you feel?'

'Ve-v-v-ery we-e-e-ll-ll,' Biegler said with chattering teeth, '. . . a-a-a b-b-blank-k-ket.'

'Reason partly clouded, partly preserved,' said the Hungarian staff doctor. 'Body much emaciated, lips and nails should be black. . . . This is the third case I've had of people dying of cholera without black nails and lips. . . .'

He leaned over Cadet Biegler again and continued in Hungarian: 'The second response above the heart has ceased . . .'

'A-a-a-a b-b-blan-k-k-ket,' said Cadet Biegler with chattering teeth.

'What he's saying now are his last words,' said the staff doctor in

Hungarian to the medical N.C.O. 'Tomorrow we'll bury him with Major Koch. Now he'll fall into a coma. Have you got his documents in the office?'

'They'll be there,' answered the N.C.O. calmly.

'A-a-a b-b-blank-k-ket,' Cadet Biegler moaned after them with chattering teeth as they were going away.

In the whole ward there were five people in sixteen beds. One of them was a corpse. He had died two hours before, was covered with a sheet and had the same name as the discoverer of the cholera bacillus. He was that Major Koch who according to the staff doctor would be buried tomorrow with Cadet Biegler.

Cadet Biegler got up on his bed and saw for the first time how people died of cholera for His Imperial Majesty, for of the four remaining two were dying. They struggled for breath and turned blue, trying to get something out, but it was not possible to identify what they said or the language they were trying to say it in. It was like the rattle of a gagged voice.

The other two with their conspicuously stormy reactions to their convalescence were reminiscent of people suffering from typhoid delirium. They shrieked unintelligibly and threw their emaciated legs out from underneath the blankets. Over them stood a bearded medical orderly, who spoke Styrian dialect (as Cadet Biegler recognized) and tried to calm them: 'I've had cholera like that, my fine gentlemen, but I didn't kick at my blankets. Now you're all right. You'll get leave when . . .

'Don't fling yourself about so,' he roared at one who kicked at his blanket so that it went over his head. 'It's not allowed here. Be glad you've got a temperature. It means that at least they won't carry you off to the sound of music. You're both high and dry now.'

He looked around.

'Over there another two have died. That's what we expected,' he said good-humouredly. 'Be glad that you're quit of it all. I must go for some sheets.'

Returning after a short time he covered with sheets those who had just died and who had completely black lips, took out their black-nailed hands which in their last agony of suffocation they had held on their erect penises, and tried to put their tongues into their mouths. Then he kneeled by the beds and started praying: 'Holy Mary, Mother of God . . .' And while doing so the old orderly from Styria looked at his recovering patients, whose delirium meant a reaction to new life.

'Holy Mary, Mother of God,' he was repeating, when a naked man suddenly tapped him on the shoulder.

It was Cadet Biegler.

'Listen,' he said, 'I . . . had a bath . . . that's to say, they gave me a bath. . . . I need a blanket . . . I'm cold.'

'This is a special case,' said the staff doctor half an hour later to Cadet Biegler who was resting underneath a blanket: 'You are a re-convalescent, cadet. Tomorrow we shall send you to the reserve hospital at Tarnov. You are a carrier of cholera germs. . . . We have made so much progress that we know all about it. You belong to the 91st regiment . . .

'The 13th march battalion,' answered the medical N.C.O. for Cadet Biegler, '11th company.'

'Write down the following,' said the staff doctor: 'Cadet Biegler, of the 13th march battalion, 11th march company, 91st regiment, to the cholera barracks in Tarnov for observation. A carrier of cholera germs . . .'

And thus it was that from an enthusiastic warrior Cadet Biegler became a carrier of cholera germs.

2

In Budapest

At the military station in Budapest Matušič brought Captain Ságner a telegram from headquarters sent by the unfortunate brigadier who had now been transported to a sanatorium. It was unciphered and contained a similar message to the one at the last station: 'Quickly finish cooking and march towards Sokal.' And then followed: 'Incorporate baggage train in Eastern group. Intelligence service abolished. 13th march battalion to build bridge across river Bug. Further details in newspapers.'

Captain Ságner went off at once to the station command. He was received by a small fat officer with a friendly smile.

'He hasn't half been carrying on, that brigadier of yours,' he said, roaring with laughter, 'but we had to send you all that lunacy, because we've got no orders yet from the division to stop delivering his telegrams to the addressees. Yesterday the 14th march battalion of the 75th regiment passed through and the battalion commander got a telegram here that each man should be given six crowns as a special reward for Przemyśl. At the same time he got the order that out of these six crowns every man should deposit in the office here two crowns for the war loan. . . . According to reliable information your brigadier has got paralysis.'

'Sir,' said Captain Ságner, turning to the station commander, 'according to regimental orders and our schedule we're going to Gödöllö. The men have to get fifteen dekas of Emmentaler cheese here. At the last station they should have got fifteen dekas of Hungarian salami, but they didn't get anything.'

'I'm afraid they'll get nothing here either,' the major replied, continuing to smile pleasantly. 'I know nothing about any order of the kind *for the regiments from Bohemia*. Anyhow, that's not my affair. Apply to supply command.'

'When are we leaving, sir?'

'There's a train in front of you with heavy artillery bound for Galicia. We shall send it off in an hour, captain. On the third track there's a hospital train. It's leaving twenty-five minutes after the artillery. On the twelfth track we've a munitions train. That's leaving ten minutes after the hospital train. Twenty minutes after that your train will be going.

'That's to say, if there are no changes,' he added, continuing to smile so that Captain Ságner found him utterly revolting.

'Excuse me, sir,' asked Ságner, 'will you be so good as to explain to me how it comes about that you know nothing of any order of the kind for the issue of fifteen dekas of Emmentaler cheese *for the regiments from Bohemia*?'

'That's secret,' the station commander at Budapest replied, continuing to smile.

'I've made an ass of myself,' thought Captain Ságner to himself, as he left the building of the station command. 'Why the devil did I go and tell Lieutenant Lukáš to collect all the commanders with all the men and go with them to the supply detachment to draw fifteen dekas of Emmentaler cheese per head?'

But before Lieutenant Lukáš could implement Captain Ságner's order and instruct the men of the battalion to proceed to the stores to draw fifteen dekas of Emmentaler cheese per head, Švejk appeared before him together with the luckless Baloun.

Baloun was trembling all over.

'Humbly report, sir,' Švejk said with his usual ease, 'the matter I've come about is extremely important. I would be most grateful, sir, if we could settle *the whole affair somewhere on the side*, as my pal Špatina of Zhoř once said, when he was a witness at a wedding and suddenly in church had to . . .'

'Well, what's the matter, Švejk?' Lieutenant Lukáš broke in. He was already missing Švejk as much as Švejk was missing him. 'Let's go a little further away then.'

Baloun walked behind them and continued to tremble. This giant had completely lost his equilibrium and was swinging his arms in frightful and hopeless despair.

'Well, what is it, Švejk?' asked Lieutenant Lukáš, when they had gone on to the side.

'Humbly report, sir,' said Švejk, 'it's always better to confess to something before it gets out. You gave a certain order, sir, that when we came to Budapest Baloun should bring you your liver pâté and some rolls.'

'Did you get that order or not?' said Švejk, turning to Baloun.

Baloun began to swing his arms about even more violently, as though he wanted to ward off the blows of an attacking enemy.

'This order,' said Švejk, 'could not unfortunately be carried out, sir, because I've eaten up that liver pâté of yours myself . . .

'I ate it up,' said Švejk, nudging the horrified Baloun, 'because I thought the liver pâté might go bad. I've read several times in the newspapers how a whole family has been poisoned by liver pâté. Once at Zderaz, once at Beroun, once at Tábor, once at Mladá Boleslav, once at Příbram. All of them succumbed to the poison. Liver pâté is the worst muck . . .'

Baloun, trembling all over, stood at the side, put his finger down his throat and vomited at short intervals.

'What's the matter with you, Baloun?'

'I'm sp-sp-ewing, sir . . . pewing, sir,' the unfortunate Baloun called out during the intervals. 'I – I ge-ge-guzzled it, ge-ge-guzzled it my-s-s-s-elf.'

Bits of tin foil and pâté came out of the luckless Baloun's mouth.

'As you see, sir,' said Švejk, losing nothing of his composure, 'every bit of the guzzled pâté comes up like oil on the surface of the water. I wanted to take the blame myself, but the bloody fool has gone and given the show away. He's quite a decent chap really, but he guzzles everything that's given to him. I once knew a man like him, who was a bank messenger. They could trust him with thousands of crowns. Once he drew money in another bank and by mistake they gave him a thousand crowns too much and he returned it on the spot. But if they sent him to buy some smoked ham for fifteen kreutzers he guzzled half of it on the way. When it came to food he was so greedy that when the officials sent him to get sausages, he cut them on the way with his pocket knife and stuck the holes together with sticking plaster. The plaster for five sausages cost him more than a whole sausage itself.'

Lieutenant Lukáš sighed and went away.

'Would you like to give me any orders, sir?' Švejk called after him, while the luckless Baloun continued to stick his finger down his throat.

Lieutenant Lukáš dismissed him with a wave of his hand and went off to the supply stores, in the course of which the strange idea came to him that if soldiers ate their officers' liver pâté Austria could not win the war.

Meanwhile Švejk took Baloun away to the other side of the military track and consoled him by saying that they could both go together, have a look at the town and bring back some Debrecen sausages for the lieutenant, since in Švejk's mind the concept of the capital of the Hungarian kingdom was naturally bound up with the concept of a special kind of sausage.

'But the train might go without us,' bleated Baloun, in whom insatiable hunger was combined with extreme stinginess.

'When you go to the front,' said Švejk, 'you're never left behind, because every train which leaves for the front thinks twice before bringing only half a trainful to its destination. But I understand you very well, Baloun. You're an old skinflint.'

But they didn't go anywhere because the signal for getting into the train suddenly sounded. The men of the various companies returned from the supply stores to their vans with empty hands once more. Instead of fifteen dekas of Emmentaler cheese, which should have been issued here, each one of them got a box of matches and a postcard, published by the War Graves Commission in Austria (Vienna XIX/4,

Canisiusgasse). Instead of fifteen dekas of Emmentaler cheese each one found himself with the West Galician warriors' cemetery at Sedlisk, with the memorial to the unfortunate Landwehr men, built by the scrimshanking sculptor, the one-year volunteer Sergeant-Major Scholz.

Outside the staff carriage too there was unusual excitement. The officers of the march battalion were collected around Captain Ságner who was excitedly explaining something to them. He had just returned from the station headquarters and had in his hand a very confidential, genuine telegram from brigade staff, containing a long-winded message of instructions and directives on how to carry on in the new situation in which Austria found itself on 23 May 1915.

Brigade had telegraphed that Italy had declared war on Austria-Hungary.

Already in the officers' club in Bruck an der Leitha there had been a lot of loose talk at lunches and dinners about the queer dealings and goings-on of the Italians but, when all was said and done, nobody expected that the prophetic words of that bloody fool Cadet Biegler would be fulfilled, when once at dinner he pushed away his plate of macaroni and said: 'The time to eat this will be when we are at the gates of Verona.'

After having studied the instructions which he had just obtained from the brigade, Captain Ságner gave the order for the alert to be sounded.

When all the men of the march battalion were assembled, they were drawn up in a square and Captain Ságner in an unusually exalted voice read them the order which he had received by telegram.

'With unexampled treachery and greed the King of Italy has forgotten the fraternal obligations which were binding on him as an ally of our Monarchy. From the outbreak of the war, when he should have stood at the side of our brave armies, the treacherous king played the role of a masked trickster, acting with duplicity and all along maintaining secret contacts with our enemies. This treachery culminated on the night of 22/3 May in his declaration of war on our Monarchy. Our supreme commander is convinced that our ever valiant and glorious armies will answer this contemptible treachery of a faithless enemy with such a blow that the traitor will come to recognize that by starting war against us in this shameless and treacherous fashion he has encompassed his own destruction. We believe firmly that with the help of God the day will soon dawn when the plains of Italy will see once more the victors of Santa Lucia, Vicenza, Novarra and Custozza. We want to win, we must win and win we certainly shall!'

After that came the usual 'Three cheers!', and the army got into the train once more, but in low spirits. Instead of fifteen dekas of Emmentaler cheese they had the war with Italy round their necks.

In the van where Švejk was sitting with Vaněk, Chodounský, Baloun and Jurajda, an interesting conversation began about Italy's entry into the war.

'There was a case like that in Táborská Street in Prague,' began Švejk. 'A shopkeeper called Hořejší lived there. A little way away on the other side of the street a shopkeeper called Pošmourný had his shop and between them both was a greengrocer called Havlasa. Well, the shopkeeper, Hořejší, once had the idea of joining up with the greengrocer, Havlasa, against the other shopkeeper, Pošmourný, and began to negotiate with him for the merger of the two shops under a single sign: "Hořejší and Havlasa". But Havlasa went to Pošmourný and told him that Hořejší was ready to give him twelve hundred crowns for his greengrocer's shop and wanted him to go into partnership with him. But if Pošmourný gave him eighteen hundred, he would rather go into partnership with him against Hořejší. And so they made a bargain and Havlasa was for some time round Hořejší's neck and acting as though he were his best friend, when in fact he was false to him all the time. When it came to the question of when they should go into partnership he always said: "Yes, we'll do that soon. I'm only waiting until the customers' families come back from their summer holidays." And when they came back, everything was really arranged for them to join forces as he had always promised Hořejší. But when Hořejší went down one morning to open his shop he saw over his rival's shop a big inscription, a giant sign: "Pošmourný and Havlasa".'

'We had a case like that with us too,' said the idiotic Baloun. 'I wanted to buy a heifer in the neighbouring village. I had the agreement all tied up but then a butcher from Votice came and snatched it away from me under my very nose.'

'Now that we have a new war again,' Švejk continued, 'now that we have one enemy more, now that we have a new front again, we'll have to be economical with our munitions. "The more children there are in the family, the more the rods are used," as grandpa Chovanec at Motol used to say, when for an all-in sum from the parents he gave all the children in the neighbourhood a good licking.'

'I'm only afraid,' said Baloun, trembling all over, 'that because of Italy the portions will be reduced.'

Vaněk pondered for a moment and said gravely: 'That might very well be the case, because our victory will now take rather longer.'

'Now we need another Radetzky,' said Švejk. 'He knew a thing or two about the Italian countryside: he understood very well where was the weak spot in the Italian defence, what had to be taken by storm and from which side. You see, it's not so hard to get in somewhere. Anyone can do that, but getting out again needs real military skill. When a chap gets in somewhere, he has to know about everything that's going on around him, so as not to find himself in a jam suddenly – what's called a catastrophe. Once at home in the house where I used to live before, they caught a thief in the attic. When he got in the bastard noticed that the builders were just repairing the air-shaft, and so he tore himself away from his pursuers, knocked down the house-portress, and dropped down the ladder into the air-shaft, from which he couldn't get out at all. But there wasn't a single path papa Radetzky didn't know. No one could catch him anywhere. There's a book where it's all written about that general, how he ran away from Santa Lucia, how the Italians ran away too and how he only realized that he had actually won on the second day when he couldn't find any Italians and couldn't see them through his telescope. And so he came back and occupied abandoned Santa Lucia. After that he was promoted marshal.'

'Well, Italy's a fine country, it certainly is!' said Jurajda. 'I was once in Venice and I know the Italian calls everybody a pig. When he gets angry everyone is a *porco maledetto*. For him even the Pope is a *porco*, even *Madonna mia è porco* and *Papa è porco*.'

Vaněk on the other hand spoke very favourably about Italy. At his chemist's shop in Kralupy he also manufactured lemon juice, which he made out of rotten lemons, and he always used to buy the cheapest and rottenest lemons from Italy. Now it would mean the end of the transport of lemons from Italy to Kralupy. There was no doubt that the war with Italy would bring various surprises, because Austria would want to take her revenge.

'It's easy to say "take her revenge",' Švejk said with a smile. 'A chap thinks he's going to take his revenge, but in the end it's the fellow he's chosen as the instrument of his vengeance who pays for it. When I lived years ago at Vinohrady, a house-porter lived on the ground floor and provided board for a petty official in a bank. This official went to a pub in Kramerius Street and had a quarrel there once with a gentleman who had an institute for the analysis of urine at Vinohrady. That gentleman never thought of or spoke of anything else except that institute and all the time carried about with him little test-tubes for urine. These he thrust under people's noses, urging them to make water and have their urine analysed, because the happiness of the man and his family depended on it and it was so cheap that it only cost six crowns. All the guests who came to the pub, as well as the landlord and his wife, had their urine analysed. Only that petty official still resisted, although the gentleman continually followed him to the urinal and when he came out said to him anxiously: "I don't know, Mr Skorkovský, but somehow I'm not very happy about your urine. You'd better make water into the test-tube, before it's too late!" Finally he persuaded him to do so. It cost that petty official six crowns and the gentleman made him suffer for it, as he did all the people in the pub, not excluding the landlord whose business he ruined, because with every analysis he produced he always enclosed a report which stated that it was a very serious case, that no one in that state should drink anything but water; they shouldn't smoke, they shouldn't get married and they should only eat vegetables. And so that petty official, like all the rest, got furious with him and chose the house-porter as the instrument of his vengeance, because he knew he was a really nasty customer. And so one day he told the gentleman who carried out the urine analyses that the house-porter had not been feeling well for some time and asked him to go and see him next day at seven o'clock and test his urine. And so he went there. The house-porter was still sleeping when the gentleman woke him up and said to him in a friendly way: "My respects, Mr Málek. I wish you a good morning. Here's a test-tube for you, please. Be so kind and make water into it and my charge is six crowns." And what a shindy there was! The house-porter jumped out of bed in his pants, seized the gentleman by the throat and threw him at the cupboard so that he inlaid him in it! And when he pulled him out of the cupboard again he seized a knout, went out as he was in his pants and chased him down Čelakovská Street with the gentleman yelling just like when you tread on the tail of a dog. In Havlíček Avenue the gentleman jumped on to a tram and the house-porter was caught by a policeman, fought with him and because he was only in his pants and everything was peeping out, they threw him into the cart for drunks and carried him off to the police station. When he was in the cart he went on roaring like a bull: "You bastards, I'll teach you to analyse my urine." He was in jug for six months for public violence and for insulting the police. Afterwards when the sentence was pronounced he committed the further offence of insulting the Ruling House, and it's very likely that he's still in jug today. And this is why I say that if ever a chap wants to take his revenge on anybody it's always the innocent party who pays for it.'

Meanwhile Baloun was furiously thinking about something till he finally asked Vaněk in a panic: 'Excuse me, sergeant-major, please could you be kind and tell me, do you *really* think that because of this war with Italy we shall get smaller rations?'

'Yes, it's as clear as daylight,' answered Vaněk.

'Jesus Mary,' shrieked Baloun. He plunged his head into his hands and sat quietly in the corner.

And this was how the discussion about Italy in the van came to a final end.

In the staff carriage the discussion about the new war situation created
by Italy's entry into the war would certainly have been very dull in the
absence of the famous military theorist, Cadet Biegler, if he had not
had a substitute in -the person of Lieutenant Dub of the 3rd
company.

Lieutenant Dub was in civil life a schoolmaster and teacher of
Czech, and already at that time manifested an unusual alacrity for
expressing his loyalty to the crown on all possible occasions.

For essays he set his pupils themes from the history of the house of
Hapsburg. In the lower forms his pupils were frightened by the
Emperor Maximilian, who climbed on to a cliff and could not get down,
or Joseph II as the ploughman or Ferdinand the Benign. In the higher
classes the themes were of course more sophisticated, as for example
the exercise for the seventh form: 'Emperor Franz Joseph I, patron of
the arts and sciences', which caused a member of the seventh form to

be expelled from all secondary schools in the Austro-Hungarian empire for writing that this ruler's most glorious act was the building of the Emperor Franz Joseph I Bridge in Prague.

He always took good care to see that all his pupils sang the Austrian national anthem with great enthusiasm on all royal birthdays and at other similar Imperial ceremonies. In society he was unpopular, because people knew that he was a nark as well, and informed on his colleagues. In the town where he taught he was one of the members of a triumvirate of the biggest idiots and mules, consisting of the district hejtman, the headmaster of the grammar school and himself. In this narrow circle he learnt how to talk politics within the framework of the Austro-Hungarian Empire. Now too he began to reason with the voice and accents of a fossilized schoolmaster:

'All things considered I was not at all surprised at Italy's entry into the war. I expected it already three months ago. It had become obvious that Italy had been growing extremely arrogant latterly as a result of her victorious war with Turkey over Tripoli. In addition she relies too much on her navy and on the mood of the population in our maritime provinces and in the South Tyrol. Why, even before the war I discussed this with our district hejtman and urged that our government shouldn't underestimate the irridentist movement in the south. He said I was quite right, because any sensible man who had the preservation of our empire at heart should have realized long ago where our excessive lenience towards such elements was leading us. I remember well how about two years ago I said in a conversation with the district hejtman that Italy – it was at the time of the Balkan War during the affair of our consul Prochaska – was only waiting for the first opportunity to give us a treacherous stab in the back.

'And now it's come!' he shouted in such tones as though everyone had quarrelled with him, although while he was talking all the regular officers present were only thinking that as far as they were concerned this blithering idiot of a civilian could go to hell.

'It's true,' he continued in milder tones, 'that in most cases in our school essays they forgot our former relations with Italy, and those great days of our glorious victorious armies in 1848 and 1866, which are still mentioned in brigade orders to this day. But I at least always did my duty, and even before the end of the school year, that is to say at the very beginning of the war, I set my pupils the following essay: "Our heroes in Italy from Vicenza to Custozza, or . . .".'

And the idiotic Lieutenant Dub added solemnly in German: '. . . Blood and life for the Hapsburgs! For an Austria inviolate, united and great. . . .'

He paused and obviously expected that the others in the staff carriage would talk about the new situation, and he could show them once more how he had known five years ago that Italy would one day treat her ally like this. But he was completely disappointed, because Captain Ságner, to whom Matušič had brought the evening edition of *Pester Lloyd* from the station, looked into the paper and said: 'Look here, that Weiner girl who we saw in Bruck in a guest performance appeared here yesterday in the Little Theatre.'

And this was how the discussion about Italy ended in the staff carriage . . .

As well as those who sat in the back of the train Matušič and Batzer judged the war with Italy from the purely practical point of view, as once years ago while they were still in regular service they had both taken part in manoeuvres in South Tyrol.

'It'll be an awful sweat having to climb up those mountains,' said Batzer. 'Captain Ságner has a whacking great pile of cases. It's true I come from the mountains, but it's another story when you take a gun under your coat and go and see if you can't pot a hare on Prince Schwarzenberg's estate.'

'That's of course if they cart us down to Italy. I can't say it appeals to me either to go flying over mountains and glaciers carrying orders. And the grub down there! Why, it's only polenta and oil,' said Matušič gloomily.

'And why should they shove us of all people up on to those mountains?' said Batzer, getting angry. 'Our regiment's already been in Serbia and the Carpathians. I've already traipsed about the mountains with the captain's cases. Twice I've lost them; once in Serbia, another time in the Carpathians in some skirmish or other, and maybe now it's coming to me a third time on the Italian frontier. And as for the grub down there . . .' He spat. Moving nearer to Matušič he said to him in a familiar manner: 'You know, at home in Kašperské Hory we make sort of small dumplings out of raw potatoes. We boil them, dip them in egg and roll them well in breadcrumbs. After that we fry them with bacon.' He pronounced the last word in a mysteriously solemn tone.

'But they're best with sauerkraut,' he added in a melancholy voice. 'They can chuck their macaroni down the rears.'

And that was how the conversation about Italy ended here . . .

As the train had already been standing at the station for over two hours, there was only one opinion in the other vans and that was that it was probably going to be re-routed and sent to Italy.

This appeared to be confirmed too by the fact that strange things had been happening with the train in the meantime. Once more all the men were driven out of the vans, sanitary inspectors arrived with the disinfection corps and sprayed all the vans with lysol. This was very badly received, especially in those vans where the army bread was being carried.

However, orders are orders, the sanitary commission had given the order that all the vans of train number 728 had to be disinfected and so the piles of army bread and sacks of rice were quite happily sprayed with lysol. This indicated that something special was afoot.

After that the men were driven into the vans again and driven out again half an hour later because an aged general came to inspect the train. He was so old that Švejk quite naturally thought of a name for him. Standing in the rear line he remarked to Vaněk: 'That old boy's a death-watch.'

Escorted by Captain Ságner the old general proceeded along the line and stopped in front of a young soldier. In order somehow to inspire some enthusiasm in the men he asked him where he came from, how old he was and whether he had a watch. The soldier had in fact got one, but because he thought he might possibly get another from the old gentleman, he said he hadn't, whereupon the old death-watch, giving the same kind of super-idiotic smile which Emperor Franz Joseph used to give when he spoke to a mayor in some town or other, said: 'That's good, that's good,' whereupon he condescended to ask the corporal who was standing next to him whether his lady wife was well.

'Humbly report, sir,' bawled the corporal, 'I'm not married,' whereupon the general with his patronizing smile repeated: 'That's good, that's good.'

Then the general in his senility asked Captain Ságner to show him how the men numbered in twos, and a little later there could be heard: 'One – two, one – two, one – two.'

The old death-watch was delighted with this. He even had at home two lads whom he made line up in front of him and number by themselves: 'One – two, one – two' . . .

Austria had masses of generals like that.

When the inspection was successfully over the general did not spare his praise when speaking to Captain Ságner, and the men were allowed to dismiss and move freely about the station area, because the news had come that they would not be leaving for another three hours. And so they wandered up and down and stared about them, because on the station there were quite a lot of people and here and there some of the soldiers cadged a cigarette.

It was evident that the first flush of enthusiasm, which had shown itself in the festive welcome for the trains at the stations, had faded considerably and declined to the point of beggary.

A deputation from the Society for the Reception of Heroes presented itself before Captain Ságner. It consisted of two frightfully jaded ladies, who handed over a gift for the train, in fact twenty boxes of sweet-smelling mouthwash pastilles, which were an advertisement for a Budapest sweet factory. The boxes were beautifully finished in metal. On the lid was painted a Hungarian Honvéd clasping the hand of an Austrian Landstürmer, while over them blazed the crown of St Stephen. Around them was the inscription in German and Hungarian: 'For Emperor, God and Fatherland.'

The sweet factory was so loyal that it gave precedence to the Emperor over the Almighty.

Every box contained eighty pastilles, so that about five pastilles fell to three men. Apart from that the care-worn and jaded ladies brought a huge bundle of printed copies of two prayers written by the Arch-bishop of Budapest, Géza of Szatmár-Budafal. They were in German and Hungarian and contained the most frightful imprecations on all enemies. They were written with such passion that the only thing missing in them was the trenchant Hungarian expression: '*Baszom a Kristus Máriát!*'[1]

According to the venerable archbishop the merciful Lord ought to cut the Russians, British, Serbs, French and Japanese into mincemeat, and make a paprika goulash out of them. The merciful Lord ought to bathe in the blood of the enemies and murder them all, as the ruthless Herod had done with the Innocents.

His Eminence, the Archbishop of Budapest, used in his prayers such beautiful sentences as for instance: 'God bless your bayonets that they may pierce deeply into your enemies' bellies. May the most just Lord direct the artillery fire on to the heads of the enemy staffs. May merciful God grant that all your enemies choke in their own blood from the wounds which you will deal them!'

That is why it should be repeated once more that the only thing missing in these little prayers was: '*Baszom a Kristus Máriát!*'

When both ladies had presented all this they expressed a desperate wish to be allowed to be present when the gifts were distributed. One of them even had the nerve to mention that she would like on this occasion to address the warriors, whom she referred to as 'our brave men in field grey'.

Both appeared frightfully offended when Captain Ságner turned down their request. For the time being their charitable alms found their

1. 'Fuck Christ and the Virgin Mary!'

way to the vans where the stores were kept. The venerable ladies passed down the line of soldiers and one of them could not resist patting a bearded soldier on the cheek. He was a man called Šimek from Budějovice, and having no idea of the ladies' exalted mission he let fall the following remark to his comrades after their departure: 'The

whores here are pretty fresh, I must say. It might be different if a monkey like that was anything to write home about but she's as scraggy as a stork. She's got nothing to show but her hocks, and looks like God's martyrdom. And an old hag like that has the cheek to try to start something with soldiers like us.'

There was a lot of bustle on the station. The Italian affair had caused some panic, because two trains with artillery had been kept back and sent to Styria. There was also a transport of Bosnians here, who for some unknown reason had already been waiting two days at the station and had been completely forgotten and lost. For two days these Bosnians had not drawn any rations and were going about cadging bread all over Új-Pest. And so you could hear nothing but the agitated voices of the forgotten Bosnians who were gesticulating violently and all the time cursing: '*Jebem ti boga, jebem ti dušu, jebem ti majku.*'[1]

Then the 91st march battalion were made to fall in again and go back to their vans. After a short time however Matušič returned from the station command with the news that they would be leaving in three hours' time. Because of this the men were again let out of the vans. Just before the departure of the train Lieutenant Dub came into the staff carriage in a great state of excitement and asked Captain Ságner to have Švejk clapped in gaol instantly. Lieutenant Dub, well known at his school as an old-established informer, loved getting into conversation with soldiers. In doing so he endeavoured to probe their opinions, seeking at the same time for an opportunity to teach them and explain to them why they were fighting and what they were fighting for.

In the course of his round he caught sight of Švejk behind the station building. He was standing by a lamp and looking with interest at a placard issued by a charity war lottery. The placard showed an Austrian soldier pinning to the wall a wide-eyed bearded Cossack.

Lieutenant Dub tapped Švejk on the shoulder and asked him how he liked the placard.

'Humbly report, sir,' answered Švejk, 'It's bloody silly. I've seen lots of asinine placards but never such tripe as this.'

'What don't you like about it?' asked Lieutenant Dub.

'What I don't like about this placard, sir, is the way that soldier there handles the arms entrusted to him. You know, he could easily break the bayonet on the wall and anyhow the whole thing is quite unnecessary. He would be court-martialled for it, because that Russian has his hands up and is surrendering. He's been taken prisoner and prisoners have to be treated decently, because after all they're human beings too.'

And so after that Lieutenant Dub decided to go on probing Švejk's views and asked him: 'So I suppose you're sorry for that Russian, aren't you?'

'I'm sorry for both of them, sir, for the Russian because he's spiked and for the soldier because he'll be gaoled for it. You know, sir, he certainly must have broken his bayonet in doing it. It's no good. You see it looks like a stone wall where he's thrusting his bayonet, and steel is brittle. Once, sir, before the war when I was in regular service we

1. Serbian oaths meaning literally: 'Fuck God, your soul and your mother.'

had a lieutenant in our company. Not even an old sweat of a sergeant-major could use such language as that lieutenant did. On the parade ground he used to say to us: "When it's 'attention', you bloody swine, you've got to roll your eyes like a cat shitting in the straw." But otherwise he was a very decent fellow. Once at Christmas he went mad and bought a whole wagon of coconuts for the company, and it's from that time that I know how brittle bayonets are. Half the company broke their bayonets on those coconuts and our lieutenant-colonel had the whole company clapped into gaol. For three months we weren't allowed out of the barracks and the lieutenant himself got house arrest . . .'

Lieutenant Dub stared in rage at the serene face of the good soldier Švejk and asked him angrily: 'Do you know me?'

'Yes, I know you, sir.'

Lieutenant Dub rolled his eyes and stamped: 'I tell you, you don't know me yet.'

Švejk answered once more with the serene calm of someone making a report: 'I know you, sir, humbly report. You are from our march battalion.'

'You don't know me yet,' Lieutenant Dub shouted again. 'You may perhaps know me from the good side, but wait till you know me from the bad side. I'm nasty. Don't imagine I'm not. I make everyone cry. Very well, then, do you know me or don't you know me?'

'I know you, sir.'

'I tell you for the last time that you don't know me, you mule, you. Have you any brothers?'

'Humbly report, sir, I have one.'

Infuriated at the sight of Švejk's calm unruffled expression, and unable to control himself any longer, Lieutenant Dub shouted out: 'And your brother must certainly be as big a bloody mule as you are. What was he?'

'A schoolmaster, sir. He was in the army too and passed the officers' exam.'

Lieutenant Dub looked at Švejk as though he wanted to run him through with his sabre. Švejk bore his furious look with dignified composure, so that for the moment their whole conversation ended with the word: 'Dismiss!'

Each of them then went his own way and had his own thoughts.

Lieutenant Dub thought he would ask the captain to have Švejk clapped into gaol, and Švejk for his part thought that he had seen many idiotic officers in his time but such a bloody ass as Lieutenant Dub must surely be unique in the regiment.

Lieutenant Dub, who had on this very day resolved that he must educate the men, found a new victim behind the station. There were two soldiers there from the regiment, but from another company, who

were haggling in the dark in broken German with two prostitutes, dozens of whom were roaming about the station.

As Švejk went away he heard clearly from the distance the shrill voice of Lieutenant Dub: 'Do you know me? . . . But I tell you, you don't know me! . . . But wait till you get to know me! . . . You know me perhaps only from the good side! . . . I tell you, wait till you get to know me from the bad side! . . . I'll make you cry, you bloody mules! . . . Have you any brothers? . . . Then they must be as big bloody mules as you! . . . What were they? . . . From the baggage train? . . . Very well then. . . . Remember that you're soldiers. . . . Are you

Czechs? . . . Do you know that Palacký said that if Austria had not existed we would have had to create it. . . . Dismiss! . . .'

Lieutenant Dub's round of inspection did not have an altogether positive result, however. He stopped some three more groups of soldiers and his educational attempts to 'make the men cry' proved a complete fiasco. The quality of the material being taken off to the front was such that Lieutenant Dub could read from the expression of every one of them that they all certainly had a very unpleasant opinion of him. He was stung in his pride and the result was that in the staff carriage before the departure of the train he requested Captain Ságner to have Švejk clapped into gaol. He tried to justify the need to isolate the good soldier Švejk by his extraordinarily arrogant behaviour, characterizing Švejk's honest answer to his last question as 'malicious remarks'. If this sort of thing were allowed to go on the officers' corps would lose all respect in the eyes of the men. Certainly none of the officers could have any doubts about that. Long before the war he had himself talked with the district hejtman about how every officer must endeavour to preserve a certain authority over his subordinates.

The district hejtman had been of the same opinion. Especially now in wartime the nearer one came to the enemy the more the soldiers should be kept in a state of terror. For this reason he asked that Švejk should be given disciplinary punishment.

Captain Ságner as a regular officer hated all these reserve officers from various branches of civilian life and therefore warned Lieutenant Dub that complaints of this nature could only be made in the form of a report and not in the odd fashion of a costermonger haggling about the price of potatoes. As for Švejk himself the first échelon of authority under whose jurisdiction he fell was Lieutenant Lukáš. A matter like this could only be done by report. From company it would go to battalion and the lieutenant was no doubt well aware of this. If Švejk had done something wrong, then he should go on company report, and if he appealed, on battalion report. But if Lieutenant Lukáš had no objections and would accept Lieutenant Dub's statement as an official notification for punishment, he would have nothing against Švejk being summoned and questioned.

Lieutenant Lukáš had no objection to this, but only observed that he knew very well from what Švejk used to tell him that Švejk's brother was in fact a schoolmaster and a reserve officer.

Lieutenant Dub wavered and said that he was asking for punishment only in the broader sense, and it was possible that the man in question, Švejk, could not express himself and that it was only his replies which left an impression of arrogance, malice and lack of respect for his superiors. Moreover, it was clear from the man's whole appearance that his intellect was clouded.

And so the whole storm passed over Švejk's head without his being struck by lightning.

In the van, which combined the functions of both office and battalion stores, the quartermaster sergeant-major of the march battalion, Bautanzel, very condescendingly handed out to two writers from the battalion a handful of mouthwash pastilles from the boxes which were supposed to be distributed to the men. It was common practice that everything destined for the men had to go through battalion office and be subject to similar manipulations.

This was something so normal everywhere in wartime that when after an inspection somewhere the finding was that there was no stealing going on, every one of the quartermaster sergeant-majors in all the offices was none the less under suspicion of having exceeded his budget and of being guilty of other fiddles to put the books straight.

And so here too, when they were all stuffing themselves with these pastilles so as at least not to waste the filth when there was nothing else to filch from the men, Bautanzel spoke about the unhappy conditions during this journey: 'I've already done two march battalions but I've never known such a rotten trip as this. My God, on those earlier journeys, even before we got to Prešov we had masses of everything you could think of. I had salted away ten thousand cigarettes, two whole Emmentaler cheeses and three hundred tins. Later when we marched to the trenches at Bardějov, the Russians who occupied Mušina cut off our communications with Prešov and you should have seen the trade we did! For the sake of appearances I gave up about a tenth of it to the march battalion and said it was the result of economies I had made. The rest I flogged in the baggage train. We had a Major Sojka over us and he was a swine if there ever was one. He was no hero and liked best of all to swan about with us in the baggage train, because up above bullets were whistling and shrapnel bursting. And so he kept on coming to see us on the excuse that he must make sure that the cooking for the men was in order. Usually he came down to see us whenever there was a report that the Russians were preparing something again. He trembled all over and had to drink rum in the kitchen before he could make an inspection of all the field-kitchens. They were grouped around the baggage train, because it wasn't possible to carry the cauldrons up to the trenches and the mess portions were carried up there by night. At that time we were living in such conditions that you couldn't really speak of any officers' mess. The only

road to the base which was still free was occupied by the Germans from the Reich. They'd seized all the best things which were sent to us from the base and guzzled them themselves, so we never got anything. All of us in the baggage train were left without officers' mess portions. During all that time I only succeeded in salting away one pig for ourselves in the office, which we had smoked, and to prevent Major Sojka finding out about it we had it hidden an hour's journey away with the artillery, where I had a friend who was sergeant-major.

'Whenever the major came to see us he always started to taste the soup in the kitchen. It's true there was not much meat to cook, only such pigs or skinny cows as we could scrounge in the neighbourhood. The Prussians made strong competition for us and when requisitioning cattle always paid twice as much as we did. So during the whole time we laid siege to Bardějov, I couldn't salt away on the sale of cattle more than a little over twelve hundred crowns. And into the bargain at that time we didn't give money but mostly vouchers with the battalion stamp on them, particularly later, towards the end, when we knew that the Russians were not far to the east of us in Radvaň and not far to the west in Podolín. It's really an awful job dealing with people like that living in that region who can't read or write and can only sign with three crosses. Of course, Supply Headquarters were in the know, so when we asked them for money I couldn't enclose forged receipts to prove I'd paid them. You can only do that where the people are better educated and know how to sign their names. And on top of all that, as I've already said, the Prussians always outbid us and paid in cash, but when we arrived at a village people looked at us as though we were brigands.

'And then Supply Headquarters issued instructions that receipts signed with crosses would have to be submitted to Field Accountant Control, and there were masses of those accountant bastards loafing around. Usually a bastard like that would come to us, wolf up our food and drink and go and inform against us the next day. That Major Sojka was always walking around our field-kitchens and, God's truth, believe me, he once took out of the cauldron the meat for the whole fourth company, he did. He started with a pig's head, which he said was underdone, and had it cooked for a bit longer. It's true that at that time we weren't cooking very much meat. There were about twelve decent portions of meat of the old size for the whole company, and he ate them all up. Then he tasted the soup and made a row saying that it was just like water and what sort of a state of affairs was this when meat soup hadn't any meat in it? He had the soup thickened and chucked into it my last macaroni, which I'd been saving up for ages. But what annoyed me much more was that in that browned flour there got swallowed up two kilos of finest quality butter which I'd been saving ever since the time when there had still been officers' mess portions. I had it on a shelf over my bunk, and he swore at me asking who it had belonged to. I told him that according to the last order of the division out of the budget for the men's victualling every man was entitled to a bonus of fifteen grammes of butter or twenty-one grammes of lard. And because the stocks of butter were not sufficient they had to be stored until the bonus of butter could be given in its full weight. Major Sojka got into a great rage, started to shout that I was obviously waiting till the Russians came, took away our last two kilos of butter and said it must be put into the soup at once, as there was no meat in it. And so I lost the whole stock and, believe me, that major always brought me bad luck whenever he appeared. He gradually developed such a nose that he knew at once about all my stores.

'Once I had managed to save from the men's rations an ox liver and we were going to stew it when he suddenly went and pulled it out from underneath my bunk. When he started shouting at me I told him that the liver was meant for burying, that in the morning it had been diagnosed and condemned by a blacksmith in the artillery who had gone through a veterinary course. The major took with him one of the men from the baggage train and they cooked the liver in the cauldrons up in the mountains underneath the cliffs. But that was his funeral, because when the Russian artillery saw the fire they shot at the major and his cauldron with an eighteener. Afterwards we went and had a look round, and no one could tell whether it was the ox's liver or the major's that was lying about on those cliffs.'

Later the news came that they would be leaving in about four hours' time. The track leading up to Hatvan had been blocked by trains carrying the wounded. Moreover, the rumour spread round the station that near Eger a hospital train carrying sick and wounded had collided with another train carrying artillery. Relief trains from Budapest were on their way.

Soon the imagination of the whole battalion began to work. People talked of two hundred dead and wounded and said the collision was pre-arranged so that the fiddle with the patients' provisioning shouldn't be discovered.

This provoked sharp criticism of the inadequate catering for the battalion and of thefts in the office and in the stores.

Most people were of the opinion that Quartermaster Sergeant-Major Bautanzel shared fifty-fifty with the officers.

In the staff carriage Captain Ságner announced that according to schedule they should now actually be already at the Galician frontier. At Eger they were due to draw a three days' ration of bread and tins for the men, but Eger was still ten hours away. It was in fact so full of trains with wounded after the offensive at Lwów that according to a telegram there was not a single loaf of army bread or tin left there. He had received orders to pay out 6 crowns 72 hellers per man instead of bread and tins. This was to be issued with their pay in nine days' time, that is to say if they got the money from brigade by that time. There was only a little more than twelve thousand crowns in the till.

'It's a bloody rotten trick of the regiment to send us out into the world in such a wretched state,' said Lieutenant Lukáš.

A whispered colloquy began between Ensign Wolf and Lieutenant Kolář to the effect that Colonel Schröder in the last three weeks had paid sixteen thousand crowns into his account in the Wiener Bank.

Then Lieutenant Kolář explained how economies are made. You filch six thousand crowns from the regiment and put them in your pocket. With inescapable logic you then order all kitchens to deduct three grammes of peas from every man's ration in every kitchen.

In a month that makes ninety grammes per man so that in the kitchen and in every company a store of at least sixteen kilos of peas should have been saved and the cook has to show this.

Lieutenant Kolář talked with Wolf only in general terms about certain cases which he had noticed.

But it was certainly true that the whole military administration was bursting at the seams with cases like this. It started with the quartermaster sergeant-major in some unfortunate company and ended with the hamster in general's epaulettes who was salting something away for himself for a rainy day when the war was over.

War demanded valour even in pilfering.

The controllers of supplies looked at each other affectionately, as if to say: 'We are one body and soul, we steal, old chap, we cheat, brother, but what can you do? It's hard to swim against the tide. If you don't salt it away someone else will, and people will say that the only reason why you've not salted anything away is that you've already salted enough.'

A gentleman with red and gold stripes on his trousers came into the carriage. It was again one of those generals travelling on inspection over all railway routes.

'Sit down, gentlemen,' he nodded affably, pleased that he had again surprised a train which he had not expected to find there.

When Captain Ságner wanted to make a report to him, he only waved his hand. 'Your transport is not in proper order. Your transport is not sleeping. Your transport should already be asleep. When transports stand at a station the men in them have to be asleep at 9 p.m. as in barracks.'

He spoke curtly: 'Before nine o'clock the men have to be taken out to the latrines behind the station. After that they have to go to bed. If not they commit a nuisance on the track during the night. Do you

understand me, captain? Repeat that to me. Or rather, don't repeat it to me. Just do what I ask. Sound the alarm, drive the men to the latrines, sound the retreat and lights out, control who is not sleeping and punish them! Yes. Is that all? Issue supper at six o'clock.'

He was speaking now of something which belonged to the past, something which no longer happened, which was, as it were, round some other corner. He stood there like a phantom from the world of the fourth dimension.

'Issue supper at six o'clock,' he continued, looking at his watch which showed ten minutes past eleven at night. 'At half past eight alarm, latrine shitting, then bed. For supper at six o'clock – goulash with potatoes instead of fifteen dekas of Emmentaler cheese.'

Then he gave the order 'stand to'. Again Captain Ságner had the alarm sounded and the inspecting general, watching the battalion falling in, strolled with the officers and talked to them all the time as though they were idiots and couldn't immediately understand. As he did so he pointed at the hands of his watch: 'Very well, now, look! At half past eight shitting and half an hour later bed. That's quite sufficient. In this time of transition the men have a thin stool anyhow. But I put the main stress on sleep. It fortifies them for further marches. As long as the men are in the train they must rest. If there's not enough space in the vans they must sleep *in shifts*. A third of the men can lie comfortably in the vans and sleep from nine to midnight and the others can stand and look at them. Then the first shift who have slept can give up their places to the next shift who will sleep from midnight to three o'clock in the morning. The third shift sleeps from three to six and then there's reveille and the men wash. No jumping out of the vans when – they're – in – motion! Station patrols along the train so that no one jumps out when – it's – in – motion! If the enemy breaks a soldier's leg ... ' The general tapped himself on the leg: '... that's something praiseworthy, but crippling yourself by uselessly jumping out of a van when the train is in full motion is a penal offence.'

'So this is your battalion?' he asked Captain Ságner, looking at the sleepy figures of the men, many of whom could not control themselves and having been whipped out of sleep were yawning in the fresh night air. 'It's a yawning battalion, captain. The men must go to bed at nine.'

The general took up a position in front of the 11th company, where Švejk stood on the left flank and yawned terribly, but while he was doing it he was good-mannered enough to hold his hand before his mouth. But from underneath his hand there resounded such a roar that Lieutenant Lukáš trembled all over in case the general should pay closer attention to it. It struck him that Švejk was yawning on purpose.

And the general, as though he knew it, turned round to Švejk and went up to him: 'Czech or German?'

'Czech, humbly report, sir,' Švejk replied in German.

'Goot,' said the general, who was a Pole and knew a little Czech, although he pronounced it as though it were Polish and used Polish expressions. 'You roars like a cow doess for hiss hay. Shot op! Shot your mog! Dawn't moo! Haf you already been to ze latrines?'

'Humbly report, I haven't, sir.'

'Vy didn't you go and sheet wiz ze ozer mens?'

'Humbly report, sir, Colonel Wachtl always used to tell us on manoeuvres at Písek, when during the rest period the men crept in among the corn, that a soldier mustn't think all the time only about shitting. A soldier must think about fighting. Besides, humbly report, what would we do in those latrines? There would be nothing to squeeze out of us. According to our march schedule we ought to have got supper at several stations, but instead we got nothing at all. It's no good going to the latrines on an empty stomach!'

Švejk, explaining the situation to the general in simple words, looked at him somehow so trustingly that the general sensed a wish on their part that he should help them. If the order was given that they should go to the latrines in march formation, then that order should have some internal build-up.

'Send them all back to the vans,' said the general to Captain Ságner. 'How did it come that they didn't get any supper? All the transports going through this station must get supper. This is a provisioning station. It's not possible otherwise. There is a definite plan.'

The general said this with an assurance which meant that although it was already approaching eleven o'clock at night, supper should have been served at six o'clock, as he had already previously observed, so that there was nothing to be done but to keep the train another night and day until six o'clock in the evening, so that the men could have goulash and potatoes.

'When you are transporting an army in wartime,' he said with enormous gravity, 'there's nothing worse than to forget about its provisioning. It's my duty to find out the truth and to see how it looks in the station commander's office, for you know, gentlemen, sometimes it is the transport commanders themselves who fail in their duties. When I inspected the station of Subotište on the Bosnian southern railway I discovered that six transports had not got supper because the transport commanders had forgotten to ask for it. Six times they cooked goulash and potatoes at the station and no one asked for it. And so they poured it away in masses. Gentlemen, there was a pit full of potatoes and goulash there, and three stations further on the soldiers from the transports which had just gone by those masses and mountains of goulash in Subotiště were begging on the station for a piece of bread. In this case, as you see, it was not the fault of the military administration.'

He made an impetuous gesture with his hand: 'The transport commanders were not up to their duties. Let's go into the office.'

They followed him, wondering why it was that all generals went off their heads.

At the station command it turned out that really nothing was known about the goulash. It was true that today meals should have been cooked for all transports passing through, but then the order had come to subtract from the army catering accounts 72 hellers for every soldier, so that every detachment which passed through would have a credit of 72 hellers per man, which they would get paid out by the supply office on the next pay-day. As far as bread was concerned the men would get half a loaf at Watian.

The commander of the provisioning point was not afraid. He told the general straight out that orders changed every hour. It often happened that he had messing prepared for the transports and then an ambulance train would arrive, refer to higher orders and that was the end of it. The transport was then confronted with the problem of empty cauldrons.

The general nodded his head in agreement and observed that conditions were definitely improving and that at the beginning of the war it had been much worse. One could not expect everything to go right all at once. Experience and practice were of course required. In fact theory stood in the way of practice. The longer the war lasted the more things would be put into order.

'I can give you a practical example,' he said with obvious delight that he had hit upon something outstanding. 'Two days ago transports passing through the station of Hatvan got no bread at all, whereas you will be able to draw your rations of it there tomorrow. Let's go now to the station restaurant.'

In the station restaurant the general began to speak again about the latrines and to say how ugly it looked when there were cactuses everywhere on the track. Meanwhile he ate beef steak and all of them imagined that he had a cactus in his mouth.

He laid so much stress on latrines that you would think that the victory of the Monarchy depended on them.

As for the new situation with Italy he asserted that it was in our army's latrines that our undeniable superiority in the Italian campaign lay.

Austria's victory crawled out of her latrines.

To the general everything was so simple. The road to military glory ran according to the recipe: at 6 p.m. the soldiers get goulash and potatoes, at half past eight the troops defecate it in the latrines and at nine they go to bed. In the face of such an army the enemy flees in panic.

The general grew meditative, lit a cigar and looked for a very long time at the ceiling. He was trying to think what else he could say now he was here and how he could further educate the officers of the transport.

'The core of your battalion is sound,' he said suddenly, when everyone was expecting that he would continue to look at the ceiling and say nothing. 'Your complement's in perfect order. That man I was talking to, with his frankness and military bearing, offers the best hope that the whole battalion will fight to the last drop of blood.'

He paused and looked once more at the ceiling, leaning against the back of his chair and continuing in this position, while only Lieutenant Dub, obedient to the slavish instincts of his soul, looked at the ceiling too. 'But your battalion requires that its good deeds should not be buried in oblivion. Your brigade's battalions already have their history and yours must continue with it. But what you need is a man to keep exact records and write up the history of the battalion. All the strands of what every company in the battalion has done must go to him. He must be an intelligent fellow, not a mule or a cow. Captain, you must appoint a battalion historian in your battalion.'

Then he looked at the clock on the wall, the hands of which reminded the whole sleepy company that it was time to go.

The general had his inspection train on the track and asked the gentlemen to accompany him to his sleeping-car.

The station commander sighed. The general had forgotten to pay for his beef steak and bottle of wine, and the commander had to pay for it himself again. Every day there were several visits like this. They had already cost him two wagons of hay which he had had to shunt on to a side line and sell to the firm of Löwenstein, the army corn suppliers, as standing corn is sold. The army had bought these two wagons back again and he had left them standing there for all eventualities. Perhaps he would sometime have to sell them back to the firm of Löwenstein again.

But all the army inspectors who passed through this main station of Budapest used to tell each other that the station commander there always had good food and drink.

In the morning the transport was still standing at the station, the reveille was sounded and the soldiers washed out of their mess-tins at the pump. The general and his train had not yet left and he went personally to inspect the latrines, where according to Captain Ságner's order of the day to the battalion the men went 'by sections under the command of the section commanders' to give the major-general pleasure. To give Lieutenant Dub some pleasure too, Captain Ságner informed him that he would be the inspecting officer that day.

And so Lieutenant Dub supervised the latrines.

The extensive long latrines with their two rows accommodated two sections of one company. So now the soldiers sat neatly on their haunches, one beside the other over the dug-up pits, like swallows on telephone wires when they prepare for their autumn flight to Africa.

Every one of them had his trousers down and his knees showing, every one had his belt round his neck as though he was going to hang himself any moment and was just waiting for the order.

The whole procedure was manifestly characterized by iron military discipline and efficient organization.

On the left flank sat Švejk, who had got there by mistake and was reading with interest a scrap of paper torn from some novel or other by Růžena Jesenská:

> ... ensive finishing school, young ladies unfortunately ...
> ... ontent not quite certain, but perhaps more rea ...
> who were mostly reticent, and uncommunicative, lo ...
> ... rved lunch in their apartments, or perhaps would ha ...
> devoted themselves to those doubtful delights. And if ...
> ... ed a man and only grief and sorrow for her hon ...
> ... ently she was getting better, but she did not want ...
> as they themselves would have wished. Successfully
> ... othing was more welcome to young Křička than ...

When he managed to tear his eyes away from the scrap of paper he looked involuntarily at the exit from the latrines and was astounded. There stood the major-general of the night before in his full glory. He was accompanied by his adjutant and beside them stood Lieutenant Dub who was eagerly explaining something to them.

Švejk looked around him. All the men went on sitting calmly over the latrines and only the N.C.O.s were somehow rigid and motionless.

Švejk sensed the gravity of the situation.

He jumped up just as he was, with his trousers down and belt round his neck, and, having used the scrap of paper in the very last moment, he roared out: 'Halt! Up! Attention! Eyes right!' and saluted. Two sections with their trousers down and their belts round their necks rose over the latrines.

The major-general smiled affably and said: 'At ease! Carry on!' Lance-Corporal Málek was the first to give an example to his section and resume his original posture. Only Švejk continued to stand and salute, because from one side he was being approached menacingly by Lieutenant Dub and from the other by the major-general with his smile.

'I seess you last night,' the major-general said on observing Švejk's strange posture; whereupon the infuriated Lieutenant Dub turned to the major-general and said in German: 'Humbly report, sir, the fellow is feeble-minded and a well-known idiot. He is an unparalleled imbecile.'

'What are you saying, lieutenant?' the major-general roared suddenly at Lieutenant Dub and let fly at him, saying that the very opposite was true. It was a case of a man who knew his duties when he saw his superior officer, and of an officer who did not see him and ignored him. It was just like in the field. The ordinary soldier assumes command in time of danger. And it was Lieutenant Dub himself who should have given the order that soldier gave: 'Halt! Up! Attention! Eyes right!'

'Haf you viped your arsch?' the major-general asked Švejk.

'Humbly report, sir, everything is in order.'

'Von't you sheet no more?'

'Humbly report, sir, I've finished.'

'Vell, now pull your hoses op and shtand at attention again!' Because the major-general pronounced the word 'attention' rather louder, the men who were nearest started getting up over the latrine.

The major-general waved to them affably and said in a gentle, fatherly voice: 'No, no! At eess! At eess! Jost go on!'

Švejk in his full splendour was already standing in front of the major-general, who delivered a short address to him in German: 'Respect for superiors, knowledge of service regulations and presence of mind mean everything in wartime. And if added to that we have courage, there is no enemy we need fear.' Turning to Lieutenant Dub, he prodded Švejk's belly with his finger and said: 'Make a note of this: when you get to the front this man must be promoted at once and at the next opportunity his name should be put forward for the

Bronze Medal for meticulous execution of duties and perfect knowledge of. . . . But you know what I mean. . . . Dismiss!'

The major-general went away from the latrines, while Lieutenant Dub gave orders in a loud voice so that the major-general could hear: 'First section up! Form fours! . . . Second section . . .'

Meanwhile Švejk went away and when he passed Lieutenant Dub he saluted as was right and proper, but Lieutenant Dub said all the same, 'As you were!' and Švejk had to salute again and hear once more: 'Do you know me? You don't know me! You know me from my good side, but wait till you get to know me from my bad side! I'll make you cry!'

At last Švejk went off to his van thinking: 'Once when we were still in the barracks in Karlín there was a lieutenant called Chudavý and he used to say something quite different when he got angry: "Lads, when you see me, always remember that I am a swine to you and I'll go on being a swine to you as long as you stay in the company."'

When Švejk passed the staff carriage, Lieutenant Lukáš called to

him to tell Baloun to hurry up with the coffee and close the tin of milk properly again so that it wouldn't go bad. Baloun was making coffee for Lieutenant Lukáš on a small spirit stove in Vaněk's van. When Švejk walked up to pass the message on he realized that while he had been away the whole van had been drinking coffee.

Lieutenant Lukáš's tins of coffee and milk were already half empty and Baloun who was sipping coffee from his cup dug about with his spoon in the tinned milk to make the coffee better.

Jurajda and Vaněk both promised that when the next supply of tinned coffee and milk came they would make it up to Lieutenant Lukáš.

Švejk was also offered coffee but declined it saying to Baloun: 'An order has just come from army staff that every batman who embezzles his officer's tinned milk and coffee will be hanged without delay within the next twenty-four hours. I have to convey this to you from the lieutenant who wants to see you immediately with the coffee.'

The panic-stricken Baloun tore out of the hands of Chodounský the portion of coffee which he had just poured for him a moment ago, put it on the stove to be heated up a little more, added some tinned milk and rushed off with it to the staff carriage.

With goggling eyes he served the coffee to Lieutenant Lukáš. As he did so the thought went through his head that Lieutenant Lukáš must be able to read in his eyes how he had treated his tins.

'I was held up,' he stammered, 'because I couldn't open them.'

'I suppose you've gone and spilt the tinned milk, haven't you,' asked Lieutenant Lukáš, drinking his coffee, 'or you've gorged it on a spoon like soup? Do you know what you're in for?'

Baloun sighed and moaned: 'Humbly report, I have three children, sir.'

'You'd better look out, Baloun. I must warn you once again about your voracity. Hasn't Švejk said anything to you?'

'He said I could be hanged in the next twenty-four hours,' Baloun answered in mournful tones, trembling in every limb.

'Don't quake in front of me here, you idiot,' Lieutenant Lukáš said with a smile, 'but try to reform. Put your greediness out of your head and tell Švejk to look around in the station or in the neighbourhood for something good to eat. Give him these ten guilders here. I shan't send you. You'll only go when you're crammed full to bursting point. Didn't you eat up my tin of sardines? You say you didn't? Then bring it here and show it to me!'

Baloun told Švejk that the lieutenant had sent him twenty crowns to find something good to eat on the station. Then with a sigh he took out of the lieutenant's case the tin of sardines and in low spirits carried it to the lieutenant for inspection.

The poor fool had been happily hoping that Lieutenant Lukáš might have already forgotten about the sardines, but now that dream was over. The lieutenant would probably keep them in his carriage and deprive him of them. He felt as if he had been robbed.

'Humbly report, sir, here are your sardines,' he said bitterly as he gave them to their owner. 'Should I open them?'

'All right, Baloun, don't open anything but take them back to where they belong. I only wanted to be sure that you hadn't looked at them. You see, I thought that when you brought me my coffee you had a greasy mouth. Has Švejk already gone?'

'Humbly report, sir, he has,' said Baloun, cheering up. 'He said that you would be satisfied, sir, and that everybody would be envious of you, sir. He went somewhere outside the station and said that he knew the whole countryside here as far as Rákospalota. If by any chance the train should go off without him he would get himself on to a motor column and catch us up by car at the next station. We shouldn't worry about him, he knew what was his duty, even if it meant taking a fiacre at his own expense and driving after the train to Galicia. The money could be deducted from his pay afterwards. You definitely don't need to have any worry about him, sir.'

'Go away,' said Lieutenant Lukáš sadly.

They brought the news from the office of the command that they would be leaving by 2 p.m. via Gödöllö–Aszód and that at the various stations they would draw two litres of red wine and a bottle of cognac for the officers. They said it was a stray consignment intended for the Red Cross. Whatever it may have been it was a gift from heaven and there was joy in the staff carriage. The cognac had three stars and the wine was Gumpoldskirchen.

Only Lieutenant Lukáš was rather uneasy all the time. An hour had already passed and Švejk had still not come. Half an hour later a strange procession emerged from the office of the station command and approached the staff carriage.

At the head walked Švejk, grave and sublime, like one of the early Christian martyrs being dragged into the arena.

On each side of him marched a Hungarian Honvéd with fixed bayonet. On the left flank was a sergeant from the station command and behind them a woman in a red skirt with accordion pleats and a man in boots with a round hat and a black eye. He carried a live hen which was squawking in a terrified way.

They were all getting into the staff carriage, but the sergeant bawled in Hungarian at the man with the hen and the woman to stay where they were.

Seeing Lieutenant Lukáš, Švejk started winking at him very significantly.

The sergeant wanted to speak with the commander of the 11th

march company. Lieutenant Lukáš took from him a document from the station commander. He read it and turned pale:

To the commander of the 11th march company of the Nth march battalion of the 91st infantry regiment for further action.

This is to present infantryman Švejk, Josef, according to his own statement the orderly of the same march company of the Nth march battalion of the

91st infantry regiment, accused of the crime of larceny, committed against the married couple István in Isatarcsa in the region of the station command.

Grounds: Infantryman Švejk, Josef, having taken possession of a hen which was running behind the house of the married couple István in Isatarcsa in the region of the station command and belonging to the married couple István [in the original was a gloriously formed new German word: 'Istvángatten'], and having been stopped by the owner, who tried to take the hen away from him, obstructed the owner of the hen, István, in this and hit him across the right eye. He was detained by the patrol, which had been called, and was marched off to his detachment, the hen being at the same time returned to the owner.

Signature of the duty officer.

When Lieutenant Lukáš signed the receipt for Švejk his knees shook under him.

Švejk stood so close that he could see that Lieutenant Lukáš had forgotten to write in the date.

'Humbly report, sir,' Švejk put in, 'today is the twenty-fourth. Yesterday was 23 May, the day Italy declared war on us. While I've been in the country, people have been talking about nothing else.'

The Honvéds went away with the sergeant and there remained below only the István couple who still wanted to get into the carriage.

'If you happened to have another five guilders on you, we could buy that hen. The rogue wants fifteen guilders for it, but he's adding another ten for his black eye,' said Švejk in his narrative style. 'But I think, sir, that ten guilders for an idiotic eye like that is pretty steep. At The Old Lady they broke turner Matěj's whole jaw and six teeth with a brick for twenty guilders, and at that time money had much greater value than it has today. Why, even the public executioner, Wohlschläger, charges only four guilders for hanging people.

'Come here,' Švejk motioned the man with the black eye and the hen, 'and you, you old hag, keep where you are!'

The man got into the carriage. 'He knows a little German,' observed Švejk, 'understands all the swear words and can himself swear pretty well in German.

'Very well then, ten guilders,' he said to the man in a mixture of German and Hungarian, 'five guilders hen, five eye. Five florins, you see, cockadoodledoo, five florins peep peep, yes? This is the staff carriage, you thief. Give me the hen!'

He thrust ten guilders into the surprised man's hand, took the hen from him, wrung its neck, and then pushed him out of the carriage, giving him a friendly and very forceful handshake: 'Cheerio, you old bastard, bye bye! Now get back to your old frump before I knock you down.

'And so, sir, you see that everything can be settled peacefully,' said Švejk to Lieutenant Lukáš. 'It's always best if everything passes off without a scene and a lot of fuss. Now Baloun and I are going to cook you such a wonderful chicken soup that you'll smell it all the way to Transylvania.'

Lieutenant Lukáš could no longer control himself and knocked the wretched hen out of Švejk's hand. Then he shouted: 'Do you know,

Švejk, what a soldier deserves who in wartime robs the peaceful population?'

'Honourable death by powder and lead, sir,' Švejk answered solemnly.

'It's the rope you deserve, of course, Švejk, because it was you who

first started to plunder. You scoundrel, you're a ... I really don't know what to call you. You've forgotten your oath. You give me a sick headache.'

Švejk looked at Lieutenant Lukáš with an inquiring glance and quickly replied: 'Humbly report, I've not forgotten the oath which our warrior people have to take. Humbly report, sir, I swore solemnly to my most illustrious prince and lord, Franz Joseph I, that I would faithfully and obediently serve him and also His Imperial Majesty's generals and indeed all my superior officers. I swore to honour them and protect them and to carry out all their orders and instructions in all services against any enemy whoever it might be and wherever the will of His

Imperial and Royal Majesty should demand it, on the sea, under the sea, on land, in the air, by night and day, in battles, in assaults, in fights and in all other enterprises and in all places whatsoever.'

Švejk picked the hen up off the ground and went on, standing at attention and looking straight into the eyes of Lieutenant Lukáš. 'I swore to fight valiantly and manfully every hour and on every occasion, never to abandon my army, my banners, my flags or my guns, never to enter into parley with the enemy, always to conduct myself as the army laws demand and as befits a good soldier, that I may live and die with honour, so help me God, Amen. And, humbly report, I didn't steal that hen, I didn't commit robbery. I behaved correctly in full knowledge of my oath.'

'Will you drop that hen, you mule,' Lieutenant Lukáš roared at him, taking the papers and hitting the hand in which Švejk held the late lamented hen. 'Look at these documents. Do you see it here in black and white? "This is to present infantryman Švejk, Josef, according to his own statement the orderly of the same march company . . . for the crime of larceny . . ." Now tell me, you brigand, you hyena – no, I'm going to murder you one day after all, *murder* you, do you understand? – tell me, you thieving blockhead, how could you have stooped so low as this.'

'Humbly report,' said Švejk affably, 'it definitely must be a question of a little mistake here. When I got your order to scrounge something good to eat somewhere and buy it for you, I began to wonder what could be the best for you. Behind the station there was absolutely nothing, only salami made of horsemeat and some dried donkey's meat. Humbly report, sir, I thought it all over very carefully. In the field something very nutritious is needed so that one can withstand the war strains better. So I wanted to give you a *grandiloquent* pleasure. I wanted to make chicken soup for you, sir.'

'Chicken soup,' the lieutenant repeated after him, grasping his head with his hands.

'Yes, humbly report, sir, chicken soup. I've bought some onions and five dekas of noodles. Here it all is, sir. In this pocket I've got the onions and in the other the noodles. We've got salt in the office and pepper as well. Nothing else was needed but to buy a hen. And so I went behind the station to Isatarcsa. It's actually a village, not like a town at all, in spite of it being written in the first street Isatarcsa *town*. I went through one street with gardens, then a second, a third, a fourth, a fifth, a sixth, a seventh, an eighth, a ninth, a tenth, an eleventh until finally in the thirteenth street at the very end, behind a house where the meadows begin, a flock of hens was walking about and feeding. I went and picked out the biggest and heaviest one. Please look at it, sir, it's pure fat. You don't need to feel it. You can see at one glance that they must have stuffed it with grain. And so I took it quite openly in the presence of the population, who shouted something at me in Hungarian. I held the hen by the legs and asked one or two people in Czech and German who the hen belonged to, so that I could buy it from them, when suddenly a man and a woman rushed out of that house at the end and the man began swearing at me first in Hungarian and then in German, saying I had robbed him of a hen in broad daylight. I told him not to shout at me, as I'd been sent to buy it for you, and I explained to him what the situation was. And while I was holding that hen by the legs, it suddenly began to flap its wings and wanted to fly away, and as I was only holding it quite lightly it knocked my hand up and tried to sit on its master's nose. And he at once began shouting that I'd given him one across the jaw with the hen. And then that woman started shrieking something and continued to screech at the hen: "Puta, puta, puta, puta." And at that very moment some silly fools who didn't understand what was happening called the patrol on me, the Honvéds, and I asked them to go with me to the station command so that my innocence would come to the surface like oil on the water. But it was quite impossible to talk to that lieutenant who was on duty there, even when I'd asked him to make inquiries of you whether it was true or not that you'd sent me to buy something good. He started shouting at me that I should shut my mug, and that as it was he could see in my eyes a strong branch with a stout cord hanging from it. He was obviously in a very bad temper, when he told me that a soldier who was as well fed as I was must obviously steal and rob. He said that there had been lots of complaints at the station. The day before yesterday, he said, someone had lost a turkey somewhere round about, and when I said to him that at that time we were still in Raab he said that an excuse like that wouldn't hold water with him. And so they sent me to you and on top of that a corporal I hadn't noticed bawled at me and asked me whether I'd realized who I was talking to. I told him that he was a corporal and that if he'd been in the Rifles he'd have been patrol commander and if he'd been in the artillery he'd have been a senior gunner.'

'Švejk,' said Lieutenant Lukáš after a moment, 'you've already had so many peculiar incidents and accidents, so many little "mistakes" and "errors" as you call them, that the only release for you from all your misadventures would be a stout piece of rope round your neck and full military honours in square formation. Do you understand?'

'Yes, humbly report, sir, a square out of a so-called closed battalion consists of four, exceptionally three or five, companies. Is it your order, sir, that I should put more noodles into the soup from this chicken and make it thicker?'

'Švejk, my orders are that you and your hen are to clear out or I'll knock you on the head with it, you bloody idiot ...'

'As you order, sir, but humbly report I couldn't find any celery or carrots either! I'll put pota ...'

Švejk did not have time to say 'toes' but flew out of the staff carriage together with his hen. Lieutenant Lukáš drank a wineglass of cognac in one gulp.

Švejk saluted outside the windows of the carriage and departed.

After a happily concluded struggle with his conscience Baloun was just about to open the tin of sardines belonging to his lieutenant when Švejk appeared with the hen. This naturally caused a flutter among all those present in the wagon, and all looked at it as though they wanted to ask the obvious question: 'Where did you pinch it?'

'Bought it for the lieutenant,' answered Švejk, taking the onions and noodles out of his pockets. 'I wanted to make him a soup out of it, but he doesn't want it and has given it to me instead.'

'Didn't it peg out of natural causes?' asked the quartermaster sergeant-major suspiciously.

'No, I wrung its neck myself,' answered Švejk, taking a knife from his pocket.

Baloun looked at Švejk with an expression of gratitude mingled with respect and began silently to prepare the lieutenant's spirit stove. Then he took some cups and went off to get some water.

Chodounský came up to Švejk and offered to help him pluck the hen, whispering in his ear confidentially: 'Is it far away from here? Do you have to climb over into a yard or is it out in the open?'

'But I bought it.'

'Oh, shut up, be a good sport. We saw how they took you away under escort.'

He helped enthusiastically with the plucking of the hen none the less. In the great and glorious preparations he was joined by Jurajda, who sliced the potatoes and onions for the soup.

The feathers thrown out of the van attracted the attention of Lieutenant Dub, who was on his round of inspection of the vans.

He shouted inside that whoever was plucking a hen should present himself and in the door appeared the happy face of Švejk.

'What's this?' Lieutenant Dub shouted, picking up from the ground the head of the decapitated hen.

'Humbly report,' answered Švejk, 'it's the head of a hen of the breed called Black Leghorns. They lay very well, sir, as much as 260 eggs a year. Would you please kindly look what a rich ovary it has.' Švejk held the hen's bowels and other intestines under Lieutenant Dub's nose.

Dub spat, went away and returned after a while.

'Who is that hen for?'

'Humbly report, it's for us, sir. Just look how much fat it has.'

Lieutenant Dub went away murmuring to himself: 'I will see thee at Philippi.'

'What did he say to you?' Jurajda asked Švejk.

'We've only arranged a meeting somewhere at "Philips". These smart gentlemen are generally queers.'

The occultist cook asserted that only aesthetes were homosexuals. It derived from the very nature of aestheticism.

Vaněk then told how pedagogues in Spanish monasteries violate children.

While the water in the cauldron on the stove began to boil Švejk mentioned how they had once entrusted a whole colony of orphaned Viennese children to a tutor and how he had violated every one of them.

'It can't be helped. It's a passion, you see. But it's worst of all when women get it. Some years ago in Prague II there were two abandoned women, divorced because they were whores. They were called Mourková and Šousková and one evening when the cherries were blooming in the alley at Roztoky they got hold of a hundred-year-old impotent organ-grinder, dragged him to a wood at Roztoky and violated him there. And there's nothing they didn't do to him! In Žižkov there is a Professor Axamit and he used to dig there, searching for the barrows of people in crouch burial, and he really dug out a few. And those ladies dragged that old organ-grinder to one of those barrows, violated him there and really wore him out. And Professor Axamit came the next day and when he saw something lying in the barrow he jumped for joy, but it was only the organ-grinder who had been tortured and martyred by those divorced ladies. Around him there was nothing else but pieces of wood. And five days afterwards the organ-grinder died and those Jezabels had the cheek to go to his funeral. That's perversion if you like.

'Have you put any salt in it?' Švejk asked, turning to Baloun, who had taken advantage of the general interest in Švejk's story to filch something and put it into his rucksack. 'Show me what you're doing there.

'Baloun,' said Švejk solemnly, 'what do you want with that chicken leg? Now look at him, the bastard. He's pinched that chicken leg from us so as to cook it himself secretly afterwards. Do you know, Baloun, what you've done? Do you know what the punishment is in war when someone robs his fellow comrades in the field? He's bound to the barrel of a gun and shot into the air with a shell. Now it's too late to sigh. When we meet the artillery somewhere at the front you'll report to the nearest chief gunner. Meanwhile you'll do some punishment drill. Get out of the van!'

The unhappy Baloun got out and Švejk sat at the door of the van and commanded: 'Attention! Easy! Attention! Eyes right! Attention! Eyes front again! Easy!

'Now you will stand and do unarmed drill. Right turn! Man! You're a cow! Your horns should be where your right shoulder was before. As you were! Right turn! Left turn! Right incline! Not like that, you ox! As you were! Right incline! Now, you see, you mule, that you can do it. Left incline! Left turn! To the left! To the front! Front, you bloody fool! Don't you know what's your front? Forward march! About turn! Kneel! Down! Sit! Up! Sit! Down! Up! Down! Up! Sit! Up! Easy!

'Now you see, Baloun, it's good for your health, as well as for your digestion.'

Crowds began to collect around them and broke into cheers.

'Be good enough to make way,' shouted Švejk. 'He's going to march. Now, Baloun, pay attention, so I don't have to say "As you were!" I hate bothering soldiers unnecessarily. Now:

'Direction – railway station! Look where I'm pointing. Forward march! Section, halt! Halt, for the love of Christ or I'll have you put in jug! Section, halt! At last you've stopped, you bloody fool. Shorten step! Don't you know what "shorten step" means? I'll teach you till you're blue in the face! Full step! Change step! Mark time! You elephant, you! When I say "Mark time!", then you must move your shanks up and down on the spot.'

Now there were already at least two companies gathered there.

Baloun sweated and had no idea what was happening to him, but Švejk went on giving orders:

'In step! Section, to the rear, march! Section, halt! Double! Section, quick march! Slow march! Section, halt! Easy! Attention! Direction – railway station, double march! Halt! About turn! Direction van! Double march! Shorten step! Section, halt! Easy! Now you can rest for a moment! And then we'll start again. Where there's a will there's a way.'

'What's happening here?' It was the voice of Lieutenant Dub who had come running up in alarm.

'Humbly report, sir,' said Švejk, 'we are practising a little so that we shouldn't forget our drill and waste precious time.'

'Get down from the van,' Lieutenant Dub ordered. 'I've really had enough of this. I'm sending you to the battalion commander.'

When Švejk appeared in the staff carriage, Lieutenant Lukáš left it by another door and went out on to the platform.

When Lieutenant Dub told Captain Ságner about the good soldier Švejk's strange tomfoolery, as he called it, the latter was in a very good mood because the Gumpoldskirchen had indeed been first-class.

'I see, so you don't want to waste precious time,' he said with a knowing smile. 'Matušič, come here!'

The battalion orderly received instructions to summon the sergeant-major of the 12th company, Nasáklo, known to be the greatest tyrant, and to equip Švejk at once with a rifle.

'This man here,' Captain Ságner said to Sergeant-Major Nasáklo, 'doesn't want to waste precious time. Take him behind the van and give him an hour's rifle drill. But no pity and no respite, mind you! The main thing is – one order smartly after the other: order arms, shoulder arms, order arms!

'You'll see, Švejk, that you won't be bored,' he said to him as he went away. And a moment later from behind the van a harsh order resounded ceremoniously between the tracks. Sergeant-Major Nasáklo, who had just been playing vingt-et-un and had held the bank, bawled out into the wide spaces of the heavens: 'Order arms! Shoulder arms! Order arms! Shoulder arms!'

Then there was silence for a short time and the happy and meditative voice of Švejk could be heard saying: 'I learnt all that years ago on regular service. When it's "order arms", then the rifle rests on the right hip. The point of the butt is in a straight line with the point of the toe. The right arm is naturally stretched and holds the rifle so that the thumb hugs the barrel. The other fingers must hold the butt by its front part. And when it's "shoulder arms" the rifle hangs freely on its sling over the right shoulder, the mouth of the barrel upwards and the barrel at the back . . .'

'Now you bloody well put a sock in it!' Sergeant-Major Nasáklo went on with his commands. 'Attention! Eyes right! Herrgott, what a mess you're making of it . . .'

'I'm at "shoulder arms", and at "eyes right" my right hand slips down the sling and clasps the neck of the butt. I throw my head to the right. When it's "Attention!" I take the sling again with my right hand and my head looks straight at you.'

And again there resounded the voice of the sergeant-major: 'Trail arms! Order arms! Trail arms! Shoulder – arms! Fix bayonets! Unfix bayonets! Sheath bayonets! Prepare for prayer! Finish prayer! Kneel down for prayer! Load! Shoot! Shoot half-right! Target staff carriage! Distance 200 paces! Ready! Aim! Fire! Easy! Aim! Fire! Aim! Fire! Easy! Sights normal! Cartridges in pouch! Easy!' The sergeant-major rolled a cigarette.

Meanwhile Švejk looked at the number on the rifle and said: '4268! It's the same number a railway engine in Pečky had on track no. 16. They should have taken it away for repairs to the depot in Lysá nad Labem but it didn't go so easily, because, you see, sergeant-major, that engine-driver, who should have taken it away, had a very bad memory for figures. And so the track supervisor called him to his office and said to him: "On track no. 16 there's an engine no. 4268. I know you have a bad memory for figures and if I write any figure down on paper you lose the paper. Now listen carefully and as you're not good at figures I'll show you that it's very easy to remember any number you like. Look: the engine that you are to take off to the depot in Lysá nad Labem is no. 4268. Now pay careful attention. The first figure is four, the second is two, which means that you have to remember 42. That's twice two. That means that in the order of the figures 4 comes first. 4 divided by 2 makes 2 and so again you've got next to each other 4 and 2. Now, don't be afraid! What's twice 4? 8, isn't it? Well, then, get it into your head that 8 is the last in the series of figures in 4268. And now, when you've already got in your head that the first figure is 4, the second 2 and the fourth 8, all that's to be done is to be clever and remember the 6 which comes before the 8. And that's frightfully simple. The first figure is 4, the second is 2, and 4 and 2 are 6. So now you've got it: the second from the end is 6 and now we shall never forget the order of figures. You now have indelibly fixed in your mind the number 4268. But of course you can also reach the same result by an even simpler method . . ." '

The sergeant-major stopped smoking, goggled his eyes and could only stutter: 'Cap off!'

Švejk went on solemnly: 'So he then began to explain to him the simpler method of how to remember the number of the engine 4268. 8 minus 2 is 6. And so now he already knew 68. 6 minus 2 is 4. So now he knew 4 and 68, and only the two had to be inserted, which made $4 - 2 - 6 - 8$. And it isn't too difficult either to do it still another way by means of multiplication and division. In this way the same result is reached too. "Remember," the track supervisor said, "that twice 42 is 84. The year has 12 months. Very well, then, subtract 12 from 84 and you have 72 left. Take away from that the 12 months and

you have 60. We're sure about the 6 and cross out the nought. Now we know 42, 68, 4. When we've crossed out the nought we also cross out the last four, and we again get quite easily 4268, the number of the engine which is due for the depot in Lysá nad Labem. And, as l told you, it's quite easy by division. We calculate the co-efficient by the customs tariff!" Aren't you feeling well, sergeant-major? If you like I can easily start with perhaps "Prepare to fire salvo! Load! Aim! Fire!" Oh, hell! The captain shouldn't have sent us to do this in the sun! I must go and fetch a stretcher.'

When the doctor came he found that it was a case of sunstroke or acute inflammation of the lining of the brain.

When the sergeant-major recovered consciousness Švejk stood by him and said: 'Let me finish my story. Do you really imagine, sergeant-major, that that engine-driver managed to remember the figures? He muddled them all up and multiplied them all by three, because he remembered the Holy Trinity. And so he never found that engine. It's still standing there on track no. 16.'

The sergeant-major shut his eyes again.

And when Švejk returned to his van and was asked why he had been away so long he answered: 'Who teaches another the "double" must himself do a hundred "shoulder arms".' In the back of the van Baloun was trembling. During Švejk's absence, when part of the hen was cooked and ready, he had eaten up half Švejk's portion.

Before the train's departure it was caught up by a mixed military transport with various detachments in it. They were either latecomers, soldiers from hospitals trying to catch up with their detachments, or other suspicious individuals returning from special duties or arrest.

Among those getting out of this train was the one-year volunteer, Marek, who had been accused of mutiny because he had refused to clean the latrines, but the divisional court had acquitted him, the proceedings had been quashed and so he now turned up in the staff carriage to report to the battalion commander. The volunteer had up till now belonged nowhere, because he had been continually taken from one arrest to another.

When Captain Ságner saw him and took from him the documents which concerned his arrival and had a very secret minute on them: 'Politically suspect! Caution!', he was not exactly delighted, but fortunately he remembered the latrine general, who had made the interesting recommendation that a 'battalion historian' should be added to the battalion's strength.

'You're very negligent, you one-year volunteer,' he said to him. 'In the volunteer school you were a thorough devil and instead of trying to do well and get promoted, as your intelligence deserved, you just drifted about from arrest to arrest. The regiment must really be ashamed of you, volunteer. However, you can rectify your faults if you carry out your duties in the proper way and so take your place again in the ranks of good warriors. Devote your efforts to the battalion and do so with love. I shall see what I can do with you. You're an intelligent young man and certainly have the talent to write in a good style. Let me tell you something. Every battalion at the front needs a man who can make a chronological survey of all the events of the war which distinguish a battalion's performance on the fields of battle. All the battalion's victorious campaigns, all the significant and glorious moments which it experiences and in which it plays a leading and eminent role, should be recorded so that they will gradually form a contribution to the history of the army. Do you understand me?'

'Humbly report, I do, sir. It's a question of episodes from the life of all units. The battalion has its history. On the basis of the history of its battalions the regiment compiles its history. The regiments make the history of the brigade, the brigades make the history of the division and so on and so on. I'll do my very best, sir.'

Marek placed his hand on his heart.

'I shall set down with true love the finest hours of our battalion, especially at this time, when the offensive is in full swing and when it's going to be tough and our battalion will strew the battlefield with the corpses of its heroic sons. I shall conscientiously record the course of all the events which will have to happen, so that the pages of the history of our battalion may be full of laurels.'

'You will be attached to the staff of the battalion, volunteer. You will note carefully who has been recommended for decorations, you will record – of course according to our own directives – the marches which will particularly illustrate outstanding examples of the warlike spirit and iron discipline of our battalion. This is by no means an easy task, volunteer, but I hope that you have enough talent for observation, so that when you have received from me certain directives you will be able to exalt our own battalion above other formations. I am sending a telegram to the regiment that I have nominated you "battalion historian". Report to Quartermaster Sergeant-Major Vaněk of the 11th company so that he can find room for you in the van. There's still plenty of room there. Tell him to come and report to me. Of course you will be included in the lists of the battalion staff. This will be done by a battalion order.'

The occultist cook was sleeping. Baloun was still trembling, because he had already opened the lieutenant's sardines. Vaněk had gone to see

Captain Ságner, and Chodounský, who had secretly laid hands on a bottle of borovička somewhere on the station, had drunk it up and was now singing in a sentimental mood:

> 'While I still erred in my sweet dreams,
> Then all the world seemed true,
> And faith alone breathed in my breast.
> With love my eye flamed too.
>
> But when the whole world seemed to me
> As false as Judas' lie,
> My love and faith did fade away
> And I first learned to cry.'

Then he got up, went to Vaněk's table, and wrote on a piece of paper in large letters:

I herewith humbly request that I should be appointed and promoted battalion horn-player.

Chodounský, telegraphist.

Captain Ságner's conversation with Vaněk did not last too long. He did no more than inform him that provisionally the battalion historian, volunteer Marek, would be accommodated in the van with Švejk.

'I can only say this much to you, that that fellow Marek is, if I can put it in this way, suspect. Politically suspect. My goodness! There's nothing very remarkable in that today. Who is there who doesn't have that reputation? There are various suspicions like this. However, you do understand what I mean, don't you? I'm just telling you so that if by chance he should say something which, well, you understand what I mean, you will immediately sit on him so that I shan't have any trouble about it. Just tell him that he's to stop all talk of that kind and that will settle it. I don't mean that you should come running to me at once. Settle it with him in a friendly fashion. A friendly talk like that is always better than a stupid denunciation. In short I don't want to hear anything, because . . . well, you understand. . . . A thing like that always reflects on the whole battalion.'

And so when Vaněk returned he took Marek aside and said to him: 'Old man, you're under suspicion, but that doesn't matter. Only be careful what you say in front of that telegraphist, Chodounský.'

Hardly had he finished saying this when Chodounský came staggering in and fell into the arms of the quartermaster sergeant-major. He was sobbing out in drunken tones what perhaps was meant to be a song:

> 'When all the world abandoned me,
> Upon thy breast I sank my head.
> Upon thy heart, so warm and pure,
> Bitter, despairing tears I shed.
> A little flame burst in thine eye
> Like tiny stars which gleam and shine.
> I heard the whisper of coral lips:
> "I'll never leave thee. Thou art mine."'

'We'll never leave each other,' howled Chodounský. 'Whatever I hear on the telephone I'll tell you at once. I shit on my oath.'

In the corner Baloun crossed himself in horror and began to pray aloud:

'Mother of God, be not deaf to my anguished prayers, but hearken mercifully unto me. Console me with Thy love, help me, miserable sinner, who calls to Thee with living faith, firm hope and ardent love in this vale of tears. Oh, heavenly Queen, by Thy intercession help me to continue to walk in the grace of God and under Thy protection till the last days of my life.'

The merciful Virgin did in fact take him under her protection, for a little later the volunteer drew out of his poor haversack several tins of sardines and distributed one to each of them.

Baloun resolutely opened Lieutenant Lukáš's case and put back into it the sardines which had fallen from heaven.

But when the others had opened their tins and were enjoying their sardines Baloun succumbed to temptation, opened both the case and the sardines and gobbled them up voraciously.

And then the most merciful and sweet Virgin turned her face from him, because at the very moment when he was drinking up the oil from the tin Matušič appeared in front of the van and called up: 'Baloun, you've got to bring the sardines to your lieutenant.'

'Now you're going to get your face knocked in,' said Vaněk.

'You'd better not go to him empty-handed,' Švejk advised. 'At least take these five empty tins with you.'

'What have you done that God should punish you so?' said the volunteer. 'There must have been some enormous sin in your past life, surely? Didn't you perhaps commit sacrilege and eat up your vicar's ham when it was hanging in his chimney? Or maybe you drank the sacramental wine in his cellar? Or did you steal the pears in his orchard when you were a boy?'

Baloun tottered away with a desperate expression on his face, full of hopelessness. His agitated expression was heartbreakingly eloquent: 'When will all this suffering take an end?'

'This is all because you've lost touch with the Lord, my friend,' said the volunteer when he heard the luckless Baloun's words. 'You don't know how to pray properly for the Lord to take you away from this world as soon as possible.'

To this Švejk added: 'Baloun still can't decide to entrust his soldier's life, his military mentality, his words, his deeds, his soldierly death to the mercy of the maternal heart of the Almighty, as my Chaplain Katz used to say, when he started to get tipsy and by mistake jostled a soldier on the street.'

Baloun moaned that he had already lost faith in the Lord, because he had prayed so often for God to give him strength and somehow contract his stomach.

'It didn't start with this war,' he groaned. 'It's already an old disease, this voracious appetite of mine. Because of it my wife and children used to go on pilgrimages to Klokoty.'

'I know that place,' observed Švejk. 'That's near Tábor and they have a very rich Madonna with false diamonds there, and once a sexton from somewhere in Slovakia wanted to rob her. He was a very pious man. Well, he came there and thought that he'd perhaps get on better if he were first purified of all his old sins. And so he went to confession and confessed among other things that he was going to rob the Madonna the following day. He could hardly say Jack Robinson and finish praying those three hundred paternosters, which the priest gave him so that he shouldn't run away in the meantime, when the sextons came and took him straight off to the gendarmerie station.'

The occultist cook began to dispute with Chodounský whether it was a violation of the seal of confession which cried out to high heaven or whether it was something hardly worth talking about, when it was a question of diamonds which were false. In the end, however, he proved to Chodounský that it was all *karma*; in other words predestined by fate as long ago as the distant unknown past, when this unfortunate sexton from Slovakia had still been a mollusc on some other planet. And it had also been predetermined long ago, when that priest from Klokoty was perhaps still an echidna or some kind of marsupial, now extinct, that he must violate the seal of confession, although from the legal point of view absolution can be given according to canonic law even where monastery property is concerned.

To this Švejk added this simple observation: 'Why, of course, no one knows what he'll be up to in a few million years, and he shouldn't tempt providence. When we were still serving in Karlín in the Reserve Command, Lieutenant Kvasnička always said, when he taught us: "Don't imagine, you dung-eaters, you idle cattle and swine, that military service will end for you in this world. We shall meet each other again after death, and I'll make such a purgatory for you that you'll be completely cuckoo, you bastard scum, you." '

Meanwhile Baloun, who went on thinking in his hopeless despair that they were now talking only about him and that everything had to do with him, went on with his public confession: 'Not even Klokoty cured my inordinate greed. After my wife and children came back from the pilgrimage they immediately set about counting the hens. One or two of them were missing. But I couldn't help it, really. I knew that we needed them in the household for their eggs, but I went out, looked at them and suddenly felt an awful void in my stomach. After an hour I was all right again, but one of the hens was gnawed to the bone. Once when they were at Klokoty to pray that papa shouldn't guzzle up anything while they were away and cause fresh damage, I walked about the courtyard and suddenly my eye fell on a turkey. That time it might easily have cost me my life. Its thighbone stuck in my throat and if it hadn't been for the fact that my apprentice, quite a young chap, managed to get the bone out, I wouldn't be sitting here with you today, or have lived to see the world war. Yes, yes. That apprentice of mine was a smart nipper. He was small, chubby, dumpy, well-fed – . . .'

Švejk came up to Baloun: 'Show me your tongue!'

Baloun put out his tongue at Švejk, whereupon the latter turned to everyone who was in the van. 'I knew it. He even guzzled up his own apprentice. Confess, when was it that you did it? Once when your wife and children were at Klokoty again, wasn't it?'

Baloun wrung his hands and cried: 'Let me be, my friends! And to think that on top of everything else I should get this from my comrades.'

'We don't condemn you for it,' said the volunteer. 'On the contrary, you'll obviously make a jolly good soldier. When the French besieged Madrid in the Napoleonic wars the Spanish commander of the fortress at Madrid ate his own adjutant unsalted rather than be starved into surrendering the fortress.

'That was certainly a sacrifice, because an adjutant who was salted would have been definitely more digestible. Tell me, quartermaster sergeant-major, what's the name of our battalion adjutant? Ziegler? He's such a scraggy fellow that you wouldn't get enough portions out of him for a single march company.'

'Look!' said Vaněk, 'Baloun has a rosary in his hands.'

And, indeed, Baloun in his infinite grief sought salvation in the small beads of the rosary manufactured by the firm of Moritz Löwenstein of Vienna.

'It's from Klokoty too,' said Baloun sadly. 'Before they brought it to me, two goslings had gone, but that's no meat. It's only mush.'

A little later the order came through the whole train that they would be leaving in a quarter of an hour. Because nobody believed it, it happened that in spite of all precautions some men went wandering off. When the train moved off eighteen men were missing, including Sergeant-Major Nasáklo of the 12th march company. Long after the train had disappeared beyond Isatarcsa, he was still haggling with a prostitute in a shallow hollow in a small acacia grove behind the station. She wanted five crowns from him, whereas he was proposing as payment for the service already performed either a crown or a few smacks in the face. In the end, however, a settlement was reached in favour of the latter and with such vehemence that hearing the lady's screams people began to run up there from the station.

From Hatvan towards the Galician Frontier

THROUGHOUT the rail journey of the battalion which was to reap military glory when it marched from Laborce through Eastern Galicia to the front, strange, more or less treasonable conversations took place in the van in which the volunteer and Švejk were travelling. The same thing was happening in the other vans as well, although perhaps to a lesser extent. Even in the staff carriage dissatisfaction reigned because in Füzesabony an army order had come from the regiment reducing the ration of wine for each officer by an eighth of a litre. Of course the men were not forgotten either. Their ration of sago was reduced by one deka per head, which was all the more curious in that no one had ever seen any sago in the army at all.

None the less, Quartermaster Sergeant-Major Bautanzel had to be told of it and felt himself frightfully insulted and cheated, which he expressed by saying that sago was a rare commodity today and he could have got at least eight crowns for one kilo of it.

It was at Füzesabony that it came out that one company had lost its field-kitchen, because at this station the goulash and potatoes on which the 'latrine general' had placed such stress were at last to be cooked. Investigations revealed that the wretched field-kitchen had not left Bruck with them and probably to this very day it still stands somewhere behind shed 186, abandoned and cold.

A day before the departure the kitchen staff belonging to that same field-kitchen had been imprisoned in the guard-house for overexuberant behaviour in the town and had managed to arrange to remain incarcerated there until their march company was safe on its way through Hungary.

The kitchenless company was therefore assigned to another field-kitchen, which of course did not occur without a row. A violent disagreement arose among the men who were drafted from both companies to peel potatoes, one party having stated firmly to the other that they were not such bloody fools as to go and sweat their guts out for the others. Finally it turned out that the cooking of goulash and potatoes was in fact nothing more than a manoeuvre so that the men could gradually get used to the eventuality that when goulash was being cooked in the field in the face of the enemy the order 'general retreat!' might suddenly come, the goulash be poured away and no one get even a lick of it.

And so this was a kind of rehearsal, not tragic in its consequences, but none the less quite instructive, for at the very moment when the goulash was about to be distributed, the order came, 'into the vans', and the train went off to Miskolc. But even there no goulash was distributed, because a train with Russian vans stood on the track there. And so the men were not let out of the vans and their imagination soon got to work: the goulash would be distributed only when they got out of the train in Galicia, where it would be pronounced sour and unfit for consumption and poured away.

And so they took the goulash farther on to Tiszalök and Sambor, and when no one any longer expected that any goulash would be distributed the train stopped at Sátoraljaújhely, where fires were again lit under the cauldrons and the goulash was again heated and at last distributed.

The station was crowded. Two munitions trains had to be sent off first and after them two artillery transports and a train with pontoon detachments. It was certainly true to say that at this station trains were collected with troops from every possible unit of the army.

Behind the station Honvéd hussars were giving hell to two Polish Jews whose hamper of spirits they had plundered. They were in high humour and instead of paying for it were hitting them across the jaw. This was apparently permitted because quite close by their captain was standing and smiling affably at the whole scene, while behind the storehouse a few other Honvéd hussars were putting their hands under the skirts of the dark-eyed daughters of the same Jews who had been beaten.

There was also a train here with a detachment of aircraft. On other lines there stood trucks with the same objects, such as aircraft and guns but badly smashed. They were shot-down aircraft and howitzers with their barrels smashed. And so while everything fresh and new went up to the front, these remnants of glory travelled back to the base for repair and reconstruction.

To all the soldiers who crowded round the smashed guns and aeroplanes Lieutenant Dub of course explained that they were war booty. It did not escape his notice either that Švejk was again standing in a group near by and relating something. And so he went up there and could hear the discreet voice of Švejk saying: 'Whatever way you look at it, it's war booty after all. At first sight it looks a bit tricky

when you read here on the gun carriage "Imperial and Royal Artillery Division", but probably it was like this: the gun fell into the hands of the Russians and we had to win it back. Booty like that is much more valuable because...

'Because,' he said solemnly, when he observed Lieutenant Dub, 'nothing must ever be left in the hands of the enemy. That's like what happened in Przemyśl or with that soldier who had his field-flask torn off by the enemy in an engagement as long ago as in the Napoleonic wars. The soldier went by night into the enemy's camp and brought the field-flask back again. It was worth it, because during the night the enemy had drawn rations of spirit.'

Lieutenant Dub said nothing more than: 'See you make yourself scarce, Švejk, and I don't find you here again.'

'Just as you order, sir.' And Švejk went away to another group of vans, and if Lieutenant Dub had heard what he said afterwards he would certainly have jumped out of his uniform, although it was a completely innocent biblical saying: 'A little while, and ye shall not see me, and again a little while, and ye shall see me.'

After Švejk had gone Lieutenant Dub was, on top of all this, so stupid that he drew the soldiers' attention to a shot-down Austrian plane which had 'Wiener Neustadt' clearly marked on its metal ring.

'This one we shot down from the Russians at Lwów,' said Lieutenant Dub. His words were overheard by Lieutenant Lukáš, who came up and added aloud: 'And during the operation both Russian airmen were burnt to death.'

Then he walked on without a word, thinking to himself that Lieutenant Dub was a prize ox.

Behind the other van he ran into Švejk and tried to avoid him, because from Švejk's expression on seeing him it was clear that the man had a great deal on his chest which he wanted to unload on to him.

Švejk came straight up to him: 'Humbly report, sir, Company Orderly Švejk asks for further orders. Humbly report, sir, I've already been looking for you in the staff carriage.'

'Listen, Švejk,' said Lieutenant Lukáš, in a snubbing and unfriendly tone, 'do you know your name? Have you already forgotten what I called you?'

'Humbly report, sir, I've not forgotten a thing like that, because I'm not a volunteer Železný. Long before the war, when we were in the Karlín barracks, there was a colonel by the name of Fliedler von Bumerang or something erang.'

In spite of himself, Lieutenant Lukáš could not help smiling at the 'something erang' and Švejk went on: 'Humbly report, sir, that colonel of ours was half your height. He wore a long beard like Prince Lobkovic so that he looked like a monkey, and when he got angry he jumped twice as high as he was tall, so that we called him the india-rubber fossil. It happened to be the first of May and we were on alert. The evening before in the courtyard he delivered a great speech to us saying that the next day we must all remain in the barracks and not move a step outside, so that in case of need on highest orders we could shoot all the Socialist scum. And so if any soldier had extended leave of absence and instead of returning to the barracks stretched it out until the next day he would be committing high treason, because a drunken bastard like that wouldn't be able to hit a man when salvos were shot, but would shoot up into the air. So that volunteer Železný returned to his room and said that the india-rubber fossil had had a good idea after all. And it was quite true, you see: the next day they wouldn't let anybody into the barracks and so it was best not to come at all and, humbly report, sir, that is exactly what the smart fellow did with great gusto. But that Colonel Fliedler was such a lousy swine, God help us, that the next day he went all over Prague and looked for anybody from our regiment who might have dared to leave the barracks. Somewhere near the Powder Tower he had the luck to run into Železný and immediately let fly at him: "I'll give you hell! I'll teach you! I'll make it bloody hot for you!" He said a great deal more like this and dragged him off to the barracks. And the whole way he said to him all sorts of ugly threatening things and kept on asking him his name. "Železný, Železný. You'll shit for this. I'm delighted I've caught you. I'll teach you the first of May! Železný, Železný, now I've got you, I'll clap you into gaol – yes, into a lovely gaol." But it was all the same to Železný. And so as they went along Poříč, past U Rozvařilů, Železný jumped off into the carriage entrance of a house, ran away through a passage and cheated the india-rubber fossil of the enormous pleasure of clapping him in gaol. The colonel was so furious over his escape that in his rage he forgot the delinquent's name, got it mixed up, and when he came back to the barracks began to jump up to the ceiling. The ceiling was low and the duty officer was very surprised that the old fossil was suddenly speaking broken Czech and shouting: "Clap Měděný into gaol! Don't clap Měděný into gaol! Clap Olověný into gaol! Clap Cínový into gaol!"[1] And it was in this way the old fossil bullied his staff, keeping on asking them whether they had caught Měděný, Olověný and Cínový, and he even called up the whole regiment, but Železný, whom everybody knew about, had been drafted into the medical section because he was a dentist. And then one day a man from our regiment succeeded in stabbing in the pub U Bucků a dragoon who had been running after his girl. So they formed us into a square and everyone had to come on parade, even

1. 'Železný' means in Czech 'iron', 'měděný' 'copper', 'olověný' 'lead', and 'cínový' 'tin'. The colonel could not get the name right.

the sick, and if anyone was very ill, he was held by two others. And so there was no help for it: Železný had to fall in in the yard and they read us the regimental order that dragoons were soldiers too and it was forbidden to stab them, because they were our "comrades-in-arms". A one-year volunteer translated this and our colonel glowered at us like a tiger. First he went to the front line, then to the rear, then round the whole square, when suddenly he discovered Železný, that mountain of a man who was so colossal, sir, that it was really frightfully funny when he brought him into the middle of the square. The volunteer stopped translating and our colonel started jumping in front of Železný like a dog jumping at a horse and all the time he roared: "You can't get away from me now. You can't escape anywhere. Now I say again that you're Železný. I've kept on saying you were Měděný, Cínový, Olověný. He's Železný, the bloody bastard Železný. I'll give you Olověný, Cínový, Měděný, you bastard, you swine, you Železný!" And then he gave him four weeks' clink, but a fortnight later his teeth began to ache and he remembered that Železný was a dentist. And so he had him brought out of arrest to the medical department and wanted to make him pull his tooth out. Železný took about half an hour pulling it out so that they had to wash the old fossil about three times, but somehow or other he got tamed and let Železný off that second fortnight. And so that's what happens, sir, when a superior officer forgets the name of his subordinate. But a subordinate must never forget the name of his superior, just as that colonel used to tell us. He said we'd never forget for the whole of our lives that we had once had a Colonel Fliedler. – Wasn't that story perhaps a little too long, sir?'

'You know, Švejk,' Lieutenant Lukáš answered, 'the more I listen to you the more convinced I am that you don't respect your superior officers at all. A soldier ought only to speak well of his superiors, even years and years afterwards.'

Lieutenant Lukáš was obviously beginning to enjoy the conversation.

'Humbly report, sir,' said Švejk in an apologetic tone, 'Colonel Fliedler has been dead for a long time, but if you wish it, sir, I'll of course only sing his praises. He was a perfect angel to the soldiers, sir. He was as good as St Martin, who used to give geese to the needy and hungry at Martinmas. He shared his dinner from the officers' mess with the first soldier he met in the yard, and when we were tired of dumplings he ordered for us in the mess "grenadier march"[1] with pork. But it was at the manoeuvres that he really showed his generosity. When we came to Dolní Královice he gave orders that the whole brewery there should be consumed at his expense, and when

he had a birthday he treated the whole regiment to roast hare in cream sauce with bread dumplings. He was so good to the men, that once, sir . . .'

Lieutenant Lukáš tapped Švejk gently on the ear and said in a friendly voice: 'Well, get along now, you bastard. Drop all that about him.'

'Very good, sir!' And Švejk went away to his van. Meanwhile in front of the battalion train where all the telephone instruments and wires were locked up in a van the following scene was taking place: a sentry stood there because by orders of Captain Ságner everything had

1. Steamed potatoes, buttered noodles and browned onions.

to be kept on field alert. Consequently sentries were posted on both
sides of the train according to the value of the transport and received
their passwords from the battalion office.

On that particular day the first part of the password was 'copy' and
the second 'Hatvan'. The sentry at the van with the telephones, who
had to remember this, was a Pole from Kolomyje, who by some
strange mischance had got to the 91st regiment.

Of course he could not know what 'copy' was, but because he had
some faint idea of mnemonics he managed to remember all the same
that the word began with a 'c', and when Lieutenant Dub, who was
duty officer, came up to him and asked him the password of the day, he
proudly answered 'coffee'. Of course this was only natural, because
a Pole from Kolomyje could not forget the morning and evening
coffee in the camp at Bruck.

And when he shouted out 'coffee' once again, and Lieutenant Dub
came nearer and nearer to him, he remembered his oath and that he
was on sentry duty, and called out menacingly 'Halt!' When Lieutenant Dub took two more steps towards him and still wanted him to say
the password, the sentry aimed his rifle at him and not having perfect
command of the German language shouted out in a strange mixture of
Polish and German: 'I'm going to shit. I'm going to shit.'

Lieutenant Dub understood and began to edge away, calling out:
"Commander of the guard! Commander of the guard!"

Then Sergeant Jelínek appeared, who had escorted the Pole to his
post, and asked him what the password was. Lieutenant Dub did
the same and the desperate Pole from Kolomyje replied to those
questions with a roar which resounded all over the station: 'Coffee,
coffee.' There were lots of transports there and men began to jump
out of all of them with mess-tins and there was a frightful panic which
ended in the worthy sentry being disarmed and led off to the arrest van.

But Lieutenant Dub harboured certain suspicions against Švejk,
when he saw that he was the first to climb out of the van with his
mess-tin. He was ready to bet his life that he had heard Švejk shout:
'All outside with mess-tins, all outside with mess-tins.'

After midnight the train moved off to Ladovce and Trebišov, where
it was met at the station in the morning by a society of Hungarian
veterans who had confused this march battalion with the march
battalion of the 14th Hungarian Honvéd regiment, which had only
just passed through the station during the night. Obviously the

veterans were tight and woke up the whole train with their cater-wauling: '*Isten áldmeg a király.*'[1] A few more nationally conscious individuals leaned out of the vans and replied to them: 'Come and kiss our arses. *Eljén!*'[2]

Thereupon the veterans roared until the windows shook: '*Eljén! Eljén a tizenégyedek regiment!*'[3]

Five minutes later the train went on to Humenné. Here were already clearly visible traces of the fighting when the Russians had advanced to the valley of the Tissa. Primitive trenches stretched along the slopes, here and there a burnt-out farm could be seen, and a rapidly built shed nearby indicated that the owners had come back again.

When later at about lunchtime they reached Humenné, where the station showed the same traces of fighting, preparations were made for lunch and the men in the transport could in the meantime catch a glimpse of a public secret, and observe how after the departure of the Russians the authorities treated the local population, who were rela-ted to the Russian armies in speech and confession.

On the platform surrounded by Hungarian gendarmes stood a group of arrested Ruthenians from Hungary. It included priests, teachers and peasants from far and wide in the region. All of them had their hands tied behind their backs with cord and were fastened to each other in pairs. Most of them had broken noses and bumps on their heads, since immediately after their arrest they had been beaten up by the gendarmes.

A little further away a Hungarian gendarme was amusing himself with a priest. He had tied his left foot with a cord, held the cord in his hand and forced him with his rifle butt to dance a czardas. Then he tugged at the cord so that the priest fell on his nose, and as the priest had his arms tied behind his back he could not get up but made desperate attempts to turn on his back, perhaps to be able to raise himself from the ground. The gendarme laughed so heartily at this that tears ran from his eyes, and when the priest tried to get up he gave another tug at the cord and the priest was on his nose again.

At last a gendarmerie officer put an end to this and ordered the prisoners to be taken away to an empty barn behind the station until

1. 'God save the King.'
2. 'Hail!'
3. 'Hail to the 14th regiment!'

the train had passed. There they were to be beaten and pounded without anyone being able to see it.

This episode was a topic of conversation in the staff carriage and generally speaking most of the officers condemned it.

Ensign Kraus thought that if they were traitors they should at once be hanged on the spot without further maltreatment. On the other hand Lieutenant Dub was in full agreement with the whole scene and turned the conversation at once to the Sarajevo assassination, explaining that the Hungarian gendarmes at the station of Humenné were avenging the death of the Archduke Franz Ferdinand and his wife. To add weight to his words he said that he used to subscribe to a journal (Šimáček's *Four-Leaved Clover*) and that already before the war the July number, writing about this assassination, had said that the unparalleled crime of Sarajevo left a wound in people's hearts which would long remain unhealed. The wound was the more grievous because the crime caused the death not only of the representative of the executive power of the state but of his faithful and beloved consort too. Thus by the destruction of these two lives a happy, exemplary family life had been broken up and children, who were universally loved, were made orphans.

Lieutenant Lukáš only muttered to himself that no doubt here in Humenné the gendarmes had subscribed to Šimáček's *Four-Leaved Clover* with its touching article. Suddenly all this began to nauseate him and he felt nothing but an urge to get drunk so as to get rid of his *Weltschmerz*. He got out of the carriage and went to look for Švejk.

'Listen, Švejk,' he said to him, 'do you know where there is a bottle of cognac to be had? I'm not feeling very well.'

'Humbly report, sir, it's the change of weather. Maybe when we get to the battlefield you'll be feeling even worse. The farther one gets away from one's original military base the fainter one feels. A gardener in Strašnice, Josef Kalenda by name, once left his home in the same way. He went from Strašnice to Vinohrády[1] and called at the pub, At the Stop, but at that time he still felt all right. But as soon as he came to the water tower in Korunní Avenue, he called at every pub along the avenue as far as the Church of St Ludmila, and then he began to feel some lassitude. However, he was not put off by that, because the evening before in Strašnice at The Terminus he had bet a tram-driver that he could walk round the world in three weeks. And so he began to

1. Both districts of Prague.

go farther and farther away from his home until he came to The Black Brewery on Charles Square and from there he went to the Malá Strana to St Thomas's Brewery and then to the restaurant, U Montágů, and even higher to the pub, The King of Brabant, and then to The Beautiful View and from there to the brewery at the Strahov Monastery. But at that point the change of climate stopped doing him any good. He got as far as Loretta Square and there got such a fit of homesickness that he fell on the ground and began to roll about on the pavement crying: "Oh, no, no. I'll not go any further. As for that trip round the world," (if you'll excuse me, sir) "I don't care a bloody – spit." But if you like, sir, I'll rustle up some cognac for you, only I'm afraid that the train might start before I come back.'

Lieutenant Lukáš assured him that they would not be leaving for two hours and that cognac was being secretly sold in bottles just behind the station. Captain Ságner had already sent Matušič there and he had brought him a bottle of quite respectable cognac for fifteen crowns. Here were fifteen crowns and he should go, but not tell anybody that it was for Lieutenant Lukáš or that it was he who sent him, because strictly speaking it was forbidden.

'You can be assured, sir,' said Švejk, 'that everything will be all right, because if there's anything I love it is forbidden things. You see, I've always been mixed up in something forbidden without my even having known about it. Once in the Karlín barracks they forbade us . . .'

'About turn – quick march!' Lieutenant Lukáš interrupted him.

And so Švejk went behind the station repeating to himself on the way all the elements of his expedition: the cognac must be good and so he must taste it beforehand; it was forbidden and so he must be cautious.

Just as he was turning behind the station he met Lieutenant Dub once again. 'What are you fooling around here for?' he asked Švejk. 'Do you know me?'

'Humbly report,' answered Švejk, saluting. 'I don't want to get to know you from your bad side.'

Lieutenant Dub turned stiff with shock but Švejk stood unmoved, keeping his hands all the time at the peak of his cap. Then he continued: 'Humbly report, sir, I want to know you only from your good side so that you shouldn't make me cry as you said to me last time.'

Lieutenant Dub's head went dizzy at such audacity and he could only utter an indignant yell. 'Get away, you bastard! I'll have something to say to you later.'

Švejk went away behind the platform and Lieutenant Dub, having pulled himself together again, set out after him. Behind the station immediately by the road stood a row of rush baskets placed upside down, on which there were straw-plaited dishes, and on these dishes there were various delicacies which looked entirely innocent, as though all these good things had been intended for school children on an outing. Lying there were sweets of spun sugar, wafer cornets, little piles of acid drops and here and there on one or two trays slices of black bread with pieces of salami quite definitely of equine origin. Underneath, however, the baskets harboured various kinds of alcohol, bottles of cognac, rum, jeřabinka and other liqueurs and spirits.

Immediately behind the ditch bordering the road was a hut where all this business with illicit drinks was actually transacted.

The soldiers first of all started the dealings at the baskets, and a Jew with long curls drew out of the bottom of the basket an innocent-looking bottle of spirit and took it under his kaftan to the wooden shed, where the soldier hid it unostentatiously in his trousers or under his tunic somewhere.

It was here that Švejk went, while all the time Lieutenant Dub with his detective talent watched him closely from the station.

Švejk began straight away at the first basket. First he picked out some sweets, which he paid for and put in his pocket, while the gentleman with the long curls whispered to him: 'I've got some schnaps too, your honour.'

The negotiation was rapidly completed. Švejk went into the shed but did not hand over the money until the gentleman with the long curls had opened the bottle and let Švejk taste the contents. Švejk was satisfied with the cognac and returned to the station, having shoved the bottle under his tunic.

'Where have you been, you bastard?' said Lieutenant Dub, blocking his way to the platform.

'Humbly report, sir, I've been to buy some sweets.' Švejk fumbled in his pocket and brought out a handful of dirty, dusty sweets: 'May I offer you some, if they don't disgust you, sir. I've already tasted them and they're not bad. They've got a pleasant, special taste like plum jam, sir.'

Under his tunic were outlined the round contours of a bottle.

Lieutenant Dub slapped Švejk on the tunic: 'What are you carrying there, you bastard? Take it out!'

Švejk drew out the bottle with its yellow contents and its clear and explicit label, 'Cognac'.

'Humbly report, sir,' answered Švejk unintimidated, 'that I pumped a little drinking water into an empty cognac bottle. I still have a frightful thirst after that goulash we had yesterday. Only the water in that pump is rather yellow as you can see, sir. There must be some iron in it. Water with iron in it is very healthy and good for you.'

'If you really have such a thirst, Švejk,' said Lieutenant Dub, smiling devilishly and desiring only to prolong as long as possible a scene in which Švejk must finally be the loser for ever, 'go on and drink but drink properly. Drink the whole of it at one draught!'

Lieutenant Dub had already planned in advance how Švejk would take a few gulps and then be unable to go on, and how then he, Lieutenant Dub, would have a glorious victory over him and would say: 'Give me that bottle too, so I can drink a little. I am thirsty also.' He could imagine the expression on that bastard Švejk's face at that frightful moment for him, and then he would make a report and so on.

Švejk uncorked the bottle, put it to his lips, and gulp by gulp it disappeared down his throat. Lieutenant Dub stiffened. Švejk drank the whole bottle before his eyes without batting an eyelid and threw away the empty bottle across the road into the pond. Then he spat and said, as though he had drunk a glass of mineral water: 'Humbly report, sir, that water really had a taste of iron. In Kamýk nad Vltavou there was a pub-keeper who made water with iron in it for his summer guests by throwing old horseshoes into the well.'

'I'll give you old horseshoes! Come and show me that well where you got the water from!'

'It's only a little way from here, sir, just there behind that wooden shed.'

'March in front, you scum, so I can see whether you can walk straight!'

'This is really very strange,' thought Lieutenant Dub. 'You can't see anything on that miserable bastard.'

And so Švejk marched ahead, putting his fate into the hands of the Lord, but all the time something told him that there must be a well there, and so he was not a bit surprised when he actually found one.

There was even a pump there and when they got to it and Švejk began to pump, yellow water spurted out from it, so he could announce ceremoniously: 'Here is that iron water, sir.'

A panic-stricken man with long curls appeared and Švejk asked him in German to bring a glass as the lieutenant wanted to drink.

Lieutenant Dub lost his head so completely that he drank up the whole glass, after which there spread over his mouth the flavour of horse urine and manure. Then, driven completely silly by what he had experienced, he gave the long-curled Jew five crowns for that glass of water and turning to Švejk said: 'What are you standing here gaping for? Clear off home.'

Five minutes later Švejk appeared before Lieutenant Lukáš in the staff carriage and with a mysterious gesture beckoned him to come out of it. Outside he said to him: 'Humbly report, sir, in five, at the latest in ten, minutes I shall be completely gone, but I'll be lying down in my van. I would only beg you, sir, if you would be so kind as not to call me for the next three hours at least and not give me any orders, sir, until I've slept it off. Everything's in order, but Lieutenant Dub caught me. I told him that it was water and so I had to drink the whole bottle of cognac before him to show him that it really was water. Everything is all right, I haven't given anything away, just as you wished, sir, and I was also very cautious indeed. But now, humbly report, sir, I'm already beginning to feel it. My legs are starting to have pins and needles. Of course, beg to report, sir, I'm used to boozing because when I was with Chaplain Katz . . .'

'Get out of my sight, you brute!' Lieutenant Lukáš shouted, but without any anger. Lieutenant Dub, however, became fifty-per-cent more repugnant to him than before.

Švejk got cautiously into his van and lying down on his greatcoat and pack said to the quartermaster sergeant-major and the others: 'Once upon a time a man got sozzled and asked not to be disturbed . . .'

After these words he rolled over on his side and began to snore.

The gases which he emitted by belching soon filled the whole compartment, so that Jurajda, inhaling the atmosphere through his nostrils, declared: 'God! It certainly reeks of cognac here.'

Marek, who after all his tribulations had finally attained the rank of battalion historian, was sitting at a folding table.

He was engaged in writing up in advance the heroic deeds of the battalion, and it was obvious that he derived great pleasure from his look into the future.

Vaněk watched with interest how the volunteer was busily writing and laughing heartily in the process. Then he got up and leant over his shoulder. Marek started to explain to him: 'You know, it's enormous fun writing a history of the battalion in advance. The main thing is to proceed systematically. In everything there must be system.'

'A systematic system,' observed Vaněk with a more or less contemptuous smile.

'Oh, yes,' the volunteer said nonchalantly, 'a systemized systematic system of writing the battalion's history. We can't march off straight away with a magnificent victory. Everything must go gradually according to a definite plan. Our battalion cannot win this world war all at once. *Nihil nisi bene*. The main thing for a conscientious historian like me is first to draw up a plan of our victories. For example, here I describe how our battalion – this will perhaps be in two months' time – nearly crosses the Russian frontier, which is very strongly defended by, let's say, the Don regiments of the enemy, while a number of enemy divisions surround our positions. At first sight it looks as if it's all up with our battalion and that the enemy will make sausage-meat of us. But at this very moment Captain Ságner gives the following order to our battalion: "It is not the Lord's will that we should perish here. Let's flee." And so our battalion starts to flee, but when the enemy division, which has encircled us, sees that we are actually running after them, they begin to retreat in panic and fall into the hands of our army's reserve without firing a shot. It is at this point really where the whole history of our battalion begins. From unimportant events, to speak like a prophet, Mr Vaněk, far-reaching things develop. Our battalion goes from victory to victory. It will be interesting to read how it attacks the enemy when he is asleep. For this we obviously need the style of the *Illustrated War News*, which was published by Vilímek during the Russo-Japanese war. Well, as I said, our battalion attacks the camp of the enemy while he is asleep. Each man of us seeks out an enemy and with all his force thrusts a bayonet into his chest. The finely sharpened bayonet goes through him like a knife through butter. Only here and there a rib cracks. The sleeping enemy jerk convulsively in their death spasms. For a moment they roll and goggle their eyes, but they are eyes which no longer see anything. Then they give the death rattle and their bodies stiffen. Bloody saliva appears on their lips, and with this it's all over and victory is on the side of our battalion. Or it will be even better in, say, three months' time, when our battalion captures the Tsar of Russia. But we'll talk about that later, Mr Vaněk. Meanwhile I must prepare in advance small episodes which testify to the battalion's unexampled heroism. I'll have to think out an entirely new war terminology for it. I've already invented one new term. I intend to write about the self-sacrificing resolution of our men, who are riddled through and through with splinters of shrapnel. As a result of an explosion of an enemy mine one of our sergeants, shall we say, of the 12th or 13th company, has his head blown off.

'By the way,' he said, hitting himself on the head, 'I nearly forgot, sergeant-major, or if we're to talk on civilian terms, Mr Vaněk, that you must get me a list of all the officers and N.C.O.s. Give me the name of a sergeant-major of the 12th company. – Houska? Good.

Houska now will have his head blown off by that mine. His head flies off, but his body still marches one or two steps forwards, takes aim and shoots down an enemy plane. It's quite obvious that in the future these victories and their repercussions will have to be celebrated within the family circle at Schönbrunn. Austria has very many battalions, but there is only one battalion like ours, which distinguishes itself so much that in its honour a small intimate family celebration is held in the Imperial Household. I visualize it in the following way, as you can see in my notes: the family of the Archduchess Marie Valerie moves from Wallsee to Schönbrunn for this celebration: the function is a purely private one and takes place in the hall next to the Monarch's bedroom, which is lit with white candles, because, as is well known, they do not like electric bulbs at the court in case there should be a short circuit, to which the old monarch has strong objections. The ceremony in honour and praise of our battalion starts at six o'clock in the evening. At this moment His Majesty's grandchildren are brought into the hall, which is actually part of the suite of the late Empress. Now it's a question as to who will be present besides the Imperial Family. The Monarch's general adjutant, Count Paar, must and will be there, and because during such family and intimate receptions someone occasionally feels faint (by which of course I don't mean that Count Paar himself should vomit), the presence of the personal doctor, the Counsellor of the Court, Dr Kerzl, will be required. For the sake of decency, to ensure that the court footmen shouldn't permit themselves any liberties with the ladies-in-waiting present at the reception, the Marshal of the Court, Baron Lederer, the Chamberlain, Count Bellegarde, and the principal Lady-in-Waiting, Countess Bombelles, will appear. The latter fulfils the same role among the ladies-in-waiting as madame does in the Prague brothel, U Šuhů. As soon as these exalted gentry are assembled the Emperor is informed and appears accompanied by his grandchildren. He sits down at a table and proposes a toast in honour of our march battalion. After him the Archduchess Marie Valerie makes a speech in which she pays a special compliment to you, quartermaster sergeant-major. Of course, according to my notes our battalion will suffer heavy and severe losses, because a battalion without dead is no battalion at all. I shall still have to prepare a new article about our fallen. The history of a battalion should not consist merely of dry facts about victories, of which I have already recorded in advance some forty-two. You, for example, Mr

Vaněk, will fall by a small stream, and Baloun, who's staring at us here in such an extraordinary fashion, will die an entirely different death. It will not be by bullet, shrapnel or shell. He will be strangled by a lassoo, thrown down from an enemy plane at the very moment when he is wolfing his lieutenant's dinner.'

Baloun stepped back, waved his hands despairingly and remarked dejectedly: 'I'm sorry, you know, but I can't help my nature! Even when I was in regular service I used to turn up some three times for mess in the kitchen until they put me in gaol for it. Once I had boiled rib of beef for dinner three times and because of that I was in quod for a month. May God's will be done!'

'Don't be afraid, Baloun,' the volunteer consoled him. 'In the history of the battalion there'll be no mention of the fact that you perished when you were guzzling grub on the way from the officers' mess to the trenches. You'll be mentioned together with all the men of our battalion who fell for the glory of our Empire, as for instance Quartermaster Sergeant-Major Vaněk.'

'What kind of death are you preparing for me, Marek?'

'Don't rush me, please, sergeant-major. It doesn't go as quickly as all that.'

The volunteer thought for a moment: 'You're from Kralupy, aren't you? Then write home to Kralupy that you are going to be missing without a trace, but write cautiously. Or would you prefer to be seriously wounded and remain lying beyond the barbed-wire entanglements? You could lie beautifully like that with a broken leg the whole day. In the night the enemy lights up our positions with his searchlights and notices you; he thinks you're spying and begins to riddle you with shells and shrapnel. You have performed a tremendous service for the army, because the enemy has had to expend on you as large a quantity of munitions as would have been needed for a whole battalion. After all these explosions your bits float freely in the air over you and, penetrating it with their rotations, sing a paean of glorious victory. In short everybody will have his turn, everyone of our battalion will distinguish himself so that the glorious pages of our history will overflow with victories – although I really would much prefer them not to overflow, but I can't help it. Everything must be carried out thoroughly so that some memory of us will remain until, say, in the month of September there will be really nothing left whatsoever of our battalion, except these glorious pages of history which will carry a message to the hearts of all Austrians, making it plain to them that all those who will never see their homes again fought equally valiantly. And I've already written the end, you know, Mr Vaněk – the obituary notice. Honour to the memory of the fallen! Their love for the Monarchy is the most sacred love of all, for death was its climax. Let their names be pronounced with honour, as for instance the name of Vaněk. Those who felt deepest of all the loss of their breadwinners may proudly wipe away their tears. Those who fell were the heroes of our battalion.'

Chodounský and Jurajda were listening with great interest to the volunteer's exposition of the forthcoming history of the battalion.

'Come closer, gentlemen,' said the volunteer, turning the pages of his notes. 'Here is page 15. "The telephonist, Chodounský, fell 3 September together with the battalion cook, Jurajda." Now listen further to my notes: "Exemplary heroism. The former, at the sacrifice of his life, protects the telephone wires in his cover when left at his telephone for three days without relief. The latter, observing the danger threatening from an enemy encirclement of our flank, throws himself at the foe with a cauldron of boiling soup, scattering terror and scaldings in his ranks." That's a splendid death for both of them, isn't it? One torn to pieces by a mine, the other asphyxiated by poison gas which they put under his nose, when he had nothing to defend himself with. Both perish with the cry: "Long live our battalion commander!" The High Command can do nothing else but daily express its gratitude in the form of the order that all other units of our army should know of the courage of our battalion and follow our example. I can read you an extract from the army order which will be read out in all units of the army and which is very like the order of the Archduke Karl, when he stood with his army in 1805 before Padua and got a frightful drubbing the day after. Listen to what people will read about our battalion as a heroic unit, which is a glowing example for all armies. ". . . I hope that the whole army will follow the example of the above-named battalion, and in particular adopt its spirit of self-confidence and self-reliance, its unshakeable invincibility in danger and its qualities of heroism, love and confidence in its superior officers. These virtues, in which the battalion excels, will lead it on to glorious deeds for the victory and blest happiness of our Empire. May all follow its example!" '

From the place where Švejk lay a yawn resounded and he could be heard talking in his sleep: 'Yes, you're right, Mrs Müller, people are all alike. In Kralupy there lived a Mr Jaroš who manufactured pumps and he was like the watchmaker Lejhanz from Pardubice, as like as two pins. And Lejhanz again was strikingly like Piskora of Jičín, and all four together resembled an unknown suicide whom they found hanged and completely decomposed in a lake near Jindřichův Hradec, just underneath the railway line, where he probably threw himself under the train.' There resounded another yawn and it was followed by: 'And then they sentenced all the others to a huge fine, and tomorrow, Mrs Müller, please make me some noodles with poppy-seed.' Švejk turned over on the other side and went on snoring, while between Jurajda and the volunteer a debate started about what would happen in the future.

Jurajda thought that even if at first sight it might seem nonsensical that just for a joke a man should write about what was going to happen in the future, it was nonetheless certain that even a joke like this often had in it some prophetic elements, when under the influence of mysterious forces the inner eye broke through the veil of the unknown. From that moment on Jurajda's conversation became nothing but veils. In every other sentence there appeared his veil of the future, until finally he went over to regeneration or the renewal of the human body. He brought in the capacity of infusorians to renew their bodies and ended with the statement that if anyone broke off the tail of a lizard it would grow again.

To that Chodounský remarked that people would have the time of their lives if they could do what the lizards could with their tails. Take war, for instance, when anyone's head or other parts were torn off. How frightfully glad the military administration would be, because there would then be no disabled soldiers. An Austrian soldier whose legs, arms and head went on growing again and again would be certainly more valuable than a whole brigade.

The volunteer stated that today, thanks to advanced war technique, it was possible successfully to divide the enemy into, say, three diagonal parts. There was a law about the renewal of the bodies of stentors of the family of the infusorians, according to which every dismembered part grew again, acquired new organs and became an independent stentor. By this analogy, after every battle it took part in, the Austrian army would be trebled or increased tenfold, and from every severed leg would grow a fresh infantryman.

'If Švejk heard you,' said Vaněk, 'he would certainly quote us some example of it.'

Švejk reacted to his name, mumbled 'Present!', and went on snoring after having uttered this expression of military discipline.

In the half-open door of the compartment appeared the head of Lieutenant Dub.

'Is Švejk here?' he asked.

'Humbly report, sir, he's sleeping,' replied the volunteer.

'When I ask for him, one-year volunteer, you must at once jump up and call him.'

'I can't, sir, he's asleep.'

'Then wake him up! I'm surprised, volunteer, that that did not occur to you at once. You must show more keenness towards your superior officer. You don't know me yet, do you? But wait till you get to know me!'

The volunteer began to wake Švejk.

'Fire, Švejk! Fire! Get up!'

'When the Odkolek mills were on fire that time,' Švejk muttered, turning again on to the other side, 'the fire brigade came all the way from Vysočany . . .'

'Please be good enough to see, sir,' the volunteer said affably to Lieutenant Dub. 'I'm trying to wake him but it's really not possible.'

Lieutenant Dub got angry. 'What's your name, volunteer? – Marek? – Ah ha, so you're that volunteer Marek who's all the time been sitting in gaol, are you?'

'Yes, sir, I've spent my one-year course – so to speak – in gaol and have been re-degraded. That means that since my release from the divisional court, where my innocence was proved, I have been appointed battalion historian while retaining the rank of one-year volunteer.'

'You won't be it long,' roared Lieutenant Dub, who was now quite red in the face. This change of colour gave the impression that his face was swelling after being slapped. 'I shall take care of that!'

'Please, sir, may I be sent on report?' said the volunteer gravely.

'Don't play with me!' said Lieutenant Dub. 'I'll teach you report! We'll see each other again and then I'll give you hell, because you'll get to know me, whereas now you don't yet know me!'

Lieutenant Dub went angrily away from the van, forgetting all about Švejk in his agitation, although a short time before he had had every intention of calling him and saying to him: 'Breathe on me!'

as a last means of establishing Švejk's illicit alcoholism. But now it was of course too late, because when he returned to the van half an hour later they had in the meantime distributed black coffee and rum to the men. Švejk was already up and at Lieutenant Dub's call jumped out of the wagon like a mountain goat.

'Breathe on me!' Lieutenant Dub roared at him.

Švejk breathed out on to him the whole storehouse of his lungs, like a hot wind carrying to the fields the fragrance of a distillery.

'And what do you smell of, you bastard?'

'Humbly report, sir, I smell of rum.'

'And so you see, you bloody scoundrel,' Lieutenant Dub called out triumphantly. 'I've got you at last!'

'Yes, sir,' said Švejk without any sign of disturbance. 'We've just drawn our rations of rum for the coffee and I had drunk the rum first. If, sir, there is a new order that coffee should be drunk first and rum afterwards, then please excuse me. It won't happen again.'

'And why were you snoring then when I was in the van half an hour ago? Why, they couldn't even wake you!'

'Humbly report, sir, I couldn't sleep the whole night because I was remembering that time when we were still doing manoeuvres in Veszprem. At that time the mock first and second army corps went through Styria and West Hungary and surrounded our fourth corps, which was in camp in Vienna and the surroundings, where we had fortifications everywhere. But they out-flanked us and got as far as the bridge which the sappers were making from the right bank of the Danube. We were supposed to launch an offensive and the armies from the north and later from Osijek in the south were supposed to come to our assistance. They read out in the order of the day that the third army corps would march to our aid, so that when we advanced against the second army corps they shouldn't smash us to pieces. But it was all no use; just as we were about to win they sounded the end of the manoeuvres and those who wore white armbands had won.'

Lieutenant Dub said nothing and went away shaking his head in embarrassment. But a moment later he came back again from the staff carriage and said to Švejk: 'You'd better all of you remember that a time will come when you will be whining before me!' He could not manage to say more and went away again to the staff carriage, where Captain Ságner was just interrogating an unfortunate man from the 12th company who had been brought to him by Sergeant-Major

Strnad. Starting already now to worry about his safety in the trenches this man had carried away from somewhere in the station the door of a pigsty which was reinforced with metal plating. Now he stood there panic-stricken with staring eyes and excused himself by saying that he had wanted to take it with him to his place of cover to shield himself against shrapnel.

Lieutenant Dub used the opportunity to deliver a lengthy sermon on how a soldier ought to conduct himself and what his duties were towards his fatherland and the Monarch, who was the supreme commander and highest military authority. Of course if there should be elements of this kind in the battalion they must be eradicated, punished and clapped into gaol. All this claptrap was so disgusting that the captain tapped the guilty man on the shoulder and said to him: 'Well, well, you obviously didn't mean anything bad, but don't do anything like it again. It was foolish of you. Put the door back again where you took it from and get to hell out of it!'

Lieutenant Dub bit his lip and thought to himself that the preservation of discipline in the battalion, which was on the point of collapse, depended only on himself. And so he went round the whole area of the station once more, and near a depot, where there was a large inscription in Hungarian and German that smoking was forbidden, he found a soldier sitting and reading a newspaper which covered him so completely that it was impossible to see his shoulder straps. Lieutenant Dub shouted at him 'Attention!', because it was a man from a Hungarian regiment which was stationed in Humenné in reserve.

Lieutenant Dub gave him a shaking. The Hungarian soldier stood up and did not even consider it proper to salute. He merely stuck the newspaper in his pocket and went off towards the road. Lieutenant Dub followed him as though in a trance, but the Hungarian soldier quickened his pace and then, turning round, put his hands up above his head in a mocking gesture so as not to leave Lieutenant Dub in any doubt that he had at once recognized him as belonging to one of the Czech regiments. After that the Hungarian trotted out of view among the huts close behind the road.

To show that this scene did not concern him Lieutenant Dub went majestically into a small shop by the road, pointed in some confusion to a large reel of black thread, put it into his pocket and paid for it. Then he returned to the staff carriage, where he made the battalion orderly call his batman Kunert, to whom he gave the thread and said: 'I have to see to everything. I know you've forgotten the thread.'

'Humbly report, sir, we've got a whole dozen.'

'Then show them to me immediately and be back here again with them at once. Do you imagine I believe you?'

When Kunert returned with a whole box of reels of thread, white and black, Lieutenant Dub said 'Now look here, you bastard. Carefully observe the threads which you brought and this big reel of mine. See how your threads are thin and how easily they break. Now look at mine. You've got to work very hard before you can break it. When we're in the field we don't want any rags. In the field everything must be solid. Very well, then, take away all those threads again and wait for my orders. And remember, next time don't you dare to do on your own anything which comes into your head, but come and ask me before you buy anything. And you'd better not wish to get to know me. You don't know my bad side yet.'

When Kunert went away Lieutenant Dub turned to Lieutenant

Lukáš: 'My batman is a very intelligent fellow. Occasionally he makes a mistake but otherwise he catches on to it quite well. The best thing about him is his absolute honesty. When we were in Bruck I got a parcel containing several roast goslings from my brother-in-law in the country, and, believe me, he didn't touch them at all. As I couldn't eat them so quickly he preferred to let them get rotten and stink. Of course it's a matter of discipline. An officer must give his soldiers proper training.'

Lieutenant Lukáš purposely turned to the window so as to make it plain that he was not listening to this idiot's claptrap. He said: 'Yes, it's Wednesday today.'

Lieutenant Dub, feeling the need to say at least something, turned to Captain Ságner, whom he asked in a quite familiar, comradely tone: 'Look, captain, what do you think . . .?'

'Excuse me for a moment,' said Captain Ságner, and went out of the carriage.

Meanwhile Švejk was talking to Kunert about the latter's master.

'Where have you been all the time when there wasn't a trace of you?' Švejk asked.

'But you know very well,' said Kunert. 'All the time I have bother with that old lunatic of mine. Every minute he calls you to him and asks you about things that aren't your business at all. He even asked me whether I was a friend of yours and I told him that we see very little of each other.'

'That was awfully sweet of him to ask about me. I like him very much, that lieutenant of yours. He's so kind, so good-natured, a real father to the soldiers,' said Švejk solemnly.

'Well, that's what you think,' objected Kunert. 'But I tell you, he's a bloody swine and a first-class idiot too. I'm fed up with him. He's always on at me.'

'Not really?' said Švejk in surprise. 'You know, I thought that he was really such a decent chap. It's funny the way you speak about your lieutenant, but perhaps it's natural. All batmen do the same. Take Major Wenzl's. He never says anything about his master except that he's a bloody idiotic fool. Or take Colonel Schröder's. Whenever he talked about his master he never called him anything else but a pissed bastard and a stinking shit. This is because every batman learns it from his master. If the master himself didn't swear, the batman wouldn't repeat it. When I was in regular service in Budějovice there was a Lieutenant Procházka there. He didn't swear very much: he only used to say to his batman: "You lovely cow, you." His batman, who was called Hibman, never heard any other word of abuse from him. And of course Hibman got so used to it than when he went back to civil life he used to say to his papa, mamma or sisters: "You lovely cow, you", and he said the same thing to his fiancée with the result that she broke with him and had him up for insulting her honour, because he had said it to her and her papa and mamma in public at a dance. And she never forgave him and before the court she stated that if he had called her a cow somewhere in private she might perhaps have been ready to consider a reconciliation, but as things were it meant a European scandal. Between ourselves, Kunert, I'd never have thought that of your lieutenant. He made such a nice impression on me the first time I spoke to him. He was like a smoked sausage, all fresh from the chimney, and when I spoke to him the second time he seemed very well read and a man of sensibility. Where do you actually come from? Direct from Budějovice? I'm always glad when someone comes direct from somewhere. Where do you live there? In the arcades? That's good. At least it's cool there in the summer. Have you got a family? A wife and three children? You're lucky, my friend. At least you'll have somebody to mourn you, as my dear Chaplain Katz always used to say in his sermons. And it's true of course, because I once heard a colonel talk like that when he was making a speech to the reserves at Bruck, who were going from there to Serbia: every soldier who leaves a family behind him and falls on the battlefield severs all his family ties – or rather his exact words were these: "If he iss a corpse, zen he iss a corpse of ze family. Ze family tice are gebroken, but he iss all ze more hero, because he hass zacrificed hiss life for ze greater family, for ze Vaterland." Do you live on the fourth floor? On the ground floor? Of course, I'd forgotten that in the square in Budějovice there isn't a single four-storied house. Are you going away already? Ah I see, your lieutenant is standing in front of the staff carriage and looking this way. Should he by chance ask you whether I've talked about him, of course tell him I have and don't forget to say how nicely I spoke of him, how I said that I'd rarely met an officer who behaved in such a friendly and fatherly way as he does. Don't forget to tell him that I consider him very well read and also say that I think he's very intelligent. Tell him too that I warned you to be good and to obey his slightest whim. Will you remember that?'

Švejk got into the van and Kunert went back again to his hole with the threads.

A quarter of an hour later they went on towards Nová Čabyna over the burned-out villages of Brestov and Veliký Radvaň. It was clear that they had had pretty tough fighting there. The Carpathian hill-sides and slopes were furrowed with trenches running from valley to valley along the railway track with its new sleepers, on both sides of which were huge shell craters. The track followed the upper reaches of the Laborec and here and there across the streams flowing into it could be seen new bridges and the charred beams of those they had replaced.

On the way to Medzilaborce the whole valley was furrowed and the earth piled up as though armies of giant moles had been working there. The road behind the river was dug up and destroyed, and alongside it could be seen the vast trampled expanses left by the armies which had rolled over them.

Storm and rain had uncovered the torn shreds of Austrian uniforms lying on the edge of the shell craters.

Behind Nová Čabyna entangled in the branches of an old burnt-out pine there was hanging the boot of an Austrian infantryman with a piece of shin-bone.

Where the artillery fire had raged one could see forests without leaves or cones, trees without crowns and shot-up farmsteads.

The train went slowly over the freshly-built embankments so that the whole battalion could take in and thoroughly savour the delights of war. At the sight of the army cemeteries with their white crosses gleaming on the plains and on the slopes of the devastated hills all could prepare themselves slowly but surely for the field of glory which ended with a mud-bespattered Austrian cap fluttering on a white cross.

After Humenné the Germans from Kašperské Hory, who sat in the rear vans, grew powerfully silent. As recently as at the station of Milovice they had still been bawling as they came in, 'When I come, when I come, when I come back again . . .'

They understood that many of those whose caps were on the grave-stones had sung like them of how nice it would be when they returned home and stayed there for ever with their sweethearts.

In Medzilaborce the stop was behind the smashed and burnt-out station. Twisted beams jutted out from its charred walls. The new long wooden shed, which had been quickly built to replace the burnt-out station, was pasted over with posters in all languages: 'Subscribe to the Austrian war loan.'

Another long shed housed the Red Cross depot. Two nurses and a fat military doctor stepped out of it. The nurses laughed uproariously at the fat military doctor, who was giving an imitation of various animal sounds for their amusement and was making an unsuccessful attempt to grunt.

At the bottom of the embankment in the valley of the river lay a smashed field-kitchen. Pointing to it Švejk said to Baloun: 'Look, Baloun, what we must expect in the near future. The men's mess portions were just on the point of being issued and at that very moment a shell flew in and made this kind of a mess.'

'It's frightful,' sighed Baloun. 'I never imagined that anything like this was in store for me. But it's all the fault of my cursed pride because, miserable brute that I am, I bought some kid gloves in Budějovice last winter. I thought I was too fine to put on my peasant paws the old gloves which my late papa used to wear and so I kept on hankering after those kid gloves from the town. Papa had to be satisfied with boiled peas but I couldn't stand peas at any price, I would touch nothing but poultry. I even turned up my nose at ordinary roast pork too; my old woman used to have to cook it for me with beer, God forgive me!'

Overcome with despair Baloun began to make a general confession: 'I blasphemed against the saints and martyrs. At Malše in a pub and in Dolní Zahájí I beat up the chaplain. I just managed to believe in God, I won't deny it, but I had doubts about St Joseph. At home I tolerated all the saints; only the picture of St Joseph had to be removed, and now God has punished me for all those sins of mine and for my immorality. All those immoral acts I committed in the grinding room! How often I swore at my papa and made his life a burden to him. How I bullied my wife.'

Švejk thought for a moment: 'You're a miller, aren't you? Then you ought to know that though the mills of God grind slowly they grind exceedingly small – if it was all because of you that the world war broke out.'

The volunteer joined the conversation: 'With all that blaspheming, Baloun, and your refusal to recognize all saints and martyrs you certainly did a bad service to yourself, because you must know that our Austrian army has been for years a purely Catholic army and finds its most glorious example in our supreme war leader. How can you be so brazen as to go into battle carrying in your heart the poison of hatred against some saints and martyrs, when the Ministry of War introduced Jesuit sermons for the officers at garrison commands and when we have witnessed the glory of the military resurrection? Are you sure you understand me, Baloun? Do you realize that you're committing a crime against the glorious spirit of our glorious army, as in the case of St Joseph, of whom you said his picture was not allowed to hang in your home? But surely, Baloun, you know that he's in fact the patron saint protecting all those who shirk military service. He was a carpenter and you know very well our expression: "Let's see where the carpenter has left a hole."[1] How many people let themselves be taken prisoner with this slogan. Surrounded on all sides, they saw the inevitability of it, and tried to preserve themselves, not out of any egoistic considerations, but just as members of the army, so that afterwards when they were released they could say to His Imperial Majesty: "We are here and we await your further orders." Now do you understand that, Baloun?'

'No, I don't,' sighed Baloun. 'I have a very thick head. For me you've got to repeat everything ten times.'

'Couldn't you manage with a little less?' asked Švejk. 'If so I'll try to explain it to you once again. Here you've been hearing that you have to act according to the spirit prevailing in the army, that you must believe in St Joseph and that when you are surrounded by the enemy you must look out for where the carpenter has left a hole, so that you can preserve yourself for His Imperial Majesty and for further wars. Now perhaps you understand and you would do best to confess to us in rather more detail what immoral acts you were actually up to in that grinding room. But don't you dare tell us anything like that story about the girl who went to the priest for confession and afterwards when she had confessed various sins blushed and said that every night she committed immoral acts. Now when the priest heard that, you can imagine how his mouth began to water at once, and he said: "No, feel no shame, my dear daughter. I am here in the place of God, and you can tell me the fullest details of your immoral acts." And then she burst into tears and said that she was ashamed, because it was such

---

1. Czech saying, meaning: 'Let's clear off!'

a frightfully immoral act, and he explained to her once more that he was her spiritual father. In the end after long reluctance she started to tell how she used to undress and creep into bed. And then again he could not get a word out of her and she only started to cry all the more. And he said once more that she shouldn't be ashamed, that man was by his very nature a sinful vessel but the grace of God was infinite. So she decided to speak and told him amid tears: "When I undressed and got into bed I began to pick the dirt out between my toes and smell it." And that was all her immorality. But I hope, Baloun, that in the grinding room you didn't do that and that you'll tell us something more substantial, a really immoral act.'

It turned out that Baloun according to his own description had committed immoral acts with peasant women in the grinding room, but his immorality consisted only in his adulterating their flour, which in his simpleness of mind he called immorality. The most disappointed man of all was Chodounský, who asked Baloun if he really hadn't been up to something with the peasant women on top of the flour sacks in the grinding room, whereupon Baloun swung his arms and replied: 'I was too stupid for that.'

The men were informed that lunch would be taken beyond Palota in the Lupkovský Pass, and the battalion quartermaster sergeant-major got out and went to the village of Medzilaborce accompanied by the cooks of all the companies and Lieutenant Cajthaml, who was responsible for the battalion's provisioning. Four men were assigned to them as patrol.

They returned in less than half an hour with three pigs tied by the back legs, a howling family of a Ruthenian, from whom the pigs had been requisitioned, and the fat military doctor from the Red Cross shed who was passionately explaining something to Lieutenant Cajthaml, while the latter was only shrugging his shoulders.

The whole dispute came to a climax outside the staff carriage, when the military doctor began to tell Captain Ságner straight out that those pigs were assigned to the Red Cross hospital. But the peasant would not admit this and demanded that the pigs should be returned to him. He insisted that they were his only property and that he certainly could not hand them over for the price which they had paid him.

Saying this he tried to thrust into Captain Ságner's hand the money which he had got for the pigs and which he was holding. The peasant woman held Captain Ságner's other hand and kissed it with that servility which has always distinguished this region.

Captain Ságner was quite scared by all this and it took a moment before he was able to push the old peasant woman away. But it was of no avail. In her place young forces came up and began to suck his hands again.

Lieutenant Cajthaml announced in a businesslike tone: 'That bastard has twelve more pigs and he was paid quite correctly according to the last division order, no. 12420, catering section. According to that order, paragraph 16, pigs are to be purchased in places outside the war zone at a price of not more than 2 crowns 16 hellers per kilo of live weight. In war-affected areas for every kilo of live weight there are to be added 36 hellers, which means 2 crowns 52 hellers per kilo. There is an additional note saying that, should there be cases documented where in war-affected areas farms have preserved intact their full complement of pigs and other stock and they can be delivered for purposes of catering units which are passing through, payment can be made for the requisitioned pork at the same rates as in places outside the war zone with a special extra payment of 12 hellers per kilo of live weight. If this situation is not completely clear a commission should at once be set up on the spot, consisting of the prospective purchaser, the commander of the military unit passing through and that officer or quartermaster sergeant-major (if it is a question of a smaller formation) who has charge of the catering.'

Lieutenant Cajthaml read all this from a copy of the divisional order which he always carried about on him. So he already knew almost by heart that in the front zone the price per kilo of carrots was increased by 15.30 hellers and the price of cauliflower for the officers' messing department by 1 crown 75 hellers.

Those who had drawn up these orders in Vienna imagined the front zone to be a land flowing with carrots and cauliflowers.

Lieutenant Cajthaml read this out of course in German to the enraged peasant and asked him if he understood it. When the latter shook his head he shouted at him: 'Do you want to have a commission then?'

The peasant understood the word commission and nodded his head affirmatively. And while his pigs had been dragged off only a moment ago to the field-kitchen for execution, he was now surrounded by bayoneted soldiers assigned on requisition duty. The commission set off for his farm to establish whether he should get 2 crowns 52 hellers per kilo or only 2 crowns 28 hellers.

Hardly had they reached the road leading to the village when there resounded from the field-kitchens the triple dying squeals of the pigs.

The peasant understood that it was all up and shouted out in desperation: 'Give me 2 Rhine guilders for each pig!'

The four soldiers ringed him in closer, and his whole family knelt down in the dust of the road and obstructed the way for Captain Ságner and Lieutenant Cajthaml.

The mother and her two daughters embraced the knees of both, calling them benefactors, until the peasant shouted at them in the Ruthenian dialect of the sub-Carpathian Russians and told them to get up: let the soldiers gorge themselves on the pigs and come to a sticky end.

And so that was the end of the commission, but because the peasant suddenly began to be obstreperous and threaten them with his fist, he was beaten by one of the soldiers with a rifle-butt so that his sheep-skin coat resounded with the blow. Then the whole of his family made the sign of the cross and fled together with their father.

Ten minutes later the battalion quartermaster sergeant-major together with the battalion orderly, Matušič, were enjoying pig's brain in their van and while the former valiantly stuffed himself he said waspishly to the writers from time to time: 'You'd like a bite, wouldn't you? Well, my boys, this is only for the higher ranks. The cooks get the kidneys and liver, the quartermaster sergeant-majors the brain, head and neck, and the writers only double the ordinary men's portion of meat.'

Captain Ságner had already issued an order for the officers' mess: 'Roast pork with caraway seed. Select the top-quality meat so that it isn't too fat!'

And so it happened that when in the Lupkovský Pass the mess portions were given to the men, every soldier found in his portion of soup two tiny pieces of meat and whoever happened to be born under an unlucky star found only a piece of skin.

In the kitchen there prevailed the usual military nepotism which rewarded all those who were close to the ruling clique. The batmen appeared in the Lupkovský Pass with greasy lips. Every orderly had a stomach like a boulder. Things happened which screamed to high heaven.

Marek caused a scene in the kitchen, because he wanted to be fair, and when the cook put into his mess-tin of soup a fair-sized slice of roast joint with the remark 'This is for our historian', he declared that in the army all men were equal. This met with general support and provided a good excuse for swearing at the cooks.

The volunteer threw the slice of meat back, saying firmly that he didn't want any favouritism. This was not understood in the kitchen where they thought that the battalion historian was not satisfied, so the cook took him aside and told him that if he came afterwards when the mess portions had been distributed he would get a piece of leg.

The writers' muzzles were also shiny with grease, the medical orderlies snorted with affluence and all around this scene of cornucopia lay the traces of the most recent battles. Cartridge cases were lying about everywhere as well as empty tins, shreds of Russian, Austrian and German uniforms, parts of smashed carts, long bloody strips of gauze bandages and cotton wool.

Where the station had once stood there was now only a heap of rubble and an unexploded shell had lodged itself in an old pine tree. Everywhere could be seen splinters of shrapnel and somewhere in the immediate neighbourhood the corpses of soldiers must evidently have been buried, because it smelt frightfully of putrefaction.

And as the troops passed through and camped in the neighbourhood there could be seen everywhere little heaps of human excrement of international extraction belonging to all peoples of Austria, Germany and Russia. The excrement of soldiers of all nationalities and of confessions lay side by side or heaped on top of one another without quarrelling among themselves.

A half-smashed water reservoir, a wooden hut of a railway watchman and everything of any kind which had any walls were riddled with rifle bullets like a sieve.

To complete this impression of the delights of war, clouds of smoke were rising behind a hill not far away, as though a whole village was burning there and was the centre of large-scale military operations. In fact they were burning the cholera and dysentery huts to the great satisfaction of those gentlemen who were concerned with the setting up of that hospital under the patronage of the Archduchess Marie, and of those brigands who had salted away tidy sums by fiddling accounts for non-existent cholera and dysentery huts.

And now one group of huts was the victim for all the others, and in the stink of the burning straw mattresses there rose to high heaven all the thuggery of archducal patronage.

Behind the station the Germans from the Reich had lost no time in setting up on a rock a monument to the fallen Brandenburgers with the inscription 'The Heroes of the Lupkovský Pass' and a huge Reich German eagle cast out of bronze. On its plinth it was expressly stated that the emblem was made out of Russian guns captured during the liberation of the Carpathians by German regiments from the Reich.

In this strange atmosphere, to which they had not yet got accustomed, the battalion was resting in the vans after lunch and Captain Ságner and the battalion adjutant were exchanging cipher telegrams with the brigade base without being able to reach an understanding on the further advance of the battalion. The messages were so inaccurate that it looked as if the battalion should not have come to the Lupkovský Pass at all, but have travelled in a completely different direction from Sátoraljaújhely, because in the telegrams there was mention of the places: 'Csap – Ungvár, Kis-Berezna – Uzsok'.

Ten minutes later it turned out that the staff officer sitting at the brigade base was an utter nitwit, because a ciphered telegram came in asking whether they were the 8th march battalion of the 75th regiment (military cipher G.3). The nitwit at the brigade base seemed amazed at the answer that they were the 7th march battalion of the 91st regiment and asked who ordered them to go to Mukačevo along the military track road towards Stryj, when the march route was across the Lupkovský Pass towards Sanok in Galicia. The nitwit was awfully surprised that the telegram had come from the Lupkovský Pass and sent the ciphered message: 'March route unchanged, direction Lupkovský Pass – Sanok, where await further orders.'

After Captain Ságner's return there was talk in the staff carriage of some people having lost their heads and certain hints were dropped that if it had not been for the Reich Germans the East Army Group would have lost their heads completely.

Lieutenant Dub tried to defend the idiocy of the Austrian staff and burbled something to the effect that the terrain here was pretty devastated by recent battles and that it had not been possible to put the railway track into the required order yet.

All the officers looked at him pityingly as if to say: 'This gentleman can't help being a bloody fool.' Encountering no opposition Lieutenant Dub started to burble more about the magnificent impression which this devastated scenery left on him, since it proved the striking power of the mailed fist of our army. Again no one answered him, whereupon he repeated: 'Yes, to be sure, of course, the Russians fled here in complete panic.'

Captain Ságner resolved that at the next opportunity when the situation was really dangerous in the trenches he would send Lieutenant Dub as officer on patrol for reconnoitring the enemy's positions beyond the barbed-wire entanglements. He whispered to Lieutenant Lukáš, when they were both leaning out of the window of the carriage: 'These damned civilians are a bloody headache. The intellectuals among them are the biggest bastards of them all.'

It looked as if Lieutenant Dub would never stop talking. He went on to explain to all the officers what he had read in the newspapers about those Carpathian battles and the fight for the Carpathian passes during the Austro-German offensive on the San.

He spoke about it as though he had not only taken part in those battles but had even directed all the operations himself.

It was especially repulsive when he uttered sentences of this kind: 'Then we went towards Bukovsko to secure the line Bukovsko-Dynov, keeping contact with the Bardějov group at Velká Polanka where we smashed the Samara division of the enemy.'

Lieutenant Lukáš could not stand it any longer and remarked to Lieutenant Dub: 'And of course you talked about this already before the war with your district hejtman.'

Lieutenant Dub gave Lieutenant Lukáš an ugly look and left the carriage.

The military train stood on an embankment and down below some metres under the slope lay various objects thrown away by the retreating Russian soldiers, who must have retreated along this ditch. Here were rusty teapots, saucepans and cartridge pouches. Side by side with these various things lay rolls of barbed wire and more bloody strips of gauze and cotton wool. At one place a group of soldiers was standing over the ditch and Lieutenant Dub noticed at once that Švejk was there explaining something to them.

And so Lieutenant Dub went up to join them.

'What's happened here?' he said in a stern voice, standing directly in front of Švejk.

'Humbly report, sir,' answered Švejk for all of them, 'we're having a look.'

'And what are you having a look at?' shouted Lieutenant Dub.

'Humbly report, sir, we're having a look down into the ditch.'

'And who gave you permission to do that?'

'Humbly report, sir, it was the wish of our Colonel Schröder from Bruck. When we were about to leave for the battlefields he said good-bye to us and told us in his speech that when we walked over deserted battlefields we all of us ought to examine very carefully how the fighting took place and see what could be of use to us. And in this ditch we can see everything that every soldier has to throw away when he retreats. We can see here, humbly report, sir, how stupid it is when a soldier drags about with him all sorts of useless things. He's need-lessly encumbered with them. It tires him unnecessarily and if he carts such a weight about with him he can't easily fight.'

The hope suddenly dawned in Lieutenant Dub's breast that he would at last manage to have Švejk brought before a wartime drum-head court-martial for treasonable anti-war propaganda, and so he asked quickly: 'And so you think that a soldier should throw away cartridges like these lying about here in the ditch or bayonets like those I see there?'

'Oh, of course not, oh no, humbly report, sir,' Švejk answered, smiling affably. 'But please look down here at that abandoned metal chamberpot.'

And under the embankment there was indeed lying provocatively a rusty chamberpot of beaten enamel among chips and fragments of other pots. All these articles, which were no longer suitable for domestic use, had been stacked up here by the station master as material for discussion for archaeologists in future ages who, when they discover this settlement, will be quite crazy about it and children in the schools will be taught about the age of enamel chamberpots.

Lieutenant Dub stared at this object but could not do otherwise than confirm that it really was one of those disabled war veterans which had spent their green youth under a bed.

This made a tremendous impression on everyone and when Lieu-tenant Dub said nothing Švejk piped up: 'Humbly report, sir, once there was a lot of fun with a chamberpot like that at Poděbrady spa. I heard about it in a pub at Vinohrady. At that time, you see, they'd started publishing in Poděbrady a provincial rag called *Independence*. A Poděbrady chemist was the main person behind it, and they made a certain Ladislav Hájek of Domažlice editor. And that chemist was such a queer fish that he used to collect old pots and other bits and pieces until he had a whole museum of them. And that Hájek of Domažlice once invited to Poděbrady spa a friend of his who was also a journalist, and they both got thoroughly pickled together, because they hadn't seen each other for a whole week. And the journalist promised his friend that in return for this binge he would write a feuilleton for *Independence*, that independent journal on which he was dependent. So he went and wrote a feuilleton about a collector who found in the sands on the bank of the Elbe an old metal chamberpot, thought it was the helmet of St Wenceslas, and made such a fuss about it that Bishop Brynych of Hradec came to look at it with a procession and banners. Then the chemist of Poděbrady thought that the feuilleton was about him and so both of them, he and Mr Hájek, had a row.'

Lieutenant Dub was dying to push Švejk down the embankment but he controlled himself and shouted at all of them: 'I tell you, you're not to waste your time standing and staring here! None of you know me yet, but wait till you get to know me . . .

'Švejk, you stay here!' he said in a frightful voice, when Švejk and the others were about to return to the vans.

They remained standing in front of each other and Lieutenant Dub was thinking hard what frightful thing he could say to him.

But Švejk cut in: 'Humbly report, sir, if only the weather would keep. It's not very hot in the daytime and the nights are really quite pleasant so that this is the most suitable time for warfare.'

Lieutenant Dub drew out his revolver and asked: 'Do you know what this is?'

'Humbly report, sir, I do. Lieutenant Lukáš has one like it, you know.'

'Then don't forget it, you bastard,' Lieutenant Dub said with gravity and dignity as he put his revolver back. 'You should know that something very unpleasant can happen to you if you continue with these propagandas of yours.'

Lieutenant Dub went away repeating to himself: 'Now I really put it well: "These propagandas of yours", yes, "these propagandas of yours".'

Before Švejk got into his van again he walked about for a short time muttering to himself: 'In what class should I put him?' And the more he thought about it the more clearly it came to him that his classification should be: 'A semi-fart.'

In the army vocabulary the word 'fart' had been in favourite use from time immemorial and in the main this honourable title was bestowed on colonels or senior captains and majors, and it indicated

a degree higher than the commonly used term: 'Bloody old man'. Without the adjective 'bloody' the appellation 'old man' indicated friendly appreciation of an old colonel or major who blew his top a lot but at the same time was fond of his men and protected them from other regiments, particularly when it came to other patrols rounding them up in pubs when they had not been given 'extended leave'. An 'old man' looked after the interests of his soldiers and insisted that their messing was in order, but he always had some kind of bee in his bonnet, was always on about something – and so he was 'the old man'.

But when the 'old man' gave the officers and men a lot of unnecessary hell, thought up night operations and other things like that, he became the 'bloody old man'.

From 'bloody old man', if he attained the highest degree of bloodiness, bullying and blockheadedness, he became a 'fart'. This word was full of meaning, and great was the difference between a 'fart' in civilian life and a 'fart' in the army.

The former, the civilian, was also a superior official and was given this name by messengers and subordinates in government offices. He was a bureaucrat and Philistine, who, for example, would complain that the draft was not properly dried with blotting paper and so on. He was a thoroughly oafish and bloody phenomenon in human society, because a mule like that at the same time pretended to be decent, wanted to understand everything, could explain everything and took offence at everything.

Anyone who has served in the army naturally understands the difference between this kind of phenomenon and the 'fart' in uniform. Here the word meant an 'old man' who was bloody, really bloody, and who made a thorough bastard of himself about everything, but all the same stopped before any obstacle. He did not like the men and wrangled with them without result. He could not gain any of the authority which the 'old man' and the 'bloody old man' enjoyed.

In some garrisons, as for example at Trento, instead of 'fart' the men used to say 'our old shit'. In all cases it was applied to an elderly person and when Švejk inwardly christened Lieutenant Dub 'a semi-fart' he quite logically diagnosed that in both age and rank, and in fact in everything whatsoever, Lieutenant Dub lacked fifty per cent of the quality of being a 'fart'.

Returning to his van with these thoughts in his head he met the batman, Kunert, who had a swollen face and muttered something unintelligible about how he had just run into his master, Lieutenant Dub, who had suddenly out of the blue socked him many times across the jaw, because allegedly he had proof that he was friendly with Švejk.

'If that's the case,' said Švejk calmly, 'we'll go on report. The Austrian soldier may permit himself to be hit in the face only in certain cases. But that master of yours has exceeded all bounds. As old Prince Eugène of Savoy used to say, "As far as so far." Now you must go yourself on report and if you don't I'll swipe you a few myself to teach you what discipline in the army means. In the barracks in Karlín there was once a lieutenant called Hausner and he had a batman too and swiped him across the jaw and kicked him. Once this batman had had so many across the jaw that he was knocked quite silly and he went on report and, getting mixed up, stated there that he'd been kicked. And so that master of his was able to prove that he was lying, since on that particular day he had not kicked him but only socked him on the jaw. As a result the good batman was jugged for three weeks for bringing a false charge.

'But that doesn't affect the case,' Švejk continued. 'It's just the very same thing as the medico Houbička always used to say, that when you cut someone up in the pathological institute it comes to the same thing whether he hanged or poisoned himself. But I'll go along with you. In the army a few socks on the jaw are no laughing matter.'

Kunert had been knocked stupid and let himself be led by Švejk to the staff carriage.

Leaning out of the window Lieutenant Dub roared out: 'What do you want here, you bastards?'

'Comport yourself with dignity,' Švejk urged Kunert, and pushed him forward to the carriage.

In the corridor Lieutenant Lukáš appeared with Captain Ságner behind him.

Lieutenant Lukáš, who had already had so much to do with Švejk, was frightfully surprised, for he no longer looked as good-naturedly solemn as usual; his face lacked its accustomed good-humoured expression and instead boded some new unpleasant developments.

'Humbly report, sir,' said Švejk, 'the matter's going on report.'

'For God's sake don't be a bloody fool again, Švejk. I'm fed up with that.'

'Would you mind permitting me, sir,' said Švejk. 'I am your company orderly. You are, sir, if you will kindly allow me to say so, the company commander of the 11th, if you please, sir. I can understand, sir, that this appears horribly strange, but I know too that Lieutenant Dub is under your command.'

'You've gone completely crazy, Švejk,' Lieutenant Lukáš interrupted. 'You're tight. You'd better go away! Do you understand, you bloody fool, you bastard, you.'

'Humbly report, sir,' said Švejk, pushing Kunert in front of him. 'It seems just like when in Prague they tried to use a protecting rail to stop people being run over by trams. The inventor himself fell a victim to the experiment and afterwards the City Council had to pay his widow compensation.'

Captain Ságner, not knowing what to say, nodded his head in agreement, while Lieutenant Lukáš looked desperate.

'Everything must go on report, sir,' continued Švejk inexorably. 'You told me already in Bruck, sir, that when I was company orderly I had other duties beyond just carrying out orders. You said I had to keep myself informed about everything that was happening in the company. On the basis of this instruction I would like to inform you, sir, that Lieutenant Dub has struck his batman across the jaw for no reason at all. Humbly report, sir, I might not have told you this. However, I saw that Lieutenant Dub is assigned to your command and I said to myself that it must go on report.'

'This is an odd business,' said Captain Ságner. 'Why are you pushing Kunert forward like this, Švejk?'

'Humbly report, sir, everything must go on report. He's been knocked silly. He had his jaw struck by Lieutenant Dub and he's not capable of going on report by himself. Humbly report, sir, you should look at him and see how his knees shake. He's got no life in him, because he has to go on report. And if it hadn't been for me he wouldn't probably have gone on report at all, like a chap called Kudela from Bytouchov. When he was in regular service he kept on going on report again and again until he was finally transferred to the navy, where he became a cornet and was later declared a deserter on an island in the Pacific. There he got married and talked also with the traveller Havlasa, who had no idea he was not a native. . . . It's of course extremely distressing when someone has to go on report just because of a few stupid swipes across the jaw. He didn't want to come here, because he said he wouldn't come here. Altogether he's been so bashed about and knocked so silly that he doesn't even know what swipes on the jaw he's complaining about. He wouldn't have come here at all. He didn't want to go on report. He would have let himself be swiped lots more times and lots more again. Humbly report, sir, look at him. He's all in a shit because of it. But on the other hand he really ought to have complained at once that he had got those swipes, but he was afraid to do so because he knew that it was better, as a poet once wrote, "to be a modest violet". He works for Lieutenant Dub, you see.'

Pushing Kunert in front of him Švejk said to him: 'Don't be all of a flutter like the aspen leaves of an oak!'

Captain Ságner asked Kunert to tell him how it had actually happened.

Kunert, however, shaking all over, asserted that they could ask Lieutenant Dub. He had never struck him across the face.

Continuing to tremble all over, the Judas, Kunert, even went so far in the end as to maintain that the whole thing was an invention of Švejk's.

Lieutenant Dub put an end to this embarrassing affair by appearing suddenly and roaring at Kunert: 'Do you want to get a few *more* across the jaw?'

The case was then completely clear and Captain Ságner told Lieutenant Dub quite simply: 'From today on Kunert is assigned to the battalion kitchen and as to the question of a new batman for yourself you'd better apply to Quartermaster Sergeant-Major Vaněk.'

Lieutenant Dub saluted and as he went out said to Švejk: 'I'm willing to bet that you'll be hanged one day.'

When he had gone Švejk turned to Lieutenant Lukáš and said in a gentle, friendly tone: 'Once in Mnichovo Hradiště there was a gentleman like that too and he spoke to another chap in the same way and got the answer: "We'll see each other on the execution ground."'

'Švejk,' said Lieutenant Lukáš, 'you really are a bloody fool, but don't you dare say as you usually do: "Humbly report, sir, I'm a bloody fool."'

'Remarkable,' said Captain Ságner as he leant out of the window. He would have liked to go away from the window, but had no time to do so because disaster appeared in the shape of Lieutenant Dub who stood under it.

Lieutenant Dub started by saying that he was very sorry that Captain Ságner had gone away and had not listened when he gave the reasons for the offensive on the Eastern front.

'If we are to understand this giant offensive,' Lieutenant Dub called up to the window, 'we have to realize how the offensive developed at the end of April. We had to break through the Russian front and found the line between the Carpathians and the Vistula the most convenient place for this break-through.'

'I'm not disputing it with you,' answered Captain Ságner drily, and left the window.

When half an hour later the journey towards Sanok continued Captain Ságner stretched himself out on the seat and pretended to sleep, so that in the meantime Lieutenant Dub might forget his hackneyed conclusions about the offensive.

In Švejk's van Baloun was missing. He had in fact begged and obtained permission to wipe the goulash cauldron clean with a piece of bread. He was now in the van with the field-kitchens in an unpleasant situation, because when the train started to move he flew headlong into the cauldron and his legs stuck out of it. However, he got used to this position and from inside the cauldron the licking of his lips could be heard. It was like a hedgehog chasing beetles. Later Baloun's pleading voice could be heard: 'For God's sake, chaps, be kind and throw me a piece of bread. There's an awful lot of sauce here still.' This idyll lasted until the next station where they arrived with the cauldron of the 11th company so spotlessly clean that the metal inside it gleamed like a mirror.

'God bless you, chaps,' said Baloun, thanking them heartily. 'It's the first time that fortune has smiled on me since I've been in the army.'

Nothing could have been truer. In the Lupkovský Pass Baloun managed to get two portions of goulash. Lieutenant Lukáš expressed his pleasure that Baloun had brought him an untouched portion from the officers' mess and left him a good half of it. Baloun was serenely happy, swung his legs which he stuck out of the train, and suddenly the whole war seemed to him something domestic and cosy.

The company cook began to tease him and say that when they came to Sanok another supper and one more lunch would be cooked to make up for the fact that throughout the journey they had had nothing. Baloun only nodded his head in assent and whispered: 'You'll see, chaps, that the Lord will not abandon us.'

Everybody laughed heartily at this and the cook sitting on the field-kitchen began to sing:

> 'Upida! Upidee!
> God won't abandon us, not he!
> If he chucks us in the dirt,
> He'll scrape us out, that's a cert.
> If he chucks us in the wood,
> He'll bite us out. I'm sure he could.
> Upida! Upidee!
> God won't abandon us, not he!'

Beyond the station of Szczawne new military cemeteries began to appear again in the valleys. Beneath Szczawne a stone cross with a headless Christ could be seen from the train. He had lost his head when the track was blown up.

The train increased its speed, hurrying down the valley to Sanok.

The horizons grew larger and at the same time the groups of destroyed villages on both sides of the landscape became more and more frequent.

Near Kulaszne a Red Cross train could be seen down in the stream. It had plunged down the railway embankment and been smashed to pieces.

Baloun goggled at this and was particularly astonished at the sight of the parts of the engine thrown around below him. The funnel was rammed into the railway embankment and stuck out of it like a twenty-eighter.

The phenomenon also aroused attention in the van where Švejk was. Jurajda got most excited by it: 'What, is it allowed to fire at Red Cross vans?'

'It's not allowed, but it can be done,' said Švejk. 'It was a perfect shot, and they will apologize afterwards, of course, and make the excuse that it was night time and the red cross couldn't be seen. There are lots of things in the world which are not allowed to be done but can be done. The main thing is that everybody should try to do what he's not allowed to do so that it can be done. During the Imperial manoeuvres at Písek an order came that soldiers on the march were not allowed to be trussed. But our captain had the idea that they could be, because an order like that was frightfully ridiculous. After all, anyone could see that a soldier who was trussed couldn't march. And so he didn't evade the order, but quite simply and sensibly had the trussed soldiers thrown into the trucks of the baggage train and in this way it was possible to go on marching with them. Or consider another case which happened in our street five or six years ago. A man called Mr Karlík was living on the first floor. One storey above there lived a good man called Mikeš who was a student at the conservatoire. He was very fond of women and among others began to run after the daughter of Mr Karlík, who had a carriers' business and a confectionery shop as well as a bookbinding firm under a completely different name somewhere in Moravia. When Mr Karlík learnt that the student was running after his daughter he went to see him in his flat and said to him: "You're not going to marry my daughter, you gutter-snipe. I shan't give her to you!" "All right," Mr Mikeš replied, "if I can't marry her what do you expect me to do? Do you expect me to break myself in half?" Two months later Mr Karlík called on him again and brought his wife with him. They both said to him with one accord: "You bastard, you've robbed our daughter of her honour." "Of course I have," he answered them. "I've taken the liberty of making a whore of her, madam." Then Mr Karlík started shouting at him quite gratuitously that he'd told him that he must not marry her and that he wouldn't give her to him, but Mr Mikeš answered quite correctly that he was not going to marry her and that at that time they had never discussed what he could do with her. There had been no bargaining about that. He would keep his word and they shouldn't worry as he wouldn't marry her. He was a man of character and not a straw in the wind. He would keep his word because when he said something it was sacred. And if he were persecuted for it it wouldn't matter to him because he had a clean conscience. His late mamma on her very death-bed had asked him to swear that he would never tell a lie in his life, and he had given her his hand of honour in promise and an oath like that was a valid one. In his family no one at all had told lies, and at school he had always had the best marks for moral conduct. And so you can see from that that lots of things aren't allowed but yet can be done, and that "though our ways may be different, let our endeavours be the same." '

'Dear friends,' said the volunteer, who was eagerly making notes, 'every cloud has a silver lining. This Red Cross train which was blown up and hurled half-burnt down the embankment enriches the glorious history of our battalion by adding a new heroic act for the future. I visualize that perhaps on 16 September, as I've already noted down, one or two ordinary soldiers from every company of our battalion led by a corporal will volunteer to blow up the enemy's armoured train which has been firing at us and preventing us crossing the river. Disguised as peasants they honourably discharge their mission.

'What do I see here?' the volunteer exclaimed, as he looked into his notes. 'How did our Mr Vaněk get here?

'Listen, sergeant-major,' he said, turning to Vaněk, 'what a fine little article there will be about you in the battalion history. I believe you've been already mentioned once, but this will be definitely finer and more substantial.' He read out in an exalted voice:

'HEROIC DEATH OF QUARTERMASTER SERGEANT-MAJOR VANĚK

'The plan to blow up the enemy's armoured train was a bold one and among others Quartermaster Sergeant-Major Vaněk volunteered to take part, disguised like the others in peasant costume. He was temporarily stunned by the explosion and when he recovered he found himself surrounded by the enemy. They immediately sent him off to their division staff, where face to face with death he refused to give any information about the position and numbers of our forces. Since he was in disguise he was condemned to be hanged as a spy, but in view of his high rank the sentence was commuted into one of death by shooting. The execution was carried out at once at the wall of the cemetery and brave Quartermaster Sergeant-Major Vaněk asked that his eyes should not be bandaged. When asked whether he had any wish he replied: "Convey my last greeting to my battalion through one of your truce negotiators. Say I die in the conviction that our battalion will continue to go forward on its path of glory. Also tell Captain Ságner that according to the last brigade order the portion of tins is increased daily to two and a half tins per man." So died our Quartermaster Sergeant-Major Vaněk. With his last dying sentence he instilled panic into the enemy who had thought that in stopping us from crossing the river they would cut us off from our supply points, quickly starve us out and sow demoralization in our ranks. The fact that before his execution he played Kaufzwick with the enemy staff officers is a testimony to the composure with which he faced death. "Give the sum I've won to the Russian Red Cross," he said, as he stood and looked down the muzzles of the firing squad. This noble magnanimity brought tears to the eyes of the military representatives present.

'Excuse me, Mr Vaněk,' the volunteer continued, 'for having taken the liberty of disposing of the money you won. I had been considering whether it shouldn't perhaps be given to the Austrian Red Cross, but in the end I assumed that from the humanitarian point of view it was all the same, provided it was given to some humane institution.'

'Our late sergeant-major could have given it to the Soup Institute of the City of Prague,' said Švejk, 'but it's better as it is, because probably with that sum the lord mayor might have bought a sausage for his elevenses.'

'Well, of course, they steal everywhere,' said Chodounský.

'And most of all in the Red Cross,' said Jurajda furiously. 'In Bruck I once knew a chef who cooked for the nurses in their hut and he told me that the matron and all the head nurses sent home whole trunks of Malaga and chocolate. This is what opportunity brings with it. It's the self-determination of man. Every man in the course of his eternal life undergoes countless changes and has to appear once in this world as a thief in certain periods of his activity. I've gone through this period myself.'

He took a bottle of cognac out of his pack.

'Here you can see the indisputable proof of my assertion,' he said, opening the bottle. 'Before our departure I took this bottle from the officers' mess. It is a cognac of the very best brand and was supposed to be used for icing on Linzertorte. But it was predestined that I should steal it, just as I was predestined to become a thief.'

'And it really wouldn't be a bad thing at all,' Švejk interposed, 'if we were predestined to be your accomplices. In any case I have a presentiment that we are.'

And the predestination proved to be a fact. The bottle was passed round in spite of the protests of Quartermaster Sergeant-Major Vaněk, who maintained that the cognac should be drunk out of the mess-tins and be fairly shared between them, because there were five men to one bottle, which, being an odd number, meant that it could easily happen that one person might drink one swig more than the others; whereupon Švejk put in: 'That's true, but if Mr Vaněk prefers there to be an even number he might like to withdraw from the circle – to avoid any unpleasantness or dispute.'

Vaněk then took back his proposal and made another suggestion which was a generous one, that the donor, Jurajda, should put himself in the position where he could drink twice, but this caused a storm of opposition, because Vaněk had had one swig already when he tasted the cognac on opening the bottle.

In the end the volunteer's proposal that they should drink in alphabetical order was accepted. He justified it by saying that what a person was called was really a question of predetermination too.

The bottle was finished by Chodounský who came first in alphabetical order. As he did so he cast a menacing glance at Vaněk, who reckoned that as he was the last he would have one swig more. But this was a bad mathematical error on his part, because there were twenty-one swigs.

After that they played ordinary three-card Zwick. It turned out that whenever the volunteer bought a card he accompanied the action with pious quotations from the Scripture. When he bought a knave he called out: 'Oh Lord, let me have this knave this summer too that I may plough and dung him, that he bear me fruit.'

When they criticized him for having the audacity to buy an eight, he called out in a great voice: 'Either what woman having ten pieces of silver if she lose one piece doth not light a candle and sweep the house and seek diligently till she find it? And when she hath found it she calleth her friends and her neighbours together, saying, "Rejoice with me; for I have bought an eight and received as well the king and ace of trumps!" So please give me the cards. You've all of you burst.'

Marek had indeed great good fortune at cards. While the others were trying to out-trump each other, he always out-trumped their out-trumpings, so that they burst one after the other and he grabbed stake after stake. He called out to those who had lost: 'And in the places there will be great earthquakes, and tribulations of famine and pestilence, and there will be great miracles from heaven.' In the end they had enough of it and stopped playing when Chodounský lost his pay for half a year in advance. He was crushed by this, and the volunteer demanded an I.O.U. from him so that Quartermaster Sergeant-Major Vaněk would pay Chodounský's pay packet to him.

'Don't be afraid, Chodounský,' Švejk comforted him. 'If you have any luck you'll fall in the first action and Marek won't get any pay packet from you. Just sign for him.'

The mention of his falling in battle upset Chodounský very much and he said firmly: 'I can't fall, because I'm a telephonist and telephonists are always in covered positions. Telephone wires are only put up or tested for faults after the action.'

The volunteer gave it as his opinion that telephonists were, on the contrary, exposed to great dangers, as it was mainly on them that the enemy concentrated their artillery fire. No telephonist was safe in his cover. If he were ten metres under the ground the enemy artillery would find him none the less. That telephonists died like flies was proved by the fact that when he left Bruck they were just opening the twenty-eighth course for telephonists.

Chodounský stared in front of him in dismay, which moved Švejk to make the friendly and good-natured remark: "You can't help it. It's all a dirty business anyway.' Chodounský answered affably: 'Shut up, auntie.'

'I shall look for the letters "ch" in my notes for the history of the battalion . . .' Marek observed. 'Chodounský, Chodounský, h'm, aha, here we are: "Telephonist Chodounský buried by a mine explosion. Telephones to the staff from his tomb: 'I'm dying and I congratulate my battalion on its victory!'"'

'Surely that's good enough,' said Švejk, 'or do you want more still? Do you remember that telephonist on the *Titanic*? After the ship had already sunk he went on telephoning down to the flooded kitchen to ask when lunch would be served.'

'It doesn't matter to me,' said the volunteer. 'If you like, Chodounský's dying words can be completed by his final call on the telephone: "Give my last greetings to our Iron Brigade!"'

4

Forward March!

WHEN they came to Sanok it turned out that in the van with the field-kitchen of the 11th company, where the bloated Baloun was farting with bliss, they had been quite right in thinking that supper would be served and that as well as supper there would even be an issue of army bread for all those days when the battalion had got nothing. When they got out of the vans they also found out that it was in Sanok that the staff of the 'Iron Brigade' was located, to which, according to its baptismal certificate, the battalion of the 91st regiment belonged. Although the railway connection to Lwów and northwards to Mościska was undisturbed it puzzled people why the staff of the Eastern sector had made dispositions for the 'Iron Brigade' with its staff to concentrate its march battalions 150 kilometres behind the lines, when the front then ran from Brody to the Bug and along the river northwards to Sokal.

This very interesting strategical question was cleared up in a frightfully simple way when Captain Ságner went to report the arrival of the march battalion to the brigade staff in Sanok.

The officer on duty was the brigade adjutant, Captain Tayrle.

'I'm extremely surprised, Captain Ságner,' said Captain Tayrle, 'that you did not get any definite information. The march route is fixed. Of course you should have reported to us beforehand the line of your advance. According to the dispositions of the High Command you've come *two days too early.*'

Captain Ságner blushed slightly, but it did not occur to him to repeat all those ciphered telegrams which he had been receiving throughout the journey.

'I must say, I'm really surprised, captain, that you . . .' said Adjutant Tayrle.

'I would expect,' Captain Ságner answered, 'that as a fellow-officer you would address me less formally.'

'Just as you like, old man,' said Captain Tayrle, 'but tell me, are you a regular or a civilian? Regular? Well, that's another story then. . . . You never can tell, you know. We've had so many bloody fools passing through – reserve lieutenants. When we retreated from Limanowa and Kraśnik all those "extra-lieutenants" lost their heads as soon as they saw a Cossack patrol. At the staff we don't think much of parasites like them. Some stupid bastard who's passed the army I.Q. test in the end goes and gets himself on to the regular list or passes an officers' examination when he's a civilian. Of course he goes on being a bloody fool of a civilian all the time. When war comes he shows he's no lieutenant at all – just a cowardly shit!'

Captain Tayrle spat and patted Captain Ságner on the back in a familiar way: 'You'll stay here for about two days. I'll show you all the sights. We'll have some dancing. We've got some lovely little whores here – "angel whores". And we've also got a general's daughter who used to be a Lesbian. So we all dress up in women's clothes and you'll see what she can do! But she's such a skinny sow that you'd never imagine it of her. But she knows a thing or two, old man! She's a bloody bitch – but of course you'll find that out for yourself!

'Excuse me,' he suddenly broke off, 'I must go and spew again. It's the third time today already.'

To prove how gay it was here, he told Captain Ságner when he came back that this was the result of a party last night, in which the sappers' unit had taken part.

Captain Ságner very quickly got acquainted with the commander of this unit, who also had the rank of captain. An enormously tall man in uniform suddenly crashed into the office. He was in a daze, did not notice the presence of Captain Ságner and said to Tayrle quite familiarly: 'What are you doing, you old swine? You certainly sewed up our countess marvellously yesterday.' He sat down on a chair and said, laughing uproariously and striking himself over the calves with a thin cane: 'When I remember how you spewed into her lap . . .'

'Yes,' said Tayrle. 'We had a very jolly evening yesterday.' It was only then that he introduced Captain Ságner to the officer with the cane and they all of them left the office of the administrative section of the brigade and went into a café which had very recently grown out of a former beer-cellar.

When they went through the office Captain Tayrle took the cane from the commander of the sappers' unit and brought it banging down on to a long table, round which twelve military writers fell into line by order. These were the chaps who had an eye for easy safe jobs behind the lines. They had large satisfied bellies and 'extra' uniforms.

Trying to show off in front of Ságner and the other captain, Captain Tayrle said to these twelve fat apostles of scrimshanking: 'Don't think that I keep you here just to fatten you. You bloody hogs, you'd better jolly well guzzle and booze less and run around more.

'Now I'll show you another training trick,' Tayrle told his companions.

He struck the table again with the cane and asked the twelve: 'When are you going to burst, you hogs?'

All the twelve answered in unison: 'At your orders, sir!'

Laughing at his own crass idiocy and stupidity Captain Tayrle went out of the office.

When they all three sat in the café Tayrle ordered a bottle of jeřabinka and called some young ladies who happened to be free. It turned out that the café was really nothing but a brothel and because none of the young ladies were free Captain Tayrle got exceedingly angry, swore at madame in the coarsest terms and shouted out: 'Who's with Miss Ella?' When the answer came that a lieutenant was with her, his vituperations increased.

It was in fact Lieutenant Dub who was with Miss Ella. When the march battalion was already in its sleeping quarters in a secondary school, he had summoned all the men of his unit and warned them in a long speech that the Russians, when they retreated, had set up brothels everywhere and staffed them with personnel infected with V.D. so as to cause the Austrian army heavy losses through this trick. He accordingly warned his men against visiting such places. Because they were in the front zone he would himself verify by personal inspection of these houses whether his order had been obeyed or not. Anyone who was caught would be brought before a drumhead court-martial.

And so Lieutenant Dub went to verify by personal inspection whether his orders had been obeyed, and for this reason he obviously chose as the point of departure for his journey of inspection the sofa in Ella's cubicle on the first floor of the so-called 'Town Café'. He was having a very good time on this sofa.

Meanwhile Captain Ságner went back to his battalion. Tayrle's company had dispersed. There was a search for Captain Tayrle at the brigade staff where the brigadier had been looking for his adjutant for over an hour.

New orders had come from the division and they had to determine finally the march route for the 91st regiment which had just arrived. According to the new dispositions, the march battalion of the 102nd regiment was to go by the route originally chosen for the 91st.

Everything was in a great muddle. The Russians were retreating very hastily in the north-east tip of Galicia so that some Austrian detatchments got mixed up with each other and in some places units of the German army drove wedges into them. The chaos was completed by the arrival of new march battalions and other military detachments. And in sectors of the front, which were farther in the rear, the same thing occurred as for example here in Sanok, where there unexpectedly arrived the reserves of the German Hanoverian division under the command of a colonel with such an ugly look that the brigadier was thrown into a state of complete confusion. The colonel of reserves of the Hanoverian division showed the dispositions of his staff, according to which his men had to be quartered in the secondary school, where at this very moment the battalion of the 91st had just been billeted. For the accommodation of his staff he requested the evacuation of the building of the Cracow Bank where the staff of the brigade were quartered.

The brigadier got into direct contact with the division and described the exact situation. After that the evil-eyed Hanoverian spoke to the division, as a result of which the brigade received the following order: 'The brigade is to evacuate the town at 6 p.m. in the direction of Tyrawa Wołoska – Liskowiec – Stara Sól – Sambor, where they are to await further orders. They will be accompanied by the march battalion of the 91st regiment which will afford them protection. The dispositions have been worked out in the brigade according to the following plan: the vanguard will leave at half past five in the direction of Tyrawa, preserving a distance of $3\frac{1}{2}$ kilometres between the southern and northern flank cover. The covering rear guard will leave at a quarter past six.'

And so there was a great flap in the secondary school and the only person missing at the conference of the officers of the battalion was Lieutenant Dub. Švejk was given the task of trying to find him.

'I hope you'll find him without any difficulties,' said Lieutenant Lukáš to Švejk, 'because there's always something going on between the two of you.'

'Humbly report, sir, may I ask for a written order from the company? This is just because there always *is* something going on between the two of us.'

While Lieutenant Lukáš copied out on a loose leaf of his notebook an order saying that Lieutenant Dub was to come at once to the school for an officers' conference, Švejk went on to say: 'Certainly, sir. As usual you don't need to have any worries. I shall find him, because soldiers are forbidden to go into brothels and he will certainly have gone into one to verify by personal inspection that none of his platoon wants to be brought before a drumhead court-martial, which is his usual threat. He himself declared to the men of his platoon that he would go through all the brothels and then woe betide them, because they would get to know him from his bad side. By the way, I know where he is. He is in that café just opposite, because all the men watched to see where he would go first.'

'The Combined Halls of Entertainment and Town Café', the establishment mentioned by Švejk, was divided into two parts. Anyone who did not want to go through the café went round the back, where an old lady was sunning herself. She spoke German, Polish and Hungarian and the gist of her remarks was as follows: 'Come along, soldier boy, we've got lovely young ladies here.'

When the soldier boy came in, she led him along the corridor to a reception hall and called to one of the young ladies, who came running up in her slip. She asked for the money in advance, which madame cashed on the spot, while the soldier boy took off his bayonet.

The officers went through the café. The route for these gentlemen was more complicated because it led through the *chambres séparées* at the back of the café where there was a choice of another category intended for the officers and where the slips were of lace, and wine or liqueurs were drunk. Madame would not allow anything to be done here. It all had to take place in the cubicles upstairs. In one of them Lieutenant Dub, in his pants, was rolling about on a sofa enjoying this particular form of paradise which was full of bugs, while Miss Ella related to him the tragedy of her life, which was entirely imaginary, of course, as always happens in these cases. She told him that her father was a manufacturer and she herself had been a schoolmistress at a girls' grammar school in Budapest, and had done this out of blighted love.

On a small table behind Lieutenant Dub within the reach of his hand was a bottle of jeřabinka and glasses. The facts that the bottle was half-empty, and that Ella and Lieutenant Dub were no longer in control of their speech, were incriminating proof that Lieutenant Dub could not carry his liquor. Judging by his speech it was evident that he was already mixing everything up and thought Ella was his batman, Kunert. He called her by Kunert's name and threatened his imagined batman in his usual way: 'Kunert, Kunert, you animal, wait till you get to know me from my bad side . . .'

Švejk was expected to undergo the same procedure as all the other soldier boys who went round the back. However, he amiably tore himself away from a girl in a slip, whose screams brought the Polish madame running up. She denied brazenly to Švejk that she had any lieutenant as a guest.

'Don't shout at me like that, madame,' said Švejk affably, smiling sweetly at her, 'or else I'll sock you one on the jaw. In Prague where I lived they once beat up a madame in Platnéřská Street so much that she didn't know where she was. At that time it was a son who was looking for his father, who was called Vondráček and had a tyre business. That madame was called Křovánová. When they brought her round and asked her at the first-aid station what her name was, she said that it was something that began with "Ch". And may I ask your honourable name, please?'

The honourable matron set up a frightful wail, when Švejk, after saying this, pushed her aside and advanced gravely up the wooden staircase to the first floor.

Downstairs appeared the owner of the brothel himself, an impoverished Polish nobleman, who ran up the stairs after Švejk and tried to drag him back by the tunic, shouting at him in German that the rank and file were not allowed to go upstairs, that it was reserved for the officer gentlemen and that the men's place was on the ground floor.

Švejk let him know that he had come here in the interests of the whole army, that he was looking for a certain lieutenant, without whom the army could not proceed to the field, and, when the Pole became more and more aggressive, Švejk knocked him down the staircase and continued upstairs to inspect the locality. He verified that all the cubicles were empty except the one at the very end of the passage. Here he gave a knock, pressed the latch and half opened the door. The squealing voice of Ella could be heard: 'Engaged', and immediately afterwards the deep voice of Lieutenant Dub, who perhaps thought that he was still in his room in camp: 'Come in!'

Švejk entered, advanced to the sofa and handed Lieutenant Dub the loose leaf from the notebook. Looking askance at the various articles of uniform thrown on the corner of the bed, he announced: 'Humbly report, sir, you are to dress and, according to the instructions which I'm handing you, report immediately at our barracks in the secondary school. We have a big military conference there!'

Lieutenant Dub goggled the tiny pupils of his eyes at him but told himself that he was not so tipsy as to fail to recognize Švejk. He immediately imagined that they were sending Švejk to him on report and so he said: 'I'll deal with you immediately, Švejk. You'll see – what – will – happen – to – you . . .

'Kunert,' he shouted at Ella, 'pour – me – another – one!'

He took a drink and tearing up the written instructions laughed: 'That's an – apology? With us – no apologies – are of any use. We – are in the army – and not – at – school. And so – they – have caught you – in a brothel? Come – here – to me – Švejk – come – nearer – I – am going to give you – a few – swipes – across – the jaw. In – what – year – did Philip – of Macedon – defeat – the Romans? You don't – know that – do you – you stallion!'

'Humbly report, sir,' Švejk continued inexorably, 'this is the highest order from the brigade. The gentlemen officers are to put their clothes on and go to a battalion conference. We're leaving, you know, sir, and only now will they decide which companies will be advance guard, flank guard and rear guard. Now they're going to take a decision on this and I think, sir, that you too will have something to say about it.'

This diplomatic speech went some way towards reviving Lieutenant Dub and he began now to feel sure that he was not in the barracks after all. But out of caution he still asked: 'Where am I?'

'You have the honour to be in a brothel, sir. God moves in a mysterious way.'

Lieutenant Dub gave a heavy sigh, got down from the sofa and began to look for his uniform, which Švejk helped him to do. When he had finally dressed they both went out, but a little later Švejk returned for a moment. Taking no notice of Ella, who attributed an entirely different significance to his return and out of unrequited love immediately climbed back into bed, he quickly drank the jeřabinka remaining in the bottle and went out again after the lieutenant.

In the street Lieutenant Dub's head again became befuddled, because

it was very hot. He talked to Švejk a lot of nonsense without any connection. He said that he had at home a postage stamp from Heligoland,
and that immediately after passing his school-leaving examination they
had gone to play billiards and had not taken their caps off to their

class master. To every one of his sentences he added: 'I think you
follow me.'

'I certainly do,' Švejk answered. 'You talk rather like a tinsmith
called Pokorný in Budějovice. Whenever people asked him: "Have you
bathed this year in the Malše?" he answered: "I haven't, but there'll
be a lot of plums this year." Or they asked him: "Have you eaten any
mushrooms this year?" and he answered: "I haven't, but the new
Sultan of Morocco is said to be a very good man."'

Lieutenant Dub stopped and managed to get out of himself:
'Sultan of Morocco? He's a back number now.' He wiped the sweat
from his forehead and looking at Švejk with misty eyes murmured:

'I've never sweated like this even in winter. Do you agree? Do you follow me?'

'Yes, I do, sir. When we were at The Chalice an old man used to come there who was a retired official of the district council, and he asserted exactly the same thing. He always said he was surprised at the difference between the temperature in summer and winter. He thought it very strange that people hadn't yet realized it.'

At the school gate Švejk left Lieutenant Dub who reeled on the stairs up to the assembly hall, where the military conference was taking place. He immediately reported to Captain Ságner that he was completely drunk. Throughout the conference he sat with his head in his hands and during the discussion occasionally stood up to cry out: 'Your opinion is correct, gentlemen, but I am completely drunk.'

When all the dispositions had been worked out and Lieutenant Lukáš's company had to go as vanguard cover, Lieutenant Dub gave a sudden jerk, stood up and said: 'I recall, gentlemen, our form master in the first year of the grammar school. Hip hip hurrah, hip hip hurrah, hip hip hurrah!'

It occurred to Lieutenant Lukáš that for the time being the best thing to do would be to make Kunert lay Lieutenant Dub on the couch in the physics cabinet next door, where there was a guard posted to see that no one stole the already half-plundered collection of minerals. The units marching through were continually warned about this by the brigade.

This measure dated from the time when a Honvéd battalion, which had been billeted in the school, began to rifle the cabinet. The Honvéds had taken a particular fancy to the collection of minerals, the gaily-coloured crystals and pyrites, and had stuck them into their packs.

On one of the white crosses in the military cemetery there is the inscription: 'László Gargany'. A Honvéd who plundered the school collections and drank up all the methylated spirit from a jar in which the various reptiles were being preserved now sleeps his last sleep there.

In wiping out the human race the world war did not hesitate to use methylated spirit intended for preserving reptiles.

When all the others had gone away Lieutenant Lukáš had Lieutenant Dub's batman, Kunert, brought to him. He took away his lieutenant and stretched him out on the sofa.

Lieutenant Dub was suddenly like a small child; he took Kunert by the hand and began to look at his palm, saying that he could divine from it the name of his future wife.

'What's your name? Take out of the breast pocket of my tunic my notebook and pencil. You're called Kunert, aren't you? Well, then, come here in a quarter of an hour's time and I'll leave you here a piece of paper with the name of your lady wife.'

No sooner had he said this than he started to snore, but again he seemed to wake up and began to scribble in his notebook. He tore out what he had scribbled and threw it on the ground. Putting his finger mysteriously to his lips he babbled: 'Not now, but in a quarter of an hour's time. You'd better look for the paper blindfold.'

Kunert was such a well-meaning ox that a quarter of an hour later he actually appeared, and when he had unfolded the paper he read from Lieutenant Dub's hieroglyphics: 'The name of your future wife will be: Mrs Kunert.'

Švejk, when he showed this to him a moment later, told him to keep this piece of paper carefully. Documents of this kind from military gentlemen ought to be respected by everyone. In army life it had never been the case before that an officer corresponded with his batman and called him 'Mr'.

When all the preparations had been made for the departure according to the given dispositions, the brigadier, who had been so smartly dislodged by the Hanoverian colonel, made the whole battalion fall in in the usual square formation and made a speech to them. He loved making speeches and, when he did so, muddled everything up, and when he had nothing more to say he remembered the field post:

'My men,' he thundered out to the square, 'now we are nearing the enemy's front, from which we are only separated by a few days' march. Up till now on the march you have not had the opportunity, my men, of informing the dear ones whom you have left behind of your addresses, so that those far away from you may know where they are to write, and you may have pleasure from the letters of your dear bereaved ones.'

He got himself so tied up that he couldn't find a way out and repeated countless times: 'The dear ones whom you have left behind – your dear relatives – your dear bereaved ones' etc., until he finally broke out of the vicious circle by calling out vociferously: 'And that is why we have the field post at the front!'

The rest of his speech gave the impression that all these people in their grey uniforms should let themselves be killed with the greatest joy just because field posts were installed at the front, and if anyone had both his legs torn off by a shell it would be a beautiful thing for

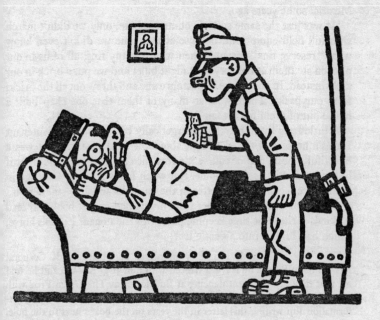

him to die with the thought that his field post number was 72, and that perhaps a letter was lying there from home, from his dear ones far away, with a package containing a piece of smoked pork, bacon and home-made biscuits.

Then, after his speech, when the brigade music struck up the national anthem, three cheers were given for the Emperor, and these various groups of human cattle, which were destined for slaughter somewhere beyond the Bug, set out successively on the march, unit by unit, according to the dispositions made.

The 11th company left at half past five for Tyrawa Wołoska. Švejk trudged behind with the company staff and the ambulance, while Lieutenant Lukáš rode round the whole column, going to the rear every now and then to check on the ambulance, where on a cart under canvas they carried Lieutenant Dub to new heroic deeds of an unknown future. Lieutenant Lukáš also whiled away the journey by talking to Švejk, who patiently carried his pack and rifle and was telling Vaněk how fine it was when they marched on manoeuvres near Velké Meziříčí some years ago.

'It was just the same sort of country as here, only we didn't march with full field-equipment, because at that time we didn't even know what "reserve tins" meant. When we drew any tins, all of us in our platoon ate them at the very next night billet and we put a brick in our sacks instead. In one village inspectors came and threw out all the bricks from our packs. There were so many of them that one chap built a house out of them for his family.'

A little later Švejk marched energetically by the side of Lieutenant Lukáš's horse and talked to him about the field posts: 'That was a beautiful speech, and of course it's very nice for anyone at the front if he gets a kind letter from home. But when I was serving years ago in Budějovice I got only one letter in the barracks and I've still kept it.' Švejk took out a greasy letter from his stained pocket book and read it aloud, at the same time keeping pace with Lieutenant Lukáš's horse, which had broken into a gentle trot:

'You bloody bastard, you dirty murderer and blackguard! Corporal Křiž came to Prague on leave. I danced with him at U Kocanů and he told me that they say you went dancing at Budějovice at The Green Frog with a stupid tart, and that you've completely thrown me over. For your information I'm writing this letter in the rears on the board next to the hole. It's all over between us. Your former Božena. What did I want to add? Yes, that corporal knows how to do it and he's going to give you hell, because I've asked him to. And what else did I want to say? Yes, when you come home on leave you won't find me among the living.'

'Of course,' Švejk continued at a gentle trot, 'when I came on leave she was still among the living and very living they were! I found her at U Kocanů too. Two soldiers of a foreign regiment were helping her to dress, and one of them was so very "living" that he was quite publicly putting his hand under her bodice just as though, humbly report, sir, he wanted to pluck the bloom of her innocence, as Věnceslava Lužická says,[1] or as a young girl of about sixteen once said with loud sobs to a schoolboy when he pinched her in the shoulder at

1. An authoress of novels for young ladies.

dancing class: "Sir, you have rubbed off the bloom of my virginity."
Of course everybody laughed and her mamma who was looking after
her took her out into the passage in the Union and gave the stupid
ninny a good kicking. However, I must say, sir, that I came to the
conclusion that the country wenches are all the same more sincere than
those worn-out young misses in the towns who go to dancing classes.
When years ago we were in camp at Mníšek I used to go dancing at
Starý Knín and went around with a girl called Karla Veklová, but she
didn't like me very much, I'm afraid. One Sunday evening when I took
her to the lake, we sat on the dam and when the sun was setting I asked
her whether she loved me. Humbly report, sir, the air was so balmy,
all the birds were singing and she replied with a horrible laugh: "I
love you about as much as a piece of straw in my arse, because you're
such an idiot." And I really was an idiot, such a frightful idiot that I
used to stroll with her, humbly report, sir, in the fields amid the
standing corn where there wasn't a living soul and we never sat down
once. I kept on showing her all that cornucopia and, stupid ass that I
was, all I did was to tell that peasant wench that this was rye, this was
wheat and that over there was oats.'

And as though confirming the remark about the oats there resounded
somewhere in front the voices of the company singing in unison. They
continued the song which Czech regiments sang when they marched
and bled for Austria at Solferino:

> 'And when the night was black,
> The oats jumped out of the sack.
> Hey, diddly dee,
> Every wench is free!'

And the others immediately joined in:

> 'Is free, is free, is free,
> And so why shouldn't she
> Plant a burning kiss
> On that cheek or on this?
>
> Hey, diddly dee,
> Every wench is free,
> Is free, is free, is free,
> And so why shouldn't she ...'

After that the Germans started singing the same song in German.
This is an old, old soldiers' marching song which the *soldateska* used

to sing in all languages perhaps as long ago as in the Napoleonic wars. Now it resounded hilariously on the dusty road on the way to Tyrawa Wołoska in the Galician plain, where on both sides of the road as far as the green hills in the south, the fields were trampled on and destroyed under the hooves of horses and the soles of thousands and thousands of soldiers' heavy boots.

'Once we made the same mess at the manoeuvres near Písek,' said Švejk, looking about him. 'We had with us an Imperial Archduke. He was such a fair gentleman that when for strategic reasons he rode with his staff through the corn, the adjutant behind him at once calculated all the damage he'd caused. A peasant called Pícha was not at all pleased at this visit and refused to accept from the government eighteen crowns compensation for the hectare of land which had been trampled down. You won't believe it, sir, but he wanted to go to law, sir, and he got eighteen months for it.

'But I think, sir, that in fact he ought to have been grateful that someone from the Imperial House came to see him on his land. Another peasant, a more conscientious one, would have dressed all his girls in white dresses like bridesmaids, put bunches of flowers in their hands and stationed them on his estate. And each of them would have had to welcome the exalted gentleman, like I've read they did in India, when the subjects of a ruler allowed themselves to be trampled on by that elephant.'

'What on earth are you talking about, Švejk?' Lieutenant Lukáš called down to him from his horse.

'Humbly report, sir, I mean that elephant which carried on his back that ruler which I read about.'

'You've certainly got an explanation for everything, Švejk,' said Lieutenant Lukáš and rode on ahead. There the column was already getting broken up. After the rest in the train the unaccustomed march in full and complete equipment resulted in them all getting sore shoulders, and everyone tried to make himself as comfortable as he could. They shifted their rifles from one side to the other. Most of them no longer carried them by their slings but had them thrown over their shoulders like a rake or fork. Some thought they would get on better by marching in the ditch or on the meadows where the ground under their feet felt softer than on the dusty road.

Most of them went with bowed heads and all suffered from enormous thirst, because in spite of the sun having already set it was just as sultry and stifling as if it had been mid-day and no one had a drop of water left in his field-flask. It was the first day of the march and this unaccustomed situation, which was a kind of prelude to greater and greater hardships, made all of them weaker and fainter the farther they went. They stopped singing and started to guess among themselves how far it could be to Tyrawa Wołoska, where they thought they would be spending the night. Some sat down for a time in the ditch and so as not to make a wrong impression undid their boots and acted at first glance like somebody who has put his puttees on wrong and tries to rewind them so that they will not pinch him on the march further on. Others shortened or lengthened their rifle slings or opened their packs and went through the objects contained in them, trying to persuade themselves that they were doing it to distribute the load better and to prevent the pack straps pulling on one or other of their shoulders. When Lieutenant Lukáš approached them they got up one after the other and reported that something was hurting them, if indeed the cadets or sergeants had not caught a glimpse of Lieutenant Lukáš's mare in the distance and already hounded them on.

Lieutenant Lukáš, as he rode by, asked them in a friendly tone to get up, telling them that it was another three kilometres to Tyrawa Wołoska and they would be able to rest there.

In the meantime Lieutenant Dub recovered consciousness through the constant shaking of the two-wheeled ambulance cart. He had not come round completely but he could already raise himself and lean out of the cart to call to the staff of the company. They were walking freely around, because all of them, beginning with Baloun and ending with Chodounský, had put their packs into the cart. Only Švejk went bravely ahead carrying his pack, holding his rifle by the sling across his chest in dragoon fashion, smoking his pipe and singing as he marched:

> 'When we marched to Jaroměř,
> Believe it, folks, or not,
> We reached the town at supper-time
> And got it on the dot.'

More than five hundred paces in front of Lieutenant Dub clouds of dust rose on the road out of which there loomed the figures of soldiers. Lieutenant Dub, whose enthusiasm had returned to him, leaned his head out of the cart and began to shout at the dust on the road: 'My men, your noble task is a heavy one. Difficult marches are ahead. You will all of you experience deprivations and hardships of every kind. However, I am convinced that I can confidently rely on your pluck and grit.'

'You shit,' Švejk put in poetically.

Lieutenant Dub went on: 'For you, my men, there is no obstacle so powerful that you cannot overcome it. Once more, my men, I repeat to you that I am not leading you to easy victory. It will be a hard nut for you to crack, but crack it you will! You are the heroes of whom historians wrote.'

'Stick your finger down your throat,' Švejk put in poetically again.

And as though Lieutenant Dub had heard this he suddenly began to vomit into the dust of the road with his head bent down and when he had spewed it all out he shouted once more: 'On, soldiers, on! Hurrah!' Then he fell on to Chodounský's pack again and slept till Tyrawa Wołoska, where by order of Lieutenant Lukáš, who had a very long and difficult talk with him, they finally put him on his feet and took him out of the cart. He then recovered so much that he was able at last to declare: 'From a logical point of view I've committed an act of folly, which I shall redeem when we are face to face with the foe.'

He was not of course yet completely himself, because when he went back to his platoon he told Lieutenant Lukáš: 'You don't know me yet, but wait till you get to know me . . .!'

'If you want to know what you've done, you can get the information from Švejk,' Lukáš replied.

So before returning to his platoon Lieutenant Dub went to see Švejk and found him in the company of Baloun and Vaněk.

Baloun was just telling them that in his mill at home he always used to keep a bottle of beer in the well. The beer was so cold that it set his teeth on edge. In other mills in the evening they drank beer to wash down cottage cheese, but he, in his gluttony, for which the good Lord had punished him, always guzzled a sizeable piece of meat after it. Now God in his justice had punished him with tepid stinking water from the wells at Tyrawa Wołoska. As a protection against cholera they had to pour into it citric acid, which they had had distributed to them only a moment ago when the well water was issued to them by companies. Baloun expressed the view that the citric acid was no doubt intended to starve them. It was true indeed that he had managed to get a little to eat at Sanok and that Lieutenant Lukáš had even left him again half a portion of veal which he had brought him from the brigade, but it was dreadful because he had thought that when they came here and there was rest and night quarters they would cook something as well. He had been quite convinced of this when the cooks fetched water for the cauldrons, and had at once gone to the kitchens to ask about it. The answer he got was that they had only received an order to draw water for the time being and any minute another one might come ordering them to pour it away.

At this very moment Lieutenant Dub came up and, being very uncertain of himself, asked: 'Are you having a chat?'

'Yes, we are, sir,' Švejk answered for all of them. 'And our chat is in full swing. It's always best to have plenty of chat. Just now we're chatting about citric acid. No soldier can do without a chat. That's how he forgets all his tribulations.'

Lieutenant Dub told him to come a little of the way with him, because he had a few questions to ask him. When they were on one side he asked him in a frightfully uncertain voice: 'Isn't it me you're chatting about?'

'Oh no, sir, not at all, never, sir, only about citric acid and smoked pork.'

'Lieutenant Lukáš told me that I am supposed to have done something wrong and that you know all about it, Švejk.'

Švejk said very gravely and with great emphasis: 'You haven't done anything at all, sir. You were only visiting a house of ill fame. But it was most likely a mistake. It was just the same as what once happened to a tinsmith called Pimpr from Kozí Square in the Old Town of Prague. Whenever he went to buy metal sheets in the town they always used to search for him and always found him in the same kind of establishment, either at U Šuhů or at U Dvořáků, just as I found you. On the ground floor there was a café and upstairs there were tarts as in our case here. You were probably where you were by mistake, sir, because it was so hot and when someone's not used to drinking in hot weather like that he gets drunk on ordinary rum, to say nothing of jeřabinka, sir. And I got an order to deliver you a summons to come to the conference before we left and I found you with that tart upstairs. Because of the heat and the jeřabinka you didn't even recognize me and lay on the sofa without any clothes on. You didn't kick up a shindy there and you didn't even say: "You don't know me yet." A thing like this can happen to anybody when it's hot. Some people love doing it as a regular thing, while others just get into it by pure accident. If you had known old Vejvoda, sir, a builder's foreman from Vršovice – he once took it into his head that he wouldn't drink any drink which would make him drunk. And so he had his last wee dram for the road at home and set out on a journey to find some non-alcoholic drinks. He called first of all at a pub called At the Stop, had a quarter-litre of vermouth there and started his unobtrusive inquiries of the landlord about what sort of stuff those total abstainers actually drank. He was quite right in thinking that pure water was rather cruel fare even for total abstainers. The landlord then explained to him that total abstainers drink soda water, mineral water, milk and then various kinds of alcohol-free wines, cold clear soup and other beverages without spirit. Of this wide range of drinks it was the alcohol-free wine which most appealed to Vejvoda's taste. He asked one more question: whether there also existed spirits without alcohol. Then he had another quarter-litre of vermouth, talked with the landlord about how it was a real sin to get tight very often, whereupon the latter told him that he could endure everything in the world except a chap who goes and gets himself sozzled in another pub and only comes to him to get sober with a bottle of soda water and perhaps makes a terrible row as well. "Get sozzled in my pub," said the landlord, "and you are my man, but otherwise I won't have anything to do with you." Old Vejvoda finished his vermouth and went out to continue his journey until he came – just imagine it, sir – to a wine shop at Charles Square which he also used to visit from time to time. He asked there whether they didn't have wines without spirit. "Sorry, Mr Vejvoda," they told him, "we don't have any wines without spirit, just vermouth or sherry." Somehow or other old Vejvoda felt ashamed and so he had a quarter-litre of vermouth and a quarter-litre of sherry, and as he sat there he met one of those total abstainers. They got talking and drank another quarter-litre of sherry, and in the end it turned out that the gentleman knew a place where they served wines without spirit. "It's in Bolzanova Street," he said. "You get there down the steps and they have a gramophone there." In reward for this cheering information old Vejvoda ordered a whole bottle of vermouth and then they both walked to the place in Bolzanova Street, which was down the steps and where they had a gramophone. And it was quite true that they only served fruit wines there, not only free of spirit but without alcohol either. First of all each ordered a half-litre of gooseberry wine and then a half-litre of redcurrant wine, and when they had drunk another half-litre of spirit-free gooseberry wine they began to feel pins and needles in their legs after all the vermouth and sherry they had had before. And they began to shout that they must be given official confirmation that what they were drinking there was spirit-free wine. They were total abstainers and if they didn't get this at once they would break everything up including the gramophone. Finally the cops had to drag both of them up the steps again to Bolzanova Street. And they had to put them in the drunks' cart and chuck them into the isolation cell. Both had to be sentenced for being drunk and disorderly when they were total abstainers.'

'Why are you telling me this?' shouted Lieutenant Dub, who had been completely sobered up by this speech.

'Humbly report, sir, it's not really to the point, but I thought that while we were having this nice chat . . .'

At that moment it suddenly occurred to Lieutenant Dub, who had now nearly completely recovered, that Švejk had insulted him once again, so he shouted at him: 'One day you'll get to know me! What about the way you are standing?'

'Humbly report, I'm standing wrong. Humbly report, I've forgotten to put my heels together. I'll do it at once.' And Švejk was already standing at the best possible 'attention'.

Lieutenant Dub tried hard to think what he should say next but in the end confined himself to the remark: 'You'd better look out and see that I don't have to speak to you again,' and then he added a modified version of his old saying: 'You don't know me yet, but I know you.'

When Lieutenant Dub left Švejk he thought to himself in his state of hangover: 'Perhaps it would have had a greater effect on him if I'd said to him: "I've known you for a long time, you bastard, and from your bad side." '

Lieutenant Dub then had his batman Kunert called and ordered him to look for a jug of water.

To Kunert's credit let it be said that he spent a long time in scouring all Tyrawa Wołoska for both the jug and the water. In the end he managed to steal a jug from the vicar and filled it with water from a well which was completely nailed over with planks. To do this he had of course to tear off one or two of them. The well was in fact boarded up because the water in it was suspected of being typhus-infected.

Lieutenant Dub, however, drank up the whole jug without any further effects, which only confirms the saying: 'A good pig can swallow
anything.'

It was a mistake to think that they might perhaps spend the night at
Tyrawa Wołoska.

Lieutenant Lukáš called Chodounský, Vaněk, Švejk and Baloun. His
orders were quite simple. They should leave their equipment by the
ambulance cart, set out straight away to Mały Polanec by a path over
the fields and then go along the stream down in a south-easterly
direction towards Liskowiec.

Švejk, Vaněk and Chodounský were to be a billeting party. They
were to find night billets for the company which would follow them in
about an hour, or at the most an hour and a half. As for Baloun he was
ordered to roast a goose at the house where Lieutenant Lukáš would
spend the night. The other three had to keep an eye on him and see he

did not wolf up half of it. Apart from this Vaněk and Švejk had to buy a pig within the limits of the quantity of meat allotted to the company. At night they were to make goulash. The night billets for the men must be up to the required standard: they should avoid lousy hovels so that the men could have a really proper rest, because the company would set out from Liskowiec as early as half past six in the morning over Krościenko in the direction of Stara Sól.

The battalion was no longer short of cash. The brigade supply office at Sanok had paid out to it advances in respect of the slaughter that was to come. In the company till there was more than a hundred thousand crowns and Vaněk had already received the order that when they were finally somewhere at their destination, by which they meant the trenches, he should settle accounts and pay the men the sums which were indisputably owing to them for the bread rations and the mess portions which they had not been issued with.

And while these four set out on their journey the local vicar appeared at company headquarters and distributed to the men leaflets with 'The Song of Lourdes' in all languages according to their nationality. He had a bundle of these songs, which had been left here by a high military clerical dignitary, who passed through ravaged Galicia in a car with some tarts. The local vicar was to distribute them to the military units which passed through.

> Where the river flows deep down in the dell
> The angels' message rings out on the bell.
> Ave, ave, ave Maria! – Ave, ave, ave Maria!
>
> The maiden Bernarda was led by the Lord
> Down to the bank through the fresh green sward. – Ave!
>
> There she sees on the rocks in a glow of grace
> A sublime being with a holy face. – Ave!
>
> Lovely she looks in her raiment of white
> With a cloud-coloured girdle, simple and bright. – Ave!
>
> She holds a rosary in hands serene,
> Our merciful and most gracious Queen. – Ave!
>
> A change comes over Bernarda's face.
> It is lit by the glow of Our Lady's grace. – Ave!
>
> She kneels and prays, and the Virgin sees,
> And addresses to her these words of peace. – Ave!

'My child, I conceived, spotless and true,
And shall now be the guardian for all of you. – Ave!

My pious people pass in procession.
They worship me and find salvation. – Ave!

In this dell I shall build a marble dome
In token that here I shall make my home. – Ave!

This bubbling spring calls thee down from above.
It shall be the gage and pledge of my love. – Ave!'

O glory to thee, most merciful dell,
In thee the Mother of God shall dwell. – Ave!

There in the rock is the cave of Thine.
Thou hast given us paradise, merciful Queen. – Ave!

Since this glorious and radiant day
Men and women come here to pray. – Ave!

Worshippers Thou shalt have in throngs.
Look down upon us and right our wrongs! – Ave!

O star of salvation, show us the way
To the throne of God, that we may pray! – Ave!

Most holy Mother, hold us dear
And shed Thy mercy on Thy children here!

In Tyrawa Wołoska there were many latrines and scattered all over them could be found the leaflets with 'The Song of Lourdes'.

Corporal Nachtigal, who came from somewhere near Kašperské Hory, had bought a bottle of spirit from a frightened Jew. Now he gathered together some of his comrades and they all started to sing 'The Song of Lourdes' after the German text without the refrain 'Ave!' and to the tune of 'Prince Eugène'.

It was a bloody awful journey when it got dark and those four, whose duty it was to find night accommodation for the 11th company, got to a spinney above a brook which was supposed to lead to Liskowiec.

Baloun, who found himself for the first time in a situation where he was going somewhere into the blue, and to whom everything, the darkness, the fact that they were going ahead to look for night billets, seemed suddenly extraordinarily mysterious, was seized by a frightful suspicion that things were not as they should be.

'Chaps,' he said quietly, as he stumbled along the path above the brook, 'they've sacrificed us.'

'What do you mean?' Švejk roared at him almost inaudibly.

'Oh chaps, don't let's make such a shindy,' Baloun begged in a whisper. 'I feel it in my bones. The enemy'll hear us and at once start shooting at us. Oh, I know it. They've sent us forward to see whether the enemy's there, and when they hear the firing they'll know at once that it's not possible to advance any further. Chaps, we're the *avant-garde* as Corporal Terna once taught me.'

'Well, go on *avant* then,' said Švejk. 'We'll follow you nicely and you can protect us with your body as you're such a giant. When you're shot, let us know, so that we have time to lie flat on the ground. You're not much of a soldier! He's afraid someone's going to shoot at him! But every real soldier ought to enjoy that frightfully. He must know that the more the enemy shoots the more ammunition he uses up. Every shot which the enemy fires at you reduces his fighting capacity. And he's glad too that he can shoot at you, because he doesn't have to drag his cartridges about with him and can run much easier.'

Baloun gave a heavy sigh: 'But I've got a farm at home.'

'Oh, damn that farm,' Švejk advised him. 'It's much better for you to give your life for His Imperial Majesty. Didn't they teach you that in the army?'

'They only mentioned it,' said the idiotic Baloun. 'They only took me to the drill-ground and after that I didn't hear anything any more about it, because I became a batman. . . . If only His Imperial Majesty would feed us better . . .'

'You're a bloody gluttonous pig. A soldier shouldn't be given any food at all before an engagement. We were told that years ago in the school by Captain Untergriez. He always used to say to us: "You bloody bastards, if there should be a war and you should get into a battle, you mustn't gorge yourselves before it. A chap who's overgorged and stops a bullet in his belly is done for at once, because all the soup and army bread fly out of his guts after a shot like that, and a soldier who stops one gets an inflammation and is finished at once. But if he's got nothing in his stomach then a shot there doesn't mean anything to him. It's just like when a wasp stings you, a pure pleasure."'

'I digest very quickly,' said Baloun. 'Nothing ever stays very long in my stomach. Just imagine, chaps, I might eat a whole dish of dumplings with pork and cabbage and half an hour later I don't shit out of me more than two or three soupspoons. The rest gets lost inside me. Some people say for instance that when they eat chanterelles they come out of them whole just as they went in. You can wash them and cook them again in sour sauce, but with me it's the opposite. I stuff myself so full with chanterelles that anyone else would burst, and when I go to the rears afterwards I just fart out a little yellow gruel like a baby. The rest gets lost inside me.

'You won't perhaps believe me,' Baloun told Švejk confidentially, 'but fishbones and even plum stones get dissolved in me. Once I purposely counted them. I ate seventy plum dumplings with their stones and when my time came I went behind the huts, poked about in it with a stick, separated the stones and counted them. Of those seventy stones more than half got dissolved inside me.'

A quiet long-drawn sigh escaped Baloun's lips. 'My old woman used to make plum dumplings out of potato-dough, to which she added a little curds to make it richer. She always preferred to sprinkle them with poppy seeds rather than with cheese, but I liked the opposite so that once I smacked her face because of it.... Oh, dear, I wasn't capable of appreciating my domestic bliss.'

Baloun stopped, licked his lips, rolled his tongue over his palate and said sadly and softly: 'You know, old man, now I don't have them I believe my wife was right and that they are better with poppy seed. Then I always imagined the poppy seeds stuck in your teeth but now I think if only they did.... Yes, my wife suffered lots of trouble with me. How often she wept when I insisted that she put more marjoram in the jitrnice and I always used to biff her one. Once I beat her up so much, poor thing, that she lay in bed for two days and it was all because she wouldn't slaughter a turkey for me for dinner and said that a cockerel would be good enough.

'Yes, old chap,' Baloun began to cry, 'if only I had jitrnice even without marjoram and cockerels now! Do you like dill sauce? You see, we always had rows about it and today I'd drink it like coffee.'

Baloun slowly forgot his fears of an imaginary danger and in the dead of the night, while they were still going down towards Liskowiec, he continued to tell Švejk with emotion what he had not appreciated before and would now like to eat, until his eyes were full of tears.

Behind him walked Chodounský with Vaněk.

Chodounský was saying to Vaněk that in his opinion the world war was bloody nonsense. The worst thing about it was that if a telephone wire was cut anywhere he had to get up in the night and put it right

and what was even worse was that when there had been a war before
searchlights had not been invented. But nowadays, just when you were
mending those bloody wires, the enemy picked you out at once with
searchlights and set their whole artillery on you.

Down in the village, where they had to find night billets for the
company, it was dark and all the dogs started barking. This forced the
expedition to stop and consider what they should do to cope with the
brutes.

'What about going back?' whispered Baloun.

'Oh, Baloun, Baloun, if we reported what you've just said you'd be
shot for cowardice,' said Švejk.

The dogs barked more and more the farther they went, and they
started to bark even to the south beyond the river Ropa as well as in
Krościenko and several other villages, for Švejk shouted out into the
night quiet:

'Down – down – down,' as he used to shout at his dogs when he had
a dog business.

The dogs only barked all the more, so that Vaněk said to Švejk:

'Don't shout at them, Švejk, you'll set the whole of Galicia a-bark.'

'Something similar happened to us on manoeuvres in the region of
Tábor,' Švejk answered. 'We marched in the night to a certain village
and the dogs started making an enormous racket. The region all round
is fairly heavily populated so that the barking spread from village to
village, always farther and farther on, and when the dogs in the village
where we camped, who had already stopped barking, heard this barking from far away, perhaps even as far away as Pelhřimov, they
started to bark again, and after a while there was nothing but barking
over the whole area of Tábor, Pelhřimov, Budějovice, Humpolec,
Třeboň and Jihlava. Our captain was a very nervous old man and
couldn't stand the barking of dogs. He couldn't sleep the whole night
but walked up and down asking the patrols: "Who's that barking?
What's that barking?" The soldiers humbly reported that it was dogs
who were barking, and this infuriated him so much that those of us
who were then on patrol got confined to barracks when we returned
from manoeuvres. After that he always chose out a "dog command"
and sent them ahead. It had the task of informing the inhabitants in the
village where we were going to stay overnight that no dog must be
allowed to bark in the night otherwise it would be liquidated. I was
also on one of those commands and when we came to a village in the

region of Milevsko I got mixed up and told the mayor that every dog-owner whose dog barked in the night would be liquidated for strategic reasons. The mayor got frightened, immediately harnessed his horses and rode to headquarters to beg mercy for the whole village. They didn't let him in, the sentries nearly shot him and so he returned home,

but before we got to the village everybody on his advice had tied rags round the dogs' muzzles with the result that three of them went mad.'

They went down to the village after general acceptance had been accorded to Švejk's doctrine that dogs in the night fear the lighted points of cigarettes. Unfortunately none of them were smoking cigarettes, so that Švejk's advice had no positive effect. It turned out, however, that the dogs were barking out of joy, because they remembered with affection the troops who passed through and always left something behind for them to eat.

From a long way off the dogs sensed the approach of creatures who always left behind them bones and horse carcasses. Suddenly, as though they had come from nowhere, four huge dogs appeared and sprang on Švejk in a friendly fashion with their tails erect.

Švejk stroked them, patted them, and spoke to them in the dark as though they were children:

'So at last we're here. We've come to you to go bye-byes, to have our yum-yum. We'll give you delicious bonies and crusties, and the next morning we'll go on towards the enemy.'

In the cottages in the village, lights began to go on, and when they started to knock on the door of the first cottage to find out where the mayor lived, they heard from inside the squealing and shrill voice of a woman, who said in what was neither Polish nor Ukrainian that she had a husband in the army, her children had smallpox, the Russkies had taken everything away from her and that her husband before he went to the front ordered her not to open the door to anyone in the night. Only when they lent weight to their assault on the door by assuring her that they were 'billeteers' was the door opened by an unknown hand. When they got inside it turned out that it was actually here that the mayor lived. He vainly tried to persuade Švejk that it was not he who had imitated the squeaky woman's voice. He excused himself by saying that he slept in the hay and that when someone suddenly awoke his wife from sleep she didn't know what she was saying. As for night billets for the whole company the village was so teeny tiny, he said, that there was no space even for one soldier. There was no place to sleep at all. There was nothing to buy either. The Russkies had requisitioned everything.

Perhaps their gracious lordships would condescend to come with him to Krościenko. There were big farms there and it was only three-quarters of an hour away. There was plenty of room there. Every soldier could cover himself with a sheep skin and get a mess-tin of milk, as they had lots of cows there. The water was good there too. The officer gentlemen could sleep in the castle, but here in Liskowiec there was nothing but penury, the itch and lice. He himself had once had five cows, but the Russkies had requisitioned them all, so that even when he wanted milk for his sick children he had to go to Krościenko.

As though in confirmation of this the cows mooed next door in his cow-shed and a shrill woman's voice could be heard shouting at those unfortunate cows and wishing that the cholera would seize them.

However, the mayor did not let himself be disturbed by this and went on putting on his high boots:

'The only cow here is the one belonging to my next-door neighbour Vojciek. It's the one you have just heard mooing, my gracious lords. It's a sick and miserable cow. The Russkies took away her calf. Since then she doesn't give any milk, but the landlord doesn't like to slaughter her. He hopes that the Mother of God from Częstochowa will put everything right again.'

While he said this he put on his sheepskin coat:

'Let's go to Krościenko, my gracious lords. It isn't even three-quarters of an hour. What am I saying, sinner that I am? It won't even be half an hour. I know a way over the brook and then through the birch grove past the oak. . . . The village is a big one, and they've got very powerful vodka there in their pubs. Let's go, my gracious lords! Why delay? The soldier gentlemen of your glorious regiment must be able to go to bed in order and comfort. The Royal and Imperial soldier who fights with the Russkies undoubtedly deserves a clean bed and comfortable sleeping quarters . . . and here? Lice, the itch, smallpox and cholera. Yesterday in our cursed village here three peasants turned black from cholera . . . the most merciful Lord has placed a curse on Liskowiec . . .'

At this moment Švejk waved his hand majestically.

'Listen, my gracious lords,' he said, imitating the voice of the mayor. 'I once read in a book how in the Swedish wars, when orders had been given to billet the men in some village or other, the mayor began to make excuses and wouldn't give them help and so they hanged him on the nearest tree. And today in Sanok a Polish corporal told me that when the billeting party come the mayor has to summon all the members of the council, and they go with them into each cottage and say quite simply: "Three men can go here, four there, the officers will be billeted at the vicarage and everything must be ready in half an hour."

'My gracious lord,' said Švejk, turning solemnly to the mayor, 'tell me where is your nearest tree?'

The mayor did not understand the word 'tree' and so Švejk explained to him that a 'tree' was a birch, an oak, a pear-tree, an apple-tree, in short anything that had strong branches. The mayor again failed to understand, but when he heard the names of fruit trees he got startled because the cherries were already getting ripe and so he said he had no idea about anything like trees but there was an oak in front of his house.

'All right,' said Švejk, making with his hand the international sign

for hanging. 'We're now going to hang you in front of your house, because you must be aware that there's a war on and that we have orders to sleep here and not in any Krościenko. You won't change our strategic plans, you bastard. You're going to swing just as it happened in that book about the Swedish wars. . . . There was a case like that, gentlemen, once on the manoeuvres at Velké Meziříčí . . .'

At that moment Vaněk interrupted Švejk:

'You can tell us about that afterwards, Švejk,' he said, and turning to the mayor added: 'Very well, then, pull up your socks and produce the billets!'

The mayor began to tremble and stammered something about how he meant it for the best for their gracious lordships, but if there was no other way he could perhaps find something in the village so that all the gentlemen would be satisfied. He would immediately fetch his lantern.

When he went out of the room, which was very sparsely lit by a small paraffin lamp under the image of a saint, who was twisted on the picture like the most wretched cripple, Chodounský suddenly exclaimed:

'Where's Baloun got to?'

However, before they could look about them, the door behind the stove, which led somewhere outside, quietly opened and Baloun slipped in through it. He looked round him to see whether the mayor was there and said, sniffing as though he had a heavy cold:

'I've beed in the larder. I found somethig. I've god my moud idto id and now id's all stuck to my deed. Id isn'd sald or sweed. Id's bread dough.'

Vaněk shone the electric torch on him and all were able to convince themselves that they had never yet seen in their lives an Austrian soldier in such a filthy mess as he was. After that they got frightened because they saw that Baloun's tunic was blown up as though he were in the last stage of pregnancy.

'What's happened to you, Baloun?' Švejk asked him pityingly, prodding his bloated belly.

'It's the gherkins,' Baloun rattled, struggling for breath through the dough, which he couldn't get either up or down. 'Careful, they are salt gherkins. I ate three of them in a rush and I've brought you the others.'

Baloun began to take out from under his tunic gherkin after gherkin and handed them round.

The mayor stood in the doorway with his light. Seeing the scene he crossed himself and whined:

'The Russkies have robbed us and now our people do the same.'

They all went out to the village accompanied by a pack of dogs which clung obstinately to Baloun and jumped up at his trouser pocket, where he had a piece of bacon also obtained from the larder but kept secret from his comrades-in-arms due to his greediness.

'Why are the dogs running after you?' Švejk asked Baloun, who answered only after long reflection:

'They sense in me that I'm a good man.'

What he did not say was that he had his hand on the bacon in his pocket and that one of the dogs was continually snapping at it ...

When they went round to look for billets they discovered that Liskowiec was a big settlement which had indeed been drained of everything by the war havoc. It had not suffered any fires, it is true, as miraculously enough neither warring parties had included it in their sphere of operations, but on the other hand the population of nearby villages which had been destroyed, such as Chyrów, Grabów and Hołubla, had been settled in it.

In some of the huts there lived as many as eight families in the greatest penury after all those losses which they had suffered through the predatory war, when a whole epoch of it hurled itself over them like the devastating waves of a flood.

The company had to be billeted in a small devastated distillery at the other end of the village, where half a company could be put into the fermenting room. The rest were billeted by tens in various farms where the rich nobility had refused to shelter the miserable riff-raff who had lost their homes and land and been reduced to beggary.

The company staff with all the officers, Vaněk, the batmen, the telephonist, the ambulance, the cooks and Švejk were billeted at the vicarage with the vicar, who had not taken in a single one of the destitute families from the neighbourhood either, although he had plenty of room.

He was a tall thin old gentleman in a faded and greasy cassock who out of stinginess hardly ate at all. He had been brought up by his father to detest Russians, but at once lost his hatred for them when they retreated and the Austrian army came and devoured all his geese and chickens. The Russians had not touched these, when several shaggy Cossacks from beyond Lake Baikal had been billeted on him.

His hatred for the Austro-Hungarian army increased still more when the Hungarians came to his village and took away from him all the honey from his beehives. Now he looked with loathing at his unexpected guests and it gave him pleasure to be able to walk past them, shrug his shoulders and say again and again: 'I've got absolutely nothing. I'm a complete beggar. You won't find even a crust of bread here, gentlemen.'

The man who was the saddest of all at this was Baloun, who nearly burst into tears at such penury. In his head he always had a vague idea of a roast sucking-pig with flesh which crackled and smelt like honey. All this time he was slumbering in the vicar's kitchen, where from time to time a lanky youth peeped in who worked for the vicar as servant and cook and had strict orders to keep an eye on the whole house and see that nothing got stolen.

Baloun could find nothing in the kitchen either except a little bit of paper with a pinch of caraway seed which was lying in a salt-cellar. He stuffed it into his mouth and its aroma awoke in him savoury hallucinations of sucking-pig.

In the courtyard of the small distillery behind the vicarage the flames blazed under the cauldrons of the field-kitchen. The water was already boiling but there was nothing to boil in it.

The quartermaster sergeant-major and the cook went up and down the whole village vainly scouring it for a pig. Everywhere they got the same answer that the Russkies had eaten everything up or taken it away.

They also woke up a Jew in a pub who began to tear his long curls and express desperate regret that he could not help the soldier gentlemen. In the end he made them buy from him an old centenarian of a cow, a scraggy living carcass, which was only skin and bones. He asked a horrific price for it, tore his beard and swore they would not be able to find a cow like it in the whole of Galicia, in the whole of Austria and Germany, in the whole of Europe, in the whole world. And all the time he howled, wept and swore solemnly that it was the fattest cow which had ever come to the world at Jehovah's bidding. He swore by all his ancestors that people came riding all the way from Wołoczyska to look at that cow, they talked about it in the whole region as a marvel, it wasn't really a cow at all but the most succulent of buffalos. Finally he knelt down before them and hugging their knees one after the other cried out:

'Kill the poor old Jew if you like, but don't go away without his cow.'

He confused all of them so much by his screaming that in the end they carried off that sorry beast to the field-kitchen, although any knacker would have refused it. But long afterwards, when he had already got the money in his pocket, he went on weeping before them and complaining that they had completely ruined him and destroyed

him and that he had been utterly beggared by selling such a magnificent cow so cheaply. He begged them to hang him for committing in his old age an act of such utter folly that his forefathers would turn in their graves.

After he had been grovelling in the dust before them he suddenly shook off all his self-pity, went home and said to his wife in the privacy of his room:

'My Elsa, my Elsakins, those soldiers are fools and your Nathan is a clever one.'

They had a lot of trouble with that cow. At times it looked as if it would not be possible to skin it. In flaying it they broke the skin several times and underneath appeared muscles as twisted as a dried-up hawser.

Meanwhile they dragged in a sack of potatoes from somewhere and began hopelessly to cook those sinews and bones, while nearby in a smaller kitchen the cook in utter despair tried to make officers' mess portions out of a piece of that skeleton.

This wretched cow, if that phenomenon of nature deserved the name of cow at all, remained indelibly impressed upon the memory of all who were there, and it is almost certain that if afterwards before the battle of Sokal the commanding officers had reminded the men of the cow from Liskowiec, the 11th company would have hurled itself with fixed bayonets at the enemy to the accompaniment of frightful bellows of rage.

The cow was such a disgrace that it was not even possible to make beef soup out of it. The longer the meat was cooked the more firmly it clung to the bones and grew into them. It grew as ossified as a bureaucrat who spends half a century pasturing on official red tape and devours nothing but official documents.

Švejk, who as courier maintained unbroken communication between the staff and the kitchen so as to ascertain when the meal would be cooked at last, announced to Lieutenant Lukáš:

'Sir, it's come out like porcelain. The cow is so tough that you could cut glass with it. When the cook, Pavlíček, tasted the meat with Baloun, he broke off his front tooth and Baloun lost his back molar.'

Baloun solemnly advanced before Lieutenant Lukáš and, stammering, handed him the broken tooth, which was wrapped up in 'The Song of Lourdes':

'Humbly report, sir, I've done what I could. I broke the tooth when we tried the officers' mess portions to see if it was possible to make a beefsteak out of the meat.'

At these words a melancholy figure rose from an armchair by the window. It was Lieutenant Dub, who had been brought in on an ambulance cart in a state of complete ruin.

'Please be quiet,' he said in despairing tones. 'I'm ill!'

He sat down again in the old chair in every crack of which there were thousands of bugs' eggs.

'I'm tired,' he said in a tragic voice. 'I'm sick and suffering. Please don't speak of broken teeth in my presence. My address is: Smíchov,

Královská 18. If I don't live to see tomorrow's day please see that my family are informed of it and that their feelings are spared. Don't forget to note on my gravestone that before the war I was a schoolmaster in an Imperial and Royal grammar school.'

He started to snore gently and could no longer hear the verse which Švejk quoted from an elegy for the dead:

> 'O Thou who saved the Virgin's soul
> And led the robber to his goal,
> Guide me to heaven and save my soul.'

After this Vaněk ascertained that the wonderful cow would have to be cooked two hours longer in the officers' kitchen. There was no question of there being any beefsteak from it and instead they would make goulash.

It was decided that before they sounded the signal for mess the men should be allowed to have a nap, because in any case supper would not be ready before morning.

Vaněk fetched a bundle of hay from somewhere, placed it beneath him in the vicar's dining-room, nervously twisted his moustache and said quietly to Lieutenant Lukáš who was resting above him on an old sofa:

'Believe me, sir, that in the course of the whole war I've never seen a cow like that . . .'

In the kitchen Chodounský was sitting by the lighted stump of a church candle preparing in advance a stock of letters for home so that he wouldn't have to bother about writing any when the number of their field post had been finally decided. He wrote:

Dear darling wife, fondest Boženka,

It is night time and I think incessantly of you, my treasure. I picture you thinking of me as you look at the empty bed beside you. You must forgive me if all sorts of thoughts spring into my mind. You know very well that I have been on military service in the field since the very beginning of the war and that I've already heard all sorts of things from my comrades who have been wounded and gone on leave. When they came back home they would rather have been in their graves than find that some rascally scamp had been at their wives. It's very painful for me to have to write this to you, darling Boženka. I wouldn't perhaps be writing like this but you know very well yourself that you confided to me that I was not the first man who knew you really well and that Mr Kraus from Mikulášská Avenue had you before me. When I think this very night how in my absence that lousy wretch might make some demands on you, I'm ready, darling Boženka, to strangle him on the spot. For a long time I've kept this to myself, but when I think that he might once more run after you, my heart turns to stone and I must warn you of one thing and that is that I will not have living with me a bitch who has gone a-whoring after all and sundry and brought a slur on my name. Pardon me, darling Boženka, for these sharp words, but take care I don't find out anything bad about you. If I do I shall be forced to hack the guts out of both of you because I'll stick at nothing even if it costs me my life. I kiss you a thousand times. Give my love to papa and mamma,

Your Tonouš

N.B. Don't forget that *I gave you my name!*

He went on writing further letters for the stock.

My dearest Boženka,
When you get these lines you will know that we already have behind us the great battle in which the fortunes of war turned in our favour. Among other things we've shot down about ten enemy planes and one general with a big wart on his nose. In the thick of the fighting when shrapnel burst over our heads I was thinking about you, dear darling Boženka, what you might be doing, how you were and what was the news at home. I often remember how we went together to St Thomas's beer hall, how you led me home and how next day your arm ached from all that effort. Now we are advancing again and so I have no more time to continue my letter. I hope you have been faithful to me, because you know very well that in this respect I'm a devil. But it's already time for the march. I kiss you a thousand times, dear Boženka, and you must hope that everything will turn out well.

Your loving Tonouš

Chodounský began to nod and fell asleep at the table.

The vicar, who could not sleep and all the time walked up and down in the vicarage, opened the door to the kitchen and for economy's sake blew out the burning stump of the candle beside Chodounský.

In the dining-room no one was sleeping except Lieutenant Dub. Vaněk, who had received in the brigade office at Sanok a new budget for the catering of the troops, was studying it carefully and found that the nearer the army got to the front the more the portions were reduced. He even had to laugh over one paragraph of the order in which it was forbidden to use saffron and ginger in making soup for the men. There was also a note appended to the instructions that in the field-kitchens the bones had to be collected and dispatched to the division stores at the base. It was rather vague because no one could know which bones were meant – the bones of human beings or of other slaughtered livestock.

'Listen, Švejk,' said Lieutenant Lukáš, yawning with boredom, 'before we start eating, you could perhaps tell me a story.'

'Oh dear,' Švejk answered, 'before we get any food I'd have time to tell you the whole history of the Czech nation, sir. But instead I know only a very short story about a postmaster's wife from the district of Sedlčany, who after the death of her husband took over the post office. I straightaway thought of her when I heard that speech about these field posts, although it has absolutely nothing to do with field posts.'

'Švejk,' said Lieutenant Lukáš from the sofa, 'you're starting to talk frightful tripe again.'

'I certainly am, humbly report, sir. The story really is frightful tripe. In fact I don't know how anything so tripish could come into my head or how I could talk of such a thing. Either it's my natural idiocy or else it's memories of my youth. There are, as you know, sir, people with various natures on our globe. And that cook Jurajda was after all right that time in Bruck when he was drunk and fell into the ditch, and when he couldn't get out and shouted from it: "Man is destined and chosen to know truth, that he may with his spirit rule the whole universe in harmony, that he may continually develop and educate himself and gradually rise to higher and higher spheres and more intelligent and affectionate worlds." When we wanted to drag him out he scratched and bit. He thought he was at home and it was only when we threw him back again into it that he began begging us to drag him out of it.'

'But what happened to that postmistress?' Lieutenant Lukáš cried in desperation.

'She was a very good woman, the only thing was that she was a bit of a bitch, sir. She carried out all her duties at the post office but she only had one fault, and that was that she thought everybody was persecuting her and had a down on her. And so after her day's work she denounced them to the authorities according to how the circumstances came about. Once she had gone in the early morning to the wood to pick mushrooms and had observed carefully how when she went past the school the schoolmaster was already up. He had greeted her and asked her where she was going so early in the morning. When she had told him that she was going to pick mushrooms, he had said that he would follow after. From that the silly old woman concluded that he had some indecent intentions towards her and afterwards when she saw him actually coming out of the bushes she took fright, ran away and at once wrote to the local school council denouncing him for having tried to rape her. The schoolmaster was summoned before a disciplinary board, but to prevent a public scandal the school inspector himself came to look into the case. He spoke to the sergeant of the gendarmerie and asked him to give his view whether that schoolmaster was likely to have done such a thing. The sergeant of the gendarmerie looked into the documents and said that he was incapable of it, because once already he had been accused by the priest of running after his niece, whom the priest used to sleep with, and the schoolmaster had obtained from the district doctor a certificate confirming that he'd been impotent since he was six, when he fell with wide-open legs from the loft down on to the shaft of a haycart. And so that bitch went and denounced the sergeant of gendarmerie, the district doctor and the school inspector for having all of them been bribed by the schoolmaster. They all of them took her to the courts where she was found guilty, but she appealed on the grounds that she was mental. She was examined by the medical experts and they issued an official certificate that although she was feeble-minded she could hold any office in the State service.'

Lieutenant Lukáš exclaimed:

'Jesus Mary!' and added afterwards: 'I'd like to say something to you, Švejk, but I don't want to spoil my supper', after which Švejk said:

'I warned you, sir, that what I was going to tell you was frightful tripe.'

Lieutenant Lukáš only waved his hand and said: 'You've dropped so many pearls of wisdom, Švejk.'

'Not every man can have wisdom, sir,' said Švejk convincingly. 'Stupid people have to exist too, because if everyone were wise then there would be so much good sense in the world that every other person would be driven crazy by it. If for instance, humbly report, sir, everyone knew the laws of nature and could calculate the distance of the heavenly bodies, then he would only be a trouble to those around him like a man called Mr Čapek who used to come to The Chalice, and whenever he went out of the pub on to the street at night he looked at the stars in the sky and when he came back went up to everyone and said to each of them: "Today Jupiter is shining beautifully. You've got no idea, you bastard, of what you've got over your head. Talk about distances! If they were to shoot you out of a gun with the speed of a shell, you lousy brute, you'd still have to fly for millions and millions of years to get there." When he said this he was so coarse and rude that afterwards he himself usually flew out of the pub with the usual speed of a tram, perhaps, sir, at about ten kilometres an hour. Or take for instance, sir, the ants . . .'

Lieutenant Lukáš raised himself on his sofa and put his hands together in prayer:

'I'm really surprised at myself for always talking to you, Švejk. After all, I've known you for so long, Švejk . . .'

Švejk nodded affirmatively:

'It's a question of habit, sir. It's due to the very fact that we have known each other for so long and that we've gone through a lot together. We've suffered a lot together and if we got into trouble it was always by a pure fluke. Humbly report, sir, I think it's fate. What His Imperial Majesty ordains, he ordains well. He brought us together and I wish nothing better for myself than to be able to be a really great help to you sometimes. Aren't you hungry, sir?'

Lieutenant Lukáš, who had meanwhile stretched himself out on the old sofa again, said that Švejk's last question was the best ending to this lamentable conversation, and that he should go and ask what had happened to the mess. It would certainly be better if Švejk could go out for a little and leave him, because the tripe which he kept on hearing from him exhausted him more than the whole march from Sanok. He would like to go to sleep for a bit, but he couldn't.

'It's all because of the bugs, sir. There's an old saying that vicars breed bugs. You'll not find anywhere so many bugs as you do at vicarages. In the vicarage in Horní Stodůlky the vicar, who was called Zamastil, even wrote a whole book about bugs. They were crawling on him even when he was preaching.'

'Well, what did I say, Švejk? Are you going to the kitchen or not?'

Švejk went out and behind him Baloun came out on tiptoe from a corner like his shadow . . .

When in the morning they left Liskowiec for Stara Sól and Sambor they carted in the field-kitchen with them the wretched cow which was still not cooked enough. It was resolved that they should cook it on the way and that they would eat it at the rest pause halfway between Liskowiec and Stara Sól.

For the journey they made the men black coffee.

Lieutenant Dub was again carried on the ambulance cart because he felt still worse after yesterday. The man who suffered most from him was his batman, who had continually to run beside the cart, while Lieutenant Dub shouted at him without cease that he had not looked after him at all yesterday and that when they reached their destination he would settle with him. Every moment he asked for water and when he drank it he vomited it up again.

'Who – what are you laughing at?' he shouted from the cart. 'I'll teach you. Don't play with me. You'll get to know me!'

Lieutenant Lukáš rode on horseback accompanied by Švejk, who marched sprightly forward, as though he could hardly wait for the moment when they were to fight the enemy. All the time he talked:

'Have you noticed, sir, that some of our people are really like flies? They have hardly thirty kilos on their backs and yet they can't stick it. They ought to be given lectures like the late Lieutenant Buchánek gave to us. He was the man who shot himself because of the advance which he got out of his future father-in-law for his marriage and which he spent on other tarts. And then he got another advance from another future father-in-law and was a bit more economical with it. He slowly lost it at cards and left the tarts alone. But he couldn't hold out for long and had to find a third future father-in-law for an advance. With this third advance he bought a horse, an Arab stallion, not a thorough-bred . . .'

Lieutenant Lukáš jumped down from his horse.

'Švejk,' he said in a menacing tone, 'if you start talking about a fourth advance I'll chuck you into the ditch.'

He jumped back on to his horse and Švejk went on solemnly:

'Humbly report, sir, there was no question of a fourth advance, because he shot himself after the third one.'

'At last,' said Lieutenant Lukáš.

'Not to forget what we've been talking about,' Švejk went on, 'the sort of lectures which Lieutenant Buchánek always used to give us whenever soldiers collapsed during the march ought, in my modest opinion, to be given to all the troops. He gave the order for "rest", made us all line up like chickens round a hen and began to explain to us: "You bastards, you're quite incapable of appreciating the fact that you're marching on this globe, because you're such uneducated scum that it's enough to make a chap vomit when he looks at you. You should be made to march on the sun! A man who weighs sixty kilos on our miserable planet weighs over seventeen hundred there. That'd do you all in. You'd have to march carrying in your packs over 280 kilos or about three quintals, and your rifle alone would be one and a half quintals in weight. You'd be groaning with your tongues hanging out like exhausted hounds." We had with us an unfortunate schoolmaster and he was so bold as to break in: "If you'll excuse me, sir, on the moon a man of sixty kilos weighs only thirteen kilos. On the moon we'd be able to march better because our packs would only weigh four kilos. On the moon we should not be marching at all, we should be floating in the air."

' "Tut! tut! That's really awful," the late Lieutenant Buchánek said. "You seem to be asking for a sock on the jaw, you lousy bastard. You can be glad I'm going to give you just an ordinary earth sock, because if I were to give you a moon sock with your light weight you'd fly as far as somewhere in the Alps and be smashed up there. If I were to give you a heavy sun sock your uniform would be changed into pea soup and your head would fly somewhere to Africa." And so he gave the Jimmy Knowall an ordinary earth sock, and he started blubbing and we went on marching. But during the whole march he blubbed and talked, sir, about human dignity or something like that, complaining that they were treating him as if he were a dumb creature. After that the lieutenant sent him on report and they gaoled him for fourteen days. He had six more weeks to serve but he didn't serve them because he got a rupture. Somehow or other they made him twist on the horizontal bars in the barracks and he couldn't take it and died as a malingerer in the hospital.'

'It's really very peculiar, Švejk,' said Lieutenant Lukáš, 'that as I've already told you so many times, you have a habit of speaking in a specially disparaging way about the officers' ranks.'

'Oh, no, I don't,' Švejk answered sincerely. 'I only wanted to tell you, sir, how in the old days in the army people drove themselves to ruin. That man whom I was talking about thought that he was more educated than the lieutenant. With his talk about the moon he wanted to lower him in the eyes of the troops, so because of that he got that earth sock on the jaw. And everybody sighed with relief. No one minded. On the contrary all were only glad that the lieutenant had made such a good joke about his earth sock: that's what you call "saving the situation". A chap has to have a sudden bright idea and then it's all right. Opposite the Carmelite Convent in Prague, sir, there used years ago to be a shop with rabbits and other birds kept by a Mr Jenom. He started walking out with the daughter of a bookbinder called Bílek. Mr Bílek didn't approve of the acquaintance and announced publicly in the pub that if Mr Jenom asked for the hand of his daughter he'd knock him down the stairs in a way the world had never seen. Mr Jenom then had a good drink to get his courage up and went to see Mr Bílek all the same. The latter welcomed him in the hall with a large knife which they used for trimming books and which looked like a chopper. He thundered at him and asked him what he wanted, and at that moment the good Mr Jenom farted so loudly that the pendulum on the grandfather clock stopped. Mr Bílek burst out laughing, shook his hand at once and from then on it was just: "Welcome, dear Mr Jenom – please come in, do take a seat – if you haven't cacked your trousers? You see I'm not such a bad chap after all. It's true I wanted to chuck you out but now I see that you're quite an agreeable gentleman. You're a rarity indeed! I'm a bookbinder and I've read many novels and stories, but I've never read in any book yet of a future bridegroom introducing himself in this way." Mr Bílek laughed so much that he nearly burst his sides and kept on saying with considerable relish that he felt as though they'd known each other since the day of their birth and were born brothers. He immediately offered him a cigar, sent for beer and sausages for him, called his wife and introduced him to her, giving her all the details of the fart. But she only spat and walked out of the room. After that he called his daughter and told her: "This gentleman has come to ask for your hand in such and such circumstances." The daughter immediately burst into tears and said she didn't want to know him, and had no wish even to see him, so there was nothing else for them both to do but drink up the beer, eat up the sausages, and part. Afterwards it brought shame upon Mr Jenom in that pub where Mr Bílek used to go, and in the end all over that quarter of the city people had no other name for him but "Shitter Jenom", and everywhere they talked about how he had tried to "save the situation".

'Human existence, beg to report, sir, is so complicated that the life of a single individual is nothing more than a bit of rubbish in comparison. Before the war a police sergeant called Mr Hubička used to come to The Chalice at Na Bojišti. Another regular guest there was an editor who collected stories of broken legs and people who were run over or committed suicide and reported them in his newspaper. He was a merry gentleman and happened to be more often at the police station than in his editorial office. One day he got the police sergeant, Hubička, completely drunk and they exchanged clothes in the kitchen, so that the police sergeant was in mufti and the editor became the police sergeant. All he did was to cover up the number on his revolver and set out on patrol in the streets of Prague. In Resslova Street behind the former Wenceslas prison he ran into an elderly gentleman in top hat and fur coat, who was walking in the middle of the night arm in arm with an elderly lady in a fur wrap. Both were hurrying home and not exchanging a word. He rushed up to them and shouted into the gentleman's ear: "Don't make such a shindy or I'll have you up!" Imagine, sir, what a shock they had! In vain they explained to him that there must be some mistake, because they were both returning from a dinner at the governor's. They had gone in their carriage as far as the National Theatre and now they wanted to take some fresh air. They lived not far away at Na Moráni: he was a senior counsellor in the governor's office and the lady was his wife. "You won't fool me," the disguised editor shouted at him. "All the greater shame on you if you are, as you say, a senior counsellor in the governor's office and behave like a young hooligan. I've been watching for a long time how you've been banging with your stick at the roller blinds of all the shops on your way and how your, as you call her, 'wife' has been helping you in it." "But I don't have any stick, as you can see. It must have been somebody else before us." "I should say you haven't," said the disguised editor, "when as I saw with my own eyes you broke it there round the corner on the head of an old woman who goes round the pubs with roast potatoes and chestnuts!" The lady was not even able to cry and the senior counsellor got so angry that he began to speak of "insolent rudeness", whereupon he was arrested and handed over to the next patrol in the district of the police station in Salmova Street. The disguised editor told the patrol that the couple should be taken off to the police station. He himself was from the police station at Svatý Jindřich and was on an official errand to Vinohrady. He had caught them both when they were disturbing the night peace and were involved in a night brawl. In addition they had committed the offence of abusing the police. He would finish his business at the police station at Svatý Jindřich and

come in an hour's time to the police station in Salmova Street. And so they were both of them taken away by the patrol and locked up until the next day while they waited for that police sergeant who had in the meantime returned by roundabout ways to The Chalice at Na Bojišti. There he woke up the police sergeant, Hubička, and told him very delicately everything that had happened, that an investigation would be made and if he didn't keep his mug shut . . .'

Lieutenant Lukáš seemed to be already tired by the conversation and before he urged his horse into a trot to get in front of the vanguard he said to Švejk:

'If you were to go on talking until evening, the longer you went on the more rot you'd talk.'

'Sir,' Švejk called out after the departing lieutenant. 'Don't you want to know how the story ended?'

Lieutenant Lukáš got into a gallop.

Lieutenant Dub's condition improved so much that he got out of the ambulance cart, gathered round him the whole staff of the company and began to instruct them as though in a haze. He delivered an enormously long speech which weighed on them all more heavily than their ammunition and rifles.

It was a hash-up of various parables.

He began: 'The soldiers' love for their officers makes unbelievable sacrifices possible. But that's not the point. On the contrary, if this love does not come natural to the soldier it must be forced on him. In civil life compulsory love like, shall we say, a school janitor's love for the teaching staff, lasts only as long as the external power which imposes it. In the army, however, we observe precisely the contrary, because an officer must not allow a soldier the slightest relaxation of the love which binds him to his superior officer. This love is no ordinary love: it is in fact respect, fear and discipline.'

All this time Švejk walked beside him on the left and as Lieutenant Dub spoke he had his face constantly turned towards him in 'eyes right' position.

At first Lieutenant Dub did not notice this and went on with his speech:

'This discipline and obligation to obey, the compulsory love of the soldier for the officer, is succinctness itself, because the relationship between soldier and officer is a perfectly straightforward one – the one obeys, the other commands. Long ago we read in books on military science that military laconism, military straightforwardness are those very virtues which every soldier must acquire. For, whether he likes it or not, he must love his superior officer, who in his eyes must be the greatest, the most perfect and completely crystallized embodiment of a firm and flawless will.'

It was only now that he noticed Švejk's 'eyes right' fixed on him. It was extremely disagreeable to him, because he suddenly felt that he was getting muddled in his speech and could not get out of the rut of the soldier's love for his superior officer. And so he shouted at Švejk:

'What are you gawking at me for?'

'By your own orders, humbly report, sir. Once you yourself were good enough to warn me that when you speak I must follow your lips with my eyes. As every soldier must carry out the instructions of his superior officer and remember them for all future occasions I have to do this too.'

'Look the other way,' Lieutenant Dub shouted. 'Only for God's sake not at me, you stupid bastard. You know I don't like it and I can't bear to see you. I'll give you such hell . . .'

Švejk turned his head to the left and went on walking so stiffly beside Lieutenant Dub that the latter shouted out:

'Where are your eyes when I'm talking to you?'

'Humbly report, sir, by your own orders, I'm now doing "eyes left".'

'Oh, my God,' sighed Lieutenant Dub, 'what a cross you are to bear! Look straight in front of you and think this about yourself: "I'm such an idiot that if anything happens to me no one will be the worse." Will you remember that?'

Švejk looked in front of him and said:

'Humbly report, sir, am I expected to reply?'

'Don't you dare behave like this!' Lieutenant Dub roared at him. 'Don't you dare speak to me like that! What do you mean by it?'

'Humbly report, sir, I'm thinking only of your orders at a station once when you rebuked me and told me that I shouldn't answer when you had finished speaking.'

'And so you're frightened of me?' said Lieutenant Dub in delight. 'But you haven't yet learned to know me. You're not the only one to have trembled in front of me, remember that! I've succeeded in taming other bastards and so you'd better shut your mug, stay quietly behind, and keep out of my sight!'

And so Švejk stayed at the back by the ambulance and rode comfortably on its two-wheeled cart to the next rest halt, where at last everyone got what they'd been waiting for – the soup and meat from the miserable cow.

'This cow ought to have been soaked in vinegar for at least a fortnight, or if not the cow, the man who bought it,' said Švejk.

From the brigade a courier came riding up on horseback with a new order for the 11th company that the march route would be changed to the direction of Felsztyn. Wojałycze and Sambor should be left out, as it was not possible to billet the company there, because they had two regiments from Poznań there already.

Lieutenant Lukáš immediately made new dispositions. Vaněk and Švejk were ordered to look for night billets for the company in Felsztyn.

'Now don't you get up to any mischief on the way, Švejk,' Lieutenant Lukáš warned him. 'Above all, mind you behave decently to the civilian population.'

'Humbly report, sir, I'll try my best, though I had a frightful dream, when I was dozing a bit towards morning. I dreamt about a washing trough which was dripping water the whole night in the corridor of the house where I lived, until the water ran over and soaked the landlord's ceiling. And he at once gave me notice that very morning. There actually was, sir, a case like that in real life: in Karlín behind the viaduct . . .'

'Oh, cut out your stupid stories, Švejk, and look with Vaněk at the map to see where you've got to go. Now here you see these villages. From this village here you must go to the right towards the stream and then follow its course until you come to the nearest village. From there, at the spot where the first brook flows into it, which will be on your right hand, you must go along a path through the fields up the hill due north. Then you can't lose your way until you get to Felsztyn. Can you remember that?'

Švejk set off with Vaněk and followed the march route.

It was just after midday. The land was breathing heavily in the heat and a rotting stink came out of the badly heaped pits containing buried soldiers. The two men came to the region where the fighting had taken place during the advance on Przemyśl and where whole battalions had been mowed down by machine-guns. The havoc made by the artillery could be seen in the small spinneys along the stream. On the wide spaces and slopes there were some maimed stumps sticking out of the ground instead of trees and this wilderness was furrowed with trenches.

'It seems to be a bit different here from around Prague,' said Švejk, to break the silence.

'At home the harvest's already over,' said Vaněk. 'We begin first in the Kralupy region.'

'There'll be a very good harvest here after the war,' said Švejk after a while. 'They won't have to buy bone flour. It's a great advantage for the farmers when their fields are covered with the dust of a whole regiment; in other words it's a very good means of livelihood. The only thing which worries me is that the farmers shouldn't let themselves be cheated and sell these soldiers' bones unnecessarily for bone charcoal in the sugar refineries. In the barracks at Karlín there was a lieutenant called Holub. He was so learned that everybody in the company thought he was an idiot. You see, because of his learning he never learnt to swear at the soldiers and considered everything only from the academic point of view. Once the soldiers reported to him that the army bread which they had drawn was not eatable. Another officer would have flown in a passion at such insolence, but not he. He remained quite calm, didn't call anybody a pig or a swine, and didn't sock anybody on the jaw. He only called all his men together and told them in his pleasant voice: "First of all, my men, you must realize that the barracks aren't a delicatessen shop where you can choose pickled eels, sardines and sandwiches. Every soldier must be intelligent enough to swallow any ration he draws without complaining about its quality. And he must have enough self-discipline not to make a fuss about the quality of what's put before him. Just imagine, my men, if there were a war. The soil in which you'd be buried after the battle wouldn't care a hoot what kind of bread you were gorged with before you died. Mother Earth would decompose you and eat you up boots and all. In this world nothing is allowed to vanish completely. Out of you, my men, there'll grow new corn for bread rations for new soldiers who again like you perhaps won't be satisfied, will start complaining, and then come up against someone who'll clap them in gaol until kingdom come, because he's got the right to do that. Now, my men, I've explained everything to you nicely and I believe I need not remind you again that whoever comes and complains a second time will thank his lucky stars later when he's allowed out again into God's light." "If he'd only swear at us," the soldiers said to each other, and they didn't at all like all those refinements in the lieutenant's speeches. And so once they chose me from the company and asked me to go and tell him that they all liked him but it's not the army if people don't swear at you. And so I went to his house and asked him to cut out all this refinement; that the army must be as tough as nails and soldiers are used to being reminded every day that they're bastards and swine. If they aren't they lose respect for their superior officers. At first he defended himself, spoke about intelligence and said that the times had gone by when the birch rod ruled, but in the end he accepted it, gave me a sock on the jaw and threw me out of the door so as to bolster his prestige. When I told the others the result of the negotiations they were all very pleased, but the very next day he went and spoiled it all. He came to me and said in the hearing of all of them: "Švejk, I lost my temper yesterday. Here's a guilder for you. Go and drink my health. One's got to know how to treat the men." '

Švejk looked at the countryside.

'I think we're going wrong,' he said. 'The lieutenant explained it to us quite well. We've got to go uphill, then down, first to the left and then to the right, and then again to the right. After that to the left – but we're going straight ahead all the time. Or have we gone through all that while we were talking? I can certainly see here before me two roads to Felsztyn. I suggest we take the one to the left.'

Vaněk, as is always the case when two people find themselves at a crossroads, started insisting that they must go to the right.

'My path,' said Švejk, 'is more comfortable than yours. I shall walk along the little brook where forget-me-nots grow and you'll be fooling around in the waste land. I stick to what the lieutenant said, that we can't lose our way and if we can't lose our way then why should I climb up any hills? I shall stroll comfortably over the meadows, put a nice little flower on my cap and pick a whole bunch for the lieutenant. Anyhow, we shall see which of us is right and I hope we part here good friends. This is the kind of country where all paths must lead to Felsztyn.'

'Don't be crazy, Švejk,' said Vaněk, 'According to the map we've got to go to the right here, as I say.'

'A map can be wrong,' answered Švejk, going down to the valley of the brook. 'Once a pork butcher named Křenek from Vinohrady walked home at night from U Montágů on the Malá Strana and tried to find his way with a street plan of Prague and in the morning he got to Rozdělov near Kladno. There they found him quite stiff in the rye where he had fallen down in exhaustion. If you insist on your opinion and won't accept any advice, sergeant-major, we must part and we shall only see each other again at our destination in Felsztyn. Just look at your watch so that we know which of us gets there first. And if any

kind of danger should threaten you just fire into the air so that I know where you are.'

In the afternoon Švejk came to a small lake where he ran into an escaped Russian prisoner who was bathing there. At the sight of Švejk he immediately ran away as naked as he was when he came out of the water.

His Russian uniform was lying underneath the willows and Švejk was curious to know how it would suit him, so he took off his own and put on the uniform worn by the unfortunate naked prisoner, who had escaped from a transport which had been billeted in a village behind the wood. Švejk wanted to see his reflection in the water and so he walked such a long way along the dam of the lake that he was caught by a patrol of field gendarmerie, who were looking for the escaped Russian prisoner. They were Hungarians and in spite of his protests they dragged him off to the staff command at Chyrów where they put him among a transport of Russian prisoners, who were being sent off to work on the reconstruction of the railway line in the direction of Przemyśl.

Everything happened so quickly that it was only the next day that Švejk realized the situation and wrote with a piece of charcoal on the white wall of the schoolroom where the detachment of prisoners was billeted: '*Here slept Josef Švejk of Prague, company orderly of the 11th march company of the 91st regiment, who as a member of a billeting party was taken prisoner in error by the Austrians near Felsztyn.*'

Part IV

THE GLORIOUS LICKING CONTINUED

I

Švejk in a Transport of Russian Prisoners

AND so when Švejk, clad in his Russian greatcoat and cap, had been taken for a Russian prisoner escaping from a village near Felsztyn, and was writing his despairing screams in charcoal on the wall, no one took any notice, and when at the transit point in Chyrów, as crusts of hard maize bread were being distributed, he tried to explain everything in detail to a passing officer, one of the Hungarian soldiers guarding the transport of prisoners prodded his shoulder with his rifle butt and said: '*Baszom az élet!* Get into line, you Russian pig!'

All this was in line with the way the Hungarians treated their Russian prisoners, whose language they did not understand.

And so Švejk went back to the ranks and turning to the nearest prisoner said:

'That chap there's carrying out his duties, but he's exposing his life to great risk. What if the rifle happened to be loaded and the safety-catch released? Then when he was beating somebody over the shoulder with it and had the barrel pointing at himself, it might quite easily go off, all the ammunition in it would fly into his mouth and he'd die in the act of carrying out his duties. In a quarry in the Šumava workers stole sticks of dynamite to have a supply to break up tree-stumps with in the winter. The guard in the quarry got the order to search every labourer when he came away from work and he did it with such gusto that he at once seized the first quarry-worker he saw and beat him over his pockets so violently that the sticks of dynamite inside went off and both of them were blown up sky-high. It looked as though in their very last moment they had their arms round each other's necks.'

The Russian prisoner looked at Švejk in full understanding of the fact that he could not understand a single word of what he said.

'No understand. I Crimean Tartar. *Allah achper*,' the Tartar said. Then he sat down, crossed his legs on the ground, folded his arms on his chest and began to pray, half in Russian and half in Tartar: '*Allah achper, Allah achper – bezemila – arachman – arachim – malinkin mustafir.*'[1]

'Well now, so you're a Tartar, are you?' said Švejk with compassion. 'Well, you're a fine customer then! How could you with your double-Dutch be expected to understand me then and I you, if you're a Tartar? Hm – do you know Jaroslav of Šternberk?[2] You don't, do you, you Tartar bastard? Well, he thrashed your arses below Hostýn. And then you Tartar bastards turned tail and fled head over heels out of Moravia. Obviously in your textbooks they don't teach you the same things as they used to teach us. Do you know Our Lady of Hostýn? Of course you don't! Well, she was there too. You'd better look out, you bastard of a Tartar. They'll baptize all of you now you're prisoners here.'

Švejk turned to another prisoner:

'Are you a Tartar too?'

The person addressed understood the word Tartar, shook his head and said half in Russian: 'No Tartar, Circassian, Circassian born and bred. I chop off heads!'

It was Švejk's luck that he found himself in the company of these various representatives of the Eastern peoples. The transport comprised Tartars, Georgians, Osetins, Circassians, Mordvins and Kalmyks.

But it was his ill luck that he could not make himself understood by any of them and was dragged off with the others to Dobromil, from where the railway line running through Przemyśl in the direction of Niżankowice was to be repaired.

In the office at the transit point of Dobromil the prisoners were registered one by one. This was a difficult process because of all the 300 prisoners who were driven to Dobromil not a single one understood the Russian of the sergeant-major who sat there at a table. This man had once reported that he knew Russian and was now acting as an interpreter in Eastern Galicia. Some three weeks ago he had ordered a German-Russian dictionary and conversation book, but they had not come yet, and so instead of Russian he spoke only broken Slovak. He had picked up only a smattering of this language when he represented

---

1. 'Great Allah, Great Allah – merciful – have pity – have mercy – simple soldier.'
2. According to legend the Virgin appeared in a vision to Jaroslav of Šternberk just before the battle with the Tartars beneath the hill of Hostýn in Moravia in 1240. The Tartars were routed.

a Vienna firm in Slovakia and sold images of St Stephen, fonts for
holy water and rosaries.

He was quite aghast at these outlandish figures with whom he could
not make himself understood. And so he went out and roared in
German at a group of prisoners: 'Who knows German?'

Švejk stepped forward from the group and with a happy face rushed
towards the sergeant-major, who told him to follow him at once into
the office.

The sergeant-major sat down at his registers, which were a heap of
forms about the prisoners' names, origin and nationality, and an
amusing conversation in German began:

'You're a Jew, aren't you?' he started.

Švejk shook his head.

'You don't need to deny it,' the sergeant-major interpreter con-
tinued assertively. 'Every single one of you prisoners who has known
German has been a Jew and that's that. What's your name? Schweich?
Now look, why do you deny it, when you've got such a Jewish name?
In Austria you don't need to be afraid of admitting it. In Austria there
are no pogroms. Where do you come from? Oh, I see, Praga. I know.
I know. It's near Warsaw. Only a week ago I had two Jews here from
Praga near Warsaw. And what's the number of your regiment? 91?'

The sergeant-major took the classification list and looked through
its pages: 'The 91st regiment comes from Erevan in the Caucasus. Its
base is in Tiflis. Your eyes pop out, don't they, when you see that we
know everything here.'

Švejk's eyes really did pop out in surprise at the whole thing and
the sergeant-major continued with great gravity, giving Švejk his
half-smoked cigarette: 'This is rather different from that *machorka*
shag of yours, isn't it? – I'm the big chief here, Jew boy. When I say a
word, everybody's got to tremble and crawl on their hands and knees.
In our army we have a very different kind of discipline from yours.
Your Tsar's a bastard but ours is a clever chap. Now I'll show you
something, so that you can see what our discipline's like here.'

He opened the door to the next room and called out: 'Hans
Löfler!'

The answer came: 'Present!' And a goitrous soldier stepped into
the room. He was a Styrian and had the expression of a blubbering
idiot. He was the maid-of-all-work at the transit point.

'Hans Löfler!' the sergeant-major ordered. 'Take my pipe there, put it in your mug like a dog fetching a stick and run round the table on all fours until I say "Halt!" And while you do it you must bark, but you mustn't let the pipe fall out of your mug. If you do I'll have you trussed.'

The goitrous Styrian went down on all fours and started to bark.

The sergeant-major looked triumphantly at Švejk: 'Didn't I tell you, Jew boy, that we had discipline?'

And the sergeant-major looked delightedly at the expressionless face of the soldier from an Alpine hut somewhere. 'Halt!' he said finally. 'Now sit up and beg and bring me my pipe! – Good, and now yodel!'

The office resounded with the roar: 'Holariyo, holariyo . . .'

When the performance was over the sergeant-major took four cigarettes out of the drawer and gave them magnanimously to Hans, after which Švejk began to explain to him in his broken German that in one regiment an officer had an obedient batman like that who did everything his master wished, but when he was asked once whether, if his master ordered him to do so, he would eat his excrement out of a spoon, he said: 'If my lieutenant ordered me to do that I'd eat it according to his orders, always provided I didn't find a hair in it. If I did, it would disgust me frightfully and I should be sick at once.'

The sergeant-major laughed: 'You Jews have quite good stories, but I'm ready to bet that the discipline in your army isn't as good as ours. But to come to the point – I appoint you in charge of the transport. By the evening you'll write down for me the names of all the other prisoners. You'll draw the mess portions for them. You'll divide them up by tens and personally go bail that none of them escapes. If anybody escapes, Jew boy, we'll shoot you.'

'I'd like to speak to you, sergeant-major,' said Švejk.

'Now don't haggle,' the sergeant-major answered. 'I don't like that and if you do I'll send you off to a camp. You seem to have acclimatized yourself jolly quickly here in Austria. You want to speak with me privately? . . . The nicer one is to you prisoners the worse it is. . . . Now, clear off quick! Here's some paper and a pencil. Make the list . . . ! What else do you want?'

'Humbly report, sergeant-major . . .'

'Get to hell out of it! Can't you see I'm busy?' The sergeant-major's face assumed the expression of a man who was utterly overworked.

Švejk saluted and went back to the prisoners, thinking to himself that all his patience in aid of His Imperial Majesty would one day no doubt bear fruit.

But it was, of course, a hard job to compile the list, as it took a long time for the prisoners to understand that they had got to give him their names. Švejk had experienced much in his life, but all the same

these Tartar, Georgian and Mordvin names simply would not stick in his head.

'No one will ever believe,' thought Švejk, 'that anyone could ever have names like these Tartars here: Muhlahaley Abdrachmanov – Beymurat Allahali – Djeredje Cherdedze – Davlatbaley Nurdagaljev and so on. After all we've got much better names at home. Think of that vicar at Živohošť who was called Vobejda.'[1] And again he went on walking along the ranks of the prisoners who shouted out one by one their surnames and first names: 'Djindraley Hanemaley – Babamuley Mirzahali,' etc.

1. 'Loafer' in Czech.

'Make sure you don't bite your tongue,' Švejk said to each of them with a friendly smile. 'Isn't it much better to be called like our people are – Bohuslav Stěpánek, Jaroslav Matoušek or Růžena Svobodová?'[1]

When after frightful suffering Švejk had finally listed all these Babula Halleis, Hudji Mudjis etc. he decided he would make one more try and explain to the interpreter sergeant-major that he had been the victim of an error. However, as had happened many times already on the journey, when they drove him in among the prisoners his appeals for justice were in vain.

Already before this the interpreter sergeant-major had had a drop too much and by now he had completely lost his capacity for judgement.

He had spread out before him the advertisement pages of a German newspaper and was singing the words of the advertisements to the music of the Radetzky March: 'A gramophone in exchange for a perambulator. – I buy broken pieces of white and green sheet glass. – If anyone wants to learn book-keeping he should do the written course in accountancy' etc.

Some of the advertisements were not suitable for a march tune, but the sergeant-major exerted himself to the utmost in an endeavour to overcome this and beat out the time with his fist on the table and stamped his feet. The tips of his moustache, which were sticky with kontušovka, stuck out on both of his cheeks as though someone had stuck a dry brush of gum into them. His puffy eyes noticed Švejk, it was true, but there was no reaction to this discovery except that he ceased beating with his fist and stamping his feet. To the tune of '*Ich weiss nicht, was soll es bedeuten* ...'[2] he drummed out another advertisement with his fingers on the chair: 'Karolina Dreger, mid-wife, respectfully offers her services to honourable ladies for all eventualities.'

Then he began to sing more and more softly until finally he stopped altogether and stared motionless at the whole space of advertisements in the newspaper. This gave Švejk the opportunity to talk about his own misfortunes, for which his sentences of broken German were barely adequate.

He started by saying that he had after all been quite right when he said they should have walked along the stream to Felsztyn, and it was not his fault if an unknown Russian prisoner escaped from captivity

1. Names of Czech writers of the time.
2. The beginning of the famous Lorelei song.

and went to have a swim in the lake. He, Švejk, had had to walk along the lake. It had been his duty to do so, when he was a member of a billeting party and had to take the shortest route to Felsztyn. The Russian ran away as soon as he saw him and left all his uniform in the bushes. Švejk had heard that the uniform of fallen enemies could be used at the

front for purposes of espionage, and so as an experiment he put on that cast-off uniform just to see how it would feel to be in a foreign uniform.

Having tried to explain his little mistake, Švejk realized that his efforts had been utterly in vain, since before he even reached the part about the lake the sergeant-major had long since fallen asleep. Švejk approached him and touched him familiarly on the shoulder, which was enough to cause him to fall on to the floor, where he went on sleeping peacefully.

'Excuse me, sergeant-major,' Švejk said, saluted and left the office.

Early in the morning the army building command changed its dispositions and decided that the group of prisoners to which Švejk belonged should be sent direct to Przemyśl to renew the track from Przemyśl to Lubaczów.

And so everything was just as it was before and Švejk continued his odyssey among the Russian prisoners. The Hungarian guards drove all of them on at a brisk tempo.

On a village green where they had a rest they met a detachment from a baggage train. An officer was standing in front of a group of carts and looking at the prisoners. Švejk jumped out of the ranks, posted himself in front of the officer and called out to him in German: 'Sir, humbly report . . .' He said no more, because two Hungarian soldiers immediately struck him in the back with their fists and thrust him among the prisoners again.

The officer threw him a cigarette stump, which another prisoner quickly picked up and finished smoking. Then the officer explained to a corporal who was standing next to him that in Russia there were colonies of Germans and they had to fight as well.

Later, throughout the journey to Przemyśl Švejk had no opportunity to complain to anyone that he was in fact the orderly of the 11th march company of the 91st regiment. He could only do this in Przemyśl, where in the evening they were driven to a fortress in the inner zone which was completely destroyed except for the artillery horses' stables.

Inside the stables the heaps of straw were so lice-ridden that the lice moved over the short stalks as though they were not lice at all but ants carrying material to build their nest.

The prisoners were each given a little black dishwash made out of nothing but chicory and a piece of stale maize bread.

Then Major Wolf, who was at that time in charge of all the prisoners working on the reconstruction of the fortress at Przemyśl and its surroundings, took charge of them. He was a man who did things thoroughly. He had with him a whole staff of interpreters who selected building specialists from the prisoners according to their abilities and previous training.

Major Wolf had the fixed idea that the Russian prisoners tried to conceal their literacy, because it used to happen that when he asked them through an interpreter 'Can you build a railway?' all of them gave the stereotyped answer: 'I don't know anything about anything.

I've never heard of anything like that. I've always lived honestly and decently.'

When, however, they all stood lined up before him and all his staff, he first of all asked them in German if any of them understood that language.

Švejk stepped forward resolutely, stationed himself in front of the major, saluted and reported that he did.

Major Wolf, visibly pleased, at once asked Švejk if he happened to be an engineer.

'Humbly report, sir,' answered Švejk, 'I'm not an engineer but the orderly of the 11th march company of the 91st regiment. I've been taken prisoner by us. It happened like this, sir . . .'

'What did I hear you say?' Major Wolf roared.

'Humbly report, sir, what happened was . . .'

'You're a Czech,' Major Wolf went on shouting. 'You've put on a Russian uniform.'

'Humbly report, sir, yes. It's perfectly correct. I'm really very glad indeed, sir, that you've at once appreciated my position. Perhaps our men are already fighting somewhere and I shouldn't like to be kicking my heels about here for the duration of the war. Let me please explain it properly to you, sir, once more.'

'That's enough,' said Major Wolf, and, calling two soldiers, he gave them the order to take the man off at once to the guard-house. And he himself followed slowly after Švejk, gesticulating violently while he talked with the officer accompanying him. In every one of his sentences there was something about 'Czech dogs', but at the same time from his words the other officer had the feeling that the major was delighted that it was his keen eye that had discovered one of those shady customers, about whose treasonable activities abroad the commanders of military detachments had received confidential reports for some months already. It had been ascertained that some deserters from Czech regiments, forgetting their oath, were joining the ranks of the Russian army and were now working for the enemy, affording him above all useful espionage services.

The Austrian Ministry of the Interior was still in the dark about whether a military organization of Czech deserters on the Russian front existed or not. Nothing definite was yet known about revolutionary organizations abroad and it was only in August that the battalion commanders on the line Sokal–Milijatin–Bubnów received the confidential report that the former Austrian professor Masaryk had fled abroad, where he was carrying out propaganda against Austria. A stupid ass from the division appended to it the following order: 'If captured he should at once be brought to division staff!'

I hereby bring this to the attention of President Masaryk, so that he may know what pitfalls and traps were laid for him between Sokal, Milijatin and Bubnów.[1]

At that time Major Wolf had no idea at all of what was being hatched against Austria by the deserters, who when they later met in Kiev or elsewhere and were asked 'What are you doing here?' answered cheerfully: 'I have betrayed His Imperial Majesty.'

It was only from secret reports like the above that he knew of the existence of these deserters and spies, one of whom they were taking off to the guard-house after he had fallen so easily into his trap. Major Wolf was a rather vain man and he pictured in his mind the praise he would get from his superiors and the decoration he would receive for his vigilance, foresight and intelligence.

By the time they reached the guard-house he was convinced that when he asked the question 'Who of you knows German?' he had done it on purpose, because when he inspected the prisoners it was this very one who at once appeared suspect.

The officer who was accompanying him nodded his head in agreement and said that they would have to report the arrest to garrison command for further action and bringing the accused before a higher court-martial, because it would definitely not be right to do as the major suggested, examine him in the guard-house and then hang him immediately behind it. He would be hanged of course, but by the due process of law, as laid down by court-martial procedure, so that before he was hanged the link with other criminals could be established with the help of a detailed cross-examination. Who could tell what else might come out of it all?

Major Wolf was overcome by a sudden fit of obstinacy. A latent brutality filled him and he announced that after the cross-examination he would have this deserter spy hanged at once on his own responsibility. This is something he could well afford to do, because he had friends in high places and nothing mattered very much to him. They should deal with the man here as they would have done at the front.

1. This 'personal message' from Hašek to President Masaryk has been omitted from recent editions of *The Good Soldier Švejk*.

If they had caught him immediately behind the battlefield, they would have interrogated him and hanged him on the spot without any fuss. Moreover, the captain must surely know that in a war zone the commanding officer, *any* commanding officer from captain upwards, had the right to hang any suspicious individual.

Major Wolf of course had got things slightly wrong when he spoke of the competence of officers to hang people.

In East Galicia the nearer they came to the front the more this competence was delegated to lower and lower ranks, until in the end there were cases where even a corporal in command of a sentry patrol ordered a twelve-year-old boy to be hanged because he had aroused his suspicions by cooking potato peelings in a tumble-down hut in a deserted and ransacked village.

The dispute between the captain and the major rose in intensity.

'You have no right to do that,' the captain shouted excitedly, 'He will be hanged on the basis of a legal verdict of a court-martial.'

'He's going to be hanged without any verdict at all,' Major Wolf hissed.

Švejk, who was being led in front of them and heard the whole of this conversation, said nothing to his escort except: 'Six of one and half a dozen of the other. We had the same sort of discussion at the pub Na Zavadilce in Libeň, when we couldn't decide whether, as soon as there appeared in the doorway a certain hatter named Vašák, who always made a nuisance of himself during the music and dancing, we should throw him out at once, or do it when he had had a glass of beer, paid for it and drunk it up, or whether we should give him the boot after he had danced the first dance. The landlord suggested we shouldn't chuck him out until the middle of the show, to give him time to run up a bill. Then he would have to pay up and leave at once. And do you know what that bastard did? He never turned up at all. What do you think of that?'

Both soldiers, who were from somewhere in the Tyrol, answered simultaneously: 'Nix Czech.'

'Do you understand German?' Švejk asked calmly in that language.

'Jawohl,' they both answered, upon which Švejk observed: 'That's good. You're lucky! At least you won't get lost among your own folk.'

In the course of these friendly conversations they all reached the guard-house, where Major Wolf continued his dispute with the captain about Švejk's fate, while Švejk sat modestly on a bench in the back.

Finally after all Major Wolf came over to the captain's view that the man should swing only after the longer procedure which is so sweetly called 'the process of law'.

If they had asked Švejk what he thought about it, he would have said: 'I'm very sorry, sir, because you have a higher rank than the captain, but he is the one who is right. Every hasty action only does harm. Once at a Prague district court one of the judges went mad. For a long time no one noticed it in him until it suddenly erupted during a libel action. A chap called Znamenáček met on the street a chaplain called Hortík, who had boxed his son's ears during religious instruction, and he said to him: "You bloody bastard, you dirty scum, you religious maniac, you filthy hog, you presbytery goat, you debaucher of Christ's teachings, you hypocrite and charlatan in a cassock!" And so the chaplain sued him. That mad judge was a very religious man. He had three sisters and they were all vicarage cooks and he had been a godfather to all their children. And so he got so infuriated that he suddenly lost his reason and roared at the accused: "In the name of His Majesty the Emperor and King you are condemned to death by hanging. There is no appeal." Then he called to the warder: "Mr Horáček, take this gentleman out and go and hang him there, you know, where they beat the carpets, and after that come back here and you'll get a tip!" Of course Mr Znamenáček and the warder stood rooted to the spot, but the judge stamped his foot and shouted at them: "Are you going to obey or not!" The warder was so frightened that he had already begun to drag Mr Znamenáček down, and if it hadn't been for the defending counsel who intervened and called an ambulance I don't know how it would have fared with Mr Znamenáček. And even when they were putting the judge into the ambulance he was still shouting: "If you can't find a rope, hang him with a bedsheet. We'll credit it to you in the half-yearly returns ..." '

And so Švejk had to sign a report drawn up by Major Wolf to the effect that as a serving member of the Austrian army he had in full knowledge of the consequences and without constraint changed into Russian uniform and been detained behind the front line by the field gendarmerie when the Russians retreated. And after that he was sent under escort to the garrison command.

All of this was holy truth, and Švejk, as an honest man, could not object to it. When the report was being drawn up he tried several times to supplement it by adding a statement which might perhaps

have explained the situation more precisely, but the major was at once ready with the order: 'Shut your mug. We're not asking your opinion about that. The case is quite clear.'

After that Švejk simply saluted and said: 'Humbly report, I'm shutting my mug and the case is quite clear.'

After they had brought him to garrison command, they took him away to some hole which had formerly been a rice store as well as a boarding-house for mice. Grains of rice were still scattered everywhere on the floor, and the mice were not at all afraid of Švejk and gaily ran about picking them up. Švejk had to go and fetch a straw mattress and when he looked around in the darkness he found that a whole family of mice had instantly moved into it. There was no doubt at all that they were trying to make a new nest here in the ruins of the glory of the rotten Austrian straw mattress. Švejk began to hammer on the locked door. A corporal came, who was a Pole, and Švejk asked to be transferred to other quarters, because otherwise he might lie on the mice in his straw mattress and cause damage to crown property, because everything in the military stores was crown property.

The Pole understood something of what he said and threatened Švejk with his fist in front of the closed door. Mentioning something about 'a shit-hole' he went away muttering angrily about cholera, as though Švejk had insulted him in some way.

Švejk passed a quiet night, because the mice made no great demands on him and obviously had their own programme for the night, which they celebrated in the store room next door. Military greatcoats and caps were stored there and the mice bit through them with great confidence and in great security, because it was only a year later that the quartermaster's office remembered to introduce into the military stores crown-property cats without pension rights, which were entered in the administration records under the heading: 'Imperial and Royal military store cats.' The rank of cat was in fact only a revival of an old institution which had been abolished after the war of 1866.

Earlier, in the reign of Maria Theresa, cats had been introduced into the military stores in wartime, when it was on the wretched mice that the gentlemen from the administration were blaming all their fiddles with uniforms.

But in many cases the Imperial and Royal cats failed to do their duties, and so it happened that once in the reign of Emperor Leopold six cats which had been assigned to the military stores at Pohořelec were hanged by the verdict of a court-martial. I can imagine that on that occasion all those who had had anything to do with the military stores laughed smugly in their sleeves . . .

With Švejk's early-morning coffee they pushed into his hole a man in a Russian cap and greatcoat.

The man spoke Czech with a Polish accent. He was one of those scoundrels who served in the counter-espionage of the army corps which had its headquarters in Przemyśl. He was a member of the military secret police and did not trouble much about any refined preliminaries before proceeding to grill Švejk. He began quite simply: 'I've got into a fine mess as a result of my carelessness. I served in the 28th regiment and immediately deserted to the Russians. Then I was stupid enough to get caught. I volunteered to go on advance patrol for the Russians . . . I served in the 6th Kievan division. Which Russian regiment did you serve in, old man? I have a feeling we must have met somewhere in Russia. I knew many Czechs in Kiev, who went to the front with us, when we went over to the Russians. I can't remember their names now or where they came from. Perhaps you can remember someone you were in contact with then? I'd very much like to know who there was from our 28th regiment.'

Instead of replying Švejk laid his hand anxiously on his visitor's forehead, felt his pulse, finally led him away to a little window and asked him to put out his tongue. The scoundrel made no resistance to this procedure, imagining that it was a case of certain conspiratorial signs. Then Švejk started to hammer on the door, and when the guard came to ask why he was making such a row, he asked him in Czech and German if they would call a doctor at once, because the man they had put into the cell with him was suffering from hallucinations.

It was no good. No one came to fetch the man. He remained there quite calmly and continued to babble something about Kiev and how he'd certainly seen Švejk there marching with the Russian soldiers.

'You must certainly have been drinking water from the marshes,' said Švejk, 'like a young man, Týnecký, whom I used to know a long time ago. He was quite a sensible chap otherwise, but suddenly out of the blue he set out on a journey and got as far as Italy. He didn't talk about anything else but Italy and said there was a lot of marshy water there, but otherwise nothing else worth seeing. And he too got fever from that marshy water. It attacked him four times a year – on

All Saints, St Joseph's, Peter and Paul and the Assumption of the Virgin. When he had these attacks, he thought he knew people who were completely strange and unknown to him, just like you. In a tram he might address someone, saying he knew him and that they had met on the station in Vienna. All the people he met on the street he'd seen either on the station in Milan or had sat with them in the Rathaus cellar in Steyr over a glass of wine. If, when this marsh fever came over him, he happened to be sitting in a pub, he knew all the guests. He'd seen all of them on a steamer when he sailed to Venice. There was only one remedy against it, and that was the one which a new male nurse used in the Kateřinky. He also had to look after a mental patient who did nothing else the whole day but sit in a corner and count: "One, two, three, four, five, six," and then again from the beginning: "One, two, three, four, five, six." He was a professor. That nurse nearly jumped out of his skin with fury when he found that that madman couldn't get beyond six. He started first by being nice to him and tried to get him to say: "Seven, eight, nine, ten." But what a hope! The professor didn't take any damned notice of him. He went on crouching in the corner and counting: "One, two, three, four, five, six," and then again: "One, two, three, four, five, six!" Then the nurse suddenly flew off the handle, jumped at his patient and when he got to the word "six" socked him one on the jaw. "Now you've got seven," he said, "and here's eight, nine, ten." And he got as many socks as there were numbers. The professor suddenly put his hands to his head and asked where he was. When they told him he was in the madhouse he immediately remembered everything and how he had got to the asylum all because of a comet, which he had reckoned would appear in a year's time on 18 July at 6 a.m., but they had proved to him that it had burnt itself out several million years ago. I knew that nurse. When the professor recovered completely and was released, he took him on as his servant. The only work he had to do was to mete out to the learned professor four socks on the jaw each morning. And he always discharged this duty conscientiously and precisely.'

'I know all your friends from Kiev,' the mercenary of the counter-espionage continued indefatigably. 'Didn't you have with you a very fat man and also a very thin one? I can't remember what their names were or from what regiment they came . . .'

'Don't worry about that,' Švejk consoled him. 'It can happen to anyone that he doesn't remember all the fat and thin people there are

and what their names are. Thin people are of course harder to remember, because there are more of them in the world. And so they
form a majority as the saying goes.'

'Old man,' the Imperial and Royal scoundrel said in a plaintive tone,
'you don't trust me. But after all we must both expect the same fate.'

'That's why we're soldiers,' said Švejk nonchalantly. 'It was for that
our mothers bore us – so that we could be made mincemeat of when we
were put into uniform. And we do it gladly, because we know that
our bones won't rot in vain. We shall fall for His Imperial Majesty
and His Royal Family, for whom we won Herzegovina. Out of our
bones they'll make bone charcoal for sugar refineries. Lieutenant
Zimmer told us about that years ago. "You pack of swine," he said,
"you barbarous hogs, you useless indolent monkeys! You twist your
shanks about as if they weren't worth anything. If you fall in the war,
they'll make half a kilo of bone charcoal out of each of them. Out of
every man jack of you there'll be more than two kilos, shanks and
paws together, and in the sugar refineries they'll filter sugar through
you, you bloody oafs. You haven't an inkling how useful you're going
to be to your descendants after your death. Your boys will drink
coffee with sugar which was filtered through your shanks, you godforsaken half-wits, you." It made me think a bit and he asked me what
I was thinking about. "Humbly report," I said, "I've been thinking
that the bone charcoal which is made out of you officer gentlemen must
be much more expensive than what's made out of us ordinary soldiers."
For that I got three days' solitary confinement.'

Švejk's companion beat on the door and had some discussions with
the guard, who called to the office.

After a while a staff sergeant-major came to fetch him away and Švejk
was left alone.

As he went out the reptile pointed to Švejk and said loudly to the
staff sergeant-major: 'It's my old mate from Kiev.'

For a whole period of twenty-four hours Švejk remained in solitude
except for those moments when they brought him something to eat.

During the night he came to the conviction that the Russian military greatcoat was warmer and more copious than the Austrian one
and that it isn't too unpleasant if in the night a mouse sniffs at the ear
of a sleeping man. To Švejk it appeared like a tender whisper, from
which he was woken in the grey light of morn when they came to fetch
him.

To this day Švejk cannot make out what kind of court it was before which he was dragged that depressing morning. That it was a court-martial there was no doubt. Even a general was sitting there, not to speak of a colonel, a major, a first and second lieutenant, a sergeant-major and an infantryman, who did nothing else but light the other persons' cigarettes.

Švejk was not asked many questions.

It was the major who showed rather more interest and spoke Czech.

'You are guilty of treason against His Imperial Majesty,' he barked at Švejk.

'Treason? Jesus Mary, when?' Švejk cried out. 'The idea that I should have committed treason against His Imperial Majesty, our most serene monarch, for whom I have already suffered so much!'

'Cut out that tomfoolery,' said the major.

'Humbly report, sir, treason against His Imperial Majesty is no tomfoolery. We men of the army have sworn an oath of loyalty to His Imperial Majesty and, as they sang in the theatre, "In loyalty my vow I have fulfilled".'[1]

'It's all here,' said the major. 'Here are the proofs of your guilt and of the truth.' He pointed to a voluminous bundle of papers.

The man whom they had put into Švejk's cell had produced the main material.

'And so you still refuse to confess?' the major asked. 'After all, you've confirmed yourself that you voluntarily changed into Russian uniform, although you were a serving member of the Austrian armed forces. I ask you for the last time: did you do this act under compulsion?'

'I did it without any compulsion.'

'Voluntarily?'

'Voluntarily.'

'Without any pressure?'

'Without any pressure.'

'You know that you're lost?'

'I know. They're certainly already searching for me in the 91st regiment. But will you permit, sir, a small observation on how people voluntarily put on other people's clothes. Sometime in July in 1908 a bookbinder Božetěch from Příčná Street in Prague was bathing at Zbraslav in the old channel of the Berounka. He left his clothes in some

1. Quotation from *Dalibor*, the opera by Bedřich Smetana.

willow bushes and was enjoying himself immensely in the water when later a gentleman came and joined him there. They got talking, frolicked together, squirted water at each other and ducked each other until evening. Then the stranger gentleman went out of the water saying that he had to go to dinner. Mr Božetěch remained sitting in

the water a little longer and then went to the willow bushes for his clothes. In their place he found some tramp's rags and a piece of paper. It contained the following message:

'I thought about it a long time: ought I to do it – or oughtn't I, when we were having such fun together in the water? So I tore off the petals of a marguerite. The last petal I tore off was "I ought!" and so I swopped togs with you. You needn't be afraid of putting them on. They were deloused a week ago in the district gendarmerie station at Dobříš. Next time be more careful about who you go bathing with. In the water every naked man looks like a member of parliament and may well be a murderer. You did not know who you were bathing with either. But the bathe was worth it. Now towards the evening the water is at its best. Run in once more so that you can come to your senses again.

'Mr Božetěch could do nothing else but wait until it got dark. Then he put on those tramp's rags and set out in the direction of Prague. He avoided the district road and went by paths across the fields, where he fell in with the gendarmerie patrol from Chuchle. They arrested him as a tramp and took him the next morning to the district court in Zbraslav, because anyone could say that he was Josef Božetěch, bookbinder from 16 Příčná Street, Prague.'

The clerk, who did not understand much Czech, took it that the accused was giving the address of his accomplice and asked once more in German: 'Is that correct? Prague no. 16, Herr Josef Bosetech?'

'I don't know if he still lives there,' Švejk answered, 'but he lived there at that time in 1908. He bound books jolly well, but it took him a long time, because he had to read them first and then bind them according to their contents. If he gave a book black edges, that meant that no one need read it. Then you knew at once that the novel would end very badly. Would you perhaps like to have still more details? Oh, by the way – he used to sit every day at U Fleků and tell people the contents of all the books which they had just sent to him for binding.'

The major went over to the clerk and had a whispered exchange with him. The latter then crossed out in his records the address of the new alleged conspirator, Herr Bosetech.

After that the strange court proceedings continued, following the fashion of the summary courts-martial held by the presiding general, Fink von Finkenstein.

Just as some people have a hobby of collecting matchboxes, so this gentleman's particular hobby-horse was to hold summary courts-martial, although in the majority of cases they were contrary to military regulations.

This general used to say that he did not need any judge advocates, that he would call the court together and in three hours every bastard must be swinging. As long as he was at the front there was never any lack of summary courts-martial.

Just as some people must regularly play a game of chess, billiards, or mariáš every day, so this excellent general had to hold summary courts-martial daily. He presided over them and with great solemnity and joy checkmated the accused.

If anyone wanted to be sentimental he could write that this man had many dozens of people on his conscience, especially in the East, where, to quote his own words, he fought with the Great Russian propaganda among the Ruthenians of Galicia. From his own point of view, however, we cannot say that he had anybody's life on his conscience.

A conscience simply did not exist for him. If on the verdict of his summary court-martial he sent a schoolmaster, a schoolmistress, an Orthodox priest or a whole family to the gallows, he returned peacefully to his quarters just like a keen mariáš player returns contentedly home from the pub and recalls how they called 'flek' and how he answered 're', how they called 'supre' and he 'tutti', how they called 'boty' and how he won everything and had a hundred and seven.[1] He regarded hanging as something simple and natural, a sort of daily bread, and in passing the sentences he often forgot His Imperial Majesty and even omitted to say: 'In the name of His Majesty you are condemned to death by hanging,' but declared: 'I condemn you.'

Sometimes he even saw the comic side in hanging and once wrote about it to his wife in Vienna:

... or for example, my darling, you cannot imagine what a good laugh I had recently when a few days ago I sentenced a teacher for espionage. I have a trained man who does the hanging. He's already had considerable practice. He's a sergeant-major and does it as a sport. I was in my tent when this sergeant-major came to see me after the verdict and asked me where he should hang the teacher. I told him to do it on the nearest tree. Now conceive the humour of the situation. We were in the middle of the steppe, where we could see nothing else far and wide except grass, and there wasn't a tree for miles. Orders are orders, and the sergeant-major took the teacher with him under escort and went to look for a tree.

He did not get back until the evening and had the teacher with him still. He came to see me and asked me again: 'What am I to hang this bastard on?' I swore at him and told him that he knew my orders: on the nearest tree. He said that he would try it next morning, and next morning he came to me white in the face and said that the teacher had disappeared in the early hours. I found it so funny that I forgave all those who had been guarding him and I even made the joke that the teacher must obviously have gone to look for a tree himself. So you see, my darling, we're not bored here in any way and you can tell little Willi that papa sends him a kiss and that he'll soon send him

1. There are various possible declarations which can be made in mariáš. One is 'a hundred and seven' which means that the player must win 100 points and take the last trick with the seven of trumps. When the declaration has been made the other players can double or multiply. If a player says 'flek' he means he will double. If another says 're', he means he will quadruple. 'Supre' multiplies 8 times, 'tutti' 16 times and 'boty' 32 times.

a live Russian which he can ride on like a pony. And that reminds me, my darling, of another comic incident. We recently hanged a Jew for espionage. The rascal happened to cross our path during our journey, although he had no business there, and gave the excuse that he was selling cigarettes. And so he swung, but only for a few seconds, because the cord broke and he fell down. But at once he recovered consciousness and shouted at me: 'Excellency, I'm going home. Now you've hanged me and according to the law I can't be hanged twice for one offence.' I burst out laughing and we let the Jew go. We have a lot of fun here, my darling . . .

When General Fink became commander of the garrison fort of Przemyśl he did not have the same opportunities of arranging circus shows like these and that was why he was very glad to seize on Švejk's case.

And so Švejk stood in front of this tiger, who sat at the head of the long table and smoked cigarette after cigarette. He ordered Švejk's confession to be translated to him and nodded his head in approval, as he listened to it.

The major proposed that, since the accused affirmed by his statements that he belonged to the 11th march company of the 91st regiment, they should telegraph to the brigade for information where that regiment now was.

The general opposed this and said that it would hold up the summary character of the proceedings and defeat the object of the whole institution. They had after all a complete confession on the part of the accused that he had put on Russian uniform, and they had in addition an important piece of evidence where the accused had admitted that he had been in Kiev. He proposed therefore that they should retire for discussion, so that the sentence could be pronounced and carried out immediately.

But the major insisted that it was necessary to establish the identity of the accused, since the whole matter was of unusual political importance. By doing this they might come on to the track of further contacts between the accused and his former comrades from his unit.

The major was a romantic dreamer. He went on to say that it was not enough merely to condemn the man but it was necessary to look for the threads. The sentencing itself was only the result of a definite investigation which involved threads and those threads. . . . He got rather tied up in those threads, but everyone understood him and nodded their heads in agreement, including even the general, who was so

enamoured by the threads that he imagined that he could hang new
summary courts-martial on them. And so he no longer protested against
the idea of verifying at brigade headquarters whether Švejk actually
belonged to the 91st regiment and in the course of what operation of
the 11th march company he went over to the Russian side.

During the whole period of this debate Švejk was in the corridor
under the guard of two men with bayonets. Afterwards he was again
brought before the court and once more asked to which regiment he in
fact belonged. Then they transferred him to the garrison gaol.

When General Fink returned home after the unsuccessful summary
court-martial he lay down on the sofa and considered how he could
expedite the whole case.

He was fully convinced that the answer would come soon, but none
the less the proceedings would lack that speed which had otherwise
distinguished his courts-martial, because afterwards they would have
to offer the condemned man spiritual consolation and that would unnecessarily hold up the execution for two hours.

'It doesn't matter,' General Fink thought to himself. 'We can offer him spiritual consolation in advance before the verdict and before we get the information from the brigade. He'll swing anyway.'

General Fink summoned Chaplain Martinec before him.

This was an unfortunate catechist and chaplain from a village in Moravia who had had such a brute of a vicar over him that he preferred to join the army. He was a sincerely religious man who with pain in his heart remembered his vicar who was slowly but surely going down the drain. He remembered how the vicar used to swill slivovice like a fish and how once in the night he had insisted on putting into the chaplain's bed a vagabond gipsy girl whom he had picked up near the village when he was lurching out of a wine-cellar.

Martinec imagined that by having the duty of offering spiritual consolation to the wounded and dying on the battlefield he would redeem even the sins of his depraved vicar, who returning home at night had countless times woken him up and told him:

'Jan, Jan, my dear boy! A buxom wench is the joy of my life.'

His hopes were not fulfilled. They threw him about from one garrison to another, where he had nothing more to do than preach to the soldiers once a fortnight before mass in the garrison church and resist the temptation of the officers' club, where the conversations were such that in comparison his Moravian vicar's buxom wenches seemed like an innocent little prayer to a guardian angel.

Now he was usually summoned to General Fink during major operations on the battlefield when some victory of the Austrian army was to be celebrated, for General Fink was just as delighted to arrange festive drumhead masses as summary courts-martial.

That blackguard Fink was such a devout Austrian patriot that he refused to pray for the victory of the Reich German or Turkish arms. When the Reich Germans won a victory over the French or British anywhere he saw to it that it was ignored at the altar.

But every unimportant victorious skirmish between an Austrian reconnoitring patrol and a Russian advance patrol, which the staff blew up into a terrific soap-bubble defeat of a whole Russian army corps, provided General Fink with the occasion for festive services, so that the unfortunate Martinec had the impression that the general was not only commander of the fortress but also supreme head of the Catholic Church in Przemyśl.

General Fink also decided the order of service at such masses and would always have preferred something like a Corpus Christi with the octave.

When at mass the exaltation of the host was over, it was also his habit to gallop up to the altar on the parade ground and call out three times: 'Hurrah – hurrah – hurrah!'

Martinec, who was a pious and honest soul, and one of those few who still believed in the Lord, did not like going to see General Fink.

After the garrison commander had given him all his instructions he always had something strong poured out for him and afterwards told him the latest stories from the most stupid booklets which were published for the troops by the German comic paper *Lustige Blätter*.

He had a complete collection of such booklets with idiotic titles like: *Humour in the Haversack for Eyes and Ears, Hindenburg Stories, Hindenburg Mirrored in Humour, The Second Haversack Full of Humour, Loaded by Felix Schlemper, From our Goulash Gun, Succulent Shrapnel from the Trenches,* or the following rubbish: *Under the Double Eagle* and *Wiener Schnitzel from the Imperial and Royal Field-Kitchen, Warmed up by Artur Lokesch*. Sometimes he even sang to him out of his collection of gay army songs 'Victory must be ours!', while all the time continuing to pour out something strong and forcing Martinec to drink and caterwaul with him. Then he went over to telling smutty stories and with heavy heart Martinec remembered his vicar who was in no way inferior to General Fink where coarse words were concerned.

Martinec saw to his horror that the more he went to see General Fink the more morally debased he grew.

The unfortunate man began to take pleasure in the liqueurs which he drank with the general, and slowly but surely the general's conversation began to appeal to him. He began to entertain lecherous thoughts and, because of the kontušovka, jeřabinka and the cobwebs on the bottles of the old wine which General Fink served to him, he gradually began to forget the Lord, and the women from the general's stories began to dance before his eyes in between the lines of the breviary. His dislike of his visits to the general slowly began to wear off.

The general took a fancy to Martinec, who had at first appeared to him to be like a St Ignatius of Loyola, but who later gradually adapted himself to the general's environment.

One day the general invited two nurses from the field-hospital, who in fact did not work there but were only entered on the books for their wages and who increased their incomes by high-class prostitution, as was the custom in those difficult times. He summoned Martinec, who had already fallen so deep into the claws of the devil that after half an hour's fun he enjoyed both ladies one after the other, and got into such a state of rut that he slobbered all over the cushion on the sofa. Afterwards he reproached himself for a long time for having acted so dissolutely, although he was not able to make amends for it even when on his return that night he kneeled by mistake in the park in front of the statue of the builder and mayor of the town, the Maecenas Mr Grabowsky, to whom the city of Przemyśl owed a great debt in the eighties.

Only the stamping of the military patrol broke in on his ardent words: 'Do not judge Thy servant, for no man will be justified before Thee, if Thou dost not forgive him all his sins. I beg Thee that Thy verdict be not severe. I beg Thy help and entrust my soul into Thy hands, O Lord.'

From that time on, whenever he was called to General Fink he made various attempts to renounce all earthly pleasures and gave the excuse that he had a stomach upset. He considered this lie necessary so that his soul might be spared hellish sufferings, for he knew only too well that army discipline demanded that when a general said to a chaplain: 'Have a good booze, old man,' he must booze out of pure respect for his superior officer.

Sometimes of course he did not succeed, especially when the general after the glorious field services organized even more glorious gargantuan feasts at the expense of the garrison budget. Afterwards in the accounts department they somehow managed to sew it all together so that they could get a rake-off too. After these happenings the chaplain always imagined that he was morally buried before the face of the Lord and reduced to a quaking jelly.

Then he went about as though in a daze and without losing faith in God in this chaos began seriously to wonder whether he should not regularly flog himself every day.

It was in just such a mood that he now appeared in answer to the general's invitation.

General Fink went to meet him beaming all over with joy.

'Have you heard of my summary court-martial?' he called to him delightedly. 'We're going to hang one of your people.'

At the words 'your people' Martinec looked in anguish at the general. He had already many times rejected the assumption that he was a Czech and explained time without number that their parish in Moravia had two communities, a Czech and a German one, and that he often had to preach one week for the Czechs and another for the Germans. And because in the Czech district there was no Czech school but only a German one, he had to teach in German in both districts and therefore was no Czech. This piece of logic had once provoked a major at the table into observing that that chaplain from Moravia was really a shop with mixed groceries.

'Sorry,' said the general, 'I forgot. He's not one of your people. He's a Czech, a deserter, a traitor who has worked for the Russians and is going to hang. Meanwhile, purely as a matter of form, we are establishing his identity. But it doesn't matter. He'll hang at once as soon as we get the answer by telegram.'

Seating the chaplain beside him on the sofa the general continued gaily: 'When I hold a summary court-martial everything must be done to match its summary nature. That's my principle. When at the beginning of the war I was near Lwów I managed to have a bastard hanged only three minutes after the verdict. He was a Jew of course, but we once hanged a Ruthenian only five minutes after discussing his case.'

The general smiled good-humouredly: 'Neither of them happened to need spiritual consolation. The Jew was a Rabbi and the Ruthenian an Orthodox priest. The case we have now is of course quite a different one. Here it's a Catholic we're going to hang. I hit on the capital idea of offering him spiritual consolation beforehand, so as not to hold matters up afterwards, as I say, so as not to hold matters up.'

The general rang the bell and gave the following order to his servant: 'Bring two from yesterday's battery.'

And a moment later he filled the chaplain's glass with wine and said affably: 'Console yourself a little before you offer spiritual consolation ...'

At this frightful time from the barred window behind which he sat on a straw mattress Švejk's song rang out:

> 'We're the boys who make the noise,
> Win the hearts of all the tarts,
> Draw our pay and then make hay!
> Hey, diddle de dee. One, two, three!'

2

Spiritual Consolation

In the literal sense of the word Chaplain Martinec did not walk in to
see Švejk but floated into his cell like a ballerina on the stage. Heavenly
yearnings and a bottle of old Gumpoldskirchen made him as light as
a feather at this moving moment. He imagined that in this grave and
holy moment he was drawing nearer to God, when in fact he was drawing nearer to Švejk.

They shut the door behind him and left the two alone. The chaplain
said enthusiastically to Švejk, who was sitting on the bunk: 'My dear
son, I am Chaplain Martinec.'

On his way to Švejk this form of address had seemed to him to be
very suitable and somehow paternally touching.

Švejk got up from his bunk, shook hands energetically with the chaplain, and said: 'I'm very glad to meet you. I am Švejk, the orderly of the 11th march company of the 91st regiment. Recently they transferred the nucleus of our regiment to Bruck an der Leitha, so please make yourself comfortable beside me, Your Reverence, and tell me why you've been put into gaol. You have after all the rank of an officer and so you are entitled to officers' arrest in the garrison. You certainly should not be put here, because that bunk is full of lice. It sometimes happens of course that people don't know where prisoners properly belong either because there's been a muddle in the office or by pure chance. Once, sir, I was sitting in the regimental gaol in Budějovice when they brought a probationary cadet into my cell. A probationer like that was something like a chaplain, neither fish nor fowl nor good red herring. He roared at the men like an officer, but when anything happened they locked him up with the common rank and file. These probationers were such mongrels, sir, that they were not accepted in the N.C.O.s' mess. They had no right to go to the men's mess, they were too senior for that, and the officers' mess again wasn't suitable for them. We had five of them and to begin with they only lived on cheese in the canteen because they never got portions from the mess. But then Lieutenant Wurm got to know about them and forbade them to go there, because he said it was not compatible with a probationary cadet's honour to patronize the men's canteen. And so what could they do? They were not allowed into the officers' canteen. And so they just hung in the air and for a few days endured such a calvary that one of them jumped into the river Malše, and another ran away from the regiment and two months later wrote to the barracks that he was Minister of War in Morocco. After that there were four of them, you see, because the one who had jumped into the Malše was fished out again alive. In his excitement when he jumped into it he had forgotten that he knew how to swim and had passed a swimming test with honours. They put him into a hospital and didn't know what to do with him there, whether to cover him up with an officers' blanket or a men's one. But they found a way round and gave him no blanket at all. Instead they wrapped him up in a wet sheet, so that after half an hour he begged to be sent back to the barracks. And that was the man they put in with me when he was still completely wet! He sat there about four days and was very happy indeed because he at last got messing there. It's true it was prisoners' messing, but he could at least be sure of getting it. On the fifth day they came for him and half an hour later he returned for his cap and wept with joy. He said to me: "At last they have taken a decision about us. From today probationary cadets will be locked up in the guard-house with the officers and we shall pay extra to the officers' mess for our messing. We shall be admitted when the officers have finished their food. We shall sleep with the men, get our coffee from the men's mess and draw our tobacco rations with the men too." '

It was only now that Martinec had recovered sufficiently to be able to break in upon Švejk with a sentence, the contents of which had no relevance whatsoever to the preceding conversation: 'Yes, yes, dear son, there are things between heaven and earth of which it behoves us to think with glowing heart and confidence in the infinite mercy of God. I come, dear son, to offer you spiritual consolation.'

He paused, because all that seemed somehow inappropriate. On the way he had composed a complete draft of a speech, in which he had intended to bring the unfortunate man to the contemplation of his life and to the realization that he would be forgiven in heaven above if he would only repent and show real sorrow.

Now he was wondering how to go on, but Švejk anticipated him by asking whether he had a cigarette.

Martinec had not yet learned to smoke; it was the only thing he had retained of his former way of life. Once or twice when he was with General Fink and had had a drop too much he tried to smoke a cigar, but at once everything came out of him and he had the impression that his guardian angel was warningly tickling him in the throat.

'I don't smoke, dear son,' he answered Švejk with unusual dignity.

'I'm surprised,' said Švejk. 'I've known many chaplains and they smoked like the distillery in Zlíchov. I can't really imagine a chaplain who doesn't smoke or drink. I've only known one who didn't puff and he preferred to chew tobacco rather than smoke it, and when he was preaching he spat it out all over the pulpit. Where do you come from, Your Reverence?'

'From Nový Jičín,' answered the Imperial and Royal Reverend Martinec in a dejected tone.

'Then perhaps, sir, you once knew a Růžena Gaudrsová. Two years ago she was employed in a wine restaurant in Platnéřská Street in Prague and suddenly brought paternity actions against eighteen persons because she'd given birth to twins. One of those twins had one blue and one brown eye and the other had one grey and one black. And so she assumed that four gentlemen with eyes like that, who had visited the wine restaurant and had business with her, had been involved. And then one of the twins had a lame leg, like a city councillor who also used to go there, and the other had six toes on one foot, like a parliamentary deputy who was a daily guest there. And just imagine, sir, eighteen guests used to go to that wine restaurant and those twins had a small birthmark after each one of all those eighteen whom she kept company with either at home or in a hotel. In the end the court decided that in such a queue of people the father was anonymous and then finally she laid the blame on the proprietor of the wine restaurant where she worked and sued him. But he proved that he had been impotent for twenty years as a result of an operation for an inflammation of his lower extremities. After that they sent her under escort, sir, to you at Nový Jičín, and from that you can see very well that whoever strives for power usually gets a lemon. She should have stuck to one man only and not said in court that one of the twins was by the deputy and the other by the city councillor or by this person or that. You can always reckon up the birth of a baby. On such and such a date I was with him in the hotel and on such and such a date the child was born. That's of course if it's a normal birth, sir. In "transit hotels" like that you'll always get a witness for ten crowns, either a waiter or a chambermaid, who'll swear that he'd actually been with her that night and that when they went down the stairs together she said to him: "And what if something happens?", and he answered her: "Don't be afraid, my silly pet, I'll look after the baby." '

The chaplain thought for a moment and the whole of his spiritual consolation seemed to him now rather difficult, although he had had all worked out beforehand what he would say to his dear son and how he would say it. He had planned to speak of the supreme mercy on the day of the last judgement, when all army criminals would rise from their graves with ropes around their necks and because they had repented would be received with mercy like the robber in the New Testament.

He had prepared what was perhaps one of the most beautiful spiritual consolations and it was going to be in three parts. First of all he would explain that death by hanging is easy if a man is completely reconciled with God. Army law punishes the delinquent for his treason against His Imperial Majesty who is the father of his warriors. One must therefore regard the smallest offence of any warrior as an act of parricide and sacrilege to the father. After that he intended to go on and develop his theory that His Imperial Majesty was Emperor by the grace of God and was appointed by him to direct secular affairs, just as the Pope was appointed by him to direct spiritual affairs. Treason against the Emperor was treason against the Lord himself. And the army criminal must expect not only the rope but eternal punishment and eternal perdition as well. If, however, because of the requirements of military discipline secular justice could not quash the sentence and had to hang the criminal, everything was not yet lost as far as the other punishment in eternity was concerned. A man could improve his position by means of an excellent move – by repentance.

The chaplain pictured this very moving scene as something which might help him in heaven by obliterating all the traces of his activities and actions in General Fink's apartment in Przemyśl.

To start with he would shout at the condemned man: 'Repent, my son! Let us kneel together! Repeat after me, my son!'

And then this stinking lousy cell would resound with the prayer: 'O God, whose quality it is always to give grace and to forgive, I earnestly beg Thee for the soul of this warrior, whom Thou hast commanded to leave this world by the sentence of a summary court-martial in Przemyśl. Grant that this infantryman by his piteous and total repentance be spared from suffering the torments of hell and that he may partake of the everlasting joys.'

'If you allow me to say so, Your Reverence, you've been sitting like a stuck pig for five minutes as though you'd lost your capacity for speech. Anyone can see on you that this is the first time you've been in gaol.'

'I have come for spiritual consolation,' said the chaplain gravely.

'It beats me why you keep harping on this spiritual consolation, sir. I'm awfully sorry, sir, but I don't feel strong enough to be able to offer you any consolation at all. You're not the first or the last chaplain to get himself behind bars. And moreover, to tell the truth, sir, I don't have the eloquence to offer consolation to anyone in such a difficult situation. I once tried, but it didn't turn out very well. Now, come and sit down nicely here next to me and I'll tell you all about it. When I used to live in Opatovická Street, I had a friend called Faustýn, who was a porter in a hotel. He was a very decent fellow, very fair and hard-working. He knew every girl on the streets, and you could come to see him, sir, in the hotel at any time during his night duty and just tell him: "Mr Faustýn, I'd like a girl", and he would at once ask you very conscientiously whether you wanted a blonde, a brunette, a short one, a tall one, a thin one, a fat one, a German, a Czech, a Jewess, a married one, a divorced one, a widow, an intelligent one or an unintelligent one.'

Švejk nestled up to the chaplain in a familiar way and putting his arm round his waist continued: 'Let's say now, sir, that you had said: "I'd like a blonde with long legs, a widow without intelligence." Well, in ten minutes you'd have had her in bed with you with her birth certificate as well.'

The chaplain began to feel hot all over and Švejk went on talking, clasping the chaplain to him like a mother: 'And you wouldn't have guessed, sir, what a feeling for morality and decency Mr Faustýn had. He didn't take a single kreutzer tip from those women whom he bargained with and delivered to the rooms. And if ever one of those women forgot and wanted to slip him something, you should have seen how furious he got and how he started to shout at her: "You filthy bitch, you, when you sell your body and commit mortal sin don't imagine that ten kreutzers of yours are going to make any difference. I'm no bawd, you impudent whore, you. I only do this out of compassion for you, so that when you've sunk so low you won't have to display your shame to passers-by in public, be caught in the night somewhere by a patrol and spend three days scrubbing the floors of the police headquarters. Here at least you're warm and no one sees how low you've fallen." But he compensated himself at the expense of the guests when he refused to accept money like a bawd. He had his tariff: blue eyes cost ten kreutzers, black eyes fifteen. And he always made out a detailed bill on a piece of paper which he presented to the guest. Those were very reasonable agent's prices. For a woman without intelligence there was a surcharge of ten kreutzers because he took the view that a vulgar piece like that provided more fun than an educated lady. Well, once towards evening Mr Faustýn came to see me in Opatovická Street. He was in a very excited state and not at all himself, as though they had only a moment ago dragged him out from underneath the protecting rail on a tram and stolen his watch in the process. At first he didn't say a word, and then he drew out of his pocket a bottle of rum, took a swig at it, offered it to me and said: "Drink." And then we didn't say anything until we'd drunk up the whole bottle, when he suddenly said: "Old man, please do something for me. Open the window on to the street. I'll sit on the ledge here. You take me by the legs and throw me down from the third floor. I need nothing more in life. I've now got this last consolation that there's a true friend who can see me off out of this world. I can't go on living in it. Honest as I am, I have been accused of procuring like a bawd from the Jewish quarter. After all, our hotel's a first-class one. All the three chambermaids and my wife have police books and don't owe the doctor a single kreutzer for his visits. If you have any affection for me at all throw me down from the third floor and give me this last consolation." I told him to climb out on to the window-ledge and I threw him down on to the street. . . . Don't be afraid, Your Reverence.'

Švejk stood on the bunk and pulled the chaplain up with him: 'Look, Your Reverence, I seized him like this and – whizz bang, down he went!'

Švejk lifted up the chaplain and dropped him on the ground again, and while the horrified chaplain picked himself up from the floor Švejk went on saying: 'So you see, sir, that nothing happened to you, and nothing happened to him, to Mr Faustýn either, although it was three times as high. Mr Faustýn was completely tight and forgot that I was living on the ground floor in Opatovická Street and not on the third floor as I used to a year before, when I lived in Křemencova Street and he used to come and see me there.'

From the floor the chaplain looked up in alarm at Švejk, who stood over him on the bunk and waved his arms.

It flashed on the chaplain that he was dealing with a madman and so he stammered: 'Yes, my dear son, it wasn't even three times as high.' Then he shuffled slowly backwards to the door, began suddenly to bang on it and uttered such frightful shrieks that they at once opened it for him.

Švejk saw through the barred window how the chaplain hurriedly rushed across the courtyard escorted by a guard and gesticulating in a lively manner.

'And now they're probably taking him to the mental ward,' thought Švejk, as he jumped down from the bunk and marched around singing:

> 'I'll never wear that ring you gave me.
> Lor lummy, why ever not?
> When I get back to my reg-i-ment
> I'll load it in my gun . . .'

A few minutes later they reported to General Fink that the chaplain had come.

The general was again entertaining many guests among whom an eminent role was played by two pleasant ladies, not to speak of wine and liqueurs.

Here were met together all the officers who had formed the board of the summary court-martial, except the ordinary infantryman who had lit their cigarettes in the morning.

The chaplain floated into the gathering like a phantom in a fairy story. He was pale, tense and dignified like a man who is conscious that he has had his face slapped for no fault of his own.

General Fink, who had latterly behaved very familiarly to the chaplain, drew him beside him on the sofa and asked him in a drunken voice: 'What's the matter with you, old spiritual consolation?'

At the same time one of the gay ladies threw a cigarette at the chaplain. 'Have a drink, old spiritual consolation,' General Fink said again, pouring him out some wine in a large green goblet. As he did not start drinking at once, the general began to pour the wine down him, and if the chaplain had not imbibed very valiantly he would have made a nice mess over him.

It was only then that the inquiries began about how the condemned man had conducted himself while the spiritual consolation was being offered. The chaplain stood up and said in tragic tones: 'He's gone mad.'

'That must have been a brilliant spiritual consolation!' the general said with a loud guffaw, upon which all the others had fits of frightful laughter and both ladies began once more to throw cigarettes at the chaplain.

At the end of the table the major nodded in his chair. He had already taken a drop too much and now he woke up out of his apathy, quickly poured a liqueur into two wine glasses, made his way through the chairs to the chaplain and forced the confused servant of God to drink 'to brotherhood'[1] with him. After that he rolled back to his place and went on with his forty winks.

With this toast to 'brotherhood' the chaplain fell completely into the clutches of the devil, who stretched his arms out to him from all the bottles on the table and from the looks and smiles of the gay ladies who

1. Drinking 'to brotherhood' was a formal preliminary to the use of the second person singular in addressing someone or calling someone by his Christian name.

put their legs on the table opposite him, so that Beelzebub was even peering at him out of lace frillies.

Up to the very last moment the chaplain had not lost the conviction that his soul was at stake and that he was a martyr.

This he expressed in his meditations which he addressed to the general's two batmen who carried him into the next room and laid him on the sofa: 'A sad but exalted spectacle is opening up before your eyes, when with an unprejudiced and pure mind you recall so many famous sufferers who became victims for their faith and who are known by the name of martyrs. In my case you can observe how a man can feel exalted over all his sufferings, when justice and virtue dwell in his heart, and armed with these he wins a glorious victory over his most frightful sufferings.'

Then they turned his face to the wall and he immediately fell asleep.

He had very disturbed slumbers.

He dreamt that in the daytime he was carrying out the duties of a chaplain and in the evening he was porter in the hotel in the place of Faustýn, whom Švejk had thrown out of the window from the third floor.

Complaints against him came to the general from all sides on the grounds that he had brought a guest a brunette instead of a blonde, and that instead of a divorced lady with intelligence he had supplied a widow without intelligence.

He woke up in the morning sweating like a pig and with a queasy stomach. It occurred to him that his vicar in Moravia was an angel compared with him.

3

Švejk back in his March Company

THE major who acted as judge advocate at the court proceedings with Švejk the previous morning was the same figure who at the general's evening party drank 'to brotherhood' with the chaplain and snoozed.

One thing was certain: no one knew at what hour and in what state the major left the general that night. They were all of them in such a condition that no one noticed his absence. The general was even confused about who of the company was speaking. The major had already been more than two hours away when the general, twirling his moustaches and smiling in an idiotic way, called out: 'Very well said, major.'

In the morning the major could not be found anywhere. His greatcoat hung in the hall, his sabre was on the hook and the only thing missing was his officer's cap. They thought he had perhaps gone to sleep in the W.C. in the house somewhere, and so they looked through all the W.C.s but failed to find him anywhere. Instead they discovered on the second floor a lieutenant who had been one of the general's guests and who was fast asleep in a kneeling position with his mouth in the hole, sleep having overtaken him just as he was vomiting.

The major seemed to have vanished from the face of the earth.

But if anyone had happened to look through the barred window into where Švejk was locked up they would have seen that under Švejk's Russian military greatcoat two persons were sleeping on one bunk and two pairs of boots were peeping out.

The boots with spurs belonged to the major, those without to Švejk.

Both men lay cosily together like two kittens. Švejk had his paw under the major's head and the major was embracing Švejk's waist, snuggling up to him like a puppy to a bitch.

There was nothing mysterious about this. The major was duty-conscious and that was all.

You must certainly have had the experience of sitting and drinking with someone the whole night until late the next morning, when suddenly your drinking companion puts his hands to his head, jumps up and shouts: 'Jesus Mary, I ought to have been in the office at eight o'clock.' This is the so-called fit of duty-consciousness which comes on as a by-product of a guilty conscience. A person who is seized by such a noble fit is not easily deflected from his sacred conviction that he must at once go to the office and make up for what he missed there. These are the hatless apparitions whom the porters in the offices catch in the corridor and tuck up on the sofa in their hole so that they can sleep it out.

And this was the sort of fit that had seized the major.

When he woke up in his chair it suddenly occurred to him that he must at once interrogate Švejk. This fit of official duty-consciousness bobbed up so quickly and suddenly and was implemented so promptly and decisively that no one noticed the major's disappearance.

But all the more conspicuously was the major's presence felt in the guard-house of the army gaol. He erupted there like a bomb.

The sergeant-major on duty was sleeping at the table and around him the rest of the men slumbered in various positions.

The major with his cap on one side let off such a volley of oaths that all stopped in the midst of their yawns and their faces acquired a grimacing expression. It was not a pack of soldiers who stared at him so hopelessly and so grotesquely but a pack of grinning apes.

The major struck the table with his fist and shouted at the sergeant-major: 'You indolent bastard, I told you a thousand times that your men are a pack of swinish shits.' Turning to the goggling men he shouted: 'Men! There's imbecility staring out of your eyes even when you're asleep, and when you're awake, you bastards, you look as if each one of you had wolfed up a truck of dynamite.'

After that there followed a long and copious sermon about the duties of all the men on guard and finally the order that they should at once open up for him the cell where Švejk was held, as he wanted to subject the delinquent to a new interrogation.

And so this was how the major got to Švejk's cell in the night.

He arrived there at the stage when everything was, so to speak, ripening within him. His final outburst was his order that the keys of the prison should be handed over to him.

In a last despairing recollection of his duties the sergeant-major refused to comply. This at once made a grandiose impression on the major.

'You swinish pack of shits!' he shouted into the courtyard. 'If you'd given me the keys I'd have shown you!'

'Humbly report, sir,' the sergeant-major answered, 'I am obliged to lock you up and to put a guard over the prisoner for the sake of your own safety. When you want to leave, sir, please just knock on the door.'

'You bloody half-wit,' said the major, 'you baboon, you camel, do you really imagine that I'm afraid of any prisoner and you have to station a guard to protect me when I'm going to interrogate him? Bloody hell! Lock me in and clear out quick!'

In the opening over the door in the barred lantern a petrol lamp with a short wick emitted a faint light which barely sufficed to enable the major to find Švejk who, awake and standing in military position by his bunk, patiently awaited what would actually come out of this visit.

Švejk remembered that the best thing to do would be to give the major a report and so he called out energetically: 'Humbly report, sir, one gaoled man and otherwise nothing to report.'

The major suddenly could not remember why he had come there and so he said: 'At ease! Where have you got that gaoled man?'

'Humbly report, it's me, sir,' said Švejk proudly.

The major however ignored this reply, for the general's wine and liqueurs were producing in his brain the final alcoholic reaction. He yawned so frightfully that any civilian would have sprained his jaw. In the case of the major, however, this yawning shunted his thoughts into those recesses of the brain where human beings preserve the art of song. Without any ceremony he fell on to Švejk's mattress on the bunk and screamed out in the tones of a slaughtered pig just before its final end:

> 'O Tannenbaum, o Tannenbaum,
> Wie schön sind deine Blätter!'[1]

He repeated this several times, punctuating the song with incomprehensible shrieks.

Then he rolled over on to his back like a small bear, made himself into a ball and began to snore at once.

'Sir,' Švejk said, waking him, 'humbly report, you'll get lice.'

It was no good. The major was dead to the world.

Švejk looked at him tenderly and said: 'Well, then, to bye-byes, old

1. This famous German folk song hardly needs translation: 'O fir tree, O fir tree, how lovely are thy leaves.'

toper,' and covered him with his greatcoat. Later he crept in beside him and it was in this position they found them next morning snuggled together.

At about nine o'clock, when the hunt for the major reached its climax, Švejk got up and thought it appropriate to wake him. He

shook him several times very thoroughly, pulled the Russian great-coat off him, until finally he sat up on the bunk and looking dully at Švejk tried to find out from him the solution to the enigma of what had actually happened to him.

'Humbly report, sir,' said Švejk, 'they've come here several times from the guard-room to make sure you're still alive. And so I've taken the liberty of waking you up now, because I don't know how long you generally sleep and I wouldn't like you to oversleep. There was once a cooper in a brewery at Uhříněves who always slept until six o'clock in the morning and should he happen to oversleep only a quarter of an hour more to a quarter past six, he went on sleeping until noon and did this for so long that they kicked him out of his job. After that he got angry and abused the church and a member of our Ruling House.'

'You dotty, no?' said the major in broken Czech, not without a touch of hopelessness, because he had a terrible hangover from the previous night and still could not find an answer to the question why he was actually sitting there, why people kept on coming here from the guard-room and why this fellow who was standing in front of him was drivelling such nonsense which was completely Greek to him. It all seemed frightfully queer. He remembered vaguely that he had already been there once in the night, but what on earth was the reason?

'I already be here night?' he asked in a tone of some uncertainty.

'According to instructions, sir,' Švejk answered, 'as I understood from your words, sir, humbly report, you came to interrogate me.'

And then it all suddenly dawned on the major and he looked at himself and behind him as though he were searching for something.

'Please don't worry about anything, sir,' said Švejk. 'You've woken up exactly as you were when you came in here. You arrived here without a greatcoat and without a sabre but with a cap. Your cap is over there. You see, I had to take it from your hand because you wanted to put it under your head. An officer's parade cap, sir, is like a top hat. There's only one man who could go to sleep on a top hat and that was a Mr Karderaz at Loděnice. He stretched himself out on a bench in a pub and put his top hat under his head. He used to sing at funerals, you see, and went to every funeral in a top hat. He put his top hat nicely under his head and impressed it on his mind that he musn't squash it. Then throughout the night in some way or other he kept the full weight of his body off it so that it wasn't damaged at all but rather benefited from it, because when he turned from one side to the other he slowly brushed it with his hair till he had completely ironed it.'

The major, who was now already grasping the whys and wherefores, continued to look dully at Švejk and could only repeat: 'You dotty, no? I now here. I go away.' He got up, went to the door and hammered on it.

Before they came to open it he had time to say to Švejk: 'If telegram no come that you're you then you hang!'

'Thank you very much indeed,' said Švejk. 'I know, sir, that you're taking very good care of me and if by any chance, sir, you should have caught one on this bunk you can be assured that if it's a small one and has little red buttocks it's a male. And if there's only one and you don't find a long grey one with reddish stripes on its belly then it's all right, because otherwise there would have been a pair and these bastards breed frightfully, even worse than rabbits.'

'Drop that,' the major said dejectedly in German to Švejk, when they opened the door for him.

In the guard-room the major made no further scenes. He just stiffly ordered them to get him a droshky, and during its vibrations on the wretched cobbles of Przemyśl he had only one thought in his head and that was that even if the delinquent was an imbecile of the first water he was probably only an innocent bastard after all. As far as he personally was concerned there was nothing else for him to do except either shoot himself as soon as he came home or send for his greatcoat and sabre from the general's apartment, take a bath in the town baths, stop at Vollgruber's wine-cellar afterwards, put his appetite in order again and book by telephone a ticket for the performance in the town theatre that evening.

Before he reached his apartment he decided on the latter.

But in his apartment a small surprise awaited him. He arrived just at the right moment ...

In the corridor stood General Fink, who was holding the major's batman by the collar, manhandling him frightfully and roaring at him: 'Where have you put your major, you swine? Speak, you animal!'

But the animal did not speak, because he was blue in the face through the general suffocating him.

As he came in upon this scene the major saw that the unfortunate batman was firmly holding under his arm his greatcoat and sabre, which he had obviously brought from the general's vestibule.

The scene began to give the major a great deal of entertainment and so he stood in the open doorway and went on looking at the suffering of his faithful servant, who had the precious quality of having drawn on to himself the major's dislike on account of his various pilferings.

The general let go of the blue-faced batman only for a moment in order to take a telegram out of his pocket. He then began to pound the batman across the mouth and lips with it and to shout at him: 'Where have you put your major, you swine, where have you put your

major *judge advocate*, you bastard, so that you can hand him a telegram on an official matter?'

'Here I am,' Major Derwota called from the door. The association
of the words 'major', 'judge advocate' and 'telegram' reminded him
again of his duties.

'Ah,' shouted General Fink, 'so you're coming back, are you?'
There was so much malice in his tone that the major did not reply but
stood there irresolutely.

The general told him to follow him into the sitting-room and when
they sat down at the desk he threw on to the table the telegram with
which he had pounded the batman's face and said to him in a tragic
voice: 'Read it! This is your work.'

While the major read the telegram the general got up from his chair,
ran up and down the room, knocked over the chairs and stools and
shouted: 'But I'll hang him none the less!'

The telegram read as follows:

Infantryman Josef Švejk, orderly of the 11th march company, got lost on
the 16th of this month on the route Chyrów–Felsztyn while on an official
journey to look for billets. Send Infantryman Švejk to brigade headquarters
at Wojałycze without delay.

The major opened the drawer of his desk, drew out a map and reflected that Felsztyn was forty kilometres south-east of Przemyśl and
so it was a frightful mystery how Infantryman Švejk could have come
across a Russian uniform in an area more than 150 kilometres away
from the front, since the forward positions stretched along the line
Sokal–Turze–Kozlów.

When the major informed the general of this and showed him on
the map the place where according to the telegram Švejk had got lost
a few days ago, the general bellowed like a bull, because he felt that all
his hopes of having a summary court-martial had dissolved in smoke.
He went to the telephone, called up the guard-room and gave orders
that they should at once bring the prisoner Švejk to him in the major's
apartment.

Before the order was carried out the general amid a volley of frightful oaths gave full rein to his annoyance countless times: he should
have had him hanged on his own responsibility without any further
investigations.

The major opposed this view and said something to the effect that law and justice must go hand in hand. He spoke eloquently in re-sounding periods about justice and the law courts, judicial murders and everything he could possibly think of, because after the night before he had a ghastly hangover which he felt an urge to relieve by talking.

When they at last produced Švejk, the major demanded an explana-tion from him of what had happened near Felsztyn and the facts about the Russian uniform.

Švejk duly explained this and corroborated it with a few examples from his chronicle of human suffering. When afterwards the major asked him why he had not stated this under cross-examination before the court, Švejk answered that no one had in fact asked him how he got into Russian uniform and that all the questions had been: 'Do you admit that you voluntarily and without any pressure put on enemy uniform?' Since that was true he could not say anything else but: 'Of course – yes – certainly – it was like that – undoubtedly.' This was why he had rejected with indignation the accusations made in the court that he had betrayed His Imperial Majesty.

'The fellow is a complete imbecile,' said the general to the major. 'Only a bloody idiot would put on a Russian uniform left on the dam

of a lake by goodness knows whom and then get himself drafted into a party of Russian prisoners.'

'Humbly report, sir,' Švejk said, 'you are right. I do sometimes notice myself that I'm feeble-minded, especially towards evening when . . .'

'Shut up, you ox,' the major said to Švejk and turned to the general to ask what they should do with him.

'Let his brigade hang him,' the general decided.

An hour later the escort took Švejk to the station to conduct him to the staff of the brigade in Wojałycze.

In the gaol Švejk left behind him a small memorial of himself, having scratched on the wall with a piece of wood a list in three columns of all the soups, sauces and main dishes which he had eaten in civil life. It was a kind of protest against the fact that for twenty-four hours they had given him nothing whatsoever to eat.

The following document accompanied Švejk to the brigade:

In accordance with instructions contained in telegram number 469 the infantryman Josef Švejk, a deserter from the 11th march company, is forwarded to the brigade staff for further action.

The escort itself, which consisted of four men, was a medley of nationalities. It was made up of a Pole, a Hungarian, a German and a Czech. The last-named, who had the rank of a corporal and led the escort, tried to show his importance towards the prisoner who was his fellow-countryman by letting him feel his frightful superiority. When for instance Švejk expressed the wish at the station that he might be permitted to urinate, the corporal told him quite rudely that he could urinate when he came to the brigade.

'Very well,' said Švejk. 'You'll have to give me that in writing, so that when my bladder bursts it is established who is responsible for it. There is a law about that, corporal.'

The corporal, who was a simple cowman, was frightened by the word bladder and so the whole escort ceremoniously led Švejk to the W.C. on the station. Throughout the journey the corporal gave the impression of being a brutal fellow and he looked so stuck-up that you might have thought he was going to get at the very least the rank of commander of an army corps the very next day.

When they were sitting in the train on the line Przemyśl–Chyrów, Švejk remarked to him:

'Corporal, when I look at you, I'm always reminded of a certain Corporal Bozba, who used to serve in Trento. The first day they promoted him corporal he began suddenly to increase in girth. First his cheeks started to swell and then his belly blew up so that the next day his crown-property trousers weren't big enough for him. But what was worst of all was that his ears began to grow long. So they sent him to the sickroom and the regimental doctor explained that it was what usually happened to corporals. At first they blow up and with some corporals this passes over quickly, but this case of his was a very serious one and he might burst, because it was spreading from his star down to his navel. To save him they had to cut off his star and then he went down again.'

From that moment Švejk vainly tried to keep up a conversation with the corporal and to explain to him in a friendly way why it was a common saying that a corporal was a disaster for a company.

The corporal did not answer except to make dark threats about which of them would be the one to laugh when they came to the brigade. In short Švejk's fellow-countryman did not prove to be much good, and when Švejk asked him where he came from he answered that it was no business of his.

Švejk tried all kinds of methods on him. He told him that this was not the first time he had been led under escort and that he had always had a grand time with all those who had escorted him.

The corporal remained silent and Švejk went on: 'Well, now, I think, corporal, that some disaster in the world must have struck you if you've lost your power of speech. I've known many gloomy corporals but such a godforsaken disaster as you are, corporal – please excuse me and don't be angry that I'm saying it – I've never yet seen. Tell me frankly what's worrying you and perhaps I can advise you, because a soldier who is being led under escort always has more experience than those who are guarding him. Or do you know what, corporal? What about your telling us a story so that the journey can pass more pleasantly? Perhaps you could tell us something about what it looks like in the part of the country you come from, whether there are lakes there or whether there are the ruins of an old castle there and, if there are, you could tell us the legend about them.'

'I've had enough of this,' shouted the corporal.

'Then you're a happy man,' said Švejk. 'Many people never have enough.'

The corporal enveloped himself in complete silence after he had spoken his last word: 'In the brigade they'll explain it all to you and I shan't bother myself about you any more.'

There was very little fun in the escort altogether. The Hungarian talked with the German in a peculiar way, because the only words he knew in German were *Jawohl* and *Was?* When the German explained something to him, the Hungarian nodded his head and said: '*Jawohl*', and when the German stopped talking the Hungarian said: '*Was?*' and the German started again. The Pole in the escort behaved like an aristocrat. He took no notice of anyone and amused himself on his own by blowing his nose on the ground, very cleverly using for this purpose the fingers of his right hand. After that he gloomily smeared it with the butt of his rifle and in a well-bred manner wiped the sticky butt of the rifle on his trousers, muttering all the time: 'Holy Mother of God.'

'You aren't very clever at it,' said Švejk to him. 'At Na Bojišti there lived in a cellar apartment a crossing-sweeper called Macháček. He used to blow his nose on the window and smear it round so cleverly that he made out of it a picture of Libuše prophesying Prague's glory.[1] For every picture like that his wife gave him such an honorarium that he had a mug like a barn door. But he wouldn't give it up and went on perfecting himself in it. It was the only pleasure he had, you see.'

The Pole did not answer and finally the whole escort was plunged in deep silence, as though they were going to a funeral and were thinking pious thoughts about the late lamented.

It was in this state that they approached the brigade staff at Woja-łycze.

Meanwhile at the brigade staff there had been very considerable changes.

The command of the brigade staff had been entrusted to Colonel Gerbich. This was a gentleman of great military talents, which had gone to his legs in the form of gout. But he had some very influential friends in the ministry who saw to it that he did not retire but could knock about in the various staffs of the larger military units, draw increased pay together with various kinds of war bonuses and remain in each place until in a fit of gout he committed some act of complete asininity. Then he was again moved somewhere else and usually it was a kick upstairs. At lunch he never talked to the officers about anything except his swollen toe, which sometimes attained such frightful dimensions that he had to wear a special big boot.

At meals it was his favourite occupation to tell everybody how his toe oozed and continually sweated, so that he had to have it in cotton wool, and that these exudations smelt like sour oxtail soup.

This was why whenever he was transferred to another job the whole officers' corps always said a heartfelt goodbye to him. Otherwise he was a very jovial gentleman and behaved quite affably to the junior

1. Libuše, the legendary prophetess, was the first ruler of the Czechs and is the subject of Smetana's opera of that name.

officers, to whom he recounted the good things he used to drink and eat before he was attacked by gout.

When they brought Švejk to the brigade and, at the orders of the officer on duty, escorted him together with the necessary documents before Colonel Gerbich, Lieutenant Dub was sitting in the office.

During those few days since the march from Sanok to Sambor Lieutenant Dub had experienced one more adventure. Beyond Felsztyn the 11th march company met a transport of horses which were being led to the Dragoon Regiment in Sądowa Wisznia.

Lieutenant Dub himself hardly knew how it had happened that he had wanted to demonstrate his equestrian skill to Lieutenant Lukáš and how he had jumped on to a horse which disappeared with him down the valley of a stream, where they afterwards found him so firmly planted in a small bog that even the cleverest gardener would not have been capable of doing it. When with the help of ropes they dragged him out Lieutenant Dub had no complaints. He only groaned in a low voice, as though his last hour had come. As they marched by the staff of the brigade, they took him there and settled him in a small military hospital.

A few days later he recovered so that the doctor could say that they should rub his back and belly two or three times more with tincture of iodine after which he could go back to his unit.

Now he was sitting in Colonel Gerbich's office and was chatting with him about various illnesses.

When he saw Švejk he shouted out in a loud voice, because he knew all about his mysterious disappearance on the way to Felsztyn: 'So we've got you back again! Many go away as brutes and return as even bigger monsters. You're one of those, I suppose.'

For the sake of completeness it would be appropriate to add that Lieutenant Dub, as a result of his adventures on horseback, had suffered a slight concussion of the brain and therefore we must not be surprised if coming close to Švejk he called upon the Lord to struggle with Švejk and shouted out in verse: 'Father, look, I urge Thee. The cannons smoke and boom. The bullets whistle past me with a terrifying zoom. Lord of battles, Father, help me against this rogue! ... Where have you been such a long time, you bastard? What's that uniform you've got on?'

It must also be recorded that the gout-stricken colonel had everything arranged very democratically in his office when he had no attacks. Officers and N.C.O.s of all ranks came to visit him to listen to his opinions about his swollen toe with its flavour of sour oxtail soup.

During the periods when Colonel Gerbich did not suffer attacks his office was always full of the most diverse ranks, because in such exceptional circumstances he was very gay and talkative and was glad

to have listeners around him to whom he could tell his dirty stories. This gave him a lot of pleasure and gave the others the satisfaction of being forced to laugh at his chestnuts, which were probably in circulation as long ago as the time of General Laudon.[1] It was very easy to serve under Colonel Gerbich at such times. Everybody did what they liked and wherever the colonel turned up in any staff everybody knew that people would flog and fiddle in every kind of way.

And so now, in addition to Švejk, who was brought before him, the

1. The renowned Austrian general in the eighteenth century who defeated Frederick the Great and was the subject of many army songs.

colonel's room was crowded with officers of the most varied ranks who waited to see what would happen, while the colonel studied the document addressed to the brigade staff and composed by the major from Przemyśl.

But Lieutenant Dub continued his conversation with Švejk in his usual charming way: 'You don't know me yet, but when you get to know me, you'll be dead stiff with horror.'

The colonel was completely flummoxed when he read the document from the major at Przemyśl, because the latter had dictated it when he was still under the influence of slight alcohol poisoning.

Colonel Gerbich was in a good mood none the less, because yesterday and today the unpleasant pains had eased and his toe was as quiet as a lamb.

'Well, what have you actually done?' he asked Švejk in such an affable tone that a dagger went through Lieutenant Dub's heart and impelled him to reply in the place of Švejk:

'This man, sir,' he said, presenting Švejk, 'pretends to be a half-wit for the sole purpose of concealing his rascality under the mask of imbecility. I am not acquainted with the contents of the document which has been sent with him, but none the less I presume that the blackguard has again committed some offence but this time on a larger scale. If you would allow me, sir, to familiarize myself with the contents of the document, I could surely give you, should you wish it, certain pointers to the way he should be handled.'

Turning to Švejk he said to him in Czech: 'You're sucking my blood, aren't you?'

'I am,' answered Švejk with dignity.

'So you can see what he's like, sir,' Lieutenant Dub continued in German. 'You can't ask him any questions. You can't talk to him at all. One day the scythe must strike against the stone and he will have to be punished in an exemplary fashion. Allow me, sir . . .'

Lieutenant Dub buried himself in the document which had been drawn up by the major from Przemyśl and when he had finished reading it he called out triumphantly: 'Now it's amen for you, Švejk. What have you done with your crown-property uniform?'

'I left it on the dam of the lake when I was trying on these rags to see how a Russian soldier feels in them,' answered Švejk. 'It's really nothing more than a misunderstanding.'

Švejk began to tell Lieutenant Dub all the troubles he had had on account of this misunderstanding and when he had finished Lieutenant Dub roared at him:

'It is only now that you're really going to know me. Do you know what it means to lose crown property, you scoundrel, to lose your uniform in wartime?'

'Humbly report, sir,' answered Švejk, 'when a soldier loses his uniform he has to draw another one.'

'Jesus Mary,' shouted Lieutenant Dub. 'You hound, you reptile, how much longer are you going to play the fool with me? Do you want to serve another hundred years after the war?'

Colonel Gerbich, who up to this moment had remained sitting calmly and composedly at his table, suddenly grinned in a frightful way because his toe, which up to that time had been very quiet, was suddenly transformed by a fit of gout from a gentle and peaceful lamb into a roaring tiger, an electric current of six hundred volts, a limb which was being slowly crushed to rubble by a hammer. He just waved his hand and roared in the frightful voice of a man who is being slowly roasted on a spit: 'Get out everybody! Give me a revolver!'

Everyone already recognized the symptoms and so they all rushed out, including Švejk, whom the guard dragged out into the passage. Only Lieutenant Dub remained. The moment seemed to him a very favourable one to settle scores with Švejk and so he said to the grimacing colonel: 'Allow me to observe, sir, that this man . . .'

The colonel mewed and threw an inkpot at him, whereupon the horrified Lieutenant Dub saluted and said: 'Of course, sir,' and disappeared through the door.

After that roars and howls resounded from the colonel's office for a long time until finally the painful lamentations ceased. The colonel's toe was suddenly transformed back into a peaceful lamb. The fit of gout had passed. The colonel rang the bell and ordered Švejk to be brought back to him.

'Well, what's the matter with you?' he asked Švejk, as though a load had fallen from his shoulders. He was as free and happy as though he were rolling in the sand at the seaside.

Švejk smiled affably at the colonel and told him his whole odyssey; how he was the orderly of the 11th march company of the 91st regiment and how he had no idea how they could get on without him.

The colonel also smiled and then issued the following orders: 'Write out a railway warrant for Švejk via Lwów to Żółtańce, where his march company is due to arrive tomorrow, and give him a new uniform out of the store and 6 crowns 82 hellers for messing en route.'

When later, dressed in a new Austrian uniform, Švejk left the brigade staff to go to the station, Lieutenant Dub was hanging about the staff headquarters and was not a little surprised when Švejk reported to him in a strictly military fashion, showed him his documents and asked him solicitously whether he should take any message from him to Lieutenant Lukáš.

Lieutenant Dub could utter no word except: 'Dismiss!' When he looked after the disappearing figure of Švejk he muttered under his breath: 'You'll get to know me in time, Jesus Mary, you will ...'

At the station of Żółtańce Captain Ságner's whole battalion was assembled except for the rearguard of the 14th company which had got lost somewhere when they marched round Lwów.

Arriving at the small country town Švejk found himself in a completely new environment because it was possible to observe from the general bustle that it was not very far from the front where people were massacring each other. All around the artillery and baggage trains had their encampments. Soldiers of various regiments came out of every house. Like an elite among them all Reich Germans were strolling about and aristocratically offering the Austrians cigarettes from their lavish supplies. In the Reich German field-kitchens in the square there were even whole barrels from which they tapped beer for the men, who fetched rations of it for their lunch and supper. The neglected Austrian soldiers with their bellies distended by filthy concoctions of sweet chicory hung around them like greedy cats.

Groups of Jews with hanging curls and in long kaftans pointed to the smoke clouds in the west and gesticulated with their hands. Everywhere they were shouting that on the river Bug the villages of Uciszków, Busk and Derewiany were on fire.

The thunder of guns could be clearly heard. They shouted that the Russians were bombarding Kamionka Strumiłowa from Grabów, that fighting was going on along the whole of the Bug and soldiers were stopping refugees who wanted to go back to their homes across the Bug.

Everywhere disorder and confusion reigned and no one knew for certain whether the Russians had not started a new offensive and halted their continuous retreat along the whole front.

Every moment field gendarmerie patrols brought to the main head-quarters of the town some frightened Jewish soul who was accused of having spread mendacious and false news. There they beat the wretched Jews until they were covered with blood and released them to go home with their hindquarters lacerated.

It was into this chaos that Švejk arrived and in this country town that he started his quest for his company. Already on the station he had nearly come into conflict with the transit command guard. When he came to the table where information was provided for soldiers looking for their units a corporal shouted at him from the table whether he didn't perhaps want him to go and look for his company for him. Švejk told him that he only wanted to know whereabouts in the town the 11th march company of the 91st regiment was billeted. 'It's very important for me to know where the 11th company is,' Švejk stressed, 'because I am its orderly.'

Very unfortunately a staff sergeant-major sat at the next table. He jumped up like a tiger and roared at Švejk: 'You blasted swine, you are an orderly and you don't know where your march company is!'

Before Švejk could answer, the staff sergeant-major had disappeared into the office and a moment later he brought out from it a fat lieu-tenant who looked as worthy as the owner of a large sausage factory.

The transit commands tended to be the collecting grounds for wild vagabond soldiers who might spend the whole war looking for their units and knocking about from one transit point to another. They would have liked most of all to wait in long queues by those tables at the transit commands, where there was the inscription: 'Payment for messing.'

When the fat lieutenant came in, the sergeant-major shouted out in German: 'Attention!' and the lieutenant asked Švejk: 'Where are your documents?'

When Švejk had shown them to him and the lieutenant was satis-fied as to the correctness of his march route from the staff of his brigade to his company in Żółtańce he returned them to Švejk and said patronizingly to the corporal at the table: 'Give him the informa-tion he requires,' and again shut himself in the office next door.

When the door closed after him the staff sergeant-major took Švejk by the shoulder and leading him to the door gave him the following information: 'See that you clear out of here quick, you stinking bastard!'

Švejk found himself once more in the chaos and started to look for someone whom he knew from the battalion. He walked for a long time on the streets until in the end he staked everything on one card.

He stopped a colonel and asked him in his broken German if by

any chance he knew where his battalion and company were quartered.

'You can speak Czech to me,' the colonel said. 'I'm Czech too. Your battalion is quartered nearby in the village of Klimontów behind the railway. It's not allowed in the town because people from one of your companies fought with the Bavarians in the town square the very day they arrived.'

And so Švejk set off to Klimontów.

The colonel called after him, put his hand in his pocket and gave him five crowns to buy cigarettes with. Then he said a friendly goodbye to him and went away from him, thinking to himself: 'What a nice lad.'

Švejk continued his journey to the village and thinking about the colonel drew the inference that twelve years ago in Trento there was a Colonel Habermaier who behaved just as nicely to the soldiers but turned out in the end to be a homosexual, because in the baths near the Adige he had tried to violate a cadet probationer, using 'service regulations' as blackmail.

Walking slowly, and absorbed in these gloomy thoughts, Švejk reached the nearby village and had little trouble in finding the staff of his battalion because, although the village was very extensive, there was only one decent building in it, a big elementary school, which the Galician local administration had built in this purely Ukrainian area as part of an intensive drive to make the community more Polish.

The school had gone through various phases during the war. Various Russian and Austrian staffs had been quartered there and the former gymnasium had been turned into an operating theatre at the time of the great battles which decided the fate of Lwów. They cut off legs and arms and carried out skull trepanning there.

Behind the school building in the garden was a huge funnel-shaped crater caused by the explosion of a shell of heavy calibre. In the corner of the garden stood a very large pear-tree and on one of the branches hung a piece of cut rope. Not long ago the local Greek Catholic vicar had been hanged on it as a result of a denunciation by the head-master of the local Polish school, who accused him of being a member of the group of Old Russians and of having during the Russian occupation celebrated a mass in the church for the victory of the arms of the Russian Orthodox Tsar. It was in fact not true, because the accused had not been there at the time but had been undergoing a cure for his gallstones at a small spa in Bochnia Zamurowana, which was untouched by the war.

Various elements played their part in the hanging of the Greek Catholic priest: nationalism, religious strife and a hen. Shortly before the war the unfortunate vicar had killed in his garden one of the head-master's hens which was pecking up the melon seeds he had just sown.

After his death the vicarage building stayed empty and it could be said that everyone took something away in memory of him.

One Polish peasant even took home the old piano, the top board of which he used for repairing the door of his pigsty. Some of the furniture was chopped up by the soldiers, as was the custom, and it was a stroke of luck that the stove in the kitchen was not ruined. It was big and had an excellent cooker, because the Greek Catholic vicar was no different from his Roman Catholic colleagues and enjoyed his yum-yum. So he liked to have many pots and pans on the cooker and in the oven.

Thus it became a tradition that all units of the army which passed through here used this kitchen for cooking for their officers. Upstairs in one big room was a sort of officers' club. The tables and chairs were collected from the inhabitants of the village.

That very day the officers of the battalion were having a banquet. They had clubbed together and bought a pig and Jurajda was making a pork feast for them. He was surrounded by various hangers-on from those ranks who served the officers, among whom the quartermaster sergeant-major played a prominent part. He advised Jurajda how to carve the pig's head so that a piece of its snout was left for him.

The eyes which goggled most were those of the insatiable Baloun.

He had the same lustful and longing look as cannibals must have when they see a missionary roast on a spit and the fat runs down and gives out a pleasant smell when it is being fried. Baloun felt like a dog leading a milk-cart when a boy from the delicatessen shop goes past with a basket of pieces of freshly smoked meat on his head. A string of smoked sausages hangs out of the basket over his back and the dog would jump and snap at it, were it not for the nasty straps in which it is harnessed and its horrible muzzle.

The initial phase of the jitrnice was the preparation of the sausage-meat, and here it lay on the baking board – an enormous embryo smelling of pepper, fat and liver.

And Jurajda with his rolled-up sleeves was so solemn that he could have served as a model for a painting of how God created the world from chaos.

Baloun could not contain himself and began to sob. Then his sobs grew into a heart-rending wailing.

'What are you bellowing like a bull for?' Jurajda asked him.

'It reminds me of home,' Baloun answered sobbing, 'how I was always at home at such times as this and never wanted to send a hamper even to my best neighbour. I always wanted to wolf it all myself, and so I did. Once I filled myself up so much with jitrnice,

blood sausage, pig's head and trotters that everyone thought I was going to burst, and they drove me up and down and round the court-yard with a whip just like a cow that's blown up after eating clover.

'Mr Jurajda, please let me scoop up a little of this sausage-meat, and after that I don't mind if they truss me. Otherwise I shan't be able to stand the suffering.'

Baloun got up from the bench and swaying as if he were drunk stepped towards the table. He stretched out his paw in the direction of the heap.

Then there came a tough struggle. It was only with the greatest difficulty that all those present could prevent him from hurling him-self at the sausage-meat. None the less, when they were dragging him out of the kitchen they were not able to hold him and in his despera-tion he managed to have a grab at the pot with guts which were being prepared for filling with the sausage-meat.

Jurajda was so angry that he threw a whole bundle of sausage-sticks at the fleeing Baloun and roared after him: 'Go and stuff your-self on sausage-sticks until you burst, you bastard.'

By that time the officers of the battalion were already assembled upstairs and were waiting solemnly for that marvel which was being born in the kitchen below. In the meantime, for want of other alcohol they drank a crude corn spirit coloured yellow with onion peel juice, which the Jewish merchant maintained was the most delicious and most genuine French cognac which he had inherited from his father, who in his turn had had it bequeathed to him by his grandfather.

'You bastard, you,' said Captain Ságner on this occasion, 'if you go on saying that your great-grandfather bought it from the French when they retreated from Moscow, I'll have you clapped in gaol until the youngest in your family becomes the oldest.'

While after every sip they cursed the enterprising Jew, Švejk was already sitting in the battalion office, where there was no one else except Marek who, as the battalion historian, was using the sojourn at Żółtańce to write up a stock of victorious battles which would obviously break out in the future.

For the time being he was making certain preliminary notes and when Švejk came in he had just written down: 'If in our mind's eye we conjure up all these heroes who took part in the battles at the village of N, where alongside our battalion there fought a battalion of regiment N and another battalion of regiment N, we shall find that our Nth battalion displayed the most brilliant strategic abilities and contributed undeniably to the victory of the Nth division, the object of which was the final consolidation of our position in sector N.'

'And so I'm back again, you see,' said Švejk to the volunteer.

'Allow me to smell you,' said Marek, pleasurably touched. 'Hum, you certainly stink of the dungeon-hole.'

'As usual,' said Švejk, 'it was only a matter of a small misunderstanding. And what are you doing?'

'As you see,' answered Marek, 'I'm making a rough cockshy about the heroic defenders of Austria, but somehow or other it doesn't hang together and the result's pure drivel. I am stressing the letter "N", which has attained extraordinary perfection in both the present and the future. In addition to my former talents Captain Ságner has discovered in me an unusual gift for mathematics. I have to control the battalion accounts and I've come to the conclusion so far that the battalion is completely in the red and is only waiting for the time when it can reach a settlement with its Russian creditors, because most stealing takes place after a defeat or a victory. However, it makes no difference whatsoever really. Even if we were wiped out to the last man the documents of our victory are still in existence here, because in my capacity of battalion historian I am honoured to be able to write: "Again fortune has turned against the enemy at the very moment when he was thinking that victory was in his grasp. A sortie by our soldiers and a bayonet attack are the matter of a moment. The enemy flee in despair and throw themselves into their own trenches. We bayonet them without mercy so that they abandon their trenches in disorder leaving wounded and unwounded prisoners in our hands. It is one of the most glorious moments." Whoever survives all this will write a letter home by field post: "They caught it square on their arses, dear wife! I am well. Have you weaned our little brat yet? Only, don't teach him to call strangers 'papa' because that would be difficult for me." Afterwards the censorship will black out the words "Caught it square on their arses", because no one knows who got it and it could be liable to various interpretations owing to its not being clearly expressed.'

'The really important thing is to speak unequivocally,' Švejk said. 'When the missionaries were at the church of St Ignatius in Prague in 1912 there was a preacher there who said from the pulpit that he would probably not meet anybody again in heaven. There was present at that evening spiritual exercise a tinker named Kulíšek and after the service he said at a pub that that missionary must have been up to quite a lot in his time, if he could declare in the church like at a public confession that he wouldn't meet anybody again in heaven. Why did they allow such people up into the pulpit? People ought always to speak clearly and distinctly and never in any kind of conundrums. At U Brejšků there was a head cellarman years ago and when he was sozzled and went home after his work he had the habit of stopping at a night café and drinking toasts with strangers. And he always said at each toast: "We'll . . . on you, and you'll . . . on us . . ." and because of that he once got such a swipe across the jaw from a respectable gentleman from Jihlava that when the café proprietor swept up the teeth the next morning he called his daughter who went to the fifth class of the elementary school and asked her how many teeth a grown-up man had in his mouth. Because she couldn't tell him he knocked out two of her teeth and on the third day got a letter from that head cellarman in which he apologized for all the unpleasantness he had caused and said he had not wanted to say anything coarse but that the public didn't understand him, because what he had in fact meant to say was just this: "We'll have a down on you and you'll have a down on us." Anyone who speaks ambiguously has got to think carefully before he opens his mouth. A straightforward chap who calls a spade a spade seldom gets a swipe across the jaw. But if he happens to get one several times, then he's careful and prefers to keep quiet when he's in company. It's true that people think that a fellow like that must be up to some trick or other, and that he often gets beaten up too, but that's what his deliberation and self-control bring him. After all, he has to reckon that he's on his own and that he has against him a lot of people who feel they've been insulted by him, and if he started to fight with them he'd get twice as much in return. A chap like that has got to be modest and patient. In Nusle there is a certain Mr Hauber and once on a Sunday on the road at Kundratice they stabbed him with a knife by mistake, when he was returning from a trip to Bartůněk's Mill. He came home with the knife stuck in his back and when his wife took off his coat she drew it cleanly out of his back. That same afternoon she was using it to chop the meat for goulash, because it was made out of Solingen steel and beautifully sharpened and their knives at home were all saw-edged and blunt. After that she wanted to have a whole set of such knives in her household and she kept on sending him every Sunday on a trip to Kundratice, but he was so modest that he never went further than to U Banzetů at Nusle, where he knew that when he was sitting in the kitchen old Banzet would chuck him out before anyone could lay hands on him.'

'You haven't changed at all,' the volunteer said to him.

'I haven't,' answered Švejk. 'I haven't had the time to. They even wanted to shoot me, but that was not the worst. I've not had any pay since the twelfth.'

'And you won't get it here either, because we're going to Sokal, and the pay will only be issued after the battle. We've got to economize. If I reckon that the fighting will break out in a fortnight, they'll save 24 crowns 72 hellers on every fallen soldier, including the bonus.'

'And what's the news here otherwise?'

'First our rear-guard got lost, then the officers' corps is having a pork feast at the vicarage, and the men are dispersed all over the village and are committing all sorts of immoralities with the local female population. This morning they trussed a soldier from your company because he climbed up to the attic after a seventy-year-old woman. The fellow is innocent because in the order of the day it was never stated up to what age it's permitted.'

'Of course the chap's innocent,' said Švejk, 'because when an old woman like that climbs up on a ladder he can't see her face. We had just the same sort of case at the manoeuvres near Tábor. One of our platoons was quartered in a pub and a woman was scrubbing the floor in the hall when a fellow called Chramosta came up to her and spanked her on her – what should I say? – her petticoat. She had a very well developed petticoat and when he spanked her on it she didn't register at all. He spanked her a second time and then a third time and she still didn't register, as though it didn't concern her. And so he resolved to start operating, but she went on calmly scrubbing the floor around. Afterwards she turned round to him, looked him straight in the eyes and said: "Ever been had, soldier?" The woman was over seventy and she told this story all over the village. . . . And now I'd like to ask you whether during my absence you haven't been gaoled too?'

'There was no opportunity,' Marek apologized, 'but on the other hand as far as you're concerned I have to inform you that the battalion has issued an arrest warrant for you.'

'It doesn't matter,' Švejk put in. 'They're quite right to have done so. The battalion had to do it. It had to issue an arrest warrant for me.

It was their duty, because no one knew where I was for such a long time. That was no hasty act on the part of the battalion.... Well, did you say that all the officers are at the vicarage having a pork feast? Then I must go there and present myself to show that I'm back again. I am sure that Lieutenant Lukáš has anyhow been very worried about me.'

Švejk set off for the vicarage with a firm military step, singing:

> 'Now look at me, my treasure, look at me!
> My treasure, look at me!
> See how they've made a gentleman of me ...
> A gentleman of me ...'

After that Švejk entered the vicarage and went up the stairs to the room above, from where the voices of the officers could be heard.

They were talking about everything on earth and were just going on about the brigade and the muddle there was at the staff. Even the brigade adjutant added fuel to the attack by observing: 'We telegraphed yesterday because of that fellow Švejk. Švejk ...'

'Present!' Švejk called out from the half-open door and repeated as he came in: 'Present! Humbly report, Infantryman Švejk, company orderly to the 11th march company.'

Seeing the bewildered faces of Captain Ságner and Lieutenant Lukáš, in which could be descried a certain mute despair, he did not wait for any questions and called out:

'Humbly report, they wanted to shoot me for having betrayed His Imperial Majesty.'

'For Jesus Christ's sake, what on earth are you talking about?' Lieutenant Lukáš shouted in despair. He was deathly pale.

'Humbly report, it was like this, sir ...'

And Švejk began to describe in detail what had actually happened to him.

They looked at him with staring eyes and he told his story with all possible detail, not even forgetting to mention that forget-me-nots were blooming on the dam of the lake where his misfortune had happened. When afterwards he mentioned the names of the Tartars he had got to know on his pilgrimage, like Hallimulabalibay, to which he added a whole string of names he had himself invented, like Valivolavalivey, Malimulamalimey, Lieutenant Lukáš could not stop himself from saying: 'I'll kick your backside, you mule. Go on, but be brief and to the point!'

And Švejk went on with his customary consistency, and when he came to the summary court-martial, the general and the major, he mentioned that the general squinted in his left eye and that the major's eyes were blue.

'And they looked me through and through,' he added afterwards in rhyme.

Lieutenant Zimmerman, the commander of the 12th company, threw a mug at Švejk. He had drunk out of it strong spirit bought from the Jew.

Švejk went on quite unruffled and explained how afterwards there had been spiritual consolation, and how the major slept in his embrace till the morning. Then he made a fine defence of the brigade, where he had been sent when the battalion reported him missing and demanded his return. Handing over the documents to Captain Ságner to prove that he had been cleared of all suspicion by the highest authority of the brigade he added: 'Humbly report, I take the liberty to inform you that Lieutenant Dub is in the brigade with concussion of the brain and asks to be remembered to you. May I now have my pay and tobacco money, please?'

Captain Ságner and Lieutenant Lukáš exchanged questioning glances but at that moment the door opened and they brought the steaming hot pork soup in in a kind of tub.

That was the beginning of all those delights for which they had been waiting so long.

'You godforsaken bastard,' Captain Ságner said to Švejk. He was in a mellow mood before the forthcoming treat. 'It's only the pork feast which has saved you.'

'Švejk,' Lieutenant Lukáš added, 'if anything more happens, it'll be a bad day for you.'

'Humbly report, it will have to be a bad day for me,' Švejk said, saluting. 'When a man is in the army he has to be conscious and aware of . . .'

'Clear off!' Captain Ságner roared at him.

Švejk cleared off and went down to the kitchen. There the crushed Baloun had returned and was asking if he could wait on his Lieutenant Lukáš at the feast.

Švejk arrived at the very moment when Jurajda was arguing with Baloun.

In the course of the argument Jurajda used some pretty incomprehensible terms.

'You're a *hodulus vorax*,' he said to Baloun. 'You'd go on stuffing yourself until the sweat poured out of you, and if I were to let you take the jitrnice upstairs you'd be *beelzebubbing* with them on the stairs.'

The kitchen now had quite another appearance. The battalion and company quartermaster sergeant-majors were nibbling in accordance with their rank and Jurajda's carefully elaborated plan. Out of a rusty wash-basin the battalion writers, company telephonists and one or two N.C.O.s were greedily gulping the pork soup, which had been thinned with boiling water so that they all could get a mouthful or two.

'Hallo!' said Vaněk to Švejk as he gnawed a pig's claw. 'A moment ago Marek was here and said you'd come back and had a new uniform on. That means you've got me into a pretty mess. He's been frightening me by saying that we shan't be able to get our accounts straight with the brigade because of that uniform. Your old uniform was found on the dam of the lake and we've already reported that to the brigade through the battalion office. I had entered you as drowned while bathing. You had no business to come back and make trouble for us with two uniforms. You have no idea what you've done to the battalion. Every part of your uniform is entered in our books. It's registered as an extra in the list of uniforms which I have for the company. The company has one whole uniform in excess. I've reported this to the battalion. Now we shall get a notification from the brigade that you've got a new uniform there. And because in the meantime the battalion will show in its equipment records that there's one complete uniform in excess. . . . I can imagine what that can mean: we could get an inspection because of it. Over a trifle like this Supply Headquarters would come and inspect us. If two thousand pairs of boots are lost no one worries about it at all . . .

'But we've lost your uniform,' said Vaněk tragically, sucking the marrow from a bone which had fallen into his hand, and digging out the rest with a matchstick which he used instead of a toothpick. 'For a trifle like that there's sure to be an inspection. When I was in the Carpathians there was an inspection just because the order had not been carried out that frozen soldiers should have their boots pulled off without damage to the boots. They tried to pull them off, pulled and pulled – and on two of the men the boots burst while this was being done and one of them had had broken boots even before he died. And so the mischief was done. A colonel came from Supply Headquarters and if it hadn't happened that as soon as he arrived he stopped one in the head from the Russians and rolled down into a valley, I don't know what might have come out of it.'

'Did they take his boots off as well?' Švejk asked with interest.

'They did,' said Vaněk pensively, 'but no one knew who had done it, so we couldn't show the colonel's boots in our accounts either.'

Jurajda returned from upstairs again and his first glance fell on the prostrate Baloun who sat, a miserable wreck, on a bench by the stove and gazed at his emaciated belly in frightful despair.

'You should belong to the sect of the Hesychasts,' said the learned cook compassionately. 'They too spent whole days looking at their navel until they got to imagine that a halo shone round it. After that they supposed they had reached the third degree of perfection.'

Jurajda reached into the oven and took out a small piece of blood sausage.

'Now put that into your maw, Baloun,' he said affably. 'Have a good glut until you burst. Choke yourself, you greedy guts.'

Tears came to Baloun's eyes.

'At home when we slaughtered,' he said plaintively, as he gobbled up the small piece of blood sausage, 'I always ate first a good piece of boiled pig's head, its whole snout, its heart, its ear, a bit of its liver, its kidneys, its spleen, a slice of its ribs, its tongue and afterwards . . .'

And he added in a hushed voice as though he were telling a fairy tale: 'Afterwards it was the turn of the jitrnice, six, ten pieces, and then pot-bellied blood sausages stuffed with meat and pearl barley or bread-crumbs, so that you didn't know which to bite into first, those with breadcrumbs or those with barley. Everything melted on your tongue, everything smelled so good – and you went on stuffing and stuffing.

'So I think the bullets will spare me,' Baloun went on lamenting, 'and it will be hunger that'll get me and I'll never more in my life come across such a roaster of blood-sausage meat as I had at home. As for brawn I didn't like it too much, because it only shakes like jelly and you get nothing out of it. My wife on the other hand would die to get brawn and I wouldn't let her put even a piece of pig's ear into it be-cause I wanted to wolf everything up myself in the way I liked it best. I didn't appreciate those delicacies, that good living, and once I even refused to let my old father-in-law have his pig. I slaughtered it and wolfed it all up myself and I was so greedy that I didn't even send him a tiny hamper – and afterwards he prophesied that when I kicked the bucket it would be of starvation.'

'And that's the situation,' said Švejk, from whose lips nothing but rhymes seemed to flow involuntarily that day.

Jurajda had already got over his sudden fit of sympathy for Baloun, because the latter nimbly slipped towards the stove, took out of his pocket a piece of bread and tried to dab the whole of it in the sauce, which was nestling up to all sides of the great lump of roast pork in the huge roaster.

Jurajda hit him over the hand, so that Baloun's slice of bread fell into the sauce just like a swimmer jumping from a diving board into a river.

Before Baloun had an opportunity of snatching the delicacy out of the roaster Jurajda seized him and threw him out of the door.

The crushed Baloun saw through the window how Jurajda took out on a fork the piece of bread which had become brown in the sauce, gave it to Švejk and put on it a piece of meat which he had cut off from the top of the roast, saying:

'Eat, my dear old modest friend!'

'Holy Mary, Mother of God,' Baloun lamented behind the window, 'my bread's gone down the drain.' Swinging his long arms he went to find a titbit in the village.

As he ate Jurajda's noble gift Švejk said with his mouth full: 'I'm truly glad that I'm back again among my own folk. I should really have hated it if I couldn't have gone on rendering the company my effective services.' Wiping from his chin the drops of sauce and fat which fell from the bread he continued:

'I really can't imagine what you'd have done without me if they had held me somewhere and the war had continued a few years longer.'

Vaněk asked with interest:

'How long do you think the war will go on, Švejk?'

'Fifteen years,' answered Švejk. 'That's obvious because once there was a thirty years' war and now we're twice as clever as they were before, so it follows that thirty divided by two is fifteen.'

'Our captain's batman told us that he'd heard that as soon as we occupy the frontiers of Galicia we shan't advance any further,' said Jurajda. 'Then the Russians will begin to sue for peace.'

'In that case it wouldn't be worth while having a war at all,' said Švejk emphatically. 'When there's a war on, let it be a war. I certainly won't hear of peace until we are in Moscow or Petrograd. After all, when there's a world war on it's not really worth it just to sit about on our arses near the frontiers. Let's take for example the Swedes during the Thirty Years' War. Look how far away they came from when they got to Německý Brod and Lipnice, where they made such a breach that to this very day they talk Swedish in the pubs after midnight there and don't understand each other. Or take the Prussians. They weren't exactly our next-door neighbours and yet in Lipnice they managed to leave behind them bags of Prussians. They even got as far as Jedouchov and America and back again.'

'Besides,' said Jurajda, who was today completely driven off balance by the pork feast and was in a mental muddle, 'all people are descended from carps. Take for instance Darwin's theory of evolution, chaps ...'

His further meditations were interrupted by the sudden entry of Marek:

'The devil take the hindmost,' Marek called out. 'A moment ago

Lieutenant Dub arrived in a car at the battalion staff and brought with him Cadet Biegler in his shitted bags.

'It's terrible with him,' Marek went on. 'When they got out of the car he rushed into the office. You know very well how when I went away from here I told you I was going to take forty winks. Well, I stretched myself out on a bench in the office and began happily to doze, when suddenly he hurled himself on me. Cadet Biegler roared: "Attention!" and Dub made me get up and then let fly at me: "You're surprised, are you, that I've caught you in the office in dereliction of duty? Sleeping is permitted only after the last post." Thereupon Biegler added: "Section 16 paragraph 9 of barrack regulations." Then Dub hammered with his fist on the table and shouted: "Perhaps you wanted to try and get rid of me from the battalion. Don't imagine that it was concussion of the brain I had. My skull can take anything." In the meantime Cadet Biegler went through the papers on the table and read aloud to himself from one of the documents: "Order for division no. 280." Dub, thinking that Biegler was making fun of him, because of his last sentence, that is to say that his skull could take anything, started rebuking him for his unworthy and insolent behaviour towards senior officers and is now taking him to the captain to complain about him.'

A moment later they came to the kitchen, which they had to go through if they went upstairs to where the whole officers' corps was sitting and where after the roast pork the chubby Lieutenant Malý was singing an aria from the opera *Traviata* and belching as well after the cabbage and rich banquet.

When Lieutenant Dub entered the kitchen Švejk shouted: 'Attention! Up all of you!'

Dub came very close to Švejk so that he could shout at him right in his face: 'Now you'll catch it! Now it's amen for you! I'm going to have you stuffed as a memorial for the 91st regiment.'

'Just as you command, sir,' Švejk said saluting. 'Humbly report, I once read that there was a great battle in which a Swedish king fell together with his faithful horse. They sent both corpses back to Sweden and now they both stand stuffed in the Stockholm museum.'

'Where did you get that knowledge from, animal?' shouted Lieutenant Dub.

'Humbly report, sir, from my schoolmaster brother.'

Lieutenant Dub turned round, spat, and pushed Cadet Biegler in front of him up the stairs leading to the big hall. But he could not help turning round in the door and looking at Švejk. With the inexorable severity of a Roman emperor deciding the fate of a wounded gladiator in a circus he made a gesture with a finger of his right hand and shouted to Švejk: 'Thumbs down!'

'Humbly report,' Švejk called out after him, 'I'm already putting them down!'

Cadet Biegler was in a weak state. During all this time he had gone through the various cholera stations and got fully accustomed to all the manipulations they used on him as a cholera suspect. As a result he had begun to discharge continually and involuntarily into his trousers. When at one of these observation stations he finally came into the hands of a specialist who could not find any cholera bacilli in his excrement, the latter bound his intestines with tannin, as a shoemaker binds broken shoes with pitch thread, and sent him to the nearest transit command. Although Biegler was as weak as steam over a pot the specialist pronounced him fit for service. He was a kind-hearted man.

When Cadet Biegler told him that he felt very weak he said with a smile: 'You'll still be able to carry off the Gold Medal for valour. After all, you volunteered for front service, didn't you?'

And so Cadet Biegler set out to try to earn the Gold Medal.

His steeled intestines no longer ejected a thin fluid into his trousers, but he still suffered from frequent urgent calls, so that from the last transit station to the staff of the brigade, where he met Lieutenant Dub, it was in actual fact a whistle-stop journey to all possible W.C.s. Several times he missed his train because he was sitting in the station W.C. so long that it went off without him. Several times he failed to change trains, because he was sitting in the train W.C.

But in spite of all that and in defiance of all those W.C.s which were hampering his journey Cadet Biegler none the less came nearer and nearer to the brigade.

Lieutenant Dub should have remained a few days longer under treatment at the brigade, but the same day that Švejk went off to the battalion, the staff doctor had second thoughts about Lieutenant Dub, when he learned that in the afternoon an ambulance car would be going in the direction of the battalion of the 91st regiment.

He was very glad to get rid of Lieutenant Dub, who as usual supported his various assertions with the words: 'I talked with the district hejtman about this already before the war.'

'You can kiss my arse with your district hejtman,' the staff doctor thought, and he was very grateful for the fortunate chance that ambulance cars were going up to Kamionka Strumiłowa via Żółtańce.

Švejk never saw Cadet Biegler at the brigade, because for two hours the latter was again sitting in one of the brigade officers' W.C.s. One can be bold enough to claim that Cadet Biegler never wasted his time in those places because he always rehearsed to himself all the glorious battles of the heroic Austro-Hungarian armies from the Battle of Nördlingen on 6 September 1634 to Sarajevo on 19 August 1888.

When he had pulled the chain of the water closet innumerable times and the water gushed into the pan with a roar, he shut his eyes and imagined he heard the battles' din, the assaults of cavalry and the thunder of artillery.

Lieutenant Dub's meeting with Cadet Biegler was not too delightful and no doubt explained a certain sourness in their future relations both on and off duty.

It happened that when Lieutenant Dub was vainly trying to get to the W.C. for the fourth time he shouted out in exasperation: 'Who's there?'

'Cadet Biegler, 11th march company, battalion N, 91st regiment,' came the proud reply.

The competitor announced himself in front of the door. 'This is Lieutenant Dub of the same company.'

'I'll be ready in a moment, sir.'

'I'm waiting!'

Lieutenant Dub looked impatiently at his watch. No one would have believed how much energy and tenacity was required to hold out a further fifteen minutes in such a situation in front of the door, and after that another five, and then a further five more, and after knocking, beating and kicking on the door to receive always the same answer: 'I'll be ready in a moment, sir.'

Lieutenant Dub became feverish, notably when after a hopeful rustling of the paper a further seven minutes went by without the door opening.

Into the bargain Cadet Biegler was so tactful that he still did not pull the chain.

Lieutenant Dub in a slight fever started to reflect whether he shouldn't perhaps complain to the commander of the brigade, who might then order the door to be broken open and Cadet Biegler to be taken out. It also occurred to him that it might perhaps be an act of insubordination.

Only after a further five minutes did Lieutenant Dub in fact realize that he could no longer perform anything inside the door and that his urge had long since passed. He remained however in front of the W.C. out of some kind of principle and continued to kick on the door, from which there always came back the identical reply: 'I'll be ready in a moment, sir.'

At last Biegler could be heard pulling the chain and after a short time they met face to face.

'Cadet Biegler,' Lieutenant Dub thundered at him, 'don't imagine that I am here for the same purpose as you. I have come here because you failed to report to me when you arrived at brigade staff. Are you ignorant of the regulations? Do you know to whom you have to give priority?'

Cadet Biegler searched his memory for a time to try to recall whether he had really done something which was not compatible with discipline and with the regulations concerning relations between junior and senior officers.

In this respect there was a vast vacuum and gap in his memory.

In the school no one had ever lectured to them on how junior officers should behave towards senior officers in a case like this. In such circumstances should he stop shitting in the middle of the process and fly out of the door of the W.C., holding his trousers in one hand and saluting with the other?

'Will you please answer, Cadet Biegler!' Lieutenant Dub called out challengingly.

And then Biegler remembered a very simple answer which solved everything: 'Sir, I was not informed after my arrival at brigade staff that you were here and when I had completed my business in the office I went at once to the W.C. where I remained until your arrival.'

And then he added in a solemn voice: 'This is Cadet Biegler reporting to Lieutenant Dub.'

'You know it's not just a mere trifle,' Lieutenant Dub said acidly. 'In my view, Cadet Biegler, as soon as you got to brigade staff you should have asked in the office whether by chance there wasn't any officer of your battalion or company there. We shall decide about your conduct in the battalion. I am going there by car and you will come with me. "But"? I don't want to hear any "buts" from you, please!'

In fact Cadet Biegler objected that he had obtained from the office of the brigade staff a march route which indicated that he should go by rail and that this method of travelling seemed much more suitable in view of the uncertainty of his bowels. Every child knows perfectly well that cars are not equipped for such cases. Before you go 180 kilometres you've already done it in your trousers.

Heaven knows how it happened, but when they drove off the shaking of the car had initially no effect on Biegler.

Lieutenant Dub was in complete despair at not being able to carry out his plan of vengeance.

When they drove off he thought to himself. 'Just wait, Cadet Biegler! When you find it's coming on, don't imagine I'm going to have the car stopped for you.'

It was in this sense that to the extent permitted by the speed of the car, which was eating up the kilometres, Dub started a pleasant conversation with Biegler: army cars with a fixed scheduled route must not waste petrol and cannot make any stops anywhere.

Cadet Biegler quite correctly objected that when a car stops anywhere for anything it does not use up petrol, because the chauffeur switches off the engine.

'But if it has to arrive at its destination at the scheduled time,' Lieutenant Dub continued inexorably, 'it mustn't stop anywhere on the way.'

There was no answer on the part of Cadet Biegler.

And so they raced through the air for more than a quarter of an hour, until suddenly Lieutenant Dub felt he had a very distended stomach and that it would be desirable to stop the car, get out, go into a ditch, take down his trousers and seek relief.

He controlled himself like a hero as far as the 126th kilometre, when he resolutely pulled the driver by the coat and shouted into his ear: 'Stop!'

'Cadet Biegler,' said Lieutenant Dub graciously as he jumped rapidly out of the car down into the ditch, 'now you have your opportunity too.'

'No, thank you,' Cadet Biegler answered. 'I would not like to hold the car up unnecessarily.'

Cadet Biegler, who was also at the end of his tether, said to himself under his breath that he would rather mess up his trousers than miss this marvellous opportunity of making a fool of Lieutenant Dub.

Before they got to Żółtańce Dub stopped the car twice and after the last stop he said doggedly to Biegler: 'For lunch I had bigos cooked in the Polish way.[1] From the battalion I shall make a complaint by telegram to the brigade. The sauerkraut was bad and the pork not fit for eating. The insolence of these cooks exceeds all bounds. Whoever doesn't yet know me, will soon get to know me.'

'Field Marshal Nostitz-Rhieneck, the elite of the reserve cavalry, published a paper called "What is bad for the stomach in war",' Biegler replied, 'and in it he recommended that during war troubles and strains pork should not be eaten at all. Every excess on the march is harmful.'

Lieutenant Dub did not say a word in reply. He only thought to himself: 'I'll soon deal with all your erudition, you bastard.' Then he

1. Szeged goulash made out of fat pork and sauerkraut.

had second thoughts and replied to Biegler with a very stupid question: 'And so you think, Cadet Biegler, that an officer to whom you must regard yourself as subordinate in rank eats immoderately? Didn't you want to say, Cadet Biegler, that I'd overgorged myself? I am grateful to you for this rudeness. Be assured that I shall settle accounts with you. You don't know me yet, but when you get to know me you won't forget Lieutenant Dub.'

As he said the last word he very nearly bit his tongue, because they suddenly flew over a hole in the road.

Cadet Biegler did not answer, which in its turn stirred up Lieutenant Dub, who asked rudely: 'Listen, Cadet Biegler, I think that you have learnt that you have to answer the questions of your superior officer.'

'Of course,' said Cadet Biegler, 'there is such a passage. But of course it's necessary first to analyse our mutual relations. As far as I am aware I have not yet been assigned anywhere and so there can be no question whatsoever of my being directly subordinated to you, sir. The most important thing of course is that in officers' circles questions asked by superiors need only be answered when they concern matters of duty. As we two are sitting here in the car we do not represent any battle component of any precise military unit. Therefore there is no official relationship between us. We are both going to our units, and it would certainly be no official utterance if I were to answer your question whether I perhaps meant that you have overgorged yourself, sir.'

'Have you finished, you, you . . . ?' Lieutenant Dub roared at him.

'Yes, I have,' Cadet Biegler stated with assurance. 'Don't forget, sir, that an officers' court of honour will no doubt pronounce on what has taken place between us.'

Lieutenant Dub was almost beside himself with rage and fury. When he got angry he had the special habit of talking even greater nonsense and idiocy than when he was calm.

And so he muttered: 'It will be a court-martial which will decide on your case.'

Cadet Biegler used this opportunity to give him the final knock-out by saying in the most familiar tone possible: 'You're joking, old man.'

Lieutenant Dub shouted at the chauffeur to stop.

'One of us must walk,' he gibbered.

'I shall go in the car,' Cadet Biegler answered calmly. 'As for you, old man, you can do what you like.'

'Drive on,' Lieutenant Dub bawled at the chauffeur as though in a delirium. Thereafter he enveloped himself in dignified silence like Julius Caesar, when the conspirators approached him with daggers to stab him.

And it was in this way they arrived at Żółtańce, where they came on to the track of the battalion.

While Lieutenant Dub and Cadet Biegler were still disputing on the stairs whether a cadet who had not yet been assigned anywhere had a right to draw any portion of the amount of jitrnice which fell to the officers of individual companies, down in the kitchen they were already stuffed full. They had stretched themselves out on the spacious benches, were talking about everything possible and puffing at their pipes like billyo.

Jurajda declared: 'Well, today I've made a wonderful discovery. I think it's going to make a complete revolution in cooking. You know very well, Vaněk, that I couldn't find any marjoram for the jitrnice anywhere in this cursed village.'

'*Herba majoranae*,' said Vaněk, remembering that he was a chemist.

Jurajda continued: 'No one has ever made a proper study of how in an emergency the human mind seizes on the most various means, how new horizons appear before it, how it begins to discover all sorts of impossible things, which humanity has not dreamed of up to now. . . . Well, I tried to look for marjoram in all the houses here. I ran around, searched and explained to them what it was needed for and what it looked like . . .'

'You should have gone on to describe the smell,' Švejk chimed in from the bench. 'You should have said that marjoram smells like when you sniff at an ink-bottle in an alley of flowering acacias. On the hill of Bohdalec near Prague . . .'

'But please, Švejk,' Marek interrupted him imploringly, 'let Jurajda finish.'

Jurajda went on: 'At one farm I came across an old pensioned soldier from the time of the occupation of Bosnia and Herzegovina. He did his military service in the Uhlans at Pardubice and still remembered his Czech. He began to argue with me and say that in Bohemia they put camomile in jitrnice and not marjoram. Honestly, I had no idea what to do because among all the spices which are put into jitrnice really any sensible and unprejudiced person must consider marjoram as champion: I had at once to find some substitute, which would give that striking spicy taste. And then I found in a farm hanging under the picture of a saint a wedding-garland of myrtle. They had been newly married, and the sprigs of myrtle on the garland were still fairly fresh. And so I put the myrtle into the jitrnice. Of course I had to steam the whole wedding-garland three times in boiling water so that the leaves should get soft and lose their too acrid smell and taste. Naturally, when I took away from them that myrtle wedding-garland of theirs for the jitrnice it caused a lot of heartache. When we parted they were convinced that for such sacrilege I should be killed by the very next bullet, as the garland was consecrated. But you have eaten my pork soup and not one of you realized that it smelt of myrtle instead of marjoram.'

'In Jindřichův Hradec,' Švejk put in, 'years ago a pork butcher called Josef Linek had two boxes on his shelf. In one he had a mixture of all the spices he put into jitrnice and blood sausages. In the other box he had insect powder, because he had found out several times that his clients had eaten bugs or beetles in his sausages. He used to say that as far as bugs were concerned they had a taste of the bitter almonds they put in cakes, but beetles in smoked sausages smelt like mildewy old bibles. And that was why he was so keen on cleanliness in his workshop and strewed that insect powder everywhere. But once he was making blood sausages and had a cold. And so he took the box of insect powder and shook it into the sausage-meat for blood sausages and ever since then people in Jindřichův Hradec only went to Linek for their blood sausages. They absolutely stormed his shop. And he was so cunning that he twigged that it was the insect powder that did it, and from that time on he ordered whole cases of the powder cash on delivery, after having previously told the firm from which he ordered it to write on the cases: "Indian Spices". That was his secret and he went with it to the grave. And the most interesting thing was that all those families who bought his blood sausages were free of beetles and bugs. Since then Jindřichův Hradec has been one of the cleanest cities in the whole of Bohemia.'

'Have you finished?' asked Marek, who obviously wanted to join the conversation.

'Well, I'd be ready with this particular case,' answered Švejk, 'but

I know a similar case in the Beskydy Mountains, but I'll tell you about that when the fighting begins.'

Marek began to speak: 'Culinary art is best appreciated in war-time especially at the front. Allow me to make a small comparison. In

peacetime we've read and heard of so-called iced soups, i.e. soups to which they add ice and which are very popular in North Germany, Denmark and Sweden. And you see the war came and this winter in the Carpathians the men had so much iced soup that they wouldn't touch it, although it's such a delicacy.'

'You can eat frozen goulash,' Vaněk objected, 'but not for too long – I should think a week at the most. That was why our 9th company gave up their positions.'

'In peacetime,' said Švejk with unusual gravity, 'the whole army service centred on the kitchen and various dishes. We had in Budě-jovice a Lieutenant Zákrejs and he was always hanging around the officers' kitchen and whenever any soldier did anything wrong he made him stand at attention and started off at him: "You bastard, you do that once more and I'll make a nice piece of beaten steak out of your mug. I'll stamp you into a potato mash and then make you eat it. Giblets and rice will come out of you and you'll look like a larded hare in a roaster. And so you'd better improve if you don't want people to think that I've made meat hash with cabbage out of you."'

Further explanations and interesting discussion about the use of the menu before the war for educating warriors was interrupted by a huge scream upstairs where the glorious dinner was drawing to an end.

Out of the confused chorus of voices there rang the shrieks of Cadet Biegler: 'Already in peacetime a soldier must know what war will demand of him, and in wartime he must not forget what he learnt on the parade ground.'

Then could be heard the snorting of Lieutenant Dub: 'I insist that it be noted that this is the third time I have been insulted!'

Great events were happening upstairs.

Lieutenant Dub, who as we well know cherished treacherous intentions towards Cadet Biegler in relation to the battalion commander, was received immediately on his entry with a great roar by the officers. The spirit provided by the Jew was having a wonderful effect on everybody.

One on top of the other they shouted, referring to Lieutenant Dub's equestrian skill: 'It's no good without a groom!' – 'The skittish mustang!' – 'How long did you spend among the cowboys in the West, old man?' – '*Haute école!*'

Captain Ságner quickly poured into him a glass of the cursed spirit and the offended Lieutenant Dub sat down at the table. He moved up an old broken chair beside Lieutenant Lukáš who welcomed him with the friendly words: 'We've eaten everything up already, old chap.'

The figure of that melancholy knight, Cadet Biegler, was somehow overlooked in spite of the fact that strictly according to regulations he had officially reported himself to Captain Ságner and the other officers round the table. Although all of them saw and knew him he kept on repeating several times in succession: 'Cadet Biegler has arrived at the battalion staff.'

Biegler took a full glass, sat down quite modestly by the window and waited for a suitable moment to air some of his knowledge from the textbooks.

Lieutenant Dub, who felt that the awful concoction was going to his head, knocked with his finger on the table and addressing Captain Ságner said out of the blue:

'The district hejtman and I always used to say: "Patriotism, fidelity to duty, victory over oneself, these are the weapons that matter in warfare." I am reminded of that especially today when our troops will in foreseeable time be crossing the frontier.'

*

This was the point reached by Jaroslav Hašek in dictating The Good Soldier Švejk and his Fortunes in the World War. *He was already ill and death silenced him for ever on 3 January 1923. It prevented him from completing one of the most famous and widely-read novels published after the First World War.*